TENEBRIUM

Elanor Miller

For Gage.

FLAPPERS AND FALSE GODS
BOOK ONE

In Tenebrium City, even neon lights cast shadows...

This edition was first published in 2023

Independently Published

Tenebrium is the debut novel from Scottish writer Elanor Miller
@elanormiller

Copyright © Elanor Miller, 2023

Elanor Miller has asserted her right to be identified as the author of this work in accordance with the Copyright, Designs and Patents Act 1988

The moral right of the author has been asserted

Tenebrium is a work of fiction. Names, characters, and incidents are the products of the author's imagination or are used fictitiously. Any resemblance to actual events, locales, or persons, living or dead, is entirely coincidental.

ISBN: 9798843065621

Cover Design by Celin Chen - www.celingraphics.com
Edited by Belle Manuel
Formatting and design by Damian Jackson

All rights reserved. Without limiting the rights under copyright above, no part of this publication may be reproduced, stored or introduced into a retrieval system, or transmitted, in any form or by any means (electronic, mechanical, photocopying, recording or otherwise), without the prior written permission of both the copyright owner and the publisher of this book.

PROLOGUE

Excerpt from *Of Flappers and Philosophers: A Tale from Tenebrium.*

— A Historical Journal by Anthony Oubier

The early 2420s saw fundamental disruptions to the lives of those living in Tenebrium City. The once prestigious metropolis, perched atop the first floating ocean colony, played host to several historical events that would change the lives of its many inhabitants irrevocably. The first of which was the reintroduction of Prohibition.

In a highly contested decision, Mayor Richard Howell, assisted by District Attorney Harold Williams, brought in wide-ranging "Public Control Laws" that many referred to as "Neo-Prohibition". Curfews were dictated, and a strict ban was placed on the sale and consumption of alcohol, as well as the many narcotic blends that plagued the city at the time. The controversial privatised paramilitary force, the Onyx Legion, was re-formed to enforce this new norm under the control of the District Attorney.

The second and equally unpopular change was the introduction of the "Three Strike Rule". A harsh capital punishment system that meant a third brush with the law, no matter how small the crime, would immediately and indisputedly carry the death penalty. This was the cause of several riots and many protests when petty thieves and embezzlers were sent to meet the firing squad along with rapists and murderers.

The establishment, however, was not the only culprit in instigating change. The third and most devastating event occurred in 2423, with the introduction of Styxx, a drug of unknown origins that created a city-wide epidemic. At first, users experienced a heavenly high, but the substance was highly addictive and excessive consumption turned the users rabid. Like horror movie zombies, they would tear at anything and anyone with a never-ending hunger that earned them the moniker "Ghoul". The drug was outlawed, and those who had succumbed to its effects were quarantined in the city's SubLevel, a network of tunnels running beneath the Poor Quarter, conditions in which were hardly better than sewers.

The final change was a coup of ideology. The systematic deconstruction of the government through infiltration began in the early 2420s when the Onyx Legion's legendary predecessors, the Gold Legion, a long-dormant sect, resurfaced in secret. The contentious group who believed in subjugating the poor to elevate the rich had been disbanded over a century before due mainly to their polarising views. It transpired, however, that far from dispersing, they had merely taken their beliefs underground and would continue to practise behind closed doors.

In 2422 the Gold Legion tentatively resurfaced and began to quietly amass followers once more. By mid-2425, they had succeeded in taking several positions of power through blackmail and bribery, and on October 22nd 2425, the sect revealed itself to the world, inciting a mutiny within the Onyx Legion and proclaiming mastery over the city of Tenebrium. A violent struggle between law enforcement and the sect culminated in power being restored to the government. However, little is known of what transpired.

What should be a fascinating period of study has proved elusive to this journalist-come-historian. What began on October 22nd 2425, and the events that led up to it are sparsely documented, with few willing to discuss it openly. The Neo-Prohibition laws are yet to be lifted, and as such Tenebrium City is still stuck in the never-ending jazz age that has been the norm for over a hundred years. Those afflicted by the drug Styxx are yet to be cured and, more troublingly, are still confined underground. There is next to nothing known about the drug's creation and distribution. The Gold Legion has once again been disbanded, and control of the Onyx Legion has been returned to the government. Yet, Tenebrium is a city changed, and its people remain uneasy.

I have spent several years trying to piece together this tale from Tenebrium, and what I did learn was not at the behest of any controlling power, but a rather more personal tale from two detectives who were silently instrumental in the liberation of Tenebrium City.

The story you are about to hear, while unverified, seems to provide the answers that I have spent many years searching for. Equivocal? Definitely. Unprovable? Most likely. Untruthful? That judgement I will leave up to you—my esteemed peers.

THE PAST
Two years ago...

They moved together as one, entwined and enthralled by each other. It could have been the hundredth time they had fallen into his bed, yet his touch still electrified her senses. In unison, they burned. As his lips roved her body with indecent familiarity and his hips ground out a gratifyingly punishing rhythm against hers, Thea saw her.

Cleo.

Slim, Black, and beautiful, she stood transfixed in the doorway, her mouth slack, her eyes glazed.

"Walt," Thea breathed, pushing against his bare chest. His response was a low moan as he nipped at her neck, blissfully unaware that they were no longer alone. Thea pushed against his chest more forcefully. "Walt." He raised his head from her shoulder and looked up towards the door. He stopped moving at once, frozen.

The sight of her husband's horror-struck face seemed to awaken Cleo from her stupor. Shaking slightly, she turned and fled the room without a word. Walt propelled himself off the bed and hurtled after her. Thea could hear his desperate apologies as she wrapped the sweat-slick sheet around herself and followed him into the living room.

Jazz still played softly, emanating from the gramophone in the corner. The single candle they had had dinner by burned low. Rose petals littered the floor.

Cleo had her back to Walt as Thea entered. Her shoulders shook, wracked by the tears that were surely flowing down her cheeks. *This is a nightmare,* Thea thought.

"I didn't want you to find out like this," Walt said hopelessly. He had made no effort to cover himself. He stood naked before her, his pale skin glowing in the candlelight. "Cleo, I'm sorry."

She turned to face him then.

Thea gasped. Tears were indeed marking Cleo's umber cheeks, but far from clear, they were a murky crimson. Blood coursed from her eyes, dripping onto her chest and staining the pearls that hung there knotted.

"What's happening to me?" Cleo said, her voice small and reedy as she looked from Walt to Thea and back again.

Cleo began to convulse, Walt lunged forward, but she had fallen before he could take hold of her. He dropped to his knees at her side and tried desperately to restrain her, but he could do nothing to stop her head from crashing over and over against the furrowed metal floor. Thea felt the vibrations on the soles of her feet.

Cleo began to cough and splutter, a thick froth forming at the corners of her gnashing mouth. Walt yelled to Thea, but she only half-heard him as she too dropped to her knees and tried to steady Cleo. The coughing turned to wheezing, and afraid that Cleo might be choking on her tongue, Thea thrust two fingers into her mouth and attempted to clear the blockage.

As soon as she did, however, Cleo stopped her paroxysm and clamped down hard. Thea cried out in pain; she could feel the blood from her fingers spilling into Cleo's mouth as she fought to free herself. Thea grabbed hold of Cleo's thick hair and yanked. Cleo's cry of pain was enough to allow Thea to pull her hand free and back away.

Cleo flopped to the ground and stilled. She lay motionless for a moment. Thea and Walt watched on in horror as she rose into a sitting position like a vampire from its coffin. Her lips were blackened, her skin grey, red veins pulsed under her eyes. Thea darted forward and pulled Walt to his feet, dragging him backwards.

With an eerily robotic quality, one bone, one muscle, one minuscule movement at a time, Cleo stood. Tension hung almost tangibly in the air between them. No one moved. Thea could hear the blood surging around her body as her heart beat a frantic tattoo against her ribs. *This is a nightmare,* she thought.

BOOM.

The front door was blasted off its hinges, showering the room with debris. Thea was momentarily blinded by the deluge of light that flooded the room. Walt grabbed her and pulled her away from the door. When her eyes adjusted to the light and the smoke cleared, she saw twenty or so Onyx Legion soldiers, clad head to toe in black and carrying vicious-looking stun rods, file into the room.

"Keep back," the last soldier to enter said to Walt. "Take her," he said to his men, gesturing at Cleo's crouched form. Four soldiers marched forward and grabbed her by the upper arms; she struggled and snapped as the soldiers attempted to restrain her.

"What's happening? Where are you taking her?" Walt said with all the authority he could muster while naked and unarmed.

"Addicts are to be quarantined in the SubLevel."

"She's not…There's been some mistake."

Cleo struggled more forcefully, snarls ripping from her chest. She tried to bite one of her captors, who retaliated by jabbing her savagely with his stun rod. She howled in pain.

"You bastard!" Walt yelled. "You do that again, and I swear to God I'll kill you!" He ran forward and tried to pull the now limp Cleo free. The soldier to his right

TENEBRIUM

raised his stun rod high in the air and brought the butt of the handle down hard on Walt's face. There was a sickening crunch as his nose shattered, and Walt was thrown backwards.

Thea tried to catch him, but they both fell to the ground tangled in the white sheet.

They could do nothing but watch on helplessly as Cleo was dragged away. *This is a nightmare,* Thea thought.

TENEBRIUM POLICE DEPARTMENT
TENEBRIUM PROPER
STYGIAN COLONY #6

TENEBRIUM CITY
DEPARTMENT OF JUSTICE

INTERDEPARTMENTAL COMMUNICATION
From: Helen Stevens (HR)
To: Captain Betty Charles

CONFIRMATION OF DISCIPLINARY ACTION

I am writing to you today to confirm the completion of disciplinary action against Detective Walter James and Detective Thea Williams.

Allegations of misconduct against Det. Williams and Det. James included:

1. Defying departmental regulation in reference to interpersonal relationships
2. Defying departmental regulations in reference to mentor/mentee relationships
3. Failing to attempt to gain supervisory consent to begin an interpersonal relationship
4. Allowing illicit relationship to affect the department

Allegations of misconduct against Det. Williams included:

1. Proving uncooperative during an investigation

Allegations of misconduct against Det. James included:

1. Proving uncooperative during an investigation
2. Becoming violent under questioning
3. Irrational behaviour in the workplace
4. Suspected consumption of alcohol in violation of Public Control Laws and departmental guidelines while in the workplace

OUTCOME:

Neither party denied any allegations. Both have been temporarily stripped of privileges for a period of two months. Detective James has been suspended for a period of three months. However, due to the mitigating circumstances, the suspension will take place at the same time as compassionate leave. As well as this, Detective James received a strike on his record, issued by the District Attorney, for his offences in relation to alcohol. Attempts to have this expunged by the department have been denied.

TENEBRIUM

NOTE: At the captain's request, the detectives will remain in the same department, subject to her supervision. Be warned; any further infractions will be attributed to the captain.

THE CHURCH

The church was run down, neglected. Bright, flashy lights and neon signs shone through the cracks and chips in the antique stained-glass windows. The busy sounds of a metropolitan city floated through the open doors, a testament to the fact that life never stopped moving on forward for Tenebites. Not even a set of grisly murders could slow them down.

The victim was another blonde, White female with half her face missing and no ID. She was somewhere between pretty and plain with her bobbed hair, short skirt, and long pearls. She was unmistakably a flapper, flaunting her disdain for the behaviours that were expected of her in the most fashionable way possible.

Thea knelt to examine the body more closely. Her jewellery and purse lay next to her, debunking the usual theory that this was a robbery gone wrong, which would have been simpler.

The eyeball that remained in her head looked blankly up at the ceiling as Thea searched the area for something, anything, that would give her a clue as to the perpetrator of such an awful crime. Alas, there was nothing—no fibres, no fingerprints, and nothing traceable.

Thea scanned the scene for a final time with her retinal chip and logged the footage with the TPD, hoping that when she got back to the station, she would notice something she had missed on first inspection.

She straightened up, her nose was stinging, but it wasn't the stench of death; the flapper's body was too fresh, it was acrid smoke. She could always smell Andrew Torrez before he appeared. The odour from his cheap Cuban cigars was unmistakable.

Thea turned and greeted him with a nod which he returned lazily. He looked as he always did. Dark hair slicked back, the hint of stubble peppering his pointed jaw, and shiny brogues that matched his waistcoat. He smoked like a chimney.

"Oh, look, they sent the bambina," he drawled in his smooth accent that hinted at his Mexican heritage.

"This isn't a vice case, Torrez."

"Staffing issue." He shrugged. Thea knew this was code for, "Walt didn't show up for work again." These days, it was hardly news.

On this particular night, Torrez was a rather unwilling partner. As a vice detective, he was more interested in shakedowns and back-alley dealings than murder, and though Thea knew he would never admit it, she got the sense that he didn't quite have the stomach for it. He was always green around the gills when dead bodies were involved.

"You think a ghoul did this?" Torrez asked, looking anywhere but the body at his feet.

"Styxx turns the addicts rabid. This is too clean."

"Clean, huh? Shit, Williams. That means paperwork."

Thea thought Torrez had a point. She was sure no ghoul had committed the murder, but the pool of blood slowly oozing along the lines of grout in between the stone tiles as if the floor had veins could hardly be described as "clean".

"This is your area of expertise. Put me to work," Torrez said after a moment.

"Can you catalogue her personal items?"

He nodded his assent.

One of the many things Thea liked about Torrez was the fact he didn't question her on everything. He was willing to accept that she knew things he didn't. Not something that could be said for every detective in the department.

Thea had joined the academy at seventeen. Now in her late twenties, she was still young, but in no way green. She was decorated, having one of the highest solution rates on the force. In fact, until recently, she and Walt had had the highest solution rate of any partnership in the department. Things had changed, however, and even though Walt had been back at work for over a year, their partnership had never been able to recover from the implosion of their romantic relationship. It was this that made Thea value her friendship with Torrez even more, no matter how cantankerous he could be.

"It's all logged in the database. Are we done here, Tee?"

"Yeah, Drew, we're done here."

It was time to allow the grim-sweepers to clean up the scene and catalogue any remaining evidence.

Thea could feel Torrez's eye on her as she gave the flapper a final look before the body was enclosed in the hovering shuttle. There was a little too much understanding in his gaze as he replaced his trilby hat on his head and turned up the collar of his coat against the rain.

"You see a little bit of her in all of them, don't you?" It wasn't really a question.

"Until we find her, I'll see her everywhere," Thea said.

It was the truth. Caught in a dangerous spiral of jazz and liquor, Thea's twin sister Cora had fallen into drugs and prostitution. *Everyone knows where roads like that lead*, or so Thea had been told countless times. Cora had been missing for nearly two years and was presumed dead by everyone but Thea.

Torrez smiled with uncharacteristic understanding. "Don't do anything I wouldn't do."

"That rules out very little, Drew."

"And life is so much more fun because of it." With that, he tugged the brim of his hat in Thea's general direction and left, muttering to himself about the dirty smudges the rain would leave on his expensive shoes.

PUBLIC SERVICE ANNOUNCEMENT
From the office of Mayor Richard Howell

Public Control Laws

This public service announcement has been issued to remind the citizens of Tenebrium City that the Public Control Laws, as a result of the drug epidemic, are still in effect. There have been no changes to the official guidelines, and failure to follow these guidelines, as set out by Mayor Howell, will result in strikes being added to personal records and could result in execution.

As a reminder:

1. Due to higher than usual levels of street violence, the 9 o'clock curfew is still in effect. This will be enforced by Onyx Legion patrols. Anyone found on the streets after that time without a permit will be arrested or executed.
2. The sale and consumption of alcohol and narcotics is prohibited. This will be enforced by Onyx Legion patrols. Anyone found in possession of these items without a permit will be arrested or executed.
3. Harbouring and/or consorting with ghouls outside of the quarantined SubLevel is prohibited. Anyone found to be in contact with the addict population without a permit will be arrested or executed.

<u>COMPLIANCE IS NOT OPTIONAL</u>

GIN RICKY'S COFFEE STOP

Hat down, collar up against the damp morning mist, Gin Ricky pushed his coffee cart into its usual spot outside the Tenebrium Police Department. As a known bootlegger, many of his associates thought it an odd choice of venue, but Gin Ricky was firmly of the belief "keep your friends close and your enemies closer".

He liked his spot, despite its precarious nature. It allowed him to keep his ear close to the ground. He knew who was arrested and who was released before anyone else did. He knew which detectives were working on what days and in which department. Blending into the background, he was privy to the chatter between loose-lipped officers who forgot that he wasn't just a barista.

He had to admit that there were some drawbacks to his ingenious spot. The weather, for one. He was exposed to the elements all day long, having to spend at least an hour in his tiny bathtub when he got home to bring some feeling back to his feet during the cold winter months.

Walter James, for another.

Known as Walt to his friends, Gin Ricky avoided calling the man anything if he could help it. The tall detective frequented the coffee stop every morning he was on duty. Unfortunately for Gin Ricky, today was one of those days.

Gin Ricky was kneeling down, placing empty boxes in front of his liquor cabinet in case one of the officers exiting the station caught sight of the boot-legged items within. A loud thud on the counter overhead caused him to jump. He took a moment to right the bottles he had sent flying before straightening up. He already knew what had caused the noise.

Detective James had dropped his souped-up bright silver Colt Police Positive on the counter by way of getting Gin Ricky's attention. He did this every time he came. He frightened Gin Ricky, and he knew it, and what was worse, Gin Ricky knew he knew it.

Raising himself to his full height, Gin Ricky turned to face the detective. He cut an impressive figure in his long black trench coat and fedora, but the months of self-abuse were starting to show.

Something had happened to the detective a couple of years back. Gin Ricky wasn't sure what, but it had caused a marked change in him. He had disappeared for a month or two, and when he returned, he was drawn. His angular face more so, his pale skin paler, his sharp eyes slightly sunken, and his hair overlong. The shadow of handsomeness on his face only added to the troubling picture, more of a statement of his apparent apathetic self-loathing than his attractiveness.

"A flat white, and the usual for me," the detective said, replacing the gun in its holster under his arm.

Gin Ricky nodded once, not trusting his voice not to shake. The usual was bourbon and just enough coffee to make it hot and dark.

Gin Ricky set about making the drinks and was grateful when the detective turned away for a moment to look at a poster warning of the dangers of Styxx. While the detective knew that Gin Ricky was carrying and selling contraband, he didn't want him to know just how much illegal liquor he had behind the counter.

Gin Ricky placed the drinks on the ledge that protruded from the front of the cart and waited for the detective to turn back to him. When he eventually did, Gin Ricky said, "That'll be four credits."

The detective didn't reply. He merely picked up the cups and walked away without paying.

BRIEFING

The first break in the flapper case came several days later. Thea had spent the day and most of the night responding to a litany of domestic calls and had only just settled into a tentative sleep when her Cicada rang. Cicada, or Cochlear Implanted Communication and Data Appliance, was the blanket, and rather long-winded term, in Thea's opinion, for the evolution of the mobile comms device. Many who wished to appear retro or vintage still carried devices that resembled phones, but the norm was a small implant in the ear.

The buzz from her tragus implant woke her from an unpleasant dream, and though the vibrations in her ear had rattled her skull, she was grateful for the reprieve.

"Williams, here."

"Thea, the doc has finished the autopsy on your Jane Doe," said the gravelly voice of Bill Fenske, a beat cop, and one of the good ones.

"I'm on my way."

Thea dragged herself out of bed, knowing that her lack of sleep was starting to show. She dressed hurriedly, hoping that her pin curls would last another day and called a Jonckheere transporter.

She stared out of the large bay window in her open plan living area, revelling in the moment of calm.

It never ceased to amaze Thea how alive Tenebrium City was under its blanket of yellow smog. Moving billboards were posted on most buildings, displaying advertisements or news bulletins in every colour imaginable. The translucent lanes and markers of the Slipstream Highway sat around a hundred stories up, supporting the wheel-less cars as they zoomed in between the buildings high in the sky.

People bustled on the streets in their spats and waistcoats, tassels and pearls. Even though it was barely morning, snippets of music floated up to the window from all around as if the city had a pulse—the perpetual jazz age in full swing. Dark and dangerous, corrupt, and amoral at times, Tenebrium was Thea's home. It was all she knew, and while police work was often fraught by a broken system, protecting the only home she had ever known made Thea feel empowered.

The thick glass of the window slid aside as the Jonk arrived. It was the usual model, black and white, with a fashionably aerodynamic fastback body and round doors. Walt had told Thea once that they were modelled on the ancient Rolls Royce from the Gatsby era.

Wind blasted Thea as she stepped out into the transporter, and she was more than glad to sit down in the warmth of its interior.

There was no driver, as was the norm with Jonk taxis and the Liquid Light Display control panel was already undulating with her destination. "Tenebrium Police Department, Tenebrium Proper" glowed blue on the dashboard.

One of the colony's thousand news streams played on the glass monitor that replaced the windscreen. Thea allowed herself to drift as she listened to the reports of more riots over neo-prohibition, fear and outrage over the ongoing "Ghoul Crisis", and the customary murder and missing persons features.

When Thea finally arrived at the TPD, she was dosing uneasily.

The gust of air as the Jonk's door opened stirred her back into consciousness. She disembarked reluctantly into the detective's office docking bay.

A large set of bright yellow airlock doors separated the grey steel of the docking bay from the dark wood of the bullpen within.

It was a man's man's paradise. Suspenders, cigar smoke, and "give 'em hell" attitudes abounded amongst the trilby hats and Ruhlmann desks.

The dark patterned walls were papered with wanted posters, moving evidence photos and pin-up girls, sparsely broken up with the occasional family photograph or advertising billboard. Clear screens hung from the ceiling showing multiple news feeds and teleshopping.

Thea didn't bother to stop at her desk this morning. The church Jane Doe would bring the number of victims up to five, which would necessitate a task force and a meeting. Instead, she headed straight to the conference room.

As she had predicted, the conference room was full. Nearly every detective the department had was lounging in tub chairs facing the wall-to-ceiling display waiting for the medical examiner to give his report.

For many of them, the briefing would be a waste of time. As terrible and sad as any murder was, murder was rather pedestrian in Tenebrium City, and many of the detectives had more than enough cases to be getting on with.

Thea sat down in the centre of the vacant front row, avoiding the necessity of looking at her fellow detectives. Among them was Orion Martin, a bald Black man who was a favourite among his colleagues. His measured voice was reassuring, and his smile warm. Where her colleagues sought out his company, Thea avoided it at all costs. He had been the investigating detective in the case of Cleo's abduction, and as such, he knew far too many intimate details of her relationship with Walt. He had done his best to find Cleo, which Thea was grateful for, but none of that eclipsed his part in making her and Walt's affair public knowledge. The affair was still the talk of the water cooler when gossip was scarce, even two years later.

Elanor Miller

The medical examiner shuffled in just as Torrez took up the empty seat on Thea's left. Cecil Flynn was White, and in his late fifties, a perpetually sweaty, twitchy little man with his greying hair parted sharply in the middle. He ambled over to the desk that stood before the assembled detectives and made a fuss of uplinking his notes to the evidence board.

"The latest victim appears to be another streetwalker. A siren of the night, a delicacy who will never again be sampled—"

"Show some goddamn respect, Flynn." Thea's stomach lurched; she would recognise that voice anywhere.

Walt sauntered into the room carrying two cups of coffee and dropped lazily into the seat on Thea's right-hand side.

"Y-yes, Detective James," Flynn said, tripping over his words.

The last two years had not been kind to Walt, and it was starting to show on his face. Looking at him now, it struck Thea that their twelve-year age gap had never been more apparent.

Thea was used to the rollercoaster of Walt's moods and had long since given up on asking him where he went and what he did when he disappeared for days at a time.

Without glancing at her, Walt pushed one of the coffee cups towards her. She took a sip, grateful for the burst of jittery energy the coffee would afford her.

Thea spluttered slightly as the hot bourbon seared her throat. She replaced the cup on the table and pushed it back to Walt, leaning in as she did so. "I think this one is yours." The taste of bourbon lingered unpleasantly on her tongue.

Walt made no comment. He just glared at her defiantly. Thea broke the connection first, hoping no one would notice the subtle flush she felt as blood rushed to her cheeks. She could sense Walt's eyes lingering on her profile long after she had returned her attention to the briefing.

What do you do when you have fallen in love with someone you shouldn't have fallen in love with?

The question plagued Thea often when in Walt's company. They had not been together in any sense of the word since the night Cleo had been abducted. Their relationship, as well as their partnership, and the friendship that had been the foundation for both, was damaged beyond repair. Walt was notably absent and unreliable. They shared very little with each other anymore, and yet she couldn't shake him or the feelings he stirred within her.

No matter how she felt, there were some things that were destroyed rather than broken and some things that could not be undone. Watching your lover's wife being dragged out of their home in a rabid state of addiction was just one of those things that you couldn't come back from. The guilt of that night weighed on Thea, but that was nothing compared to the change it had wrought in Walt. Undependable and reckless at best, he was far from the department hero he had once been.

"She was a vision in red," Flynn was saying. "An exquisite flower, whose petals were plucked. A goddess extinguished in her prime." He was almost panting.

"Get back on point, Doc," Thea said, disgusted. "Do we have an official cause of death yet?"

"It appears to be some kind of blast to the temple, same as the others," Flynn said, mopping the sweat from his upper lip with a soiled handkerchief. "I'm classing it as a fatal gunshot wound. My best guess is a pulse weapon of some sort. She also had traces of the Styxx variant in her system."

"That drug is making the rounds," Torrez said, a crease between his eyebrows.

"Any idea who's cooking?" asked Orion unexpectedly.

"No, and believe me, we're worried about it. It has to be corporate. It's far too advanced to be a homebrew. There are only three labs in the city capable of creating that kind of product, and they all turned up clean."

"That's disappointing," Orion muttered.

Torrez turned around in his seat to look at Orion; their eyes met, sharing some kind of unspoken communication, then Torrez turned back to the front.

"Got a name?" Walt asked Flynn.

"We have no ID as of yet. Understandably we are having trouble scanning her image into the database—her DNA wasn't filed. B-but well, she was ch-chipped."

"Chipped? Like a pet?" Thea was repulsed.

"Well, they are property."

"You really are a sick S.O.B."

Flynn blanched at the look on Thea's face.

"Is anyone else starting to think suicide?" Torrez asked with the air of a man diffusing a bomb.

"The wounds could be self-inflicted," Flynn conceded, grasping at the lifeline.

"It can't be," Thea said immediately.

"Why not?"

"Are you really going to sit there and tell me that you think five people killed themselves in the exact same way? That's one hell of a coincidence."

"Four," Walt said with a subtle challenge in his voice. "Four people. This Jane Doe had Styxx in her system."

"She can only have taken it once or twice," said Torrez, considering. "She showed no signs of addiction, and she definitely wasn't a ghoul."

"If you're right, which I doubt, maybe she killed herself before she inevitably turned," Thea said, trying the possibility on for size.

"That's still suicide, sweetheart," said Walt dismissively.

Sweetheart.

Sweetheart.

The moment of silence that followed was deafening.

"Not if she was forced to take the drug," Thea said in a voice of determined calm. "Then it becomes manslaughter minimum. But I'm just not buying that they did this to themselves—too many similarities. A sex worker committing suicide in a church? That sounds like a message to me."

"Sounds like a bad joke," said Torrez.

"Opens some new avenues of investigation, I guess," Walt said, unconvinced.

"Who's the pimp?" Thea shot at Flynn, who dropped what he was holding.

"M-Mary Pickford."

Thea was overcome with anger as she sat at her desk moments later. The nerve of him. For over a year, she had been doing both of their jobs and doing it damned well. After everything they had been through, Walt was the last person she expected to dismiss and disrespect her amongst her peers. And yet he had. He had appeared at the precinct for the first time in days and spoken to her, not like a friend, a partner, or even a former lover; he had spoken down to her as the seasoned detectives had in her first few months out of the academy. Perhaps if he had had that attitude back then, she mused, they would have been spared the mess that followed.

Centuries after the conception of detective work, research was still a huge part of the job. Thea hovered her hand over the console embedded into the mahogany of her desktop. The TPD data stream sprung to life. Floods of information composed of blue and red light floated in mid-air. Thea used her retinal chip to sift through the millions of entries until she found what she needed.

Mary Pickford was the proprietor of the high-end brothel Ward Eight. Clicking on the datasite brought up the image of a beautiful Chinese woman in her early thirties; the garish titles pronounced her to be Mary herself.

Before Thea had a chance to read any more, a hand came down atop her console, dismissing the data stream. She looked up, irritated, to see Walt dropping into the seat opposite and putting his feet up on her desk.

"We've got a B and E in Eltham. You coming?"

Thea pushed his feet off the desk as she spoke. "You need my help now, sweetheart?"

"That's some shit. You know I didn't mean anything by it," Walt said standoffishly.

"Right." Thea rolled her eyes.

"Come on, Thea. Whaddaya say?"

"You go," Thea said. She didn't have the time or energy to listen to Walt claim that he had turned over a new leaf. "I'm going to follow up on the church Jane Doe."

"You never miss a chance to needle those pompous pricks at Medicorum."

"Yeah, well, maybe if we leave them alone, they will work out how to turn ghouls back into people," Thea said, standing up.

"Thea Williams—Champion of the Underdog," he mocked.

"You used to care about helping people, too." This, he ignored entirely.

"Come on. We're partners," Walt said as if that changed something.

"We haven't been partners for a very long time."

Thea turned away from him and strode out of the bullpen.

Walt caught up with her in the narrow corridor between the break room and the captain's office. Grabbing her by the upper arm, he pulled Thea aside.

"Thea! What's eatin' you?"

"I can smell it on you! You don't have any strikes left!" Thea said, rounding on Walt.

"It's me. They won't find out. Don't turn into a bluenose on me. Never bothered you before." Walt shrugged.

"You arrogant asshole!" said Thea loudly. "You are literally playing with your life, and for what? A buzz? And yes, it did."

"Keep your damn voice down," Walt said, stepping in close.

"Sort your shit out, Walt. Because in this city, a drunk cop is a dead one. Enjoy your B and E. If you need back-up, call Torrez." She turned on her heel and marched away, leaving Walt to stare after her.

MEDICORUM

Guilt, Walt was made of it. He had so many things to feel guilty about. He felt guilty about everything that had happened on the fateful night Cleo was dragged away. He felt guilty that he had had an affair and betrayed his marriage vows. He felt guilty about his ever-growing dependence on alcohol. He felt guilty that he still had feelings for Thea, and he felt guilty about the way he was treating her.

He knew it wasn't fair that he dropped in and out of her life, disappearing and reappearing without warning, but he felt guiltier still in her company. She was a walking reminder of the biggest mistake he had made in his life. The fact that he knew he would not be able to stop himself from making the same mistake again if he had the chance only compounded the twisting feeling in his gut as he walked through the Eltham District.

Everything in the business centre for the rich and powerful was shades of white. The buildings, the pavement, the benches, and even the trees in the centre of the wide street were a glowing whitish silver. It struck Walt as cold and impersonal as if the faceless corporations whose businesses were situated there wanted people to know that they cared little for the everyman.

It didn't take him long to find Medicorum Medical Services. The building was the largest and the whitest on Main Street, a status symbol of sorts that made Walt instantly dislike it.

Inside, the reception area was yet more white. The floor was a subtly mottled marble, as were the pillars punctuating the vast space. The chairs were chrome, and the reception desk was made of a smooth opalescent glass. Delicate blue letters flashed across the outward-facing surface of the desk detailing the wait times and occupancy. Soft jazz played just audibly enough over the crowds of people that ebbed and flowed like waves.

Medicorum was a mix of all things medical. It was a research giant, a hospital, a cosmetics clinic and a bioengineering lab, a drug manufacturer and many more things it was less willing to discuss openly. Walt had heard that they were working on upgrading humans with devices that could improve everything from strength and agility to eyesight. The retinal implant SEE®, Surgical Eyesight Enhancement®, pronounced "*Seer*", that was standard for all law enforcement, and that Walt was currently using to scan the room, was evidence of the changes that technology had already brought to human bodies.

Walt pulled his detective badge from his pocket and flashed it to the receptionist allowing him to skip the politely disgruntled queue.

"Please take a seat, Detective. Dr Maxwell will be with you shortly."

The receptionist spoke in a rather robotic way that had Walt wondering if they had not already been upgraded.

Walt noted that the seats in the luxury waiting area were surprisingly uncomfortable as he lowered himself into one, almost as if to discourage waiting.

As he sat alone with his thoughts, he felt increasingly on edge, jittery. He had not dared drink the coffee he had accidentally passed to Thea, and because of this, it had now been hours since he had gotten his last fix. Hit. Dose.

He tapped his foot impatiently on his knee to compensate for the shakes he was unable to quell, and though it didn't entirely hide them, it was better than nothing.

Everything seemed to echo in his ears as if the withdrawal had heightened his senses. The sound of a pair of stiletto heels clip-clopping on the marble floor, the sound of blood dripping onto the reception counter where an injured man argued with the receptionist over his bill, the croaky laugh of an elderly woman on the phone, the subtle whoosh of the automatic doors as they opened and closed to emit visitors, patients, and staff alike. Like a drum pounding in his ears, the pressure was too much.

Walt quickly felt around in the pocket of his long overcoat for the delicate silver hip flask that had been taunting him all day. It had been a gift from Thea before they had parted, and she had branded him an alcoholic.

"Mr James?"

Walt quickly stowed the hip flask out of sight, lamenting the sip he had almost taken. Walking towards him was a tall White man in a white coat. He had a thin moustache and dark slicked back hair parted sharply to the side. He gave off an air of superiority that told Walt he was going to be difficult.

When the man reached him, Walt stood and held out a hand that was ignored.

"Dr Maxwell," the man said in a crisp, curt voice.

"Detective Walter James—"

"I know who you are, Mr James," Maxwell said dismissively. "Why are you here?"

"It's Detective James, and you called us," Walt said, crossing his arms.

"I assure you, Detective, no one here called for you."

It took Walt several minutes of waspish conversation to convince Dr Maxwell to take him to the security nerve centre. He finally conceded only when Walt suggested he come back with a warrant and a full team of investigators.

Elanor Miller

The Security Office was an endless expanse of white. The room was empty but for a large curved glass screen that seemed to float in the centre of the room.

Reluctantly, Dr Maxwell had agreed to allow Walt to examine the security feed for the building while informing him emphatically that he would not be accessing the classified research areas and there was not a warrant strong enough in the colony that would change that.

"You won't find anything, Mr James. There has been no theft. We would know if we were missing items of value."

"Then who called the precinct?"

"Maybe it was a prank. Not all citizens respect the Tenebrium Police Department as much as we here at Medicorum do," Maxwell said patronisingly.

"I'll bet," Walt said flatly. "But if you're going to prank the police department, you call in a missing persons report for "I.P. Freely", you don't call in a robbery at a high-end pharmaceutical company."

"Medical Services," Maxwell corrected.

"Right."

Walt turned away from the doctor and set to work.

Nearly an hour later, Walt was getting tired of the doctor tutting impatiently behind him and was ready to give up the investigation as a bad job when something odd happened.

He was watching sped-up footage of one of the numerous labs in the building when a scientist got up from their desk, replaced the samples they had been working on back in the storage refrigerator and disappeared. They just blinked out of existence, leaving an empty lab. Then, roughly a minute later, they reappeared at their desk.

"I wonder what would cause that," Walt said sarcastically, turning to the doctor.

"What? What have you found?" Maxwell leapt up from his chair and joined Walt at the screen.

"You see this?" Walt played the anomalous footage for the doctor. "That's a loop. Footage has been deleted and replaced with a static image of the empty lab. Still think that you haven't had a break-in?"

Maxwell stepped away from the screen and crossed to the door, which he held open for Walt.

"Thank you for your help, Mr James, that will be all."

"Excuse me? This is evidence of a crime."

"We don't need your help," the doctor said firmly.

"What are you hiding, Doc? You've got me all curious." Walt took a step towards Maxwell, who backed away towards the door.

"Your services are no longer required."

"I'm not one of your contractors, I'm an officer of the law, and a crime has been committed here."

"This is private property. Leave, or I will have you removed."

Walt crossed his arms in a clear gesture of immovability. The doctor's actions left him in no doubt that something was amiss within Medicorum.

"Fine," the doctor said, and he pressed a small circular button next to the door.

Moments later, twelve security guards entered the room. They surrounded Walt on all sides.

The security guards were wearing grey uniforms and reflective silver helmets that wouldn't have looked out of place on a motorcycle. They were all armed with pulse weapons styled like Tommy Guns, all of which were aiming at Walt's chest. Dr Maxwell stood behind them, looking self-satisfied.

"Your escort, I believe," he said smugly.

"Hands where we can see them and follow us," one of the security guards ordered.

Smirking, Walt raised his hands lazily. "Oh, sure, you've nothing to hide." The guard who had spoken stepped forward and shoved Walt roughly towards the door. "Keep moving."

"I'm goin'."

With a final smirk at Dr Maxwell, Walt allowed himself to be escorted out of the building.

WARD EIGHT

Ward Eight was the premier brothel in the Pleasure Quarter, Tenebrium's red-light district. It boasted a culture of anything goes. The official line was that there was something for everyone, but the establishment tended to be frequented by the wealthy.

The street outside was bustling with activity. Hawkers and peddlers, as well as freelance Sex Workers, had set up shop in the various inlets between buildings, all of them jostling for the attention of passers-by.

Today, however, the attention of the public was not drawn by the delights of the Pleasure District, but by the heavy paramilitary presence on the street.

The atmosphere was tense. Many protesters had gathered. Some were protesting Neo-prohibition, some protested the Three Strike Rule, while others protested the brutal presence of the Onyx Legion on the streets.

Thea kept her head down as she passed through the crowd. She didn't want to draw attention to herself or disrupt the protesters. She agreed with them, but her position forbade her from openly taking a stance. The reality was the public control measures had caused just as much harm as Styxx, and it had given people an ingrained mistrust of law enforcement.

It was lucky, Thea thought as she was jostled by the never-ending flow of human traffic, that she had been born in Tenebrium City. She was a Tenebite through and through, and as such, she was always vigilant. Thea spotted the young thief right as she was removing her hand from Thea's coat pocket. Thea just managed to catch her by the wrist as the girl, who couldn't have been older than sixteen, tried to sneak back into the crowd.

She was young, too young, her hair was overlong, but not unclean, and she had the look of someone who ate enough to survive, but never had her fill. She was probably part of one of the many "Twist" gangs, so named because of their Fagan-like penchant for using teenagers and young children to pickpocket.

"Give it back," Thea said in a low voice.

"Get off me, lady," the thief snarled, trying to pull herself free of Thea's grip.

"My credit card, give it back."

With an exaggerated pout, the thief produced a clear plastic card with a delicate silver border from where it was tucked tightly against her palm. Thea was impressed by her dexterity; it was almost like a magic trick.

Thea took the card and replaced it in her pocket, but kept hold of the struggling girl's wrist. She fished a credit chip out of her pocket and handed it to the girl, who snatched it greedily.

"Use it to buy food, okay?" Thea said, letting go of the girl, but the thief had already disappeared expertly back into the crowd by the time she had finished her sentence.

When Thea finally made it to the entrance of Ward Eight, it was oddly quiet. The brothel's door was tucked down a side alley, presumably to afford its customers some anonymity. Even so, there were usually people outside tasked with enticing customers in. Not today.

The face of Ward Eight was made from muted silver, jagged metal strips illuminated a moody red by thin neon lights that outlined each separate panel. The name of the brothel was entirely absent. If it had not been for her retinal chip, which flashed the destination at the corner of her field of vision in bright blue letters, Thea would have thought she was in the wrong place.

She examined the door. She couldn't see how she was supposed to get in. There was no handle or doorbell, nor was there any type of keypad or scanner. She raised her hand to knock, but before she had a chance to make contact with the door, a vivid hologram appeared in front of her. It depicted a life-size likeness of Mary Pickford wearing a figure-hugging red dress with feather trim. "Any gender, any species, any taste, any fetish, any time," it proclaimed in a husky voice.

The centre portion of the metal panelling blinked out of existence, and Thea stepped inside. The atrium had no doors that Thea could see. Everything was feathers and silk in shades of red or gold. The walls were damask. Several chaise longues were placed around the room. There was a small desk in one corner which the real Mary Pickford stood behind, still in her feathered dress, dripping with diamonds and pearls.

"Pick your poison. What will it be?" said Mary Pickford, looking Thea up and down, unimpressed.

"I'm Detective Williams with the TPD. I'd like to see the owner, please."

"I am she," said Mary, inclining her head slightly. "How may I help you?"

"No, you're not. Where is he?"

"I can assure you—" Mary began.

"Where's Benny?"

Benjamin Pickford was sitting behind his desk when Thea entered. He wore a handsome black suit with gold embroidery that complimented his complexion. He was an attractive Black man, tall, with angular features and full lips. He was a businessman and, as Thea knew all too well, a dangerous man.

There was a virtual catalogue on the wall of his mahogany and leather office depicting all types of people in varying stages of undress. Thea flicked through it disinterestedly, waiting for Benny to speak. When he didn't, she said, "So this is where you have been hiding out, Benny. Or should I say 'Mary'? The Sheba in the lobby is just a front, right?"

Benny leaned back in his chair and surveyed Thea over the top of his clasped hands. "What can I do for you, Detective Williams? We cater to any taste, any—"

"So I've heard." Thea paused to gauge his reaction. "We found one of your girls murdered last night."

"Not possible," said Benny, a little too quickly. "All of my assets are accounted for."

"Check again."

Benny turned away from his desk to a large clear screen that sat on the bureau behind it. Careful not to allow Thea to see what he was doing, he searched through his records. When he was finished, he turned back to face Thea. "As I told you—accounted for."

Thea pulled up the sleeve of her long tan coat and turned her hand palm up. There, on her wrist, was a tiny metal symbol embedded into the flesh. It looked like a circle containing a triangle, which in turn contained another smaller triangle. It was called an Index. Thea touched it lightly, and a prism of light erupted from the spot. A three-dimensional image of the church crime scene, complete with the gruesome corpse of the Jane Doe, hovered in the air.

Benny regarded the image with dramatic distaste, then turned his head away.

"She was not mine."

"How can you tell?" Thea pressed. "She doesn't have a face, but she did have your chip in her."

"However distasteful you may find it, that's perfectly legal," Benny said, his eyes narrowed. "Perhaps the chip was counterfeit."

"Perhaps. Have any of your staff been caught using or in possession of Styxx?" Thea said, changing tack at lightning speed. "Or is there a client you have previously suspected of dealing or possibly supplying?"

"No."

"I'm going to need to take a look at your client list, and I'd like to talk to your people," Thea said, changing tack again. She was trying to unbalance Benny and make him nervous. It was working apparently because when he replied, it was a little too surprised and betrayed a hint of fear. "Why?"

"Haven't you heard, Benny? Pillow talk is illuminating."

"They will not talk to you," said Benny, regaining his composure.

"Is that right?" Thea sat casually on the edge of the desk, watching.

Benny leaned in, his tone losing some of its usual airs and graces. "I own them, and as such, I own the right to dictate with whom they speak." Benny smiled, clearly feeling he had regained the upper hand. "It's a shame up here in the sky that the ground laws don't apply," he said, smirking.

"I'm not so sure. Being allowed to torture uncooperative suspects has certainly made my job easier." This was a downright lie. Thea abhorred the department's stance of "the ends justify the means" and had never made good on any threats to the contrary.

"Not without a warrant."

Thea stood up suddenly and was gratified to see Benny flinch. "You know, it's a nice set-up you have here."

"I've finally found my calling."

"So I see."

Thea looked at Benny curiously for a moment, then turned to exit. "Before you go," said Benny, coming around his desk to perch on it as Thea had. "I have been meaning to ask about the Onyx Legion patrols in the Pleasure Quarter."

"Above my paygrade."

"The military presence is bad for business."

"I'd have thought murder was bad for business," Thea retorted.

Benny smirked appreciatively and said, "Goodbye, Detective."

"You think of anything…" Thea let the sentence hang.

"You'll be the first to know."

Benny lived a dangerous life; he was an informant as often as he was a suspect. Thea had spent a considerable amount of her career searching him out in whatever luxurious hidey-hole he happened to be in at the time for various offences, but something about Ward Eight just didn't feel right. Benny was a criminal and a nasty bastard of a pimp, but he had always been smart enough to have others do his dirty work. Money was his ultimate goal, like most in Tenebrium. Thea was sure that if one of his girls was missing, he'd know. She was even surer that if he had killed her, they never would have found the body, but he was up to something, and she was determined to find out what.

THE SUBLEVEL

Blackness. The void. Total sensory deprivation.

The darkness was so oppressive that Cleo wasn't sure if she was blind. The rhythmic breathing of the equally condemned blended together in a deafening cacophony of drone. The heat from her fellows made Cleo feel faint, yet she stood upright, pressed against the twitching bodies of those trapped with her in the SubLevel.

The hatch opened overhead, and a square shaft of light illuminated the crossroads of tunnels. Cleo's eyes stung; the light was like a lance to the brain. Squinting, she took in the sea of ghouls that surrounded her.

They stood in their thousands like grotesque statues twitching infinitesimally; their faces turned upwards towards the light. A shadow passed over the hatch, temporarily restoring darkness, then something wrapped in a dirty blanket was heaved into the hole.

The blanket unravelled as it fell to reveal the naked body of a woman. Cleo looked at her face for the shortest moment before the body hit the ground with a sickeningly wet splatter.

There was a moment's pause before the ghouls erupted into a frenzy, converging on the body, ripping it apart in a haze of snarls and blood.

Cleo knew she was a ghoul; she also knew she wasn't like the mindless others, yet, when the blood splattered her face, she couldn't stop herself from seeking out a morsel of flesh for her own to devour and slake the ravenous hunger that burned inside her.

WARD EIGHT HAS A SECRET

Thea was stalling for time as she wandered around Ward Eight's atrium, pretending to be interested in the catalogues of kink that were strategically and subtly placed next to the many chaise longues. Mary Pickford was eyeing her beadily. Thea was trying to think of a legal reason to search the place. If Walt had been with her, he would have just gone right ahead and done it, warrant or no; that was his style—act first, ask questions later. Thea, however, tried to operate inside the law as best she could.

The wall to her left blinked out of existence just as the entrance and the wall opposite that led to Benny's office had. A maid walked through the newly revealed corridor carrying bloody sheets and looking upset.

The corridor was long and narrow, made from a dimly reflective metal. Door after door was spaced evenly along each wall. Red strip lights lined the floor giving the corridor an eerie quality.

Without a moment's hesitation, Thea headed for the newly revealed passage, Mary Pickford hot on her heels. "What the hell do you think you're doing?" Before the last word had left her lips, a scream echoed distantly from one of the private rooms.

"Probable cause," Thea said without looking at her.

As soon as Thea set foot past the false wall, she heard another scream mingled with snarls from the door nearest her.

"Get out! Get out! Now! Security!" Mary screamed, running as fast as her heels allowed. Thea ignored her.

Thea grabbed the door handle; it was locked. She stepped back, raised her leg and, making sure she put her hip into it, kicked the door—hard. It sprang open to reveal a horrific scene.

A naked male ghoul was chained to an extravagant bed by shackles at his wrists and ankles. There was blood on the sheets. A businessman was standing next to the bed, pulling on his trousers without underwear. He had jumped back as the door crashed open and tried desperately to button his fly with trembling hands.

Thea stood motionless, trying to comprehend the scene in front of her, the implications of which made her feel ill. "...My God," she almost whispered. "Do not move," she spat at the businessman who was trying to sidle out of view.

Thea grabbed Mary roughly by the arm and pushed her back out into the corridor.

"Open it," Thea said, jerking her head in the direction of the door opposite.

Mary didn't move. Thea pulled the delicate gold pin from Mary's dress and threw it at her. "Open it."

Mary caught the pin and held it up to a small sensor above the jam; there was a faint click. Thea pushed her aside and thrust the door open. This room was empty of a client, but another male ghoul was chained to a geometric cross bolted to the wall.

BREAK ROOM

Torrez leaned casually against the chrome counter in the break room, bragging to Bill about one of his many conquests. He enjoyed talking to the older man. He had a good ear and a sharp wit. Bill was a stocky White man of medium height with thinning grey hair and a rather magnificent moustache.

"So, are you going to see her again?" Bill asked in that gravelly voice of his.

"Nah, we both knew it was a one-time deal." Torrez turned and placed a cup into the coffee maker. "Milk and three." He watched as the cup filled from the bottom; the black liquid swirled, lightening slowly to a caramel colour.

"What about the guy from last month?"

"C'mon, Bill, I'm married now," Torrez said, feigning outrage.

"You've always been married."

"I'm turning over a new leaf."

Bill snorted, "Wife got you by the balls?"

"If only, Pendejo, if only," said Torrez with a roguish grin. "It's been a long time since I have indulged—"

Bill cleared his throat loudly, "Captain Charles, would you like some coffee?"

Captain Betty Charles stood in the doorway of the break room. She cut an impressive figure. She was a handsome Black woman with a penchant for ivory suits. The captain had a regal quality about her that meant Torrez couldn't help but respect her. She was a family woman with strong morals, and she didn't kowtow to the higher-ups if she could help it.

"No thank you, Bill," The captain said, then turning her attention to Torrez, "Flynn tells me we have identified the drug present in the church Jane Doe."

"Yes, Ma'am. It looks like a modified strain of Styxx. Word is the dealers are calling it Quietus. It's high-quality stuff. I can't see any street pushers carrying it."

"Any leads?"

"Not yet. We are having the same problem as we had with Styxx; we can't trace it back to a manufacturer. I'm just about to head out to meet with an informant. See if it's trickled down that low," Torrez said.

"Keep me posted."

"Will do, Captain."

"Oh, and Bill?" The captain turned to him. "Thea is looking for assistance at Ward Eight."

"Yes, Ma'am." Bill stood, nodded deferentially to the captain, and left. Torrez felt slightly awkward alone in the captain's company; she was an intimidating woman. She surveyed him as if deciding whether or not she should speak what was on her mind.

"Andrew, do you happen to know why Walter is not at Ward Eight with his partner?"

WARD EIGHT HAS MANY SECRETS

Uniformed Officers swarmed Ward Eight along with Crime Scene Investigators and grim-sweepers, just in case. The officers swept room by room, searching for more ghouls and any other dark secrets that the brothel might hold.

Thea stood with her hands on her hips in the centre of a lavish room. Everything from the curtains and bedsheets to the carpet was upholstered with black velvet and trimmed with gold. They had found two female ghouls in here; one chained to the back of the door that led to the en suite and the other chained to the bed. Both were bloody. The smell in the room was telling.

When the ghouls had been rounded up, no one had bothered to take a census. It gave Thea a heavy feeling in her stomach to think about all the families who would never know for sure what had happened to their loved ones and the ghouls whose identities were lost forever. This callous oversight also meant that they would have little chance of identifying the victims of Ward Eight. They would be treated as best they could be then forced back into the SubLevel, and there was nothing Thea could do about it.

She was repulsed and shaking with rage. Her blood boiled as she looked at Benny where he stood in the corner, held by Bill and a stocky officer Thea only knew by sight.

The injustice and the violation of it all was enough to bring her to tears, and had she been off duty, Thea would have cried; as it stood, it was taking every ounce of energy she had not to attack Benny, not to pound him into a pulp. She had known he was amoral, but she had never expected this.

"So, it's ghouls now, huh?" Thea said in a voice of determined calm.

"Any gender, any species, any taste, any fetish, anytime," Benny sneered.

Thea clenched her hands into fists so tightly she could feel her nails digging into her palms. "Benjamin Pickford—"

"Oh, I don't think so." Benny began to struggle, but Bill held on tight.

"You are under arrest for forced prostitution, false imprisonment, harbouring ghouls outside the SubLevel without a permit, and I'm quietly confident I'll be adding murder to that list." Thea pulled the handcuffs from her belt and stepped towards Benny. He stopped struggling and straightened up to look her dead in the eye. "But you'll never prove it."

Benny elbowed Bill hard in the stomach, pushed the other officer roughly to the floor, then grabbed a chair which he hurled with all his might at Thea. It caught her off guard, clattering painfully into the arms she had only just managed to raise to protect her face and causing her to fall backwards. Benny seized the opportunity and ran. Thea, getting quickly to her feet, gave chase, several officers behind her.

Benny ran through corridors and private rooms, barrelling people out of the way as he went. Thea hurtled after him.

They rounded a corner into a long dead-end corridor, or so it seemed. When Benny reached the end, he placed his palm flat against the wall, and it disappeared. Benny ran through the new opening and reached for the reader on the other side. Thea only just managed to pass through before the wall reappeared, blocking her and Benny off from the other officers.

"Someone get this wall back up!" yelled Bill's muffled voice.

Thea followed Benny into a VIP room. There was a female ghoul crouched in the corner. Benny grabbed her by the manacles around her wrists and thrust her at Thea before darting from the room.

The ghoul grabbed at Thea and wrestled her to the ground, trying desperately to bite at her with salivating jaws. Regaining control, Thea rolled so that she was on top, straddling the ghoul. She pulled her gun from its holster at her back and held it to the ghoul's gnashing face at point-blank range. For a moment, neither moved.

"Kill me..." the ghoul ground out dismally. "Please..."

Thea didn't move. She just stared, then she turned the dial on the side of her gun from blue to red, from non-lethal to deadly, and pulled the trigger.

There was a bright flash of light as Thea loosed a single pulse round, and when it dissipated, the ghoul was dead, a small smouldering hole in the centre of her forehead.

Without looking back, Thea got to her feet and ran.

She burst out into a stairwell. Benny sprang from behind the door and pushed her over the railing. Just barely, Thea managed to catch the bannister two flights down. Her shoulders burning with the pain, she hauled herself up and sprinted after Benny, who was now a floor down.

Almost at the same time, they breached the basement door. In stereotypical prohibition-style, six men smoking cigars sat around a felt-covered table playing illegal poker. They jumped to their feet as Thea and Benny crashed through the double doors, but neither paid them any mind.

Benny ran for the exit at the other end of the room; Thea pulled out her gun and fired a well-aimed shot at the door frame an inch or two to the left of Benny's head.

"Time to stop running, Benny."

Benny turned to face her, looking contemptuous. "Fine. You got me. It's a poker racket. All these joints have 'em." Benny had dropped his refined air for a much rougher no-nonsense tone.

"Cute," said Thea motioning with her gun to a seat at the poker table, "But I don't give a damn about some shitty poker game. Tell me about the flapper in the church." Benny took the hint and sat down lazily. He spat on the floor at Thea's feet.

"I didn't kill that girl."

"But you know who did," Thea said, holstering her weapon. She shot when she had to, but she found it rarely solved anything.

"Listen, bitch, it ain't worth my life. I talk—I'm toast."

"You're toast either way, Benny."

Without warning, Benny sprang from his seat and swung for Thea. She caught the punch and, using his arm as leverage, forced him face-first onto the poker table.

"Benjamin Pickford, you are under arrest," said Thea pulling two silver bracelet-like objects from her belt and attaching one to each of Benny's wrists. As soon as the clasps snapped shut, they lit up blue and pulled his wrists sharply together with a faint *ding*.

"You have the right to remain silent, though I don't suggest you use it," Thea continued, "You have the right to an attorney. If you cannot afford one, one will be appointed to you by the Tenebrium Criminal Court. You will be transported back to the TPD, where you will be detained and questioned. Do you understand?"

"Fuck you!" Benny spat.

"I'll take that as a yes."

Thea pulled Benny upright and marched him, muttering under his breath, from the room.

DECO

The rain smelled metallic. Its yellowish drops fell relentlessly from the sky, refracting the rainbow of neon lights all around. Keeping his head down, Gin Ricky wound his way through the labyrinthine streets. His destination was Deco, a known favourite of the city's wealthiest gangsters.

The restaurant had Greek-style pillars in shades of gold surrounding the entrance. Once inside, Gin Ricky was relieved of his coat and searched somewhat rigorously for concealed weapons. He allowed the search, as to decline was a death sentence, and he, the consummate survivor, was neither stupid enough nor brave enough to make any sort of aggressive move on Tenebrium's mafia.

He was ushered into the main dining room by a gorilla of a man with a face that looked like playdough as if he were routinely punched. He had a Tommy Gun on a strap hanging from his shoulder. That particular style of pulse weapon had come back into fashion when neo-prohibition was introduced and was favoured by private security and the mob alike.

The refectory had a black and white chequered floor with huge crystal chandeliers hanging from the ceiling. The round tables were covered with white cloths.

On the far side of the room, the largest table was occupied by a portly White man with iron-grey hair. He wore a white shirt and waistcoat in the exact shade of silver as his slick locks. There was a gold pocket watch chain attached to a strained button. Behind him stood four heavily armed men in brown suits and hats that conspicuously obscured their faces.

"Take a seat, Ricky," Dill Kelly said, gesturing with a greasy hand. Gin Ricky complied.

He didn't like being called just "Ricky". When he had started out as a bootlegger, some of his partners had thought Gin Ricky was a good alias, apt even, and really, he didn't mind it that much as it wasn't too much of a departure. It also afforded him a modicum of mystique. His real name was Ri Jin-woo; his parents were Korean, and he was proud to share that heritage, but just Ricky made him sound like every other criminal on the street. He, of course, would never say any of this out loud to a man as dangerous as Dill Kelly, so Gin Ricky just sat in silence, waiting for the mobster to speak.

But Dill Kelly didn't. He just continued to eat an especially rare steak with indecent fervour. "Mr Kelly…"

"Shut up."

"Yes, Mr Kelly."

Dill eyed Gin Ricky for a moment as he wiped a trickle of pinkish-red liquid from his chin, then reached down and pulled something from his pocket. Gin Ricky flinched.

"Relax, Ricky," said Dill darkly. "It's just your permits."

Dill passed the folded slip of paper over the table. Gin Ricky snatched it in his haste to be out of the unsettling man's presence.

"Ouch."

Dill showed his hand to Gin Ricky. There was a small thin paper cut on his thumb, bleeding sluggishly. "Lick it clean." Dill Kelly held out his thumb. Gin Ricky froze. Surely Dill wasn't serious? The silence that followed was icy, yet Gin Ricky felt beads of sweat forming on his forehead. "Lick. It. Clean."

Breathing heavily and thinking he had no other choice Gin Ricky leaned forward. He parted his lips, extended his tongue, and…

Dill Kelly pulled his hand back, grinning. He proceeded to suck his own bleeding thumb, then wipe it on a soiled napkin, chuckling. Gin Ricky let out an audible sigh and sat back.

"No more selling to cops. All right?" Dill was still chuckling.

"Y-yes, Mr Kelly." The comment threw Gin Ricky. How did he know? And which instance was he talking about? Gin Ricky prided himself on his ability to play all sides for profit and gain, but if the mob got a hint of his extracurricular activities, he was dead.

"Don't worry. You haven't displeased me that much," said Dill, misinterpreting Gin Ricky's panicked expression. "Now get the fuck outta here."

Gin Ricky did not need to be told twice. Clumsily he got to his feet and bolted for the door where he collided with something hard. He looked up from the floor to see Detective Andrew Torrez standing over him, looking unimpressed.

A PRECARIOUS ARRANGEMENT

Torrez looked down at the bootlegger Gin Ricky where he sat dishevelled on the floor. He had run into Torrez and sort of bounced. He wasn't surprised to see him, though he had been surprised to collide with him.

"Still dealing in illegal permits, I see," Torrez called over to Dill Kelly, where he sat at an overladen table.

Gin Ricky got to his feet, his beady eyes travelling between Torrez to Dill Kelly like he was watching a tennis rally. "Go," Torrez said, jerking his head towards the exit. Gin Ricky scrambled to his feet and bolted.

Torrez strolled leisurely into the room and took up the seat opposite Dill without waiting to be asked. Dill Kelly reminded Torrez of a boar, rotund and dangerous. He was covered in grease, and his suit that probably cost more than Torrez was paid in a month, was dappled with stains from his meal.

"Are you here to bust me, Detective?"

"One day, Dill, but not today," said Torrez, looking Dill's bodyguards up and down. "I'm here to ask you a few questions about a new drug on the streets, involved in a few murders in the Pleasure Quarter."

"Quietus," said Dill, putting down his knife and fork at last.

"You peddling?"

"Not my business, but I'm sure I could find a name or two for you," said Dill, shrugging. He motioned to a waiter in the corner whom Torrez had not noticed when he entered. The haughty looking young man trotted forward and filled Dill's glass with wine, he then filled the empty glass that sat in front of Torrez.

"Much appreciated. You got a beat on its origins?"

"I'll ask around. Not many places in the city capable of producing that kind of product. Probably corporate," Dill Kelly said slyly.

"Great minds." Torrez nodded.

"Could be tricky…"

Torrez had seen this coming. Nothing was ever free when you were dealing with the mob.

"You'll get your cut." Torrez took a long drink of wine, swilling it around his mouth. He let out a faint *ahh* of appreciation as he swallowed. He pulled a small gold case from his inside breast pocket, opened it, pulled out a cigarillo, and lit it. "How's the wife?" Torrez asked as he replaced his cigar case inside his jacket.

"Pregnant and well cared for."

"Amen to that. Congratulations," said Torrez raising his glass.

"Thank you, and you?"

"She's not pregnant or happy. Says I work too many hours with too many dangerous folks." Torrez shrugged.

"She's got a point, Drew."

"Yeah, I suppose she does," Torrez conceded. "So, what you got for me? Any foxes in the henhouse?"

Dill straightened in his chair. "You sell to one cop, and he goes running to Mommy in vice."

"Who did you sell to?" said Torrez, unable to keep the surprise out of his voice.

A smile played across Dill's lips. He had the upper hand, and he knew it. "That's not the deal."

Torrez flicked his cigarillo away and reached for his gun, as did Dill. "I think our meeting is over, Drew. I tolerate your presence just as you tolerate mine. Let's leave it at that."

Torrez looked at Dill's thugs, well aware he was outnumbered in a big way. "I still want those names."

"And you'll get them. Now get out."

HER NAME WAS STARLA

The second-floor dressing room was reserved for those who would fetch the highest price. It was lavish, with its built-in hot tub, spacious steam showers and couches that resembled beds. This appearance of care and respect vanished immediately when Thea looked at the people who used it. They all seemed defeated, Thea thought, as she watched Bill un-cuff Benny, then re-cuff him to a chair.

As far as Thea was concerned, sex work was work as long as it was undertaken out of choice as opposed to necessity. She saw no difference between sex work and any other job in the entertainment industry. It was clear, however, that choice was not offered at Ward Eight.

Only three of Ward Eight's "courtesans" had agreed to talk to the police, and even as they sat huddled in front of Thea and Benny, they looked as if they were having second thoughts. There were two women and one man. The women were both sultry redheads, one tall and one petite; they were so similar, Thea wondered if they were sisters. Their male colleague was extremely handsome and extremely well-muscled. All refused to give their names. All glanced nervously at Benny.

"Ask them if they mind talking to me. And Benny, ask real nice."

"Go ahead. Tell the bitch whatever she wants to know."

The taller of the redheads spoke first. "Mr Pickford came to us and offered to set our families up for life if we started taking Styxx. We all got problems, but I'd rather starve than become one of those things. So, I said no. Never heard any more about it. I knew some of the others were considering it, but...I couldn't. This city robs you of so much. My sanity is all I got."

"Thank you, and I'm sorry," Thea said sympathetically. This was yet another thing she couldn't fix. It was legal to own people in the colonies. They had to agree to sign over their freedom, and desperate, starving people did.

"I don't need your pity," the tall redhead said, holding her head high. Thea nodded once.

"The ghoul you shot used to be Starla," said the male courtesan. A single tear fell on his cheek; he wiped it away, his face becoming set.

Thea felt her chest constrict. She genuinely believed that she had done Starla a kindness, but the memory of it would have her rattling around in her own head for a long time to come.

"That wasn't her real name," he continued stonily. "She was my...I loved her. Anyway, her daughter was really sick, and I tried to help, but it wasn't enough... She needed credit bad, so..." He broke off, unable to continue.

"So, she agreed," Thea finished the sentence for him sadly.

"See! I didn't do nothing. I still take care of that kid," Benny reckoned.

"You are a leech," said Thea, getting to her feet. "Preying on the vulnerabilities of desperate people." She took a step forward with every word. "You've done plenty."

SHE'S GOOD

By early evening Walt was tired of trying to dig up dirt on Dr Maxwell and Medicorum. Both the man and the company were so squeaky clean it was suspicious, but Walt could sift through the TPD data stream no longer. His eyes were itchy, and his hip flask was empty; he was starting to feel on edge again.

With an overly aggressive swipe of his hand, he dismissed the data stream and got to his feet. Walt wasn't sure if he could get truly drunk anymore, or perhaps he was never really sober. Either way, he felt buzzed.

He made his way to the break room and poured himself a triple redeye which he gulped down. The bitter coffee caused him to gag slightly. He was a mess, and he knew it.

Walt poured another triple redeye. As the tar-like liquid hit the back of his throat, he retched loudly.

"You okay there?"

Walt spun around. Torrez was standing in the doorway.

"I'm fine."

"Right. Did you catch the news?"

Torrez nodded to one of the screens on the wall. It showed Thea loading Benjamin Pickford into the back of a transporter. Torrez turned up the volume.

"In a shocking turn of events," the reporter was saying. "Detectives discovered a dark secret within Ward Eight, one of the Pleasure Quarter's most popular adult venues..."

"She's good," Torrez said, watching Walt.

"Yeah, she is." Walt turned and walked away.

THAT PARTICULAR NICHE

The interrogation room was entirely metal. It was cold and uncomfortably bright. Benny sat naked on a straight-backed chair, goose pimples puckering his flesh. Thea lounged on the wall opposite, sipping coffee.

They had been like this for nearly an hour.

"Irtezah Jafri?"

"I got nothin'."

"Dorothy Park?"

"Never heard of her."

"Jaqueline Ruth?"

"Not ringing any bells."

"Cora Williams?"

"Sounds cute. She single?"

"I'm really not in the mood to play games with you, Benny."

She hadn't been surprised that he had nothing to say about any of the other missing persons. Whatever his involvement, Thea was sure that he wasn't at the top of the ladder. He was, however, guilty in the extreme when it came to the ghouls, and he was never going to be able to talk his way out of that. He was going to jail for a very long time.

Thea finished her coffee then walked slowly over to Benny. She sat in the seat opposite.

"You got the hots for me or something?" Benny asked, gesturing to his naked body.

"Your clothes are evidence. My apologies." In truth, it had been Torrez's idea to try to set Benny on edge.

"Couldn't have given me something else?"

"What can I say? I'm enjoying the view."

"I knew it!"

"Cold out, is it?" said Thea exaggeratedly, drawing her eyes downward.

"You know what? Fuck you, man."

Thea snickered. "All right, let's talk about Ward Eight."

"People are property whether you like it or not." Benny shrugged.

"I don't like it."

"Nothing you can do about it, sister," Benny said as if he was teaching Thea a life lesson. "It's the law around here. I mean, weren't you born in the ocean colonies?"

Thea nodded. "I was born right here in Tenebrium City."

"Then why are you acting like some bleeding-heart dry-lander?"

It was true; Thea did have more than the average amount of distaste for the dystopia that was Tenebrium City. It galled her that other people didn't seem to feel the same way. Tenebrium was brutal and cold, uncaring as a population.

"Who are you hiding from?" Finally, Thea had achieved the upper hand. Benny looked genuinely surprised by the question.

"'Scuse me?"

"Mary Pickford. It's not like you to hide in the shadows."

"It's good for business. Better a madam than a pimp. Y'know, optics. My clients prefer a feminine touch. I'm forward-thinking."

"How practical." Thea stood up and moved behind Benny. He shifted nervously in his seat. "Let's talk about Starla and the other workers you turned into ghouls."

"I didn't force my people into nothing!" said Benny, turning where he sat to keep Thea in view.

"'Your people'. Oh yeah, I'm sure they had plenty of choice in the matter."

"You're kinda judgey for a cop, you know that? My people have it good. You think I'm a bastard? You have no idea what goes on in some of the other joints in town. I never made them take it. And I took care of the ones who did."

"You don't surrender your freedom because you've 'got it good'," said Thea. She knelt down and tugged Benny's handcuffs. "You do it because you're desperate. A feeling you're about to become very well acquainted with."

"Look, it was only supposed to be a one-time deal," said Benny quickly. "A big client offered me huge piles of credit if I could cater to his...darker tastes. Turned out that particular niche—wasn't so niche."

"Who's the client?" said Thea, sitting back down.

"I can't tell you," Benny said fearfully.

"You were the one who pointed out that up here, the rules are different. Maybe we should put them to good use." She had no intention of laying a hand on him, no matter how appealing the thought was, but he didn't know that.

"You're gonna beat me while I'm chained up? Figures. You cops are all the same." Benny was attempting nonchalance, but his eyes betrayed his nerves.

"You want to talk about being chained up?"

"All right! All right. Keep your ass in your seat. I don't know. I don't know who he is. I never saw him. He entered masked, left the same way."

"Okay."

"Okay?"

"You can't tell me something you don't know. The woman in the church, who is she?"

"Her name was Eve," Benny sighed.

"Just 'Eve'?" Thea leaned forward in her seat.

"So... I pick up a stray off the streets now and then," said Benny leaning forward conspiratorially. "Might not be above board, but at least they ain't sleeping rough. I'm doing a public service."

"Oh, yeah, you're a real Good Samaritan. You gave her the drug?" said Thea.

"No, no. She was one of my best. Would have been a waste. Truth is, I was thinking of letting her go."

"Why? If she was one of your best."

"I caught her freelancing. Couldn't find the client, though. She hid her tracks well."

Right on time, there was a knock at the door, and Torrez entered. He had removed his suit jacket and rolled up his sleeves. It was a nice touch, thought Thea. "Busy, Querida? Can I borrow your suspect?"

"Be my guest," Thea said, getting to her feet.

"Hey, hold on now..." said Benny, sizing Torrez up.

Torrez sat down in the seat Thea had vacated and clasped his hands on the table. "My name is Andrew Torrez. I'm a detective in the vice department. I'd like to ask you a couple of questions if you don't mind."

"So, you're good cop, huh?"

Torrez glared at Thea, where she stood leaning against the wall. It was a good approximation of disapproval.

"Who supplied you with Styxx?" said Torrez, keeping his tone light.

"I want to make a deal," said Benny, leaning back and crossing his arms.

"We just want your supplier. There isn't much you can offer us that's gonna get you out of this one," Thea said incredulously.

"I got a cop for a client." Benny had dropped his ace in the hole. He grinned in a self-satisfied sort of way. Thea and Torrez glanced at each other, all pretence lost.

"Fuck." Thea had absolutely no doubt who that cop was. She stormed from the room, leaving Benny to Torrez's questionable mercy.

"I want a name," Torrez said fiercely, all politeness gone.

Benny laughed tauntingly, enjoying the chaos he had sown. Without warning, Torrez yanked hard on the chain attaching Benny's handcuffs to the table, pulling him forward so their faces were inches apart.

"Give me the name!"

Benny smiled widely. "Guess you aren't good cop after all."

THE QUADRANT

The Quadrant was a dismal place. It was home to Tenebrium's most unwanted. The poor and the homeless lived there in abject poverty. The streets were narrow, and the buildings soot-blackened. The high-rise housing was cramped and dilapidated. Those unfamiliar with the area would have been forgiven for attributing the damage to bomb blasts; several buildings had gaping holes in their walls, and few had windows anymore.

Small camps had been set up in and around the most crumbling of buildings. Canvas tents and makeshift walls made of fabric combined with the many hawkers and peddlers gave The Quadrant the look of an exotic bazaar.

This couldn't have been further from the truth, however. The people there were starving, barely able to survive day to day. Order was kept by police beat-pounders and Onyx Legion soldiers who patrolled in heavily armed pairs.

The Onyx Legion was not only present to keep the peace; the SubLevel gates loomed large at the south edge of the Poor Quarter, like an oppressive shadow that reminded everyone present of the lost souls trapped within.

Gin Ricky kept his head down as he moved through the streets, careful to avoid detection. Creeping through the claustrophobic alleys, he came to a small unguarded section of the gate. The black metal was rusted in places, and the stones in the surround were crumbling. With trembling fingers, Gin Ricky pulled a small brown paper package from his coat and slid it through the bars.

Down below in the SubLevel, Cleo shuffled forward and picked up the package.

NO DOPE FIEND

It was nearing midnight when Walt made his way to the canteen for what felt like his fiftieth coffee. He was tired and irritable, but Dr Maxwell had annoyed him. Walt was like a bloodhound when he caught the scent of something, he wouldn't give up until he got to the bottom of the mystery. Or at least that was what he had been like before.

The coffee machine beeped, letting Walt know that his java fix was ready. He picked up the cup and was about to bring it to his lips when the door burst open.

Thea stormed into the room in a towering rage. Her dark hair was flying around her beautiful face, which was contorted with anger. Before Walt could ask her what was wrong, she grabbed an old-fashioned newspaper from the nearest table and hurled it at him. The scalding hot coffee he was holding slopped down his front.

"Thea! What the hell?" Walt yelped. He could feel the burn forming on his chest; the sodden fabric of his shirt clung to it.

"You're buying drugs from these low-lives now?"

Walt couldn't remember the last time he had seen her this angry. He was almost surprised that sparks weren't flying from her eyes. "It's not what you think," he said, mopping himself with a paper towel.

"I idolised you! Looking at you now, I can't for the life of me remember why."

That hurt.

"You used to care about helping people," she said, advancing on him. "But now, you're no better than the people we arrest. You'll do anything for a quick buzz and an easy lay."

"I'm not sleeping with anyone, and I'm no dope fiend," said Walt defiantly.

"You are a cop. The rules are simple—no blow, no booze, no brothels. If they catch you drinking and taking drugs and paying for sex—you're dead. Firing squad, dead. What about that isn't sinking into your thick skull?"

"I don't care!" The admission burst out of him before he could stop it.

Thea blanched, but before she could reply, Bill peeked his head into the canteen. "Thea?"

"What?" Thea snapped.

Bill's eyes widened in shock. He took in the obvious tension between the pair. "The captain wants a word."

"You'd better not keep her waiting," Walt said. Thea glared at him for a moment, then turned on her heel and left.

In the minutes that followed, Walt felt like dirt scraped off the bottom of someone's boot as he traded small talk with Bill to cover the awkward moment.

THE PAST
Three years ago...

Jupiter Jazz was Tenebrium's most popular and most exclusive club. Anyone who was anyone made it their business to be seen in the place, lest they lose their chic image. The exterior was composed of black glass spaced and stacked like tiles, each bordered by orb-shaped light bulbs that let off a warm buff coloured glow; they looked like vanity mirrors from Hollywood's long-forgotten Golden Age.

The interior was nothing short of opulent. It was a labyrinthine spectacle of glass and neon. It was a maze of mirrors that meant everything, and nothing, could be seen all at once. Booths were set out strategically, some with small personal bars and others surrounding the dance floor at the centre of the maze. The inside layout changed frequently, meaning even those who had found the dance floor once in a night may still have trouble finding it again.

Thea, in spite of her dislike of excess, liked the place; it wasn't somewhere she often ran into her judgemental colleagues, and luckily Torrez knew the owner. Apparently, they had had a "thing", and despite the end of their tryst, Torrez was still welcome "anytime" in the VIP section.

The booth they had chosen tonight was closer to the dance floor than they usually favoured, but Thea knew exactly why. Torrez was on the prowl.

He talked, joked, and laughed, always remembered whose round it was, and was completely attentive to the conversation, but his eye roved the dance floor looking for a paramour for one night only. It was for this reason that Thea was especially glad to have run into Bill and his husband, Amir.

Amir was a tall, slim man of Pakistani descent with a pointed nose and kind eyes. He was deaf, which would usually make visiting a club an annoyance for him as he preferred to lip read, but as Thea watched him and Bill on the dance floor, their arms around each other like they were the only two people in the world, she felt sure he was having a better night than she was.

"I see you eyeing me, Jolene," Torrez said out of the corner of his mouth; his eyes were focused on a handsome Black man with short hair and a six-pack that could be seen through his waistcoat.

"Don't call me that," said Thea flatly. "And I'm pretty sure the woman grabbing his dick is his fiancé—she's wearing a ring."

"Nice spot, Detective, but she's giving me the eye, too. Three's company," Torrez said with a wink. He flashed the couple his most dazzling smile, and it was most definitely appreciated.

"Please, Drew," Thea pleaded as the couple beckoned Torrez to join them. "I hate lying to Marielena."

"Because lying to Cleo is so much fun," said Torrez, firing up at once. Drinking often shortened his usually non-existent temper. "I'm a dog, I know that, but for me, it's just sex. What's your excuse?"

"Your 'it's just sex, it takes two to tango' shit doesn't fly with me. There is nothing wrong with being promiscuous if everyone involved is on the same page—"

"Everyone is. Anyone I'm with knows exactly what I want from them, and I know what they want from me."

"No, they aren't. You're married, you don't get to be just you, and Marielena didn't sign up for this."

"Don't talk to me like you're better than me."

"You're right," Thea muttered. "I'm a mistress. There is no 'better' here."

All the anger faded from Torrez's face.

"I'm sorry, Querida."

"Don't apologise. You're right."

"It's not the same," Torrez said, leaning closer.

"But it is. It really is. What we are doing is wrong, but..."

"Do you love him?"

Thea didn't answer. She didn't need to. They both knew the truth.

"Does he know?" asked Torrez, ignoring the couple who were trying to regain his attention.

"God, I hope not."

"Thea," he said sympathetically.

"It's complicated. He was my teacher, my mentor, my boss, my partner and now—" Thea shook her head. "Now, I don't know what he is."

"Complicated."

"Complicated." Thea nodded in agreement.

After a quiet moment, Torrez let out a low chuckle.

"What?"

"You used to hate each other," he said as if it was unfathomable now.

"He called me 'Rookie' for a solid six months. Refused to use my name until I'd earned my badge." Thea smiled at the memory, not because it was pleasant, but because it was like remembering another life.

"That man's an asshole."

"Yup." Thea laughed. "I'm gonna scram. You do whatever you want. If anyone asks, I'll tell them you were with me. Tell Bill and Amir I said 'bye'."

"You sure?" Torrez asked, taking her hand and giving it a reassuring squeeze. "Four's a crowd."

Thea drained her glass and took her coat from the back of her chair. "Be good." She kissed Torrez on the cheek.

When Thea glanced back on her way to the door, Torrez had already joined the couple on the dance floor. He was sandwiched between them, his arms around the handsome Black man, kissing him passionately while the fiancé had her hand down the front of his trousers.

REPRIMAND

The captain's office was a classy affair in tones of deep brown and rich red. Betty sat behind her expansive Dfrêne-style desk with her arms folded as Thea entered.

"You wanted to see me, Captain?"

"Sit down."

Thea sat down in the chair opposite, unable to shake the feeling she had been summoned to the principal's office.

"Are you all right?" Captain Charles asked, showing genuine concern.

"I'm fine, ma'am," Thea lied. In truth, she was still reeling from her encounter with Walt. The captain gazed at Thea appraisingly. "Hundreds of years since Emily Davidson, and women like you and me still have to fight tooth and nail for a place in this world."

"I'm not sure I'm following, Captain."

"You remind me of myself at your age. You're young, you're brash, and you feel like you have a lot to prove," said the captain smiling slightly.

"I don't have anything to prove," Thea said, firing up at once.

"That's my point exactly. You're still young, but you're a woman, and you certainly aren't green. What you did today was reckless, and you know it," the captain said sternly. Thea had been waiting for this. "We never go in alone. Where was Walt?"

"Medicorum, as per your request. I only went to Ward Eight to interview Mr Pickford," said Thea without a beat. "Had I suspected that I would end up in a physical altercation, I wouldn't have gone alone. It was a miscalculation on my part."

The captain raised an eyebrow and surveyed Thea through narrowed eyes, it was clear she suspected there had been more at play. She wasn't the captain of the detective squad for nothing. "Things went your way today. They won't always."

The captain stood. She moved over to an impressive carved sideboard and poured herself a glass of water from the cooler that sat on top of it.

"Trying to cut back on the coffee," she said absently. "Would you like anything?" Thea shook her head. Betty inhaled deeply before ploughing on, "We're cutting Benjamin Pickford loose."

"That is...No! No way!" Thea was blindsided.

"The order came from above," the captain continued quickly. "It's out of my hands."

"What about the ghouls? They were—are people. They are someone, somewhere's family."

"I understand your need to catch the bad guy on this one, after what happened to your sister; I really do, but..."

"This has nothing to do with that," said Thea, needled by the mention of Cora.

The captain sighed and sat back down behind her desk. "It's been two years since her disappearance, Thea. Out of respect for you, I haven't closed the case, but it's beyond cold. I'm not blind to the similarities here. This case, it must have opened some old wounds. I'm not telling you to give up hope; I'm not even telling you to stop investigating, but I am telling you that you have a job to do first and foremost."

"Taking a stand against forced prostitution isn't my job?" Thea said acidly.

"I'm going to be honest with you, and I'm sorry, but the DA doesn't care. He's far more interested in the Pleasure Quarter murders."

Thea signed and shook her head.

"Listen to me, Thea," the captain said imploringly. "Play this right. Mr Pickford has friends in high places, it would seem, but more than likely, the DA wants the collar for himself. It's nearly election season, after all. You have to be smart. Toe the line until you see an opportunity. You'll catch Benjamin Pickford. People like him always slip. Just make sure you're there when he does. Watch him, but for now, let him go."

The battle here was already lost. "Understood," said Thea, far from finished with Benny.

"This job is a thankless one. It will consume you if you let it. You're a great detective. I'd hate to see that happen."

Thea nodded and got to her feet.

"Be careful out there."

"I will," Thea said, leaving the office and closing the door behind her.

HOW TO LOSE FRIENDS

Having finally managed to politely excuse himself from Bill, Walt made his way to the bathroom on the twenty-eighth floor. It was rarely frequented and rather rundown. The grey-green tiles were marked with graffiti, and many of the stall doors were hanging off their hinges. It would have been more at home in a high school than at a police station.

Walt's hands shook as he splashed his face with cold water. He stared in the mirror at his red-eyed visage as if hoping to find answers in his reflection—none came to him.

Hating himself as he did it, Walt dug around in his coat pocket for his hip flask. Pulling it out of his pocket, he fumbled the cap open and brought it to his lips. He took a long swig savouring the burn in the back of his throat. He was about to take another gulp when the door to the bathroom was pushed roughly open. Walt tried quickly to hide the flask from view, but it was too late; Torrez had seen it.

"Go right ahead. You're no use to me when you got the jitters."

Obstinately, Walt took a long draft before shoving the flask back into his inside jacket.

He could see Torrez watching him as he pulled some drops from his pocket and dripped them into his right eye first, then the left. "Don't look at me like that," Walt said, blinking rapidly. "I get enough shit from Thea."

"Then maybe you should listen to her. That particular torch is gonna burn you." Torrez crossed his arms over his chest.

"You need something, Torrez?" said Walt impatiently.

"I've got a bone to pick with you."

"Oh, yeah? And why's that?"

"Two ends of the supply chain, Benny Pickford and Dill Kelly both have a cop as a client. Now, Benny, he straight up told me you tried to buy drugs from him, a lot of them. I'd bet money, that if pressed, Dill would say the same. What do you think?" Torrez spoke with the arrogance of someone who already knew they'd won. "Poor Thea, her hero is well and truly gone, isn't he?"

Lunging forward, Walt grabbed Torrez by the lapels and thrust him hard against one of the long mirrors in the bathroom. It shattered on impact. "Don't talk to me about Thea," Walt growled, their noses inches apart. "How do you think she will react when she finds out you're dirty?"

Torrez smiled, he had wanted a reaction, and he'd got one. "Shady deals are part of my job. Out of the two of us, who do you think she trusts more these days? I'm not worried."

Walt disregarded this. "Have you taken this to the captain?"

"Not yet," said Torrez.

"Whatever you have, delete it," said Walt, slamming Torrez into the wall again.

"The hookers and booze, I get..."

"You are going to forget about it, Torrez. Or we are going to have a much less friendly conversation." Walt released Torrez and stalked from the room, a perfect storm inside his mind.

12A

The TPD lobby was a beautiful chalcedony cavern with geometric accents.

Benny stood, fully dressed, in front of Thea, waiting impatiently to have his handcuffs removed. It had been with a vindictive smile that Thea had travelled to work that morning, having left Benny to stew overnight in the cells, and it was with a subtle smirk that she removed his handcuffs.

Thea leaned over the reception desk and grabbed a thin glass plate tablet which she thrust at Benny. "Sign here." Rubbing his wrists, he did so.

"I told you, you were never gonna lock me up," Benny gloated.

"Yeah, then you sang like a canary."

"You still don't got me."

"Maybe not," said Thea smiling at the expression on Benny's face. "But that doesn't mean I can't confiscate funds."

"What?"

"Section 12a of the Tenebrium Criminal Code— 'any and all funds gained through illegal activity or in its proximity can be reclaimed by law enforcement as property of the city'."

"Nice try. My business is legit," said Benny, regaining his self-assured smile.

"Is it? Harbouring ghouls outside the SubLevel is a crime. Congratulations, Benny, you're broke." It wasn't her finest moment, but damn if it didn't feel good.

Benny stepped in so close to Thea that they would have been nose to nose had he not been nearly a foot taller than her. "I'll get you, bitch," Benny growled, looming over Thea.

Thea stared him down, daring him to make a move, but he didn't. Benny shoved the tablet back at her and walked away. "Stay out of trouble," she called after him.

"You know you just painted a target on your back, right?" the receptionist behind the counter said as Thea handed back the glass tablet. She smiled broadly and walked away.

VIRTUAL EVIDENCE

The vindictive and petty happiness Thea felt as a result of her small victory over Benjamin Pickford was short-lived. It was quickly replaced by a feeling of aimlessness. With her best lead in the wind and unlikely to surface any time soon, regardless of what the captain said, Thea had exhausted all avenues of investigation. What was she to do now? She couldn't give up; she wouldn't.

The case had struck a chord with her in a way that she couldn't ignore. The sheer brutality and exploitation of the murders ensured that she wouldn't rest until they were solved. Not to mention the fact that the victims were around the same age as her sister. They all had the same type of job and frequented the same places, they had all been vulnerable in the same way, and Thea detested those who preyed on the weak.

It occurred to Thea as she rode the elevator back up to the bullpen, that the only thing she could do was go over everything they had, from the beginning, and hope that she found some clue, some new piece of evidence that could lead to a culprit.

She rode the elevator past the detectives' office all the way up to the two hundred and fifty-seventh floor. When the elevator stopped, it caused her stomach to jolt uncomfortably.

The doors opened into a narrow, clinically white hallway. It was so bright it was almost painful to look at. There was a single door at the end of the corridor. It was a gleaming polished red. A slim black glass sign on the wall above read: "VIRTUAL EVIDENCE".

Thea walked quickly to the door, hoping no one else was using the VR suite. She was pleased to find it empty.

The Virtual Evidence room looked like a large empty warehouse, glossy and impossibly white. Thea raised her hand in mid-air, and as if summoned by the proximity of her fingers, a keypad appeared. Thea typed in her code and waited.

TENEBRIUM

"Detective Thea Williams. No active cases," said the cool, monotone voice of the computer system.

"Not possible," said Thea, re-typing her code.

"Detective Thea Williams. No active cases," the computer repeated. Thea typed in another code. "Displaying last archived footage," the computer droned.

Instantly the room transformed into the church crime scene. Thea stepped forward and watched her virtual self enter the church and speak to Bill. "Nothing traceable. No witnesses," the virtual Bill said, shaking his head.

The real Thea knelt down to examine the flapper's body more closely as the virtual one was joined by a virtual Torrez. The real Thea ignored their conversation. She couldn't stop staring at the wound in the woman's skull, morbid perhaps, but there was something not quite right about it. The spatter pattern was wrong, it was difficult to tell because of the large pool of blood that had formed around the body by the time they had arrived, but the tiniest of flecks that had not been engulfed by it seemed to imply something had exploded out the way, not in the way.

Squinting, Thea noticed a tiny crescent-shaped indentation at the flapper's temple. It was strange, she thought, that that had not appeared on the autopsy report. It wasn't much, but it was something.

It was with a renewed sense of purpose that Thea made her way to the morgue. She peered through the small glass window in one of the double doors; the medical examiner was nowhere to be seen.

Thea sidled into the room. "Flynn? You here, Doc?" she called just in case. There was no reply.

Sure she only had a small amount of time before Flynn returned, Thea crossed quickly to his computer. Unlike her desk, he was graced with a large glass screen depicting the TPD emblem, underneath which were the words "RESTRICTED ACCESS". There was a keypad on the desk; Thea typed in her code. "Detective Thea Williams. Access denied," came the computer's voice once more. Thea wasn't altogether surprised; she tried another code. "Detective Walter James. Access denied."

Thinking quickly, Thea rifled through the papers on Flynn's desk. It always surprised her how some of the older detectives also liked to work "old school" with good old-fashioned paper.

About to give up her search, Thea noticed a large coffee mug on the shelf above the desk, next to a picture of Flynn's disappointed looking wife. Thea flipped the mug over and was gratified to find yet another relic from the past; a post-it note with a six-digit code sticking to the bottom.

"Idiot."

Excitement bubbling in her stomach, Thea typed the code. "Senior Medical Examiner Cecil Flynn. Access granted." Elated, Thea scrolled through the files until she found what she was looking for, but when she tried to open the file, "Security level raised, please enter a unique passcode."

"Computer," Thea said, touching her tragus implant. "Tell me the file numbers for the last three bodies brought in."

"Not listed. Manual search required."

Ahhhmmmmm.

A faint moan flitted through the vents in the room marked "COLD STORAGE", setting Thea instantly on edge.

She pulled her gun from her belt and moved cautiously to the door. In her excitement and single-mindedness, she hadn't noticed that it was ajar. She peered through the gap, holding her gun tightly, ready if it was needed. She was repulsed by what she saw.

Flynn had his back to her, half leaning over the corpse of a dead woman. His left hand fondled the dead woman's breast, his right shoulder jerked repeatedly, his trousers and underwear around his knees.

Pulling the door wide, Thea marched into the room and grabbed Flynn by the back of his lab coat and pulled. He stumbled backwards. Caught in his trousers, Flynn was unable to stop himself; he fell to the ground, landing in a crumpled heap. He tried to cover himself, but his left hand was stuck in his rumpled coat.

"I knew you were a creep, Flynn, but this…" Thea said, towering over him.

"Detective Williams…I—" Flynn spluttered, reaching up to touch Thea's arm.

"Touch me with that hand, and you lose it." Flynn dropped his hand at once. "Who revoked my clearance for the church Jane Doe?"

"I did," said Flynn. He looked close to tears.

"Why?"

"The order came from above."

"How high?"

"All the way up."

"The rest of the files? Photos? Samples taken from the scenes? Autopsy reports?"

"Classified. There's nothing I can do."

"Shit." Thea turned away from Flynn. She needed a moment to think; she also couldn't stomach the sight of him exposed and pathetic, his perversions laid bare. "You disgust me," Thea said, turning back and kneeling so they were eye to eye. "You are a vile creature. Castration? Too kind. Now, this can go one of two ways for you. Whatever you find, you bring it to me first. I don't care how you do it; write it in tea leaves if you have to."

"But—"

"You're already playing with only half the deck. You come to me with whatever you find, from now on, or I go straight to the captain. Understand?"

Flynn nodded, looking thoroughly miserable. Thea was not keen on the idea that he was not going to be punished or the fact he would still be allowed access to his porn of choice, but she couldn't see any other way of keeping herself involved in the investigation. She would never say it to Flynn, but she wasn't entirely sure that his behaviour was a firing offence.

A ROCK AND A HARD PLACE

Walt had no choice. Things were unravelling. Someone was going to find out his secret. He had to do something. He had to tell Thea before someone else did. This would impact her. If he was caught, there was no way anyone would believe that she didn't know.

Their relationship was strained, to say the least. The space between them was filled with things that should have been said and so many things that shouldn't, but their affair was still the gossip of the office. People still looked at them whenever they were together, with that subtle glint in their eye that said, "We know."

But how could he tell her? How could he tell her that he had been lying to her for nearly two years? Would she understand the reason he had done all the questionable things he had been forced to do in the name of doing what was right? Or would she finally and forever eject him from her life? Deep down, he knew the latter to be true, but maybe, just maybe, she would understand.

Walt touched his tragus implant. "Computer, locate Detective Williams."

"Detective William is in the Morgue," said the computer in his ear.

Walt couldn't imagine what she'd be doing in there with autopsy reports and case files accessed easily at their desk terminals, but he made his way there, nonetheless.

When Walt arrived at the morgue, he could hear a commotion inside. The door to cold storage was open. Keeping his distance, he listened as Thea confronted the medical examiner. He smiled approvingly as she threatened to out him. She hadn't always had an edge; that had come later.

Moments after, Thea came marching out of the morgue, nearly colliding with him. She didn't even break stride. "We need to talk," Walt called as she walked away.

"Not now," she said without looking at him.

Walt let her go. If he had any chance of keeping her on side, she needed to be in a better mood than this.

He knew Thea wouldn't like him acting the white knight, but he couldn't help himself. Walt swept into the morgue, his long coat billowing. The door to cold storage was still open, and he could see Flynn getting to his feet and pulling up his trousers.

The M.E. jumped as Walt came marching towards him. "You betray her, I'll kill you myself. And if I catch you doing anything but examining bodies in here, I'll feed you dick first to the ghouls." Walt nearly laughed at the look on Flynn's face; he appeared to be near fainting.

Satisfied that he had made his point, Walt left.

PARENTING

Thea was barely aware of what she was doing as she demanded a transporter from Toby, the garage clerk. "Business or pleasure?" they asked, unfazed.

"Anything you have."

Toby handed her a hexagonal button reminiscent of an old British fifty pence piece. The police Jonks looked like prohibition-era cars, the only noticeable difference being that they floated a good foot off the ground and didn't have wheels. The insides, however, were ultra-high-tech.

Getting inside the nearest one, Thea placed the button in the centre of the steering wheel. The engine purred into life, and the Jonk floated slightly higher off the ground.

Without so much as a thank you to Toby, Thea zoomed out of the garage and joined the Slipstream Highway.

The District Attorney's building was hugely tall and thin. Geometric, like a rough shard of silver hematite, the building was beautiful.

Thea didn't trouble herself with the parking garage when she arrived. She landed the Jonk on the pavement right in front of the main entrance, much to the anger and chagrin of the security guards posted there.

Holding her badge out in front of her as if it produced a forcefield, Thea barged through the crowds of security and workers, and made her way to the DA's private elevator.

The elevator opened into an elegant waiting area that, in Thea's opinion, screamed wasted money. A stunning secretary sat behind a smooth desk. Ignoring the woman, Thea crossed to the door marked "H. Williams, District Attorney."

Flustered, the secretary got to her feet and moved as quickly as her tight dress would allow to intercept Thea. "DA Williams is not receiving at the moment, ma'am," she said in a sensual voice that had absolutely no effect on Thea.

"He'll see me."

"He's in a private meeting."

"Not anymore."

Thea sidestepped the helpless secretary and flung the door wide.

Thea's father, District Attorney Harold Williams, was sitting in his chair behind his desk, a woman straddling his lap. While they both appeared to be fully clothed, Thea had no illusions about what was happening.

Harold was unperturbed by the interruption, in fact, he smiled as if glad to see Thea. "Leave us for a moment, my darling," he muttered into the ear of his date. Straightening her skirt, the woman stood.

For something to do, Thea looked around the room. It was as she remembered; dark and filled with expensive leather furniture. Priceless artworks adorned every wall. When she risked a glance at her father, the woman was walking towards the door, her eyes downcast, and Harold was zipping up his fly. "I wasn't expecting you," he said, smiling genially.

"Clearly," Thea scoffed.

"But I'm glad you're here. We need to talk."

"You took away my security clearance," Thea said, shutting down whatever conversation her father had hoped to have.

"No, I put a dangerous case out of your reach," Harold said evenly.

"That's not for you to decide."

"The hell it isn't. I'm your father," said Harold, firing up at once.

Thea knew his temper only too well, though he liked to hide it from his peers.

He closed his eyes for a moment, composing himself. "I swear to you, my people are doing everything they can to catch the killer," he went on smoothly. "But you must leave this alone now. It's dangerous. I've already lost one daughter."

"Don't you dare," spat Thea, overcome by a wave of anger that matched her father's. "Don't even say her name. Not to me. You couldn't even be bothered to come to her memorial. You don't get to use her as an excuse."

"Pressing matters needed my attention," said Harold, completely unabashed.

"This is my case. Nobody cares about these people, but I do. Just because they work in the Pleasure Quarter, it does not make them any less human. They deserve justice, too."

"You'll receive a strike, Thea."

"First time for everything," Thea shot back.

"True, your career could survive the fallout from this," Harold said slyly. "But could Walter's? I've heard he has used up all his strikes. Another toe out of line, and it's the firing squad for him."

"Is that a threat?"

"No, my dear," continued Harold in a placating tone that Thea saw right through. "It's a warning. I heard about today. Anything could have happened to you. I just want you to be safe."

"Bullshit," Thea said bluntly. "You want the collar for yourself, and you thought I wouldn't put up a fight. But unlike you, I haven't forgotten that it's my job to protect people."

"I never planned for you to follow me, to serve at such a young age," Harold patronised. "But you were stubborn, headstrong. Still are, it seems."

"I didn't follow you," said Thea, affronted. "You don't serve—you're the DA. You're a glorified politician, and the only thing you protect is your bank balance."

"Thea, I am your father. You will show me respect."

"Call it like it is. You want the arrest. It's election season."

"I am doing what's best for you, and I will hear no more of it. I love you; I just want you to be safe," said Harold as if that settled it.

"Say 'Hi' to Mom when you're done here."

"We have no secrets, she and I. You could come home, you know."

"I'll pass."

"Thea."

"Let's not, Dad. You've done quite enough parenting for one day."

Thea left the office without giving her father a chance to reply. Back in the waiting room, her father's paramour was sitting delicately as if waiting for a meeting. "He's all yours," Thea called to her.

SPIRALLING

French 75 was a beautiful speakeasy. The walls were bare brick, and the tables were made from old wooden beer barrels topped with chrome. A jazz singer with a feather in their hair and a tasselled dress sang softly in the corner.

It was one of Walt and Thea's old stomping grounds. They may have parted ways, but both ended up there when they had been victim to bad days. Thea called that feeling "the jazz blues", Walt smiled at the memory.

He was sitting at a corner table nursing a coffee he had made Irish. Thea sat at the bar. She hadn't noticed him where he sat in the moody darkness.

"I'm sorry, Detective," the put-upon bartender was pleading. "You're wearing your badge—I can't serve you."

Walt watched as Thea pulled her badge roughly from her belt and stowed it in her pocket. "What badge? Tequila, please."

Unable to argue, the bartender poured a healthy measure of amber liquid into a glass and passed it over to Thea, who drained it in one long swallow.

"Practising what you preach, I see," Walt said, sliding into the seat beside her.

"Rough day." She didn't look at him.

"How rough?"

Thea raised a hand and beckoned the put-upon bartender, who refilled her glass without comment.

"Slow down. You haven't had a drink in years," Walt said. Thea ignored him.

"The DA took my clearance, took our clearance, for the Pleasure Quarter murders." She sounded tired and world-weary. So often, she appeared older than her twenty-eight years.

"Money talks, I guess, and so do voters. But there's plenty of good to be done in this town."

"I lost today." Thea drained her second glass.

"This is about Cora, isn't it? She's gone, Thea. You have to move on," Walt said sagely.

"As long as it doesn't affect my work, the captain is willing to look the other way while I investigate," said Thea resolutely.

"Is that what you want me to do? Look the other way?"

"I do it for you every day," Thea said pointedly.

"You're letting your sister's disappearance consume you," said Walt seriously.

"Am I." It wasn't a question. "And how are you coping with the death of your wife?" Walt didn't say anything; he just looked at her. He supposed he had deserved that. "My father knows something about what happened to Cora," Thea ploughed on. "I'm not letting this one go just yet. But you should. Going against the DA would mean your last strike."

"I'm not leaving you to deal with this shit alone."

"I don't need you to protect me." Something passed between them as they looked at one another. Thea turned away and signalled the bartender for another drink.

"I know. But I want to." Before he knew what he was doing, Walt raised a hand and touched Thea's face softly, rubbing his thumb over her cheek. She looked unsure. Walt leaned in; he couldn't stop himself. Their lips touched for the briefest of blissful moments before Thea pushed him away. "Fuck you," she said, getting to her feet and pulling on her coat.

"I know I've—"

"Fuck. You."

"I'm sorry, I shouldn't have done that." It was too late. She was halfway to the door.

Walt drained the newly filled glass, dropped some credit chips on the counter and followed Thea out.

It was pouring outside. The cobbles were slick. Thea was only a metre or two ahead. "Thea, wait," Walt called to her.

She turned around immediately; she looked close to tears. "I've had enough," she said almost to herself. "This apathetic, self-destructive spiral that you're on is exhausting to watch."

"I'm sorry."

"You're the one who slammed that door shut, not me."

"I know," he said quietly.

"I'll see you…whenever you show up next."

"I'll walk you home," said Walt, taking a step towards her.

"Don't bother." Thea turned her back on him and, bowing her head against the rain, started her journey.

Walt watched her out of sight, then turned to make his own way home. Whether it was physically or metaphorically, he felt that they were always going in different directions, and there was nothing either of them could do to change it. The best thing they could do for each other was to move on. But Walt couldn't. He was trapped between what was right and what he wanted.

Walt wound his way through the cramped streets. Shadows passed behind him. He peered over his shoulder. Figures loomed out of dark alleyways and alcoves.

They were Onyx Legion soldiers, but why they were watching him, he wasn't sure, or particularly keen to find out.

Walt quickened his pace.

The buzz from his tragus implant caused him to jump as Torrez's unimpressed voice sounded in his ear. "I cleared those records for you, asshole. Lucky for you, the brass doesn't want to admit we picked up Pickford. I don't know what your deal is, but you are in deep waters, my friend."

"Torrez," Walt sighed with relief, continuing to walk. "Thank you."

"And Walter? You put hands on me again—I'll beat the shit out of you."

"Fair enough."

A click in his ear told Walt that Torrez had hung up.

Walt walked on. At the end of the road, three Onyx Legion soldiers blocked his path. Walt considered turning away and finding another route home or even calling for a Jonk taxi, but the soldiers who had been lurking in the shadows had stepped into the light of the street. They blocked all exits.

Walt pulled his badge from his belt and held it up as he came level with the three masked soldiers at the end of the street. They raised their guns as he approached.

"You're breaking curfew."

"Easy there, boys," Walt said, showing his hands and the badge held therein.

"Best be on your way then, Detective," said the tallest soldier, stepping aside to create the narrowest of paths for Walt. As the soldier had surely intended, Walt had to squeeze between him and his nearest comrade. Walt could sense the danger in the situation. Once clear of them, he quickened his pace and didn't look back.

COMPUNCTIONS

Thea's apartment was cold when she arrived home, soaked to the bone. Her skin tingled as it always did when exposed to the acidic yellow rain. She shivered as she removed her coat and headed straight for the soothing heat of the shower.

Misted glass separated the bathroom from the main living area. The room was square and entirely black, the floor, the tiles and the porcelain. Thea slipped out of her sodden clothes and stepped into the large shower. "Hot, steam, high pressure."

Hot water erupted around her, warming her to the core. No longer cold, Thea couldn't push away thoughts of what had happened at French 75.

It had been a chaste kiss, filled with none of the passion she and Walt had exuded before their lives had fallen apart. It'd had a desperate quality to it that went both ways. She had tried everything to stop feeling the way she felt about Walt, but he was under her skin.

She had kissed him more times than she could count in the past, sweetly, passionately, lovingly, and even though it had been a long time since they had kissed last, it had felt, for the briefest of seconds, like they had never parted— and that was exactly the problem. Nothing had changed. The two years since they had last been intimate seemed non-existent. Far from being reopened, the old wounds had never really closed. But much, much more than infidelity stood between them now.

Thea remembered how Walt had looked at her after Cleo was dragged away. Something had changed behind his eyes. He had pushed her away after that, and he had been cruel about it. To have kissed her like that was a betrayal; it was a moment of weakness that set them right back to where they were.

Thea rested her head on the cold tile. The whole situation was such a mess. She felt ashamed of herself. She missed Walt the way he had been, carefree and courageous, quick-witted and quick to laugh, sexy, and free of the burden of crippling guilt. To hope would get her nowhere, that Walt was gone. He had been replaced by a Walt that never laughed, and showed little care for the job that had defined him, an addict drowning in self-loathing.

With that gloomy thought, Thea stepped out of the shower and readied herself for bed. Sleep, when it eventually came, was fitful and restless.

THE PAST
Three years ago...

Thea knew he was watching her. Walt hadn't moved from the floor next to the coffee table where they had made love. He pulled himself into a sitting position, leaning against the couch with one arm behind his head and watched her unashamedly as she sashayed into the bathroom, his enjoyment evident.

She had barely started the water in the shower when he appeared at the door. He watched her, his eyes bright, as she stepped under the torrent.

Steam blurred the glass as she revelled in the feel of the water on her electrified skin. It wasn't long before he joined her. He slipped into the shower behind her as she was wetting her hair. Walt pulled her close to him, her back to his chest as he kissed her neck while his hands caressed her body. Thea turned to face him, bringing his lips to hers. He wrapped his arm around her waist; his free hand found her face and stroked her cheek.

Thea brought her hand up to hold his.

The effect was immediate; it was like she had been doused in cold water. She felt his wedding ring under her fingers, and guilt overtook her desire for him.

He dropped his hand, knowing what had bothered her.

She turned away from him, the moment lost.

THE SWORD OF DAMOCLES

Walt stepped quickly inside his apartment and closed the door, shaking the rain out of his hair as he did so.

A light clicked on behind him.

Walt didn't turn immediately. He strained his ears, trying to get a sense of the danger. Out of the corner of his eye, he could see a figure. He wondered if he could unholster his gun without being caught. Slowly and carefully, Walt reached across his body to his shoulder holster.

"There's no need for that. Set it down on the side," said the voice of Thea's father.

Sighing, Walt turned and placed the gun on the counter near the door. Harold Williams was sitting in Walt's favourite armchair on the west side of the large open room, his legs crossed at the knee. He hadn't come alone either.

Two Onyx legion soldiers were standing beside Walt's kitchen island near his dining table, another two stood next to his bookcases on the wall opposite, and the remaining two flanked Harold. Walt could see Thea in her father's face, and he didn't like it. They had the same pale skin, and his brown eyes with the subtlest hint of gold were so similar to hers, that Thea could have been looking at him. That was where the similarities ended as far as Walt was concerned, however, where Thea was warm and caring, her father was cold and calculating.

"Would you like a drink?" Harold said, pouring himself a generous measure from the crystal decanter that sat on a spindly-legged table next to the armchair.

"You're gonna offer me my own liquor?" Walt stepped further into the room, making sure to keep all six soldiers in sight.

"As I'm sure you know, my daughter is very stubborn."

Walt let out a short, sharp laugh.

"Indeed," Harold continued. "I'm trying to keep her safe, Walter. I know that's what you want, too." Harold paused to give Walt a chance to speak; when he didn't, "She's deeper than she knows into some very dangerous business. Make sure she leaves the Pleasure Quarter murders to my people, and I'll wipe your strikes. The proverbial sword of Damocles will no longer be hanging over your head."

"And if I don't?"

"I'm going to be frank," said Harold leaning forward in his chair. "I don't like you. You took advantage of my daughter."

"Excuse me?"

"You were her mentor, her teacher. She looks up to you, and that clouds her judgement. You are too old for her, too broken," Harold looked Walt directly in the eye when he said the last.

"Thea may be young, but she's quick, smart, intuitive, a real bearcat, and she's more woman than any dame I've met," Walt said defiantly. "She puts her mind to something, there's no changin' it. She won't listen to me—or you. If you know something about what happened to Cora, you owe it to the daughter you still have to tell the truth."

"Neither of my daughters are your concern."

Harold raised a hand signalling his men. The two who were standing beside the bookshelf and one of the soldiers standing in the kitchen moved forward. The trio pulled long batons from their belts; Walt recognised them instantly as stun rods. He hated stun rods.

Walt took off his coat and threw it aside, unbuttoned his waistcoat and rolled up his sleeves. He moved into the clear space between his couch and the wall of bookcases and took up a boxing stance.

The first soldier was taller than his fellows and broader by half. A bruiser. He sauntered lazily towards Walt. When in range, he swung his stun rod like a baseball bat aimed at Walt's head. Walt weaved deftly underneath the blow and delivered a heavy hit to the body, followed by a thunderous hook to the face. The bruiser was knocked out cold.

The second and third soldiers, one slim and one shifty, looked at each other. They circled like wolves in opposite directions, searching out an opening.

The tension was causing adrenaline to pulse through Walt's body, but that was just fine by him.

Slim was over eager as he closed the distance between Walt and himself. Walt jammed his attempt to jab him with the stun rod by sheer proximity, simultaneously striking with his elbow. The blow caught Slim on the jaw and sent him reeling back. Shifty moved forward to assist. As Walt raised his fist to strike at Slim, Shifty jabbed Walt viciously between the shoulder blades with his stun rod.

Walt tumbled forward into Slim, the jolt causing his muscles to seize painfully. Walt used the momentum to grab hold of Slim and, torquing his hips, throw him bodily at Shifty. Shifty ducked unsteadily out of the way, and Slim collided forcefully with the wall and fell to the floor unconscious.

Walt advanced on Shifty, pressing his advantage. The soldier backed into the dining table. He grabbed a chair and slung it at the still advancing Walt, who caught it and brought it down in a devastating blow that sent Shifty to the land of nod.

Elanor Miller

There was a moment of stunned silence punctuated only by Walt's heavy breathing. The remaining soldiers rallied. They touched knuckles with themselves like boxers, causing their gloves to glow blue and sparks to fly. As a unit, they barrelled towards Walt.

The first soldier to reach Walt swung a heavy haymaker at Walt's body, but he was too fast for him and intercepted the blows with a much more precise jab-cross combo. The second soldier threw another heavy haymaker that Walt only just managed to slip before the final soldier was able to make contact.

His sparking gloves grazed Walt's hastily raised guard. The moment of connection sent a wave of electricity through Walt's body that threw him off his feet. Walt hurtled through the air colliding heavily with a bookcase and slumping to the ground.

Walt felt as though his heart had momentarily stopped beating. He could feel the burn forming on his forearms where the gloves had touched him. The stun gloves were deadly. He couldn't let them touch him again.

Realising the danger, Walt got shakily to his feet. The first soldier to attack was upon him in seconds; he aimed a kick at Walt's body. Walt caught his leg and hammered down on his knee hard. The soldier let out a yell that did not altogether mask the sickening crunch as his leg broke. Walt cast him aside and turned just in time to see the second soldier throw a careless hook. Walt blocked with his stinging forearm and retaliated with a heavier hook that sent the soldier reeling back. The final soldier had backed away, trying to gain some distance. He alone among his peers had kept his head.

Walt closed the gap between them at a run, catching the soldier by surprise. He grabbed him by the lapels and headbutted him in the face sending them both careening to the ground. The soldier's head snapped audibly against the concrete floor, and he moved no longer.

Dizzy, breathless, and seeing black spots, Walt struggled to get to his feet. The only remaining soldier kicked Walt savagely in the ribs, sending him back to the ground. The soldier lent down and dragged a lagging Walt to his feet. Face to face once more, he threw a relentless string of combinations at Walt, who parried desperately.

With Walt distracted by the deadly stun gloves, the soldier kicked him hard in the stomach, sending him hurtling into the wall.

Dazed, Walt saw the soldier step forward to deal the final, fatal blow. Walt slipped to the side, causing the soldier to miss. The power of his punch, combined with the gloves, embedded his fist in the concrete. Walt seized the opportunity and broke the trapped arm at the elbow by way of hyperextension. Then, without a beat, he grabbed the soldier's head and rammed it repeatedly into the wall. He stopped when he had no strength left. The soldier slid awkwardly down the wall leaving a bloody trail in his wake.

Battered and bleeding, sure it was broken ribs that were making it hard to breathe, Walt spat a mouthful of blood on the floor and turned to face Harold.

Harold was still sitting comfortably in Walt's chair. He looked at him impassively and perhaps, slightly impressed.

TENEBRIUM

"You gonna send someone to collect these?" said Walt, wincing as he inhaled. "I'm assuming you don't want me to call this in."

Walt leaned over and picked up a towel from the floor and slung it over his shoulder. "You can show yourself out."

"Convince her, Walter."

Smiling in spite of himself, Harold watched as Walt waved an unconcerned hand over his shoulder and limped out of the room. Moments later, Harold heard the sound of running water. He chuckled to himself as he stood and righted his suit jacket. He stepped over two of his men on the way to the door. In different circumstances, he thought, he might have liked Walter James.

CAUGHT

Torrez wrapped his coat tighter around himself against the crisp cold morning. He rubbed his hands together as he waited for Gin Ricky to make his coffee. He had an uneasy feeling in his stomach. He wasn't exactly the straightest arrow in the department, but tampering with evidence was a striking offence. His record was clean, and he'd like to keep it that way, thank you very much.

The problem was that he had a streak of loyalty in him. Granted, it was to Thea, not Walter, but Torrez was sure that if Walter was taken down, he would drag Thea down with him.

Gin Ricky cleared his throat, and Torrez turned just in time to see him putting his cup of coffee on the counter.

"How much?"

"On the house, with Mr Kelly's compliments."

They shared a meaningful look before Gin Ricky turned away and began to wipe the counter.

Torrez lifted the cup to see a small piece of paper hiding there. Torrez slipped it off the counter and moved away from the coffee stop. Sure that no one was nearby, Torrez unfolded the paper.

It was a handwritten list of names. This was the list Dill had promised him. Names of people who had bought or sold Quietus. Torrez scanned the list and saw a few of the usual and expected suspects. Right at the bottom of the list in capital letters was the one name he had been looking for and the one he had sincerely hoped wouldn't be there. "WALTER JAMES".

"You stupid son of a bitch."

YOUR MOVE

Thea wished she had put on a warmer coat as she patrolled The Quadrant alone. Once again, Walt had not turned up for work, and Torrez was busy with his own caseload. "Quad Duty" or a "Sub Shift" was widely recognised as a mild punishment. If a detective was asked to cover for the beat cops and patrol the Poor Quarter as opposed to solving cases, it was safe to say that they were on someone's "Shit List". Thea knew the whys of it and had no regrets.

As usual, The Quadrant was alive with activity. The many hawkers and peddlers were doing their best to attract the attention of those passing through on their way to the industrial district. Foot traffic was heavy, and Thea often had to squeeze through opportunistic gaps in the crowds.

It was with a sense of unease that Thea made her second pass of The Quadrant. There was something in the air that she couldn't quite put her finger on. The Onyx Legion soldiers seemed twitchy, and that never boded well.

"Thea," a voice called through the crowd.

Thea scanned the sea of people and spotted Walt limping towards her. He looked awful. His face was badly bruised. He had a large cut on his lip and one to match on his right cheek. Both of his eyes were blackened. The closer he got, she could see that he was holding his side and walking as if every step pained him.

"What the hell happened?" said Thea, taking him by the chin and turning his head side to side to examine the damage. Walt winced.

"Walked into a doorknob," he quipped weakly.

"You look like shit. Who did this?"

"It's nothing. Really. You'll be more pissed if you know."

Thea gazed upon Walt, dissatisfied.

"About yesterday..." Walt let the sentence trail off.

"Don't." Thea was not prepared for that conversation.

There was a moment's silence between them.

"Shall we?"

They had been patrolling for barely a moment when a shot rang out, piercing the early morning air. Thea set off at a run, following the direction of the sound; Walt limped behind.

"TPD! Get out of the way!" he bellowed as the hordes of people showed little intent to let them pass.

They found themselves at the gates to the SubLevel. Four legion soldiers were peering through the bars that kept the tunnel entrances separate from the Poor Quarter. The area was quiet. Far fewer people were passing by, and those that did kept their eyes resolutely on the ground. Three of the soldiers were laughing as one of them took pot-shots at a young male ghoul who was pulling at the bars.

The ghoul appeared to be so far gone he couldn't speak, but the pain in his eyes was unmistakable. "Aw, look at it. It's almost cute the way it growls. Like a dog in a bear trap."

Walt charged past Thea, but she ran after him and grabbed him by the arm, pulling him back. He yelped in pain. It appeared he had broken ribs on top of his other injuries.

"Get off me," Walt snarled. Thea didn't let go.

"You can't," she implored. "We patrol the streets, not the gate. That's military jurisdiction." Walt tried in vain to shake Thea off. "You could be executed for interfering with the Legion without a warrant," she said desperately.

Walt made yet another attempt to rid himself of Thea, but she clung on. "Look at what those scumbags are doing!" he said.

"If you want to arrest them, I will. But you better be prepared for the fallout," Thea said, letting go of his arm.

"You're right. Let's call for back-up and get a warrant."

Walt allowed Thea to lead him a small way away, then pushed her hard and sprinted off towards the gate. Thea collided painfully with a street vendor's cart and sank to the ground. Her ribs singing, she scrambled to her feet and chased after Walt.

When she caught up with him at the gate, he had his gun levelled to the back of the soldier who had been doing the shooting's head, and his fellows had their guns trained at Walt. "Call off your men," Walt barked.

"I can't do that. Next move is yours."

Without thinking about what she was doing, Thea ran forward. Thea put an arm over Walt's shoulder and around his neck and used the other to tug on his gun arm. She pulled him back so she could speak into his ear. "If you kill him, nothing changes except you end up dead, too."

"They are worse than any ghoul," said Walt in a pained voice that Thea felt in her chest.

"You can't help anyone if you're dead. You say you don't care if you live or die. Prove it then, pull the trigger and let the others gun you down. Or, we could leave now and come back in a position to do something." Thea was all but begging.

Walt didn't move. Then, he sagged slightly, leaning back and resting his cheek on the top of Thea's head. Slowly he lowered his gun. Thea let out a breath she hadn't been aware she was holding. "Let's go," she whispered.

"Ma'am—" one of the soldiers began, but he was cut off mid-sentence by Walt, who had thrown a heavy cross at his face. The soldier stumbled back, and his comrades cocked their guns and refocused their aim on Walt.

"That's some death wish you got there," the soldier said, dabbing his bloody lip.

"Back off, or I call Bastion and tell him exactly what his soldiers get up to at the gate."

The soldiers baulked at the mention of their commander.

"Come on," she added to Walt.

The soldiers didn't lower their guns, but they made no move to stop Walt and Thea as they backed away.

THE PAST
Two years ago...

"Did you find her?" Walt asked, getting to his feet as soon as Bastion entered the living room.

Bastion didn't say anything. He looked at Walt, standing amongst the chaos of the night before, wearing only a pair of trousers, with his own blood still coating his face and chest. He was worried about what his answer would do to the man. He and Walt were as good as brothers, he had known him all his life, but he had never seen him like this.

"You need to get yourself cleaned up. Your nose looks broken."

"Did you find Cleo?"

"We should sit."

"Tell me."

Heaving a deep sigh, Bastion said, "I tried to find her, but it's chaos out there. The Onyx Legion is stretched thin trying to round up everyone who took that fucking drug. Some of my guys grabbed her, but I swear to you, it wasn't on my orders."

"Where is she?" Walt advanced on Bastion, a slightly mad glint in his eye.

"I don't know for sure, but if she showed signs of addiction, she's in the SubLevel."

"How do we get her out?"

"We don't. And even if we could get to her, she's not her anymore. I'm sorry, buddy. She's gone."

"You're their commander. There must be something we can do. If you won't help me, I'll find her myself."

"It's not 'won't', it's 'can't'. There's nothing to be done. The mayor ordered a quarantine. I know you don't want to hear this, but she's gone, Walt."

"Get out," Walt said bluntly, turning his back on Bastion.

"I'm sorry."

"Get out!" Walt bellowed.

Worry over his oldest friend weighing heavily on his mind, Bastion turned and walked away.

Once outside, he used his Cicada to call Thea.

"Hello?"

"I know things are terrible right now, but he needs you."

RED

Thea was furious as she returned to patrolling The Quadrant. She was furious at Walt, at the Legion, and at the injustice of it all. As soon as they were out of sight of the gate, Thea separated from him. She needed a moment to think and calm down, or she was likely to add another bruise to his already crowded face.

"I'm sorry."

"You should be."

"They're scum."

"And we can't do anything about it because of you!" yelled Thea, unable to stop herself. "If we report them now, they report you. All you had to do was keep your cool, keep your head, but instead, you committed yet another strikeable offence. We've all lost things, Walt. You can't keep acting like this."

"I should have protected her, but instead, I was with you, and now I can't protect them either. I can't fix what I broke." All the fight seemed to leave Walt, and he appeared somehow smaller; even as he stood at his six-foot-something, he seemed diminished.

Thea turned away from him and let herself be engulfed by the crowd. How long could she allow herself to be handcuffed to a drowning man?

They patrolled in silence for the rest of the morning and into the afternoon. Thea was aware of Walt in her peripheral vision, but she was careful not to look at him. A welcome distraction came in the form of the food vendors who had set up shop around The Quadrant. Multiple carts were erected, side by side, all offering hot food, all of which smelled delicious. Thea had been tempted to order some Trdelník from a cart marked "The Czech Kitchen", but the queue around it was too long, and the ever-moving crowd kept pushing her forward.

A small someone brushed past her, and she felt a sharp pain in her side. "Ow," she said aloud, reaching forward to grab the arm of a bright red coat.

"Get off me, lady!"

It was the pickpocket she had stopped in the Pleasure Quarter outside Ward Eight. She was remarkably better groomed than when Thea saw her last, and her coat appeared new and, more importantly, warm, but there was still that inescapable air of neglect that all the street kids had.

"Here," Thea said, handing her a credit chip. "Use it to buy food, okay?"

The young thief snatched the credit chip and wrenched herself free from Thea's grip in one fluid motion before disappearing back into the sea of bodies.

Thea hadn't felt it at first, distracted as she was by the young pickpocket, but there was something warm and wet trickling down her ribs. She brought her hand to her side; her fingers came away bloody. Lifting her arm to inspect the damage, Thea saw a two-inch gash in her coat as if she had been stabbed with a short sharp blade.

She was starting to feel fuzzy when Walt noticed she had stopped walking. "Thea?"

"I'm okay," she said, waving him away. She made to close the gap between them, but her legs couldn't hold her weight, and her vision was blurring.

The last thing Thea saw before she fainted was Walt darting forward to catch her as the ground seemed to be rising up to meet her.

SUBSTANCE UNKNOWN

Thea was falling. Walt saw it in slow motion as if it was part of a ballet. He darted forward and caught her just before she hit the ground.

Keeping her in his arms, he knelt down. She was bleeding. Her skin was pale, and there was a slight sheen on her forehead. Her lips were parted softly, her breathing shallow. Walt touched the gash on her side as gently as he could. He brought his fingers to his lips and dabbed the blood on his tongue. He spat it out immediately. It tasted like acid, with a hint of spice. Poison.

Walt knew the hospital was no good. They would never make it in time. He got to his feet, holding Thea tightly to him and ran. He could feel panic trying to creep up on him, mingled with fear, but he pushed those thoughts away.

He ran in a blur, hardly aware of anything but Thea's limp weight in his arms. He ran far past his usual endurance, ignoring the screaming in his muscles, the throbbing of his head and the sharp stabbing pain in his side. His broken ribs threatened to break through the skin, but Walt didn't care.

When Walt arrived at Thea's apartment, who knew how many minutes later, he kicked the door open without breaking his stride. Inside, he carried Thea over to her wide couch and placed her down gently. She moaned groggily.

Walt dashed into her bathroom. He knew it had to be here somewhere. Crouching, he riffled through the cupboard under her sink, throwing things all over the floor in his haste to find what he searched for. Finally, wedged at the back of the cupboard behind the pipes, he found a MedKit. It was a stupid place for it, really, and if it hadn't been there...but it was. Breathing slightly more easily, he stood.

He had been so intent on saving Thea that he hadn't noticed them at first. But Walt saw them now. Two ghouls leered at him in the bathroom mirror, naked, with small circular discs on their temples that glowed a subtle blue.

Thea came to on the couch. She felt sick and heavy. Her nerves were on fire, they screamed at her, but she didn't have the energy to cry out. She felt weak. The warm wet patch at her side was growing. She was bleeding out.

A shadow moved in the corner of her vision. A ghoul was creeping towards her. It moved with the eerie roboticism of a wind-up toy. Thea tried to move, but her body wouldn't comply no matter how hard she willed it to.

She could hear the ghoul's ragged breathing now. Or was it her own? With an effort that would have had her screaming in agony if she could have, Thea managed to roll herself onto the floor, landing in the small gap between her coffee table and the couch.

The ghoul was close now, almost upon her. Thea used every ounce of determination she had, fuelled by the basest of desires to survive, to drag herself along the floor. She grabbed onto the runner on the coffee table by mistake. As soon as she pulled on the fabric, the contents of the table tumbled down on top of her.

The ghoul dropped to the floor like a sack of potatoes and began to crawl after her. A gnarled hand found her ankle and dragged her backwards. She reached out for anything that she could use for a weapon, and her hand found the heavy earthenware bowl her sister had given her.

SMASH.

It took Walt a moment to register what was happening to him. He felt his feet leave the ground. He felt the pain as something hard collided with his back, then it seemed to disappear. It was then he realised that he had been thrown through the misted glass window that separated Thea's bathroom from the main living area.

He landed heavily on a bed of broken glass, a thousand tiny needle-like pains forming a cacophony. But he had no time to worry about the latest in a long string of damages. He was on his feet before the first drop of blood-soaked his shirt.

The ghouls clambered through the hole left by Walt in the glass and set upon him again.

Thea kicked weakly as the ghoul clambered up her body. She felt its saliva land on her cheek as its crazed face drew level with hers. Using one hand at its neck to stop it from biting her, Thea used the other to swing the earthen bowl with all her remaining strength. It clattered with a dull *thunk* into the ghoul's temple, knocking it sideways.

This was her opportunity. With a huge effort, she clambered to her feet and stood over the ghoul. She lifted the bowl above her head and brought it down, hard. There was a horrendous cracking noise as the ghoul skull shattered, and it moved no more.

Unable to stand any longer, Thea fell backwards. She gasped for a breath that wouldn't come, and then darkness took her again.

Stepping over the battered corpse of the ghoul who had thrown him through the window, Walt dived for its partner. He managed to wrestle it into a chokehold, and with a tremendous effort, he snapped its neck.

Walt doubled over panting, he was finding it difficult to breathe, and his vision was spotty. He looked over to Thea. She was on the floor, a dead ghoul next to her. All pain and injuries forgotten, Walt dashed to the bathroom and retrieved the MedKit.

He dropped to his knees at Thea's side as he had done with Cleo the night she was dragged away. He put two fingers to her jugular. No pulse.

"No, no, no, no. Don't you dare. Don't you fucking dare."

Walt ripped the MedKit open and pulled out a lance-shaped chrome instrument with a digital display. He jabbed it into Thea's neck. "Analysing." The cold voice came through Walt's tragus implant.

"Come on, come on."

"Analysis complete. Substance unknown."

Walt had no idea what the correct antidote was, so he did the only thing he could think of. He loaded a large gauge needle with Adrenaline and stabbed it hard into Thea's chest.

Nothing happened.

"This isn't happening. This isn't happening. Don't do this to me, Thea. Please."

Still, nothing happened.

"Fuck, fuck, fuck."

A hopeless feeling of despair was spreading through Walt, numbing him to everything else. His chest ached like he'd been shot. He cradled Thea tightly to him, muttering pleas over and over again.

Walt's eyes stung as she lay lifeless in his arms, then as the realisation that she was gone hit him like a wrecking ball, tears fell unchecked, soaking his face. He rocked her back and forth, back and forth, begging her not to leave him, but no matter how hard he tried, he couldn't ignore the fact she was getting colder and colder.

Without warning, Thea sat bolt upright, dragging a gasping breath into her lungs. She spluttered into his chest as Walt held her to him, fresh tears of joy dripping into her hair.

THE PAST
Three years ago...

Walt couldn't remember the last time he had laughed so hard. His stomach hurt, and his ribs ached as he and Thea wandered aimlessly through the vibrant neon jungle of Tenebrium's streets. Music blared all around them and the drone of chatter fluttered by, completely ignored by them, who were so engrossed in each other. Walt felt like he was a teenager again, unable to wipe the grin from his face.

They reached a docking junction that allowed Jonks to park at street level, and Walt stopped dead. His face lit up as he eyed a beautiful transporter. It was red with black accents, and its aesthetic pseudo wheels were a bright gleaming silver.

"Oh man, oh God, oh man," he said, nearly dancing on the spot. "She is a thing of beauty."

"I'm sure we could rent one if you want," Thea said, grinning at his boyish glee.

"I don't want to rent one—I want to buy one!" he said, affronted.

"Nobody owns a Jonk anymore," She laughed incredulously.

"Look at the wheels, not a mark on 'em! Bet she drives like a dream," Walt said seriously, bending over to examine the rims.

"She? So, what are you gonna do? Have the only apartment in Tenebrium with a garage? Park it in your living room?"

"You're too young to understand; when I was a kid, this thing was a symbol. You had your own transporter, and you'd made it. My dad would go on and on about owning one of these beauties; he finally got one when I was eleven, and man, we would drive it everywhere. We upgraded every bit of that thing." Walt peered in the driver's side window. "Just look at that interior. Bet she could go zero to eighty in seconds. Convertible, too."

Walt turned to look at Thea. She was staring at him with a wide, unapologetic smile on her face that he couldn't help but mirror. "What?" he asked a little self-consciously.

"You're a dork! Who knew?"

"We are renting one. That's the only way you'll understand."

"Right now? It's two a.m.!"

"Hell yeah, right now."

Walt pulled Thea close and kissed her hard, his arms encircling her. "Come on," he said, taking her by the hand and pulling her over to the nearest Rental Portal. "We are going for a ride."

THE MORNING AFTER

"Yeah, this is dispatch. Whaddya need?"

"I need... Thea is..."

"Walt? That you? You okay, buddy?"

"Thea's hurt. It's bad. I need Medicus, and an ambulance, and every cop you got."

Six minutes later, Thea was pried from Walt's protesting arms. Her apartment was alive with activity. The Medicus arrived in an ambulance and immediately set to work. Officers, detectives—including Torrez, forensics, and grim-sweepers arrived and formed a crime scene where they meticulously catalogued evidence. Ten minutes after that, Thea crashed again.

Walt watched on in a kind of horrified daze as Thea's body jerked and contorted. The electricity from the defibrillator coursed through her, but showed no signs of having any effect.

Walt was dimly aware that everything hurt. In any other circumstances, he would be the one that was receiving medical treatment, but he found he didn't care about his injuries right now. Any pain was eclipsed by the sick feeling of fear in his stomach and the tearing sensation in his chest.

Torrez sat beside Walt on Thea's blood-stained couch. He was talking in a low, worried tone, but Walt wasn't taking in a single word.

"Walt. Walt. Walter." Torrez shook Walt by the shoulder. "I think you need to see a doctor, Cabron."

"I'm fine," Walt muttered absently, watching as the Medicus shocked Thea again.

"No, you're not."

"Not until I know Thea is okay."

A faint *beep* issued from the medical equipment the Medicus had brought. "We have a rhythm, but it's faint. We need to get her to a medical facility."

"What's going on?" Walt tried to get to his feet, but he couldn't quite coordinate his body. Torrez pulled Walt's arm around his shoulder and helped him stand.

The amount of effort that the manoeuvre cost them was hardly worth it. All they could do was watch as Thea was placed onto a hovering stretcher and guided to the doorway. "Wait. I'm coming with you," Walt called to one of the Medicus.

The woman was tall and lean with cropped hair and a look in her eyes that said she did not suffer fools gladly. When she spoke, however, it was in a gentle and almost apologetic tone. "I'm sorry, Detective James, but we have specific orders from the District Attorney not to allow you to accompany her."

"Fuck that. Just try and stop me."

"Walt, you can barely stand," Torrez muttered so only Walt could hear.

"You really think I'm going to stay here?"

"I don't think you have a choice. If I let go of you, you aren't standing anymore. You need a doctor. Hell, you need to go to medical services. You should be on a stretcher, too. You're only conscious out of sheer belligerence right now. We aren't finished here. There is nothing you can do for her. Don't let this be how her father gets you."

"We need to get going," the Medicus said, reminding Walt and Torrez that she was there. "Please don't try to stop us."

"Let them go. You can't help her there. Here, you can help me find who did it."

Walt gritted his teeth as he watched the Medicus take Thea away. He felt helpless, scared in a way he couldn't quite process. It was like he was standing on the edge of an impossibly high cliff.

"All right," Torrez said after a moment. "Take me through it."

"Watch it for yourself. Technically we're on duty. My chip recorded everything."

Torrez eased Walt back down onto the couch, then brought up the TPD database and began to search for the footage of what had transpired that evening.

Torrez used his Index to search through the TPD archive and, having found what he was looking for, projected the footage in mid-air. He watched it gravely, concentrating hard.

Walt couldn't bear to watch. The scene would be imprinted on his memory for as long as he lived. He didn't need to see it again. He felt increasingly uncomfortable as the footage neared its climax. He heard himself sobbing and uttering pleas to gods he didn't believe in, fully aware of just how desperate he sounded. To distract himself, he watched what the other officers were doing.

The room was a mess. Blood that must have been his mingled with the pile of broken glass that had been the misted window; a crime scene investigator was bagging pieces. Grim-sweepers were loading the ghouls into body bags and carting them away. It would take hours to process the scene.

"Hey Walter, what the hell is that?"

Walt turned reluctantly to see what Torrez was talking about. Hovering in mid-air was a flickering Walt who had an equally holographic ghoul in a chokehold. Torrez had paused the footage and zoomed in on the ghoul's grotesque face.

"You see that? On the ghoul's temple?" Torrez pointed to a small metallic disk that glowed a faint blue, nestled in the shaggy hair on the side of the ghoul's head.

"What is it?" Walt was fading. He was getting tired, he knew sleep would constitute passing out, but now that the adrenaline was wearing off, he was struggling to keep his eyes open. When Walt looked back at Torrez, he had unzipped a body bag containing one of the ghouls. With tweezers and a steady hand, Torrez extracted the unknown object from the corpse and placed it in a small, clear evidence bag.

"What is it?" Walt asked, fighting sleep as best he could.

"I think it's a microchip."

PICK YOUR SIDE

Torrez had seen it coming. Whether it had been due to his injuries or the shock and worry over what had happened to Thea, Walt collapsing shortly after they had discovered the microchip had not been a surprise.

Torrez had called another ambulance and helped load a feebly protesting Walt inside.

"Don't worry, we both know you are too stubborn to die."

Torrez found himself admiring Walt for the first time in a long time. He really would do anything for Thea, he fought hard for the things that mattered to him, and that was something even a "love 'em an' leave 'em" type like Torrez could understand. Torrez didn't love anyone enough to die for them, but he admired those who did.

Torrez peered around Thea's apartment. He liked to give the appearance of being cool, calm and collected, and at this point, he had mastered the illusion, but staring at the blood and the broken glass was sobering. Thea could die, and he would lose his only true friend, the only person that he would, perhaps, take a non-calculated risk for, other than his wife.

As such, it was with a sense of regret that he pocketed the microchip. Leverage won out over friendship on that day.

ESCAPE

The heat inside the SubLevel tunnels was intense. The walls seemed to sweat, and the air was humid. Every breath Cleo took felt like she was inhaling more water than oxygen, but she pushed on.

The package Gin Ricky had given her had afforded her a clarity she hadn't felt in years. She was more herself. Whatever had been in the squat round bottle had brought her back to lucidity. She was starting to remember.

The more she walked, the more tired she became, but she knew she must be nearing the gates. The walls of the tunnels became thicker and smoother, and she began to notice small vents at the tops that allowed the simulated daylight to peer through the darkness.

She was nervous now and excited, the prospect of freedom eclipsing any fear of what might happen when she was outside. She made her way to the southmost wall. As Gin Ricky had told her, the walls there were not made from single impenetrable slabs of concrete like the rest, but old rounded bricks reminiscent of cobblestones.

The wall looked as though the gates had been built against another long-dormant structure, a surviving portion of which had been enveloped into the SubLevel as it had grown over the decades. The mortar in between the bricks was crumbling. With a shaking hand, Cleo pushed against a particularly old looking brick; it moved slightly. In trepidation, she pulled the crude tool she had fashioned from a discarded rib bone and began to pick at the deteriorated mortar like an archaeologist excavating.

Slowly she removed brick after brick from the wall until she had made a small hole, just large enough for her to crawl through. And she did.

The city was bright, loud and uncaring. It hadn't changed. No one paid Cleo any notice as she crept through the streets. She dipped and ducked out of the sight of any legionaries she saw, but they too seemed oblivious to her escape.

The freedom was heady. Cleo wanted to dance and skip, sing and shout, but she didn't have time to enjoy it yet; she had to get out of sight.

A hand shot out of a deep-set doorway and pulled her into the shaded alcove. The man who had grabbed her pressed a finger to his lips. She wasn't sure why, but she obeyed his command and stayed quiet. He was oddly familiar to her muddled brain.

His dark eyes were hooded, and his lashes straight and long. He had high cheekbones and thin lips. His glossy straight black hair wasn't what was fashionable in its stylings, but it suited him the way it was loosely tied back. His features were set into an expectant grimace.

"I'm going to get you back to your family," he said simply.

If Gin Ricky had only one opportunity to gain her trust, he had used it well. There wasn't a sentence in the world that could have made Cleo happier at that moment. What she had dreamed about for what felt like an age had happened; Walt had come for her.

SEE

Thea had never set foot on the earth's surface. She was born in the colonies and had spent her entire life in Tenebrium City. If she were to set foot on earth, however, this was exactly how she would have imagined it. She knew there were cities on the planet's scorched surface, gigantic unforgiving metropolises, but there were also forests and mountains and ruins. You could touch the grass and dip your toes in the ocean, or so she had dreamed.

Thea stood in one such forgotten city. It was a ghost town reclaimed by nature. She was surrounded by once-grand buildings that had long since crumbled into ruins. The sun blared, bright and warm, filling her with a sense of comfort that was alien to her. The pale blue sky brought joyful tears to her eyes, for she had never seen it before, encased as Tenebrium was by its blanket of yellow smog. Vivid green vines wound their way unchecked in and out of windowless frames, and lush foliage-covered most of the concrete faces.

Thea walked through the lost city with a sense of awe. It was so beautiful. The ground beneath her feet was cracked and uneven, yet in some places, still bore the signs of road markings whose meanings were known only to time.

She wasn't sure how long she wandered at her leisure through the calm jungle streets; she didn't care much either. She would have been happy to dwell there forever. She could hear running water. *A swim would be nice*, she thought idly.

She turned down another long street; it was straight and wide. Perhaps it had been this city's Main Street once. In the middle of the road, a giant fissure had opened, deep and broad. The sunlight danced on the crystal surface of the impossibly clear water that filled it.

Thea quickened her pace, excited to feel the water's cooling caress, then stopped dead. A woman was standing at the water's edge. Without pausing, the unknown woman raised her arms gracefully above her head and dived into the water. Thea laughed; she couldn't help it. The freedom of it all was invigorating.

But the woman didn't resurface.

Fear began to dampen Thea's contentedness. The woman had been under the water for too long. If Thea didn't do something, she would surely drown. Throwing caution to the wind, Thea ran as fast as her legs could carry her. When she reached the pool's edge, she was horrified to see that the woman was floating face down just below the surface.

Thea jumped into the pool with none of the woman's grace and was surprised to find that the water was only waist-deep. She saw an endless cavern below, and yet, Thea stood upright, the water barely touching her navel. Wading, Thea made her way to the woman and turned her over. Thea yelped. It was her... or was it?

"Cora?"

With no idea how she got there, Thea suddenly found herself on the banks of the shallow pool. Soaking wet and cold now, she faced her twin sister.

"Do you see?" Cora asked, her eyes a blank milky white.

"See what? Cora, where have you been? Are you all right?"

"Do you see?"

Suddenly, the skies darkened, and thunder rumbled deafeningly loud. Cora's lips moved soundlessly. Thea was transfixed, rooted to the spot, unable to move. Rain poured, and lightning pierced the sky. An agonising scream sounded painfully loud, and the darkness claimed Thea again.

WORST CASE SCENARIO

The room was clinical and impersonal. It was far too bright to allow sleep, not that she could have even if she had wanted to. Athena thought her heart was going to break in her chest as she looked at Thea, lying there, covered in wires and breathing through a tube.

It was a mother's worst nightmare to see her child so hurt. She was awash with emotions. She was angry and frightened, suspicious, and worried to the point of sickness. No one, her husband included, would tell her how Thea had come to be in such a sorry state. The doctors refused to talk to her about anything that might give her clues as to the why of it all, at her husband's behest, no doubt, and she hadn't dared call the police department. To circumvent Harold would mean punishment. Nothing physical; he never had and never would raise a hand to her, but there were other ways in which he could show his displeasure, and she was still paying for her last transgression.

The door opened softly.

"Mrs Williams?"

Athena Turned to look at Dr Howard. He was a spindly-legged White man with a ratty face, when he spoke, however, it was with the calming assurance of someone who knew exactly what they were doing. His confident and smooth voice was rather juxtaposed with his appearance.

"When will she wake up, Doctor?" Athena had asked this question every time he had entered the room, which in the last six hours was many.

"Mrs Williams, your daughter has been through one hell of an ordeal. I'm not going to sugarcoat it, as doing so helps no one. I'd like you to be prepared for what may happen."

"Are you saying she might not wake up?" Athena clutched her chest.

"It's possible, but it's not what I'm concerned about presently. Your daughter went into respiratory arrest several times. The damage that may have been done to her brain during that time can't be ascertained until she wakes, if she wakes. More than this, however, she was stabbed with—forgive me the melodrama—a poison blade. Now, the wound itself is shallow and will heal quickly. The poison, however, is a variant of Styxx—"

"What do you mean? Is she a ghoul?"

"No, definitely not. The problem that you need to be aware of is that this drug appears to be addictive in the extreme. She was administered a small amount, and it was enough to cause adverse effects, but not enough to cause her to change. That means if she does wake, she may experience withdrawal so severe that her body won't be able to cope with it. So, you see, asleep is exactly how we would like to keep her until the drug is out of her system. If not, the havoc it may wreck could be fatal."

"My god," Athena whispered.

"I'm sorry to lay all this at your feet, but I want you to be prepared. We can't put her in a medically induced coma as there is no way of knowing what effect mixing the drugs may have. For now, all we can do is pray that she stays asleep a little while longer."

THE RIGHT THING?

Torrez felt guilty. It was not a feeling he was accustomed to. He had never pretended to have honour, at least not in the same way Thea had it and Walt used to have it, but he did pride himself on having a personal code of sorts. When your bread and butter was liars and thieves, an "if you can't beat 'em, join 'em" attitude was essential. There were, however, lines that even Torrez wouldn't cross. Still, it was with an uneasy feeling in his gut that he asked Orion Martin to pull up Walt's bank records.

Being several years north of sixty, although he didn't look it, Orion no longer acted in the field. Instead, he was the keeper of the TPD archives. He was a master of all the information that was in the TPD database and some that wasn't. He was not an easy man to circumvent. It was well known that anyone who made a request of the archive had better have a damn good reason for doing so.

"What possible reason could you have for needing that information?" Orion demanded predictably.

"It's about the attack on Thea, Walt's fine with it."

"Well, if he's given his permission, you won't mind bringing him down here to corroborate that, will you?"

"Usually, I would have no problem, but I can't—he's in the hospital."

It was with a suspicious look in his eye that Orion turned from Torrez and began hunting for the records he wanted.

The archive was a holodeck, similar to the virtual evidence suite. It appeared like a Victorian library, candlelit, with massively high varnished wooden shelves, ladders for perusing the hard to reach volumes and woven rugs, but all the leather-bound books were actually files and directories that allowed Orion access to nearly everything in Tenebrium.

Orion returned to Torrez less than a minute later.

"Ready when you are," Orion said, still regarding Torrez shrewdly.

Elanor Miller

Torrez lay his wrist upright on the impressive wooden desk that Orion liked to sit behind. Much like a librarian checking out a book, Orion used a small silver handheld device to scan over Torrez's Index, which acted as a dock as well as a link to the database. There was a flash of light, a small beep, and that was that.

"You're all done. You can access the information at any data point, using your desk or any of your portable database devices or your implant."

"Yeah, yeah, I know the drill. Thanks, Orion."

Ten minutes later, Torrez was sitting at his desk. He waited for the bullpen to clear and brought up the new records on the console embedded there.

Tenebrium Central Bank
Walter James
Account Number: 0000236479852358622

Transactions
January – March

T	03012425	Enertec Power	300.00c	2869.53c	3544125	T
	07012425	French 75 Speakeasy	16.00c	2569.53c	4687925	
E	07012425	Willis & Wills	500.00c	2069.53c	1742751	E
	08012425	Gin Ricky's Coffee Stop	50.40c	2019.13c	5468896	
N	10012425	Green's Grocers	87.95c	1931.18c	1857548	N
	10012425	French 75 Speakeasy	26.50c	1904.68c	1874348	
E	13012425	569859 ATM	750.00c	1154.68c	5484659	E
B	20012425	Gin Ricky's Coffee Stop	12.00c	1142.68c	3215214	B
	20012425	Gin Ricky's Coffee Stop	50.00c	1092.68c	3214854	
R	20012425	Gin Ricky's Coffee Stop	08.00c	1084.68c	4897844	R
I	20012425	French 75 Speakeasy	14.65c	1070.03c	4548782	I
	01022425	Gin Ricky's Coffee Stop	12.60c	1057.43c	3578782	
U	02022425	Tenebrium City (PS)	+3156.75c	4214.18c	4520.	U
	03022425	Green's Grocers	117.98c	4096.20c	7899123	
M	03022425	Enertec Power	300.00c	3796.20c	5248781	M
C	05022425	Deco	89.37c	3706.83c	9870128	C
	06022425	Gin Ricky's Coffee Stop	25.26c	3681.57c	7985412	
E	07022425	Willis & Wills	500.00c	3138.57c	1876488	E
	08022425	French 75 Speakeasy	57.08c	3124.49c	6548452	
N	11022425	Gin Ricky's Coffee Stop	90.00c	3034.49c	8741555	N
T	12022425	W8	235.36	3009.13c	2186765	T
	13022425	Gin Ricky's Coffee Stop	21.02c	2988.11c	3478751	
R	14022425	Gin Ricky's Coffee Stop	56.97c	2931.14c	3484534	R
A	15022425	Gin Ricky's Coffee Stop	168.00c	2763.14c	5487415	A
	17022425	French 75 Speakeasy	79.64c	2683.50c	8745148	
L	21022425	Green's Grocers	110.47c	2573.03c	1278797	L
	25022425	231184 ATM	1250.00c	1323.03c	9845878	
B	02032425	Tenebrium City (PS)	+3156.75c	4479.78c	4520.	B
A	03032425	Enertec Power	300.00c	4179.78c	4578777	A
	07032425	Willis & Wills	500.00c	3679.78	4987322	
N	10032425	Green's Grocers	145.63c	3534.14	7897888	N
	12032425	895655 ATM	1500.00c	2034.15	3878787	
K	27032425	W8	250.00c	1784.15	6660616	K

Torrez wasn't sure what he had expected to find. He wasn't even sure what to make of what he had found. Walt appeared to pay his bills on time and drink too much; that was clear. Torrez hadn't needed the bank statement to glean that little insight. His many trips to visit Gin Ricky were hardly irregular for a police officer either; whether it be for the artisan coffee or the information that could be purchased for the right price, most detectives on the force were likely to have the Coffee Stop on their bank statements. Taking credit out from an ATM, while suspicious in large amounts, wasn't a crime either.

Two of the transactions Torrez knew only too well, as he had frequented the place many times himself. A widowed single man with a yin for a dame he couldn't have was exactly the kind of fellow you would expect to find in a brothel from time to time.

All in all, Torrez was not disappointed, for he had no desire to help Walt nail himself to the wall, but he was dissatisfied. He, like most detectives, didn't like a mystery he couldn't solve. He had found nothing to corroborate Benjamin Pickford's assertion that he had done business with Walt in a manner other than the expected, and other than a single trip to a popular restaurant, he found nothing that could tie him to Dill Kelly conclusively. While Torrez was sure that there was more to the story, he could do no more about it short of tailing Walt.

Instead, he turned his attention to the small metallic chip that was still nestled in his coat pocket. He had done his due diligence; it was time to focus on what he wanted.

MAKING A SCENE

The scene was a mess. The large open plan space bore all the markers of a violent incident. There were three body bags lined up near the main door containing the bodies of three ghouls. The grim-sweepers had planned to take them away, but a last-minute order from the powers that be had meant that they were to be processed at the scene. All Nazia and her team could do was wait for a coroner to arrive and take them away. Corpses were not in their wheelhouse.

The large square panel of opaque glass that allowed light from the living space to pass into the bathroom had been shattered from the inside; several members of the team were busy cataloguing and collecting the pieces. Photographers and data technicians recorded every inch of the scene as fingerprint specialists scanned all surfaces.

Nazia herself was working on the living room area with two others. She hated crime scenes. The aftermath of the violence on display was a stark reminder of what people were capable of. She couldn't pretend that the attack on one of their own hadn't shaken her because it had. She didn't know Detective Williams personally, but she, like the rest of the team, felt for her and her family.

Nazia's parents didn't approve of her job in forensics. Her mother, in particular, thought it was a dirty job unbecoming to a lady, but Naz disagreed. To her, being even the smallest cog in the machine of justice was worthwhile.

That was what she had to remind herself of as she sifted through a lumpy pool of quickly coagulating blood between the stained sofa and the overturned coffee table. It was brain matter. She grimaced. The area in which she worked had until recently been home to the corpse of one of the ghouls. Evidently, the ghoul had had its skull shattered with an earthenware bowl that Regis, the tech who was working next to Naz, was bagging.

Hiding in the pool of blood, skull fragments, and grey matter was a small metallic chip. Unlike the others, it didn't seem to light up. The force that had shattered the ghoul's skull seemed to have damaged it. By her count, it was the third they had found, one for each ghoul.

"This is a closed scene," Nazia called, for there had been a loud knock at the door. No reply came. The knock sounded again. "This is a closed crime scene, authorised access only."

BOOM

The explosion sent Nazia flying through the air like a ragdoll. She felt her arm break as she landed on it badly. Her ears rang, and her eyes watered as she squinted through the smoke. She tried to speak, to call to her team, but the breath she inhaled caught in her throat. She coughed, splattering the floor with blood.

She saw blurred figures moving in the gloom, she wanted to call out to them, to beg for their help, but no words came. Through streaming eyes, Nazia could see pairs of black boots moving around the scene, but her mind, overloaded as it was, couldn't make sense of it. *They are contaminating the scene*, she thought blearily as the pain in her arm seared.

The room was lit up by flashes of light, and dull bangs filtered through the ringing in her ears. When she realised what was happening, it was too late. A pair of boots stopped so close to her face that she could count the eyelets on the laces. Something cold and metal was placed to her temple, and Nazia thought no more.

IN MY ARMS

Walt was warm and comfortable, or rather he would have been comfortable in the soft, cosy bed if his head hadn't pounded and every breath he took didn't cause a sharp shooting pain across his chest.

He opened his eyes slowly, then closed them again. The light in the room was overwhelming. Walt was groggy, and he couldn't quite piece together what was happening. It felt as though his mind was working in slow motion. Where was he? He opened his eyes again.

The room was oppressively bright. The walls were an excruciatingly glossy ivory. Walt looked down at his body. He was encased in white linens and had several intravenous lines extending out from his left arm. There were bandages around his ribs, and when he brought his hands to his face, he felt stitches there on his cheek and forehead.

He was in a hospital, but he still couldn't remember how he had gotten there. He glanced around some more. There was a digital sign on the back of the heavy door that stated his name and condition. His clothes were carefully folded on a pale grey leather chair opposite the bed. His shirt and waistcoat were both bloodstained.

The realisation hit Walt like a punch. Memories from the previous night flooded back like he was living them again.

The blood on his clothes was Thea's.

Walt's heart dropped into his stomach as the fear and misery hit him anew. The brief reprieve unconsciousness had bestowed was over; he had to find Thea. He had to know that she had survived.

Walt sat up and immediately felt the urge to vomit. Unable to stop himself, he did so, lurching over the side of the bed. The murky liquid splattered the floor as Walt retched again. The pain in his ribs was intense enough to make him faint, but he fought to keep hold of consciousness. With a great effort, he slowed his breathing, and after a moment, the black spots in his vision cleared.

Walt pulled the tubes from the crook of his arm and was surprised by the comical spurt of blood that issued from the hole. He held his arm aloft for a few seconds, and the bleeding slowed.

On shaky legs, Walt shambled over to the chair where his clothes lay and dressed quickly with fumbling fingers. He picked up his holster, complete with gun, that had been hidden beneath the pile of clothes and checked his pockets. His badge was still there, as was his lockpick, wedding ring, and hip flask. It sloshed around tauntingly, and Walt couldn't resist. He had been through so much, who would judge him for taking a draft now? He ignored the niggling voice in the back of his head and took several large gulps of bourbon.

Imbued with liquid courage, Walt limped out into the corridor. He felt better than he deserved having benefited from what seemed like some very expensive medical care. There was no one around. He appeared to be in an empty wing, of which hospital he had no idea.

It didn't take him long to find the elevator. He couldn't be sure that Thea was in this hospital, but he thought it seemed likely that the Medicus would have brought them both to the same place, considering they had been injured in the same incident.

He tapped his foot impatiently as he waited for the elevator, which arrived in seconds that felt like hours. The gold doors opened wide to reveal a spacious box with a beautiful woman standing inside. She was so lifelike it took Walt a moment to realise that she was a hologram.

"Which floor?" The hologram asked, smiling placidly as Walt stepped inside.

"Can you give me information on a patient's whereabouts?"

"Which floor?"

"That's a no. Reception, I guess."

The ride down was short, uncomfortably short. The elevator moved at such a speed that Walt felt like his brain was trying to escape through his ears, but it was over so fast he didn't really have time to react to the sensation.

The doors opened wide, revealing an all too familiar white marble atrium. He was at Medicorum Medical Services, not a hospital at all. He didn't have insurance. He was devil may care that way, but someone must have paid his bill. Medicorum didn't do freebies or payment plans. Several signs strategically placed around the reception area made that abundantly clear as they pronounced in bold "NO CREDITS – NO CARE".

Walt pushed the strangeness of the situation out of his mind. He didn't have time to wonder how he came to be at the medical services or who had paid for his stay, he needed to find Thea.

Pulling out his badge, Walt forced his way to the front of the long queue that had formed in front of the reception desk.

"Can I help you, Detective?" asked the young man behind the counter, slightly alarmed. He couldn't have been older than eighteen, and he looked younger still, like a slightly overgrown schoolboy.

"Is there a Thea Williams here?"

"Patient or staff?" the youth asked mechanically.

"Patient," Walt snapped. "Is she here?"

The young man was flustered as he brought up the patient records on the clear glass screen in front of him. There was a small beep and an error message coruscated red on the screen, though Walt couldn't read the faint letters backwards. The receptionist paled as his eyes moved over the message.

"There is a Thea Williams here," the receptionist's voice was thin.

"Where? What floor? What room?" Walt demanded.

"Are you Detective James?"

"Yes, has she asked for me?"

The receptionist made a face as though his worst fears had been confirmed. "No, I don't think she has woken up, but you're on the restricted list."

"What the hell does that mean?"

"Her father...I mean, the District Attorney...Mr Williams gave the medical staff a list of people who we're not allowed to admit as visitors or give any information out to. Your name is on the list. It's the only name on the list," the receptionist looked as though he might burst into tears.

Walt stared at him for a moment. "Fine."

The receptionist visibly relaxed.

Walt vaulted over the counter and landed next to the receptionist's chair. "Oh my... Sir, you can't be back here." Walt peered over the young man's shoulder and read Thea's information from the screen, along with the notice advising that he, Walt, be removed by force if necessary, should he try to gain access to Thea's room. In the mood he was in, he dared them to try.

"Thank you for your help," said Walt, hopping back over the counter.

Walt knew he would pay for that little manoeuvre later as he jogged back to the elevator. Ignoring the protestation of his ribs, he got into the nearest one.

"Which floor?"

"Seventy-seventh. Nightingale Ward." The irony did not escape Walt.

The elevator doors opened into a rather more expensive corridor than Walt had been privy to. Where his had been clinical and white, with no personal touches, the passage that led to the Nightingale Ward was styled like that of an expensive mansion, with its polished dark wood floor, gleaming rose gold floral wallpaper and glittering chandeliers.

In fact, it seemed like oddly decadent décor for a ward that presumably would see its fair share of blood and other unpleasant fluids, likely to stain.

There were two suited and booted guards posted outside a door halfway down the corridor. They didn't turn as the elevator doors opened; they just stared resolutely ahead. This gave Walt time to size them up. He was in no shape to be involved in any more fisticuffs, but he wasn't naïve enough to assume that just because he wasn't prepared for it, it wouldn't happen.

The guard closest to him was female and of medium build. She was on the taller end of average height, and she held herself with a poise that made Walt think she would be fast and slippery. Her long hair was swept into a wavy ponytail that fell to the middle of her back. Her male companion was shorter than Walt by an inch or two and broader. Yet he was lean, his muscular physique was visible even through the layers of his suit.

Walt stepped cautiously into the corridor. He had no plan of action, and none more sophisticated than the truth came to him.

"I want to see Thea," Walt said matter-of-factly when he drew level with the female.

"You're not on the list," she said without looking at him. There was no sneer in her voice, nothing personal, all business.

"Let me through. I just want to see her."

"You're not on the list."

"This isn't a nightclub, my... someone I care about very much has been hurt, and I am asking you politely to let me through." Walt gritted his teeth, willing his voice to be pleasant and respectful.

"You're not on the list."

Walt lunged forward and found himself on the ground before he knew what had happened. The female guard had swept his legs from underneath him, then went back to her position at the door. He'd been right; she was fast.

Wincing, Walt got gracelessly to his feet. He took two steps backwards until he reached the wall opposite the guards. He leaned back, crossed his arms, and prepared to wait. Injured as he was, the guards would no doubt best him in seconds, but they had to leave sometime.

They had been stuck in their Mexican standoff for only a few tense minutes when the elevator doors opened again, and Harold stepped out.

His greying hair was perfectly arranged around his heart-shaped face. He was dressed immaculately as was his norm, with a subtlety that, in any other circumstance, Walt would have admired. There was nothing flashy about Harold, and yet his status was evident and indisputable.

"You can't see her. I warned you there would be consequences if you didn't do as I asked." Harold walked leisurely towards Walt, every bit the man who held all the cards.

"Did you do this to her? Is your office that important to you?" Walt stepped off the wall to face Harold head-on.

"Watch your words. She's my daughter," Harold said, his voice dangerously low.

"That's not a no. I want to see her."

"Well, you can't, and unless she recovers and regains the ability to make poor choices—you won't."

Walt was repulsed by this man who could use his daughter as leverage, as a bargaining chip and as a carrot dangled in front of those whom he wanted to control.

Walt grabbed Harold by the lapels of his expensive jacket and slammed him hard into the wall. There was a crunch as Harold's back left an indentation in the plaster. Walt's breath was ragged as he fought his barely contained rage. The guards rushed forward, but Harold signalled them with one wagging finger to wait.

"Think very carefully about your next move, Detective," Harold said. He leaned forward and sniffed the air with over-exaggerated flair. "Is that alcohol I smell on your breath?" His smile was cruel.

Walt let out a roar and punched with every ounce of strength he possessed. His fist broke through the wall an inch to the left of Harold's head. Walt pulled his bleeding hand from the hole and stepped back from Harold, feeling like a volcano that was about to erupt.

"I knew you had a brain in there somewhere beneath all that testosterone."

"She died in my arms." The confession was devastating. "She died. In. My. Arms."

Something passed between them then as the two men looked at one another. Harold's smug expression softened slightly when his eyes met Walt's. "She hasn't woken up yet," Harold said so quietly Walt almost missed it. "She was dead for several minutes, and there were complications because of the drug... they aren't sure if she will..." Harold appeared unable to finish. For the first time since Walt had met him, he looked not like a politician, but a father. "I won't let you see her. You have caused her enough pain. If you want to help, leave. Let her move on with her life. You are a sinking ship, don't drag her down to the depths with you."

Walt didn't say anything, he just looked at Harold, scrutinising his face. Then, he turned and walked away.

SURVIVOR

Benny had done many questionable things in his life, and he was sure he would pay for every single one of them at some point, but he would be damned if it would be today.

He had dragged himself up. He had built Ward Eight from nothing and whatever people might say about the practises that took place inside its walls, he was proud of what he had achieved. It was the closest to legitimate business he had ever come. He wasn't fool enough to think that with all his friends, enemies and those who fit somewhere in between that he could escape the criminal lifestyle, but he had sworn to himself a long time ago that he wouldn't let it be all he was.

And for a while, he had succeeded. He had been the proprietor of a brothel and nothing more, but his greed got the better of him as it always did. He was in so deep he could no longer see the surface.

He was surprised to find that he truly regretted the part he played in the attack on the detective. The news that she had survived may have signed his death warrant, but he couldn't pretend that there wasn't a strange sense of relief buried underneath the fear. Perhaps it was her attitude; they operated in systems that couldn't be reconciled, but there was something respectable about her search for justice. Secretly, Benny thought Tenebrium needed more people like her and fewer people like him, but he was resigned to his place and dwelling on it wouldn't help him out of his current predicament.

No matter how he looked at it, his time in Tenebrium was done. He would have to start again somewhere new. He'd done it before, and he could do it again.

Still, it was with a heavy heart that Benny packed his "go bag".

He made his way from his private quarters in the penthouse that sat atop Ward Eight and down into his office. He quickly emptied his desk and the safe hidden behind the portrait of Mary Magdalene. Looking at it gave him a chuckle every time.

"You really fucked up this time, didn't you, Benny?"

A tall man in a gold mask stood in the doorway of the office, blocking the exit with his impressive bulk. Benny had never known his name, but he knew exactly what his coming meant.

Benny dropped the bag he was holding and backed as far away as he could.

"It's good to see you." He kept his tone casual, but his heart was pounding as if trying to escape his chest.

"You've rather screwed the putsch, haven't you?" The man's voice was low and commanding. It had a resonance to it that he could manipulate to convey great warmth and charisma, but it could also convey danger in a very real way.

"It's not my fault the bitch survived."

"Then why are you running?"

"I'm not, not from you," Benny lied seamlessly. "The pigs raided us. Found the ghouls."

"I'm well aware. It's all over the news. Chester is very disappointed."

"Tell that sick freak that he and his friends will have to get their kicks somewhere else."

The man stepped into the room. He moved over to Benny's desk and sat in one of the black leather wingback chairs opposite. It groaned under his weight.

"Tell him yourself." Benny couldn't see it, but he was sure there was a wicked smile under the mask.

"Yeah, right, sure. I'll do just that," said Benny, picking up his bag and continuing to throw his possessions inside pell-mell. The man chuckled.

"The detective is getting too close. See to it that she tragically succumbs to her injuries. Personally. No more sending two-bit flunkies to do your dirty work."

"You want me to go to the hospital and kill her? That was never the deal. The place will be swarming with cops."

"She's in the way. The Gold Legion wants her gone."

"What about the DA? She's his daughter."

"He will come to understand. It's all part of the plan. You will do this. I know you gave the twists Quietus. You will tie up the loose ends you created."

Benny, who prided himself on being able to talk his way out of anything, was dumbfounded. When he had agreed to aid The Gold Legion in their master plan to take control of Tenebrium, he had only been concerned about the money, but the darker and frankly crazier the plans had gotten, the colder his feet had become. He had been leaving breadcrumbs for the police for a while now.

Thinking quickly, he realised that if the man knew he had staged the church crime scene, he would be dead. However, he did know that he had planted Quietus on Detective Williams. He had intended her to die, to keep himself ingratiated with the Gold Legion, but he had hoped that the other police would start to piece together what was happening. He really had no choice.

"Fine. I'll do it."

"That's settled then," the man said, getting to his feet and straightening his tailored jacket. "I'm glad we are back on the same page." The man reached out a hand that Benny reluctantly shook.

As soon as their hands connected, Benny felt a red-hot pain in his arm. He dropped to his knees and tried desperately to wrench himself out of the man's enormous grip, but the man held fast. "Punishment and insurance in equal measure, you know how it goes."

True enough, Benny was well acquainted with this technique; he used it on his courtesans often.

Finally, the man relinquished his grip. "I'll expect the deed to be done by tomorrow. See you soon, Benjamin. Or perhaps not, should you fail." And he left.

Benny clutched his arm to him. It felt like he had been scolded by boiling water. When the pain had subsided to more of an itch, he rolled up his shirt sleeve. He recoiled when he saw what was there. The veins in his arm seemed to have turned to gold. His hand was beginning to feel cold and numb. Whatever the man had done to him was spreading fast.

The sooner he got rid of the detective, the better. He was taking no chances.

DOWNRIGHT SUICIDAL

Walt could have called a Jonk, but he needed to clear his head. He made his slow and winding way to the TPD, Harold's words ringing in his ears all the while. *You have caused her enough pain...* Thea's father was right. He had made so many mistakes. Too many.

It wasn't just Harold's words rattling around the inside of his skull like it was an echo chamber that was bothering Walt. Ever since he had woken up, the previous night's events had played over and over in his head. He was missing something obvious, he was sure of it, some clue buried in the back of his mind trying to get out.

When he arrived at the precinct, Torrez was standing at the reception desk filling in a report. Walt knew that he shouldn't be in the building, and judging by the look on Torrez's face when he caught sight of Walt, Torrez was thinking the same thing.

That was when it hit him.

Torrez.

Torrez had told Walt that the ghouls had had chips on their temples, and Torrez himself had taken one from a body. Walt had a vague and hazy memory of Torrez bagging a chip and putting it in his pocket. Why would he pocket evidence unless he intended to withhold it? And where would it be now if he had? Was it important enough that he would still be carrying it on his person?

"Whoa, Walter. You can't be here," said Torrez, meeting Walt halfway across the lobby and barring any further progress. "I gave the captain your Seer footage. You are a material witness in the attempted murder of a police officer. You know the drill. You have to go home."

"Torrez. Drew. We don't always see eye to eye, but I know you mean well. So, I mean no disrespect when I say get the fuck outta my way."

Torrez pressed his lips into a grim line. "Go home."

Walt knew he was right, but he suddenly found that he had a burning desire to do something reckless, to find an outlet for the rage and hurt that had been seething inside him since he had left Medicorum.

Walt stepped so close to Torrez that he could feel his breath on his face.

"What? You want a kiss? Listen, you are in no condition to do this," said Torrez with the slightest hint of a sneer. "I get it. It's been a bad couple of days..."

"It's been a bad couple of years. Last chance, Torrez."

"Last chance, huh? Go home. Let us do our jobs."

Before Torrez knew what had happened, Walt's fist collided with the side of his face. He did a sort of pirouette on the spot and stumbled back. When he straightened, Torrez looked at Walt, making it clear that if he wanted to go a few rounds, Torrez was only too happy to oblige.

Walt went for a tackle, but Torrez got there first. Diving at Walt, he caught him around the middle, taking them both to the ground. Quickly, Torrez clambered so he was on top and began to punch Walt mercilessly.

Walt used his arms to cover his face, but he was more concerned by Torrez's weight bearing down on his broken ribs. He couldn't breathe. Walt bucked his hips, throwing Torrez off balance and twisted his body so that Torrez fell to the side. Walt scrambled over to Torrez and began to punch every inch of him that he could reach with his left hand while searching his jacket pockets with his right.

Torrez easily pushed Walt away and got to his feet, but it didn't matter; Walt had found what he was looking for. Using all the strength he could muster, Walt stood, breathing heavily. The two men faced each other, neither wanting to back down. Walt got the impression that Torrez was happy to have an excuse to lay into him, probably in payback for his recent behaviour. Walt needed an outlet, and if Torrez was happy to volunteer, so be it.

A crowd had gathered, but none of those watching seemed sure of what to do. Both Walt and Torrez outranked the uniformed officers who stood among the bystanders, making them unwilling to intervene.

"Come on, Walter. You're a wreck. No wonder your life is falling apart. Go home and get a grip. You're pathetic, and you're a drunk. Everyone knows it. Thea knows it. I'm glad she can't see you like this." Torrez had been looking for a button to press, and he had found several.

Walt had done what he needed to. He had found the chip, he could stop now, but he didn't want to. All Walt could see was red. Torrez's words rang in his ears, but it wasn't his voice that taunted him.

...You have caused her enough pain already...

Walt ran at Torrez and grabbed him by the throat. He squeezed his hands together, choking Torrez, who spluttered trying to drag air into his lungs, his eyes wide with shock.

...Let her move on with her life...

Walt didn't see the blow, but he felt it in every inch of his body when Torrez's knee collided with his groin. Walt let go of Torrez's neck at once and dropped to the ground, a horrible sick feeling in his stomach.

...You are a sinking ship. Don't drag her down to the depths with you...

He had no idea what he was doing. Before his mind had processed what was happening, it was too late. He had pulled out his gun and aimed it at Torrez.

"What the hell is wrong with you? You're acting like a fucking crazy person," said Torrez, raising his hands and backing away. His voice sounded hoarse. "Come on, Walt, this is suicide. We both know you aren't going to shoot me."

"That's enough."

The captain was standing inside the elevator, which had just arrived in the lobby. She looked livid. "Have you lost your minds? Torrez, clean yourself up and get back to work. James, with me."

Numbly, Walt dropped his gun. The clatter it made as it hit the ground caused several of the onlookers to jump, and one young officer let out a yelp. Torrez picked it up and took it with him when he left, muttering under his breath. Walt only dimly registered what was happening.

Mechanically, he followed the captain back into the lift.

He felt sated, like he had gotten rid of the energy that had been building up since he had watched Thea being taken away by the Medicus, but he also felt worse than ever. He felt vindicated yet ashamed, high on the adrenaline, but fearing the crash.

The elevator ride to the captain's office was one of the most awkward Walt had ever experienced. He and the captain stood in silence while he stared straight forward, the chip held tightly in his palm. He could feel her eyes on him. When he chanced a look at the captain, her expression had softened a minute amount. She seemed guarded, almost expectant, like a woman walking on eggshells. He realised he must look terrible; she was afraid he was going to—What? Collapse? Explode? She was a good woman, he thought. She could be blunt, harsh even, but she took a personal interest in her subordinates.

When they entered her office a few moments later, the captain sat down behind her desk. Walt took the seat opposite without being asked.

"How's Thea?" the captain asked without preamble.

"I don't know. Not good. Her father wouldn't let me see her. She hasn't woken up yet. She might not. That's all he told me," Walt said in a jumble. He found that talking with the captain about something so personal was difficult.

"I'm very sorry to hear that. Thea is…well, she's Thea," said the captain with a small smile. "This must be very hard for you. I'm sorry for that, too."

Walt met the captain's gaze fully for the first time since they had met in the atrium.

"The crime scene at Thea's apartment has been destroyed, and the team of CSI's that were working there are dead," Betty said, surprising Walt. He had been expecting to be read the riot act for his little performance in the lobby.

"I don't understand."

"There was a fire."

"How is that possible?" Walt was nonplussed.

"The fire department hasn't made its report yet, but I wouldn't rule out a cover-up."

"Why are you telling me this?"

"I'm not blind. My hands may be tied, but I can see the things that are happening in this city. I don't think that it's a coincidence that the first real lead that we had in the Pleasure Quarter murders was released by order of the DA, or that the investigating officer was attacked, or that the scene of said attack was destroyed. Do you?"

"No, I don't."

"Good." The captain clasped her hands and touched them to her face. She looked at Walt for a moment, taking in his injuries. "Hand over your badge and gun."

"What?"

"Your badge and your gun, now."

"You can't—"

"The hell I can't," the captain said, leaning forward, daring him to cut her off. "What you just did was downright suicidal. You attacked a fellow officer. You threatened him with a firearm. You're goddamned lucky that I'm not arresting you. We both know another strike would be the end of you, and maybe that's what you want, but I'm not here to facilitate your suicide. If you are hell-bent on self-destructing, I refuse to help you do it.

"If I let you stay on as a detective, sooner or later, the way you're going, you'd make a mistake that I can't protect you from. Strikes come easy in this city. I know you've had a tough couple of years, but none of that is an excuse to behave the way you just did. I need the man who was tipped to be the next lieutenant, who went above and beyond, not a man so blinded by his own self-loathing that he can't see he still has plenty to lose. I hope you can sort yourself out; I really do. But not here."

"Captain..." Walt began pleadingly, but he had no idea what to say.

"You can call me Betty. You're fired, effective immediately."

THE PAST
Eighteen months ago...

Boulevardier Casino was owned by the mob. Everybody knew it. It was a dangerous place, where losing cost more than just money. Patrons either had to be impossibly wealthy to play there, or suicidal. There were no second chances and no IOUs. If a player couldn't pay up, their debts would be collected in flesh.

The bar, however, was legendary. Guests needn't gamble and risk their lives for a good time; there were plenty of other delights to keep them occupied.

Cigar smoke created a mist that further dimmed the warm orange light cast by the many chandeliers that hung low over the circular booths fitted with soft red velvet. Holographic strippers danced on every tabletop.

The bar was full of people drinking, laughing, and flaunting their sexuality. A live jazz band played for those kicking it on the dance floor, and rooms were available for those who wished for more intimate experiences.

Walt sat at the bar, drunk as was the norm for him these days, watching a group of six men as they sat around a felt-covered table in the dingiest corner of the bar playing high stakes poker. He drained the glass that sat on the counter in front of him and ambled over to the men.

"You can't afford this game, Detective," Dill Kelly said from the depths of the gloom where he had been hidden.

"You still owe me from the last time, so how about I sit in?" said Walt, edging closer to the table.

His progress was halted by a tall White man in a grey suit, who put his hand on Walt's chest by way of a warning. Walt recognised him as Lewis Avery, one of Dill's hired henchmen; they had traded blows before.

"We have no business, you and I. You are a cheat, and I don't play with cheaters," Dill said, not looking up from his cards.

Walt made to move past Avery, who rebuffed him again with the same hand to the chest.

"Hey, fuck that," Walt spat. "You callin' me dirty?"

"You used your retinal chip to scan cards, and I was kind enough to let you keep your thumbs as a favour to Torrez, so let's just leave it at that, shall we?" Dill said, finally deigning to glance in Walt's direction.

More forcefully this time, Avery pushed Walt backwards, clearly intending to escort him out.

"You wanna go, pretty boy?" Walt threatened.

"You are drunk, Detective," Dill said, throwing his cards on the table impatiently. "Last warning. Go home."

"Who's gonna make me, huh?" Walt stepped so close to Avery that they were nose to nose. "This bruno?" Walt shoved Avery hard enough to make him take a step back. "Is it gonna be you? Huh?"

Dill sighed in a resigned sort of way. "Try not to kill him, Lewis."

Without a beat, Avery punched Walt hard in the face, quickly followed by a mean uppercut to the gut. Walt doubled over, seeing stars and coughing. He spat blood on the floor and straightened up, smiling.

"That's what I'm talking about," Walt said, rolling up his sleeves and advancing on Avery.

It was absolute chaos. Avery's attack on Walt seemed to spark something primal as the entire venue erupted into an all-out brawl. Yet it seemed not to affect the mood; partiers partied, drinkers drank, and dancers danced as chairs were broken over backs and bottles were smashed over heads.

Avery threw Walt roughly over a table, and he landed upright in a booth, surprised and disappointed to find himself no worse for wear. His reprieve was short-lived. Avery grabbed him around the neck in a rear naked choke and dragged him over the back of the seats. Walt elbowed him thrice in the side, and Avery let go of the wheezing Walt to clutch his own ribs.

Before he had had time to recover, Walt hooked Avery squarely in the jaw, following up quickly with a lazy kick that knocked Avery to the ground. Walt leant down and grabbed the front of Avery's shirt, half lifting him from the patterned carpet. He raised his fist high, ready to deliver a punishing blow—

CLICK.

Something cold and hard was pressed to the back of his head. It was a gun, cocked and ready to fire, held by Dill Kelly's blood-soaked hand.

"Enough."

Walt was dragged into a back room and held while Dill took out his displeasure on him with his fists. Then, lagging and dizzy, he was taken through the kitchens and thrown into the alley at the back of the casino. He landed painfully in a dirty puddle, badly beaten and bloody, barely able to lift his head from the murky water.

"Pussy," he drawled, blood dripping from his mouth and nose.

Walt tried to stand, but he couldn't. His body wasn't following his commands. It still wasn't enough; he hadn't paid enough.

"You just don't know when to quit, do you?"

So, it had been Avery who had ejected him from Boulevardier. Walt hadn't been fully conscious when he was moved.

He rolled over, it was all he could do, and gave Avery the finger.

"Spin on it."

Avery let out a crack of laughter. "You first." And he kicked Walt hard in the stomach.

Walt choked back vomit.

"Had enough yet?" Avery asked, lazily circling Walt.

"That little love tap?" Walt rasped belligerently. "That was nothing."

"You really have a death wish, don't you?"

"Nah," Walt panted, struggling to stay conscious. "You just hit like a dame."

Avery looked down at Walt with something close to pity in his eyes, but he began to kick and stomp on him nonetheless.

Every blow was devastating.

Walt was sure this would be the end of him, yet it was the most peace he had experienced in weeks. It felt right. It felt like exactly what he deserved.

"Hey!" came a voice he recognised from somewhere far away.

Walt looked blearily towards the mouth of the alley and saw Thea standing there, gun raised. She was a vision.

"Get away from him," she commanded.

Avery lifted his leg, and Walt was sure his punishment was going to begin anew, but Avery just rested his foot on the centre of Walt's chest.

"This here ain't something you need to worry your pretty little head about. Keep walking." The threat in Avery's voice was obvious.

"Maybe you didn't hear me," Thea said, coming closer and pulling her badge from its perch at her waist. "Get back."

"Ooh," Avery mocked. "Baby's got a badge."

"Baby's got a gun. Back, the fuck, off."

Avery looked from Thea to the gun she had levelled at his chest.

"Fine, he's all yours," he said, shrugging and walking back to the casino door. "Good luck, kid."

Walt heard the door snap shut, and then he let blackness claim him.

"Walt? Walt? Can you hear me?"

He was propped against the rough brick wall of Boulevardier. He was still drunk, wet, and in pain. He couldn't have been unconscious for more than the minute or two it had taken Thea to drag him there.

"Thea?"

"Can you stand? We need to get you off the street. What were you thinking? Are you trying to get yourself killed?"

"I didn't need your help," he slurred, batting away the hands that were checking the cuts on his face.

"One of your pupils is blown," Thea said, worry mixing with exasperation.

"You shouldn't be here."

Thea ignored this and tried to pull Walt to his feet, he pushed her away roughly, and she stumbled.

"Don't touch me," he spat, holding a hand to keep her from helping him as he struggled to stand. "The thought of your hands on me makes me sick."

Thea dropped the arms that had been reaching out to him.

"Great. That's just great. Real nice, Walt," she said, her eyes glassy.

"I didn't ask for your help. I never do."

Finally upright, he leant, panting against the wall, unable to coordinate himself enough to walk yet.

"If it wasn't for me, you would be dead a hundred times over."

She was right, and in that moment, he hated her for it.

"Stop trying to save me!" he blurted angrily.

"Someone has to," she shot back, her temper rising.

"I don't want you," he yelled far louder than he had intended. "I don't want to be saved by you."

Thea stepped back, and Walt instantly regretted the outburst. It wasn't true, at least not wholly. He both loved and hated her, but how could he explain that?

"Fine."

"I didn't mean..."

"You're a mean drunk, you know that?"

"I'm—"

"You feel guilty. I get it, and I'm sorry about what happened, I truly am, but sooner or later, you are going to have to stop punishing me for something that *we* did. And stop punishing yourself for something you can't change. Cleo is gone; you need to find a way to live with that."

"I still want..." He let the sentence trail off.

"I called you a Jonk. Go to a Medicus before anyone sees you like this, and you lose your badge for good."

She turned away and left him staring helplessly after her.

GUESS WHO'S COMING FOR DINNER

The bathroom was small and grubby. Not unclean exactly, but rundown. The bathtub was deplorably small, and the edge of the sink overlapped it slightly, making it still more cramped inside. The toilet was dated in the extreme; it didn't even have an automatic flush. The black and white tiles were cracked in places, and the grout in between them was crumbling and grey.

Sweat stung in Gin Ricky's eyes as he held the bathroom door tight shut. Why hadn't he fixed the lock? The pounding from the other side sent shooting pains into his shoulder as Cleo slammed the full weight of her body against it, over and over.

He hadn't expected the effects of the drug to wear off so quickly. When he had brought Cleo to his tiny apartment, she was as lucid as she had ever been, but over the course of the day when he had been out working, the drug had evidently worn off.

He could hear her snarls as she threw herself repeatedly at the door. Gin Ricky, of course, had some Quietus in his apartment, but it was, unfortunately, in the living room with Cleo.

"I can get you what you need," he called irritably through the door.

The reply was more snarls.

Thinking quickly, Gin Ricky pulled the small wicker cabinet that sat next to the bath in front of the door, hoping it would buy him a moment or two. He rummaged through the drawers in his sink and found what he was looking for.

The small glass phial was filled with a fine iridescent power that looked like gourmet salt. Pixie Dust was a powerful hallucinogenic that also had the qualities of a pharmaceutical-grade sedative; it happened to be Gin Ricky's drug of choice. The blend he held in his hand was one of his own design.

With every pounding thump, the small cabinet moved an inch or two away from the door. Gin Ricky clambered on top of the toilet lid and crouched down facing the threshold. He unscrewed the cap of the phial and poured its entire contents into the palm of his hand, and waited.

The next assault on the door pushed the cabinet just far enough away that Gin Ricky could see Cleo's bloody face and hands curled into claws. The hit after that caused the cabinet to move enough so that, if she'd had a mind to, she could have slipped through the gap. The hit after that threw the door wide open and sent the cabinet skittering across the floor.

Cleo advanced with demonic fervour, her arms held in front of her. Thick black saliva coated her teeth and dribbled down her chin. His knees shaking, Gin Ricky waited until she was less than a foot away from him before he raised the hand filled with powder to his mouth and blew.

The powder created a dense cloud in the air between them, and Cleo could have done nothing to stop herself from inhaling the Pixie Dust. She coughed and spluttered, sending globules of spit flying through the air, then slowly sank to the ground. Her eyes remained open, but her mind was clearly elsewhere.

There was no way of knowing how long the effects of the Pixie Dust would last. Covering his nose and mouth with a handkerchief, Gin Ricky sprinted from the bathroom and into the living room. Stepping over crate after crate of bootlegged liquor, he opened his own personal cabinet and pushed the bottles out of the way, causing a number of them to fall, spilling their contents on the threadbare carpet. Far more pressing was what was behind the bottles; a slim metal case that sat flush with the back of the cabinet.

Gin Ricky pulled it from the shelf and put his thumb on the fingerprint reader. The case popped open. Inside was a small stout bottle. He dropped the case and took the bottle back to the bathroom. He undid the cap and poured the clear contents into Cleo's mouth.

Nothing happened, she was still under the influence of the Pixie Dust, but Gin Ricky breathed easily once more. When she did come to, she would be Cleo again, and she would be rational, for a short time anyway.

MISE-EN-SCENE

Walt's Cicada wasn't working. He wasn't sure whether this was due to the electric shocks from the stun weapons used by the Onyx Legion soldiers on Harold's payroll, or the numerous blows to the head he had received in the last seventy-two hours, but either way, his tragus implant was no longer making or receiving calls. He irritably added it to his mental list of problems, far nearer the bottom than his current issues, including Thea, his firing, Torrez, the possible criminal charges that he would no doubt face when one of the techs at the TPD watched the full days footage from his Seer implant which, inconveniently, was still working and saw his little episode at the SubLevel gate, and the Pleasure Quarter murders.

Walt felt an odd sense of detachment from the majority of his problems. He knew that he should fear the consequences of the scene he had made at the SubLevel gate, there was, after all, the very real possibility that it would result in his execution, but he found he didn't care. He knew that he should feel guilty about his altercation with Torrez and should be worried about his firing that, if the SubLevel incident didn't bring charges, could also result in a strike, but he just wasn't.

While his self-loathing and apathy had increased, so had his resolve. Walt was unable to do anything for Thea at present, and that knowledge was driving him mad. It meant that he was singularly focused on finding out who had attacked her and solving the larger mystery. He would do anything to distract himself from the aching feeling in his chest that had nothing to do with his broken ribs.

When Walt arrived at 2319 Belvedere, he was not surprised to see that Thea's entire floor had been evacuated. A popup hotel had been erected in the street outside the tall chromatic building, and from the music and laughter that was coming from inside, Walt assumed no one was particularly put out by the inconvenience, especially as they could claim back their expenditures in the line of their civic duties.

As the elevator door opened onto Thea's floor, Walt had to cover his nose and mouth. The smell was indescribable, like a roast left in the oven too long, but so much worse. The corridor bore the marks of an explosion at the very end. The farthest door had been blown from its hinges, the carpet was blackened, and the wooden panelling on the walls was blistered. Fire department investigators were moving around the corridor and, from what Walt could see, inside Thea's apartment.

"Hey, fellas. How's the investigation going?" Walt called.

Several of the investigators turned around. They were all wearing yellow-ish suits stained with patches of soot and silver face masks shaped like convex hexagons.

"Authorised personnel only, pal. The homeless shelter is downtown," said the nearest yellow suit.

Ignoring the slight on his evidently bedraggled appearance, Walt made to pull his badge from his pocket before remembering it wasn't there.

"I'm Detective James, but if I ever find myself sleeping rough, I'll remember that."

"Oh, sorry, Detective. Jeez, you look awful." The tactless investigator removed his mask. He was middle-aged, White, and weather-beaten, though he spoke with the candour of a much younger man. Walt got the impression he was immature and sloppy.

"That happens when you're attacked by ghouls," he said dryly.

"You were here before the blast?"

"Yeah, mind if I take a quick look around?"

"Eh, sure. Officers were here earlier, though. We are still trying to recover some of the bodies. It's a real mess in there."

"How many dead?"

"Four CSI and three ghouls that were dead before the explosion, but some of your guys took the body bags earlier."

"Everything on the level?"

"Gas explosion, from what I can tell."

"None of the buildings in this district are connected to gas mains. In fact, less than ten percent of buildings in the city are. I checked." Walt smirked at the expression on the investigator's face. "I'll take that look around now."

Walt walked past the investigator, leaving him dumbfounded.

Inside, Thea's apartment was unrecognisable. It was like a blackened square crater. The furniture was destroyed. Nothing could be salvaged. Even if Thea did recover from the ordeal, she would still have to start again.

The investigators had marked out the positions of the four bodies with blinking red buttons that flashed with semi-transparent numbers. The bodies were charred and fragile, the bones had bowed and melted in places due to the heat. Their placement did nothing to corroborate the notion that the fire was a setup, but there was also nothing that explained it.

No matter how many times Walt looked over the scene, he could find nothing out of the ordinary. The place was so distorted that had he not known it as well as he knew his own apartment, he would have been lost inside. Just as he had given up hope of finding any leads, a glimmer of something small caught his eye.

Underneath the charred mass that had been the kitchen island, the edge of a brassy cylindrical object glinted in the light cast by the evidence markers. Walt got down on his hands and knees and retrieved the suspicious item.

It was a shell casing from a large calibre bullet. Walt recognised it to be from an assault rifle that was commonly used by the Onyx Legion. He scoured the scene for more, but the fake gas explosion had done its work, and the legionaries who had been present had covered their tracks well.

With nothing left to do at Thea's apartment, Walt resolved to go home and change, then find a way to speak to the medical examiner about the chips on the ghouls and the clear murder of the TPD CSIs. After that, he had a bone to pick with a friend in the Onyx Legion.

Page 3 of 3
LOCATION:
2310 Belvedere
Tenebrium Central
Tenebrium Proper
TC 257

TENEBRIUM FIRE DEPARTMENT
SINCE 2137

INCIDENT REPORT

Company/Business: No.
Private Residence: Yes.
Owner/Proprietor: Detective Thea Persephone Williams.
Owner/ Proprietor present at time of incident? No.
Injuries due to incident? Yes.
Fatalities due to incident? 7.

FD notified of incident at approx. 10:20 pm, by Mrs R. Hernandez (neighbour), who heard a large explosion from apartment 2310. Responders arrived at scene at approx. 10:35 pm. Property was ablaze. Responders were unable to enter due to the severity of fire. Responders brought fire under control at 00:35. Safety protocols were followed, and after adhering to Safe Entry procedures, responders were able to begin the search for casualties. After an extensive search carried out on 1/05/2425, 7 fatalities were confirmed, and their bodies were recovered from the scene, as well as the bodies of 3 ghouls who had predeceased the fire.   Note: As the scene of the fire was also an active crime scene, the TPD has its own open investigation into the incident. This has no effect on the conclusions drawn in this report.
CONCLUSION
After investigating the scene for a period of 3 days, 1/05/2425-3/05/2425, the FD has concluded that the explosion and resulting deaths were the direct result of a faulty gas main. See File#210-545-08
No evidence of foul play.
No evidence of negligence.
Did the building meet all relevant health and safety codes? Yes.
Were all relevant checks and servicing requirements met? Yes.
INCIDENT DESIGNATED AS ACCIDENTAL DUE TO UNAVOIDABLE CIRCUMSTANCES

Report completed by: Fire Chief Lionel Irons
Verified by:
Enertec Engineer: N. Goldberg
Independent Investigator: H. Proops
Responders present at scene: M. Ramirez, A. Khan, T. Willson, T. Jones, X. Chen and P. Ford

THIS IS YOUR 9 AM WAKE UP CALL

"Thea? Thea? Doctor, she's waking up!"

"Miss Williams, can you hear me?"

Thea could, but she kept her eyes tight shut. The lights wherever she was were so bright that they were blaring orange through her closed eyelids. She felt groggy, like she could sleep for days if the voices would just stop.

"Miss Williams, are you with us?"

Reluctantly, Thea opened her eyes. A doctor with a pointed rodent-esque face was bearing down on her, his eyes narrowed with concern. There was something in Thea's throat, she began to cough and tried to pull it out, but the doctor stilled her hands with his.

"Let me get that for you," he said, gently removing the long clear plastic tube from her mouth. "Nice of you to join us, Miss Williams. How are you feeling?"

Hospital, Thea thought, clarity returning with every second.

"Awful," she answered truthfully.

"That's to be expected. You have suffered quite an ordeal. Now, as I've explained to your mother..."

Thea was only half paying attention as the doctor carried out a neurological exam; she already knew what had happened to her and what the consequences would be. She had been poisoned with Quietus, and the comedown would be hellish.

She was far more concerned about the implications of the attack than anything else. She remembered everything that had happened with painful acuity. She replayed the events in her head, already searching for answers.

Who had attacked her? Why had she been poisoned? Who sent the ghouls? Was it because she was getting close to something that some dangerous people wanted to be kept secret? How did Cora factor into the grander scheme?

While not one for portents and omens, she was convinced that her dream had meant something, that her unconscious mind was putting together the pieces while her conscious mind slept.

"Thea? Thea?" Her mother's voice brought her back to the present. The doctor had left, and Athena was looking at her, concern etched on her face.

"How long have I been—"

"Nearly five days, but—"

"Where's Walt?"

"I paid his bill and visited him while he was still unconscious. He looked poorly when I saw him. He was discharged yesterday against doctors' orders. Your father has forbidden him to see you. Now Thea, really. You need rest."

Thea ignored her mother's protestation and sat up. She pulled the tubes from her arm and the electrodes from her chest. Taking a brief inventory, her throat was scratchy from the intubation tube, her head hurt, and the wound on her side was tender. Her chest was sore as if something was pressing down on it. Her mind was fuzzy, she felt tense and on edge, irritable.

"No, Mom, what I need is to leave."

"You're shaking, Thea. You need to get back into bed."

Thea looked down at her hands, she was indeed trembling. Her fingers quivered, and her body felt odd, her skin tingled, and she felt clammy. She was twitchy and moody, and she knew exactly why.

That put a kink in Thea's plans. She needed to be on an even keel, with her wits about her to investigate, yet she couldn't just sit around and wait for another murder or another attack. Walt, she reasoned with her reckless side, managed to cope with varying degrees of success while under the influence of both alcohol and withdrawal.

Before she could finish her dangerous train of thought, however, there was a knock at the door. Thea hurriedly pulled the covers around herself as her mother moved to emit the visitor.

"I'm not interrupting, am I?"

"Never, Bast. How are you?"

"Very well, Mrs Williams, thank you for asking."

"We haven't seen you in so long. You should join us for dinner sometime."

"I'd love that. How's Thea?"

"Ask her yourself." Athena opened the door wide so Bastion Tyrus could see into the room.

"I'll let you and Thea chat. Perhaps you can convince her to stay until the doctors discharge her."

Bastion stepped aside to let Athena sidle past him, closer than was necessary, in Thea's opinion. Her mother lived a bland and relatively simple life, she wouldn't grudge her small pleasures. Bastion was a fine-looking man, after all. He was particularly tall, Black and well-muscled. He had sharp cheekbones that gave his face a regal quality and long, thick dreadlocks that were pulled back into a ponytail.

"Ignoring orders, now there's a surprise," Bastion said, closing the door behind him. He walked over to the side of Thea's bed and hugged her. His warm body felt like a salve.

They hadn't seen each other in a while. Bastion was Walt's oldest friend; they were more like brothers, and as such, the lines of Thea's friendship with him had blurred after Cleo's death.

But here and now, a friendly face was what she had needed. Her mother loved her, there was no doubt about it, but her worldview was limited. She was uptight and only saw what she wanted to. She didn't, or perhaps wouldn't, acknowledge the darker parts of life that didn't fit in her perfect fantasy of how things should be. Thea's theory was that she had married young and spent too much time with people who were paid to be her friends. Her mother's life was insular.

"I hear you got your ass handed to you," said Bastion grinning, letting go of Thea and sitting on the edge of her bed. He looked good; he usually did. His hair, which was such a dark shade of brown that it was almost black, was a lot longer now, and he hadn't had dreadlocks the last time they had seen each other, but he was the same Bastion. Sweet, charming, always able to express himself, and unafraid to share his feelings.

"That's a way to describe it."

"Ooh, half a smile. You must be sick."

"How did you know I was here?"

"Walt asked me to check in on you. If it wasn't for your father's embargo, he'd be here himself."

"How is he?"

"He's Walt. He looks like shit, but he's doing his thing. I know you guys are on the trail of some bad guy or another, but at least one of you needs to take the time to get better, and Walt's already left, so it's on you to be the sensible one. How you feeling?" Bastion reached out and took Thea's hand, he squeezed it gently.

"On edge, and apparently, this is only the beginning, so maybe another day or two of hospital sedatives will do the trick. Before I forget, what hospital am I in?"

"You're not. This is Medicorum Medical Services. Is that a problem?" he asked, for Thea had winced. She wasn't keen on the place, something about it gave her the creeps.

"It's fine, doesn't matter. I love paying exorbitant bills."

"I'm sure Daddy will pay for it anyway."

"I may be sick..."

"Yeah, yeah. You'll kick my ass. I can see it now, six-foot-six soldier killed by tiny cop."

Thea laughed, then regretted it instantly; the movement had caused a searing pain in her side where the knife had penetrated.

"You remember what happened?" Bastion asked seriously.

"Some of your guys were firing at ghouls through the gate."

"What?" Bastion's whole aspect changed. He went from an old friend to a commanding officer in seconds. "What do you mean? Who? Where? Did you get unit numbers? They attacked you? I'll have their heads."

"You can't discipline them. I just need you to be on the lookout in case it happens again," said Thea rubbing her hands up and down her arms in an effort to stop the odd tingling sensation that was causing the hairs there to stand up.

"What do you mean? What does this have to do with your attack? If the Onyx

Legion or any of its soldiers had a hand in what happened to you or Walt, I will see to it that they are punished, corporally or dismissed."

"Thank you," said Thea with a wistful smile. "But you can't. Walt and a small squad had an altercation. If you investigate too heavily…"

"Damnit, Walter. Can you at least tell me when? So I can try to get those soldiers off SubLevel rotation."

"It was morning. Walt will remember more. I was… out of it."

"You're sure they had nothing to do with the poisoning?"

"I suppose we shouldn't rule anything out, but I don't think so. I think whoever it was knew I had a Sub Shift, and the legionaries were just incidental. They didn't know we were there until Walt put a gun to the back of one of their heads."

"Fuck. I'll check no one reported it and clear the records if they have. Walt has survived enough shit, I'm not having him die over this."

"Still cleaning up his messes."

"Since we were kids. You're one to talk. Besides, he'd do it for me. He has. More times than I can count. The last while has been hard for him. He's done some stupid things, but the man's my brother. I won't give up on him, and you shouldn't either."

"It's not that I've given up on him; I haven't. It's not that simple," Thea said, struggling to find words that encompassed the complicated mess that was her relationship with Walt. "He still cares, I know that, and I know he saved my life, but I can't count on him. I think he blames me for what happened with Cleo."

"He doesn't blame you—he blames himself. That, I know for sure."

"I think being around me makes him feel worse, and I don't want that, but no matter what we do, we don't seem to be able to get away from each other. We don't talk anymore. We don't anything. It's like we're in limbo. But none of that matters right now."

"The case comes first."

"People are being turned into ghouls and brutally murdered. My numerous personal problems can take a back seat."

"He and I don't talk much either, not since Cleo. I tried to investigate the Onyx Legion's part in it, but I came up empty. If we let him push us away, he'll have no one. Think about that before you kick his reprobate ass to the curb."

Thea nodded and looked away so that Bastion wouldn't see the tears pooling in her eyes and threatening to fall down her cheeks.

"I'll let you get some rest. Stay here, at least for another day. I know you feel responsible for the cases you're on, but you need to get better before you can get back out there. Tenebrium needs its best detective working at a hundred per cent. I'll see you soon, Williams." Bastion gave Thea a quick peck on the cheek and left.

Now that she was finally alone, Thea let herself crumble.

IN AND OUT

Walt wasn't a victim. He was a lush, a juicer, a boozehound, a liar, and a coward, too afraid to face his demons. He was coasting, existing, doing the bare minimum that could still be classified as living. He could pinpoint the exact moment in his life when he had gone past the point of no return, and it hadn't been when Cleo was taken away, or when he had turned to alcohol to drown his sorrows, when he had begun to neglect his duties as a detective, or when he had pushed Thea away, and it definitely hadn't been his firing. No, that was just the last in a long list, his chickens finally coming home to roost.

The beginning of the end for the man Walt always wanted to be, the hero he envisioned, the superstar detective that had been a champion of the department, was when he had compromised his principles. The beginning of his affair with Thea was the first in a long line of questionable decisions that had led him to this point.

Neither of them had wanted it to happen; in fact, they had both fought it for a long time. Walt had even gone as far as to try to get her assigned to another mentor, but whether by fate or unfortunate coincidence, they had ended up together in all senses of the word. It was, to Walt's mind, this first bend of his internal morals that had snowballed and ended him up in his present mess, because it was the little things, the small chips, cracks, and pieces that he lost along the way. It had been a slow decline, not a freefall.

He was no longer a detective. It struck Walt with painful clarity as he stood staring at the TPD building that he had truly and completely hit rock bottom. He had been stripped of the thing that had been the linchpin of his identity for so long; he felt naked in the desert. He had lost everything that mattered to him, and it had all been done by his own hand. As bereft as he felt, he had no one to blame but himself; it was sobering—though, only metaphorically.

It felt strange to attempt to break into the police department. He had gotten so

TENEBRIUM

used to being able to come and go freely. He had been suspended once before, and on that occasion, he'd had no desire to return to the building, in fact, he'd had no desire to return to anything. Now that he was actively and genuinely pursuing his duties as a detective, it was peculiar that he was having to do so in secret.

Walt ruled out entering through the main doors. The fact he had pulled a gun on Torrez in the middle of the atrium was surely still fresh in people's minds. The likelihood of him going unnoticed was slim. He had considered getting a Jonk to drop him off in the detective office docking bay, but that ran the risk of coming face to face with Torrez himself or the captain. She may not have cut him off from the TPD database yet, as was the norm when an officer was fired, but he doubted her precarious favour would tolerate trespassing. No, what Walt planned to do was use the old fire escape at the back of the building.

The back of the Tenebrium Police Department building was far less well maintained than the front. Large dumpsters lined the alleyway between the TPD and the SWAT garage that neighboured it. They were all yellow or blue and marked with signs ranging from "Office Waste" to "Corpse Disposal". The smell was pungent, to say the least. Bags of miscellaneous refuse were piled up between the dumpsters giving the space the look of a shady back alley rather than the rear of a police station.

The fire escape was narrow and rusted in places, made from wrought iron and painted black. Walt pulled his newly re-filled hip flask from his pocket, took a large swig hoping to dull his fear of heights, then started his ascent.

It was around thirty stories up that Walt's acrophobia decided it would be a good time to try to enter the building. On his best day, he would not have been able to climb to the two-hundredth floor, let alone battered and exhausted as he was.

The landing had a wonderful view of the ever-moving city and a small window that led into a deserted corridor near the old paper archives. Unhelpfully the window was locked, and as the floor was rarely trafficked, Walt wasn't surprised.

He scanned over the window with his ocular implant. It showed, in glowing red letters, that the window was locked by a single magnetic deadbolt. Thankfully, Walt had just the tool to deal with it. Thinking idly that the police station should employ better security, he pulled a small metal object shaped like a drop point blade without the handle from his pocket. He placed the lockpick on the bottom of the window frame and pulled it slowly along the edge. Near the centre, he heard a faint *click* and knew that he had been successful.

Replacing the lockpick in his pocket, Walt gently pushed the window open and paused to listen for movement in the corridor. All was quiet.

Walt climbed through the window, then shut it carefully behind him. He wasn't particularly worried about running into anyone other than cleaning staff as the paper archives were almost never used. They served only as a backup should the virtual archive that formed the TPD database, presided over by Orion Martin, or the virtual evidence archive be hacked or destroyed.

With appropriate caution, he made his way to the elevator and prayed that no one was inside. When the doors opened, however, "Walter, how are you? I was real sorry to hear about Thea."

"Thanks, Bill," said Walt, clearing his throat. The doors slid shut as Walt pressed the button for the one-hundred-and-thirty-second floor.

"Any news?"

"None yet."

"Must be hard for you."

Walt was spared the need to reply as the lift doors opened a moment later, and Bill said, "Welp, this is me. See you around." Walt inclined his head. The doors shut, and the elevator continued its upward climb.

Either Bill was an excellent actor, or his firing wasn't common knowledge. Surely, Bill, like everyone else in the building, had heard about his dust-up with Torrez. Haply, Bill was showing some of his characteristic tact, and it was conceivable that many attributed the brawl to stress over the attack on Thea. Their sordid past was well known within the TPD, and it was possible his colleagues were assuming he had been given special dispensation. Whatever the case, Walt could not be seen by too many people, lest word get back to the captain, or arguably worse, Torrez.

A hundred floors above the window through which he had broken into the building, Walt showed the chip to Jasper Kinley or Irish Jaz as his friends called him. He was White and in his mid-thirties with an excitable personality that Walt usually associated with ferrets. The tech expert's eyes widened as he examined the slim octagonal metal disk.

"It's big," Jasper said quietly, holding the chip under a magnification lamp.

They were standing in the corner of his cramped and humid office, behind a row of large filing cabinets. Jasper's copper hair was sticking to his forehead, but his grey eyes were focussed.

"Big?" Walt repeated, surprised, curling his thumb around his index finger, imitating the size.

"Nowadays, yes, that's big for a microchip. Unless..."

"Unless what?"

"If it's new tech and it's this size, it's probably extremely powerful. We are talking serious hardware. Expensive to make, too. Maybe in the millions for a single one." Walt's hesitancy must have shown on his face because Jasper continued, "Think about your ocular implant or the coms device in your ear. Both can link you to the database and people all over the world, not just the colonies. And they are a tenth of the size—if that."

"So, these chips are serious business."

"Unless they are over a couple hundred years old, yes. If you could give me some more time with it, I could tell you more."

"It comes with me, I'm afraid."

"That's all I can tell you just by looking at it. If you change your mind, let me know. I would love to open it up. On the Q.T., of course."

"Thanks, Jaz. Hey, before I forget, my Cicada isn't working. Any chance you could take a look?"

"Sure. Sit up on the table, and I'll see what I can do."

Walt complied, taking off his jacket. He winced, his ribs aching.

"I have only ever had to replace one of these before, and you're on your third. You need to be more careful."

"I know, I know. It comes out of your budget." Walt waved a hand dismissively as he lay down on the leather recliner, rather like a dentist's chair.

"With yourself. You need to be more careful with yourself."

"Working on it."

Jasper seemed unconvinced.

After Jasper had repaired his Cicada, Walt had an idea. While he was there, he was going to pay Flynn a visit and see if the cockroach knew anything.

Walt met no one as he walked through the corridors he knew so well. When he arrived at the morgue, he peered through the reinforced square glass window. It gave a perfect view of Flynn's desk.

The medical examiner was sitting behind it, eating a dry-looking and slightly battered sandwich.

"Flynn," said Walt loudly, bursting through the door and causing the skittish ME to jump.

"Walter... eh, Detective James," Flynn said as he picked his lunch up from the floor. "What can I do for you?"

"You're not going to eat that, are you?" asked Walt, eyeing the sandwich from atop a wrinkled nose.

"I assure you the floor in here is spotless." Flynn sat the sandwich back on the cluttered desk. "Did you need something?"

"I just wanted to see how the autopsies were coming on the ghouls taken from Detective William's apartment."

"What ghouls?"

"The ghouls that were collected from the scene by our guys. Unless we have another morgue I don't know about, they must have been brought here."

"I have the bodies of four crime scene investigators, but no ghouls. If they were meant to arrive, they never did. I think the DA is dealing with them." Flynn turned away in what Walt thought was a pathetic attempt at indifference.

Walt moved further into the room and leaned against a clean and empty autopsy table, knowing full well that it would agitate Flynn. The ME looked over at Walt, his eyes sweeping his position on the table, but said nothing.

"Have you completed the autopsies on the crime techs?"

"Yes."

"Anything to share?"

"No." Flynn's voice shook. "It's not your case... conflict of interests..."

"Weird, I'd have thought you'd have plenty to say." Walt paused, watching Flynn. When the man continued to stare silently, Walt went on, "No? I'll talk then. Are you still getting freaky with the corpses in cold storage? If that got out, it might even be a strikeable offence. How clean is your record? Even if it isn't, the damage it could do to your reputation... I'm thinking that you've probably got some skeletons in your closet. Maybe in your bed. Rather fond of the old cold embrace, ain't ya? Does your wife know? Do you make her have a cold bath before you—"

"Enough, Detective," said Flynn, throwing up his hands. "You've made your point."

"Have I?"

"The autopsies are not conclusive. The fire damage is severe. I can only surmise that the deaths are a direct result of the fire." Flynn gave Walt a sly look. "You were fired."

"What's your point?" Walt stood and stepped closer to Flynn, his hands in his pockets, an eyebrow raised.

"I-I don't have one," said Flynn, taking a step back.

"Thought not. Has any evidence been brought to you from the scene for cleaning or sampling?"

"None."

"Thanks for the help, Doc. Tell anyone I was here, and… well, you get it."

CHIT CHAT

Dill Kelly's penthouse apartment was a thing of beauty. A statement in and of itself. A constant high-class reminder that he had status and position. Torrez longed for the same kind of power and influence. He had planned to lie in wait for Dill and strike a deal, but the temptation to snoop was not easily ignored.

Torrez wandered through the grand rooms imagining himself living there. The penthouse's circular main area was more like a palace with its glazed dome ceiling that flooded the room with light. The walls were black bean veneer inlaid with golden figures from Greek mythology. The entire polished floor was mother of pearl, and the furniture was teak, upholstered with ivory leather, all of which sat atop a magnificent terracotta and cream rug with a luxuriously thick pile.

The envy Torrez felt was maddening. Did he not work hard? Had he not paid his dues? Was he not entitled to this kind of living? Why did Dill, a dirty criminal, deserve more than he who fought for justice? Granted, Torrez thought, he had not walked the straightest of lines; but didn't the ends justify the means in a city like Tenebrium? Where it took extra determination and a real desire to do good to fight through the corruption and make a difference. He had made a difference...hadn't he?

"Are you staying for dinner, Drew? Mrs Kelly does so enjoy your company."

Torrez wheeled around; he had been so busy admiring the bookshelves filled with rare first editions that he hadn't heard the elevator doors open

Dill was dressed in his usual grey suit with matching waistcoat. The chain of a golden pocket watch hung from one of his buttons and disappeared into his pooched pocket. His manner was open and friendly, amused even, but Torrez was sure that he sensed the darker intent Torrez was possessed of.

"Actually, this isn't a social call. I'd like to speak to you in private."

"As you wish. Follow me."

Dill led Torrez into a comfortable study. It was more minimalist than Torrez had expected, but no less grand. The entire east wall was made up of mismatched shards from broken mirrors in shades of gold, bronze, and the usual silver. The desk was lacquered black wood, and the chair that sat behind it was an opulent leather wingback with bronzed studs.

Dill didn't ask Torrez to sit, nor did he take up his impressive throne. He poured himself a glass of bourbon and then perched on the edge of his desk.

"What can I do you for?" Dill swilled the amber liquid around in his glass, then took a swig.

"You lied to me."

"I ain't your wife, complete honesty was never part of the deal."

"I'm a cop—"

"Second. You're one of us first, ain'tcha?"

"Well, see, that's why I wanted to talk. You live like a king while I'm out here like a pauper. I think I've done enough cleaning up after you. I think it's time you start treating me like part of the inner circle."

"Oh, you do, do you? You know, this is disappointing to me. I thought you knew the score. I tell you what the higher-ups want, you do as I say, and maybe, maybe, if I see fit, I cut you a piece of the pie."

"There's no maybe. You deal me in, or I'm going straight."

"Hardly a threat. Working legit or not, you don't have dick on me, Drew."

"It's funny, when I'm not running around covering up for mobsters, I'm actually pretty good at the whole detective thing. I did some digging and greased the right palms, and I put a little scenario together. Maybe you'll help me fill in the blanks."

"Do tell."

"All right, and you'll have to bear with me here, someone—that bit I'm not so clear on—makes this powerful and presumably cheap new drug; Styxx. It's illegal, so they have to use a bootlegger to transport it around the city. Once there, it's passed to an entrepreneurial individual who distributes it through his many strip clubs and the brothel that he is a silent partner in, it starts to do well, and he begins to get some of his pushers to start peddling it, too. It wasn't properly tested, and it created a pandemic. Suddenly, all distribution stops. Loose ends are tied up, and everyone pretends they have no idea what happened to those poor ghouls, but then a new strain appears, and fingers are pointed, cops start investigating again, and it becomes a problem. Am I at all close?"

"You've forgotten how to play poker—you don't give away the farm."

"I'm not finished. To try and clean up the mess, the guilty parties weaponize ghouls using these little adorable silver chips. Then they destroy the crime scene, the ghouls and the chip, killing or at the very least scaring off and stymying the detectives investigating."

"You have no proof; you just said it yourself."

"But what if one of those chips survived?"

STRANGE BEDFELLOWS

Thea was climbing the walls. She had never experienced anything quite like it. She was so tired that she could barely lift her head, and yet she couldn't sleep. The withdrawal had hit her all at once with the force of a ton of bricks. She had seen it in others more often than she could count, but she had never truly grasped how it felt. It was like she was on fire. Her eyes burned, her skin seared, the pins and needles were so intense that she thought she must be bleeding. As quickly as the fire came, it would disappear, and she would be so cold that she could have been naked in the snow.

Without relief, her stomach churned, her abdominal muscles were strained from the number of times she had vomited. She was anxious, paranoid, and irritable in the extreme.

She had barely registered the news that her apartment was gone, she had chased her mother away with her sniping, and her father hadn't deigned to visit. The doctors and nurses came in and out in a blur, changing her IV and bringing food she couldn't bear to eat.

Thea was hearing things; her sister was crooning in her head. There was a tap, tap from the drums, and then the spotlight from the little jazz bar she sang at came on. It was too bright. Thea couldn't see. The silhouette on the stage was blurred. It didn't look like Cora, it was too tall, too broad.

"Detective."

Hands were pulling Thea away, but she didn't want to go.

"Detective."

She fought against them, but the singing was growing quieter, and the jazz bar was melting away.

"Bitch, I need you to wake the fuck up." The hands were shaking her hard. It was painful, and her neck was straining. "Detective!"

Benny Pickford was in her hospital room.

All at once, Thea was completely aware. She knew exactly what was happening and where she was—in danger.

Thea kicked out at Benny, catching him in the chest and scrambled back up the bed as far as she could until she hit the wall. Benny regained his balance as Thea darted off the bed towards the dresser which held her clothes and, more importantly, her gun.

She plunged her hand into the drawer and pulled out her Colt 2411. She pointed it straight at Benny, centre mass, then paused, surprised.

Benny looked awful.

There was a thin film of sweat covering every inch of his skin. He was ashen-faced and unsteady on his feet.

"What's wrong with you?"

Benny chuckled in a pained, hoarse sort of way. "There isn't enough time in the world to answer that question."

"Why are you here?"

"I need your help."

"That's a laugh." Thea lowered her gun, she no longer had the strength in her arms to hold it up, but she didn't let go of the trigger.

"I'll tell you everything I know about the ghouls, and the murders, and Styxx. I'll tell you about the Gold Legion, but I need your help."

"The Gold Legion is dead. You're lying."

"Bitch, I wish I was."

With difficulty, Benny removed his suit jacket, then his waistcoat, then his shirt. At first, Thea was confused, sceptical even, but soon all became clear.

It was as if the blood in his veins had turned to pure gold. His entire hand was aurulent. It looked dead and heavy like a statue's. Whatever was causing the affliction was spreading up his arm like teardrops running upwards.

"Still think I'm lying?"

"You need a doctor." Thea threw her gun onto the bed and reached for the call button, but before she could grasp it, Benny threw it across the room. It smashed as it hit the wall falling to the floor in pieces.

"No. Some of them are here. If they see me talking to you, I'm dead, and all the info you need is gone."

Sneaking out of the hospital was not going to be an easy task. Between the police officers patrolling the floor and the guards Thea's father had placed outside the door, few options were left to them.

"How did you get in here?"

"I have ways."

"Of course."

"We're just going to go out the way I came in."

"And if they challenge us?"

"You're armed, aren't you?"

Thea didn't reply. Instead, she picked her gun up off the bed. She dressed quickly, taking little notice of whether or not Benny was looking. He owned a brothel, she had nothing he hadn't seen a million times before.

"All right, let's go. I think I know someone who can help you. You first," Thea said, nodding towards the door.

Benny was palpably sweating now. It had soaked through his jacket, and he rubbed his eyes repeatedly as the salty liquid stung them. Thea was impressed with how easily he could assume his Ward Eight persona. He went from a perspiring mess to calm and collected in seconds. He fixed his collar, mopped his brow, and headed to the door.

Benny stepped out of the room and left the door ajar. Thea could hear him shooting the breeze with the guards. She put her hands in her coat pockets to hide the shakes and followed after Benny.

The guards in the hallway did a double-take as she stepped out of the room. "Miss Williams," said the guard on the right, a tall blonde. "You have to stay put."

"I'm really sorry about this."

Thea pulled her gun from her pocket and fired two shots lightning-fast. Both guards dropped to the floor unconscious.

"I didn't think pigs carried non-lethal weapons," said Benny.

"Most don't," said Thea. "Personal choice. Don't worry," she turned the dial on the side from blue to red. "It does both. Let's go."

Thea and Benny dragged the guards as best they could into Thea's now-vacant room and shut the door.

Both struggled as they made their way down the stairs, avoiding the elevators and as many staff and visitors as possible. Benny's arm seemed to be heavy and cumbersome. Whatever was slowly crawling up his skin was making him weak, and even though they were travelling downstairs, he became quickly tired.

Thea was jittery and clumsy. She would lose and regain control of her body from one second to the next. Her hearing was acute to the point of pain, and she too felt weakened.

The lobby was swarming with police and personal security. The DA's men patrolled in pairs, much like the way they patrolled the SubLevel gate. The unis sat in groups in the waiting room huddled together, but no less alert. All seemed to be focusing on the entrance, tasked with stopping unwanted entry more than unwanted exits.

"Which way?" Thea asked.

Benny led Thea out of the elevator and to the left to a set of large double doors, the sign above which read "Staff Only". Just beyond the doors was a fire exit.

Walking neither too quickly nor too slowly, they made their way towards the doors making every attempt to look as inconspicuous as possible.

As Thea had predicted, there was a biometric scanner next to the door. "We'll need to wait for someone to come out."

"No, we won't," said Benny. He closed his eyes for a moment, and when he opened them, they were no longer a rich brown, but a startling blue. He looked directly at the scanner, which emitted a red beam of light, there was a small *beep*, and the doors swung open.

"You coming?"

Elanor Miller

Amazed, Thea followed Benny through the door towards the fire exit.

THE PAST
Three years ago...

Thea felt sick. She had only just managed to pull the armoire door shut as Cleo had entered the bedroom. It was so clichéd, the mistress hiding from her lover's wife in a closet. Thea was ashamed of herself. She felt dirty, she felt guilty, she felt stupid.

She could hear Walt chatting airily with Cleo as if nothing had happened. What if Cleo was home for the day? What would they do then? Would she have to hide all night? It was easier to contemplate these problems than to think about what would happen should Cleo find her.

The armoire was made of dark wood and filled with Walt's suits; his shoes piled up at the bottom were making it impossible to find a comfortable way of sitting or crouching. She supposed that she deserved no less.

Thea's knees were starting to ache, and she was cold. She had only managed to grab her underwear and trousers before diving out of sight. It had been quite the task to put them on in such a cramped space. Now, as she sat in the dark listening to the man she loved laugh with his wife over lunch, she felt like a fool. What were they doing? It was ridiculous. Walt was married. He was twelve years older than her. He was her mentor and her partner. He was married.

Long after her legs had gone numb, Thea heard Cleo bid Walt goodbye. The front door slammed shut, but still, Thea waited. It wouldn't do for Cleo to have forgotten something and come back. She had hidden for what felt like hours, what difference would a few more minutes make.

An aeon later, or so it felt to Thea, Walt opened the armoire door slowly. Blood flushed Thea's cheeks; she was mortified. She got to her feet with as much dignity as she could muster and stumbled out into the bedroom without looking at Walt. She grabbed her shirt from where she had kicked it under the edge of the bed and put it on.

Neither said a word.

Thea got down on her hands and knees and groped under the dresser for her hastily hidden shoes. She grabbed them, straightened up and then threw the shoes against the wall. Walt didn't flinch. Still, he said nothing; he just watched her, his face a mask she couldn't read.

"This has to stop," Thea said finally.

"I know."

YOUR MEN

French 75 was quiet, which suited Walt. It would be early evening before the nightlife really kicked off. As it stood, the speakeasy was all but empty. A young couple canoodled in a booth near the bar where Walt sat next to a pair of habitual lounge lizards. The couple laughed and smiled, clearly lost in each other. Walt ignored them bitterly and raised his hand to call for another drink.

In the early hours of the morning, on the brink of collapse, Walt had had to concede to sleep. He'd gone home, showered and changed, slept for an hour or two, then headed to Medicorum, where he had been refused at the door.

Walt felt stymied. Without the avenues that were usually available to him, he had no way, or at least no legal way, to follow up on any of his suspicions. He had no jurisdiction or authority, and unless the bodies of the ghouls could be located, there wouldn't ever be any proof of anything other than an unfortunate, yet random, attack on an unlucky detective.

Walt gulped back the cheap liquor that the bartender poured him as soon as the glass landed in front of him.

"Another."

"You have exceeded the maximum amount allowed on a single tab, sir."

Walt lent over to the register and swiped his Index over its face; it made a happy little *beep*.

"Excellent. Another drink coming right up," said the bartender turning away to fetch a bottle. It hadn't taken much to convince him that Walt was no longer law enforcement; he had believed it with insulting ease.

Someone sat down in the seat next to Walt.

"You're not supposed to be drinking," said a warm and measured voice that Walt knew to be Bastion Tyrus.

"I'm not a cop right now. I was fired," he said without looking at Bastion.

Bastion sighed audibly. "What did you do this time?"

"Long story. I'm in no mood to chat, Bast. So, if you wouldn't mind…" Walt walked his fingers in mid-air. Bastion waited, ignoring Walt's abrasiveness. Unable to stand his best friend's scrutinising gaze, Walt said finally, "I attacked Torrez, choked him, pulled my gun on him, and broke into the police station though they might not know that yet."

"You're suicidal now. Wonderful," Bastion said dryly.

"I mean it, Bast…"

"I went to see Thea for you." Walt turned to look at Bastion, whose expression was slightly smug. "She seems all right, climbing the walls, but that's not unlike her."

Walt said nothing, the relief he felt was indescribable.

"I know you care about her. And I get it. Thea's nice, really nice. She's great. Strong-willed—pretty, too," Bastion continued. "But she's just a dame." Again, Walt said nothing. "Are you just going to ignore me? I dragged my ass halfway across town for you. I do have better things to do than to check up on your not-girlfriend. The Legion doesn't run itself."

"Speaking of—"

"Thea already told me about your little stunt at the gate. I'll look into it, and I'll cover your ass as always."

"That's not what I was going to say," said Walt leaning in. The place was empty, but nonetheless, he didn't want to be overheard. "Thea's apartment was torched."

"What does that have to do with the OL?" said Bastion, his eyes narrowed.

"The investigators were killed, and the crime scene was destroyed."

"That's awful."

"I found some shell casings at the scene from an OL standard rifle."

Walt watched Bastion's face trying to measure his reaction.

"You're sure?"

"No doubt about it. Your men were in her apartment. Cleaning up after whoever attacked us."

Bastion lent forward and grabbed Walt by the shoulders. "Are you absolutely sure? This is a serious accusation to make."

Walt pulled a small evidence bag out of his pocket containing the dark gold shell casing and placed it on the counter between himself and Bastion. Bastion stared down at the small piece of metal with wide eyes.

"I'm sure. You're the legion commander. You didn't know about this?"

"You think I would do this? You think I would try to kill you? Me? You are a pain in my ass, but you're my brother."

"I don't think you tried to have us killed. But I'm not convinced that you didn't send your men to clean up after Harold Williams. We all take our orders from somebody, right? Duty above all else. That's you through and through, Bast."

"I had nothing to do with this," he spat the words, affronted. "You may have lost yourself, but I never did. The OL upholds justice, we don't cover up crimes."

"Right, of course not. The DA is squeaky clean, just like the OL. Except, he's not, and they aren't, because it was your men who dragged my wife away while I watched, and it was your boss who, if he didn't order the hit on Thea, is working with the people who did."

"No. No, Harry would never; he loves Thea. They can't have been legion soldiers, my men—"

"Maybe," said Walt, loudly cutting across Bastion. "You don't have as much control over your men as you think."

"You are a paranoid sonuvabitch, you know that? And don't talk to me about your wife—I put my ass on the line for you with that one. I did what you asked; the rest is all you. The Onyx Legion, my legion, had nothing to do with this."

"Except I know it did."

"You don't trust me?" Bastion said, getting roughly to his feet. "Me?"

"I want to."

Bastion let out a clap of derisive laughter. "What happened to Cleo really did a number on you, didn't it? I'll investigate what happened to Thea, and I'll clean up your mess at the gate. When you remember who your friends are, call me."

Bastion grabbed the glass from Walt's hand, drained it, slammed it on the counter, then left.

Walt would normally think it was the height of dishonour not to trust a man like Bastion, who was more brother than friend, but that was just the problem; he knew him too well. He knew when he was lying, he knew when he was deflecting, and he knew that Bast was hiding something. He didn't want to believe that Bastion had anything to do with the attack or, knowing as he did how Walt felt about her, that he would hurt Thea, but Walt just couldn't shake the feeling in his gut that somewhere along the way something in Bastion had changed.

MISCALCULATIONS

Torrez was blindfolded. He knew this for certain. It had taken him a moment when he had awoken to realise, but he was sure of it now. Whether his eyes were opened or closed, all he could see was blackness, but if he looked as far down as possible, as if squinting at his nose, he could see a thin line of light.

After establishing he was blindfolded, he tried to establish just how bad the situation was. He was tied to a chair, another certainty. The cold metal against his bare back was giving him shivers, and the rough rope around his wrists and ankles was biting into his skin. His hands were already starting to go numb. He had been divested of his shirt and shoes, but was grateful to find that he was still wearing his trousers.

The last thing he remembered was threatening Dill Kelly. It had seemed like a calculated risk at the time; now however, Torrez felt that he had underestimated the man.

As the minutes ticked by, Torrez began to lose his composure. The fear was setting in. Struggle as he might, he could do nothing to even minutely loosen his bonds. Nervous sweat dripped down his spine, causing his skin to stick to the chair.

A door opened somewhere to Torrez's right. Every muscle in his body tensed, and his breath became ragged and shallow. He knew that it would do him no good to struggle, but he did it anyway. He was panicking. He fought so hard against the ropes that held him that he almost toppled the chair over.

"...Sounds to me like that broke down bastard isn't as washed up as you thought."

Dill's voice stilled Torrez instantly. He strained everything in his body, trying to listen, to get a sense of where the large man was.

"Just wait until Pickford kills the girl." Dill was on the phone, to whom Torrez had no idea. "The way I hear it, you take her out, he won't be a problem... Just remember, though, a man with nothing to lose is dangerous."

Silence fell. Torrez's fingers ached from holding on so tightly to the arms of the chair.

"You really fucked up, kid."

Torrez started; Dill was inches from him. He heard footsteps circling him, coming closer; there was more than just Dill in the room. "You're gonna have to pay for that. We'll talk afterwards. Hold out for me. It'll be better if you do. Stay loyal to the cause, and you might survive this."

The first blow was more of a tap, really. Torrez was so tense that when the fist collided with his gut, it didn't wind him. What followed was much worse.

Torrez wasn't sure which hit did it, but as he coughed up blood and spat it on the floor, a tooth went with the coppery liquid. It made a small *tink* as it hit the ground. His fingernails were next. No matter how collected he claimed to be, he couldn't help but scream then. He kept waiting for questions, but they never came, nor was he asked to pledge his allegiance or to swear fealty. He would have done anything to make it stop.

After they had broken a few of his fingers, they took a lighter to the soles of his feet. The pain was excruciating. Tears streaked his face as he cried out for someone, anyone, to rescue him. He passed out not long after, the smell of his own burning flesh lingering in his nostrils.

CHOPPING BLOCK

Benny was barely conscious as Thea all but dragged him down the hallway that led to Walt's apartment. She let go of him gently next to the door; he slid down the dark panelled wall sprawling on the burgundy carpet, his eyes open, but unfocused.

The small hooded lantern atop which Walt usually kept a spare key had been torn off the wall, and the key was nowhere to be found. Thea was contemplating breaking the door down before it occurred to her to check the handle. She was feeling the effects of withdrawal far more acutely now, and it was making her hazy.

The unlocked door swung wide, propelled by Thea's foot. She didn't bother to check if Walt was home; she knew instinctively that he wouldn't be. He would be working the case, or he would be drunk, possibly both.

Benny didn't have the strength to stand anymore. Thea didn't have the strength to hold him up anymore. She grabbed him by the ankles and dragged him over the threshold into the apartment, closing the door quickly behind them.

Walt's apartment was in disarray. Books, and the broken shelves that once housed them, littered the floors around the walls; their cases bare and toppled. The glimmering Damascus steel kitchen island was covered in shattered glass and debris. The dining table and chairs were scattered and upturned; one was missing its legs which lay abandoned near the couch.

Walt's glass coffee table was smashed into pieces, and the tall lamp that sat between the bedroom and bathroom doors was broken in half. The gramophone that Thea had listened to so many times before, lay discarded upside down on the floor, the brass horn bent. There were several holes in the walls, and the floor was specked with blood.

A bloody shirt had been thrown over the back of the armchair opposite the door, and a wet towel lay on the floor at its feet.

"The fuck happened here?" slurred Benny, reminding Thea he was there.

He looked ghastly. His skin was greying, and his eyes were surrounded by deep purple circles. He was sweating so much that he was leaving a puddle on the metal floor.

With shaking hands, Thea removed Benny's jacket and shirt. The gold tendrils had crawled past his elbow, had it not been killing him, it would have been beautiful, artistic even, like his right hand was dipped in gold.

"How bad is it?"

"Can you move your hand?"

A look of deep concentration strained Benny's face as Thea watched his fingers, but nothing happened.

"Not good, huh?"

"We need to stop its progress somehow..."

"Do what you gotta." Benny's eyelids slid shut, and he began to pant.

"Benny?"

"Cut it off. I'd rather have an aug arm than be dead. Do it."

"I—"

"You want what I know, you'll do it. Do it!"

"I can't," Thea said. Her palms were sweating.

"You have to!"

"You'll bleed out! I have no idea what I'm doing!"

"Just do it. It wouldn't be the first time a cop killed someone like me. If it goes wrong, no hard feelings, but I can feel it trying to strangle my heart, so you better do it quick."

"I am a mess. My hands are shaking. My head is fuzzy. My eyes can't focus. I feel like I could vomit," Thea was babbling, but she needed him to understand that she was not capable of what he was asking.

"Then congratulations on a wish fulfilled. You get to watch me die. Slowly. Karma is a bitch, huh?"

Thea got to her feet. She went to Walt's closet and grabbed a tie, then she darted back to where Benny sat. He fished around in his trouser pocket as Thea extended his arm. She tied the thin black tie tightly around Benny's bicep, cutting off the circulation. Benny's left hand grabbed her right and pushed a small white nasal spray into it.

"What is this?"

"China White. It will slow my heart rate, if not, I'll go out smiling."

Thea removed the cap from the small bottle and slid the conical tip that was revealed up his nose. He pushed in the bottom of the container and breathed deeply. "Ahhh...That's the good shit."

Thea touched her hand to her Cicada.

"Doc? It's Thea."

"Miss... I-I mean Detective Williams," came the flustered voice of Cecil Flynn in her ear. "Are you well?"

Thea ignored this. "I need your help. Bring your kit to Detective James' apartment."

"He and I..."

"He isn't here."

"I'll be there shortly."

Flynn arrived in a surprisingly short amount of time, carrying a heavy brown leather physician's bag. He was sweating as was par for the course for him, and he looked worried. He glanced around the ransacked apartment as he stepped through the door that Thea held open for him, but didn't comment.

"Are you hurt?" he asked, business-like, appraising Thea.

"Not me."

Thea led the doctor over to the couch, where Benny lay flat, his eyes closed and his breathing uneven. The gold tendrils had made their way up to the tourniquet just below his bicep.

"My God," Flynn uttered quietly. "What happened to him?"

"He wouldn't tell me, but whatever it is, it's killing him."

All blundering awkwardness disappeared as Flynn set about examining Benny. With precision and a practised hand, he took Benny's vitals and measured his condition. It wasn't until the doctor was examining his pupilar response that he paused and took a step back.

"What? What is it?" said Thea

"Is this Benjamin Pickford?"

"Yeah—"

"Detective, this is a conflict of interest in so many ways. He is a suspect in your attack. Why didn't you call this in?"

"It isn't that simple."

"I will not risk my career over this," said Flynn, drawing himself up to his full height. He turned away from Thea, grabbed his bag and began throwing his instruments back into it.

"The hell you won't. You do this, and I'll forget what I saw in cold storage. Save him, or I'll tell the captain that you are a depraved sex offender who should be in jail."

"You wouldn't," Flynn spluttered, letting go of his bag. It hit the floor with a dull *clunk*.

"I have nothing to lose if I do."

Thea could almost hear the cogs turning in his head as he weighed up his options. Benny moaned loudly as if to highlight the urgency of the situation. "You will call off Detective James. You will hold him to your silence."

"Yes. Yes, I'll make sure Walt stays quiet. Just do something."

Flynn looked at Thea for a split second, then set to work. He untied the tourniquet from Benny's upper arm. The flood of gold on his skin immediately gained another inch.

"Mr Pickford?" said Flynn, shaking Benny gently. "Mr Pickford, I'm going to need to remove your arm. I have no time to try to diagnose what has been done to you; it's spreading too quickly. Do I have your consent? Mr Pickford?" Benny moaned dismally.

"Do it," Thea said. "I know for certain he'd rather lose his arm than die here with us." Flynn's eyes found Thea's, and he nodded once.

Together they righted the dining room table and sterilised it as best they could. Thea washed it down and then doused it with top-shelf vodka. Moving in an agitated daze, she went to the linen closet in the bathroom and pulled out all the sheets she could find while Flynn set up a tray of surgical instruments, which he placed atop one of the dining chairs. She handed the square sheets to Flynn, who dressed the table. For once, he was calm and unflustered. Thea could not say the same.

With difficulty, Thea and the doctor carried Benny's dead weight and laid him on the table. Flynn draped a white sheet over him, leaving only his right arm visible.

"All right, Mr Pickford, I'm going to give you something for the pain." Flynn rummaged in his bag for a moment, then he pulled out a silver pentagonal syringe complete with a long black needle. Flynn muttered something, and the barrel of the syringe filled with a clear liquid.

"Wait!"

"Detective, we don't have time to waste."

"He's already taken something."

"Morphine?"

"No, China White...eh...Fentanyl."

"What dosage?"

"I have no idea..."

"I'd rather risk an overdose than him waking up for this."

The doctor turned back to Benny, a look of deep concentration on his face. He plunged the long needle into Benny's arm just above the tideline of gold. Benny, who had been moaning and writhing, stilled after three seconds, which Thea counted in her head.

"I'm going to need your hands here, detective," Flynn said tersely, handing a pair of latex gloves to Thea without looking at her. She took them and put them on.

"What do you need me to do?"

"Once I make my incisions, I need you to keep the site as bloodless as possible and hold the arm still so I can see what I'm doing."

Thea took a deep breath and nodded.

"All right," said Flynn, picking up a scalpel. "The first thing I'm going to do is make anterior and posterior incisions. You see how I'm going just deep enough to part the skin? Now, I'm going to deepen the incision on this side and begin ligating the major veins."

"Why are you telling me this?"

"To keep you focussed. This isn't pleasant. Dab away that blood. Thank you. I'm going to use the laser scalpel to cut away the muscle tissues. Be prepared for a slight burning smell. See? Now it's time to dissect and ligate this artery here, do you see it?"

"I think so."

"It's very important that we tie this off, so he doesn't bleed out. This thick white string here? That's his nerve. I need to pull it out a bit so I can cut it. There. So far, so good?"

"I'm fine. His breathing is even as far as I can tell."

"Time to tie off the other artery, this one is a bit bigger, so we need to be more careful. Easy does it... and there we go. Swab, excellent. Another nerve out of my way...Could you hand me that flat—ah! Yes, thank you. I don't want to catch any surrounding tissue when I cut the bone, so I'm going to use this to scrape away any remaining tissue. You see? A bit like carpentry this bit, isn't it?"

Thea nodded. Flynn's constant commentary was having the desired effect. It was causing Thea to focus on the medical whyfors and not the grisly reality of what they were doing.

"Nearly there," said the doctor, mopping his brow. He reached over the tray and picked up what Thea thought looked like a garrotte. It was a thin piece of serrated wire with a thick cylindrical handle on each end.

"Hold the arm still," said the doctor, sliding the wire under Benny's arm in line with the exposed bone.

Thea put a hand on Benny's shoulder and the other at the crook of his elbow.

Flynn began to pull the wire back and forth like a saw, slowly but surely making its way through the bone, "Careful not to breathe in any of the dust—it's poisonous."

With one final pull on the wire, the bone split in two and Benny's arm was separated from his body.

Thea took a step back from the table. The gruesomeness of what they had just done, settling in. She watched in a kind of horrified amazement as Flynn quickly and deftly sewed up the incision.

"I should put in a drain, but I don't have one in my kit. I suggest he go to a hospital—and soon. He'll need antibiotics and more tests to ensure that we have rid him of whatever ailed him. I'll leave the syringe. It's programmed with the correct dosage of morphine should he awake and be in pain."

"Thank you, Doc."

"I do not enjoy working under duress, but you did well. I trust you will uphold our bargain," Flynn said, a trace of his usual nervousness returning.

"I will."

"I was never here, then."

The doctor collected his instruments, washed them off in Walt's kitchen sink then packed them into his bag. He checked Benny's vitals one more time and then left.

Thea looked at the faux operating table where the doctor had left Benny's amputated arm. Breathing heavily and with shaking hands, she wrapped the limb in the sheet that covered Benny and placed it on the kitchen counter. She would have to dispose of it, but that was a problem for later.

Thea pulled the duvet and pillows from Walt's bed and took them into the living room. She covered Benny with the throw and put a soft pillow under his head and his stump. She looked at the ragged wound, sewn up neatly with black thread. It made her very slightly nauseous to think about it.

Turning away, Thea went and laid down on the couch. She pulled the blanket that was thrown haphazardly over the back, over herself, curled up into the foetal position and fell asleep almost instantly.

KINKS

Ric was alone on the stained bed with no memory of when Hayes Henshall had left. The damp satin sheets were twisted around his neck, and he was hanging half off the end, his shoulders touching the floor. The room was awash with gloom, the only light coming from the neon signs posted on the buildings outside. His head pounded. Hayes liked it rough, but he had never caused Ric to blackout before, and he had never just left. He paid for Ric's company, it was true, but only because he had to; they couldn't see each other otherwise. Their relationship had long since surpassed that of sex worker and client.

Ric slid off the bed onto the floor. He grabbed his underwear from the heap of clothes nearby and slipped them on, his body aching all over. It wasn't the first time that a client had gone too far, and it probably wouldn't be the last. But Hayes wasn't just a client. He turned on the bedside lamp and began searching the room. Usually, Hayes would leave payment on the dresser when he left, but there was nothing there.

"Fuck."

Ric guessed that when he had passed out, Hayes had panicked and left, but he couldn't understand why. Hayes was a doctor after all; he should have, would have, known that Ric was unconscious. Could the man who talked so often of freeing Ric so they could marry really have just left?

How was he going to explain this? The women were never far from their pimps, but the men like him were trusted to fend for themselves. Ric knew that there was going to be hell to pay if he didn't come up with the credits. The boss would never believe that Hayes hadn't paid; he was a loyal customer, and Ric was property.

A pain like a jolt of electricity shot up Ric's spine and nailed him in the back of the head. He dropped to his knees, blood spouting from his nose. The pain was blinding, so intense that Ric thought his skull was splitting and then...it was gone.

Shaking, he got clumsily to his feet. He slipped on the pool of his own blood and threw out a hand, managing to catch himself using the bedpost. Carefully, the echo of the pain in his head still causing a low uncomfortable throb, Ric made his way to the bathroom.

He opened the door; the automatic light came on overhead, drenching the room in clinical blue-white light that served only to highlight the dismal look of the place. Ric grabbed some tissue from the grubby counter and dragged it over his face. He ran the water in the sink filling the basin halfway and dunked his head. The cold water was sobering.

Surfacing, Ric looked in the cracked and tarnished mirror. He watched as his own eyes narrowed. There was something on his temple. It was circular and metal; a faint blue light emanated from the rim.

"What the hell?"

He tried to pry it from his skin, but it shocked him. As soon as his fingers made contact, the light around the edge turned red. A strange feeling like he was floating or high came over Ric, and suddenly he wasn't in command of his body.

He pulled back the shower curtain, unsure why he was doing it, but unable to stop himself. Hayes was dead in the freestanding bath. His hands bound, his throat cut. Ric wanted to scream, to cry, to hold the man he loved, but he couldn't. He wanted to run, but his body wasn't following his commands. Instead, he reached up and wrenched the shower curtain from the rail and laid it flat on the floor.

He wanted to stop, but he couldn't. He lifted Hayes' body from the bath and laid it out on the shower curtain before rolling him up in it and tying it off with the cord from the hairdryer under the sink.

All he could do was watch as his body acted of its own accord. Over and over, he screamed "NO!" inside his head. The more he tried to fight back, the sharper the pain was in his temple; it was like the disc was burning him, but he refused to allow himself to be party to a murder. His body tried to pick up the bundle that contained his lover. *NO,* he thought, and his hands paused. *Move away from the body,* he commanded himself, focusing with every ounce of brain power he had.

His body slowly straightened up and backed away towards the counter. With a herculean effort, he turned himself around to look in the mirror, all the while fighting the compulsion to give in to the silent orders that told him to take Hayes' body outside and toss it in the dumpster behind the building.

The pressure in his head was building higher and higher the longer he refused to act. He felt an electrical jolt in his temple that caused his knees to buckle, and then nothing.

MISTAKES WERE MADE

Darkness.

'¿Dónde estoy? ¿Es este el infierno?"

"Close, but no. You're still in Tenebrium City, kid."

"No puedo moverme."

"That's the drugs. It'll wear off soon. But you're gonna wish they didn't, trust me."

Darkness.

"Hazlo parar!"

"Relax, if we don't set that arm, you'll never use it again, and you can't afford a new one on a detective's salary."

Darkness.

"Mis pies están fríos..."

Darkness.

The floor was cold. That was the first thought that came to Torrez as he floated somewhere between consciousness and unconsciousness. His hands ached, and his fingers felt tender. His ribs were tightly bound, it made it difficult to breathe. His feet tingled, and his left arm was heavy. Why was he lying on the floor? He couldn't remember.

"You with me, Drew?"

Torrez opened his eyes. He was in a small dark concrete room, lying on a thin blanket on the cold, unyielding floor. His body was covered in bandages. With difficulty, Torrez sat up.

"You broke my arm," said Torrez looking over to where Dill Kelly sat in a throne-like chair that was juxtaposed to the otherwise stark room.

"You really fucked up this time."

"So why am I still kicking?"

"Because I am the one who brought you in out of the cold, and if you fuck up, it reflects on me. And Detective Williams survived our attempt to silence her."

"You tried to kill Thea?" Torrez winced as he tried and failed to get to his feet.

"Yes, and now she's in the wind. Sit down before you hurt yourself. You are going to bring me that chip and do everything you can to keep her away from the case."

"I was right, then, about all of it."

"Some of it, but it's so much bigger than you can imagine. You do this, and I'll give you what you want."

"Just like that?"

"Just like that. Mistakes were made on both sides. I should have given you more credit. But, I think I've made my point. Fail me again, and you're dead. Succeed, and well, you'll live the rest of your life like a king."

"I won't hurt Thea or anyone else."

"I never asked you to. Bring me the chip, and all will be forgiven. Welcome to the club."

QUIETUS

Cleo tossed and turned in the bed, almost strangling herself with the sheets as she writhed, gasping for breath. Sweat beaded on her skin, soaking the fabric that choked her and causing it to cling still more to her thrashing form. As the veins in her neck threatened to pop and her face got redder and redder, Cleo awoke screaming. She wrenched herself free of claustrophobic covers, ripping them in her haste to be rid of them. The light duvet wrapped snugly around her had made her feel like she was in a coffin. Throwing the tattered remains of the bed set aside, Cleo stood.

She was in a small bedroom. It was impeccably clean, but shabby. It appeared to be a child's room, or perhaps a teenager's. Various posters covered the blue walls, and there was a short bookcase filled with science fair trophies next to a writing desk.

Cleo walked unsteadily to the door, still shaken from her nightmares. It was locked.

"Is anyone there?" she called out.

There was a sharp click, and the door opened, but she didn't recognise who stood on the other side.

"Who are you? Where is my husband?" Cleo said, stepping back. "How did I get here?"

"It's me, Gin Ricky. I freed you, remember?"

"No..." she said unsurely, but he did look familiar.

"We met at Ward Eight and again at the SubLevel."

"Who are you? Where the hell am I, and what the hell is going on?" The familiar agitation that led to anger and then frenzy was itching inside her brain. A red haze was creeping into the corners of her vision. She couldn't help but notice the vein in the side of Gin Ricky's neck; it pulsed tantalisingly.

"What's happening to me?" And she was shocked to hear that her voice was more like a snarl.

"I'll tell you everything, but first, you need to take this." Gin Ricky held out another squat bottle.

"What is it?" she growled.

"Quietus. It'll take the edge off."

Cleo snatched it from him, only barely containing the urge to attack him. She gulped at the bitter liquid, retching as she swallowed it. It was like someone had poured warm water down her back. It was pleasant and soothing. The haze began to clear, and then she was falling. She felt arms catch her and carry her over to the bed. She sank into the soft mattress gratefully and succumbed to sleep.

ATONEMENT

Sitting up as best he could, Benny faced Thea. He didn't much like the way she was looking at him. It was expectant, but the mood in the room was different than he was used to. Somewhere over the last few hours, their dynamic had changed. She no longer looked at him like a nut to be cracked, but as an equal. It was unnerving.

"How you feeling?" she asked.

"Like twist caps are going to be a bitch from now on."

It was true, many things in Benny's life were going to be harder now. He would have to make adjustments. All of that seemed like a small price to pay for his life, however. He had no plans to mourn his lost limb, but he did have machinations to make those who had done this to him pay.

"I'm sure a man of your means can afford an augmentation."

"Thanks to you, I'm broke, remember."

"Actually, I didn't get a chance to process the seizure of your funds before I was attacked. I hadn't completed the requisition form, and the deadline will have passed. So, you're still filthy rich," The detective didn't try to hide the contempt in her voice.

"You don't like that I'm a pimp, you don't like that I'm rich, you don't like my clientele. You're awfully judgemental for a cop. Unless you're as squeaky clean as you pretend to be."

"I'm not." She laughed without humour. "And I don't hate that you are a pimp. I hate the way you treat people. You prey on the desperate, and you treat the ghouls like mindless beasts. You facilitate rape, and you take away people's freedom. You choose to own those who work for you, you don't have to, but you do. You make them property, objects, 'assets'. You dehumanise them. You are everything that is wrong with Tenebrium. That's why I hate you."

Benny shifted uncomfortably under Thea's unwavering gaze. He had pins and needles in the arm that was no longer there. He looked at the bandaged stump, trying to convince his brain that it was an illusion.

"Do you need more meds?" Thea asked, leaning forward in her armchair.

"Do you care? Ain't I more likely to talk if I'm in pain? Leverage and all that. If I do talk, you gonna kill me?"

"I want you in jail. I don't want you dead. But no, I don't care if you're in pain. You wanna play the tough guy? Be my guest. I have all the leverage I need. You betrayed whoever you were working for when you came here with me. There is no going back for you and considering what they did to you." Thea gestured to Benny's stump. "I think you know that."

"I'll take the morphine," Benny said after a moment.

Thea picked it up from the table next to her and threw it underhand to Benny, who caught it. "You aren't gonna play nurse?"

One corner of Thea's mouth lifted slightly in a half-smile. "I don't trust myself to stick that thing in your neck."

Benny laughed softly. He tilted his head slightly to the side and placed the syringe against his skin. There was a faint *beep,* and he felt a tiny prick, and then a pleasant warmth flooded his limbs, numbing the uncomfortable tingling in his missing arm.

Neither spoke, both seemingly content to sit while the pain relief did its work.

"You're nothing like your sister," Benny said after a while. Thea stiffened where she sat, but didn't comment. "She only worked for me for a month or two, did you know that?"

"Yeah," Thea said quietly.

"Gave me a real shock the first time you caught up with me, let me tell ya." Benny's eyelids were getting heavy. "You're identical on the outside, but she struck me as lost, unsure of herself, damaged. But not you." Benny was fading fast. "Can you sing like her? She was mesmerising."

"No. No one can," said Thea. Benny was too drowsy to look at her, but her voice sounded sad.

When Benny opened his eyes again, Thea was sleeping upright in the same high-backed armchair. She had pulled it over to the dining table that was serving as Benny's bed. She looked peaceful, her breathing even. Her high cheekbones were thrown into sharp relief by the dim lamp her head was tilted towards, and her full lips were parted the smallest amount. Her face was much softer when she was asleep. The tension that underpinned her features disappeared, and she looked her young years. It was easy to forget her age when she carried herself like someone who had experienced a much older person's suffering. The weight of responsibility pushed down on her, but as she slept, it seemed to melt away.

Benny sat up as quietly as he could. He slowly pushed the duvet off his legs and swung them quietly off the table. There was a nearly inaudible rustling behind him, more a movement of air than a sound.

"Don't even think about it."

Benny turned. Thea was pointing her gun at him, as alert as if she had never been asleep, her eyes shrewd, all gentility gone from her face.

"I'm just stretching my legs."

"You promised me information if I saved you, and I did. It's time to start talking."

Benny settled himself on the table again. He punched his pillows into a more comfortable position so that he could sit as upright as possible. It was difficult to know where to begin.

"The rich in this town think the poor and disenfranchised are a plague," he began making sure to look Thea dead in the face. "They want to subjugate them, so the rich can rise even higher. They can't see that they have already done that. The Quadrant, The Poor Quarter, it's a prison with no bars. You end up there; you're stuck for life. You start there; you ain't got a hope in hell of making it in this city.

"Only a select few get out, and I was one of them. I built myself from the ground up. I've done bad shit, you already know that, but you, with your rich daddy, can't understand what the hunger feels like. You don't know what it's like to be starved of food, starved of respect. And once I got a little bit of that power—a little piece of my own, I did anything and everything to defend it, to grow it; but no matter how much you're worth or how impressive your climb is, no matter how different you are from that starving kid, everyone still looks at you like you're an orphan in rags begging on the street."

Benny watched Thea's face soften slightly as if the thought of him as a hungry child bothered her.

"So, when a man in a gold mask came to Ward Eight and told me that he could give me position and power, that hunger I had felt in the camps, that need to prove myself, that greed that comes from knowing what it's like to have nothing took over."

"A hard life is no excuse for the things you've done," said Thea

"I'm not making excuses; I'm telling you my reasons. I didn't know he was from the Gold Legion at first. People wear masks to my place all the time, especially those who like to pretend they are above it all. The deal was simple. Be the middleman for a new drug. The manufacturers give me the drugs, and I give it to the pushers and peddlers, maybe sell a bit through my clubs. All under the table, and you only know the names of those beneath you, so nobody has anything concrete to tell the cops. Turned a tidy profit, too."

"You were selling Styxx. Did you know what it would do to those who took it?"

"No, not at first. But after a couple of weeks, some of my guys started reporting that buyers were getting violent, acting irrationally. It didn't take long to realise that the drug was highly addictive, and the withdrawals were serious shit. I didn't really start asking questions until a young guy named Melvin turned up dead. He'd been working on the street for me, good kid, hard worker. It was like he'd been mauled by an animal right behind the club. So, I checked my cameras, and I saw a woman in a business suit, she was fine one minute then she collapsed. He tried to help her, and when she came to, she ripped out his throat with her teeth and tore him apart. She was probably one of the first ghouls."

"Who was the man in the club?" Thea asked, her face unreadable.

"I never found out. But I began to ask questions of the delivery guys before all hell broke loose. One let slip about the Gold Legion, and I did some digging. I should have known better; in this city, someone is always watching. Anyway, another masked man found me, asleep in my bed this time. He stuck the barrel of a shotgun in my mouth and told me that he could give me everything I had been promised and more if I kept my mouth shut.

"I never saw his face, but as the weeks went on, he came to me more often and began to give me a little more info about how the Gold Legion planned to rise up and take power from the city and when they did, I would be given a job in the DA's office. They wanted an army, so some genius came up with the plan to extort the city's existing drug problem. Make a drug so addictive that people would do anything they wanted to get a hit, even march against the mayor. But they were too eager, it seems, and the drug wasn't properly tested. They were just as shocked as we were when the ghouls went on their rampage."

"All this death and suffering because of greed and carelessness."

"Welcome to Tenebrium City," Benny said with an ironic smile.

"What about the ghouls at Ward Eight? What about Quietus?"

"I was telling you the truth before. A client asked, and I obliged. I still had some Styxx left over. I was never stupid enough to keep selling it though I know others were. As for Quietus, I ain't got a clue. I hadn't heard hide nor hair from the legion for nearly two years until bodies started to drop. I didn't kill Eve, but I did put her body in the church, and I did inject her with Quietus after she was dead."

"Why? Why would you do that?"

"Breadcrumbs for your boys. I'm greedy, and I want power, but what use is money or station in a city that's destroyed? And that is what will happen if they get their way."

"Why did they come to you after such a long time?"

"They wanted me to kill you. You are getting close to something they don't want you to know about."

"You had me attacked?" Thea sat forward in her seat.

"I chose my life over yours. I'm not sorry. That's how I survive. I am sorry about the drug. I had managed to get my hands on some for Eve and thought that with you dead, I would be free of The Gold Legion, and when they did your autopsy, it might lead that partner of yours to the truth."

"What happened to Eve?"

"She came pounding at my door, screaming about a pain in her head and then she just dropped dead, blood pouring out of her nose and ears. I knew she had been servicing The Gold Legion on the side, that was who she was 'freelancing' for, so I hedged my bets. I don't know how she came to have that hole in her head. It wasn't like that when I left her."

"That's everything?"

"That's all I know."

"What about the Onyx Legion?"

"I think there's trouble there. Some are loyal to the city, but others are acting without orders. I think they may have defected. I can't be sure, though."

"And you have no idea who is behind all this? Who is actually part of The Gold Legion?"

"I have my suspicions. Your father knows something, I'm sure of it. I'd be looking at all the top dogs in the major businesses. Styxx usually came in unmarked cases or cases that had the labels blacked out, but once not long before the ghoul situation was labelled a crisis, someone hadn't been thorough enough, and I could read the last few letters 'O-R-U-M'."

"Medicorum. Makes sense. Why else would the place be crawling with OL soldiers?"

"What are you gonna do?"

"What are *we* gonna do? There is no going back for you. You might as well join us and try to make a difference."

"You want me locked up."

"Not right now, I don't. You are more useful to everyone here. You'll pay for the atrocities you've committed, but I'm not putting you in the hands of people who want to silence you when you could help fight for others who don't have a voice. If they really want to take the city, this is only the beginning."

"Do you believe in god?"

Thea's eyes widened momentarily. "No, I don't," she said, taken aback.

"Why?"

"I'm a detective; my world is rooted in evidence and hard fact."

"No faith, then. I believe, but I worry that I have strayed too far from the path."

"Then why do you do the things you do?"

"If I'm already going to hell, I might as well enjoy the ride. But this feels like atonement, what we're doing. Do you think it will help?"

"I don't know. I don't think I'm the right person to answer that."

THE PAST
Two years ago...

The clear cube was suspended over a deep ravine that led straight to the incinerator some one-hundred-and-twenty floors below. Cleo's eyes stung with tiredness as she watched the naked man in his glass cell. His fists were bloody as he pounded on the impenetrable walls; he had been like that for hours. Giving up finally, the man dropped to the ground, curled up into the foetal position and began to cry.

"Computer, begin recording audio log."

"Recording."

"Doctoral candidate Cleo Rose James. I have been observing subject 78152 for —" Cleo checked her watch. "—six hours. Subject is exhibiting advanced withdrawal symptoms after a single dose. Ticks, spasms and muscle contortion are all present. Styxx prototype batch GC22-10 is unsuccessful. Proceeding with termination. Damnit."

Cleo leaned forward, her hands hovering over the console in front of her, she looked at the desolate man once more before pushing a harmless looking green button. Instantly, coiling ethereal smoke began to fill the holding cell. The man scrambled to his feet, trying to outrun it, but he was cornered by its tendrils in seconds. He coughed and choked, clutching at his throat, then fell to the ground, arms and legs akimbo. He twitched for a few moments, then was still.

Cleo pressed the orange button next to the green one, and the bottom of the cell opened like a trap door. The man disappeared out of sight as he fell into the abyss.

Cleo yawned. The trial was getting nowhere, and they would run out of death row inmates soon. She drank the last cold dregs of the coffee she had left on the console hours before and stretched in her seat.

Reluctantly she got to her feet and made her way out of the lab. Medicorum's corridors were dark and deserted at this late hour, but Cleo was used to it; she paid no mind to the creeping shadows. When she arrived at Doctor Maxwell's office, the door was ajar. She knocked gently on the frame.

Chester Maxwell was sitting in his chair, tall and sharp-nosed as ever, he absently stroked his thin moustache as he read from a data stream.

"How may I help you, Cleo?" he asked, looking up with a small smile.

"I think we need to start working on a new batch of Styxx. The latest test results have shown it's more addictive, not less, and some of the subjects are exhibiting violent behaviour." Cleo rubbed her eyes, exhausted.

"How violent?"

"In the extreme."

"With these sorts of trials, there are always setbacks. It's to be expected when researching. We will work it out, don't worry." He turned his attention back to the data stream. "Good lord! Is that the time? I'm going to call it a night, and you should, too."

"I just need to send my report," Cleo said, nodding. "Then I'll head home."

The doctor dismissed the files he had been browsing, picked up his briefcase from under the handsome wooden desk and slung his navy-blue overcoat over his arm. "Goodnight," he said, taking his matching Homberg hat from the rack next to the door, putting it on and tipping it to Cleo.

"Goodnight."

Cleo turned to follow him, then stopped. She heard a commotion from the corridor beyond. She peered out. Chester had disappeared, but five Medicorum guards with their mirror-esque helmets were dragging a teenage boy towards the holding cells. She watched them out of sight, rooted to the spot.

Surely a boy that young couldn't be an inmate for testing? He had looked so lost and scared.

Cleo teetered where she stood in the doorway, undecided. Finally, curiosity won out, and with a last check to see if Dr Maxwell was really gone, she entered the office proper.

All thoughts of sleep gone, Cleo moved quickly towards the desk and sat down. With practised fingers, she pulled up the last data stream opened and began to read. She was horrified by what was in front of her plainly in black and white.

"Looking for something?"

Cleo let out a little yelp of surprise. Dr Maxwell had returned. He stood in the doorway, his arms folded. His face was impassive as he waited patiently for an answer.

"I...I accidentally deleted my last report. I need it for my own records. I sent it to you, and I was hoping to find it and email it back." The lie was feeble.

"All computers, consoles, and terminals in the labs are backed up to the remote server." Maxwell leaned against the door frame, his large body blocking any hope of an exit he didn't permit.

"I forgot. Sorry. I'm just so tired it must have slipped my mind. I've already found it and sent it back anyway."

"No harm, no foul then." Maxwell smiled, but it was cold and didn't reach his eyes.

Cleo jumped to her feet. "Well...Goodnight, sir."

"Just one moment," said Maxwell, raising a finger. "Computer, tell me the last file opened at this terminal."

Cold sweat formed on Cleo's brow; her hands started to shake.

"Data stream, communications from GL, trial progress," the computer stated clearly.

"Ah. That's unfortunate." There was an acute danger in his voice.

Cleo wanted to cry, but she was too scared to move even so much as to shed a tear.

Maxwell's face set into a grave mask she had never seen on his usually friendly features. He lunged forward and grabbed her by the hair. Cleo screamed in pain as he dragged her from the office. She could feel chunks of her tight curls coming loose from her scalp. She kicked, punched and scratched every inch of him she could reach, but Maxwell paid her no mind possessed as he was of malintent.

He let go of her finally when they entered her lab, throwing her roughly to the floor.

"You should have left well alone. Do you know how long it will take me to find someone as capable as you? As brilliant? All you had to do was your job, but that's the problem with scientists—you have keen minds. You're curious." He sounded almost manic as he rifled roughly through the neatly arranged phials in the refrigerated units that lined the walls.

"You're part of a cult! You aren't trying to help addicts; you are trying to control people."

"Trying and failing, it seems, but we'll get there. Without you, I'm afraid."

Maxwell grabbed Cleo by the arm and threw her into the chair behind her desk, it nearly toppled over. He was upon her moments later, forcing the contents of a small vial down her throat.

"No! Please!" she spluttered, trying to spit the liquid out, but Maxwell clamped a hand over her mouth.

"Don't worry, my darling. If we are lucky, you will be my first success."

Maxwell held Cleo on the chair and dragged it over to the empty cell. He tipped the chair forward, and Cleo tumbled onto the clear glass floor. Tears flooded her vision, but she could still make out the darkness below. "No!" she screamed.

Gas flooded the chamber. She began to choke and splutter; the last thing she saw as she fell into unconsciousness was Maxwell's solemn face.

Cleo was wet, drenched even. Her skin tingled as the droplets of water hit it. She opened her eyes. She was lying in a gutter, her clothes soaked as rain poured down upon her. She felt...wrong. She was finding it hard to gather her thoughts. How had she gotten here?

Cleo got shakily to her feet, her limbs felt uncoordinated, and she staggered slightly. Passers-by gave her a wide berth as she stumbled along the narrow side street. "Where am I?" she asked over and over again, but no one answered.

Using the nearest wall for support, Cleo foundered her way out of the alley and into the open. The industrial district was busy. Businessfolk pointedly ignored the poor who had spilled over from The Quadrant. Not a soul noticed as she dragged herself, stumbling and shambling through the streets. She could think of nothing but getting home. Her head sang in agony. It felt like there was an electrical storm happening inside her skull. Every flash was like a lance to her nerves. Her vision was blurred. She had to make it home to Walt.

When the familiar building came into sight, she let out a cry of relief that sounded like a snarl. She ambled through the front entrance. The door steward spoke to her, but she didn't have the energy to reply. She flung herself into the elevator and, once inside, allowed herself to slide to the floor. The journey to her storey was too short, and it took all the determination she had to crawl from the elevator. She clawed herself upright using the railing on the wall and held it tightly as she slid herself to the door of her apartment.

The door was unlocked; Walt was home. Relief washed over her. She pushed the door open and lurched into the living room.

Jazz played softly, emanating from the old gramophone in the corner that had been a wedding gift from her father. Rose petals littered the floor. Cleo could hear noises coming from the bedroom. Moaning, whispered words, laughter.

STYMIED

Walt was exhausted. Since leaving Bastion at French 75, he had been to every morgue and corpse disposal unit in the city. Not one of them had had the bodies of the three ghouls who had attacked Thea and himself pass through their establishments, which meant that they were either hidden somewhere he couldn't reach, or they had already been disposed of by nefarious means.

He had been sure that with the eyes of the police force squarely on the case that they would have been disposed of quickly, perhaps before an autopsy, but through legitimate channels. It struck him as odd that whoever was trying to cover up the attack would do something so obviously knavish.

If he had felt stymied before, it was nothing to how he felt now. There was nothing he could do without the support of the TPD. He had followed every avenue open to him and some that shouldn't have been.

It was so late it was morning, but exhausted as he was, Walt couldn't face going home. To stop trying, even for a moment to get some rest, felt like giving up. He needed his badge back. He needed to be able to go to crime scenes and investigate with the clout that being a detective provided him.

It was this thought that prompted the possibly unwise decision he made next. He was only a thirty-minute walk away from the Derngate area of Tenebrium Proper where the captain lived with her wife and three children.

Somewhat rarely for Tenebrium City, the captain lived in a townhouse. There weren't many of those buildings left as, due to overcrowding, any development built in the last century had opted for tall apartment buildings.

The house had three floors and was slightly narrow. Rectilinear flower designs filled the panes of glass in the black hardwood door.

Walt rapped smartly with his knuckles and waited. Quicker than he had expected, the door was opened by a curvaceous blonde woman. She was White and in her early forties. He had never met her before, but the look she gave Walt told him in no uncertain terms that she knew exactly who he was. "Bea, the cause of your migraines is at the door," she called over her shoulder.

Moments later, Captain Betty Charles appeared behind her wife, looking unimpressed. She was dressed casually in a loose cream jumper and matching slacks, a wine glass filled with root beer in her hand. "This won't take long," the captain said, kissing her wife on the cheek. Mrs Charles retreated back into the house. "Mr James, what brings you here?"

"I want you to reinstate me."

"No."

"You need me on this case."

"Vanity and arrogance," the captain said bluntly. "I have a department full of stellar detectives, and you think that you are the only one capable of solving the case. No, I think we will do just fine without you. You are too close to this."

"Did any of my esteemed peers find evidence of an OL coverup at Thea's apartment?"

"Did you?"

Walt pulled out the small evidence bag containing the shell casing and held it out to the captain.

"Walter!" she said, stepping in close and lowering her voice. "That's tampering with a crime scene. It's a strikeable offence for a police officer, let alone a civilian. Have you truly lost your mind?" They looked at each other for a moment. "You'd better come inside."

The inside of the captain's house was simple yet elegant. The living room was outfitted in grey-blue and gold. Two large carved black cat statues sat on either side of an impressive and welcoming fireplace. Lit and well-stoked, the fire filled the room with a flickering intimate light. The remnants of a candlelit dinner sat atop the low table.

"I'm sorry to have disturbed you," Walt said, looking around uncomfortably.

"No, you aren't, or you wouldn't have come. Sit. Speak."

Feeling like a misbehaved dog, Walt did as he was bidden. He spared no words as he told the captain everything he had discovered since he had awoken at Medicorum, including Torrez's misdeeds. "I won't deny that I have skin in this game, but I want the truth. I have no agenda that includes coverups. Can you say the same for the rest of the department?" Walt finished at last.

"In light of what you have told me, I don't think I can," said the captain. Leaning on the mantelpiece, she stared off into the fire for a moment, thinking. "But neither can I simply reinstate you. The DA wants your head, he has done for a long time, and you know exactly why. The commissioner wants you prosecuted. The only reason you haven't been yet, is that she, like I, finds the idea of indirectly causing your death abhorrent. To charge you is to walk you to the gallows."

"I never realised her majesty cared," Walt said impetuously.

"That's because you think the whole world is against you. You are so wrapped up in your own misery that you can't tell friend from foe anymore." Captain Betty Charles looked him straight in the eye as if willing her words to sink in. "No matter what you think about capital punishment, I think we'd be hard-pressed, what you did to Torrez aside, to find someone who believes that having a drinking problem and falling in love with a colleague warrants death."

"What do you want me to do?"

"I want you to stay out of it. I want you to let others handle this. I want you to live." The captain smiled ruefully. "But we both know that's not what you'll do no matter what I say."

"I need to do this," Walt said emphatically.

"No, you don't. This is a distraction because you can't cope with your feelings." Walt spluttered, but the captain ploughed on before he could respond. "I can see only one way out of this. Accept a demotion." She said it so casually.

"To what rank?"

"Officer."

"You want to put me back on the beat?" Walt yelled, jumping to his feet.

"Embarrassing? Yes. A blow to your ego? I'm sure." The captain moved away from the fire. She sat down on the impressive grey sofa and waited for Walt to join her. When he did, "But you would still be part of the TPD, and you would still be able to participate in investigations. It's what will keep you alive. Accept the demotion, or accept that you no longer have any part in the justice system."

"I was nominated to become sergeant."

"Yes, then you let your personal life ruin you. You are in a hell of your own making, Mr James, and I am going to be frank, my sympathies are limited. You continually act against your own best interests and leave those who care about you to clean up your messes. This is a chance to start again, and I sincerely suggest you take it. If you accept the demotion, it will placate the commissioner. It's a harsh thing to strip a detective first grade of his rank, but the alternative is a final strike. No one will be able to claim favouritism. All eyes are on us—optics are important here. If I am too lenient, the commissioner or higher could overrule me, and we can't risk it."

"You are putting my career back twenty years," said Walt, defeated.

"You worked your way through the ranks before, and you can do it again."

He had done it before, it was true, but it had taken the entirety of his adult life. He didn't know if he could do it again.

"When do I start?" Walt felt like he had been steamrolled.

"A wise decision, Officer James. You can collect your uniform tomorrow morning and start immediately. I'll assign you to the Pleasure Quarter murders. Torrez is the lead temporarily."

"Have we run out of homicide detectives?"

"Watch your tone. And frankly, yes, there are more murders than we can investigate. We have taken everyone we could spare from vice and bunco and moved them to homicide. There is something rotten in this city, and this is just the start of it. Watch Torrez. If he does anything untoward, I want to hear about it. I don't want to spook him by pulling him from the case, we will learn more with you keeping an eye on him."

"Roger that."

Walt bid the captain goodnight and ventured out into the early morning feeling hardly better than he had when he was fired.

SELF-PRESERVATION

Torrez had never been a fan of dentists, especially not when he had an audience. The office was pristine and clinical, and the dentist herself was pretty and kind. Dill, who was footing the bill, sat in the corner watching as Torrez had a false tooth implanted into his jaw to replace the molar knocked out by the mobster's thugs.

"Say it again," Dill demanded.

"I lied. I never had a chip. It was taken from me by a grim-sweeper. I pulled it off the body, bagged it and then turned it over as evidence." Torrez said thickly, his mouth numb.

"You better not be lying to me."

"Look at me, Dill," said Torrez, causing the dentist to tut as she had to remove her instruments from his mouth for the third time. "You think I wanna go through your hazing again? I'm a company boy now; you can be sure of that."

"Good, because next time I'll take an eye."

Torrez hoped that his lie had been convincing. Since it had been returned to him, he had checked every pocket his jacket had, but the chip was gone. It was out there in the world somewhere. Had he dropped it? Or had it been taken?

When allowed to finish her work, the dentist worked deftly and quickly. Torrez felt no pain, but he could feel the dull pressure as she fitted the implant.

"Send in the bone surgeon," Dill told the dentist. She nodded and left, apparently eager to be out of the large man's company.

The bone surgeon arrived moments later. He was nightmarish in appearance. Huge and hulking, his hands were the size of dinner plates and looked better suited to breaking bones rather than mending them. His touch, however, was gentle as he examined Torrez's broken arm, ribs and fingers.

"I can fuse these here; the breaks are nice and clean. Treatment is painful and expensive, but quick," said the surgeon. His bedside manner was pleasant.

"Don't worry about the cost," said Dill dismissively.

"How painful?" Torrez asked.

"Honestly? Very. This device," said the surgeon pulling an implement that looked like a flashlight from his bag, "Changes the composition of your bones, making them malleable, then reforms them, good as new. It's non-invasive, but it's going to feel like you've got lava under your skin."

"But it's quick, right?"

"Very."

"Do it."

"Give us a moment before you do," said Dill looking at the surgeon. If being dismissed was out of the ordinary, he didn't show it. He nodded once and left the room. Torrez tensed. He did not relish being alone with Dill when he wasn't in a position to defend himself.

"I have somewhere to be. Once you are done here, I have a job for you. The first test of your loyalty. Detective Williams—"

"I won't hurt Thea," Torrez said at once.

"You sleepin' with this broad?"

"It's not like that, never has been."

"A selfish bastard like you made a friend. Wonders never cease. You can relax, I don't want her dead. Not now anyway. Too many eyes on us. It would look suspicious. I want you to destroy her. Her reputation and her personal life. I want her out of commission, discredited. A laughing stock."

Torrez thought for a moment, his sense of loyalty warring with his sense of self-preservation. He had no desire to harm Thea, but he also had no intention of ever allowing himself to be tortured again. "How?" he asked.

"Look into the break-in at Medicorum."

"Is that it?"

"The rest will come to you, but it needs to look organic. You can't just appear with all the answers. When the time is right, swoop in for the coup de gras."

"Which is?"

"Tell her that Walter James knew."

"Knew what?"

"You'll know it when you hear it." The grin that curled Dill's mouth sent a shiver down Torrez's spine. He knew he was a contemptible coward, but he could still smell his own burning flesh and see the mangled nail beds at the tips of his fingers. As his tongue roved over his smooth new implant, he decided: better she than I.

Thea could weather the storm of her destroyed reputation; she had done it before. Torrez knew that he would not survive another ordeal like the one he had just endured, and he would do anything, even ruin his only friend, to make sure it never happened again.

TABULA RASA

The artificial lights had brightened to their fullest extent by the time Walt reached the station. Try though they might to mimic the brilliance of daylight, much like everything else in Tenebrium City, they had no warmth.

The hazy fog that Walt tended to live his life in was lifting, and the hangover headache was setting in. He was sobering up. As he usually kept himself topped up, it was a feeling he was not accustomed to. He felt the shakes setting in at the captain's home, but he wasn't stupid enough to drink in front of her.

He held his hip flask in a trembling hand; the liquid inside sloshed tantalisingly. It would be so easy to give in as he had done at every single opportunity in the past. He could drown his sorrows and give in to the blissful numbness that bourbon wrought.

What was the harm really? What could one more sip, or even a few more sips, really do in the grand scheme of things? He was a functioning alcoholic, after all. In an ideal world, he wouldn't need alcohol to feel normal or to numb the feelings he didn't want to experience, but it wasn't like it impaired his judgement or his reactions. In fact, it was the sobering up that made him jittery, not the whiskey.

Even thinking it, he didn't believe it. His drinking was a downward spiral that, on his current course, could only end one way. "Stay away from jazz and liquor!" That was what his mother always said, and she had been more than right.

No more. He could continue like this no more.

Walt thought it was funny that he came to the decision there and then. It wasn't nearly losing Thea that had done it, or losing his job. It was just that right at that moment, he didn't want to be the person he was becoming anymore. He didn't want to get to the stage where there was no coming back. He had been teetering on the precipice for months now, and he had finally decided to take a step back from the edge. Hitting rock bottom wasn't always enough, thought Walt. You had to realise you'd hit it before you could begin to climb back out.

Walt unscrewed the cap of the silver flask and poured its contents down the nearest drain. As the honey-coloured liquid spilled, Walt had to fight the irrational urge to try to lap it up. It wasn't nearly as cathartic as he had expected, but it was a start.

He would right his many wrongs, and he would earn his badge back. He could wallow in self-pity, or he could take the second chance he had been given with both hands, and that was exactly what he planned to do. It would be difficult, but he had nothing more to lose, and if he could drag himself back to an approximation of the Walt he had been four years ago, everything to gain.

Walt noted with some surprise that Gin Ricky and his cart were not in their usual spot near the entrance to the TPD. He checked his watch; it was barely six am. Perhaps it was too early. He would have to get the coffee he had been hoping to buy from the Coffee Stop from the canteen instead.

Walt paused at the entrance of the station. It was harder than he would have expected to set foot inside, no longer as a detective, but as an officer. Torrez and Thea, Orion and Harry, Clark and Fischer, O'Malley and everyone else in the bullpen, even Bill outranked him now. It made him feel small, shorter somehow. His head bowed; Walt entered the revolving door.

The lobby was quiet. The night shift didn't finish until seven a.m. which meant there were fewer officers on duty. Even so, Walt tried to avoid making eye contact as he made his way to the uniform store.

More of a cupboard; the store was operated by an excessively old woman with Cerebral Palsy named Yolande. She reminded Walt of the kind of librarian you found in children's novels: irascible and strict. She muttered under her breath as she scanned Walt to find his measurements and grumbled constantly while she located a uniform in his size. When he thanked her for the uniform she had given him, she looked him up and down, sniffed, and then all but pushed him out the door.

From there, he took the lift to the Detectives' office, dread knotting more deeply in his stomach with every floor. When the elevator opened, however, there was only a smattering of people, none of whom paid Walt any mind. He moved over to his desk and found that it had been cleared; officers didn't have desks, they were reserved for detectives. He looked over to Thea's desk, it was as it had always been, neat and impersonal, scuffed from the numerous times he had rested his feet upon it.

"Your things are in a box in the officers' lounge on top of your new locker," said a gruff voice. Bill was standing a few feet away, he had pity etched into his sympathetic expression.

Walt took a step towards Bill, then paused.

"You don't know where the officers' lounge is, do you?" Bill said, smiling.

"They refurbished the building after I was made detective," Walt said apologetically.

He followed Bill past the canteen to a short corridor. There were four handsome wooden doors, two on each wall and a fifth glass one that led to the stairwell. Each door had bronzed letters screwed into the surface; they read: "Officers' Lounge", "Showers", "On-Call", and "Shared Desks".

"Hopefully, you won't have to slum it with us beat-pounders for long," said Bill, pushing open the door marked "Officers' Lounge."

"Nothing wrong with working the beat."

"Amen."

The Officers' Lounge was larger than Walt would have expected and well furnished. The walls were a deep Sacramento green, and the floors were well-kept hardwood. Scallop-backed velvet couches were scattered throughout the room, and three screens hung from the ceiling, all currently showing "Dolls, Dames, Twists and Tomatoes"—a softcore adult network. The wall opposite the door was home to large, grey metal fronted lockers. A small cardboard box sat atop the corner locker.

"The one on the end is yours," said Bill pointing to the box.

Walt pulled the box down and examined the contents. There was nothing of value, knick-knacks, some loose credit chips and a half-empty bottle of bourbon. It was a damning indictment on the state of his life. He opened his locker and shoved the box and its contents roughly inside.

"Is the on-call room free?" Walt asked Bill, who had seated himself in front of the nearest screen and changed the channel to a sports network.

"Should be. You aren't rostered on until the evening. Get some sleep. Someone will call you if they need you before then."

Walt thanked Bill, then headed for the showers.

Steam, the room was more steam than anything else. It reminded Walt of a swimming pool. There were no cubicles, shower heads were placed on the wall at metre intervals, and in front of each was a wooden bench, complete with a shelf and mirror.

Walt wasn't exactly shy, but he was glad the room was empty. He stripped off and, for the first time since he had woken up in the hospital, took a moment to assess the damage.

His legs were battered and bruised, both his knees were swollen, and there was a large gash across his right kneecap; it was already closed and scabbing over. His stomach still bore the slight redness from the coffee scalding, and his ribs were black and purple with deep bruising that surrounded the broken ones. His face was battered; he had twin cuts on his cheek and lip, and both of his eyes had dark circles that were the remnants of having been blacked. There was a graze on top of the dent that had been left when the OL soldier had broken it with the butt of his rifle. All in all, he had looked better, but if he was honest, he had looked worse.

Just as he stepped under the shower's warm cascade, the door opened, and six officers entered. Joking and laughing, the officers who had finished their night shifts stopped abruptly when they saw Walt. Even with his back turned to them, he could feel their eyes upon him through the haze of steam.

"Hey, Murphy, are you and your friends just gonna stand there and stare at my ass all morning?" Walt called over his shoulder.

"Just didn't expect to see you here, detective," said the stocky Murphy, not a trace of embarrassment in his voice.

"Haven't you heard?" said Walt, lathering up his hair with shampoo. "I'm one of you now."

"Well, welcome to the team," said Murphy, stripping down and getting into a vacant shower.

Thankfully, it appeared that chit chat in the shower wasn't something any of the officers were particularly interested in, and ten minutes later, Walt had dried and dressed and was heading to bed in the on-call room.

He felt like he had barely set his head down when Bill shook him awake.

"We've got a case, buddy."

And so it began, Walt's first day as an officer.

THE GAUNTLET

Cleo stared at her own reflection in the small mirror mounted on the inside of the closet. She was clean. She was herself again; there was no trace of the ghoul that lurked inside on her face, and yet every time she closed her eyes, she could see the dirt on her skin and the blood of those she had devoured. She could see the veins pulsing under her eyes and taste the bits of flesh between her teeth. She felt stained inside and out.

She had been confined to the bedroom for what felt like days. At first, the small, spotless nature of the place had been a comfort; now, it was starting to feel like an echo chamber for her fractured memories. She had only snippets of the last...she didn't know how long. Vague memories of her old life mingled with the horror she was almost accustomed to living in the SubLevel.

"Are you awake?" Gin Ricky called through the locked door. "Are you hungry?"

He hadn't been back since he had given her Quietus. The initial happiness of her rescue had long since turned to dread. She wasn't in the SubLevel anymore, but she was still a prisoner.

Cleo crouched down in the corner between the bed and the wall, fear of what might be yet to come gripping her.

The key scraped in the lock. Gin Ricky opened the door, a tray of food in one hand. He walked inside and carefully placed it on the writing desk.

"You need to eat something so the Quietus doesn't knock you for such a loop."

"Why am I here? What happened to me?"

"You don't remember? Nothing at all?"

Gin Ricky sat on the bed with his back to her.

"I remember before...mostly."

"Just not how you ended up in the SubLevel?"

Cleo nodded.

"I'm not going to hurt you," Gin Ricky said with a sigh. "We can talk in the living room if that makes you more comfortable, but when we're done, you need to come back in here for my safety as much as yours. Until you get yourself steady."

"What do you want from me?"

"I'll explain. Come on." Gin Ricky picked up the food tray end exited, leaving the door wide.

Cleo stayed rooted where she was until her legs went numb. When, after a while, no one came back, and the door wasn't shut and locked again, she got to her feet and made her tentative way to the living area.

Like the rest of the tiny apartment, the living room was dowdy, but meticulously clean. Gin Ricky clearly took pride in what little he had.

He was sitting on the couch when she entered.

"Sit anywhere you like," he said, gesturing to the various mismatched chairs. "I put your food back in the oven to keep it warm. I'll go get it."

He left through a set of saloon-style doors and returned moments later with the tray. He placed it on the table then sat back down. Cleo hesitated then, deciding that she was in no immediate danger, sat cross-legged on the floor in front of her plate.

The first bite of food was heavenly. It had been so long since she had eaten anything warm, but as she ate another mouthful and then another, her stomach began to growl. As she chewed, the taste of human flesh, the feel of it in her mouth, came back to her, and she couldn't block it out. Her insides squirmed, and before she knew what was happening, she had vomited all over the wooden floor.

"It's okay," Gin Ricky said at once.

He placed a blanket around her shoulders and eased her into an armchair. Cleo watched in silence as he took a mop and bucket and cleaned up the mess. When he was done, he handed her a glass of water and once again took up his perch on the couch.

"Am I your prisoner?"

Gin Ricky frowned as if pondering his answer. "No, you aren't a prisoner, but you can't leave yet."

Cleo felt insane to even think it, but Gin Ricky didn't seem like a threat. There was something about him that made her want to trust him. Maybe it was because he had shown her relative kindness, or maybe it was because there was something sad about him. He seemed to be in pain. The long, emotional kind that's drawn out, and the longer it's felt, the more lost its victim becomes.

"What do you want?"

"I didn't seek you out. I was desperate, and you were just there."

"What are you talking about?" Cleo asked, regaining some of her confidence.

Gin Ricky rubbed his face roughly with his hands. "You don't remember me. I'm not surprised; we worked together only briefly on the Morpheus Project. I'm the one who developed the basic cocktail for suggestibility that would become the basis of Styxx and Quietus."

A flash of a clean-shaven man with short hair danced across her mind's eye. "You're Ri Jin-woo?"

Gin Ricky nodded guiltily.

TENEBRIUM

"I left because what they're attempting is morally bankrupt. I wanted no part in it. I didn't believe they were attempting to help addicts. I could tell they weren't happy, but I didn't realise who I was dealing with. I thought I'd just change company and get on with my life, but then I started to notice OL soldiers following me wherever I went. Then my apartment mysteriously caught fire. I had to protect my family, so I disappeared and became Gin Ricky. It worked, too, until about two years ago. My son was kidnapped in the middle of the night. No suspects, no leads, and the police aren't doing boo about it."

"I'm sorry."

"No note, no nothing, and when I went to Medicorum, Maxwell laughed in my face. I get a video once a month to show me he's alive. It's a warning to stay gone, to keep my mouth shut. No one will listen to me. No one cares that my son is gone." He wiped his nose roughly on the back of his hand. "I left before the epidemic. I only have suspicions. I don't have any proof. They are untouchable for someone like me. I have to get my son back. I don't know what else to do." His voice broke on the last.

"I'm sorry about your son, but I don't know how I can help you."

"You worked for Medicorum. You went missing the same day; both dragged out by the OL—I saw it on the news. It has to mean something. It has to."

"I don't remember that day. I'll help you get your son back if I can, but I just want to go home."

"You can't. You need Quietus, or you'll turn back into a ghoul, and I'm the only one who has it. But I can help you get your memories back, and maybe you'll know something or remember something about that night."

Cleo was certain she didn't need to be afraid of Gin Ricky now; she just felt pity for him. He had no grand master plans; he was just a human struggling. Just like her.

"If I do this, you'll let me call my husband?"

"Yes," he said excitedly. "If it works or not, even if you don't know anything. I'll call him or find him, just as long as you try."

The straight-backed metal chair Cleo sat on was cold, and the ropes that tied her to it chaffed the skin of her wrists and ankles. She examined Gin Ricky's face, irritated.

"I'm fine. The only time I want to rip your head off is when you keep looking at me like that."

It may have been early-onset Stockholm Syndrome talking, but as captors went, he wasn't so bad.

"I've got your next dose ready just in case."

In order to maintain her newfound lucidity, she had to take Quietus periodically, or she devolved back into a snaring ghoul hungry for flesh.

"I'm tired, and I'm sore. Can't we try again tomorrow?"

They had been at it for hours. Gin Ricky had invaded her mind over and over again with very little success. The truth was, while she wanted to help Gin Ricky get his son back, she wasn't sure she wanted to remember; bringing back the memories that might have crucial information would also bring back memories of the things that happened in the SubLevel. What happened in the SubLevel could stay in the SubLevel as far as she was concerned.

"Do you want to go home or not?" he said in the vein of a teacher scolding a pupil.

"Fine," Cleo said through gritted teeth. "Get it over with."

As he had done several times before that day, he slipped his hand back into the silver glove. It was a strange thing to behold, the Regression Gauntlet. It was made of something akin to very fine chainmail, and on the tips of each finger, there were slim spikes like acupuncture needles. On the palm, there was a circular disk, in the centre of which there was a jagged blue crystal.

"How does this work again?" Cleo asked nervously as Gin Ricky made to place his hand on her head.

"It allows me to sift through your memories as if I were browsing the contents of a hard drive. If you're repressing, I'll be able to unlock the memories. It's usually used on patients with severe amnesia. There is a chance that the recollections are gone or simply weren't created due to the effects of the drug, but I'm hoping that's not the case." Gin Ricky sounded bored, he had given this explanation many times before and each time he did, Cleo found no comfort in it.

"Ready?"

"Do it," Cleo said, taking a deep breath.

Nodding once, Gin Ricky took up his position behind Cleo. He placed his palm on the top of her head and pressed the needles into the skin, his pinkie and thumb at her temples.

It was like being struck by lightning; Cleo could feel her mind being blown wide open. She saw her tenth birthday party; she had cried with happiness when her uncle had given her a doll, only to be overcome with joy when her father gave her her first microscope moments later. She saw her first kiss, her graduation, her mother's funeral, the day she met Walt. Next was their first date; he had taken her to a small restaurant on the shore. It was the first time she had set foot on the earth's surface. She had known she loved him there and then.

She was watching her first big presentation, then their wedding. She was comforting Walt after his father died. She was sitting on the counter in her kitchen watching Walt cook dinner; he laughed as she tried to distract him. She was cuddled into Walt's chest, happily doing nothing as he read a book, absently stroking her hair. She was in the lab, noting the behaviours of human test subjects. She was shambling through the streets, "Stop!" she cried out. "That's the night! That's when it happened."

"Okay, focus. Focus on that night. What happened?" his voice came to her as dully as if she were underwater.

In her mind, she pulled herself back to the lab. "We were having no success in an anti-addiction trial. We were trying to create drugs that helped addicts get clean, but they were also trying to create recreational drugs that weren't addictive. We were failing on both counts. The subjects displayed violent behaviour, and we had to terminate them. I was suspicious."

"Keep going."

She was in Dr Maxwell's office. They were talking and then she was leaving. She felt uneasy, but she couldn't remember why.

"What's happening?"

"I'm leaving work... I'm..."

And then, she was home. There were rose petals on the floor. Music played softly from the gramophone in the corner. She felt safe. Walt would be able to help her.

She heard laughter from the bedroom. Cleo made her way towards the sound, and then, standing in the doorway, she saw her. Thea. She was in the bed that she, Cleo, shared with her husband. Walt was on top of the younger woman, his fingers leaving light red marks on her milky skin wherever he gripped or touched. They moved rhythmically, lost in each other. There was a blazing look on his face that she never saw when he looked at her. They seemed to burn together, Walt and Thea.

Walt and Thea.

Walt and Thea.

"No!" Cleo screamed aloud. The word seemed to blast from her like an invisible force. Gin Ricky yelped and removed his hand from her scalp, panting.

"Cleo—"

"I can't," she snarled, struggling against the ropes that held her. She could feel the veins under her eyes pulsing and knew they would have turned red again. "I think I need that dose."

FANCY MEETING YOU HERE

Thea was starting to worry about Walt. It wasn't unusual for him to disappear, but he hadn't been home in nearly two days. She hadn't tried to contact him in any real way other than commandeering his apartment. He hadn't tried to contact her either.

She never knew what to expect or say. She didn't know the rules of their personal engagement because he continually changed the goalposts.

Maybe he would be happy to hear from her. Maybe it would send him into another one of his dark moods. Maybe he would throw her and Benny out of his apartment. She wasn't sure that she was welcome after they had parted romantically. She had only set foot inside the place once since the spectacular implosion of their affair, but there was nowhere else to go.

After everything they had been through, it still felt like a safe place. True, he had saved her life, but that was his hero complex showing, it told her nothing about the state of play between them.

They had fallen apart after Cleo was taken away. There had been no need to make a break, the relationship had crumbled all on its own, like cliffs into the sea. Walt had spiralled and pushed her away. Cora disappeared not long after, and Thea was far too absorbed in trying to find her sister to fight for a relationship she had thought doomed in her heart of hearts.

So, Thea was surprised when she found some of the clothes she had left behind, more than two years ago now, folded neatly in the top drawer of Walt's dresser. Another message she didn't know how to interpret.

"I'm gonna need your help, Super Cop," Benny called from the bathroom.

Thea dressed quickly, then went to find out what Benny wanted. "What do you need?" she asked, peeking her head cautiously into the bathroom. He was standing in front of the mirror, holding a shirt he had appropriated from Walt's dryer and examining the stump that used to be his right arm.

"I can't do the damn buttons myself; the trousers took me an age."

Thea took the shirt gently from Benny and draped it over his shoulders. She helped him manoeuvre his arm into the sleeve and then buttoned it up. The proximity was awkward, and they both avoided looking at the other.

"Are you all right?" Thea asked; she could feel him shaking slightly.

"My choices led me to this. A lifetime worth of selfishness, cruelty, and bad decisions."

Thea said nothing.

"No words of comfort?" Benny asked in a would-be casual voice.

"Do you want me to lie to you?"

Benny stepped back to lean against the counter, and Thea sat down on the closed toilet lid.

"I'm not a good person. I've done terrible things, and I'm willing to do more to get what I want. Maybe this is karma," Benny said quietly, gazing at his reflection.

"I don't believe in karma, and I don't think the world is that black and white. Good people do bad things the same way bad people do good. If you want to be better, make a conscious effort to do better. If you want me to justify the things you've done, you're looking in the wrong place. You have my sympathies. I'm sorry that this happened to you, but it doesn't make up for anything. And if you are thinking about using it to excuse the things you're planning to do, remember you still have to go through me."

"Your sympathies appear limited."

"I'm sorry this happened to you. I can't imagine how traumatic it's been, and I wouldn't wish it on anyone, but I haven't forgotten about the things you do to those you own or the fact you own them in the first place. You tried to have me killed. We might be able to do some good for this town, but we aren't friends. I'm not here to give you a hug and tell you that it's all going to be okay."

"Well, I can't hug you back right anyway." Benny paused. The silence stretched so long that Thea stood to leave. Then, "What if I don't want to be this anymore?"

"You have to work at it, pay your dues."

"You are still itching to send me to the big house, huh?"

"It's what I do." Thea shrugged.

Thea was saved from having to say more by an incoming call. She brought her hand to her ear and answered. "Williams here."

"Thea?"

"Yeah, Hank. It's me."

"You okay? You back at work?"

"I can be. What do you need?"

"There's been a murder linked to your Pleasure Quarter case. I wasn't sure if you'd even answer, but things are getting bad out there, and we're short."

"It's fine. What's the address?"

"You sure?"

"Yeah. I'm fine."

And she was. Whether it was taking part in her first amputation or the good night's sleep she'd had, Thea was well and truly sober. The shakes had subsided, and the fog that had clouded her brain since she had woken up in the hospital had dissipated almost completely.

"Will you be okay here? I may have a lead," Thea asked Benny.

"Yeah, I feel fine. I'll do some digging of my own while you're gone. Be careful."

"You, too."

Thea hadn't been to Gradna for a long time. It was supposed to be the only entirely residential area in the Pleasure Quarter. While the homes there were privately owned, it was still well established that business was conducted as usual.

The apartments were what were known as micro-homes. Small and compact studio apartments that had originally been designed around seventy years previously with the intention of promoting modern living. Unmaintained, they had fallen into a kind of chic disrepair. Some were grungy in a fashionable way; the sort of place socialites went to prove their anarchic devotion to walking on the wild side. Others were dilapidated in the extreme, more hovels than homes.

The crime scene was the latter. The main area of apartment 3217 consisted of a stained bed and peeling wallpaper. The bathroom was a horror show.

There were two bodies. Both nude. One was a young man, whose brains were splattered across the walls, the other was a middle-aged man who had had his throat slit in the bathtub and was then wrapped up in the shower curtain. His body lay next to that of the younger man.

Orion Martin kneeled, notepad in hand, examining the scene.

"It must be the end of the world," Thea said wryly. "Detective Martin has left his archive."

"Thea, you are looking well, all things considered," said Orion, straightening up and bestowing a small warm smile. "We are undermanned, and I consented to help. I'd be lying if I said I had missed this."

"What have you got?"

"Let me know if I'm rusty. Two victims—one male in his late twenties small tattoo at the base of the neck, common among sex workers, I'm told, and a second male in his late forties, a doctor judging by his Index wrist implant. I'd put money in this being a client and a pro. The doctor was bound, placed in the bathtub and killed there, judging by the volume of blood in the tub and the splatters on the tile. He was then wrapped in the shower curtain, which is a relic in and of itself, and here's where it gets odd. He was most certainly dead before he was wrapped up, and all evidence points to the pro doing the dirty deed, but then who killed our young murderer?"

"I'm sure you have a theory."

"A less experienced detective might assume a suicide. But where is the gun? Why is there only an exit wound? I think something on his head exploded, a device of some kind, maybe an ocular implant, and that's what created the splatter, and it's why there is a faint smell of burning. How'd I do?"

"Damn good, as usual, but you have no interest in my approval. You've been a cop longer than I've been alive."

"It's good to remind the younguns that we old-timers still know a thing or two." And he had.

Why had she never considered the possibility? The first autopsy reports had been intentionally obfuscating, but she herself had noticed discrepancies in the blood splatter at the church crime scene. It seemed clear as day to her now; the murder weapon was some kind of small implant or device.

It fit in with what Benny had told her about Eve, and it explained so much of what had made the culprit hard to identify; yet posed many new questions.

"I never doubted it. Did you find any evidence of a device?"

"The techs are working with the unis, but nothing as of yet."

"Who found the bodies?"

"Building manager. This entire floor is a pay by the hour joint. He came to kick out some late leavers. A uni should be taking his statement in the hall."

The building manager was a balding White man wearing a grubby string vest and suspenders with stained pinstriped trousers. His fingers and teeth were yellowed by tobacco. He was yelling at Bill, who was trying valiantly to remain calm, but Thea could tell as he massaged his moustache that he was itching to punch the man.

"I still don't see why you need to lock down the whole floor. Every minute you and your boys are here is costing me money," the man shouted, spittle flying. "And I'll tell you another thing; I'm not paying for the clean-up job. It's not my fault some lowlifes got into it!"

"The quicker you answer my questions, the quicker I'm out of your hair. Such as it is," said Bill through gritted teeth.

"Are you dumb? I told you, the pretty boy came in first. Then his daddy, they fucked rough and then cuddled like bunnies."

"How do you know all this? You got a peephole?" Bill asked, unable to keep the disdain from his voice.

"Are there cameras in all your rooms?" said Thea, coming to stand next to Bill.

"Who's this tomato?" the manager asked Bill. He ignored Thea.

"Detective Thea Williams. Take me to your office."

The manager extended a hand to usher Thea forward. "You go first," she said, unimpressed by his perverted leer.

He led them to a door at the end of the hall marked private. The office was another full micro-home, but it had been repurposed. Every wall was covered in screens. Some even hung from the ceiling. Old fashioned television sets and monitors were piled atop one another, each showing a different room in the building. Some screens showed family living rooms, others showed parties, others still showed couples and strangers engaging in sexual activity, and one or two showed empty rooms.

"Give me the footage from 3217," Thea said, turning from the screens in disgust.

"What's it worth to ya?" the manager asked, fingering his navel and giving Thea a vomit-inducing grin.

"You seem to be under the misguided impression that you have a choice. We aren't bargaining here because you have no leverage. Give it to me or don't; it doesn't matter. I was just trying to save the techs a job—they'll find it anyway. Bill, cuff him and take him to the station if you don't mind."

"Hey, hey, hey," the manager said, backing up, his hands raised. "It's a security system. I'm doing my tenants a good turn. Keeping 'em safe like."

"Safe?" Thea said, nodding to a screen that showed the bathroom crime scene.

"We'll see how that defence works out for you," Bill said as he placed the manager in handcuffs and frogmarched him from the room.

Thea rubbed her eyes. Tenebites could always find new depths of depravity to plumb. She examined the screens for a moment before leaning down and pulling the plug on them all. One by one, they each went blank.

"Thea? What are you doing here?"

Thea wheeled around; Walt was standing in the office doorway. His face was bruised. Some looked old and were fading to a yellowish-brown, while other fresher additions were still deep purple.

"They called me in. Why are you—" But the end of her sentence was cut off as Walt all but ran forward and pulled her into his arms. He held her tightly to his chest, lifting her off the ground. He kissed the top of her head. "I thought..." He set her down and stepped back, taking her face between his hands. His thumb traced the gash on her cheek.

"Thank you for everything you did, they told me you saved my life." Thea took his hands and pulled them gently from her face. She stepped away from him, creating a distance between them.

"Why didn't you call me? I've been going crazy. Your father wouldn't let me see you. I was out for two days, and when I came to, they said you hadn't woken up, and there was a chance you never would. I only knew you were alive because of Bastion." He looked like he had been worried sick, guilt bubbled uncomfortably in Thea's stomach.

"I'm sorry, it was selfish not to let you know I was okay. I asked about you when I woke up, and they told me you had discharged yourself. That sounded like you. I figured you had gone straight back to work or—"

"A bar? That's fair," Walt finished for her, nodding jerkily. He turned his back on her and moved away slightly.

"I was going to say home," Thea said quietly. "I'm sorry I didn't call. Things just... snowballed."

"Do you remember what happened? You died, you get that, right?" Walt demanded, his voice low and fierce. "How long have you been running around for, while I've been worrying like an idiot?"

"You have some nerve to lecture me on keeping in touch." This was not how she had imagined this conversation going.

Walt turned to glare at her. "I'm an unreliable S.O.B, I don't deny it, but *this* is different."

Thea didn't want to have this conversation, and she especially didn't want to have it at work with Orion Martin in the next room. To avoid commenting, she cast her eyes around for another topic. "Why are you dressed like a flatty?" she asked, taking in his crisp new uniform.

"Because I am one. I got demoted," Walt said matter-of-factly.

"Demoted? What for?"

"I had a fight with Torrez. It was either this or my last strike."

"Hell of a fight."

"I pulled my gun on him," Walt said, not looking her in the eye.

"What is wrong with you?"

"Torrez isn't who you think he is."

"I'm not talking about Torrez," Thea said, raising a hand to indicate that she would not be waylaid. "Were you drunk?"

"What do you think? Don't ask questions you already know the answers to." Walt stared her down defiantly, then said quietly, "I didn't mean it to go that far, but he's hiding something, and I was worried about you..."

"Stop using me as an excuse."

"Ahem," came a loud pointed voice from the doorway.

Both of their heads whipped around to see Orion watching them. He looked unimpressed. The whole team must have heard at least part of their conversation. "If you two can tear yourselves away, I'd like to wrap things up here," Orion said judgementally and fairly.

NEXUS

Many people had been happy to see Thea when she had returned to the TPD. There had been clapping, hugs and tears, handshakes and back-pats, well wishes and good-natured smiles from those she only knew by sight. That hadn't been all, however. There had also been a good deal of muttering and side-eyeing. Those more prone to gossip and judgement watched carefully as Thea tried to stay as far away from Walt as possible. He himself seemed uncomfortable as his colleagues got wind of his new job role.

She was relieved when the crowd dissipated, and she was able to have a moment to herself. She was still seething from her argument with Walt and even angrier still that it had been witnessed.

Now that she was sure that a device had been the elusive murder weapon, it was with a furrowed brow and a renewed sense of determination that she entered the bullpen, ready to tackle the latest development in the case. Unfortunately for Thea, she had done all she could at the scene. Without the results from the autopsies, which hasn't been complete yet, or the footage they hoped to obtain from the illegally placed cameras, all she could do was type up her report.

"Hey, O'Malley," Thea called to the detective sitting at the adjacent desk after twenty or so minutes of writing. "Where's Torrez?"

"AWOL." He elaborated no further and went back to watching teleshopping on one of the many overhead screens. O'Malley was a squat White man with curly brown hair and wibbling jowls.

"What do you mean?"

O'Malley sighed exasperatedly. "He's not here. Ask your boy about the whys. Now quit talking over my show."

O'Malley was unpleasant as a rule. He was part of the old guard who saw Thea as a little girl who had no place on the force; his opinion, like his ire, meant nothing to her.

"How long has he been gone?"

"Are you kidding me?" he growled, turning reluctantly to Thea, who kept her face impassive. "Two days, I think. Unlike you, I'm not really up in my colleagues' business."

Thea rolled her eyes and went back to her report. She had hoped Torrez would have been the one to come and see her instead of Bastion, but perhaps he felt, due to his fight with Walt, that he had better keep his distance. It was a shame because the thing she wanted most at that moment was a friend. It made her miss her sister even more. She had not picked a career that was built to make friends. Her affair with Walt had lost her the few she had made in the academy, but she had still had Cora then, and they were as close as you'd expect twin sisters to be. With her gone and no Torrez to commiserate with, she felt alone.

The bullpen was getting busy by seven o'clock. Between six and eight p.m. was a time of crossover where the backshift, dayshift, and the nightshift were all working at the same time. It was common for detectives to work overtime, to come in early, and to work past the end of their shifts, but the department was never busier than it was for those two hours.

Thea was glad to finish her personal report just as Deandra, one of the few other female detectives in homicide, took up Walt's empty desk. She was a hard-working up and comer who deserved better than the cramped desk she had enjoyed next to the docking bay previously, but it still made Thea feel oddly unsettled to see someone new at Walt's desk.

Trading idle chit chat for a moment or two, Thea then made her way to the break room. She was starving. The food in the precinct wasn't anywhere near five stars, but it would do in a pinch.

Thea entered the canteen and then swiftly turned on her heel and left. But he had seen her. Walt followed her out into the corridor moments later.

"Thea!"

"No. No. I'm not doing this here. I'm not having another screaming match at work," she said over her shoulder as she walked away.

"Then don't scream," Walt said, grabbing her by the arm and steering her into the nearest supply closet.

The interior was small, but well maintained. There were several rows of plain metal shelving, half of which were filled with file boxes and the other half with cleaning supplies.

Walt shut the door on them and turned to face her.

Something passed between them as they both realised that it was in that very closet they'd had sex for the first time. Thea pushed the memories away, she didn't want to think about that. She wanted to be as far away from Walt as possible.

"What do you want? I'm hungry, and I just don't have the time or the energy for this," Thea said, starting for the door, but Walt blocked the way with sheer bulk.

"I feel like I'm going crazy here. Have you forgotten everything that happened?"

"Which bit? The part where you kissed me? Or the part where you nearly got us shot at the SubLevel gate? Wait, maybe you mean the part where I nearly died,"

Thea said, crossing her arms and creating as much distance between them as she could in the small space.

"You did die," Walt said so quietly Thea only just caught it.

"It changes nothing."

"Are you kidding me?" Walt yelled, making Thea start. "It changes everything."

"How?" Thea yelled back. "Is there still a killer out there? Yes. Are we still being screwed by my father? Yes. Do I still have absolutely no idea where we stand? Yes. Sounds like Tuesday to me."

They glared at each other for a moment.

"I thought you were dead. I believed it. I felt it," Walt said. "It was the worst day of my life, and that is saying something. You—"

"Don't." Thea didn't want to hear apologies or romantic admissions, not from Walt. Not when she felt so alone and so vulnerable. "I can't rely on you. And we aren't the same people we were back then. I know you still care, but it doesn't change anything for me."

Walt seemed to fill the tiny room. No matter where she looked, he was there.

"I felt you go cold," he said with a slight shiver. He reached out to her, but Thea backed up so far that she hit the wall. Not wanting to be cornered, she moved around him like he was a bomb and stood next to the door.

"Do you know how long and how hard I fought to get away from being the rookie who fucked her boss, her mentor, her partner, her married partner?"

"What does that have to do with anything right now?" Walt said incredulously.

"We had problems long before Cleo. You're only remembering the good parts. It's like you've forgotten how wrong it felt. How we let things slide and cut corners because we were so wrapped up in each other. You aren't remembering the mutters and the judgement even before we became watercooler gossip." Thea spoke so quickly that her words came out in a jumble.

"I don't care what people think, and we made a damn good team no matter how we did it," Walt said, holding his head high as if he was challenging her to disagree with these 'facts'.

"You've spent the last two years spiralling. Treating me like crap and leaving me buried neck-deep in shit. You're a drunk, Walt." He flinched at her final words; it was his turn to take a step back.

"I know I've fucked up. I have shit the bed in ways I don't even know how to begin to fix. But I watched you die, I heard your breathing stop. Maybe you don't care about me the way I care about you anymore, but I defy you to stand there and tell me you wouldn't be rattled by that, that you wouldn't go a little bit off the rails."

"That's my point! You were already off the rails, getting demoted, attacking Torrez—it's nothing new. It's almost like you want to be punished, and if it's capital, you don't care. The man I fell in love with was funny, and honest, and loyal. He faced his problems, he was always there when I needed him. When I look at you now… I don't see him anymore."

Thea could tell that Walt had been hurt by this. He seemed somewhat diminished as he turned away from her.

"I'm trying here," he said quietly, placing his hands on his hips.

"How? By trying to buy drugs from Benjamin Pickford? By using pros?"

"That's not what you think," Walt said simply. "I'm making a start. That's all I can do."

"You came to one crime scene. You did your job for one day. I've been doing both of our jobs for two years. And that's not even...it doesn't matter. I was young, and I was stupid. I let myself get dazzled by the legend that was Walter James. I'm not doing it again." Thea turned and actually had her hand on the doorknob when Walt spun her to face him.

He was angry now.

"That is bullshit!" he said, firing up at once. "Don't play the victim there. I didn't seduce you. I wasn't some creep making moves on an impressionable girl. I loved my wife. I had no interest in having an affair; I wasn't that guy. I have never been that guy. I tried to stay away from you. You kissed me. You turned up at my door. You invited yourself into my bed. I should have turned you away, and I didn't. I couldn't. I wanted you as much as you wanted me. More. But that mistake is both of ours. So don't you stand there talking to me as if I did something to you, took something that you weren't offering willingly."

His words seemed to hang between them in the air.

"You ended this. You left me," Thea spat, jabbing a finger hard into Walt's chest, her anger matching his. "You told me that the thought of 'us' disgusted you, that my touch sickened you. You made your feelings perfectly clear. Now the dust has settled, and you want to take it back, well, you can't."

"I couldn't handle the guilt. You want to call me a coward, fine. I am one. I couldn't look you in the face and not see her. Cleo didn't deserve what we did, and she didn't deserve what happened to her, and that's on me. I thought that was the worst feeling in the world; until a few days ago." He was so close now she could feel his breath on her face.

"Stop looking at me like that," Thea said suddenly, pushing Walt away. He stumbled, surprised.

"Like what?"

"Like you're drowning, and I'm air."

"To me, you are." He dropped his gaze to the floor.

"That's not all I am, though. I make you sad, too. I see it sometimes when you think I don't know you're looking. I don't want that for either of us."

"I make me sad," Walt said with a short, humourless laugh. "Not you." He leant against one of the shelves and crossed his arms loosely. "I am haunted by what happened to Cleo. When I look at you, I see that night, and it reminds me of how weak I am. The things I've thrown away and the things I've let slide. How far I am from the man I was...I barely recognise my own reflection."

"We ruined each other, and I'm only just back on my feet. I can't do it again."

"But that's not all I see when I look at you. Maybe I am forgetting the bad parts, but that spark I used to feel, that was all you, and I want it back. I'm sorry it took so long for me to realise it. It was...I knew that I'd do it all again. If I could go back, nothing would change. I couldn't stay away from you then, any more than I can now. But it felt like an even bigger betrayal after everything that happened, so I pushed you away. I know there are a lot of things that can't be undone, and I have plenty to be ashamed of, but I spent two years pretending I didn't care, and the truth is, nothing has changed for me when it comes to you. I need—we need—to move on. I'd like it to be together." Walt closed the gap between them. They were barely inches apart, but he didn't touch her; he just stood there, waiting.

"I don't know if I can," Thea said, meeting his eyes. "There is so much I haven't forgiven you for."

"I just need you to trust me."

"But I don't," Thea said, honestly. "I don't trust you anymore."

"Then let me earn it back."

Thea didn't say anything. She continued to hold his gaze as his eyes searched her face for an answer. Walt tilted his head ever so slightly and began to slowly lean forward, his lips inching towards hers. He was giving her every chance to tell him to stop, but she didn't.

As soon as their lips met, she melted into him like she had done so many times in the past. His arms entangled her; they were statuesque in the embrace for a moment, and then her hands were in his hair, pulling it, using it to crush his feverish lips against hers. He was roaming her body with his palms. They were on her back, on her waist, twisted in her hair. It was terrifying and exhilarating. It felt like acquiescence and coming home all at once.

Gently, Thea pulled away. She felt hot, breathless, she didn't want to stop, but she knew they must. He knew it too; he didn't fight her. After one last quick brush of his lips, he laid his forehead against hers and clasped his hands around her waist. "I've missed this," he muttered.

Thea listened as his breathing returned to normal. She would have been content just to stand in his arms a while longer, but the precinct wasn't the right place.

Thea looked at Walt for a moment. "Are we really doing this?"

"I'm not going anywhere, so we'd better." He smiled, it was small, but it was there.

"What?" Walt asked, a crease between his brows.

"Nothing. We have work to do."

Was it wise to restart her relationship with Walt? Probably not. They had burned each other's lives to the ground, but he made her feel so alive, and in that moment, it was exactly what she needed. It felt good to give in to weakness sometimes, to throw caution to the wind and say, "To hell with the consequences." Just like before, it could only end badly, but it was better to be hurt than to feel nothing at all.

With a last kiss, Walt ducked his head out into the corridor to check the coast was clear, then left to follow up on the footage from the crime scene, and Thea went to see Flynn on the off chance he had started the autopsies.

ELUCIDATE

Flynn wasn't in his office when Thea paid him a visit, and when she returned to the bullpen, Walt wasn't back with the footage yet. Out of tasks again, Thea headed to the canteen and was finally able to eat. She didn't care that it was a hotdog or that the bun was slightly stale, she was just happy to have warm food in her belly.

She wondered as she ate how Benny was doing alone at Walt's, whether or not he would be there when she got back, and how Walt would react to seeing him there.

After returning to her desk and finding that Walt was still not there, she made her way to the officer's lounge. She knocked gently on the door.

"Come in."

Bill was inside. He was sitting upright on one of the wide sofas with his eyes shut.

"Tired?"

"Always. You lookin' for Walter?" he said without opening his eyes.

"Always."

The corner of Bill's mouth curved slightly. "He's following up on the double homicide with Jasper. He's probably downstairs."

"Thanks. How's Amir?"

"He's good, really good. I just wish I got to see him more, but that's the job. It's hard on a relationship."

"Sure is."

Thea stepped back out into the corridor and brought her hand to ear.

"What?" came Walt's slightly confused voice through her Cicada.

"I called."

"Funny."

"Any luck?"

Barely five minutes later, Walt was sitting next to Thea, his feet up on her desk as she loaded the footage into the data stream. They watched as a handsome young White man with sandy hair entered the dilapidated bedroom. Walt paused the tape with a wave of his hand.

"We were able to confirm that the young man," Walt said, pointing at him. Thea noticed his fingers shook. "Is a sex worker who goes by the name 'Big Dick'."

"He does not."

"He does. Real name Richard Luckstrim, Ric to his friends."

"Luckstrim? As in Marcus Luckstrim? The founder of Medicorum."

"Mmhmm. He then sold it and became Tenebrium's first quadrillionaire."

"Do we know who he sold it to?"

"Brandis Haytham, but she sold it not long after, and I can't find any record of the sale or who she sold it to, but she definitely doesn't own it now—she's dead."

"I didn't have any luck either when I tried. We're going to have to petition the Mayor if we want to crack that one." Thea sighed audibly. "So, how does the son of a quadrillionaire end up on the game?"

"His father disinherited him after he gave his brother Styxx. He didn't know what it would do, far as we can tell, but his brother turned into a ghoul. He tried to rip Ric apart, and Luckstrim Senior had to shoot him."

"That's awful. How did his father take the news? Can't be easy losing both your sons."

"We can't find him. Last known address is on Colony Fourteen, but from there..." Walt shrugged.

"Do we know where Ric worked?"

"Old Fashioned. Ward Eight's direct competition."

"I wonder if that's significant."

Thea resumed the tape.

Ric looked around the room, checked the bathroom, closed the curtains and sat himself on the end of the bed. He appeared relaxed. A few moments later, something caught his attention, and he headed to the door.

"No audio?" Thea asked. Walt shook his head.

Ric passed out of sight for a small period, and when he returned into view, he was accompanied by a stocky White man with a waxed moustache wearing a lab coat.

"Do we know who the second victim is?"

"Dr Hayes Henshall. A plastic surgeon specialising in cosmetic augmentations. No priors."

Henshall allowed Ric to pull him by the hand further into the room. They were clearly comfortable with each other; Thea was willing to bet that the doctor was a regular client. Next to the bed, Ric pulled Henshall's jacket from his shoulders and placed it on the sideboard under the small square shuttered window next to a bottle of wine and two glasses. When Ric returned, Henshall grabbed him and kissed him lustfully.

The sex that followed was rough. No surface was safe, ornaments were smashed, pictures were knocked off the walls, and red marks were left on skin.

When Henshall was nearing his climax, Ric grabbed the tie the doctor had abandoned on the bedside table and tied it around his own neck, then handed the makeshift noose to Henshall, who pulled.

Ric began to go purple in the face, his eyes bulged, and then it was over. The two men curled up together under the covers, Ric with his arms around Henshall as the latter seemed to drift into a peaceful doze.

"Do we know if they were a couple?" Thea asked.

"Neither had any family for us to speak to. We're still trying to contact friends who may know."

The men stayed like that for a while, but just as Thea was thinking about fast-forwarding the footage, Henshall opened his eyes. He kissed Ric lightly on the lips and extracted himself from the tangle of covers. He walked to the bathroom and left the door ajar.

The stream went black.

"What the hell? Did the landlord scrub the tape?"

"There was a black-out. It took down all the cameras, lights and electrics in a four-block radius and lasted about seventeen minutes," Walt said.

"Let me guess, nobody saw or heard a thing. That's...convenient."

"Wait till you see what happens next."

When the picture reappeared, Henshall was nowhere to be seen. Ric was slumped over the edge of the bed, a satin sheet wrapped constrictingly around his neck. There was a small metal object on his temple that hadn't been there before.

"What's that?" Thea said, pausing the stream once more and pointing it out to Walt.

"How much do you remember about the attack?" he asked, looking at her seriously. There was a thin sheen of sweat on his face, and he was tapping his foot rapidly.

"You doing okay?"

"I haven't had a drink in a couple of days, is all," Walt said dismissively.

Thea hid her surprise. "That's really great."

Walt inclined his head the smallest amount. "What do you remember?"

"I remember the gate, and I remember someone pushing past me...and falling."

"What about when we were in your apartment?" he pressed.

"The ghouls!" she almost shouted. She remembered with shocking clarity the face of the ghoul, with its gnashing maw bearing down on her. "They had the same things on their heads. I checked the footage of the church Jane Doe. It seemed like the wound was outwards like Ric's. What if these devices are our murder weapons? But we didn't find anything at this scene." She pointed to Ric. "Someone had to enter the room with Henshall there, possibly still alive, to fit the thing."

"Sure looks that way."

"That's what the blackout was for. It's a lot of trouble to go to, though, to fit a device on a sex worker who died less than an hour later, and then have to come back to cover it up."

"So what happened to Luckstrim is a fuck-up, and the chips aren't supposed to explode?"

"It's a chip?" Thea asked, surprised.

"I managed to recover one from one of the ghouls at your apartment before it was torched. I stole it from Torrez, who stole it from the scene. And yeah, I didn't want to leave it with him, but Jasper told me it looks like an extremely powerful, extremely expensive piece of hardware."

"I think I might have an idea about what's going on here."

SMOKING GUN

Walt and Thea didn't notice Torrez where he lurked near the lifts as they rushed out of the detective's office. He was glad. He didn't think he could have faced Thea knowing what he was planning to do. The odd calm that seemed to be between her and Walt told him that they had done what he had always known they would; two people so drawn to one another could never stay parted forever. He didn't want to see her hurt again, but it made what he had to do that much easier.

While his injuries were, for the most part, healed thanks to Dill's plethora of doctors and ample funds, the trauma that had come along with the experience was making him jumpy and paranoid. Every time he looked at the mangled nail beds on the tips of his fingers, he began to shake, and his vision blurred. This nauseating feeling gave him the strength to do what he must.

There was a small brown package sitting at his desk when he arrived there. His desk, the precinct, everything about the place was now slightly alien to him. He had finally crossed the line from a cop who believed that the ends justified the means to a full-blown criminal; it was a line he could not uncross. There was no doubt he was in deep.

He wasn't surprised when he opened the thin package to find that there was a small datachip nestled between the two sides of a folded piece of paper which read:

```
A gun only smokes once it is fired.
```

Tossing the note into the trash, Torrez pressed the datachip against the silver metal Index embedded into his wrist and waited. A moment later, the data stream sprang to life, rising from the surface of his desk.

"This file has not been vetted by the TPD security system; would you like to proceed?" the station's central computer intoned in his ear.

"Yes."

The footage was dated a week previously and showed a dark and rainy night in The Quadrant. Without the neon lights that usually robbed the other districts of true darkness, it was harder to see the details of what was happening. The image changed; the bottom of the frame was now stamped with "Property of Chef Lau's – Authentic Chinese Cuisine." It showed an alley behind a restaurant that backed right onto the older portion of the SubLevel walls.

Torrez watched as the portion of the wall he could see began to crumble at the bottom. "¿Que demonios?" A hand was groping around the newly hewn opening in the wall, pulling out brick by brick until it was wide enough to fit a very small, very slim person. Torrez watched, his mouth wide, as a head covered in matted dark hair poked through the gap, followed by the body of a woman. She looked starved. Even in the darkness, Torrez could see how her collarbones and cheekbones stuck out from her dirt coated skin. As she straightened up and the light caught her face, Torrez yelped so loudly that several of those in the office turned to give him concerned looks.

He recognised her. He knew her. It was Walter's wife, Cleo. Not dead as they had been led to believe, but very much alive and roaming the city. Had her husband known all along that she was confined in the SubLevel? A smoking gun indeed. If Walt knew that she was alive and had conspired in her escape, he was ruined, imprisoned, executable even, and the devastating effect that would have on Thea was…exactly what Dill was after.

Their affair was public knowledge to the precinct, but Dill had no way of knowing about it unless someone had told him. Yet again, Torrez felt a pang of guilt. He had not divulged that secret, the only other person it was likely to have been was her father. Poor Thea.

The frame changed again, as did the lettering at the bottom. It now read: "Property of Medicorum Medical Services – any duplication or distribution of this footage and the scientific knowledge it may contain to any third party, employee, or member of the public will result in legal action."

Torrez was looking at a clinical white lab. A scientist was sitting behind their desk, working with cultures under a microscope. As they peered down the viewfinder, they made notes in the air with their hand that appeared, neatly written in cursive, on the clear pen board next to them. When they were finished, they glanced at the clock, put their samples back inside a glass-fronted refrigerator, and moved out of sight. Moments later, a figure Torrez knew all too well appeared.

Gin Ricky sidled up to the fridge the scientist had just closed and opened it. He turned away from the camera so Torrez couldn't see what he was doing. He left quickly, and the scientist returned moments later to sit and eat their lunch at their desk.

This solved the mystery of the break-in at Medicorum Walt had been investigating what seemed like an age ago, but Torrez couldn't see how it tied into the greater mystery. He was sure he would find out soon enough.

AGAIN

"Again," Cleo said, her lips pulling back to bare her teeth.

"I'm not sure the Quietus has quite taken effect yet," Gin Ricky said, backing away slightly so that his coffee table was in between them.

Cleo strained against the ropes that tied her to the metal chair; her hands curled like claws.

Gin Ricky had been hesitant to delve into her mind again and had only reluctantly agreed to put her back in the chair. On reflection, Cleo supposed that was only because it involved tying her down.

"Again," Cleo said, working hard to remove the growl from her tone. "I want to know what happened to me."

"All right, once more."

All Cleo could think of was the burning look on Walt's face as he made love to Thea. Young, smart, beautiful Thea. It wasn't that he'd had sex with someone else, though that was bad enough; it was that it was excruciatingly clear there was so much more between them than mere passion. The image would be seared into her memory forever.

And worse than this, despite it all, she still loved him. She still longed for nothing more than to be in his arms. The last two years had been so terrible that all she wanted was to go home and pick up where they left off, Thea be damned. He had always been her north star, and she needed that now more than ever. She needed something that could root her to who she was. Walt was like a way back to the time before she was a monster.

When she thought back to the weeks and months that she could remember before her sabbatical in the SubLevel and the memories Gin Ricky had helped her retrieve, she found she wasn't surprised. Walt had always had a way about him when he spoke of Thea, he wasn't aware of it, but it was as though he couldn't help but smile. Thea's exploits and triumphs, her name on his lips, made him happy, but it was a private happiness, one not shared with Cleo.

"Ready?" Gin Ricky asked nervously, slipping the gauntlet on once more.

"Do it."

Cleo almost relished the sting of the gauntlet on her scalp, like it was a tiny outward expression of what she was feeling inside.

She was staring at the shabby living room, and then she was at her desk on the night she had been exposed to Quietus. Again. She was observing the behaviour of test subjects. Again. The project was failing. Again. She was tired and desperate to head home for the night. Again. She was exchanging idle chit-chat with her boss, Dr Maxwell. Again. She watched as a teenage boy was dragged towards the cells. She was sneaking back in. This... This was new.

Cleo sat up straighter in her chair, willing herself on.

"Keep going," Gin Ricky urged her, the tips of his fingers digging in deeper.

Cleo concentrated with everything she had. Her mind was trying to jump to the next viable place in her memory, but she wasn't going to let it, she was going to see what happened to her.

She was sneaking back into Maxwell's office. She was sitting at his computer and reading his files. She was caught. Maxwell had come back and found her, she had tried to pass it off, but he knew. He grabbed her and forced her to imbibe one of the trial drugs.

Cleo couldn't stop shaking. She could feel the sticky liquid trickling down her throat as if it was happening in the present.

"We need to stop now," Gin Ricky said, trying to pull his hand from the gauntlet, but he couldn't.

Cleo tried to close her mind. She didn't need to see what happened next. She didn't want to. She wouldn't watch it again.

"That's enough," she said out loud. "I got what we need. Gin Ricky?"

"I'm trying..."

She could feel him pulling at the gauntlet, but it wouldn't relinquish its hold on her scalp.

It was happening again. She was shambling through the streets. She was at her door. Jazz played softly from the gramophone that had been a wedding present. Rose petals littered the floor. A flickering candle cast romantic light over her living room. Laughter from the bedroom. Walt on top of Thea, their bodies joined. Sweat glistened on his skin.

"No!" Cleo screamed. A wave of energy burst forth from her, blasting Gin Ricky off his feet as the gauntlet fell to the floor.

"Are you all right?" Gin Ricky scrambled to her side.

"What happened?"

"It's a prototype. I don't know. Maybe we pushed it too far."

"You were right," Cleo panted. "Maxwell took your son. I saw him being taken to the cells in the research wing."

"You did? What else?"

"Walt's in love with his partner." The tears she had held back refused to be stayed any longer.

"Walt?"
"My husband."
"Walter James is your husband?"

DELIRIUM TREMENS

"Walt, you're shaking," Thea said softly as they stood together in his kitchen.

"I'm fine," he said, folding his arms tight over his chest and tapping his foot on the ground.

The journey back to his apartment was a bit of a blur in Walt's head. He was having trouble marshalling his thoughts. Every time he tried to make a cohesive idea stick, it seemed to slip through his fingers. He had yearned for a long time for Thea to look at him the way she was now; concern shone out of her face, but far from making him feel warm, it was a sobering mirror to look into.

"Maybe cold turkey isn't the way to go."

"It's just the DTs. I'll be fine," Walt said, running his tongue over his teeth, trying to get rid of the odd metallic taste in his mouth.

"I'm worried about you."

"Stop worrying about me and start worrying about him," Walt said harshly, jabbing a figure in the direction of the living room where Benny still sat in his, Walt's, favourite chair.

Benny and Walt's official introduction had not gone smoothly. Harsh words and threats had been traded on both sides, unaided by the discovery of the severed arm that had been placed, along with the detritus from the operation, in Walt's kitchen sink. It was only when Thea returned from having disposed of the unattached limb in the basement furnace that a calm of sorts had been restored.

"I think you should sit down, man," Benny said.

"Why don't you shut up and mind your own business," Walt said, a cold sweat forming across his entire body. He knew it was the withdrawal, he knew it wasn't real, but as the walls undulated like water and giant spiders crawled from the shadows, it took all of his very limited self-control not to cry out.

He let himself be steered to the couch by Thea's gentle hand. His stomach was tied in knots, the sensation flickering between hunger cramps and a nauseousness that made him afraid to open his mouth.

"Walt, can you hear me?" Thea was leaning over him. Of course, he could hear her, he tried to tell her so, but no words came out, his throat felt stretched, painfully tight. "Fuck! Benny, I think he's going down!"

"Get him on his side!"

"Help me hold him!"

Walt felt himself being dragged from the couch. His arms and legs jerked and spasmed, but he could do nothing to stop it. He could hear a pitiful moaning, and it took him a moment to realise that it was he who was making the sound. His jaw was clenched so tightly he thought his teeth would break. He felt dizzy and panicky. Hands rolled him onto his side. He stared at the dust underneath the couch as he continued to convulse until blackness mercifully took him.

When Walt awoke, he was lying naked on his back, tucked comfortably into bed. The covers were tighter to his left, and Walt turned his head to see Thea sitting on the other side of the bed. She had a wet cloth in her hand; she had been sponging his forehead.

"You had a seizure. You've been out for a couple of hours."

"You mopped me up, huh?"

"Don't I always?" Thea wiped the wet cloth over his forehead once more before discarding it on the bedside table that had been Cleo's. "How do you feel? Do you need anything?" Worry creased her forehead.

"I feel like I'm a mess," Walt said, finding it hard to look her in the eye. Her gaze was too sympathetic, too understanding. "I'm so fucking sorry."

"Don't be. I'll take this over the alternative any day."

"I don't just mean this; I mean about everything."

"We still have a lot to work through, but now isn't the time." She was placating him.

"You deserve better; you always have."

"Luckily, that's not for you to decide. Sleep. We can talk about whatever you want when you wake up."

"Nobody really gets to go back, do they?"

Thea didn't answer. She scooted down the bed and lay her head on his chest. He wrapped his arms around her almost reflexively and held her tight, but like subtle clouds in summer skies, he knew a storm was coming.

LOST CAUSE

Thea was too warm. She was still lying on top of Walt's bed. Walt himself was wrapped around her as closely as he could be with a duvet between them. Trying carefully not to wake him, she tapped her Index; she had been asleep for around six hours.

"Get under the covers," came a soft voice in her ear.

"Have you been awake this whole time?"

Thea rolled onto her back so she could look at him. Walt propped himself up on one elbow, leaving his other arm draped loosely over her waist.

"I can't sleep," he said. "But you could do with a couple hours more, get under the covers."

"I have work to do."

"We have work to do."

"Is there any point in me trying to convince you to stay in bed?"

"Nope. Not a chance in hell that's happening."

"Getting you in there was no cake-walk. The least you could do is stay a while."

"I'm actively trying to block that out, so if you don't mind..."

"I've had plenty of practice at undressing you, don't worry about it." Thea looked away. "Sorry...I shouldn't have..."

Walt shrugged. "It's true."

"I know you well enough to see through your bravado. You're strung out."

Walt rolled onto his back and stared at the ceiling. "I am...struggling," he said finally. "I can't sleep, and all I can think about is the bottle of bourbon in my bedside drawer. You were right, cold turkey is dangerous, but if I take a drink now, even to avoid another seizure, I know I won't ever stop again." The words came out in a rush.

Thea put her hand in his; he gripped it tightly and brought it to his lips.

"Look at me." He shook his head and continued to stare at the ceiling. "What can I do?"

"I'm gonna take a shower. Will you get rid of all the bottles in the apartment, please?"

"Of course. Where are they?"

"Everywhere."

"Where do you even get your liquor?"

"Gin Ricky."

"Ah."

While Walt was in the bathroom, Thea scoured the apartment for liquor bottles. She found them in cupboards and closets, under sinks and in suitcases; several were even stashed under the couch.

"How's your boy?" Benny asked, watching Thea as she emptied the decanter next to Walt's armchair, with a pained expression.

Thea shrugged noncommittally.

"You know you have to bench him, right?"

"Sorry?"

"We don't have time for you to be taking care of him; we have to move on the Gold Legion before it's too late. I'm not gonna just sit around and wait to die while you play Florence Nightingale to a lost cause."

"First of all," Thea said, rounding on Benny. "You don't know a thing about Walt or my relationship with him so keep your opinions to yourself, and secondly, if I'm going to 'bench' a liability, it'll be you. Don't think for a second because we have an understanding that I don't know you will screw me the first chance you get. And save me your indignation, you tried to have me killed under the guise of the greater good, so I will take a jacked-up Walt over you any day."

"Believe it or not, I am in this for the long haul, but I don't blame you for being sceptical. The thing is, between the two of us, me an' him, I'm not wrestling with my demons—I own them. No matter how hard he tries, he will let you down—that's the nature of addiction. It's not as easy as just stopping. I just hope I get a chance to say I told you so: the alternative is he will have gotten you dead."

"You'll forgive me if I don't take relationship advice from a pimp."

Benny sighed loudly and raised his hands in surrender. "Fine. When you are done dumping his liquor, we'd better get down to business. But I know his type; they walk in and out of my joint every day."

TRANSCRIPT OF RECORDED CONVERSATION(S)
Subject: Det. Andrew Javier Torrez   Date: ▇▇▇▇   Case: #▇▇▇▇
Authorised by: District Attorney Harold Williams
Investigating Officer: Det. Damien O'Malley
Transcribed by: Det. Damien O'Malley

```
Date: ▇▇▇▇    Time: ▇▇▇▇
INCOMING CALL - TRACED - Dillard Kelly (Verified)
DK: Any Luck?
AT: I saw ▇▇▇▇▇▇▇▇▇▇▇▇▇▇▇▇
DK: Interesting watch, huh?
AT: What do you want me to do now?
DK: Sit on it.
AT: What the hell?
DK: The trick with leverage isn't having it; it's knowing when to use it. So, yeah,
sit on it. I'll call you when it's time.
AT: What am I supposed to do now?
DK: Go about your business. Be a good little detective and keep your nose clean.
LINE DISCONNECTED - DURATION 00:37
```

```
Date: ▇▇▇▇    Time: ▇▇▇▇
OUTGOING CALL - TRACED - Det. Thea Williams (Verified)
TW: Torrez?
AT: How you feeling?
TW: I'm okay. You?
AT: I'm sorry I didn't call sooner. I got […] tied up.
TW: I heard. You've been busy. […] Did you really steal evidence?
AT: Walter wasted no time dropping that bombshell, huh? It's complicated, Querida.
TW: Then explain it to me, Drew.
AT: You know I love you, right?
TW: What happened?
AT: God, I'm so sorry. I just need you to know I'm sorry.
TW: What have you done?
AT: Too much. Just remember, when this is over, no matter what, I never wanted to
hurt you.
LINE DISCONNECTED - DURATION 00:49
```

NOTE: The rest of the official record was destroyed during the fire of September 2427. Summarised copies can be found in the virtual evidence archive.

WE NEED TO TALK ABOUT TORREZ

Over the next few days, Thea, Benny, and Walt each recounted the information they had gathered while sitting around Walt's coffee table. Benny reiterated everything he knew about the distribution of Styxx and the introduction of Quietus, as well as his involvement in the murdered flapper in the church and his assertions that the Gold Legion was returning to power. Walt told of his suspicions of a cover-up helmed, at least partially, by the Onyx Legion, the involvement of Torrez, his suspicions about Bastion, and revealed the chip he had procured in his less than finest hour. Thea brought them both up to date with everything she had discovered about the latest victim, Ric Luckstrim.

"So," Walt said for the third or fourth time, turning the octagonal metal disk over in his hand as if it were a poker chip. "This is our murder weapon."

He was making progress in his quest for sobriety. He had eaten that morning, and his jitters were less frequent, though he still wasn't sleeping well. Thea could tell, however, every time she saw the thin sheen of sweat form on his forehead that the cravings were as strong as ever.

"Yes. We don't know precisely what it does or what it was designed for, but we know it has explosive capabilities," Thea said, taking the chip from Walt and placing it carefully on the coffee table.

"It's not what killed the ghouls in your apartment, though, and Jasper said these are expensive tech. We're talking millions of credits for a single one," said Walt.

"We can't be sure it wouldn't have if we hadn't gotten there first," Thea countered. "We can't be sure whether or not the detonation is deliberate either, but that still leaves us with three avenues to follow. Who designed it, who manufactured it and where, and who fitted it and how? We know Medicorum is involved, but we can't be certain they're working alone."

They had come to these conclusions several times during the last few days, but hadn't been able to agree on how best to proceed. Walt, ironically, prescribed caution, correctly asserting that the unknown "they" had already tried to kill Thea before; what was to stop them trying again and more actively once they discovered how much she, he, and Benny knew? Thea felt that the more time they wasted, the more innocent people could be hurt. Benny preached action.

"You guys are focussing on the wrong thing; you got murders to solve, I get it, but the big picture is the Gold Legion and its plans. We need to find out as much about the shady sons of bitches as we can," he said, irritated.

"Yes, but to be in a position to do that, we need to do our jobs, and unless we can tie them to the crime—even if we find out who they are—we can't do anything if we can't prove they've broken the law," Thea shot back.

"Getting a warrant to search Medicorum is downright impossible. They will never let us get past the front desk, and even if by some miracle we did get a warrant, they will tie us up with litigation so tight that it could be years before we get access to anything," said Walt.

"We need to find the bodies of the original victims and get the autopsies redone, get that chip examined and find out everything we can about the Gold Legion," said Thea, counting on her fingers. "And see if we can get Flynn to talk because he's the only person we can be sure is involved in the coverup."

"Not the only person, and he's the one most likely to snitch back to his bosses," said Walt. "We need to talk about Torrez."

"We need to talk to Torrez," said Thea pointedly.

"And the DA," Benny said.

"Getting a straight answer from my father is going to be difficult; Flynn answers to him, so he is the next best thing, and if he isn't scared of me, he's definitely scared of you," she nodded to Walt.

"Torrez gets a pass huh?" Walt said with thinly veiled contempt.

"He called me last night," Thea said quietly.

"What did he say?" Walt asked suspiciously. He took an ornamental gold coin out of his pocket and began to turn it over in his fingers the same way he had with the chip.

"Not a lot. He told me he loved me and that whatever happens—he's sorry."

"Sorry for what?" Walt's brow furrowed.

"I don't know. He's in trouble. He sounded scared," Thea said worriedly.

"If he is involved in this, he should be," Walt said.

"He's our friend—"

"He's your friend. To me, he's a mediocre colleague and most likely a dirty cop."

"Because you're an angel." Thea got to her feet and paced the room once. "You suspected Bastion so easily. I don't know why I'm surprised," she said as she came to face Walt. "But I am not going to just throw him to the wolves without at least trying to find out what's going on."

"You trust too easily, put too much faith in people, expect too much," Walt said bitterly.

"Are we talking about Torrez and Bastion, or you?"

Benny sighed, crossed his arms and leaned back in his chair; Thea and Walt ignored him.

Walt scoffed and said, "He stole evidence from a crime scene."

"So did you, or did the shell casing you took from my apartment just magically appear in your pocket?" Thea demanded.

"That's different," Walt said, flaring up at once and getting to his feet so Thea could no longer tower over him.

"It always is when it's you. Maybe he had his reasons. He deserves the benefit of the doubt. I owe him at least that much."

"Why, because he loves you?" Walt sneered.

"I refuse to believe you're that insecure," Thea said, pinning him with a level stare.

"He is involved with the people who hurt you, whether by choice or not. That means your safety isn't as important to him as you'd like to think it is."

"Don't patronise me. I'm a big girl. I don't need you to protect me."

Walt scoffed again, but it lacked any real derision. Running his hands roughly through his hair, he sat back down.

"Fine," he said after a pregnant pause. "You talk to Torrez, and I'll do some digging into the Gold Legion."

Thea turned away and grabbed her coat from where it sat over the back of one of the dining room chairs.

"And Thea," Walt said as she made her way to the door. "Don't tell him everything. I know you want him to be with us, but there is a chance he isn't. Don't give him ammo to hurt you with."

LIAR

Marielena Torrez was a beautiful woman. Her olive skin and dazzling green eyes, coupled with her delicate features and long dark hair, made for the kind of face you did not forget quickly.

Thea felt like a fraud in her presence. Marielena treated Thea like she was part of her family, and had Thea not been concealing knowledge about Torrez's extramarital activities, Marielena would have been a rare true friend.

As it stood, Thea sat uncomfortably in Mrs Torrez's conservatory, sipping tea and making small talk.

"This room is beautiful," Thea said, and she meant it. The ceiling and three of the walls were all composed of long panes of glass framed in white metal. Plants hung from the panes in the roof, and vines covered the glass walls. The furniture, which was ivory and gold, was camouflaged by the numerous plants in terracotta pots that sat atop the black and white patterned floor.

"Andrew brings me a new plant on our anniversary and every birthday without fail," she said, leaning over the arm of the long sofa she and Thea shared and petting one of the plants, looking at it much like a mother would her child.

"Jewellery isn't for everyone." Thea smiled, and Marielena laughed.

"Since the illness, I don't go out very often. They bring me joy. I miss going to dinner with you and Walter, the laughs we had," she said wistfully.

Five years previously, Marielena had suffered from inflammation of the brain in the form of encephalitis. While she had recovered from this, the attack on her immune system by the virus had left her with a severe case of Chronic Fatigue Syndrome. Often too dizzy and tired to get out of bed, she was all but housebound.

Thea knew she was rationalising because she cared for Torrez, but a tiny, terrible part of her felt slightly better knowing that his unfaithfulness had begun long before his wife was ill.

"Walt and I..." Thea took a sip of her tea for something to do, unsure of how to explain.

"Drew told me about... Well, what happened. I'm sorry things didn't work out for you two. I probably shouldn't say this now, but I always thought you were a lovely couple. You challenged each other, and the way Walter used to look at you—it could make a preacher blush. Oh, I am sorry, that's insensitive of me," said Marielena, blushing herself.

"Actually, we have decided to try to work things out," Thea said before she could stop herself.

"How wonderful, Thea! Indulge me. I never get to chat anymore. How's it going?" Marielena positively beamed.

"Turbulent," Thea said, setting her cup down on the live wood table. "We had a fight just before I came here."

"Passionate couples fight. It isn't always a bad thing."

"Fight, struggle, bottle things up. That's pretty much us."

"Hey, baby, where are you?" Torrez's voice came from the living room, cutting the women's conversation short and bringing with it a waft of cigarillo smoke.

"In here with Thea," Marielena called happily.

Silence was the reply.

"Andrew?" she called, unsure.

"Do you mind if I go?" Thea said, indicating the direction of the living room. "Work stuff," she added when Marielena looked concerned.

"Send what's left of him in when you're done," Marielena said, smiling knowingly. She was used to Thea being the voice of reprimand in Torrez's life. If only it would be so simple this time.

Thea got up from the gilded sofa and patted Marielena on the leg as she passed, making her way through the French doors that led to the living room.

The room was small, but well kept. The walls were exposed brick, large metal embossings of various jazz icons were spaced evenly along the east wall, and the sofa was upholstered in dark leather with rolled arms and deep button tufting all over. Several bookcases and brassy lamps were propped against the walls. Torrez was nowhere to be seen.

Thea didn't have to look for long, however. She found him in the small square, oak kitchen with a cigarillo in one hand and a bottle of tequila in the other. He was sipping directly from the glass neck.

"What kind of trouble are you in?"

"I'm fine, Querida. Just go home," said Torrez, waving a would-be airy hand. It left a smoke trail in the air.

"What happened to your nails?" Thea said in horror.

Torrez sniffed, his eyes red and watery. "Nothing, perk of the job." He took a final drag of his cigarillo, then stubbed it on the countertop.

"That's not nothing."

"Leave it alone," said Torrez, his voice shaking.

His face was strained. He looked tired, highly strung, and bruised; his bottom lip was puffy.

"Did Walt do that?" Thea said, pointing at his lip.

"He wishes. Hell, I wish, he probably would have been gentler. But no, no, he didn't. Look, Thea, things just got rough on a case..." He let the sentence trail off, then took a large gulp of tequila.

Thea took a step towards him, gently pulled the bottle from his hands and set it on the glossy black countertop.

"Talk to me, Torrez."

He turned away from her and braced his arms on the counter.

"Drew, talk to me," Thea said, putting a hand on his arm. "I know you. I can tell you're in trouble."

Slowly, his dark eyes met hers and Thea was surprised to see that tears flowed down his face. He quickly dropped his gaze and pulled his arm out of her reach.

"Drew..."

"I'm in over my head. I thought I knew what I was doing, but I don't, and I want out, but I'm afraid. This," he held up his mangled nail beds for her to examine. "Isn't even the worst of it. I don't ever want to experience that again, but I don't want anyone else to get hurt either." The expression on his face was fear mingled with guilt.

"What did you do?"

"Forget it. I'm drunk and rambling." Torrez picked up the bottle again and took a long draft. He leaned his back against the counter and folded his arms defensively, but tears continued to roll down his cheeks.

"You stole something from my apartment crime scene."

His eyes widened momentarily before he recovered himself and fixed a passive, belligerently disinterested look on his wet face.

"How did you..." He let the sentence trail off again.

"That chip—"

"Do you have it?" Torrez stepped away from his leaning perch and bared down on Thea.

"What does it do?"

"For fuck's sake, Thea," said Torrez taking her by the arms and shaking her hard. "Do you have it? And how the hell did you get it?" He was yelling in her face now.

"Take a step back, Drew," Thea warned.

"Where is the fucking chip?" said Torrez, his grip on Thea's arms painfully tight.

Thea wrenched her arms out of his clutches and shoved him hard, her hands on his chest. He stumbled backwards into the kitchen counter and knocked the bottle of tequila to the floor as he tried to steady himself. It shattered, showering both their feet in glass and alcohol.

"Walter, it was him, wasn't it? He saw me at the scene. That fucking bastard, that's why he attacked me in the precinct. Querida, you put a leash on him, and you'd have the most faithful dog in the world," Torrez said, bitterness dripping from every word.

"Do you have something to do with my case? With the attack on me?"

"I had no idea that it would...I would never...not you."

"You know something. Drew, tell me what's going on. Tell me about the chips.

If you tell me, I can help you. We can work through this together. What do you know about the Gold Legion?"

Lunging forward, Torrez grabbed Thea by the upper arm again and dragged her out of the kitchen. "Drew!" Thea yelled in protest as he yanked on her arm, pulling her through the living room and into the hall.

"You need to leave."

Torrez thrust Thea across the hall towards the front door. She stumbled slightly, then turned to look at him aghast.

"Torrez, we can help you."

"Get the fuck out of my house!" he bellowed.

Thea had never seen him like this before. The Torrez she knew was cocky, full of wise-cracks, and calm as a rule, bordering on indifferent. Now, his face was red. His eyes were bloodshot, and he looked panicked. He scared her slightly, but she didn't move.

"Leave, Thea! Get the fuck out!"

"Andrew," came Marielena's shocked voice. She appeared at the door of the living room, looking astounded and appalled. "What has gotten into you?"

"Not now," said Torrez, rounding on his wife. He was trying to sound calm and collected, but it only served to make him seem more manic.

Marielena looked between her husband and Thea, then back again. She was pale.

"It's fine, Marie. Just a stupid fight that got out of hand. I need to go anyway. Take care of yourself. I'll come by again soon," Thea said, blowing Marielena a kiss. "We'll talk later, Drew."

Thea left the apartment with her heart pumping rapidly. She ran down six flights of stairs before she stopped, her breath coming in short bursts. Torrez never behaved like that. He was scared to the point of blind panic, and for the first time in their eight-year friendship, she had truly glimpsed just how dangerous he could be. Her mind whirring, Thea left the building and headed to the station.

THE GOLD LEGION

The Gold Legion was a ghost, a dirty secret that was kept buried. It was treated more like an urban legend than a historical fact, even though it was known that the sect was the Onyx Legion's predecessor. Most of the true details of its demise weren't available to the public. It was a smear on the reputation of the establishment who were keen to keep the nitty-gritty of it under wraps. Contrary to what they intended, however, this shroud of secrecy had ensured that it was a continuing fascination for many predisposed to conspiracy theories and history, nearly two-hundred-and-fifty years later.

"What do you know about the Gold Legion? Cops always know about the shady shit," Benny said. He had picked up an irritating habit of throwing passive-aggressive questions at Walt, and it was starting to grate on the latter's nerves.

He and Walt were sitting together at Walt's dining room table, the data stream in front of them courtesy of Walt's Index. Though they had collectively gone through huge amounts of data, sources, texts, and articles, they found only passing mentions and hushed illusions to the fabled sect.

It didn't help that Walt was once again jittery and on edge. He felt slightly better of body, but that merely added to the delusions that only a true addict can possess; that perhaps just one drink would be enough, that maybe it would quash the sick feeling in his stomach and get rid of the persistent fog in his mind. In his most rational brain, he knew that this was the withdrawal talking, but that knowledge did nothing to stem his cravings.

"Bit before my time," Walt said in reply to Benny's unflattering question.

"It's a bit before the data stream's time, too, so what do we do now?"

"We have to go to the archives," said Walt, scratching his head absently.

"I ain't going anywhere near the police station, I got out of there once, but I'm sure that you pigs would try to find an excuse to keep me this time," said Benny holding his hands up.

"Reasons aren't the same as excuses. They'd hardly be carrying out an injustice. But no, not the archives at the station. The city archives."

"And where are those when they're at home?"

"The Mayor's office. City Hall."

Benny let out a crack of laughter. "Hell no. Hell no. I'm not setting foot in the Gold Legion's old headquarters."

"Rumoured. But if we want that info, we're going."

"When did we become a 'we'? You need backup—call your girl. I mean, if she'll answer after your little tiff."

Ignoring this and sighing in a resigned sort of way, Walt said, "The archives are open to the public. Anyone can walk in—"

"Off you go, then, have fun. I'll see you when you get back," Benny cut across Walt.

"But," Walt ploughed on, "Some of the archives are restricted, things of a more delicate nature, things that make the city look bad. I'm betting that the info about the Gold Legion is there, so I need you to be a lookout while I browse the city's dirty laundry."

Benny kept up a torrent of complaints as he and Walt sat in the back of a Jonk heading for City Hall.

"This just proves it," he said. "All you cops are dirty in some way. Bet you've had to wash plenty of blood off your hands."

"Says the man who was working for the GL," Walt shot back, though he privately agreed—most of the police in the city were indeed dirty in some way.

"Someone puts a shotgun in your mouth; what would you do?" Benny said, nettled.

Walt laughed self-deprecatingly. "You don't know me very well, do you?"

There were a few minutes of silence after this until the Jonk started its descent towards the street adjacent to city hall.

"No docking bay?" Benny said in surprise.

"Only in the Mayor's office on the top floor, and I think we can both agree that is a place neither of us should go."

The Jonk landed somewhat bumpier than Walt would have liked due to the narrowness of the street. To get into the right position, the transporter had to pull in at a slant, which caused the back to drop suddenly in order to level off near the ground. Walt and Benny exited the transporter and walked casually into the main street.

City Hall was a temple to the establishment. Ostentatiously built to resemble something between The Parthenon and The Library of Alexandria, it was a wonder in white marble. Nearly a hundred stories high, gargantuan Corinthian columns stood impossibly tall at the building's four corners stopping only where the magnificently carved acanthus leaves at the tops met the triangular prism that was the bronze roof. Each floor had its own smaller columns that stood ten feet tall, every one flanking a large rectangular window that outwardly reflected a pale gold. The decorations alternated between floors, depicting friezes of the greatest moments in Tenebrium's history, and huge carved statues of important figures styled like ancient gods.

"If this ain't a sign they think they are above us, I don't know what is," Benny said with a healthy amount of disdain.

Walt grunted in agreement as they passed through the large open archway that served as the entrance. Onyx Legion soldiers stood like sentries just inside. Instead of their usual stun rods, assault rifles, or brass knuckles, they held long golden spears. Walt could tell by the faint humming as he passed them that the tips were electrified.

The large atrium was tiered like an amphitheatre, with desks, lifts, halls, and doorways all leading off in various directions connected by glossy granite steps.

Several of those who worked in the building eyed Walt and Benny as they made their slow way towards the archive.

"You think they are eyeing us because they've used my services and don't want me to stop and say 'Hi', or you, because you're fucking their boss' daughter? Or at least you wish you were."

"First of all," said Walt out of the corner of his mouth. "The mayor is their boss, not the DA, and secondly, you talk about Thea like that again, and I'll knock your teeth out."

"I don't think you get to play the white knight anymore; she seems to be the only one doing the rescuing."

"Why are you trying to piss me off?" Walt said, stopping and turning to Benny. Two passers-by had to do an awkward sidestep to avoid walking into them.

"No reason." Benny said, an infuriating grin on his face.

"Then save the wise-talk until later."

Walt stalked away from Benny, who hurried to catch up.

The archive was another grand room. Open to the intricate mosaic ceiling depicting the scorching of the earth that had led to the building of the ocean colonies. It was visible across multiple floors. Millions of books on thousands of shining black shelves looked down into the centre below, where Walt and Benny stood on another intricate mosaic depicting the healing of the earth's surface, next to a gold metal monolith surrounded by wooden chairs and tables that would not have looked out of place in an aged university library.

Walt stepped up to the monolith. He was barely a foot away when it finally showed his reflection. Except it wasn't a reflection. The "him" depicted in the monolith's smooth surface was wearing grey robes, not a three-piece suit underneath a dark trench coat. It pointed to the very top floor, which was shorter than the others. Walt thought that once up there, he would be able to touch the mosaic ceiling if so inclined.

Walt looked around for a staircase or ladder, but could see no way of ascending. As soon as the problem had occurred to him, however, a solution presented itself. Just beyond the monolith, a shimmering pool of gold appeared on the floor. The "him" standing serenely in the monolith nodded towards it smiling in a contented way that made Walt uncomfortable.

"Stay here," he said to Benny, who immediately showed signs of protesting. "You have to keep watch, remember?"

"Is that thing sentient?" Benny looked at the huge gold obelisk with suspicion and fear.

"Yes. It protects the knowledge held within here so that no one can steal it or deny it, but that doesn't mean that if an OL soldier comes in and sees me up there, they won't throw us out on our asses with a beating for good measure."

"And if they realise you are snooping into the other legion…"

"Exactly," said Walt stepping into the shimmering puddle. "I won't be long." It felt oddly solid beneath his feet. He stood there for a moment and was just wondering if he had to do something when it began to rise slowly. It wasn't the most pleasant way to travel. Heights made Walt uncomfortable at the best of times, but standing on the edgeless, undulating pool as it rose higher and higher made him feel a queasiness that had nothing to do with withdrawal.

The solid puddle stopped neatly next to a gap in the railings on the top floor and Walt stepped gratefully off. The liquid lift fell back to the floor like glittering rain.

There were only ten rows of shelves compared to the many on each floor below. They were all composed of three impressive bookcases shaped like pointed archways and made of an orangish wood. All the shelves were diagonal, forming a crisscross pattern. The books on the slanted shelves were all thick leather volumes embossed with different coloured metals.

It didn't take Walt long to find the section dedicated to the Gold Legion. In truth, it wasn't a section at all, it was a single large tome bound in black leather. The cover depicted a young man with an angelic face wearing a golden crown of leaves and pronounced the title to be "The Rise and Fall of The Order of Khrysos".

Fingers trembling with anticipation, Walt opened the dusty book and began to read. The first page bore only a few words:

"Neither moth nor rust devoureth it; but the mind of man is devoured by this supreme possession."

— Pindar, Fragment 222 (trans. Sandys) (Greek lyric 5th century BC)

Elanor Miller

KHRYSOS CHILD OF ZEUS

A brief and introductory summary of the origins, rise, and fall of the Gold Legion.
By Anthony Oubier

Authors note:
No doubt, this record of mine detailing what scarce knowledge I could find about the legendary Gold Legion will go unread. The years of my life devoted to the research of that very subject, however, are not wasted. For I, at least, among the common folk, will know a fraction of the truth.

Before it became the Gold Legion, the sect, open only to the richest and most powerful, was called *The Order of Khrysos,* and it was not a sect, but a cult.

In the years leading up to The Scorching of 2189, humanity was privy to many a warning sign. Dating back to the early 2000s, many of the world's leading scientists had warned world leaders that fundamental changes had to be made in order to stop a catastrophic weather event due to the climate crisis, but few heeded their warnings. By 2107 it became clear to all that the damage was irreversible; it was only a matter of time before Mother Earth made sure that mankind paid dearly for its abuse of her.

This knowledge led to a rise in so-called "Doomsday Cults". Previously victims of mockery, those devoted to *Apocalypticism* gained a large boost in popularity. This resurgence led to the creation of several new cults, the most successful of which was The Order of Khrysos.

Khrysos, one of the many sons of Zeus described in ancient Greek mythology, was said to be the god of gold and riches. When one learns of the order's aims, it becomes clear why they chose a somewhat unknown deity as their figurehead. For the order believed in the purity of gold, and in the decade preceding The Scorching, they hoarded the precious metal setting its value above all other things, including food and shelter, so convinced as they were that it was the key to salvation.

Unfortunately, having forsaken many of the other preparations taken by their non-cultist neighbours, on November 9th 2189, when fire began to fall from the sky, a large number of the order lost their lives. Some refused to take shelter and burned where they stood praising Khrysos, while others perished under piles of molten gold.

Those who did survive, however, became the first venture capitalists of the new world. They became the first to own and rebuild "Big Business" and had a hand in restarting the stock market on the original ocean colonies. It is unclear why gold, above all things, seems to appeal to Man more than diamonds or other more practical commodities, but what of the metal that had been saved, quickly became the most coveted of currencies.

In the twenty or so years that followed, The Order of Khrysos saw a shift in ideals, parting ways with the religious devotion to worshipping gold in the literal sense to focus on the worship of profits gained through savvy business choices.

It was around this time in 2210 that the first records of the Gold Legion appeared. What scant accounts I could recover suggested that among the newer, more capitalist minded members of the order, Harlen Williams and his wife Eliza (née Maxwell) became tired of the ceremonial and ritualistic duties that were still expected of them. According to the diary of one Lance Maxwell (brother of Eliza), Harlen and his wife broke away and became the founding members of the Gold Legion.

No longer a cult, but something rather closer to the freemasonry of old, the most powerful and influential in the now blossoming ocean colonies banded together to form the Gold Legion. These leaders in their economic fields were welcomed by the governing powers of the day, and in some wealthy cities, Tenebrium among them, the now sect was more powerful than the elected officials.

Alas, it was in Tenebrium alone that the Gold Legion became more than the wealthy elite and trusted advisors to the establishment.

Enjoying their new lavish lifestyle and an unprecedented level of celebrity, as a result, Harlen and Eliza moved to Tenebrium City, which was, at the time, the most coveted of locations. It had been the first place to reintroduce agriculture outside of a lab, and it was one of the first cities in the world, let alone its colony, to see real livestock available for purchase.

Something changed for the money-minded couple, however, not long after they had settled into the city. They were introduced to Robert Luckstrim, a scientist who had loftier ideas for the sect than merely controlling the business world. This was the beginning of the end for the Gold Legion.

The Williams' and their fellows among the sect heard a sermon of such charisma and fervour that they were converted to a new, darker way of thinking. Luckstrim preached that the poor and the downtrodden were a plague in their perfect city and must be wiped out in order to make Tenebrium a haven for only those enlightened enough to be part of the legion. This, I believe, was in response to the rather more well-documented food shortages of 2217 that had begun in Tenebrium due to its ever-growing population, drawn in by the promise of a new life, and the food industry's inability to keep up with demand. The mayor at the time, Celia Short, stated that "No life is worth more than another", then proceeded to roll out a city-wide rationing scheme that saw the poorest of households receive the same as the richest.

It is written in Lance Maxwell's diary that Luckstrim often stated his disdain for the equal distribution of rations. He, a self-proclaimed god among men, was often heard voicing his contempt for having to compete for food with those he saw as unworthy.

It was then, Maxwell claims, that Luckstrim hatched a most heinous plan.

During his long and varied tenure in Tenebrium City, Luckstrim had amassed a veritable empire across several types of business, and as it happened, he owned the biggest water company in the city, which operated out of the Poor Quarter, colloquially known as "The Quadrant".

In the early summer of 2218, Luckstrim allegedly set an entire factory in The Quadrant, co-owned by six Gold Legion Members, a single task: to create hundreds of gallons of Hydrogen Cyanide. While I have no proof of this other than Lance Maxwell's word in a personal journal, one thing I can say for sure is that in 2218,

789,301 people, all of whom lived in the Poor Quarter, died over a two-day stretch between 26-28th August.

The official report states that a toxin of unknown origins entered the water supply, and while those investigating could find nothing definite on its source, it was surmised that as the Poor Quarter's water supply ran parallel with the Industrial District's waste disposal line, that somewhere along the thousands of miles of pipe there had been a leak. The inquest ruled the deaths a tragic accident.

Outwardly Tenebrium mourned and moved on; inwardly, Mayor Short heard rumours of Luckstrim's involvement and opened an investigation, most of the documentation of which was destroyed. What remains, however, paints a vivid picture.

There had been several reports from locals in the Poor Quarter of missing persons vanishing in the night and whispers of experiments being carried out on unwilling subjects. Trashcore, the waste disposal giant, seemed to corroborate this when a young worker named Hamish Vole discovered over twenty industrial waste bags containing human body parts. The bags were stamped "Luckstrim Enterprises". Cover-up or a convenient accident, I'll let you decide, but a day later, the bags were mistakenly destroyed by an unwitting employee at the city morgue, and according to Vole's mother, he sent her a letter stating that he had moved to a new city and was never heard from again. The bodies of the victims were never recovered or identified.

With no evidence, any charges that may have been brought against Luckstrim Enterprises were forgotten. Mayor Short did not forget, however. She disbanded the Gold Legion using an obscure business law that she claimed it violated. Both Harlan Williams and Robert Luckstrim were arrested days later on tax violation charges, and both would spend over a decade in prison. In their absence, their empires flourished, and both were greeted with even greater wealth and popularity upon release.

Tenebrium's elite seemed to recover quickly from the disillusion of the Gold Legion, and a roaring trade in Gentleman's clubs was achieved. The Poor Quarter was given grants to modernise the housing, and an initiative was created by the mayor's office that would provide food and medical care to those living under the breadline for years to come. Sadly, Mayor Celia Short would not live to see the good she did for Tenebrium City; She was shot on the steps of City Hall on December 25th, 2219. Her killer was never caught.

For the record, I would like to state that I believe the facts as I have reported them here to be true. Draw what conclusions you will from these. It can be argued, I'm sure, that there are explanations far more rational than a homicidal sect of crazed billionaires, however, I would caution it as unwise to underestimate the allure of power and wealth.

CRAVEN

Flynn was not at the station when Thea arrived there, nor was the body of Richard Luckstrim or any of the other victims, for that matter. The studious young Anatomical Pathology Technician was far more self-assured than the Medical Examiner when he informed Thea of this; Thea couldn't help but wonder how much he knew about his boss' predilections.

"And nobody thought to inform me that the body wasn't coming here for an autopsy?"

"That's hardly my job," the APT said snootily. He was White and relatively slim, with an English accent that told stories about his upbringing. Thea couldn't for the life of her remember his name; she would have felt guilty for this had his attitude been better.

"Don't start with me, kid. Where's the body?"

"Dr Flynn had the body diverted to the county morgue care of the District Attorney, whom I believe you are well acquainted with." The APT quelled under the look Thea gave him. "It was a direct request by Zhao, the head of the DA's Investigators office," he added more helpfully.

"Of course it was. Where's Flynn?"

Flynn, as it turned out, was having a long lunch at Roaring Third, a multi-tiered establishment that marketed itself as a one-stop-shop entertainment venue. It boasted an expensive restaurant, a casino, a speakeasy, a brothel, and a playhouse. What it was truly famous for, however, was its underground trafficking ring favoured by creeps, paedophiles, and sadistic killers. It was also rumoured that if one was looking to hire a professional assassin, Roaring Third was the place to enquire.

The entrance to the venue was styled like the glass-fronted ticket booths of old-fashioned cinemas. It was a fairly modest exterior. The tinted windows across all floors made it a mirror for the businesses surrounding it, almost camouflaging it from view unless you knew it was there. The clerk sitting at the faux ticket desk's eyes widened when they looked up and saw Thea walking towards them at a smart pace. She knew exactly why; like many detectives in the precinct, she looked like a cop. It was an undefinable thing, but whether it was her high waisted trousers, her pussy bow shirt, or the gun that was pouching her jacket, criminals could smell an officer of the law from a thousand paces.

The clerk didn't comment as she passed, making no attempt to pay the admission fee, but Thea was certain as soon as she was inside, they would tell their bosses to hide anything illegal.

Directly inside the saloon-style doors was a narrow staircase painted black. Several couples averted their eyes and tried to hide their faces as they passed Thea on the stairs. She couldn't be certain, but she was fairly sure the last pair, two women in their sixties, were her downstairs neighbours.

The staircases changed colour depending on the floor, a warm amber for the restaurant, gold for the casino, bare brick for the speakeasy, red for the brothel, and finally purple for the playhouse.

When Thea entered the theatre, there was a beautiful woman in a full bodysuit made out of a glossy red material performing on aerial silks. Thea thought as she watched her for a moment that the way she moved was far too graceful for a place like this.

It was small, supporting a maximum capacity of fifty people. Narrow tables formed the rows of the audience, with a long booth bench on the wall opposite the bar. Like the stairs that lead to it, everything was purple, except the stage, which was gold and the curtains therein, which were red.

Flynn was sitting at a small square table near the bar, eating a seafood platter with his back to Thea. As Thea stepped further into the room, she was met by the Maître D', a young Chinese woman with gloriously white-blonde hair dressed in a full tuxedo.

"Well, hello there," she said loudly, and a few heads turned. "How may I help you, Detective?"

The effect was immediate. Chairs scraped the floor as they were pushed away from tables, as several members of the audience jumped to their feet and, carelessly tossing credit chips to cover their bills, hastened towards the exit. The artist on the stage uncoiled herself from the hanging black silks and disappeared behind the velvet curtains. The bartender pulled several bottles off the top shelf and hid them from view as the lights brightened.

When the commotion died down, there were only a handful of people left, including Thea, the Maître D', the bartender, and Flynn, who was the only one who hadn't moved.

"You have your choice of table, ma'am," said the Maître D' with no trace of irony.

Thea smiled at the audacity.

She made her way over to Flynn and pulled up a chair from the adjacent table. It wasn't until she sat down that he acknowledged her presence.

"Detective Williams, please, join me."

As was the norm, he was sweating noticeably, but he put on a good show of friendly curiosity. "How are you? How is Mr Pickford? Recovering well, I hope."

"He's fine, and I'm having the time of my life chasing corpses all over the city," Thea said, leaning back in her chair.

"I-I...Well," Flynn spluttered. "Is this a new case? Are you sure you are up to it? You were never actually cleared for duty." Flynn continued to eat, but it looked pained, as though he was trying valiantly not to vomit.

"You gave Richard Luckstrim's body to the DA."

"I didn't have a choice."

"I don't doubt it. But what happened to the other bodies? Are they at the DA's office too?"

"No," said Flynn, going an uneasy shade of mint green.

"Where are they?" Thea leaned forward, her elbows on the table. For one absurd moment, she thought that Flynn was going to comment as his eyes fluttered over the now rumpled tablecloth, but he said nothing. "Where are they?" she repeated.

"I can't. It's...You don't understand what the consequences will be for me. There are other things at play here, other forces at work." A bead of sweat dripped from his nose onto his plate, he pushed it aside, and as if summoned by magic, the Maître D' cleared the table at once.

Thea waited a moment to be sure that no one was within earshot, then said, "No worse, surely, than if I let slip the things you do to the bodies in your care. I could paint quite the picture for the captain. Trousers around his ankles, hand firmly grasping—"

"You can't," Flynn spat, cutting across her. He had the cheek to look disgusted. "And you wouldn't; we made a deal. You do that, and I shall tell those who count about Mr Pickford."

"That's the thing—you don't have any bargaining power. You are complicit in what we did for Benny."

"To him."

"Exactly. If I were to tell the captain what I saw, and Benny was to tell someone at the precinct that you amputated his arm without his consent...Could what my father has threatened to do to you if you talk honestly be any worse than what would happen to an ex-law enforcement officer, who is also a sex offender, if he found himself in jail?"

"You are far from as white as you are painted," Flynn said, shaking with rage. He had the twitchy look of a cornered animal.

"I never pretended to be a paragon. You lied on the autopsy reports. What was the cause of death?"

"Massive head trauma."

"Caused by?"

"You already know." Contempt mingled with fear coated his voice like oil.

"Small metal disk?"

"Yes."

"What does it do?"

"I have no idea."

"Now would be the time to be upfront."

"I have no idea what they were supposed to do. Truly," Flynn added when Thea didn't look convinced.

"Where are the bodies?" Thea pressed on.

Flynn hesitated, looking even more nervous, though there was a defiant edge to his expression now. "Gone," he said with a strangely satisfied look at Thea.

"What do you mean 'gone'?"

"Disposed of, utilising the SubLevel." The smile he gave Thea was positively perverse.

As the realisation hit her, Thea felt sick.

"It's economical. We have run out of grave space, and why spend money on cremation when we have a ravenous population to feed." Now that he had hit his stride, he was thoroughly enjoying himself. "You must admit it's practical. Cost-effective. There is no shortage of the dead in this city."

"You're disgusting."

"So, you see, my dear," Flynn said, with an air of confidence Thea had never been privy to. "You are not fighting a single enemy. You're fighting the whole city. And you can't prove what I've told you. Take my advice. Let it go. This needn't be the hill you die on."

Meek and creepy, Thea had never seen Flynn as a threat. He didn't have a chance of physically overpowering her, and whatever he had taken part in, he was a coward; but he was dangerous and protected, that had never been more apparent.

"You're part of the Gold Legion," Thea stated. "You all are."

"Mentioning that name in this city is very dangerous," Flynn said, some of his old nervousness returning as he looked over his shoulder.

"That wasn't a 'no'."

"I've said all I will. Leave me to my drinks or have me arrested."

Thea got to her feet so quickly that her chair toppled over. The clatter seemed even louder in the deserted theatre. Flynn flinched.

She had planned to walk straight out of there, she really had, but as she passed the Medical Examiner's chair, she couldn't stop herself. She drew back her hand with all her might and struck him across the face. Her closed fist collided with his jaw sending him careering to the floor. He whimpered and coughed, clutching his cheek.

"See you around." And she left without a backwards glance.

THEY KNOW

"Did you get what we needed?" Benny called to Walt.

"Yeah," Walt called back as he stepped uneasily onto the lift and made his way to the bottom floor of the archive.

"Good, because I think we're rumbled."

Four Onyx Legion soldiers marched into the room. When they reached Benny, they fanned out, boxing him in with the monolith at his back.

"Can we help you, gentleman?" asked the only one of the soldiers not wearing a helmet. His face was oddly unremarkable, neither handsome nor ugly, neither young nor old, and his features were neither weak nor pronounced.

Walt stepped off the lift, which disappeared back into the floor and came to stand next to Benny.

"Just looking for information pertinent to an investigation," Walt said casually, flashing his badge.

"Did you find it?" The unremarkable man asked. He kept his voice light, but Walt could tell he was building up to something.

"We did, thank you. The service here is great."

"May I ask what it was you were investigating?" The unremarkable man took a step closer. Walt stood his ground.

He hummed and hawed exaggeratedly. "'Fraid not. I can't discuss an active investigation."

"That's a shame. We at the OL are always keen to assist law enforcement wherever we can."

"I'm getting bored of these pretend niceties," Walt said, dropping all pretence. Beside him, Benny drew in a deep breath. "The archive is public domain, so unless you suspect I'm bending page corners—you're here for another reason."

"Your friend doesn't look so good," the man said, nodding towards Benny.

Walt hadn't paid much attention to Benny, but now that he was looking at him, the unremarkable man was right. His lips were pale, and he was sweating.

"Maybe you and your companion should leave."

Minutes later, Walt and Benny were walking briskly out of City Hall.

"They know," Walt said under his breath.

"No shit, they know," Benny said loudly as they made their way down the front steps. Benny stopped at the bottom, panting.

"He's right. You don't look so good. Didn't the doc say you need antibiotics? You might have an infection or somethin' maybe we should take you to the hospital—"

"Tenebrium General is a hell hole," said Benny, shaking his head and pushing Walt, who had tried to take his arm, away. "I know a guy."

"All right, where?"

"I'll go myself. He doesn't like strangers."

Benny took a few steps away from Walt and stopped again. He looked as though he was trying to regain his equilibrium.

"You sure you don't want me to come with you? I'm not convinced you'll make it alone," said Walt sceptically.

"I'm dead sure," Benny said, pushing away Walt's attempts to hold him up. A passer-by or two spared them a sideways glance, but no one stopped.

"What's your problem?" Walt said, giving up the attempt. "You'd rather crawl there than accept my help?"

"You are my problem!" Benny yelled. Those nearest to them on the streets now gave both men a wide berth. To the casual onlooker, it may have looked like they were performing street theatre. "You're a liability, and I already told Thea as much. You're gonna crack under the pressure. This front you put on, this tough guy with a big mouth persona, is a load of crap. I know it, and she knows it. I'm fighting for my life here. I don't want to place it in trembling hands if you catch my drift." Benny lent forward, his breathing uneven, and put his hand on his thigh.

"A pimp who has a problem with an alcoholic? I don't buy it."

"Right, because you're just so likeable otherwise."

"Touché, but of all the cops on the force, I've had the least contact with you. So, what's gotten up your nose?"

"You think you're better than me," Benny spat.

"Well, yeah. You keep people as possessions." Walt shrugged.

"You act like I'm so much worse than you because you got a badge, but the difference between us isn't as big as you'd like it to be. Being a cop doesn't make you special, and your hands are far from clean, Detective. You wear that title like a cape, but you're only one or two bad decisions away from being right where I am. I see you watching me, looking down on me, but you've got it, too. You've got the look. That little something that appears behind a man's eyes when he knows he's going to hell. I recognise it. I see it in the mirror everyday. Thea gets to judge me; she's one of the good ones, but you? I don't think so. Glass houses, my friend."

"I'm not like you," Walt said quietly.

"No?"

"You there," a voice called from behind them.

Walt looked around, he had forgotten where he was, but the Onyx Legion soldiers who had asked them to leave were walking down City Hall's front steps towards them

"We had better leave," Walt said, taking Benny by the elbow and marching him away from City Hall. "Where's this doctor?"

"Get me to fifth and Blanchard, and I'll do the rest."

TENEBRIUM POLICE DEPARTMENT TENEBRIUM CITY
TENEBRIUM PROPER DEPARTMENT OF JUSTICE
STYGIAN COLONY #6

INTERDEPARTMENTAL COMMUNICATION
From: Gideon Arthur

INFORMATION REQUEST

I have processed your information request and attached my findings below. Please note that the request was blocked by the District Attorney's office.

Details of Request:

1. List of companies licenced to produce pharmaceuticals and augmentations, privately and commercially, on a large enough scale to support city-wide distribution
2. List of premises capable of mass chemical production, augmentation creation, and waste disposal
3. List of suppliers linked to medical services, both medicines and equipment

Reason for Request:

1. Pertinent to an active investigation (Case #124-1215JD)

Authorised by:

1. Captain Betty Charles

OUTCOME: REQUEST DENIED

Reason:

1. Data Protection.
2. Possible conflict with investigation being carried out by the DA's office.

Hi Thea,

I filed your request and have attached the results, but I don't think it will be much help. Some good news: the contractors have been liaising with finance; Hendrickson asked me to let you know that your apartment is finished. I guess TPD insurance isn't so bad after all.

Glad you're back on your feet. We should grab lunch sometime.

Gid.

WHERE WOULD I GO?

Thea felt at sea as she sat in the Jonk on her way back to Walt's apartment. She was still reeling from her conversation with Doctor Flynn, and she wouldn't quickly forget the panic in Torrez's eyes as he had thrown her from his home. Her list of allies was growing thin. The odds seemed more and more stacked against her. She couldn't trust her friends or colleagues or even her family. It appeared that it was she, Walt, and Benny against the world. It wasn't a comforting thought.

She barely registered what she was doing as she stepped out of the Jonk and into the docking bay. The corridor that led to Walt's door could have been on fire for all the attention she paid, lost as she was in her thoughts.

When she entered, she noted with some surprise that someone, probably Walt, though that didn't seem plausible in her current understanding of the man, had tidied the living area somewhat. The bookcases that sat against two of the four grey-blue walls had been righted and their shelves and books neatly replaced. The broken dining chair that, for the last week, had rested upside down on the kitchen island was nowhere to be seen. The broken glass coffee table had also been removed, and the glass shards that had littered the carpet were gone. The now battered gramophone had been put back on its perch, and the lamp that stood between doors was upright once more, though without a bulb. There was no way to hide the enormous hole in the wall near the front door, but it was much less glaring now with a bookcase tucked tight against it.

Walt was leaning against the counter in the kitchen when Thea entered, a crystal scotch glass in his hand. The liquid inside, far from its usual amber, was a bright yellow.

"It's orange juice," he said quickly, looking up as Thea shut the door behind her.

Thea took off her coat and hung it on one of the pegs beside the door. "You don't like orange juice."

"Coffee makes me jittery at the best of times." Walt raised his arm and showed her a less than steady hand. "And I don't have anything else." Walt set the glass down on the counter and stepped into the living room. "Are you okay?" he asked, tilting his head in concern.

"You were right."

"I'm sorry, what was that?" he cupped a hand around his ear.

Thea laughed feebly.

"You were right," she said. "About Torrez. He knows something. He's working for them. Whoever 'they' are. He's scared, and they hurt him. Bad. He freaked out when I mentioned the Gold Legion. He's in over his head, and I think he's just realised it. I'm worried about him. He threatened me. He threw me out, literally threw me out of his apartment. If Marielena hadn't been there, I don't know what would have happened."

Walt held out his arms to her, beckoning her into them. She went to him gladly. They stood in the middle of the room, holding on to each other for several minutes as Walt swayed gently from side to side.

"I'm sorry. I don't enjoy being right. Not about this. We'll help him if we can, and maybe he'll help us."

"Where's Benny?" she asked, her head still resting on his chest.

"He wasn't lookin' so good, so I took him to some underground clinic in the Pleasure Quarter. I suggested the hospital, but he refused. I don't blame him." Walt kissed the top of her head, then buried his face in her hair. Thea could have stayed like that forever, but she knew she had to tell him all Flynn had revealed to her, and so she did.

When she finished, they were sitting at the dining table. Walt looked repulsed and a little sad. Thea knew exactly why. If Cleo had been alive, she would have been imprisoned in the SubLevel, another unwilling, unknowing cannibal. It made it more personal somehow.

"These people," he said with contempt. "With no bodies, the chip is all we have. At least we know it's what killed them, but is it a malfunction? Or is that exactly what they're supposed to do?"

"I don't know. We have to find out who's manufacturing them."

"Benny was right about the Gold Legion," Walt said seriously.

"What makes you so sure?"

Walt shared everything he had learned from his short time in the archive.

"To me, Styxx is history repeating itself," he said. "The drug had the largest effect on the poor population, and we were headed for shortages just before it. The rich and powerful banding together to subjugate the lower class. It's not a stretch in this city; we see glimpses of it every day. If we find out who is in the Gold Legion, we'll have a much easier time identifying who made the chips and the drugs. If I were a betting man—"

"Which you are."

"I'd put my money on them not being made at Medicorum itself. If I was going to make a shady device, I'd have somewhere separate that I owned, but with no paper trail."

"This is big. A thing of this scale, it's impossible to hide all evidence. These people act like they're gods in this city of men, but they aren't. It's time we reminded them of that."

Walt nodded in agreement. "Do you think we can learn anything more from Flynn?"

"No. He's told us all he's going to. Repulsive as he is, I don't want to get him killed."

"I wouldn't feel particularly bad about that if I'm honest."

"We do this right—and he'll end up in a jail cell where he belongs. I put a request in with Gideon to try and follow the supply chain, but it was blocked by the DA's office. I thought that maybe if we could track down a supplier, a weak link, we might get enough for a warrant, but it's a no go. We will have to see if the captain can swing something for us, and I'd like to meet this Anthony Oubier if he's still alive. He knew more than anyone about the Legion before; perhaps he's following just as avidly now. Maybe you should reach out to Bastion."

Walt nodded, but didn't say anything.

"There's something else," he said, shifting uncomfortably in his seat. "When the Order of Khrysos became the Gold Legion, the founding members were Harlen and Eliza Williams."

"It's a pretty common surname."

Walt crossed and recrossed his arms, stalling.

"You think they have something to do with me?" Thea said, her brow furrowed.

"I know they do; I checked. They are your great, to the power of five, grandparents."

Thea didn't know what to say; she felt dirty. She took all her cases personally, but the knowledge that the Gold Legion originated from her family made her feel responsible for all of it. No wonder her father had wanted to keep her as far away from the case as possible; he was worried that if she kept digging, she would find out exactly what she just had and, worse, be able to tie him to it.

"Cora Artemis, Thea Persephone. I guess calling one of us Khrysos would have been too obvious."

"I know what you're thinking," said Walt. He leaned forward and took Thea's hand from where it lay on the table in his. "This isn't your fault. This has nothing to do with you. You aren't responsible for this."

"But it's still my responsibility. This is my case." Thea looked away from Walt, unsure whether she should or even could voice the thing that had been nagging at her. A stray echo of a thought in the back of her mind at first, it had grown into a fully-fledged worry over the past few weeks.

"What is it?" Walt asked.

"I think Cora's disappearance is linked to this. What if she knew something? What if my dad—"

"Few people have a lower opinion of your father than me," Walt said, tapping the semi-healed cut on the bridge of his nose. "But I refuse to believe that he would harm his own daughter. I know he's screwing with you and your career, and he's neck-deep in the Gold Legion, but that's not the same as trying to kill you or killing your sister."

Thea didn't bother correcting his implication that her sister was dead. She had always been the only one who believed that Cora was still alive and out there somewhere. She believed it still.

"He knows something about what happened to her. I can see it in his eyes every time I mention her."

"Maybe, but you didn't see him at the hospital before you woke up. His mask slipped. He was worried like a father should be." Walt rubbed his thumb over Thea's knuckles.

"I never thought I'd see you defending him."

"He's dirty—it's just a fact, he is, but I don't believe he wants to see you hurt."

Thea leaned in and kissed Walt gently, then stood up.

"Where are you going?"

"My apartment is ready," Thea said awkwardly.

"That was fast," Walt said, equally so.

"I can't stay here forever..."

"I guess not."

"Do you want to come with me to check it out?" Thea asked.

The journey to Thea's newly restored apartment was a quiet one. Though they sat contentedly together, they were both lost in thought. Thea glanced at Walt as he stared out the window with unfocused eyes at the brightly lit night. Something had clicked between them today. They had begun to overcome the strangeness of navigating a relationship with someone you had done lasting damage to. Walt had pulled through as promised. He had been reliable and comforting. He was sober. He had been everything she had wanted him to be over the last two years.

He still wasn't the same carefree Walt he had been, and he probably never would be, but this Walt, who faced his demons and was there when he said he would be, was one she could get used to.

"Are you ready?" Walt asked as the Jonk hovered outside the bay window that opened into Thea's living room. The glass slid smoothly aside to allow the alighting bridge to connect with the transporter.

"Let's go."

Very few apartments had their own docking port, most shared one with the rest of their building. Stepping into the apartment her father had bought her as a present for her sixteenth birthday suddenly felt alien. It was like a falsehood; her expensive apartment reflected her father far more than it did her.

Whoever had refurbished the place had done a very good job, almost too good. Her apartment looked exactly the same, from the furniture to the floors. The only thing missing was her personal touches. The irreplaceable things that had been destroyed by the blast, photos and keepsakes.

It was the exact same open-plan layout it had been, with the kitchen, living room, and dining room all part of one large space, though Thea had hardly expected that to change. The floors were once more beautiful glossy tigerwood, and the walls were the same shimmering off white. Her couch and chairs were still teal. Her kitchen, as ever, was black and white with gold appliances. They had even replaced the frosted glass window that Walt had been thrown through.

Her bathroom was still black marble, and her bedroom was still decorated in tones of black and amber. She opened the wardrobe; even her clothes had been replaced.

It just didn't feel right, it was like the attack, and its aftermath had been erased. What had once been her safe haven now felt like a stranger's home.

"Wow," Walt said, clearly impressed. "They did a really good job. I had forgotten how nice this place is."

Thea smiled half-heartedly. "It doesn't feel right anymore. Maybe I just need to settle back in. It looks mostly the same in here, but it's like the warmth is gone. It's not my home anymore. Does that make sense?"

Walt, who had lingered near the door while Thea reacquainted herself, moved further into the apartment. He took off his long coat and sat in the replica of the armchair that had always been his when he visited.

"Do you remember after Cleo was taken, you insisted on taking me to the hospital to get my nose seen to?" Thea met his gaze, and neither looked away.

"Yeah."

"After I got home, my apartment felt different, empty. It stopped being my home and just became the place I slept. It was tied to the terrible things that happened there. This place meant something to you because of Cora, the memories you shared with her, and if that's gone now, you don't have to stay here."

"Where would I go?"

"We were doing fine at my place," Walt said.

There was an awkward moment.

"You know I can't live there."

"I know, I'm sorry. I shouldn't have said anything," Walt said gruffly as he got to his feet. "I'd better go. If you need anything, call me."

"Or you could stay here," Thea said.

"What about Benny?"

"I don't think he'd like to witness what I have in mind, but whatever gets you going."

"Tell me what you want."

"You."

The moment stretched on, and Thea began to feel self-conscious. Perhaps now wasn't the time. But then Walt was in front of her. Apparently, an invitation was all he had been waiting for.

He didn't kiss her gently, but mercilessly, with an ardour bordering on desperation, pulling her close and pressing her body and her lips against his. He was all over her, and it was exactly what she wanted. Thea slid her hands from his face and took hold of his belt buckle. She tugged, using it to lead him by the waist to her new bedroom; he came willingly.

At the foot of the bed, Thea kicked off her shoes as she eased Walt's suit jacket from his shoulders. As soon as he was free, his mouth covered hers, and his hands found her again. He took the hem of her shirt and lifted it over her head as she fumbled with the buttons on his waistcoat.

"I hate three-piece suits," she said breathlessly as she finally stripped him of it.

Walt laughed and nuzzled her neck.

Impatient, Thea didn't trouble herself with the buttons on his shirt, she ripped it open with one jerk. She pushed him back onto the bed and quickly followed him down to the mattress.

It felt equally like the first and hundredth time as they lost themselves in each other.

BIONIC MAN

In hindsight, Benny wished he'd had Walt take him directly to the front door of Rishaan Chowdhury's clinic.

Benny liked the doctor very much. Highly educated and highly intelligent, Rishaan had forsaken a career at one of the leading medical service providers to work closer to the ground. He helped people for free and was funded only by donations. He was a rare, good man in a city of sharks, in Benny's humble opinion.

As Benny ambled down Blanchard Avenue, stopping every few feet to catch his breath, he hoped the doctor was in a giving mood. He and Rishaan had not parted on good terms when last they met.

The lights of the sign above the clinic flickered dismally, only just illuminating the words "Free Medical Care". It appeared that business was not booming for Rishaan.

With difficulty, Benny pushed the clinic's heavy door open. The interior was far less ramshackle than the outside. It was like a modest Emergency Room, with a reception desk in the centre and gurneys lining the walls.

Doctor Rishaan Chowdhary was standing filling in a patient's chart with his back to the door when Benny entered. He was an Indian man of medium height and a slightly stocky build. He wore a lab coat over a crisp white shirt and brown waistcoat that matched his slacks. He had a kindly, rounded face and very sharp eyes that, Benny knew from experience, saw everything.

"You are not welcome here," Doctor Chowdhary said, catching sight of Benny dripping with sweat on the welcome mat.

"I need your help, Rish," Benny said breathily. He removed his coat and unbuttoned his shirt to show Rishaan the purpling stump of his arm, the stitches on which were puckered, a repugnant yellow fluid seeped between them.

"We nearly lost this place because of the dirty money you fed me under the guise of donations. We were raided. They seized equipment; we are only just back on our feet, but people are afraid to come here now. That's because of you. And you think I should treat you over them?"

"I'm sorry. I'm not asking you not to treat them. I'm asking you to treat me, too." Benny slumped sideways against the wall. Rishaan looked as though he was fighting every impulse he had not to go to Benny.

"That's exactly what you're asking because, thanks to you, our resources are finite. If I treat you, the likelihood may be that I can't treat someone else."

"You're a shrewd bastard. I'll pay. Clean money. I'll fund the clinic properly this time."

Rishaan considered Benny for a moment. "Nurse," he said to the man behind the reception desk. "Please get Mr Pickford a wheelchair and take him to my treatment lab. If you are lying, mark my words, anything I do to you here can be undone."

The nurse stepped out from behind the desk and pulled a wheelchair from the stack of them beside it. The chair hovered next to him as he manoeuvred Benny into it.

The doctor's lab was a far cry from the ER. It was entirely chrome and looked far cleaner. It was home to a large operating table surrounded by counters, cupboards and fridges half-filled with the drugs, implements and equipment necessary for innumerable medical procedures.

"Can you stand?" Rishaan asked, holding the door open so Benny could glide in.

Benny tried to stand, but with only one arm, he couldn't get the leverage he needed. The doctor stepped in to assist him, and slowly they made their way over to the table.

Once Benny was lying down, the doctor adjusted the operating table so that Benny was sitting upright.

"So, explain to me in as much detail as possible what happened to your arm," Rishaan said, business-like, as he put on a pair of latex gloves. He sat down in a hovering armchair and looked patiently at Benny as if trying to make it clear he had his full and undivided attention.

"It's difficult to explain."

"Just do the best you can."

"My line of work necessitates that sometimes I deal with unsavoury characters," Benny said, shivering despite the sweat soaking his back. "Bastard shook my hand and did something to me."

"What do you mean 'did something' to you?" Rishaan asked.

"My hand turned gold. Almost literally, and it spread up my arm. I lost movement in my hand, and it went all cold and heavy, felt like metal. Listen, can you give me something for the pain? I'm itching like crazy. I feel dizzy."

"I'm going to examine you now," said the doctor, placing a pair of frameless pince-nez on the bridge of his nose. "Whoever did the deed made a good job of it," he said, peering at the stitches on Benny's stump and touching it gently. "The incision is nice and neat, but you should have had a drain inserted. The lack of it has caused an infection. I'll need to start you on intravenous antibiotics, and I'll need to clean the site, which might not be pleasant, and then I'll insert the drain."

"Do what you gotta."

Benny laid back and covered his eyes with his other arm as the doctor set to work. Rishaan deftly placed a cannula into Benny's hand and attached the line to an IV bag filled with a clear purplish fluid.

Benny felt a sharp prick as the doctor injected something near his incision, but then a pleasant numbing sensation spread from his arm to the rest of his body. He floated contentedly in and out of consciousness as the doctor treated him.

When he opened his eyes, the doctor had his back to him, filling in some paperwork on the counter opposite. Benny looked down at his arm. It was wrapped in soft, clean bandages, and there was a length of clear tubing protruding from between the swathes. It led to a small transparent bag that hung on the edge of the table, which was filled with a small quantity of a lumpy off-pink liquid.

"You may have to stay here overnight depending on how quickly you respond to treatment," Rishaan said without looking up. "And when you are ready, we can talk about fitting you with an augmentation."

"You can do that shit here?" Benny asked in drowsy surprise.

"Why do you think I'm so coveted in Eltham?" Rishaan said, raising an eyebrow. "I am, or I was, the leading engineer in the field of biomechanical augmentations until I found my true calling here."

"I'm ready to talk now," said Benny fervently.

"All right, what would you like?" the doctor once more adopted his business-like tone. He took a tablet from the desk and held the stylus in hand, ready to take notes.

"An arm, the ability to do up my own shirts."

Rishaan smiled sympathetically. "I understand, but here, with your resources—I can offer you so much more than just a working prosthetic. I can offer you a fully functional biomechanical augmentation, capable of increased strength and dexterity, and that's just the beginning." He spoke with a passion and conviction that awed Benny.

The doctor stood. He moved over to the north wall, which was bare apart from a chart that Benny assumed was used to conduct eye tests. Chowdhary lifted the chart and pressed the small button that was concealed behind it. The entire wall slid aside to reveal what looked like a mechanics workshop filled with biomechanical components, metalwork benches and engineering tools.

"This is my private collection. I help anyone I can, but materials are expensive," the doctor said, gesturing to the newly appeared portion of the lab. "That shouldn't be a problem for you, though."

"If you can do all this, why are you out here in the sticks?" Benny asked incredulously.

"When you work for a large Medical Service or pharmaceutical giant, your research is grant-based. You work on what they tell you to. You apply your theories and discoveries how they want you to. Technology is merging with biology at an alarming rate, and I didn't agree with the ethics of what they planned to do with some of my creations. So, I left billions of credits behind to help people while living in near poverty; but my conscience is clear. I haven't looked back, and I sleep peacefully every night. But that's enough about me. What you want from me is what's important at this moment."

"I want a fully functioning arm; strength would be good. Can you make it look natural? If I have augmentation instead of a prosthetic, will it be like having my arm back?"

"It will be better," Rishaan said, smiling. "This is what I gave up glory for—witnessing true happiness and having a hand in it. No pun intended."

"Will it hurt?" Benny asked nervously, the initial excitement bleeding away.

"It will be worth it, my friend."

It all happened at such a speed that, looking back, Benny would never be able to fully recount the events that led him to be strapped down on an operating table having his shoulder joint removed. Rishaan had recommended that he have his entire arm replaced as it would function better as a whole without the weakness of the original shoulder to contend with.

Benny hadn't expected to be conscious for the procedure, and as he lay there waiting for it to begin, panic set in. He was having trouble breathing, compounded by the heart monitor's beeping, which let him know exactly how fast his heart was racing.

Rishaan's face swam in and out of focus above him. "Calm down, you won't feel a thing, but when we attach the augmentation and link it to your nerves, I need you awake to test its function. It will be virtually painless, and in a few short hours, you will feel as good as new. I promise."

"No hard feelings then."

"Oh, plenty, but I'm a professional, and I am going to hold you to our bargain." The doctor smiled in a not wholly reassuring way. "We shall begin now."

At first, it wasn't so bad. Benny felt the odd tugging or quaver from time to time and found that it didn't bother him particularly; it didn't hurt. He wasn't even sure he could really say he felt it in the usual sense. It was a duller sensation than touch.

When the drilling started, Benny nearly lost it.

It was the sound and the vibration that rattled even his teeth. Still not pain, but the awareness of the pressure being exerted upon him was enough to tip him over the edge. Even with the blue sterile screen that protected the procedure from his view, the shadows cast by the doctor and his team on the other side was like a horrific theatre show.

Benny fainted when he saw his shoulder and what was left of his arm being removed in silhouette, but he awoke quickly after as the drilling resumed.

Rishaan kept up a constant, pleasant commentary to ensure Benny's wellbeing, but far from relaxing him, it made him wish the doctor would give his full attention to the procedure at hand.

The pain came when the new joint was attached. Benny could feel everything as it was melded with his flesh, but that was nothing to what he felt as it was attached to his nervous system. He hadn't bargained for the small sensor that was placed in the back of his neck to translate the signals from his brain to his arm.

When it was done, he couldn't even bear to look at the addition. He just wanted to sleep and recover, but Rishaan insisted on having him sit up and test his new hardware.

He felt heavy and lopsided. He had only been without a second arm for just over a week, but his body had adjusted somewhat.

Upon inspection, it would have been very difficult to guess that his new arm was not wholly organic. It matched his skin tone perfectly and mirrored the appearance of its brother. With a very close look, there was a seam of sorts running from his wrist to his armpit. It was a shiny black silicone that Benny guessed was how it would be opened and repaired if needed.

He flexed his new fingers. They moved as intuitively as his own fingers ever had. He leaned to the side and put his weight on his new arm, and it held with ease. He was filled with a sense of childlike wonder.

"You'll need time to adjust to your new strength, so I wouldn't grip anything you value too soon if you follow my meaning," Rishaan said with a smirk. "How does it feel? Quite the masterpiece, no?"

"It feels ...good. Better, much."

The initial shock was wearing off, and Benny was starting to feel whole again, complete.

"You will need to continue the antibiotics to clear the infection from the original amputation and take a course of anti-rejection drugs. I'll go and get them now."

As the doctor left the room, something occurred to Benny. Something that had he not been delirious may have occurred to him much earlier.

"Rish," he said, calling the doctor back.

Rishaan appeared at the door, looking expectant.

"What was your old company trying to use your augmentations for?"

He looked surprised for a moment, then said, "It wasn't the limbs; it was the chips that controlled them. They wanted to investigate whether they could be repurposed to work the opposite way. Have the chips exert control over a person. They claimed it was to aid those who were paralysed, but I witnessed some telling proposals, and so I left. Research like that is a slippery slope. But enough, I must get you your medication so you can be on your way."

"One more thing," Benny said quickly. "Who did you work for?"

"Medicorum. But leaving that place is like leaving the mob, so don't tell anyone what I told you." Rishaan said with a roguish wink.

GIDEON

When Thea awoke, it was with a sense of contentment that she wasn't used to. Walt was tucked tightly against her back. One arm under her pillow, the other draped loosely over her waist. It took her foggy, sleep-addled brain a minute or two to process the feeling she was experiencing, and then it hit her. This was the first morning-after in which she had woken up next to Walt and felt no shame. It was the first time in their long and complicated relationship that they'd had sex that wasn't illicit. Walt was a free agent, and so was she. For the first time, they could be together with no caveats and no scandals.

She looked absently around her newly decorated bedroom, not wanting to move yet, nor to wake Walt, who was still snoring softly. She didn't feel as alien in her home this morning though she resolved with herself that it was about time she moved into an apartment that had her name on the deed. Maybe she could buy the place from her father.

Thea cursed herself for being so foolish. She and her father had never had the kind of relationship where she could just go and visit him and ask him for something. No, not her father and definitely not now. There was always a deal to be made with Harold Williams, always terms to be agreed, and that was before she had discovered he was part of the Gold Legion and working directly against her in an effort to... To what? That was the question. Test drugs on unwilling citizens? Curb the population? Control the city from the shadows? The "whats" were becoming ever clearer, but the "whys" were still obscured.

"It's too early to be frowning like that," Walt said, surprising her. He kissed her shoulder and ran his hand gently over the bruise Torrez's grasping fingers had left on her arm.

Thea rolled over to face him. "I was just thinking about my dad, the things he's done, and the Gold Legion. A lot of people are going to die, and I'm not sure we can stop it."

"Is this what you dream about?"

"No. It isn't."

"When's the last time you slept for more than four hours? I know you feel responsible, but you have to take care of yourself."

"You're sober for a few days, and suddenly you're a life coach." There was no malice in her words.

Walt laughed softly. "I care, that's all. You heard from Benny?"

"Yeah, he left me a message during the night, said he'll be back soon."

"Come back to sleep then."

"I have to go to the station," Thea said, sitting up.

Walt sighed and followed suit. He checked his watch and rubbed his eyes. He looked younger and healthier than he had in a long time, though slightly exasperated at present.

"I'm going to see if I can find this Anthony Oubier; he may know something," Thea said, throwing off the covers. Walt eyed her form as she stepped out of bed.

"I'm coming too; if I'm going to get my badge back, I had better at least pretend to do my duties as a uni. I'll see what I can dig up about the food shortages a couple of years ago. It would stand to reason that those who were the most vocal about it might be our guys now. Same as last time. And I know I was reluctant, but we need to get that chip examined properly by Jaz; we need to know for sure what it does."

"Good, the time for guesswork is over. Make sure—"

"I won't let it out of my sight."

When they arrived at the station, Thea was disappointed to see that Gin Ricky's coffee cart wasn't in its usual spot outside. His coffee was smoother and richer than anywhere else she had tasted in the city, and she had been holding out for a cup. When she communicated this thought to Walt, he drew his eyebrows down in a frown.

"What's wrong?" she asked.

"He wasn't here a few days ago either. I wonder if anyone has seen him. I was hoping to have a word."

"What about?"

"Benny. He can't stay with me forever, and the Gold Legion has already tried to kill you both, so I don't think it's wise for him to stay with you. Gin Ricky's a bootlegger, but he's also a fixer of sorts. He might have somewhere safe we can hide Benny. For a price, of course."

Once inside the station, Thea and Walt parted ways in the lift. Walt exited on the detective's floor to make enquiries about Gin Ricky and the food shortages, while Thea continued on to the Information Request Office to speak to Gideon.

The lift opened into a large square room that looked, to Thea, like a press office. Its walls were a dull mauve, and several desks were lined up in uniform rows. Atop each workstation was three screens, everyone who sat behind them flicked their eyes at light speed between the neon displays looking thoroughly harassed.

All except Gideon.

Gideon was cocky and just handsome enough to back it up. This bravado was the linchpin of his otherwise weak personality. He was White and in his early thirties with loosely curled blonde hair and startlingly green eyes. His mop of curls and his slightly round face made him look like a schoolboy who had never grown up. His most irritating trait was not his overconfidence however, it was his interest in Thea.

Not a single interaction between them went by without him making some kind of verbal advance, and no matter how many times she ignored, rebuffed, or flat out told him she wasn't interested, Thea couldn't seem to shake his attentions.

"Hey, beautiful," he drawled as Thea approached his desk.

"Hey," Thea said unenthusiastically.

"Can I do something for you, or did you just miss me?" Gideon flashed Thea his most breath-taking smile. She wasn't moved.

"I'm here strictly on police business, as always."

"Shame," and he had the gall to wink as he said it.

"Listen," Thea went on exasperatedly. "About the request I filed, is there any way to compile that data without filing a petition with the DA?"

"I could do the research manually," Gideon said seriously. "But that could take days. I'd do it for you, though."

"I don't think I have days, and I'd hope, seeing as it's your job, you'd do it for anyone in the department."

"You're special, though."

"Excuse me?"

"You know I have ways of finding things out. Go to dinner with me, and maybe that information will find you quicker."

"Spare me," Thea said, her temper rising.

"Calm down," he said dismissively.

"Calm down?" Thea repeated. "Oh, I'm calm."

"I...It's just a bit of fun," Gideon said, unsure.

"For you. I find nothing about you trying to extort a date out of me in exchange for the information that helps me do my job 'fun'. Maybe other people find you charming, but I don't, and I'd appreciate it if you'd remember that."

Gideon looked for a moment like a scolded child. He rallied quickly. "What can I do for you, Detective?"

"Don't waste your time with the DA, it'll take too long. I want you to find me all you can about Anthony Oubier, address, contact details, history, everything. I need it now."

"I'll get right on it."

"Call me as soon as you find anything."

ENEMY TERRITORY

Jasper was sitting at his desk, reading a magazine about gourmet cooking, when Walt walked into his cluttered office. Had he not been wearing a light tan suit, he might have been hard to spot amongst the various computers and papers.

"Tell me you haven't damaged another Cicada?" he said, throwing the magazine aside.

"No." Walt smiled at the look on his face. "I want you to take another look at that chip."

"Really? Because I have been dying to get my hands on it. That has got to be some serious hardware."

"Really. But this is of a...sensitive nature, so off the books if it's all the same to you."

"How sensitive?"

Walt just looked at Jasper, whose eyes travelled over the faded bruises on Walt's face and the scab on the bridge of his nose. "Right," Jasper said finally. "Well, you'd better hand it over."

Walt pulled the chip from his pocket and laid it carefully on the cluttered desk. Jasper's eyes lit up like he had just won the lottery, and then his features set themselves into a mask of professional concentration.

"This could take a while," Jasper said, placing the chip under a small camera that was attached to several of the screens around his desk.

"Fine, I've got some things to follow up on in the building. I won't be long. Do not tell anyone what you are doing. Don't show it to anyone, don't take it anywhere, don't write anything about it."

"I get it. Just go."

Walt, it transpired, was not the only person to have noticed the absence of Gin Ricky. Many of the TPDs detectives had been deprived of their morning coffees with a side of information, but no one had any clues as to his whereabouts.

"What, no coffee to hide your jitters? Whatever will you do now to hide the fact you're a worthless drunk?"

Upon hearing Walt's queries, the never-pleasant O'Malley had taken the opportunity to air his grievances. Publicly. None of the detectives sat at their desks in the bullpen pretended not to have heard the jibe, but instead, they turned expectant eyes to Walt and O'Malley, awaiting the show.

"Do we have a problem here, O'Malley?" Walt asked, keeping his tone light.

"Naw, 'course not. Just my way of letting you know I've been promoted to Lieutenant." O'Malley tapped the little pin on his lapel that signified his new rank. Walt couldn't believe it. The man was a neanderthal. That job had been as good as his, not so long ago, hell, he'd been tipped for Sergeant.

"Congratulations," Walt said dryly.

"Means I get to give you your assignments, flatfoot."

Walt said nothing.

"I'm assigning you to Detective Williams. You are at her beck and call for the duration of her little murder case. You're off the beat. You're welcome."

"Great," Walt said tonelessly, waiting for the other shoe to drop.

"I thought you'd be happy. Now what we have all known for years is official; you're Thea's bitch."

Walt had to admit that O'Malley had a flair for showmanship that he wouldn't have credited the man with. Rather than looking at Walt as he spoke, he circled, talking to the now avid audience.

"We've all got dirty laundry, O'Malley. Even you," Walt said, crossing his arms and perching on the edge of the nearest desk; he was determined not to rise to any of O'Malley's taunts.

"You've been pussy-whipped by that tomato for years. She must be a real goer. Still, it's a cryin' shame to see a good man torn down by a dipped wick." He looked Walt dead in the eyes trying to gauge how much of a reaction his words had garnered. Walt could feel the vein in his temple pulsing, and his face was hot, but he remained silent, watching, waiting. "No, what gets me," O'Malley continued nastily. "Is the fact you're still being treated like you got a badge. Like you're not a disgrace to the rest of us. Can anyone think," he addressed the smirking onlookers. "Of another son of a bitch who got fired, then re-hired, and still gets to walk around like some big shot? Because I can't."

"You don't think I've paid enough? Lost enough?" Walt said quietly, speaking only to O'Malley. He wasn't going to take part in this little production if he could help it.

"Am I making you angry? Because we can fight right here. Apparently, you're immune to discipline. Pulled a gun on one of your own and got the boot for a whole day. Doesn't sit right with me."

"So, this is about Torrez? I'm sure he'll be touched by your concern. I got demoted, and as you've so sympathetically observed, I'm a mess. What more do you want?"

"Don't look like a mess to me. The way I see it, everythin' has come up roses for you. You got rid of the wife you didn't want, and now you're free to chase young tail. You break the hooker case with your side piece, and you're right back to being a detective again. It ain't right."

Walt unfolded his arms and stepped away from the desk. He was a good eight inches taller than O'Malley, and he used it to his advantage as he towered over the squat man.

"You outrank me, and that's just fine. I am more than happy to pay my dues, sir. I learned my lesson. I'm not gonna bite, not here. But if you wanna take this to the alley 'round back—I'm happy to set superiority aside and see who comes out on top." Walt's voice was low, but it carried.

O'Malley seemed to deflate slightly under Walt's scrutiny.

"So, what'll it be?" Walt said.

"You're not worth it," O'Malley said, stepping back. "You'd get praised, and I'd get a strike."

And just like that, he wanted to drink, to dull the anger coursing through him, but he knew if he gave in to the temptation, he'd never stop. His temper on the brink of being unleashed, the last thing Walt felt was happy, but he grinned broadly nonetheless, knowing it would infuriate O'Malley. "Smart. Not at all the coward's way out. Now, seeing as we are all pals again, heard much about Gin Ricky?"

O'Malley, like his colleagues, had little to tell Walt except that he also hadn't seen the man or his cart for over a week.

"Is Orion working today?" Walt said to the room at large.

His reply was general mutters. He headed to the TPD archive to see for himself.

"You done?" Walt asked half an hour later, strolling into Jasper's office and dropping heavily into an empty chair. He was still on edge. He hadn't had much luck with Orion, not because the man refused to help, but because the shortages were so short-lived, the records were sparse; the introduction of Styxx had pushed most other worries out of people's minds.

"Yup," Jasper said simply.

"Well, what does it do? What's it for?" Walt asked, sitting up straighter in his chair.

"Okay, so I was right. The materials that went into this are worth millions of credits. There is platinum, gold, palladium, ultra-rare polymers, and this bio-metal compound that I can't even identify—it's cutting edge. And that's just the stuff that makes up the chip inside."

"I thought it was a chip?" Walt said, confused.

"It is, and it isn't. It's a chip that's also a device, sort of like the chips that bordellos use to keep track of employees. But it blows them out of the water," Jasper babbled excitedly.

"So, what does it do?"

"Right, sorry. I can't test it on anyone, so this is technically a guess, but I am certain I'm right. I think the polymers are used to mimic nerve impulses, and the transmitter in the chip can receive information, but it also creates impulses which is why it's worth so much credit. And there is a processor that is linked to a private data stream which means it can manufacture the nerve impulses and radio waves based on commands sent via stream."

"I'm not following. Speak idiot to me."

"The power of suggestion, that's what this chip does." Jasper's eyes were wide in a mixture of fear and heady excitement. "It can receive orders and manufacture them into nerve impulses and brainwaves."

"Are you—? Mind control? That's insane." Walt's mind was working in overdrive as he tried to wrap his head around the fact that technology had advanced so far as to be able to control thoughts and actions.

"Mind control. This is huge, scary, but huge." Jasper was almost giddy.

"This private stream, can you find its origins?"

"No, it's encrypted way past the point of deciphering. When I tried, it pinged me to Athenium, and that was just for starters."

"What about the deaths," Walt said slowly. "How is it blowing skulls apart?"

"This thing is powerful; you think it's small, but it's not, look at your Seer or Cicada or Index, and it has the juice to create a powerful electrical surge that could easily shatter bone."

"Thank you for this."

Walt got to his feet. He picked the chip up from under the large magnifying glass that Jasper had left it under. He tucked it safely into the inside pocket of his suit jacket.

"I was never here."

"You have to tell me what's going on," Jasper said, standing up, too.

"Look at my face, or do you need to see my broken ribs, or maybe the shock burns on my chest, or better yet, the cuts on my back from the window I was thrown through. Forget the chip and forget I was here. It's safer that way." And with that, he turned on his heel and swept from the room.

YOU LIED TO ME, DREW

The ultra-white lights that Marielena used to keep her most prized plants alive were almost like the real sun that Torrez remembered from his childhood visits to his grandparents. His grandmother, like his wife, loved plants—the greener the better, but she had the benefit of the true sun living as she did on land. Torrez would have liked to see dry land, true dry land, once more before he died, and Torrez was sure that he was going to die.

He sat in the plant room in a drunken stupor. His feet were bare. Since their literal torching, he had found that he enjoyed the cold tile against his soles. His shirt was open to the waist; he had long abandoned his jacket and waistcoat. His dark hair was unruly, and his stubble was unkempt. Discarded cigarillo butts littered the floor.

Marielena had given up on talking to him as a bad job, leaving him staring at the fake sun some hours ago. He hadn't moved. He was waiting for death. Whether it came in the form of Dill Kelly or one of his henchmen, it would come.

It came as no surprise to Torrez when he heard a knock at his door. Soft and unassuming, he knew that it was for him and him alone. Marielena was likely asleep, tired from their argument; the soft knocking wouldn't be enough to wake her—she slept like the dead. Torrez was glad of this, for he had no intentions of answering the door. If they wanted him, they would have to come in and get him.

The knocking continued at polite intervals for another thirty seconds, then Torrez could hear the faint clicking that meant someone was picking the lock. He heard the door open gently and then calm, measured footsteps growing steadily louder.

"You lied to me, Drew."

So, Dillard Kelly had come to see him personally. He was almost flattered.

"I'd say I'm sorry, but we both know I'm not." Torrez drained the bottle of tequila that was sitting between his legs in three large gulps.

He turned to see Dill, a hulking figure in the doorway to the plant room. He looked oddly serene.

"Where is the chip?"

"I don't know for sure." Torrez made no effort to ready himself. He didn't reach for the gun he had left on the table in front of him, he didn't clutch the empty glass bottle now lying discarded beside him, and he entertained no thoughts of escape.

"Where do you think it is? Tell me, and I won't touch your wife, it'll just be you, and it'll be quick." Dill pulled a small silver knife from the inside pocket of his grey suit jacket. It was his signature weapon. If you were unfortunate enough to have run afoul of Dill Kelly, you had your throat slit and then you were suspended by your ankles to bleed out. He could paint quite the grotesque masterpiece, Torrez mused.

"Not in here," Torrez said simply.

"Excuse me?"

"Not in here. I'll tell you, but do the deed in the kitchen. Marielena loves this room. I don't want to ruin it for her."

"If this is some kind of last-ditch attempt—"

"I won't try anything; I just don't want to damage her plants."

"Who has the chip?"

"Walter James. He saw me take it from the crime scene and stole it back—I think. He's a detective, so, he's probably putting the pieces together as we speak. He's a tough son of a bitch. I hope he gets you." Torrez spoke with no intonation.

"I know exactly who Walter James is," Dill said through gritted teeth. "I'm the one who tipped you off about his wife, remember?"

"Guess I'm feeling a little fuzzy." Torrez wiped his nose roughly on the back of his hand.

"There are worse ways to die than drunk on top-shelf booze," Dill said quietly. "Come on, it's time. Don't make a fuss, and I promise you'll barely feel a thing."

Torrez got stiffly to his feet. The room seemed to sway as he walked slowly to face Dill.

Together they walked into the kitchen side by side, condemned man and executioner. Dill's face was set. Regret etched in his stretched features, but there was something else there too, just below the surface. Torrez was too drunk to make it out.

Dill kept his back to Torrez as he took off his jacket and laid it neatly on the counter, then rolled up his sleeves.

"Do you mind?" he asked, gesturing to the apron hanging next to the stove.

When Torrez didn't reply, Dill grabbed the red polka dot pinafore and put it on.

It's a funny thing, death. There is a real difference between thinking you've accepted it, that you're ready for it, and truly being at peace with it. As it turned out, when he was faced with his large and steak-loving doom, Torrez wasn't quite ready for the big sleep.

"Dill..." Torrez said, taking a step backwards.

"You're nervous," said Dill as he turned, gleaming knife in hand. "I understand. Close your eyes. I'll make it quick."

"Those won't hold my weight," Torrez said, indicating the copper pipes that ran along the ceiling.

Dill looked up. "Yes, they will."

Like a predator, Dill could sense when his prey was skittish. He lunged forward with the knife. Torrez managed to manoeuvre himself out of the way, but only just; the blade sliced at his billowing shirt. Unbalanced, he fell backwards, hitting the door frame. Bouncing off it, he fled into the living room.

With surprising speed for a man his age, Dill followed. Like a bull, he charged at Torrez, spearing him in the back. Torrez went careening into a glass-fronted bookcase. Shards cut at his forearms as he slid to the ground. He got to his feet just in time to see Dill bringing the knife down in a tremendous slash. He caught Dill's wrist in both hands and tried to wrestle the blade from him, but the older man was impossibly strong.

"Drew? What's going on?" came a frightened voice from upstairs.

"Don't come down."

"What's happening?" Marielena said.

"¡Permanecer allí!" Torrez yelled and his moment of distraction cost him dearly. Dill grabbed Torrez with his free hand and threw him bodily across the room. Torrez landed painfully on the coffee table, which collapsed on impact. He was winded and seeing stars, the coppery taste of blood on his tongue.

"This could have been quick and clean, Drew," Dill said, walking almost lazily towards him. "Now you are going to die knowing I'm gonna gut your wife next."

Torrez clambered to his feet. He raised his hands like a boxer, his head swimming. He punched Dill once, twice, three times, but the large man blocked all his attempts with ease. Dill raised a leg and kicked Torrez hard in the stomach, sending him flying. He crashed into the wall and slid to the floor.

"You've got augmentations," Torrez panted as he struggled to get to his feet. He felt sick.

"You like?" Dill flipped the knife in his hand and threw it with deadly precision. Torrez scrambled out of the way. The knife embedded itself in the wall exactly where Torrez's head had been moments before. "When money is no obstacle, you can do anything. You'd have found that out if you had the stones to go the distance."

Torrez crawled on his hands and knees into the plant room, Dill followed unconcerned. Torrez laboured to his feet. He grabbed a large terracotta pot containing the bamboo plant he had bought Marielena for her last birthday, raised it above his head, and brought it crashing down on Dill's skull. He didn't even blink.

Cursing, Torrez dived onto the couch to avoid another punishing blow from Dill. He knew he couldn't take many more of those. He rolled from the couch onto the floor and reached for the gun he had abandoned on the table there hours ago. Grabbing it, he got to his feet and pointed the weapon directly at Dill's heart.

A wide grin spread across Dill's face, more terrible than any threat. "Do it. See what happens."

Torrez did. He pulled the trigger over and over, but the bullets seemed to have no effect. As each pulse round hit the massive chest, it popped, no more harmful than a bubble.

"Relax, I'm wearing a vest," Dill said with a chuckle. Torrez's face must have shown the panic he was feeling, worried Dill was now indestructible. "It's nifty. It emits this sort of magnetic wave that disperses pulse rounds. Damn useless if you're firing led though."

"I'll keep that in mind," Torrez said, tossing the gun aside and casting around for another weapon. He was running out of options. He was drunk, dizzy, and hurt. He couldn't shoot Dill, he had given up his traditional pistol long ago. He had no chance of winning if they were to trade blows, but maybe, just maybe, if he was smart enough and lucky enough, he could get the upper hand.

Torrez moved out into the centre of the room; this was going to hurt, but he had to do it. He ran forward as if to flee, and as he hoped he would, Dill grabbed him around the middle. He flung Torrez with ease, sending him hurtling into one of the many windows. It shattered on impact; Torrez went clean through it, landing painfully on the balcony beyond.

His head pounded, and his stomach felt like it had vanished altogether. Carefully, Torrez made a show, that required little acting, of getting to his feet. As he scrabbled on the ground, he grabbed a long thin shard of glass and concealed it in his fist, the knife-like tip running flush with the outside of his forearm.

Dill stepped through the hole in the window he had used Torrez to make. It was now or never. Torrez rushed forward and threw a telegraphed punch at Dill, who slipped it easily. To the unaware, it must have looked like Torrez was finished, his arm overextended with no chance of returning to protect his face before Dill could land a devastating mortal blow; but instead of pulling his arm back, Torrez took advantage of its placement next to Dill's head and plunged the glass dagger into the side of his neck.

It took Dill a moment to realise what had happened as Torrez quickly stepped back, shaking. Dill blinked and opened his mouth, but nothing came out, then the blood really started to pour. Even though he had wisely left the shard where it was, the damage was done. Blood was spilling from the hole in his neck like a fountain drenching his shirt and his trousers as it made its way to the floor. It found its way to his mouth too, coating his lips as he coughed and spluttered. Dill's knees gave way next and, with a thunderous crash, he collapsed to the floor. Blood bloomed around him as he twitched, and then as the red tide ebbed, he was still.

Torrez collapsed to the ground and vomited, the contents of his stomach mixing with the pool of quickly cooling blood.

MAKE THE CALL

"For the last time, Walt is a good man," Cleo said firmly.

"I mean no disrespect, but you just told me he was having an affair with his partner."

They were sitting at opposite ends of Gin Ricky's long couch. It had become a favourite spot of theirs to hash out their plan to rescue Gin Ricky's son and make Maxwell pay for what he had done to Cleo.

"He's a good person, and he was a good husband until he wasn't. He will help us."

"That man can't even help himself. He isn't even a police officer anymore."

"What do you mean?" Cleo asked, sitting forward.

"He was fired last I heard. The man's a drunk, and as for his partner...it's not good. I overheard a couple of cleaners saying that they had a huge fight in the canteen a few days ago. He hurt you, and by all counts I can see— he isn't someone to put your faith in. I say that we give the impression that you are a hostage. Make sure he does as he says."

"We are not blackmailing Walt. He and I will have a lot to work through. I'm sure you are right, he isn't the man I remember, but he is a good person. No matter what he's done or what happened while I was gone, I know that won't have changed. He will help us."

"Even if he will, that's only the first step. I've only been as far as the commercial labs. You know your way around the building, but that isn't enough to get us to the cells. There will be security from both the GL and OL to contend with, and then there is Maxwell. I want him to pay just as much as you do."

"So, what are we going to do?" Cleo asked pointedly, knowing she had already won.

Gin Ricky gave a sort of resigned half-shrug, half-sigh.

"Fine. I'll make the call."

WE KNOW

"Mind control?" Thea said incredulously after Walt had told her everything that Jasper had told him. They were sitting once more at Walt's dining table. Thea had ordered them some Chinese food from Chef Lau's; it was her favourite place to eat whenever she was at Walt's home. She mulled over this shocking new information as she picked at her food.

"It's wild, I know," said Walt, using his chopsticks to remove the onions from his rice.

"This is a war that no one else can see coming. They've already infiltrated the government and law enforcement. Look at the havoc they wrought with Styxx, and we haven't even seen how bad Quietus can be. The GL used the chips to control the ghouls in my apartment. That much is clear, but are the killings accidental or part of the plan?" Thea said. She wasn't really asking, more thinking out loud.

"The real question is, 'are the murders failed experiments?' Because if they aren't and the chips are working as they should—we're out of time. The GL could make their move at any moment." Walt scrubbed the stubble on his chin that had turned into a beard over the last week.

"We have to do something, but I don't know what. We can't trust the TPD, though I think we should fill the captain in at some point. We can't go public; that's a great way to get ourselves killed and send the truth down with us," Thea said, rubbing her forehead.

"Do you still want to do this legally?" Walt asked pragmatically. "If you want to do this by the book, I'll back your play, but we need evidence yesterday."

"Say it—what you are really thinking."

Walt sighed then said, "Even if we get evidence, the corruption runs so deep I'm not convinced it would do any good. The DA, the TPD, Big Business, at least some of the Onyx Legion. There is so much more at stake now, thousands of lives."

"I'll do what needs to be done if that's what it comes to, but I'm not turning vigilante just yet," Thea said resolutely.

"Could you? If you had to? You've never been one to step out of bounds."

"You missed a lot the last couple of years."

A chill that had nothing to do with the room's temperature nestled uncomfortably between them.

"I'm just starting to see how much," Walt said quietly, but Thea didn't hear him, for Benny had just burst into the apartment. He was wearing his usual finery once more, a suit that Thea was sure had cost more than Walt's rent, and shoes so gleaming they were hard to look at. He was sweating and breathing heavily as if he had run a marathon, but the most surprising thing about his appearance was that he had two arms.

"You've got—"

Benny waved away Thea's unfinished remark with his new hand.

"I know what the chips do," he all but yelled.

"Slow your roll, so do we," Walt said placatingly.

"I know who invented them and who he invented them for," Benny said with the merest hint of a smug challenge in his voice.

"Who?" Thea asked, getting excitedly to her feet.

"How?" asked Walt, shoving his meal aside.

"His name is Rishaan Chowdhary, and he worked for Medicorum until he started to disagree with the direction they wanted to take his research," Benny said triumphantly.

Thea and Walt listened with rapt attention as Benny described to them what Rishaan had divulged.

"So he invented these chips to help amputees. They are what powers augmentations like mine," he waved his artificial fingers. "They translate the nerve impulses from my brain to the prosthetic—that's how it moves. Some high-ups at Medicorum thought they could make it work the other way. But Rish didn't want that, he rightly thought that it sounded like some dodgy shit. Looks like they continued the research without him."

"And figured it out. When did he leave Medicorum?" Thea asked.

"I'm not sure, I was pretty doped up," said Benny apologetically.

"What are you doing?" Walt asked Thea, who had moved around the table, to stand a little bit away from the two men.

"Putting a protection order on Rishaan."

"Is that smart?" Walt asked quickly.

"We don't have to tell anyone why."

"If we enter a protection order into the database, there's a chance the wrong kind of someone might pick it up," said Walt reasonably.

"We can't just leave him unprotected."

"If they have left him alive until now, it means that they think they might need him in the future, or they don't see him as a threat. We start pickin' him up, that'll change real fast. He's safer where he is," said Walt sagely.

"Okay. Fine," Thea conceded. "This is good. We have a witness. If we can convince him to testify, on top of the chip, we might be able to get a warrant or even launch an official investigation that the DA wouldn't be able to quash." It felt like progress at last.

"That's what Celia Short thought, and look how she ended up. We need enough evidence for an arrest warrant, not a search warrant. And you," Walt jerked his head towards Benny. "You need to lay low from now on."

"Me? I can take care of myself," Benny said, waving his new hand again. "I've been upgraded."

"You are one of the only witnesses we have, and you now have a chip inside your body. Until we make contact with Chowdhary, you can't just wander around. They already tried to kill you or had your new toy made you forget," Thea said seriously.

"Where am I supposed to go?" Benny asked.

"I've been working on that," Walt said. "I know a guy. He's been MIA, but I'll keep trying to get a hold of him. You better stay here until then."

"Super."

ALGOR MORTIS

The blood was starting to dry on the concrete balcony. Torrez was cold, and his legs were numb. He hadn't moved. He was catatonic with shock. He had killed a man, and he'd done it dirty.

Torrez had dealt with plenty of shady characters who had shot more than their fair share, but it wasn't the same. Getting up close, stabbing someone, slitting their throat, feeling their warm blood as it dripped down his fingers, feeling it cool exposed to the air, it was personal in a way that shootings could never be, almost intimate. Torrez had never realised how impersonal a gun made things, how much it trivialised the act until he had been forced to do his killing another way.

The sound of the stairs creaking brought Torrez back to himself.

"Andrew? What happened?" Marielena called.

"Stay...wait...don't come in here." Torrez's thoughts were garbled.

He struggled to his feet, still drunk, legs shaking, and stumbled back through the hole in the window into the plant room.

He wasn't quick enough.

"Dios mío," Marielena breathed as her eyes took in the smashed terracotta pots and destroyed plants, the broken window, and the body slowly cooling on the balcony. "What have you done, Drew?"

"I'm in over my head, baby. I wanted to make a better life for us," Torrez pleaded.

"What was wrong with the life we had?" Tears streaked her face.

"Had? ...He was going to kill me because I know things. Things he doesn't want the police to know."

"You are the police! At least you used to be."

Torrez reached for Marielena, but she backed away.

"Baby, please, I need you to understand," Torrez said, tears threatening to fall.

"Do you think I'm blind? I am sick, not stupid. The gifts, the nice clothes...Yo se que eres un polica sucio." She seemed beyond tears.

"I thought I was in control, but I'm not. I'm going to call this in. I have to. But I need to know if you will back me or not. Are we still an 'us'?"

"I didn't see anything."

Marielena, a look of disgust on her face that made Torrez feel hollow, moved unsteadily further into the room. She looked sadly at the damage that had been done to the plants that were her pride and joy, then sat delicately on the edge of the long couch and put her head in her hands.

"Baby..." Torrez said uncertainly.

"Make the call," Marielena said, her voice cold and detached.

Torrez turned away from her, unable to bear the chill and the distance. He touched his Cicada. "Hey Thea, can you come to the apartment? And, uhm, bring forensics...There's a body."

When Thea arrived some twenty minutes later, she brought with her Walt, Orion, O'Malley, Flynn's assistant, and an entire Crime Scene Unit, who set to work immediately. Medicus arrived not long after and began treating Marielena for apparent shock and Torrez, who had several bad lacerations, and broken ribs in his back.

Torrez didn't register what was going on around him. His mind was muddled and foggy. Whether from the concussion, shock, drink, or the inevitable adrenaline crash, he was only dimly aware as Thea took him by the elbow and led him to the staircase.

"Wait upstairs. I'll be there soon to take your statement," she said, squeezing his arm reassuringly.

Torrez didn't move right away, and another larger hand was placed on his back.

"I'll take him."

The hand gave him a gentle push, guiding him up the stairs. He and the comforting hand meandered into the master bedroom. It was a bright room in tones of cream with a false skylight that showed the true sky, blaring rays of sunshine during the day, and dotted with twinkling stars at night. Torrez was sitting on the edge of the neat bed before he realised that his companion was Walt.

"Torrez? You still with me, buddy?"

"I'm not your 'Buddy'. I know what you did," Torrez mumbled drunkenly.

"Right," Walt said offhandedly, but there was a slight stiffening of his posture. "Maybe you should lie down."

Walt put a hand on Torrez's shoulder, attempting to ease him towards the pillows, but Torrez batted it away.

"Don't touch me, asshole."

Torrez leaned over the side of the bed and began to rummage in the cabinet. He was sure there was a bottle of tequila tucked at the back. After a moment or two of blind searching, his hand closed around the neck of his prized Don Julio Real.

"C'mon, you're drunk enough as it is," said Walt trying to gently pull the bottle out of his grip.

"That's rich," Torrez spat at Walt with every bit of venom he could muster. "Fine. Take it."

Torrez uncorked the bottle and thrust it at Walt, who backed away.

"I don't want it," said Walt, raising his hands defensively and taking a step back.

"I didn't know you were capable of saying 'no'," Torrez said, taking a glug from the bottle's thin neck and slopping some of the auburn liquid down his still bare chest.

"I'm off the sauce, so please, put that away," Walt said resolutely through gritted teeth.

"I'm sure that'll last," Torrez sniggered spitefully. "You're back with Thea, right? Soon as she sees sense and dumps your ass, we both know you'll replace her with a bottle, so why wait?"

"I have some unpaid tickets, but we're not gonna settle up here. You're drunk, and you're beat up and—"

"There's a corpse on the balcony?"

A tense silence fell. Torrez slumped on the bed somewhere between sitting up and lying down. Walt stood in front of the doorway like a sentinel.

"Thea must be talking to forensics," Walt said just as the silence was starting to get to Torrez. "You can start giving me your statement if you like."

"Whatever." Torrez took another gulp of tequila. It was smooth with a hint of vanilla, and it warmed his insides.

"You know the drill. Start at the beginning," said Walt, all business.

"The beginning?" Torrez let out a slightly manic laugh. The shock was wearing off, and the fog in his brain was lifting; far from sad or guilty, Torrez was angry. "It started with you. This all started because of you! If you hadn't stolen that chip from me, none of this would have happened."

"I didn't make you dirty."

"I was tortured because of you, you son of a bitch!"

Torrez lunged at Walt with the Don Julio Real in hand. He swung the bottle hard at Walt's head, and unprepared for the attack as he was, Walt did nothing to stop it from colliding with his temple. The blow was fierce and true, and it sent Walt crashing to the ground.

"Have you ever smelled your own skin melting?" Torrez screeched. He hated Walt more than anyone in the world at that very moment. He forced Walt onto his back and clambered on top of him. Walt brought his hands up to cover his head as Torrez brandished the Don Julio bottle, but he didn't strike him with it; he tipped it and began pouring the alcohol onto Walt's face.

As soon as the first drops touched his skin, Walt began to struggle madly, coughing and spluttering. Finally succeeding in throwing Torrez from him, Walt scrambled to his feet and backed himself into a corner, breathing heavily. He was visibly shaking when Thea arrived a moment later.

Torrez knew he had done something wicked as he looked from Walt, who was wide-eyed and panting, to Thea, whose anger showed plainly in the furrow of her brow, but with the body on his balcony, the blood on his hands, and the nearly guaranteed breakdown of his marriage, he simply didn't have the energy to care.

"What the hell is going on?" Thea said, trying hard to keep her voice down.

"He attacked me," Torrez said, tossing the Don Julio bottle aside. Walt watched for a moment as the dregs spilled onto the carpet.

Thea looked questioningly at the man Torrez knew she loved.

"Not him. I just owed him." Torrez chuckled drunkenly. "Dill. He attacked me. Because I know. I know. About the chips and, and the Legion, and the things he—" Torrez jabbed a finger in Walt's direction. "—has done. You are in for a big surprise, Querida."

Thea just watched him, her eyes searching his face. Torrez found he couldn't meet her gaze, knowing he'd see betrayal and anger there. He didn't want her to see him, to truly see him. He sighed with relief as she turned away from him to focus on Walt.

Torrez watched detachedly as the pair spoke. Thea pulled a towel from the dresser and mopped the tequila from Walt's face, hair, and shirt, as she muttered words of comfort Torrez didn't care to hear.

When Thea stepped away from Walt finally, he reached out and caught her hand in his own. He brought her fingers to his lips and kissed them gently. They shared something that Torrez couldn't interpret, then Walt left.

"I'm not sorry," Torrez said petulantly.

"For what? What you just did to Walt? Or for the part you played in what happened to me? Or all the lies you've told?" Thea said, closing the bedroom door. She looked like a detective, there wasn't a trace of their personal relationship in her demeanour.

"I'll tell you whatever you want to know. It all just got so out of hand. Querida, I am out of my depth, in a hole I don't know how to climb out of. Seems lost causes are your thing, no?"

"Is that supposed to get me on your side?" Thea said bluntly. "You killed Dillard Kelly."

It was a fact.

"Yes."

"Was it self-defence?"

"Yes, it truly was. I got myself into this mess, that's me—messy, but he came here to kill me today, and I planned to let him. I really did. But he was standing in front of me with that pig sticker of his and talking about letting me bleed out hanging from the pipes in the kitchen, and I realised I wasn't ready," said Torrez, his hands together almost in prayer. "And I fought as hard as I could. I didn't want to kill him, I don't want to kill anyone, but Thea, I don't want to die."

"Tell me everything."

"I saw the way the other half lives, and I wanted it. I wanted to provide for Marielena like she deserves. That's what I told myself anyway. We're not even poor," Torrez laughed. "We have a good life, but I'm greedy. I wanted more. More men, more women, more sex, more money, more power. I wanted to change what I saw in the mirror."

"What did you see?"

"A fake. I wanted something to back up my swagger with. I wanted status because that's what this city is. It's about what you have, about excess. You, me, Walt—everyone, we are all trying to carve ourselves a place in this city of the blind. This city where no one sees anyone else. And I was mad, drunk, and I was blind, too." Once Torrez started talking—he couldn't stop. The floodgates opened, and even though he was ashamed of every word he spoke, it felt like a suffocating weight had been lifted from his chest. "It started small, a tip-off here, a payoff there. Dill promised he would let me in on the big secret. But I got impatient, I started digging, and I was horrified by what I found, the drugs, the chips and instead of reporting it, I tried to use it as an all-access pass to the club. To the big boy's table. Didn't go as planned though... He held me for hours, tortured me." The memory caused Torrez to shiver. "Burned me, beat me, cut me, poked me and after it all said you can be one of us as long as you keep quiet and even then, I still wanted to be one of them. I'd already stolen a chip from your apartment, and I didn't realise until after that Walter had stolen it back. Bastard. I knew they would kill me for losing such an incriminating thing, but I also knew I would never be able to get it back without dirtying my hands, and well, we both know I'm a coward. I signed my own death warrant." He chuckled drunkenly.

Thea had remained silent the entire time he spoke, her face impassive. His stomach ached as he longed for her to say that she understood.

"And tonight?" was all she said.

"I panicked when I realised you knew. I decided to drink myself into oblivion and wait for Dill, or one of his, to come for me. He was holding the knife, ready to strike before I realised I didn't want to die. We fought, I killed him, and I called you." Torrez's mouth was dry, and he was very drunk, but he felt lighter of the soul.

"You can't tell anyone what you know about the Gold Legion."

"Is that it? Is that really all you have to say?" Torrez demanded.

"What did you expect?" She didn't give him a chance to reply. "You had your suspicions that Dill was selling Styxx, but nothing concrete. Your suspicions were confirmed when Dill came here and tried to kill you. You got it? That's what I'm going to put in my report, you have to get it right."

"Thea!" Torrez was frustrated, his stomach was agony now, and he couldn't understand why his closest friend didn't have more to say about the ordeal he'd been through or why the only detective who hadn't compromised for the job didn't have anything to say about the many lines he had crossed.

"Drew, you are a dirty cop. You could be complicit in the deaths of thousands of people if we don't stop the Gold Legion. I could have died. Walt could have died. You want a hug? You want to talk it through over drinks like old times? Not gonna happen. I am so angry at you I can barely look at you, but I love you, and I don't want you to die, so, what happened?"

"I had a fight with Marielena, and I got drunk. I had my suspicions about Dill, but nothing concrete. I realised I must be on the right track when he showed up here and tried to kill me. I killed him in self-defence," Torrez rhymed off robotically.

"Good."

"Thea, I'm sorry," Torrez pleaded. "I never wanted you to get hurt."

"I know," she sighed. "But trust is a hard thing to earn back once you've lost it."

Torrez opened his mouth to tell Thea that he had learned his lesson, that he was sorry, that she could trust him and that he was going to prove it to her, but no words came out. He coughed slightly, feeling a tangy metallic liquid fill his mouth and then he doubled over in pain. He slid from the bed onto the floor, clutching his stomach. He brought his hand to his mouth, it came away bloody.

"Medicus," Thea yelled, coming to his side. "I need Medicus up here!"

From where he lay curled up on the floor, Torrez heard the door open and felt the vibration of feet entering the room. An oxygen mask was placed over his face. He could feel it sucking the blood from his mouth to allow him to breathe. Next, he was lifted onto a hovering shuttle. Somewhere on the journey down the stairs, he drifted into unconsciousness. The last thing he remembered was Thea's worry-stricken face.

WALT'S GHOST

The night was cold, and the smog that hung perpetually over the city clung to the pavements. The streetlights and neon signs struggled to be seen like many small lighthouses in a catastrophic storm. Thea watched the Medicus transporter that held Torrez as it rose to meet the Slipstream Highway and disappeared from view. She had wanted to go with him, to check he was all right, to tell him that she would forgive him in time, but it might have tipped the wrong people off that Torrez had flipped.

Taking her eyes from the sky, Thea looked for Walt in the mist. She could only just see him where he stood in the doorway of Torrez's apartment building.

"Are you okay?" she asked him, already knowing the answer.

"I should be asking you that," Walt said, strung out.

"I'm fine, are you?"

"I—" Walt flinched, then touched a hand to his Cicada. The incoming call had startled him.

The call was short, and when it was over, Walt said, "I may have a lead for us to follow while we wait for news on Torrez. Gin Ricky, the bootlegger, says he has some info for me."

"Info about what?"

"Let's find out."

They could have had a Jonk take them to Gin Ricky's place, but Walt had insisted that the cool night air would do him good. Thea doubted it would make much of a difference to the maelstrom inside his head, but she had agreed regardless.

Taking two quick steps, Thea caught up to Walt and slipped her hand into his. He gripped it like a vice in return.

"Torrez will be okay," Walt said with a shiver that had nothing to do with the temperature.

"I hope so." Thea couldn't bear to think about the alternative.

They walked on a few paces, Walt flexing his fingers agitatedly.

"This is just a setback," he said, though it seemed that he was reassuring himself as much as her. She could still smell the tequila that had soaked into his clothes. He must have been in hell.

"I'm not worried."

Walt stopped and turned to look at her. His eyes were slightly wild. Thea knew that he was fighting the urge to drink.

"I'm not worried," she repeated, though it wasn't strictly true.

"I don't deserve you," Walt said, taking her face between his hands.

Thea grimaced exaggeratedly. "Don't quote Torrez."

Walt chuckled reluctantly and dipped down to quickly press his lips against hers.

"I love you," he said casually, like he planned to say it for the rest of his life. He didn't give her the chance to reply. He took her hand before he had even finished the sentence and began to walk again, saying, "I think Gin Ricky lives in that dive on the corner."

Dive was right. Gin Ricky's apartment was in a stubby brown brick building of about six stories. The windows on the first three floors were either covered by fine mesh bars or had permanent metal shutters eclipsing all light from the outside. Graffiti covered the walls, and the upper floors were yellowed by the particularly dense and murky fog that hung around the place.

The entrance had the unmistakable signs of a door that was routinely kicked or rammed open; the frame was splintered, and there was a large dent around the size of a dinner plate in the centre of its red face.

The stairs inside were no better. Littered with all manner of rubbish and debris, and smelling pungently of urine, the bare and battered concrete was unsteady underfoot. It was a small mercy that Gin Ricky resided on the second floor. Thea wasn't thrilled by the prospect of climbing the crumbling flights any higher than necessary.

Gin Ricky's front door was cleaner than the others surrounding it, and the welcome mat at its foot was clear of dirt.

Walt hammered on the polished black wood harder than Thea thought was wise. It was answered moments later nonetheless by Gin Ricky. His glossy black hair was falling out of the leather string that tied it at the back, and he had a bowl of soup in his hands.

"Detective James," he said, looking pleased, but serious. "You brought Detective Williams, I see." A small crease appeared on his forehead. "Follow me."

Gin Ricky ushered the pair inside and shut the door quickly behind them. The hallway in which they stood was shabby yet spotless. Stopping at the end of the short passage Gin Ricky indicated with his hand that they should enter before him.

Walt took a step inside the living room, then froze.

"Walt?"

Thea peered around him to see what had given him pause.

It was like being hit by a train. Sitting on the windowsill, a bowl of soup in her hands, was Walt's wife—Cleo. Not dead and not a ghoul, she was as lovely as she had always been. The springy coils of her hair were longer, and she was thinner, but it was definitely her.

Thea's breaths came in shallow gulps as she looked from Walt to Cleo, and they at each other. The silence stretched on and on.

"Cleo?" Walt said uncertainly, as if he couldn't quite believe what he was seeing.

Cleo cast her bowl of soup aside, and it slopped onto the sill. She bounded across the room and threw herself at Walt, who caught her and held her tightly in his arms, swaying slightly.

"I thought...I can't believe you're here," Walt said, amazed, his eyes shining. "Where?... How?"

Cleo pulled Walt's head down and kissed him ferociously. He kissed her back. "I missed you so much," she said. Crystal clear tears streaked her face. Or maybe they were slightly pink.

"I thought you were dead. I'm so sorry."

"This isn't your fault."

Cleo kissed him again gently, then took a step back to examine him. "You look different," she said. She touched his stubble with the tips of her fingers, and ran her hands through the lengths of his hair. It would have been shorter when she had seen it last. She looked at his bruised hands and kissed each one of his knuckles. She took great care as she traced the evidence of his broken nose. Thea wondered if Cleo remembered how it had happened.

Thea felt sick. The room around them seemed to spin. She felt like an outsider, an interloper intruding on a most personal moment. She backed away slowly, needing desperately to be anywhere but there.

"Thea!" Cleo exclaimed unexpectedly. She stepped away from Walt, keeping hold of one of his hands, and pulled Thea into a tight, one-armed hug. "I'm so happy to see you," Cleo beamed. Thea's insides squirmed uncomfortably. "Been keeping him in line, I'm sure. You were always such a good friend to him. I'm glad you were there for him while I was gone." And she squeezed Thea again.

"I'm so happy you're safe," Thea said, squeezing Cleo back, hoping the wetness in her eyes would be mistaken for tears of happiness.

The implications of the situation beyond the reunion seemed to dawn on Walt as he looked at Thea and Cleo, his face pale.

Cleo took both of Thea's hands and looked her up and down much as she had Walt, like she was searching for differences from when they had last met.

"You haven't changed." She cupped Thea's face between her hands. "Still beautiful."

"How is this possible?" Walt asked in amazement.

Cleo relinquished her hold on Thea and turned to her husband. "It was all Gin Ricky. He saved me."

Gin Ricky, who had been hovering in the doorway, stepped into the room proper, taking up a spot next to Cleo.

"Where...? He...I thought you were dead." Walt took Cleo's hand and pressed her fingers to his lips. "What happened?"

"I was walking home from work, and someone attacked me. I've no idea who.

The next thing I knew, I was in the SubLevel. I don't remember much until Gin Ricky found me. My memory is spotty."

Gin Ricky cleared his throat. Thea looked around at him, but he didn't meet her eye.

"All this time." Walt's voice was weak. Cleo nodded. "How did you get out? When did you get out? How are you...you?"

"The first time I saw her was about three months ago," Gin Ricky began. "I was delivering booze to Ward Eight as usual, and there she was. Ben, the guy who runs the joint, and I were just shooting the breeze, and some OL soldiers turned up. He told me that there was a market for ghouls in the sex industry, but he hadn't been able to convince more than a couple of his people to take Styxx. So, he used his contacts at the OL to...outsource. The soldier's unloaded six or seven ghouls from this cargo Jonk, and there was Cleo among them."

Walt went white, and the muscles in his jaw twitched. "I'll kill Benny," he snarled, pulling Cleo close to him as if protecting her.

"Nothing like that happened," Cleo said placatingly. "Gin Ricky protected me."

"It took me a minute to recognise her," Gin Ricky continued. "But once I did, I couldn't just leave her. I paid Ben for time with her. I tried talking to her, but she was too far gone. I just sat with her until the soldiers came back to take her away. It was a few weeks before I could convince Ben to bring her back. He wasn't in the market to take requests for a specific ghoul. I had to convince him that I was more than the average sicko and that I had enough money to make it worth his while. Finally, he agreed, and I was able to get to her and give her Quietus."

"The Styxx variant?" Thea asked, reminding them she was there.

"It's the antithesis to Styxx. You take it, and you're fine; you stop, and you're a monster like the rest. It was just luck that was what had been used on her. It's not a cure. It won't help the others. But anyway, we talked, made a plan and staged a jailbreak."

"Gin Ricky brought me here and nursed me back to sanity."

Walt held out a hand to Gin Ricky. "Thank you," he said as they shook. "For bringing Cleo back to me."

"There's more, but now's not the time."

"I have some leads to follow up on for a case," Thea lied abruptly. She needed to be anywhere else.

"You've only just got here," Cleo said as if she was genuinely disappointed.

"You and Walt need some time to catch up. I'm really glad you're okay," she said to Cleo with a weak smile.

Thea spun on her heel and swept from the room; it took everything she had not to run.

"Thea, wait," Walt called, following after her, but when she turned back, he seemed lost for words.

"It's fine. You two need some time."

"I'll tell her everything," Walt said, taking a step towards Thea.

Thea took a step back.

"I love you," Walt said quietly, trying again to close the cavern between. "Thea, I love you."

"I'll see you later," Thea said, hiding her face from him.

"Your place?"

"Sure."

Outside in the artificial air, Thea felt selfish and dirty as she walked aimlessly, trying to calm her racing mind. Cleo was alive. Walt's wife was back. She, Thea, had hugged her and wished her well, all the while commiserating for herself. Cleo had suffered who knew what, and she, Thea, was sad that she was going to lose a man to his wife.

But then, he hadn't ever really been hers, had he.

THE PAST
Four years ago...

Thea had messed up in a big way, and she knew it. It had seemed like a good idea at the time—attend the party as a guest and question Dill Kelly in his own home—but he had made them both the moment they arrived, and Thea's careless questions had confirmed what the mobster had already suspected.

She had been arrogant and overconfident, lost in her own cleverness, and it had nearly cost both she and Walt their lives. If it hadn't been for his quick thinking and even quicker fists, they never would have made it out alive. They had been lucky, she had been lucky, but the captain would be well within her rights to suspend her or worse, and she would have no one to blame but herself. She was on her way to being a disgraced ex-cop at twenty-four. How could she have been so stupid?

She wanted to apologise to Walt, but he hadn't looked at her once on their way back to the TPD. She hadn't meant to cause him this much strife, or any strife at all. She had just gotten carried away. And now, as they waited for the captain to reign down her fury upon them, he still wasn't looking at her. He hadn't said a word since he had called the incident in. The silence was glacial.

"My office. Now," the captain said from her doorway. Thea could tell she was struggling to contain her anger even then.

With Walt still refusing to acknowledge her presence, they followed the captain into her office. The room was bright and classy, Walt made to sit in one of the chairs in front of the large desk, but the captain said, "Oh no, you are going to want to stand for this."

Thea waited, barely breathing, for the captain to let her wrath fly free.

"I am appalled," she bellowed from behind her desk. She too remained on her feet. "That two of my own could behave in such a manner. The sheer recklessness.

How dare you?! You could have been killed! I'm in a mind to suspend you both. Without pay!"

"Ma'am, it was my call. Detective James had nothing—" Thea began.

"Be quiet, Williams. Anything I hear from you at this point will only make it worse. I know it was 'your call', but Detective James is the senior officer here. He is supposed," she stretched out the word for emphasis. "To be the one calling the shots, the one of sound judgement, the mentor, but clearly, that isn't the case." She threw her hands up in the air as if at her wit's end. "What were you thinking?"

"Ma'am, I take full responsibility for what happened and will gladly accept any punishment you deem fit," said Walt deferentially.

"I should damn well think so," she paused, looking from one to the other, her face a mask of anger. "Playing spy. Two years of undercover operations ruined. I hope it was worth it because the only action you'll be seeing in the near future will be from behind a desk. If either of you ever pull a stunt like that again, so help me god, you'll do nothing but paperwork for the rest of your careers."

"It won't happen again," said Thea seriously.

The captain gave her a withering look.

"I'm separating you two. This partnership clearly isn't working. Now get out of my sight." She waved them away.

Thea looked at Walt, expecting, wanting, him to challenge this, but all he said was, "Yes, Captain," then swept from the room.

Thea followed him out into the corridor, running to keep up with his long strides.

"Walt," Thea called.

"Thea, please just go, the fuck, away."

"I'm sorry," she said, trying to keep pace with him.

"You have nothing to apologise for."

"You have every right to be angry with me."

"I'm not pissed at you." He stopped abruptly. She stopped, too. "This is on me. I let you do it. I give you free rein because..." He laughed as if at himself. "You know why. You aren't blind." His eyes flicked to her face and away again.

He started to walk once more.

"Walt."

"I can't keep doing this."

"Detective James," she said, raising her voice slightly.

He turned back to her, shaking his head.

"Fuck you calling me 'Detective' like I have any of the power here," he said, pointing at his own chest. "Like I'm in charge. Like I'm not always about five seconds away from begging you just to let me touch you."

"We're partners," Thea said, stunned. "You're married. We can't." Their chemistry was undeniable, and she had thought about it often, but always in the realms of fantasy.

"I know we fucking can't," he yelled, taking a step or two towards her. "But it's too late, you're already up here." He tapped his temple roughly.

"I'm not trying to seduce you." She wanted him, yes, but she had never planned on taking him.

"I know that, but it doesn't mean you aren't."

"What do you want me to do? What do you want?"

Walt rubbed his eyes with the heels of his hands.

"I want us separated. I want to go home to my wife and not think about you when I'm in bed with her," he said, his eyes blazing.

"Then go to her," she said, matching his ferocity.

"You're telling me to go."

"I'm telling you to go."

"I'm going."

He didn't move.

Thea walked slowly towards him, never breaking eye contact, she wanted him to know he could stop her if he wanted to, but she hoped he wouldn't.

"I don't want to want you," he said as Thea reached him. They were mere inches apart. The very air between them seemed charged.

"I'm going to hell in a fast car," he breathed, and Thea knew his resolve was crumbling. If she wanted him, all she had to do was claim him.

Thea waited, waited for what felt like an age, waited as long as she could bear it and then— she was kissing him, and he was kissing her. He invaded and overwhelmed her senses. The feel of him, the smell of him, the taste of him, it was intoxicating.

"Fuck," he moaned against her lips. "I can't stop." Thea didn't want him to.

They could have had sex right there in that corridor, and Thea wouldn't have cared, but, guided by Walt, they were moving. Thea was walking backwards, his lips never leaving hers. When their mouths finally broke apart, she was only vaguely aware that she was in a supply closet. With one hand, Walt fumbled with the buttons on the front of her blouse, the other, he reached behind himself and locked the door.

There was no going back now, but Thea wouldn't have even if she could have.

She pushed Walt into the door, crushing herself against him as they continued to kiss hungrily. His hands slipped from her waist to the back of her thighs, hinting subtly. Thea did as his touch requested and jumped lightly, wrapping her legs around his waist.

Standing, still half-dressed, they had made love against the back wall. It was quick and desperate, like they were pouring all their frustrations into each other.

When they had finished, Walt lay his head on her shoulder, his right hand still holding both of hers above her head, his breathing harsh.

"Fuck," he hissed into her neck. He pulled away, gently easing her feet back on the floor. He quickly zipped up his trousers, re-buttoned his shirt, righted his jacket and sped from the room, slamming the door behind him.

Thea stared at the closed door for a moment, the slam still echoing in her ears, then she too righted her clothing and left the closet.

MACHINATIONS

The sudden death of Dillard Kelly had come as a complete surprise. Harold Williams didn't like to be surprised. He was a man in control, a man with a plan. He behaved as if he knew everything because, in truth—he often did. The effect was a necessary one, it was how those in power kept it, but it took a lot of work to maintain the appearance of omniscience. It was tiring and dull. Being surprised gave the sharks that endlessly circled their first whiff of blood, and he couldn't have that.

He praised his sources internally as Bastion Tyrus sauntered into his office with a knowing smirk curving his full lips.

"Dill Kelly is dead," Bastion said, his eyes measuring the effect the news had had on the older man.

"I know," said Harold superciliously.

"Puts a kink in your plans, no?" Bastion still looked smug.

"Hardly," said Harold, sitting up a little straighter in his expensive chair. "I just received the contents of his data drive. Shall we review them together?"

Bastion smiled in a strained sort of way and inclined his head.

Much that was stored on the drive was nothing to be concerned about, Dill knew slightly more than they would have liked about Medicorum and the creation of Styx and Quietus, but he wasn't in any position to tell what he knew anymore. His knowledge of the Morpheus Project and the chips it created was baseline. Interestingly, Dillard had been keeping tabs on a freelance physician called Chowdhary; Harold made a mental note to investigate that more later.

He only became mildly concerned when he observed a ghoul escaping the SubLevel.

"That's Walt's wife," Bastion said, wide-eyed as he watched the footage that hung mid-air between them with rapt attention.

"That's Cleo James. She worked on the project. Maxwell had to eliminate her because she became too nosy. She's supposed to be dead." Harold slammed his fist on his desk. "If she makes her way back to her husband, she will tell him everything, and if she tells him, he tells Thea."

"What would you have me do?" said Bastion.

"It's not enough just to kill them. The dead can still talk, and they tend to shout louder than the living. People listen to the dead. We can't just kill them; we have to destroy them."

"They don't know anything," said Bastion. "Walt suspects that the Onyx Legion had a hand in the cleanup job at Thea's apartment, but he doesn't know anything for certain."

"Did you think that I was unaware you had failed to kill Benjamin Pickford?" said Harold.

For a fraction of a second, Bastion looked shocked; he rallied quickly. "I didn't expect the prick to cut his own arm off. I did what I was asked. I injected him with the nanites."

"You failed, and he ran straight to Thea. It's what any smart man would have done, and that bottom feeder is a survivor if nothing else. If you are burned by one side, you ally with the other."

"I miscalculated his determination."

"Indeed. Find out what your friends know while I clean up your mess."

"Should we bring this to Maxwell?"

"You tell him," Harold said.

Neither man liked Maxwell, and while they enjoyed his vision, they feared him. Neither had any intention of disclosing their mistakes, and both knew it.

"What do you plan to do?" Bastion asked

"Destroy them."

"Even your daughter? You've already forsaken one."

"Hail Krysos."

CLEAN SLATE

Walt's mind was blank. Or maybe he had so many thoughts that they sounded like white noise inside his head.

Gin Ricky had tactfully gone into the kitchen half an hour ago. Walt and Cleo had been sitting in silence ever since. She had perched herself on the windowsill again; Walt watched her as she gazed out at the murky streets through a crack in the metal shutters. She was still beautiful, and his heart was full of genuine joy to find her safe and well, but he couldn't ignore the writhing snake pit in his stomach.

"You look different," Cleo said finally, just as the silence was becoming too much. "Sadder."

"It's been a hard two years."

"Is that why you smell of tequila?"

Walt laughed uncomfortably. "No, that was something else."

"I don't remember the last two years of my life," Cleo said.

She sounded so lost it made Walt's chest ache. He hadn't wanted to push her, for her sake and his.

"Nothing?" Walt felt relief, then guilt.

He had to tell her.

"I remember your face, staring at me. You looked so horrified. The last time I saw that look, your father had died. Was that the night I was taken? Where were we?"

"In the bedroom."

His insides were knotted, but he had to tell her.

"I turned rabid."

"Yes."

He had to tell her.

"Then the Legion came? They dragged me away?"

"Then the Legion came."

"Thea was there, wasn't she?" Cleo said, turning Walt's insides to ice. "I think I remember seeing her…"

"You had been working late, and she and I…" He couldn't do it. "She and I had been working on a case. We were stumped and decided to have some food and talk it over." He was a bastard, and he knew it, but he didn't have it in him to break her heart twice. He deserved to be haunted by that night; she didn't.

"I know we have a lot more to talk about, about what happened to me and about Gin Ricky. He needs our help, and I'll get to that, but I'm not ready. The things I do remember aren't pleasant. I'm free. I'm here now. Can that be enough? Just for a little while?"

"Whatever you need."

"I'm not cured," Cleo said, hugging herself. "I'm not normal. There is a monster inside of me."

"I know. We'll fix it. We'll find a way."

More silence.

"It's been two years. I don't need to know what you did in that time," Cleo said. She looked at Walt expectantly. He thought he knew what she was getting at, but he wasn't willing to speak until he was sure. "You're not a monk." She smiled apologetically.

Walt looked at the floor, sure she would see the shame on his face.

"I don't care," she said, filling the silence that had almost become unbearable again. "I don't care who you were with or what you did with them. I just need to know if you still want me because I want you. I want my life back. I know it's a lot, and I know it's soon, and that life hasn't stood still, but are you still my husband? Are we still Cleo and Walt? Is there still hope for us? Will you stay with me?"

Walt loved Thea. It was one of the few things of which he was absolutely certain. He knew that no matter how much time they spent apart, or how much distance there was between them, he always would. She, for better or worse, had become as vital to him as oxygen. Walt loved Thea. But what kind of man said "No" to his wife in her time of need? He had abandoned her once before; he wasn't going to do it again. Staying with Cleo would hurt him, and Thea, but surely, she would understand. The right thing, the honourable thing, the thing that a good man, who wasn't a drunk or a cheater, would do was stay with his wife, wasn't it? So, what if he loved someone else? He had made vows to Cleo. He had loved her once; he could again.

"Yes," he said simply, holding his hand out to her.

THE LIMIT

Rishaan hated what he was about to do. He was a man that prided himself on his integrity. He knew with complete certainty that some lines could not be crossed, but what was he supposed to do? Everyone had their limit, and he had found his. He would do anything, even forsake his prized decency, to protect his husband and their son.

Feeling like a fool, he crept through the dark streets, keeping his head down. No one looked at him as he wend his way through the crowds, but that didn't surprise him much; Tenebrium was a city full of people desperate to be anywhere else.

The detective's home was on the outskirts of Tenebrium proper, not a district that Rishaan knew very well. It had more government and associated agency buildings, stores and recreational facilities than residential dwellings.

It didn't take him long to find the place he sought. The detective lived in a comparably small building of only a hundred or so stories. It was a nice building. Not expensive or flashy, but nice, respectable.

The main door was large, made from gleaming silver metal and built to withstand heavy artillery by the look of it. It was ornately carved with triangular spiral patterns. There was a slim keypad hidden within the lines. Rishaan had been given the keycode by his blackmailer and was relieved when the door opened with a pleasing beep.

He didn't take much notice of the atrium as he made his way to the narrow lift. Inside, the carpet was red, and the walls a dark lacquered wood. A small light flashing on one of the ceiling tiles told him that there was a camera watching him. He pulled the brim of his hat down lower.

The lift opened out into a wide corridor; he could see the apartment he was looking for halfway along it. The door of 1147 was new, but the jam showed signs of wear.

His heart raced, and sweat dripped down the tip of his nose as he pulled the small circular device he had been given from his pocket. Rishaan placed the strange object over the lock and waited. There was a click, a faint buzz, and then the door swung open.

The detective's apartment was pleasant, nothing compared to what Rishaan had lived in when he still worked for Medicorum, but far more agreeable than his current accommodations. This was the part he had been most worried about. Up until this point, he had been following a script of sorts, but now he was on his own.

Where did one keep a crucial piece of evidence?

Rishaan turned the apartment upside down, taking no care to hide the fact it had been searched. Surely, the absence of such a vital thing would be noticed. That was part of the reason, the other part was that he secretly hoped that the detective would expose Medicorum—even if it meant he went down with it.

He was starting to panic. What if the detective kept the thing on his person? Would he have to track this unknown Mr James down and what? Take it by force?

But then, as his mind was swirling with the impossibility of the task and his complete lack of skills to accomplish it, he saw it out of the corner of his eye. There was a slight shadow in one of the lamps mounted on the wall. A kind of dreadful excitement filled him as he walked towards it. He examined the lamp with surgical precision and, with a shaking hand, reached under the slim glass cover. He withdrew his fingers sharply; the petite metal disk was hot. He sucked the blister that had formed on the tip of his finger, then pulled a handkerchief from his pocket. He wrapped the silken material around his hand and attempted the extraction once more. With a little manoeuvring, he pulled the small object free.

It was strange that such a small thing could cause so much strife and stranger still that his life's work, his biggest achievement, was the thing threatening to destroy him. With that hopeless thought, he left the apartment and made his way back to the clinic to hand over the chip.

TENEBRIUM GENERAL

Tenebrium General Hospital was a hellhole. It was more like a warzone than a medical facility, and the patients who found themselves there were just as likely to die from being admitted as they were to survive. It was a loud and chaotic place. Overworked doctors and nurses rushed from patient to patient, most of whom were in dire condition and screaming in pain. It was a dirty place, blood and grime stained the floors and walls, and the facility was so lacking in funds that they had to reuse instruments, needles, and bandages, among other usually single-use items.

When Torrez awoke, he lay uncomfortably on top of a gurney that sat seemingly forgotten in a dingy corridor. His abdomen was heavily bandaged, and there was a drain in the incision. There was a drip in his arm and a catheter in his urethra; it wasn't pleasant.

Marielena had only stuck around long enough to get the OK from the Emergency Room, check Torrez was alive, and tell him that he needed to find somewhere else to sleep. He had been wallowing in his misery ever since.

He was a killer. Torrez had had many labels attributed to him in his life–dirty cop, cheater, asshole, among others–and most of them were true, but a killer? That was one he never hoped to gain. Being a killer felt more like a brand, seared into his memory. He'd always thought that that was the line he wouldn't cross. He had been wrong, and it only went to show how far from the straight and narrow he really was.

He supposed the dire conditions he now found himself in were the beginning of his punishment. He hadn't expected to wake up in a swanky room at Medicorum Medical Services or some other similar high-end place, healthcare was expensive, nigh on unaffordable even if the patient had a steady job as he did, but Tenebrium General was the worst of the worst. It felt like those who had dropped him there had been willing to play the fifty-fifty odds that he might not survive.

Even though he had been awake for over an hour, no doctor had come to see him yet, and he still had no idea what had happened to him. Wincing as he did so, he leaned over the side of the bed and grabbed his chart from where it hung from the railing. The chart was a creamish-grey and roughly the same size and shape as a pencil. Torrez tapped the end, and his notes sprung to life.

A concussion, three broken ribs and a ruptured spleen. So, he had been bleeding internally. That explained the headache, the queasy feeling and the pain in his stomach.

"Hey, Mexico," said an unpleasant voice.

Torrez looked up from his chart to see Detective Damian O'Malley, his bald pate shining, his ruddy face smirking, sauntering down the corridor.

"Thea sent me to check in on you," O'Malley said upon reaching Torrez's bedside.

"She must be pissed," Torrez said with a strained half-smile.

O'Malley sat down heavily on the edge of Torrez's bed, jostling him and causing him to grimace.

"Nah, she probably thought it would be too conspicuous for her to turn up, considering that the Gold Legion has tried to kill you both. Wouldn't want it to look like you're colluding against us."

Torrez's eyes widened in shock. O'Malley was positively beaming with malintent.

"Yeah, she's a hot piece, not too bright, though. And definitely not worth losing everything for. Someone should have told that to James, huh?" he laughed maliciously. "But then again, maybe you already know that. You and her never did the dirty, did you? Well, you've missed your chance. Neither of you is going to be around much longer," he paused. "Still got nothin' to say? I'm giving you my best stuff!"

O'Malley leaned over and closed his hand on Torrez's, where it had been slowly inching towards the call button. "Oh, I don't think so," he said, picking up the remote and tossing it casually over his shoulder out of Torrez's reach. "Did you really think you were the only one?"

"I'd hoped it was a slightly more exclusive club, if I'm honest," said Torrez with all the bravado he could muster.

O'Malley laughed as if he genuinely appreciated the joke.

"You must have known you were being watched, or are you really that arrogant?"

"Guilty as charged."

O'Malley looked over the side of the bed at the clear fluid-filled bags for the drain and the catheter. He smirked and wrapped his fingers around the catheter tube and gave it a gentle wiggle. Torrez tensed, his fingers gripping the bed sheets.

"What're you doing?"

"Dill Kelly entrusted you with some evidence, and my superiors would like to know what happened to it and what happened to the subject of that little escape video. And Drew, don't even think about lying; we know you know."

"I don't know where she is," said Torrez. He was suddenly very warm.

"Are you sure?" said O'Malley, giving the catheter a little tug.

Torrez yelped. "The video is on a data chip on my desk. The woman, Cleo, I have no idea where she is." Torrez was panting, his breathing coming in short, shallow breaths. He thought about lunging forward and grabbing the catheter tube himself, but he was worried that would cause O'Malley to rip it out. He had no idea what forcefully removing the inflated catheter would do, but he definitely didn't want to find out.

"Did you tell Williams or James?" Another slight tug.

"Fuck!" Torrez yowled. The feeling was awful, sharp, painful and far too intimate. It made him feel like he was going to wet himself.

"Did you?"

"No," Torrez shouted. "Dill told me to wait."

"You told that little bitch Williams everything tonight, though, didn't you?"

Wiggle, tug.

"I didn't tell her about Cleo. How could I?"

"Aww, aren't you sweet? But you did tell her about the Gold Legion, didn't you?" Twist.

"She already knew," Torrez hissed. "You haven't been as careful as you thought. You are all going to get yours, one way or another. It's just a matter of time."

"Oooh, defiant. I like it. Maybe we will, but you and your little friend, and her lap dog, aren't going to be around to see it."

Then came the sharpest tug yet. Torrez had been poised to retort, but instead, he cried out in pain and clutched his groin.

"Mr Torrez," a doctor called from the end of the corridor. "I've come to check your incision; would you like me to come back?"

"Now's fine," Torrez said with a valiant attempt at airy as relief washed over him.

"Consider yourself marked," O'Malley whispered, coiling the catheter tube around his hand again as if preparing to yank it clean out. "Get well soon."

He released the catheter tube and stood as the doctor reached the bedside.

"I'll be seeing you." O'Malley turned from Torrez and walked back the way he had come whistling tunelessly.

VISITORS UNWELCOME

Thea felt like a ghost as she unlocked the door of her apartment. It was like she had been hollowed out, and coiling dread had taken the place of her innards.

It was pitch dark inside her home, like she had stepped into the void, but Thea didn't mind—it matched her mood. But there was something off. Something not quite right about the atmosphere, the flow of the air in the blackness. Thea paused at the threshold, scanning the darkness, but it was impenetrable. Slowly and quietly, she reached around her back and pulled her gun from its holster. She raised it in front of her, and the nose made contact with something solid.

Before she could react, the gun was twisted from her grip, and she heard it clatter to the floor somewhere beside her. A slight breeze across her cheek gave her the only warning she could hope for, blinded as she was. She ducked just in time, and the blow that was meant for her collided heavily with the door. Taking her opportunity, she dropped low and swept the legs of her attacker, who went crashing to the ground with a grunt of pain.

"Lights!" she yelled, then, "Bastion?"

Warm, bright light filled the apartment revealing Bastion Tyrus sprawled ungainly at her feet.

"Thea?" he said in surprise.

"No shit, you're in my apartment." She was irritated and not quite relieved just yet.

"I'm sorry," Bastion said, sitting up. "I needed a place to hide."

"From who?"

"The Gold Legion."

Thea watched Bastion warily as he got to his feet. He had a large cut on his lip and an obvious bump forming on his forehead. The earring that usually dangled on his right earlobe had been ripped out, and blood trickled down the side of his neck.

"Talk," she said, picking her gun up from the ground and holstering it.
"Any chance of a patch job?"

Thea perched on the edge of her coffee table with a Medicus Kit at her side. She used the handheld carbon dioxide laser to close his split ear and the cut on his brow.

"So," she said, dabbing his bloody lip.

"The Gold Legion aren't a myth, but I think you already knew that."

"I'm more interested in what you know," Thea said, setting the bloody gauze down and reaching for the bruise cream.

"You've been talking to Walt. I understand why he and I are on the outs, but I thought you trusted me," Bastion said, snatching the cream from her and applying it haphazardly to his under eye. "I don't have many friends left."

"It pays to err on the side of caution these days."

"I had nothing to do with what happened to Cleo. But the OL is dirty. They did cover up the attack on you. They are marching around taking people into custody without charge, messing with police investigations and claiming jurisdiction where they have no business; they have to be stopped. It's my house, and I have to clean it. But I have no idea who's still loyal to me."

"And the Gold Legion?"

"They're taking over. A million of our citizens have been turned into monsters, and that was just phase one. Phase two is so much bigger."

"How do you know?"

"Because your father told me! He will eliminate any threat, including you. He ordered me to silence you. He already thinks you know too much. He still thinks I'm on his side, and look what he did to me because I failed to meet his standards," Bastion said, slamming the pot of cream angrily on the counter. "But once he realises that you know about everything, about the chips and Styxx and Medicorum; he will kill you and me and Walt and anyone you have so much as looked at to protect his secret."

"And what is his secret?" Thea asked shrewdly.

"Morpheus chips, they manipulate nerve impulses to control anyone who has been implanted with one. They have perfected mind control. Do you understand what that means? How bad is this going to get?"

"Yes, I understand what it means," Thea said, slightly vexed.

"You already knew all of this, didn't you? You haven't flinched, not once. I tell you your father is an evil mastermind and," his hand cut through the air. "Nothing."

Thea considered Bastion. She would have described him as a friend in the past, and before Cleo had been taken, he and Walt had been brothers, but the relationship had degraded, and she knew Walt would not approve of his inclusion. Then again, Bastion was in a position of power, one that could be useful.

"I was working a case; I still am. We found five sex workers dead in suspicious circumstances, it looks like they were all chipped, and that's what killed them. I kept pulling on the thread, and here we are."

"The pros were chipped?"

"Looks like it. Whether they were failed experiments, intended kills, or why they were chosen, I don't know, but I'll find out one way or another."

"How do we fight this? What evidence can we find that they won't destroy? Who can we tell that they won't kill?"

"I don't know." Thea shrugged. "I don't have any answers. I don't have a plan. I don't know how to fight them, but I do know that if we don't try, we're no better than them."

"Good speech. Short, to the point."

"Did it work?"

"The Onyx Legion means something to me, it's my life, and these elitist bastards are trying to take that away; I'll be damned if I let them."

Thea nodded approvingly.

"Walt isn't going to be happy about this. He doesn't want me in his life—he doesn't trust me, and he certainly doesn't want me anywhere near you." There was something in the way he said the last that Thea chose to ignore.

"I can handle Walt."

"I'll bet." There was a pause. "I'm sorry," Bastion said quickly. "I didn't mean it like that. Listen, I can't stay here, it's too dangerous. I'll find somewhere else to lay low, but Thea, you need to be careful. They want you dead, they already tried, someone ordered Pickford to kill you, and he failed. He's as good as dead."

"We're being careful."

"So, he's changed sides. It's smart. Your father is not an enemy anyone should want, but he's just as dangerous as a friend. Be safe, okay."

"You, too."

They both stood. Bastion pulled Thea into an unexpected hug. He held onto her tightly, his arms holding her close to him, as one of his hands found its way into her hair. When he let go, he left without a backwards glance.

FREE

It was freeing, freeing people. At first, the people who worked at Ward Eight were shocked, they thought that he was firing them, but once they realised that he was giving them a choice, nothing more and nothing less, the joy was overwhelming.

Benny knew that it was a small step to redemption. He knew it wouldn't keep him from jail or change any of the terrible things he had done. He was selfish and greedy, and that would probably never change, but he didn't have to cause harm, and that was where he was going to start.

He hadn't done it for gratitude, to impress anyone, or try to convince the world that he was a changed man. For the first time in his life, he had done the right thing because it was right, not because it benefited him. Benny knew he had no right to feel good about it, he had caused the suffering in the first place, but he felt fresh, like just maybe he had turned a corner.

He tucked the files he had returned to Ward Eight for into his jacket and left the place that had been his castle, knowing he might be on the other side of a jail sentence before he saw it again.

It was with a heady feeling that he made his way back to Walt's apartment. The dark Tenebrium streets didn't trouble him; he was used to it. He wasn't afraid of the dark because, in the past, the thing that had lurked there was him, or men like him. He wasn't surprised either when three Onyx Legion soldiers stepped forth from the shadows.

"Evening, gentlemen. Shall we get this over with?"

PEOPLE JUST AIN'T NO GOOD

Water dripped from the ice pack that Thea had used to calm the bruise on Bastion's face from the table where it lay onto her dark wood floors, and the gauze she had used to staunch the bleeding at his lip and ear sat discarded in a small bowl filled with saltwater. She had been about to tidy them away when there had been a soft knocking at her door.

Her breath caught in her throat; she was momentarily immobilised. She looked at the door, but made no moves towards it.

He knocked again. And again.

Thea had been in gunfights that had scared her less, but she walked to the door and opened it regardless.

Walt stood before her, his face, as it so often was, unreadable.

"Hi."

"Hi."

"Can I come in?" he asked softly.

Thea stepped aside. She felt a jolt of electricity flow through her as he swept past, their bodies barely inches apart.

"Are you hurt?" he said, pointing to the Medicus kit and the bloody gauze that were still sitting on her coffee table.

"Not me. Bastion was here."

There was an obvious shift in Walt's demeanour. "You let him in?"

Thea didn't respond.

Walt made a quick sweep around the living room as if he expected Bastion to be hiding behind the curtains.

"You can't trust him."

Thea rolled her eyes. "He was hurt."

"Is that all it took?" Walt said coarsely.

Thea took a deep calming breath. "He told me that the OL is dirty and pushing him out. He told me about the Gold Legion and the chips—apparently my father calls them 'Morpheus'."

"He told you that?"

"Yeah, he did."

"And what did you tell him?" Walt said seriously.

"Nothing, I didn't have to. He already knew," Thea said defiantly. "We need as many allies as we can get. He's on our side. The man was like a brother to you. I don't understand what happened."

"Don't you?"

"This is a good thing. You, me, and Benny isn't exactly a crack team." She moved over to the kitchen and poured herself a glass of cranberry juice.

"I've never thought of you as naïve before," Walt sniped. It echoed in the large open space.

Thea took a long draft from her glass and then set it loudly back on the counter.

"Did you just come here to insult me?" She said, trying to keep her voice level.

"No," Walt said quietly, a wry smile on his lips. He moved further into the room and took off his jacket, throwing it over a chair. Thea waited, but Walt just peered out the window, seemingly lost for words, then he sighed. "She doesn't remember anything. She doesn't remember that night. She doesn't remember what we did."

Their eyes met for the merest moment, remembering together the night that had ruined them both.

There it is, Thea thought. She folded her arms and lent against the counter, waiting. She knew what he was about to do; she had known the moment she saw Cleo.

"I love you," he declared.

"It's funny how men think that's all a woman needs to hear. Like the words are magic."

"Thea—"

"Say it."

"She's my wife," he said simply.

"Say the words. Say what you came here to say."

"I'm staying with Cleo. I'm going to give our marriage another shot. You and I; we're done." The last was barely more than a whisper.

From her vantage point in the kitchen, Walt looked so distant, so far away from her, where he stood in the middle of her living room against the backdrop of Tenebrium City as it shone bright and alive through the wide windows.

"Then go to her." The words cost her something.

"I'm not ready."

Time seemed to stand still as they just stood there together, in the purgatory of their doomed relationship, both knowing that once Walt left, there was no going back.

"This is hard," he said eventually.

"We've been here before. You should be used to it," Thea said with a weak smile.

"I need to explain. I need you to understand."

"I understand." She turned away from him. Her eyes were starting to fill with tears, but she refused to let them fall.

"I love you." His voice shook.

"Don't," she moaned.

"I love you," he said more clearly. "I love you."

"Stop saying that," Thea snapped, rounding on him. "It doesn't change anything."

"If I had a choice—" Walt began.

"You did have a choice. You've already made it."

"It's not that simple. She practically begged me to stay." He was begging too, begging her to understand.

"Do you love her? Actually, no. Don't answer that." Thea waved her hand through the air as if to swat the question away. "I don't need to know. That's none of my business."

"You know I don't. Not anymore. Not since you."

"That's worse." Thea knocked the glass into the sink, and it shattered loudly, sloshing juice over the counter. "Your wife should be more than an obligation."

"Why? Why is it worse?"

"You're staying with her out of guilt, like she's a job."

"I want to be the man that she remembers, the one you can't see anymore. The man I should have been. The man that would have protected her."

"You are so consumed by self-loathing that lying to her, pretending you love her, that you've never cheated on her, is the price you are willing to pay to feel like the old you? The Walt you could stand to look at in the mirror? That's pathetic."

"That's not fair."

"You have this idealised notion of the man that you were, you have convinced yourself that this fictional past 'you' wouldn't have cheated, wouldn't have fallen for a rookie, but he did. Sorry to break it to you, but the old you loved me, too."

"I don't blame you for the mess I'm in. It's not your fault that I'm a drunk or that I got demoted, those are my mistakes, and I own them. This is about Cleo and what she needs, what I owe her. It's about my duties as a husband."

"This isn't about Cleo or me. This is about you. You've just said as much. This is about how much *you* hate you. You're gonna go and live in a fantasy where you can pretend the last two years never happened, that you're still the TPD's star detective and everyone's favourite guy. I'm just collateral. You were never going to stay with me, and now we both know it." Thea looked him dead in the eyes and mustered all the venom she could. "They never leave their wives."

"You don't get to throw that in my face," said Walt affronted.

"We were together for over two years, and you didn't leave then either. You didn't want to be divorced or separated, the man who left his wife for his mistress. You were fine with the status quo then, and I think if you thought for a second I'd go for it, you'd be happy with it now."

"You think betraying my wedding vows wasn't eating me up inside? You think I could do that again? You think I would?"

"We could have been legit. For the first time ever, we could have just been us. It could have been you and me, and it could have been right. Now we'll never be anything more than a sleazy affair that went on too long."

"We were never just a sleazy affair. I fell in love with you. I still love you. I never stopped," Walt said, throwing his arms wide as if in defeat. "I tried to stay away, but I couldn't."

He moved around the couch to stand in front of her, the counter separating them. It might as well have been an ocean.

"But you're going to now, right? Stay away? Cut ties? Guess it's not that hard after all." Thea took a shaky breath that was almost a laugh and began to wipe the counter with a towel. "You know what the worst part is? I didn't believe you. When you said you were going to tell her, I didn't believe you. I knew you would never pick me, and I hoped anyway, like a fool. Because that's what you have done to me, made me a fool. The rest I did to myself. I knew better. I knew better than to trust you." She emphasised the last few words by pointing at Walt with her fist that still clenched the wet towel.

"You know I don't love her."

"That's just sad."

"She doesn't remember anything. Nothing. How can I tell her after everything she has been through? What kind of man would hurt his wife like that?"

"An honest one."

"You can't say anything. I know I'd deserve it, but she doesn't."

"Get out."

"But—"

"Get out," Thea screamed.

She threw the cranberry-soaked towel at him. Splotches of crimson appeared on the shoulder of his white shirt. He ignored them.

"We have to talk about this."

"You don't want to talk," Thea bellowed. "You want me to give you a pass. You want me to tell you that I understand, that it's okay, that I forgive you. Well, it's not, and I don't. You are leaving me again and asking me to lie for you in the same breath. Are you kidding? Go home. Go be a husband to a wife you don't love and pretend that it will fix what's wrong with you."

"She didn't do anything," Walt implored. "She was a wonderful wife. She wasn't cold or distant. If I had never met you, I would never have even dreamed of straying."

"Get off the cross, Walt. Someone else needs the wood."

"You don't get it—"

"Can you hear yourself? You don't get to play the martyr here. You aren't making some big sacrifice for the greater good. You are a coward. It is easier to get rid of a mistress than it is to get rid of a wife. It's that simple. You wanted us to be done—we're done. Now, please just go."

Walt, his eyes red and watery, moved around the counter. He reached out a hand to touch Thea's face.

"Do not touch me."

He dropped his hand, turned away and left.

The moment the door snapped shut, Thea slid down to the floor and cried. Great sobs wracked her body, and fat tears splashed onto the floor.

It was a long time before she calmed herself and went to bed, and even then, she didn't sleep.

To: Detective Thea Williams
From: Information Technician Gideon Arthur
CC: TPD Detectives Office Group Data Storage.
Subject: A. Oubier

Hey Thea,

I followed up on your request for information on "Anthony Oubier"- details below.

Name: Anthony Bertram Oubier
Born: January 11th, 2293 - Tenebrium native of Scottish descent
Current Address: Bedford Institute, Stygian Colony #7, Level 32
Spouse/Partner: Carol Oubier (deceased 2331)
Status: Cryogenically frozen, 2338

Note: There is an active marker on this file.
Note: There is an expired arrest warrant on this file, incomplete due to current status.

Sorry it isn't more. A lot of the files relating to Oubier are restricted at a level with far higher clearance than mine.

Hope this is enough,

Gid.

DOA

It was with a sense of weary resignation that Bill found himself at his third crime scene in as many nights, an unfavourable personal best. Two teenagers had called in a 7-6-7, possible dead body, near the Pleasure Quarter, and Bill had been the closest. Dispatch had advised that this 7-6-7 was most likely a prank due to the age and attitude of the callers. Dispatch had been wrong.

Bill's partner had called in sick, and stretched thin as they already were, he'd had no choice but to round his beat alone. He wished he wasn't alone now.

Standing at the mouth of a dark alley, it was clear that something was amiss. A rusted green dumpster had been pulled away from the wall to sit in the centre of the narrow gap between the two impossibly tall buildings, and the metal shutter to one side was dented as if something had been thrown against it. There was a dark pool slowly growing underneath the dumpster, and while it was too dark to see what colour the liquid was, Bill would have bet his life that on closer inspection, it would turn out to be red.

"Police." Bill called, raising his gun and shining his torch into the darkness. "Make yourself known."

He had no idea if there was anyone in the alley, but he thought it best to err on the side of caution. Slowly he moved to the dumpster and looked inside; nothing but rancid garbage. The smell was repugnant. The alleyway was so narrow that he had to move the dumpster out of the way to get behind it. When he did, he knew for sure that the 7-6-7 had not been a prank.

The body of a man in an expensive black and silver suit lay face down on the concrete. Both of his arms had been broken. Bill could tell this because of the horrible angle they jutted out at. Judging from the slashes on his clothes and the copious amount of blood present at the scene, he had been stabbed multiple times.

Bill knelt down to get a closer look as he brought his hand to his ear.

"Dispatch, this is Officer Fenske. I have a possible homicide in the alley between Killer Dame and Card Noir Casino, unidentified Black male."

Noticing the floral detailing on the suit, Bill moved around the body to get a good look at the face and sighed. "Scratch that, dispatch. It's Benjamin Pickford."

SPURNED

Thea had lain in bed for hours staring at the ceiling. She wanted more than anything to drift into unconsciousness, but sleep refused to claim her. The only memories she had in her new bed were ones of her and Walt, and they were tormenting her.

Their reunion had been brief, painfully so, but it had been just long enough to foster real hope, and that was the thing that caused her chest to ache. The loss of him felt like her chickens coming home to roost, but the loss of hope was devastating. She hated feeling this way and hated that it was because of a man; it made her feel like a swooning teenager. She had far more important things to worry about than Walt, and yet her mind kept making its way back to him.

Eventually, she got up and moved into the living room. Walt had left his coat thrown carelessly on the armchair that he had claimed as his.

She wanted to curl up next to it.

She wanted to burn it.

She left it where it was.

A gust of wind stirred her from her misery. She hadn't even noticed the docking bay window open. Torrez stood, framed by the luminescence of the city on the alighting platform, neither inside nor out. He was clutching his stomach. Even in silhouette, he looked awful.

"Hey, Querida," he said, his voice reedy.

"Drew!" Thea jumped to her feet and met him as he half tumbled inside. "You're bleeding." She pulled his arm around his shoulder and guided him to the couch.

"I'm fine...But you aren't." With a groan, he sat up straighter. His lips were pale, and his skin clammy. He looked slightly green. The patch of blood on the front of his shirt was too big to ignore. "O'Malley is one of them, one of the Gold Legion," he went on.

"What?" said Thea, aghast.

"He knows about Cleo—"

"How do you know about Cleo?"

"That doesn't matter," Torrez said urgently. "They are sending people after her."

"Why?"

"She worked for Medicorum, she is supposed to be in the SubLevel, she isn't a normal ghoul. Take your pick!"

"She was a medical researcher..."

"Yes, at Medicorum."

"That's why she was attacked. They wanted rid of her."

Thea got to her feet and paced the living room, willing Walt to answer her call, but as she brought her hand to her Cicada over and over, there was no reply.

"Fuck," she said. "He isn't going to answer to me."

Torrez didn't comment or question why. Thea felt a renewed rush of affection for him.

"What do you need?" Torrez asked. "What can I do?"

"You need to go back to the hospital."

"This is my fault. Let me help," said Torrez, struggling to keep himself upright.

"You can't help if you're dead," said Thea.

She pulled Torrez's hands from the wound in his stomach and unbuttoned his shirt for the bottom. As carefully as she could, she lifted the dressing there and examined the incision.

"I'm no doctor, but I think you've pulled some stitches."

"Nothing serious then," Torrez said, making a valiant effort to sit up, which caused a lethargic pulse of blood to spurt from the deep slit on his stomach.

Thea grabbed some clean gauze from the Medicus kit that had lain discarded since Bastion's visit and pressed it firmly over the wound.

"Do you have any V?" Torrez grunted. "Verve!" he yelled when Thea didn't catch on quickly enough.

"Yes, but it's dangerous, Drew."

"Gimme it. Thea, so help me, God..."

Against her better judgement, but well aware Torrez was not the only person in danger, Thea reached once more into the Medicus kit and pulled out an auto-injector and a small green bottle with a large "V" emblazoned on the label.

Torrez made quick work of filling the syringe, and without so much as a moment of hesitation, he plunged it into his thigh. The effect was immediate and slightly comical. He sat bolt upright as if hit with a jolt of electricity and jumped to his feet, the colour already returning to his face.

"Woo! That is quite the rush." Torrez checked his wounds. "Bleeding's stopped, too."

"For now. The comedown can be hellish. Promise me you will go back to a medical centre soon," Thea pleaded.

"I will. But first things first—Cleo and you."

"Fine," said Thea reluctantly. "I'm going to Walt's place to see if they've gone home. Go to Gin Ricky's and see if they're still there—I'll send you the address."

Elanor Miller

"They are after you too, Querida. Don't forget that."

INCRIMINATION

Bill hadn't seen his husband in days, and while he had hoped to go home to him that night, he knew it wasn't going to happen.

What should have been a routine crime scene had attracted a suspicious amount of attention, in his opinion. O'Malley had rushed in to relieve Orion Martin, and Onyx Legion soldiers had arrived with him to "protect the crime scene". It was a homicide in a single location with a single victim; the Crime Scene Unit should have scanned and recorded the scene, catalogued the evidence, then allowed the grim-sweepers to take the body back to the TPD morgue, but that hadn't happened. Instead, they had stood back while O'Malley alone searched for evidence pertaining to the killer, a ring of OL soldiers shielding him from view.

Bill had been standing in the rain, internally lamenting his aching knees, when O'Malley had called upon him.

"Fenske, get over here."

Reluctantly, Bill went to his side.

O'Malley was peering in the dumpster that had obscured the body from view when Bill had arrived. Where there had been nothing but trash, there was now a blood-encrusted blade sticking out of a torn refuse sack.

"You got one of those handy fingerprint scanners?" O'Malley asked, pointing at the knife.

Bill grunted affirmatively. He had long since abandoned the usual deferential manner beat cops were supposed to treat detectives with. O'Malley was a dirtbag, and Bill was too old and too experienced to be bothered about pretending otherwise.

"Well, do your damn job and scan it then."

Bill pulled the black pentagonal scanner from his pocket and affixed it to his palm. He closed his fist gently around it, and a moment later, it glowed blue.

Grudgingly, Bill leant over the edge of the dumpster and passed the scanner over the blade.

"Analysing," said an androgynous computerised voice in his ear. "Analysis complete. Fingerprint match. Detective Thea Persephone Williams."

IMBROGLIO

"Pickup, you asshole," Thea railed at Walt's voicemail as she rounded the corner onto his street.

She knew immediately that something was wrong. Tirtoff Avenue was busy like everywhere else in the city, but there were people dotted here and there that Thea recognised immediately as soldiers or cops. There was a man smoking on a stoop wearing an overcoat that didn't quite hide the bulk of his Onyx Legion armour underneath. A woman in a beautiful red dress, the cut of which was slightly too short to hide the thigh-holster she was sporting, and a pair of men wearing flak jackets over their waistcoats who, while appearing to shoot the breeze, kept glancing from the smoker, to Walt's building, and back again.

Thea had hoped that she could have gotten there before the Legion, Gold or Onyx. That way, all she had to do was go inside and explain to Walt and Cleo what was happening; now, she would have to sneak into the building and, worse still, out.

Thea slowly turned away and moved back around the corner, making sure she wasn't noticed and scanning the streets and buildings with her Seer as she walked.

The block that contained Walt's apartment building had a small square of concrete in the centre that allowed the restaurant parallel to his building to house its dumpsters, but it was sealed by a large gate making street access impossible. If she could gain access to the restaurant, she would be able to enter Walt's building from the back. She could only pray to gods she didn't believe in that as Cleo was unaware of the danger she was in, those who wished her ill would only have felt the need to watch the front entrance.

Kublai Khan's was a small Mongolian Restaurant owned by one Arban Batbold. He was affable in the extreme, with a thick head of dark hair and a seemingly permanent smile. He was more than happy to allow one of Tenebrium's finest access to the back of his premises. Thea thanked him warmly. She was genuinely grateful that this first part of what would be a very dangerous task had gone smoothly.

The back of Kublai Khan's was as Thea had expected the back of a restaurant to be. There was a fan embedded in the wall blasting warm air out from the kitchen, the door of which was propped open by an empty beer keg that doubled as a seat for those taking short smoke breaks. Two dumpsters sat open, piled high with neatly tied trash bags, and a delivery bicycle was resting in a bike rack. A slim alleyway only just wide enough to move the dumpsters along led back to the main street, though it was currently blocked by a heavy gate.

The only entrance to Walt's building from this shared space was a fire exit that was shut and, as Thea had expected, locked.

Thea's Cicada buzzed and "Torrez" flashed at the corner of her eye.

"Drew?"

"There's no one here. The place is empty. If they aren't with you..."

"We won't find her in time," Thea finished for him. "Okay. Okay," she said, pacing up and down in front of the door. "Torrez, I hate to ask—"

"Do it anyway." He was slightly too perky.

"Soldiers are staking out the front of the building, but there is a fire exit at the back. It's locked, but—"

"I'm on it. But Thea, if I get caught—I'll be shut out of the system, and they will know exactly what you're doing."

"I know."

"Well, all right then."

The fire department had access to a network that allowed them to lock and unlock all city installed fire doors. It would not be wise to be caught hacking into it, but what choice did they have?

Thea chewed her lip and continued to pace while she waited for Torrez to open the door. Finally, he said, "I think that's you, Querida. Good luck."

"Thank you. Go see a doctor, okay?"

Thea reached a nervous hand out to the round brass doorknob. It turned easily.

She was inside.

The fire exit opened into a grey concrete stairwell. Downwards led to the basement Boiler Room. Upwards to the apartments. Thea ran up six flights, then entered the residential area proper. She didn't have time or energy to run up hundreds of staircases, but the lift was dangerous; it came with stops, cameras, and the possibility of the wrong kind of company. Thankfully, when the doors opened, the elevator was empty.

Before she was ready, she was on Walt's floor. She was walking towards his door. She was knocking and then—

"Walt? Oh...Thea," Cleo said as she opened the door. She was slightly breathless as if she had run to open it. Her face fell when she saw who it was. "He's not here. Someone tossed our apartment. He's gone to the station."

They just looked at each other for a moment before Thea said, "Someone broke in—? It doesn't matter. I'm here to take you somewhere safe."

A change came across Cleo's face then. She had always had a kind and slightly wide-eyed air that made Thea think of child-like innocence, but now she looked more worldly somehow as if out of nowhere, she had developed an edge.

"They're coming for me, aren't they?" she said simply, like she had already resigned herself to it.

Thea blinked, not quite comprehending. "You know. You remember."

"When you work for Medicorum, you sell your soul. It's inevitable that you become acquainted with the devil."

Everything went black. The lights died, and they were plunged into darkness. Moments later, red emergency lights flicked on, bathing everything in an eerie incarnadine glow.

"They're here," Thea said, reaching forward and grabbing Cleo by the arm. She pulled her out into the corridor.

"What are you doing?" Cleo whispered as Thea pulled her along the hall. "Where are we going?"

Thea didn't answer. She led Cleo to an apartment three doors down from Walt's and knocked. "Police, open up. Please."

"What are you doing?" Cleo asked again.

"We have no out. No power means no elevator, which means they are coming up the stairs right now. They will have the building surrounded, so the roof is out. Hiding is all we can do. Police," Thea said, hammering on the door again. "Open up."

The door opened just wide enough that Thea could see one hazel eye.

"Detective Thea Williams."

"Mx Barker. What do you want?" The single eye looked from Thea to Cleo suspiciously.

"Mx, we need your help. May we come in?" Thea said, showing the person her badge. They ignored it.

The door opened and fraction wider, and Thea saw that Mx Barker was an elderly Native American person with warm copper skin lined by age. They had long glossy white hair in a braid that fell somewhere in the middle of their back and dark alert eyes that were in stark contrast to their advanced years.

Footsteps echoed from the stairway nearby out into the corridor; the person gave Thea a final piercing look and stepped aside.

"You two in trouble?" they asked, closing the door behind themselves and locking it.

"Something like that," Thea said noncommittally, moving quickly around the apartment marking all the possible points of entry.

"Police, are you?" Mx Barker asked, still standing at the door.

"I am. I'm Detective Thea William, and this is Cleo James. She's under my protection."

"Mx Barker will do, you don't need to know my first name. I doubt we will become bosom friends."

"Thank you for your help, Mx," Thea said, moving past them to listen at the door.

She heard a quickly stifled cough that told her the Gold Legion were just outside, then a thunderous crash. Cleo gasped, and Thea pressed a finger to her lips to quiet her. So, they had burst through Walt's door just like they had done on that awful night two years ago. Thea listened hard. There were gunshots, shouting and crashing, the sounds of splintering wood and shattering glass.

"Whoever is after you two doesn't sound too happy," Mx Barker said, though they didn't seem at all perturbed by the goings-on.

"They're gonna search the building, apartment by apartment," Thea said, ignoring Mx Barker's comment. "We can't stay here."

"Get in the bathroom and close the door," said Mx Barker in clipped tones. When it looked as though Thea was about to argue, they added, "Get."

"Mx—"

"You came in here knowing that this could happen, and it has. You have involved me whether I like it or not, but they will not burst in here and destroy my home. I won't have it. I won't leave two young women at the mercy of those in power either. Now do as you're told and get."

Thea nodded and pulled Cleo into the neat bathroom.

"We can't let them do this," Cleo whispered urgently. Her hands were shaking.

"We don't have a choice," Thea said, holding a hand up for silence.

They were in the bathroom for mere moments when they heard thunderous knocks at neighbouring doors and then finally on Mx Barker's door.

"What?" Mx Barker snapped as they opened the door.

"We have reason to believe that a ghoul has escaped the SubLevel and taken refuge in this building. For your safety, Mx, I need you to step into the hall while we search the premises."

"Premises? You mean while you search my home. Not a chance."

"Mx—"

"Don't you 'Mx' me. This is a one-bedroom apartment, and you think I'm hiding some crazed addict? Where have I put them? Under the bed? In the washing machine? Obviously, brains don't come with the badge."

"We have reports—"

"Nuts to your reports, you are not setting foot in my home."

"It's for your own safety. I really must insist."

"Insist away, but you aren't coming in unless it's through me."

Thea opened the bathroom door to the smallest crack and peered through the gap. Two Onyx Legion soldiers, one tall, one squat, were bearing down on the shrunken Mx Barker, but Mx Barker was standing firm. They radiated an odd sense of power; formidable didn't do them justice in Thea's steadily growing opinion.

The soldier's stepped back slightly to mutter amongst themselves, and Thea could tell that they were contemplating going through Mx Barker. One of the soldiers brought a hand to his holstered gun, and Thea was about to throw open the bathroom door when he said, "Very well, Mx. As you wish. But, if you see anything untoward or feel like you are in any danger, call the authorities."

"Fat chance," Mx Barker said, slamming the door in his face.

Even with the door shut, Thea distinctly heard the soldier say, "Old bat."

"Thank you," Thea said, moving back into the living room. "We owe you."

"You owe me nothing, and I want nothing from you. You can wait here until they leave, then I want you out."

And they did wait. In silence.

Thea sat on the very edge of an old rocking chair that faced the main door, ready to spring to her feet if any nefarious someones tried to enter, but no one did.

An hour later, Thea and Cleo were thanking Mx Barker and heading back towards the fire exit.

"Where are we going?" Cleo asked, panting as she ran down the stairs in Thea's wake.

"I'll figure that out once we get you out of here," Thea said without slowing.

"Thea, it's not that simple. I'll need another dose soon."

"Dose?" Thea said, stopping halfway down a flight near the sixtieth floor.

"If I don't keep taking Quietus..."

"You'll turn back into a ghoul," Thea finished for her. "How long?"

"A few hours maybe. Twelve at most."

The fire exit was ajar when they reached it, but Thea was sure she hadn't left it so.

She swore under her breath.

"What? What is it?" Cleo said worriedly, keeping close to Thea.

"I closed the door on my way in."

Cleo's eyes widened as she understood what Thea was telling her.

"Are we trapped?" she asked. Thea could see Cleo was starting to panic. It made the veins under her eyes pulse. "Thea?" she demanded, her voice rising. "Are we trapped here?"

Thea thought through their options. If the back was covered, the front certainly was and exiting via either was probably a death sentence for them both. She doubted they wanted Cleo alive after her surprising survival of their last attempt to silence whatever she may know. The roof was out too, as it was very likely that there were tactical armed transporters positioned there in case they tried to hop a Jonk from the roof. The building was flanked on either side by commercial properties with no through access. They couldn't hide in the building, and they couldn't escape by any obvious means.

"Come out, come out wherever you are," a booming voice called from all around, somehow magnified. It reverberated through her as her heart sank into her stomach.

"Yes," Thea said finally. "We are trapped."

"What are we going to do?" Cleo said with a skittish air.

Thea didn't reply. What were they going to do?

"Thea! Say something." Cleo shook her roughly.

"I'm thinking!" Thea snapped. She wracked her brain for anything that would help them get out of this impossible situation free and with their lives. "This is an old building."

"What?"

"This building is over a hundred years old, right?"

"I-I think so. Why does that matter?" Cleo had sat down on the stairs and wrapped her arms around herself.

"Detective Williams, we know you're here. On the count of ten. You come out, or we come in," the voice threatened so loudly that both women simultaneously brought their hands to their ears in pain. "One."

"There should be an underground parking structure in the basement. Move, now."

"Two, three, four, five, six, seven, eight, nine, ten."

The fire door was kicked open with such power it came off its hinges, but neither Thea nor Cleo was there to greet the soldiers as they entered the building.

SCAPEGOAT

Lewis Avery didn't enjoy visiting Medicorum. It was too clean and too quiet. He preferred the smoke and the noise of a casino or a bar, where he could indulge in some quality violence, or booze, or a bet, depending on his mood.

Whether he enjoyed it or not, however, he came when Dr Maxwell called.

The doctor was sitting behind his desk in his impressive office come laboratory. Impressionist sunrises hung in slim frames on two of the four walls. The others were lined with lab equipment and bookcases filled with experimental data in thick binders.

"The job is done?" the doctor asked, not looking up from the report he was annotating.

"The pimp is dead. I took the files he had on him. He didn't have any of our faces on record, but he did have the images of the Styxx deliveries. I took care of it," Avery said arrogantly. "Oh, and I planted the knife with the cop's prints on it."

"A yes or no answer will do in future. I find it's best not to boldly declare one's iniquitous exploits."

Avery faltered slightly. "Yes, sir," he said unsurely. There was a dangerous something in the doctor's voice that made him feel suddenly ill at ease. "Is that all?"

"Yes," said the doctor, waving an impetuous hand. "In fact, no. You've had dealings with Walter James, is that correct?"

"Played cards with him, once or twice," said Avery hedging his bets. He wasn't sure what answer Maxwell wanted, but he was sure he wanted to give the correct one.

"And the altercation where you would have beaten him to death if you hadn't been stopped." The doctor's eyes were narrowed, and his eyebrows drawn down as he surveyed Avery.

"Uh, yeah. He threatened Mr Kelly, I think."

"So, he'd have a reason not to like you very much?"

"I guess so."

"That's useful. Could you pass me the binder from the top shelf?"

"Sure," said Avery, shaken by the odd direction the conversation was taking.

He moved to the bookshelves nonetheless and reached up for the binder the doctor had indicated. He was convulsing on the ground before he realised that he was being tased, and then he was unconscious.

IT SHOULD HAVE

The subterranean garage was dark and dusty. Cobwebs were strung thickly between the long-forgotten concrete columns. Thea used the flashlight attached to her gun to navigate the gloom.

"There has to be a riser here. The transporters had to get up to street level somehow," Thea said as she squinted around the large open room.

"Thea," Cleo said, tugging at Thea's sleeve. "I need to get out of here."

"I'm working on it."

"No. I need to get out of here. This garage."

Thea had never set foot inside the SubLevel, but she was willing to bet that it was reminiscent of the dank gloom that surrounded them. She took Cleo's hand and gripped it tightly, pulling Cleo with her as she searched for an exit, letting her know that she wasn't going to leave her. Cleo's palm was damp, and she trembled, her breathing shallow and quick.

"There's a Jonk here."

Thea followed Cleo's pointing finger with her eyes and saw that there was indeed a gleaming black and red Jonckheere transporter hiding in the darkness. The Jonk's ID tags pronounced it to be new, the most recent model, and a privately-owned vehicle.

"No one owns a transporter anymore," Thea muttered. "Let's go," she added more loudly, jogging over to the Jonk.

"You don't know the start code or have the owner's fingerprints!"

"Police have a universal override. Now come on!"

Thea placed her hand on the right-side handle and waited.

"Fingerprint not recognised," the Jonk chimed in an automated singsong voice. "Please state a valid exception identity, or the system will begin anti-theft protocols."

"Detective Thea Williams, badge number 0131J, stationed at the thirty-third."

"Checking credentials," there was a pause. Thea imagined she could hear shouting and crashing from the upper floors, but it wasn't possible from the depths of the garage, then, "Accepted."

The transporter came to life, exuding light from within. Thea got inside, beckoning Cleo to do the same.

The interior was beautiful, all leather and highly polished chrome. The Liquid Light Display that shone up from the dashboard onto the windscreen was the palest of blues, so much so it was almost clear. There were only seats enough for three people along a single couch-like row situated at the back. They sat at each end, the free seat between them.

"Initiate manual controls," Thea said loudly.

The seat jacked forward, bringing Thea and Cleo barely a foot from the dashboard, as a gleaming chrome steering wheel unfolded itself on the driver's side in front of Thea. As soon as she placed her hands on the wheel, the Jonk reversed, of its own volition, from its parking space into the centre of the deserted garage and began to rise.

A shaft of light broke over them as a large circular hole opened overhead, allowing a perfect view of the Slipstream Highway high above. Below, the garage flooded with faceless soldiers clad all in black, and the Jonk had only just breached the street when they began to fire upon Thea and Cleo. The pitter-patter of bullets on the bottom of the Jonk sounded more like hailstones as they gained still more height.

The moment the Jonk was free of the garage, Thea took control. She veered hard to the right causing a group of legionaries who had been waiting on the street to dive out of the way.

Cleo gripped the edge of her seat so tightly that her knuckles paled as Thea steered them through narrow streets, tight alleys, and winding snickets. Patently, their would-be captors had not expected them to escape via transporter, and they were not quick enough to give chase. It wasn't long before Thea was able to join the Slipstream Highway heading for safety.

"Where are we going?" Cleo asked after a few minutes.

"My sister's place," Thea said distractedly as she tried to navigate the growing traffic.

"Thea?" Cleo said, sounding worried.

"What?"

"I think that black Jonk is following us."

Thea glanced out the back window and knew at once that Cleo was right. Keeping the standard tailing distance of two lengths at all times, the black Jonk was carefully shadowing their movements.

"Hold on," Thea said as she pulled the Jonk sharply into a dead end and killed the engine, hoping that the camouflage of the ever-moving tide of traffic had allowed them to escape unnoticed for the moment.

They waited in the semi-darkness, Thea was sure they hadn't shaken their pursuers, and she was right. Blinding spotlights shined down on the streets that could be seen from their tenuous hiding place and began to peer down adjoining alleyways.

Should they move? Would they be more or less likely to be caught if they stayed put? Would those chasing them think to check a dead-end where there was no means of escape but through?

The pure white light that seared her corneas was the answer. Blindly, Thea pulled straight up. She could feel the Jonk soar skywards as Cleo screamed beside her. She blinked away the bright spots in her vision just in time to see they were about to collide with another Jonk obliviously travelling on its way. Thea tugged the wheel to the left, narrowly avoiding a collision with the other Jonk, but sending them careening into a nearby building. The Jonk bounced off the brick and spun out of control, hitting a police transporter that had joined the hunt for them.

Thea swerved their new foe and, pulling sharply upwards once more, managed to join the ever-moving flow of traffic. The TPD transporter and several sleek black ones followed suit, but they were slowed by the Jonk tide.

Thea bobbed in and around, above and below the other vehicles, as those chasing them fell further and further behind. It wasn't long before they had lost them entirely and were free, for the moment, to make their way to the safe house that had been Cora's home.

Cora had lived on the outskirts of the city, where the edge of the colony and the open ocean was a visible reminder that they were still on the earth. On very clear days, the other colonies could be seen in their hundreds, huge and conical, like lightning rods embedded deep into the ocean floor.

They hadn't said a word in nearly an hour by the time Thea caught the first glimpse of the tiny apartment building that her sister had loved. It was only seven stories and made of red sandstone. It looked like something from another era. Thea's stomach filled with butterflies as she landed the Jonk in the docking station across the street. She had been paying Cora's rent for the last two years, but she hadn't been able to bring herself to step inside since the disappearance. It felt wrong to be using someone else's home as a hideout, but what choice did she have?

Thea looked up at the building. She hadn't realised she had stopped walking until Cleo said, "What's wrong?"

"Cora disappeared not long after you did. We never found her."

"This must be hard for you."

"Everything will be covered in dust. It's like admitting she's gone."

"We can take a minute," Cleo said softly. She moved to stand beside Thea and just waited. Her presence was oddly calming.

"Okay," Thea said after a moment. "Let's go."

The inside of Cora's apartment was indeed dusty. Cobwebs hung from all corners and doorways, some with the skeletal remains of unfortunate spiders curled up in the tangles. Other than the obvious signs of emptiness, it was exactly as Thea remembered it, with everything draped in shawls and crystals on every free surface. Pictures cluttered the windowsill and bookcases. The kitchen with its tiny table served as the divide between it and the living room, which was all squashy couches. Inside, Thea felt closer to Cora than she had even before she had disappeared. She would have loved to look around, to reminisce, to perhaps take some of the pictures that were scattered around the room, but now wasn't the time to reconnect with her twin.

"Stay here," Thea said to Cleo, who was examining a picture of the twins swimming in a large outdoor pool. "Don't take any calls from anyone other than me or Walt—"

"I don't have a Cicada."

"Good. I'll be back with some food, but I need to go to the station. This has gotten bigger than we can handle on our own, and we need to find you some more Quietus. I won't be long."

"Thea?" Cleo said just as Thea reached out a hand for the doorknob.

"Yeah?" she said, turning back to look at her lover's wife.

Cleo appeared to chew over what she wanted to say in her mind. "Why are you helping me?"

"What do you mean?"

Another pause.

"I'm the only thing standing between you and him. He'd still be yours if I hadn't come back."

It was like someone had poured a bucket of cold water over her; this was a conversation Thea had hoped never to have. She didn't know what to say. She'd had a suspicion that Cleo remembered more than she admitted to Walt, but it didn't matter. What could you say to a woman whose husband you had slept with? And not just once, over and over, at work, in their home, at every opportunity. What could you say to the man you love's wife?

"He was never mine."

"That never stopped you before."

Cleo might as well have slapped her in the face, but it was true, and Thea knew she deserved much worse than candour.

"It should have, and I'm sorry it didn't." She would do Cleo the courtesy of not having to hear self-gratifying apologies or excuses. Thea owed her that at least.

"I wish we could have been friends," Cleo said unexpectedly, like she had measured Thea up and found her worthy.

"Me too," Thea said, and with one final look at Cleo, she left and headed back towards the TPD.

OLD FASHIONED

"What can I get you, sir?

"Old fashioned, keep the cherry."

French 75 was bustling; every seat was taken, and those forced to stand were crammed into any and all gaps between the tables and booths. Walt was continually jostled by drinkers trying to make their way through the speakeasy. The chatter was so loud it was like white noise. Even as busy as the place was, it only took the bartender a few moments before he placed the whiskey cocktail in front of Walt.

Walt created circles on the side of the glass in the condensation with his index finger. He picked it up, smelled the sweet, rich contents then replaced it back on the counter. He was torturing himself. Ever since Torrez has doused him in tequila, the need to drink was so powerful that it was causing actual physical pain. He deserved it. He cursed himself as he watched the ice melt tantalisingly into the glistening honey liquid. He had finally had the one thing he had wanted more than anything, and he had given it up.

It helped, in a twisted way, that he had destroyed any chance of a relationship with Thea. He had left her twice now, and she was a woman who knew her worth; it was one of the many things Walt loved about her. She would never allow a third time, but knowing he had extinguished any hope for them didn't make him want her any less.

He loved Cleo, he just wasn't in love with her, but still, he owed her his loyalty, they were supposed to be a team, partners, and he was committed to being the husband he should have been from the beginning, but he thought about his feelings for Thea much as he thought of his alcoholism; addictions aren't easily conquered or ignored.

She had been calling him almost non-stop for the last couple of hours, but he wouldn't answer. Currently, it was the only step he was willing to take towards that special brand of sobriety. He didn't want to talk to her, to hear how badly he had behaved, how much of a disappointment he was, how he had shown her once and for all that the man she had loved no longer existed. He was trying desperately to be that man. Maybe in time, if he managed to honour Cleo the way she deserved, he would prove to himself that he could be that man again.

If he could stop from taking even a sip of the cocktail in front of him, maybe he would be able to stay away from Thea.

He stood up from his chair, dropped some credit chips on the bar, downed the old fashioned in one heavenly gulp, and left.

UNDER ARREST

Thea left the stolen Jonk a block or two away from Walt's, hoping the owner would be able to recover it, and decided to take the subway to the police station. It was only three stops, but she thought she was less likely to be seen or noticed there.

Steep, winding steps led down into Dunand Subway Station, the platform of which was immersed in nearly two feet of water. Some commuters huddled standing on benches, while others accepted their fates and stood miserably in the murky water allowing it to seep slowly up their trouser legs. The bottle-green ceramic tiles that lined the walls, columns, and the curved ceiling glimmered with the refracted light from the signage and the glow from the strip lights overhead. The submerged station's only saving grace was the fact that trains ran roughly every two minutes.

Thea stopped for a moment on the last dry stair, steeling herself for the cold she was about to plunge her legs into, but the water was tepid as it filled her shoes. Somehow it felt worse. The cloudy water completely obscured the concrete floor beneath it; Thea was very careful not to trip as she descended the last few stairs. Standing on the platform proper, the water reached past her knees.

The platform was quiet. None of those waiting for the train were speaking or using their various devices; they all averted their eyes, stared at the timetables hanging from above, or blankly at the posters that flashed on the walls. Thea waded further out, away from the stairs; anyone she passed seemed to shrink away from her. She glanced from bedraggled face to bedraggled face; they all looked expectant, nervous. A trill of disquiet went through her, piquing her senses, allowing her to scent imminent danger.

All at once, every light on the platform went out. Thea stood rooted to the spot, straining her ears to hear even the merest hint of what was to come. Small patches of light flared all around her one at a time, two at a time, a few here and there until the room was illuminated by hundreds of tiny lights combining into a blaze. It took Thea a moment to realise what they were. Every person on the platform, with scared looks on their faces, was using their Index to project a single bright image into the air.

Her image.

Thea stared around at her own face as it stared unblinkingly back at her from all sides. Words circled her holographic countenance; they said, "WANTED FOR MURDER," in large glowing letters.

"Detective Williams," a hugely magnified voice called, the same voice she had heard at Walt's building. The sound bounced off the tile and reverberated around the station, making it impossible to tell where the speaker was. "Surrender yourself now. You are under arrest."

"What for?" Thea called back, slowly inching her hand towards the gun at her side.

The strip lights above flickered back into life, but instead of the dull whitish-yellow that was the norm, they were an eerie red that cast just as much shadow as light.

"The murder of Benjamin Pickford."

Thea's heart stopped.

"He's not dead," Thea said with no real conviction.

She could see the speaker now. Drenched in crimson, he was dressed in the black Onyx Legion armour, but his mask was smooth, featureless, and gold. It reflected the room back at her as he walked out of the tunnel and into view. He was followed by a mix of Onyx Legion soldiers and police that Thea recognised from the TPD, Bill among them; he looked miserable.

"Come quietly, Detective. This is neither the time nor the place to make a scene."

"And if I don't?"

A shot fired from behind the gold masked man, hitting the water in front of Thea and causing it to splash her face and clothes.

"I don't have any strikes, and we don't kill for first offences. So, your threats are empty," Thea said, her voice challenging.

"But Miss Williams, you murdered Lewis Avery."

"Who?" Thea had never heard of this Lewis Avery.

"'Who?' It takes a very cold and calculating killer to forget a victim so quickly." His voice was haughty and silky in a way that made Thea want to gag.

Refracted on the water, Thea caught sight of a shadow. She dived behind the nearest pillar just in time as a series of shots rang out, hitting the place she had been standing moments before. Chaos erupted as the soldiers and cops flooded the station, and the commuters scattered. Shot after shot was fired at the pillar Thea stood behind. The tiles had shattered and fallen into the water; it wouldn't be long before the pillar crumbled under the onslaught. Thea dived out from behind it, taking carefully aimed shots at the golden masked man on her way to the pillar opposite. She didn't want to fire back blindly, surrounded as they were by innocent bystanders, but she couldn't remain where she was.

"No!" Thea heard Bill shout. "You said we were going to bring her in alive! She's one of us."

TENEBRIUM

The trains must have been stopped, Thea realised. How else could the gold masked man and his compatriots have entered from the tunnel? And before her mind had finished forming a plan, she sprinted out from her hiding place and dived onto the tracks. The water there was waist height.

Thea waded as fast as the flooding would allow her into the relative darkness of the tunnel at the opposite end, pulse rounds hitting the water all around her. A bullet skiffed the back of her hand, causing her to drop her gun. She cursed loudly in pain and frustration as it sank beneath the murk, but she didn't stop to retrieve her weapon. She flexed her fingers; it was only a graze; the damage, though it was causing a trail of blood behind her in the water, was only superficial. It had been enough though; she was now alone in the dark with no way to defend herself.

She ran blindly deeper and deeper into the gloom. The only light was cast by small bulbs spaced evenly along the tracks at her feet, but they were dulled considerably by the murky water they were submerged in. Sloshing and splashing in the distance told her that, as she was expecting, she had been followed.

Someway into the tunnel, Thea came to a fork. She went left because it was closest to her and was rewarded for her choice with a set of stairs that led onto a thin maintenance walkway out of the water that ran parallel with the tracks. She climbed the stairs gratefully, her pace quicker now she was on dry land. The metal walkway twisted this way and that with the track. Thea had no idea where she was or how she would get out of the tunnels, but that also made her hard to find.

There were several doorways set back from the path in deep inlets, but all were locked. Thea tried door after door to no avail. She was getting tired, and she knew they would catch up to her sooner or later.

"Spread out. She can't have gotten far." The words echoed slightly, far closer than was comfortable.

She was lost, she had no idea where the next platform was, and she was facing a small army of heavily armed and heavily trained combatants. It was time to thin the herd while she searched for an escape. At the next inlet, Thea stopped. She pressed her back into the wall and waited. Soon she heard swashing footsteps running along the tracks. It sounded like two people, three at most.

The clang of boots on metal told her that they had climbed the walkway. Thea readied herself, and when she caught the first glimpse of an assailant, she hit him hard in the throat with the side of her hand to stop him from crying out, then grabbed him by the flack jacket and pulled him around in an arc that ended with his face colliding with the wall she had hidden against, he was knocked out cold. He had brought a fellow, Thea saw just in time as the man, a beat cop Thea knew only as "Tinker", raised the butt of his rifle. She caught it with both hands before he could hit her with it and, after a moment of tussling, thrust it back at him, breaking his nose. He let go of the gun to hold a hand to his bleeding face. Thea showed him no mercy. Using it like a bat, she swung the rifle at his head. It connected with a horrible crunch, and Tinker joined his friend, unconscious on the floor.

Thea paused, listening for any signs of life, but heard nothing. She stepped fully out from the alcove, confident that she was safe. The moment she did so, however, a shot rang out. It missed, hitting the wall next to her, but only just. Thea vaulted over the railing and back onto the waterlogged track, moving towards her attacker. It was an Onyx Legion Soldier, a slender, but muscular White man with red hair slicked back and a large moustache that was neatly twirled at the ends. Surprised by Thea's decision to move closer, he fired wildly, missing with every shot.

When she had closed the gap between them, Thea grabbed the barrel of the gun and twisted it around, bending the redhead's wrist at an odd angle and causing him to yelp in pain. He continued to fire, the barrel of the gun getting hotter in her palm. She punched him square in the face, then kneed him hard in the stomach. He reeled back, letting go of the gun as he did so. Thea trained it upon him, he kicked water at her causing her to momentarily lose sight of him, but it was enough. He lunged forward, grabbing her behind the knees. He used his shoulder to force her backwards, sending them both under the water.

The redhead punched her hard in the stomach, winding her and causing the small amount of air she had managed to gulp before she was submerged to burst from her lungs, and then he was gone. Thea couldn't see in the roiled water. She kicked out, but hit nothing. She scrambled to her feet, spluttering as her head breached the surface. Gasping, she scanned the water for the redhead, but he was nowhere to be seen. She fired into the flood at random, but no bullets came out. The gun just sparked in her hand. Cursing, she threw it aside. Then, with an almighty splash, he was behind her, his arm around her neck, his forearm pressed under her chin, making it impossible for her to breathe as he dragged her back to the depths.

Thea kicked and punched every part of him she could reach, but to no avail. His hold on her was far too strong. She was starting to see black spots; she would lose consciousness at any moment. She thrust her hands up behind her head, and her thumbs found their target. She gouged them savagely into his eye sockets. He released her at once, wailing in agony. Thea foundered to her feet, clutching her throat and coughing. They were both above water now. Taking a moment to recover, they circled each other.

The redhead's eyes were puffy and dripping profusely. He blinked rapidly, trying to clear them, and before Thea had fully caught her breath, he darted forward, but this time she was quicker. She raised her leg and unleashed a sidekick that collided with his chest. The water removed much of the kick's power, but it was enough to stop him in his tracks. The redhead lunged at her again, fists raised, but she easily ducked his attempts to hit her. Bobbing underneath a particularly wide haymaker, Thea brought her fist up in an uppercut that connected with his jaw with such force that Thea was sure she had cracked his teeth. As he faltered, she moved in for the coup de grace, but before she could land a finishing blow, a voice called her name.

Thea whipped around to see Bill standing a ways down the tunnel. He had his gun levelled at her chest.

"Bill?"

"Don't fight. You'll only make this worse for yourself," he said, his voice shaking. "I don't want to hurt you."

"Bill, I didn't do this. I didn't kill anyone," Thea implored, raising her hands in a gesture of surrender and walking slowly towards him, all the while keeping the redhead in her sights.

"I believe you, but we work within the law. They have reason to take you in, so let them. Let the investigation pan out. The truth will clear your name," he said miserably.

"You really believe that?" Thea asked.

"I have to. If I didn't, I wouldn't be able to do my job." Still keeping his gun trained on Thea with one hand, Bill reached into his pocket with the other and pulled out a pair of handcuffs. "Please don't fight me. I don't want to hurt you," he said again.

"You think you could?" Thea said, the merest hint of a threat in her voice.

"Probably not. I'm just hoping I won't have to try," he said, disconsolate.

Sure, she could fight off Bill and maybe the next attacker and the next, but she was lost and outnumbered. Her wanted posters would be all over the news by now, and where could she go that they wouldn't find her?

Seeing that continuing to struggle would be futile, Thea held her hands out in front of her and allowed Bill to cuff her.

"I'm sorry," he said quietly as he fastened the metal ring around her wrists.

"Remember this when they execute me," Thea said bitingly.

The walk to the next platform was short and silent, Bill keeping hold of her, guiding her by the arm as the redhead followed behind, his hand never leaving the trigger of the gun he had retrieved from the water.

When the station and its platform came into full view, Thea nearly laughed. They were at Tenebrium Proper, the station closest to the TPD. The platform was lined with police and the Onyx Legion, the gold masked man standing in front of them. Thea couldn't see his face, but she imagined he was smiling a wide and malicious grin.

He helped her up onto the platform, then, holding her by the upper arm, marched her from the station to the Police Transporter that was ready and waiting outside.

"Enjoy the view from the highway," he said as he threw her roughly inside. "You won't be seeing the city lights for a while."

THIS ISN'T OVER

Walt hunkered down in the chair behind Thea's desk. Using her higher clearance to access the Data Stream, he searched the security footage near his apartment, hoping that with all the chaos of the shift change, no one would notice that he was there. So far, he had been lucky; there appeared to be some kind of incident occupying most of his colleagues, and as a result, his presence in the bullpen had gone unnoticed, or at the very least, uncommented on.

Until now.

"Officer James," the captain called loudly over the hubbub.

Walt thought for one ludicrous moment about keeping his head down and pretending he hadn't heard her, but he knew he would never get away with such a childish course of action. Heaving a deep sigh, he stood up and walked over to where she waited near the elevator. She was, as ever, dressed in ivory tones, but her face showed uncharacteristic signs of worry.

"Follow me," she said, turning on her heel and moving swiftly in the direction of her office.

"What's wrong?" Walt asked, lengthening his strides to keep up with her.

She didn't reply.

Once inside her office, Walt automatically sat in the chair in front of her desk, the captain sat in her armchair behind it. Walt could tell something serious had happened. He felt a tingle of fear prick the hairs on the back of his neck. He had received some of the worst news of his life in this chair and some of the worst reprimands. He was uncomfortably aware of the scent of bourbon on his breath.

"Thea has been arrested," the captain said without preamble. "For the murder of Benjamin Pickford, and Lewis Avery. They have added assault and resisting arrest to the bill."

Walt blinked, the information taking a moment to permeate his brain. "No," he said because it was all he could think of.

"She's downstairs in processing right now," the captain was speaking quickly, a sense of urgency clear in her tone. "Don't react."

There was a knock on the door, and Bill entered without waiting for an invitation. He looked hangdog as he avoided looking at Walt.

"Where would you like her, ma'am?" he asked the captain, his eyes resolutely on the carpet.

"Interrogation Three," the captain said, getting to her feet and walking around her desk to follow Bill back out into the bullpen. When she reached Walt, she whispered, "I believe her, but I can't help her; my hands are tied. Don't get yourself killed."

Walt trailed the captain back into the detective's office just as the elevator doors opened.

Walt inhaled sharply.

Thea was flanked on all sides by Onyx Legion soldiers, her hands cuffed behind her back. Her bottom lip was burst and bleeding heavily down her chin, neck and chest, a large bruise was purpling on her right cheekbone, threatening to black her eye and her neck was red and scratched. Far from looking beaten into submission, however, she looked alert and defiant.

Now, Walt knew what the captain meant. It was hard to stand still and watch, but he knew running forward and attempting to rest Thea from their clutches would do neither of them any good. He had to be calm, and he had to be smart.

A crowd had gathered almost like a perverse honour guard. Walt saw Torrez step to the front, his own anger and worry reflected on Torrez's face.

Thea was frogmarched roughly out of the elevator. She spat blood on the floor, causing one of the soldiers holding her to shake her as if she had misbehaved. Walt clenched his fists tightly, willing himself to wait. When they passed him, her eyes met his for a moment, but her look told him nothing, and then she was gone.

"All right, everyone. Show's over. Get back to work," the captain said, for the entire detective's office had stopped to watch Thea being taken in. They murmured amongst each other, casting suspicious looks at Walt and Torrez.

When the shock had died down and the onlookers had gone back to their various tasks, Torrez made his way over to Walt.

"You should have been there. If she hadn't been trying to save your wife, this never would have happened," Torrez said with a falsely casual smile as if they were discussing the weather. "You're never where you need to be." Torrez clapped him on the back; to anyone watching, it would have looked friendly, but it was far too forceful for Walt to misconstrue it as such.

"What do you mean she was trying to save my wife?" Walt whispered, also trying to give off the appearance that he and Torrez were just shooting the breeze.

"The GL are in the precinct."

"I know. I'm looking right at one."

"I am the least of your problems. O'Malley is one of them, and he knows Cleo is out. They're looking for her."

"What? Why?"

"Use whatever brain cells the bourbon has left you—she worked for Medicorum."

"Where is she?"

"I don't know. Thea tried to warn you, but when she couldn't, she went to protect Cleo herself. That was the last I heard from her until..." Torrez nodded towards the elevator.

"Fuck," Walt said, running a hand through his hair. "I'll fix this."

Torrez scoffed derisively. "Fix this? You did this. This is your fault. I know you've known Cleo was alive this whole time."

"Does Thea know?" Walt stepped in closer, lowering his voice.

"You scumbag," Torrez spat.

"You tell her and—"

"You'll what? You're a broke-down bastard. Get out of my face." He gave Walt a final contemptuous look and turned away from him.

The corridor that held the TPD's ten interrogation rooms was grim by design. It was cold and dark, all bare grey brick and stainless steel. It was devised to create a feeling of fear and isolation, and it succeeded. The deathly quiet could drive a person mad.

O'Malley was leaning casually against the door of Interrogation Room Three, dressed in a dark green suit his salary shouldn't have afforded. He gave Walt a self-satisfied smile as he approached.

"Where do you think you're going, Officer?" O'Malley sneered.

"When Thea gets her phone call, we both know she's gonna call me anyway, so you might as well let me through," Walt said, bearing down upon O'Malley.

"Do we, though? Do we know that? I heard a rumour your wife is back in the picture. If I were Thea, you'd be the last person I'd wanna see."

Finding buttons to press, Walt thought, was a talent of O'Malley's.

"Move, or I'll move you," Walt said, staring O'Malley down.

"Fine, fine," O'Malley said, moving aside. He projected an air of supreme indifference that worried Walt; it was never a good thing when a notorious coward suddenly came across bold. "They've charged her with resisting arrest too, just so you know." His smile was malevolent.

"What's your point?"

"Two murders, resisting arrest, and assault on officers of the law," O'Malley counted on his fingers. "That's three strikes and then some. Sounds like a hangin' case to me."

Walt lunged for O'Malley, grabbing him by his lapels and slamming him into the wall. Walt was so much taller that holding O'Malley so they were eye to eye meant that the shorter man's feet dangled inches above the ground.

"Go ahead. Then it's your third strike. The thought makes me giddy."

Walt dropped O'Malley, but didn't step back, meaning O'Malley's nose was level with Walt's chest.

"You know, I thought you were just the office jackass, but it turns out you're a sadistic son of a bitch. I'm almost impressed. And you're right, what I'm planning to do to you would cost me my last strike. Thing is, you wouldn't be around to see it," Walt paused to allow his meaning to sink in. "Let me through the door, or I'm gonna call your bluff, and I'm gonna do it with my fists."

"This ain't over," O'Malley said belligerently.

"Yeah, it is," Walt said.

O'Malley slid sideways along the wall to get away from Walt, then fished a key from his trouser pocket and inserted it into the lock of the interrogation room. He flung the door wide and stepped back.

"Get in there before I change my mind," he snarled.

Walt smiled, tickled by O'Malley's newfound impotence. He watched O'Malley to the end of the corridor, then entered the interrogation room and closed the door behind him. He barely had a chance to glance around at the chilly metal-filled interior before Thea was in his arms, hugging him, but there was a cold rigidity to her body, the connection they shared absent.

"Cleo is safe. She's at my sister's place," she whispered softly in his ear before wrenching herself free and moving back to sit behind the plain stainless-steel table. There were droplets of blood on the floor and a small pool of it on the tabletop in front of where Thea sat.

"Are you okay?" Walt asked urgently.

"I'm fine," she said, wincing. The cut on her lip was still oozing.

Walt looked Thea over, taking note of every cut and every bruise. His face must have betrayed his thoughts because Thea said, "Walt, I'm fine."

"What happened?" Walt asked, taking the seat opposite.

"They were waiting for me at Dunand. I have no idea how they found me, but they had orders to kill if necessary."

"Who hurt you?"

"The lip?" Thea gestured unnecessarily towards her face. "A gift from O'Malley in booking. He needed me in handcuffs before he was brave enough to hit me. The rest was when I was trying to lose the OL."

"Thea, I'm so sorry. This is all my fault," he said, reaching for her hand. She withdrew it from his reach.

"No. No, we are not doing this. This is not another thing you get to feel guilty about. You don't get to punish yourself for this. I made my choice just like you made yours. Save your wife. There is nothing you can do for me right now."

"You didn't have to protect her."

"Yes, I did," Thea said simply.

Walt pulled a handkerchief from his pocket and handed it to Thea. She took it and dabbed gently at her lip.

"I'm going to get you out of this," Walt said.

"I'm not the one who needs your help. Cleo is out there alone with people hunting her. Focus on saving your wife."

"I can't just leave you here," Walt said quietly.

"Yes, you can," Thea said firmly. "No one is going to kill me today. Cleo doesn't have that luxury."

"I'll keep her safe. Of course, I will," said Walt, getting to his feet. "But I'm not going to watch them walk you to the gallows."

"Go," Thea said.

Walt wanted to hold her, to kiss her, to reassure her, but he had forfeited that right. Instead, he gave her a tight-lipped smile and left.

THE PAST
Four years ago...

Thea hammered her fist against the door, a wave of anger she couldn't place flowing through her as if it had replaced her blood.

"Walt!" Thea yelled.

When the door opened, however, it was not Walt who stood before her; it was Cleo. Her hair had been styled in intricate finger waves, and she was wearing a bright red suit that only served to highlight the gleaming iridescent pearls that hung knotted on her chest.

All the anger drained from Thea to be replaced by cold shame.

"What did he do?" Cleo asked with a knowing smile.

"I—I'm so...sorry," Thea spluttered. "I was..."

"Oh, don't worry, I know what he can be like. He's very capable of inducing the kind of anger that makes you a little crazy. I'm heading to work anyway, so have at him. Walt," Cleo called over her shoulder. "Whatever you did—apologise."

Cleo grabbed her jacket from the pegs next to the door and stepped back to let Thea inside, because she felt like she had no choice; Thea accepted the invitation.

Walt was standing rigid-backed against the kitchen island, a glass of bourbon gripped tightly in his hand. He drained it as he glared at Thea with such fury that she stopped short just inside the apartment.

"Give him hell," Cleo said with a conspiratorial wink. "And don't take any of his BS." She picked up her bag and left with a final warm smile for Thea.

"What do you want?" Walt barked as soon as the door was shut, slamming the empty glass down on the counter.

"Nothing. I shouldn't have come here," Thea said, turning to the door.

"You're damn right you shouldn't," Walt spat with venom.

"Forget it," Thea said, throwing the door wide. "This was a mistake."

"You had no right," Walt said, striding towards the door and slamming it shut. "No fucking right."

Thea could feel the anger rolling off his body in waves.

"To come here, or to screw you? Because there were two of us in the closet, and I don't remember you complaining. I don't remember you saying much of anything."

"I never would have... if you hadn't," he paused as if trying to think of the right words to describe her crime. "Seduced me."

"I seduced you?" Thea was outraged. "I see your eyes on me every day. I see you watching me, looking at me when you should be looking anywhere else."

"You think I want to look at you?" he said, his breathing ragged.

"Then look away."

"I would if I could."

His words seemed to hang in the air between them. He meandered over to the kitchen and grabbed the bottle of bourbon; he screwed his face up as he took a swig from the bottle's neck.

"I hate hard liquor," he said inconsequentially.

"It's already done; the line was crossed, and I can't pretend that it wasn't. Can you?"

He turned his back to her as he said, "I have to. I'm married. I love my wife." He sounded tired, world-weary.

"I shouldn't have come here. I'll go."

"I am enthralled by you," Walt said as if Thea hadn't spoken. "Your laugh, your righteousness, your fearlessness. It's pure hedonism, but being with you, I've never felt more alive."

"You left," Thea said, moving away from the door.

"I realised what I'd done," Walt said grimly.

Walt took another swig from the bottle then placed it back on the counter. He moved away from the kitchen into the living room. The gap between them was slowly closing.

"We can't do this," Thea said, holding up her hands to halt Walt's progress towards her.

"Then why are you here?"

"You left; you didn't say anything."

"I hurt your feelings."

"You treated me like a toy to be picked up and put down at your leisure."

"Literally," Walt said with a malapert smile.

"Stop. Stop with the little jibes and the innuendos. Stop pretending to be an asshole to cover for the fact you have no idea what to do now."

"What do you want from me?"

"What do I want from—? Nothing! But I won't pretend it didn't happen. You say it'll never happen again—that's fine. I can chalk it up to the high of a near-death experience, but at least have the good grace to treat me with respect. There were two of us in that closet. I wanted you, I don't deny it, but you wanted me, too. You don't get to put this on me."

"I'm sorry," he said with genuine contrition. "The hurt it would cause Cleo if she ever found out makes me sick to my stomach." Walt wandered around the back of his armchair, hands in his pockets. "I've never done anything like this before. I'm a steady guy. I'm your boss. Worse—your mentor. You're twenty-four years old; I'm thirty-six. This should never have happened. I feel damn well ashamed, I've broken my vows to my wife, and I've disgraced my badge, but still, there's a part of me that is aching to rip your clothes off and take you on the dining room table if you'll let me."

Thea didn't know what to say. Walt usually perpetuated an air of authority, always in command and always in the right; his candidness softened his usually hard edges slightly. For now, they were not colleagues. They were not a superior and his subordinate; they were a man and a woman, and the playing field was level.

"I shouldn't have kissed you," Thea said finally.

"I'd be lying if I said I didn't want it."

"It can't happen again."

"No, it can't." Walt smiled in a resolute sort of way.

"I'm sorry for my part," Thea said.

"I'm sorry too," Walt said, leaning on the back of the chair. "I think we should allow the captain to separate us. It's for the best."

"I understand," Thea said. And she did. He was married. It didn't matter that they had an attraction to each other. It would be better for both of them if they went their separate ways.

"I'll show you out," Walt said briskly, gesturing with his hand.

Thea allowed herself to be ushered out the door.

"Goodnight, Detective James," she said with ironic deference.

"Detective Williams." Walt inclined his head slightly, the trace of a smile playing across his lips. It was so quick Thea wasn't aware of how it happened. Walt's hands were on her face pulling her lips to his. It didn't occur to her to tell him to stop.

"Do you want this?" he said, breaking away, his breathing heavy.

"Yes."

ACCUSED

Thea shivered slightly as she sat mopping her lip at the impersonal table inside interrogation room three. Evening had long since turned into night while she waited for an officer to begin her interrogation. This was a deliberate tactic employed to make a perp sweat.

The door was thrown open, clattering heavily against the brick wall. Thea jumped.

O'Malley entered, his glee evident.

"That looks sore," he said, pointing at her lip.

Thea didn't respond.

O'Malley pulled a hermetically sealed evidence bag containing a small bloody blade and placed it on the table between them.

"Know what this is?"

Thea looked at the knife, then looked away indifferently.

"It's the knife that was used to kill Benjamin Pickford," O'Malley went on when Thea said nothing. "Would you care to explain how it came to have your fingerprints on it?"

"I'm assuming you put them there because I have never seen that knife before in my life."

O'Malley gave a fake laugh, then leaned forward. "That's one option, and it's very cloak an' dagger. I like it. Another theory, and my personal favourite, is that you used it to gut the pimp."

"What respect you have for the dead," Thea said sarcastically. "Why would I kill Benny?"

"You tell me."

"I know you aren't used to doing legitimate detective work, but that's not how it works."

"Okay, I'll tell you what I think. He treats women like dirt. He abuses ghouls—you have been very vocal about your opposition to their mistreatment. And he's linked to your sister's disappearance."

"He was a person of interest. Since cleared."

"Then why did you ask him about her when you brought him in? It's in the official transcript," O'Malley said smiling.

"Get to the point," Thea said acidly.

"Am I bothering you? Making you angry? Angry enough to kill?"

"Mostly, I'm just bored."

"I'll hurry this along then. Your sister worked for Benny. You saw what it was like in his joint, the way he treated his pros, and you got mad. You could imagine all the horrible things he made her do and all the nasty little things he let be done to her."

"Thin ice," Thea said, her voice low.

"Hell, it would make me mad, too. Maybe he got cocky. You've been seeing a lot of each other. Maybe he let his guard down and let something slip. Maybe it was that he was the one who killed her—"

"She's not dead," Thea said reflexively.

"Or maybe," O'Malley continued, his grin widening. "It was just that he had used her up and tossed her away. You see red; you kill him."

"You have any evidence to back up that motive?"

"We've convicted for less."

"That's weak," Thea said through gritted teeth. "Even a jury you've paid off would have trouble swallowing that one."

"I like this new you. You used to be so righteous and by the book. Now you've seen how this city really works. You're meaner, sharper. Got rid of some of those soft edges."

"Great, now I'm sure we'll be the best of friends."

O'Malley chuckled and delved into the depths of his jacket once more. This time he pulled out a picture of a dead man, shot once in the back of the head. Thea had to try very hard to hide her shock; she knew the man. Not his name, but she would never forget his face.

"As I think you already know, this—" He tapped on the picture. "—is Lewis Avery. A thug in the employ of Dillard Kelly."

"So?"

"A couple of years ago, you stopped him beating Walt to death."

"I know I did."

"That's strong motive. You can see why I'd be asking you about him."

"That's your angle? I broke up a fight two years ago? What a load of crap. If I offed everyone who gave Walt the stink eye, I'd be a serial killer. Like I said, weak."

"I hoped you'd react like this. Honestly, I never thought you'd confess, and I'm glad. Trials like this are so drawn out and messy, so I asked for special dispensation to use extraordinary measures to extract a confession."

"There is nothing you can do to me that will get me to confess to crimes I didn't commit." Thea leant back in her chair and crossed her arms.

"You're going into virtual evidence. You can't hide the truth when you're in hell."

"I have no idea what you're talking about."

"You will."

TENEBRIUM POLICE DEPARTMENT
TENEBRIUM PROPER
STYGIAN COLONY #6

TENEBRIUM CITY
DEPARTMENT OF JUSTICE

INTERDEPARTMENTAL COMMUNICATION
From: Human Resources
To: All Staff

URGENT REMINDER – TPD BLOOD DRIVE

Due to the blood shortages being experienced throughout Tenebrium City, all staff are required to donate a minimum of two pints of blood. This is mandatory. No exceptions will be made for any reason. Those who have been told that their blood is unsuitable for donation in the past due to anaemia or other medical conditions etc., are required to have their blood re-tested at the mobile donation sites. Your direct superior will provide you with a non-negotiable donation appointment in the next seventy-two hours. Any member of staff who does not present themselves at the Blood Drive will be subject to disciplinary action.

<u>DONATION IS YOUR DUTY</u>

THE PAST
Four years ago...

The annual TPD masquerade ball was the event of the year for the cops in the city. It was technically the office Christmas party, but it had little to do with the holiday and everything to do with letting loose. This year it was to be held at The Monterey Room, a high-end hotel on the outskirts of Eltham.

The hotel was a tall rectangular building made of red and white brick. It was just as much window as wall, with frames spaced identically over all one hundred floors, each blaring light into the darkness, making The Monterey Room look like a beacon for party-goers.

Tonight, Walt had swapped his usual three-piece suit and gun holster for a black tuxedo complete with tailcoat and polished shoes. Cleo had opted for a gorgeous bronze gown of beaded satin with feathers at the bottom. She looked stunning.

Together they stepped out of the transporter and made their way inside the hotel and into the ballroom, ready for a night of music and dancing.

The interior was even more opulent than Walt had imagined. There was a faux glass ceiling, outlined in gold and painted with ambrosia trees adorned with glimmering fruits. The walls showed charcoal-blue, green, and pale-yellow frescoes depicting the Greek god Dionysus surrounded by grapes and jugs of wine. The tables that filled the room were topped with polished brass, and the chairs and booths that accompanied them were red velvet. The floor was covered with a magnificent black carpet decorated with white geometric Fleur-De-Lis. The party was already in full swing, and the flappers were out in force.

Walt checked the seating chart and found that he and Cleo were sitting right in front of the make-shift stage that had been erected at the far end of the hall. There was a full jazz band waiting patiently behind their instruments, but the microphone stand stood alone without its singer.

"This is us," Cleo said when they reached the table, holding up a little card that showed "Mr & Mrs James". The glow from the tabletop lamp illuminated her skin, and Walt was struck by how gorgeous his wife was.

"You're beautiful, Mrs James," Walt said, taking the card from her and kissing her gently. Cleo put her arms around Walt's neck, and he pulled her closer, deepening the kiss.

"If I find some mistletoe, will you kiss me like that?" Torrez said, clapping a hand on Walt's shoulder.

"Andrew," Cleo exclaimed, stepping back from Walt, genuinely happy to see Torrez. She held him at arm's length to examine his dark blue suit. "You look very handsome. No Marielena tonight?"

"She's having one of her bad days," Torrez said with a wistful smile. "Can I get you a drink? Walter?"

"I would love some champagne," Cleo said brightly.

"I'm all right for the moment," Walt said, taking his seat. His heart gave a little jump. The small card that sat in front of the empty seat to his left read "T. Williams."

He looked up and found her immediately in the crowd as if he could sense her. She was walking towards the bar to join Torrez. She had chosen a floor-length emerald-green dress made of velvet, with a slit up the side and a single row of beading that sat in the middle of her upper arms almost like a shawl. She was a vision. Thea laughed at something Torrez was saying to her and leaned in to hug him. Walt turned away.

"She looks gorgeous, doesn't she?" Cleo said, having followed Walt's eye line.

"Yeah," Walt muttered uncomfortably.

The lights dimmed all around them, and the stage was illuminated by a single spotlight. Thea and Torrez took up their seats and handed over the drinks they had purchased for the group just as the singer stepped on stage. It was Thea's twin sister Cora. She looked every bit the seductive jazz diva in her glittering silver dress with tassel trim. The chatter died down as the double bass started to play a sultry rhythm, but when Cora started to sing, she was met with awed silence. Her voice was mesmerising; it was hypnotic as she crooned. Cleo gripped Walt's hand, and he glanced at her to see wonderment etched into her features.

As Cora started to sing a more upbeat number, a mass of people took to the dance floor. Torrez led Thea to her feet, Walt followed suit with Cleo.

Cleo was a glorious dancer, and it was all Walt could do to keep up. They laughed and danced, lost in each other, until finally, Cleo said, "I need some air. I'll be back in a moment." She kissed Walt quickly then made her way towards the restrooms.

Now alone, Walt looked around and saw Thea and Torrez standing off to the side, both clearly having also tired themselves out on the dance floor. Walt made a beeline for them, but was stopped by the captain. She wore a pale champagne coloured drop hem dress.

"Walter, are you enjoying the evening?" Betty said with a warm smile.

"I am, possibly a bit too much. How's your wife?"

"Two weeks to go." The captain positively glowed with happiness.

"Have you picked a name yet?"

"We are waiting until we meet them. Then we'll know."

The captain left him moments later to go to the bar, and Walt continued to make his way over to Thea, who was still standing just off the dance floor. This time he was stopped by Cora.

She and Thea were identical on the outside, but that was as far as it went. Extremely close as sisters, they were very different people. Walt could tell by the determined look on her face that he was about to be warned off.

"Stop."

Walt tried to sidestep her, but she put a hand on his chest to halt him.

"She can do better than a married man who can't, and won't, fully commit to her. If you really loved her, you'd leave her alone. You have already made a name for yourself; she's just starting out. You're leaving a mark on her, and if you aren't careful, it's a mark that won't wash clean," said Cora with all the formidability he usually associated with her sister.

"It's not that simple."

"Yes, it is. You and your wife looked so happy dancing together. Why isn't that enough for you?"

She had got him. Walt had no answer to that. Knowing she had won, Cora slipped through the crowd to Thea. Walt watched from a distance as they hugged, and he could tell from her smile that Thea was gushing over her sister's performance. Shortly after, Torrez returned from the bar with a fresh round of drinks. Walt saw a glint in his eye that told him if Torrez had his way, he would be taking Cora home tonight. With a pang of guilt, Walt wondered if that was what he looked like when he was with Thea.

NEW MONEY

Walt had only been to Cora's apartment a handful of times. Though she and Thea had been very close, they had always had their differences, and he was one of those differences.

It was with a strange sensation in his gut that he knocked on Cora's door. It felt like he was stepping back into the past. The present crashed over him, however, when Cleo answered. She was tired and frightened. Dark circles were forming under her usually bright eyes.

"Are you all right? Did they hurt you?" Walt asked softly, stepping inside and closing the door behind him. She appeared unharmed, but Walt wanted to be sure.

"Thea?" Cleo asked, ignoring the question.

"She's in trouble."

"Then you'd better get her out of it. She saved my life, Walt."

"I will, but for now, are you all right?"

"I'm fine. There isn't anyone watching the building as far as I can tell, so I think I'm well hidden."

The living area was covered in a thick layer of dust, but the kitchen was spotless. Walt smiled; he had forgotten that whenever Cleo was stressed, she cleaned. It was a habit he had always adored because it was so at odds with the rest of her personality. Neither of them had been particularly worried about housekeeping, they were both busy with their careers, but he had always known if there was something on her mind if he had come home to find the apartment spotless.

Walt perched himself on the edge of the sofa and surveyed Cleo.

"I know you didn't want to talk before, but want in one hand, shit in the other," Walt began. "See which you get more of," they finished together.

"You don't remember what happened to you; I accept that. But you do remember why it happened, don't you?"

"Are you interrogating me, detective?"

Cleo hopped up onto the kitchen counter and crossed her legs, another habit Walt had forgotten and had loved in the past. Cleo sat cross-legged whenever she could, even on dining chairs in restaurants.

"No. I'm asking you husband to wife."

Cleo watched him for a moment chewing her lip as if she wondered what he would make of what she was about to say.

"I worked for Medicorum, not PharmaSave. I lied; it was part of my contract. It seemed like such an inconsequential lie at the time, they wanted to protect their work, and the buildings were right next to each other. I was part of Chester Maxwell's team. They—we—were trying to create drugs that made people highly susceptible to suggestion, to help with addiction, or so we were told. We were failing. It was causing extreme paranoia and violent outbursts in all those we tested it on. Batch after batch—a failure. The Gold Legion isn't just a Tenebrium City problem; Maxwell might be the head of the snake here, but even he answers to someone. His superiors wanted results, but we were running out of test subjects, so he decided to test Styxx's viability in a live environment. It was only supposed to be distributed to the Poor Quarter, but I gather that's not how it played out. I'd had a feeling that something wasn't right, that the project wasn't, as we were told, to rehabilitate dangerous offenders. I snuck into Maxwell's office and read his latest report; he was deploying to the Poor Quarter. He caught me, having already been suspicious, dosed me with the second drug we had been developing and left me to die in the street. That's everything I know."

"It's enough to bring him down," Walt said. He was elated; they finally had a name to hold accountable.

Cleo laughed in a hollow sort of way. "Maxwell will never let it get that far. I'll be dead long before then."

"I'll protect you, I promise."

"I know you will, but you are one person, and they are an army with endless resources. It's not that easy. I should be dead," she paused, playing with her fingers. "You believe me then?"

"I believe you because I know you."

Walt crossed to her. She uncurled her legs and let them hang off the counter so he could stand between them with his arms around her shoulders. He kissed her gently on the forehead.

"This isn't your fault," he muttered. "I'll be back soon. I have something I need to take care of. When will you need more Quietus?"

"Maybe tonight," Cleo said. "But I don't have any left."

"I'll be back before then. Don't worry about it."

Walt leant down to chastely kiss her lips, but she locked her legs around his waist. She deepened the kiss, her tongue exploring his mouth. He could feel himself melting into her; whatever their problems, this they had always been good at. He pulled away and stepped gently out of her grasp before they reached the point of no return.

"Not the time," Cleo said, watching him shrewdly.

"Not the time," Walt agreed. "I'll be back."

Bastion and Walt had grown up together, neither wealthy nor poor, but somewhere in the comfortable middle. Walt had never had aspirations for wealth, but even from a young age, Bast had desired to possess anything and everything he could.

His dreams had come to fruition when he had joined the Onyx Legion. He had risen quickly through their ranks, enjoying increased danger, wealth, and stability.

Bastion had made quite the life for himself, Walt thought as he made his way through the Diamond District. Every house was a mansion with its own docking bay and a grass lawn complete with trees and flowers, not things that were commonplace outside of florists and botanic gardens. Tenebrium was a city of brick and glass; nature had no place there.

Bastion's home was no different. It was a tall and broad manor made from pale stone with an abundance of columns and archways, pointed chimney tops, and Palladian windows. Small lanterns lit the front terrace where Bastion sat on a wooden recliner decked out with squashy cushions. He smoked a cigarillo as he read something from the clear glass tablet he held loosely in one hand.

"I'm surprised you still remember where I live," he said, setting his reading aside.

"I'll grant you, it's been a while," Walt said, stopping just short of the terrace. "Never liked them," he said in response to the proffered cigarillo.

"Have you come to chew me out for visiting your girl?" Bastion asked, taking a long drag and blowing a smoke ring that twisted and writhed into the air.

"I need your help, Bast." Walt said ruefully.

"You're a real bastard. You know that? You turn up here asking for help after all your jibes and mistrust, your accusations, because you know I'm a damned idiot. What do you need, brother?"

MISFIRE

Classy, Torrez thought. Harold Williams' office was so damn classy. It made Torrez dislike him even more because, if he was honest, he envied him. As Torrez sat in the expensive leather chair behind the district attorney's suggestively large desk, he was rather proud of himself. He had managed to sneak into the building unnoticed, and he knew sitting in the man's chair would cause irritation, which was exactly the effect he wanted. He hoped it would avoid drawing attention to the blood on his shirt and the sickliness he was feeling due to the stitches he had most definitely pulled. He should probably go to a medical service soon, and he would, but not yet; the Verve he had taken would tide him over a little longer.

The millions of credits worth of paintings on the walls stared down at him. As Torrez took in the beauty of each one and let the status of someone capable of owning them wash over him, he thought about taking one of the platinum fountain pens from the desk and drawing a tiny smiley face on the corner of each masterpiece. Harold would never notice, but he, Torrez, would always know.

Before he could ponder the misdeed in realms beyond the idle, however, the door opened.

Harold stopped short as he spotted Torrez nestled behind his desk. The district attorney was wet from the rain, the hat he held by his side and the tips of his trench coat were dripping large drops of water onto the dark carpet.

"Mr Torrez."

"Mr Williams."

"Is there a reason you are here, Andrew?" Harold said, shutting the door behind him.

He took off his coat, hanging it on the pegs behind the door and moved further into the room to sit at one of the long, wide, black leather couches placed on either side of the glass coffee table at which Torrez knew he took his less formal meetings.

TENEBRIUM

"Thea has been arrested," Torrez said, sitting up and managing, only just, to stifle the wince the movement caused.

"I'm well aware," said Harold, as if the fact was of no consequence.

Torrez watched as Harold draped one arm along the back of the couch and crossed his right leg over his left. Torrez leant back in reply, placing one foot on the edge of the desk defiantly.

"She's your daughter," Torrez said quietly.

"Do you have a point? Or are you planning to continue to make obvious statements?"

"They are going to execute her, and you are just going to sit here?"

"I have a trial to prepare for." Harold shrugged.

"She's your daughter, you goddamned reptile," Torrez spat, unable to master himself.

"Her choices, and the consequences she incurs, are hers to bear," Harold said, maddeningly calm.

"Is that why you never searched for Cora?"

"Careful, Andrew, you are getting dangerously close to deep waters. I'm sure you wouldn't enjoy it if I told Thea, should she survive, that you slept with her sister not long before she disappeared."

Torrez felt nauseated, but it had nothing to do with the DA's knowledge of his sex life.

"You will help your daughter. You will drop the charges, or I'll go public. I will tell anyone who will listen everything I know about Styxx, the ghouls, the Gold Legion—all of it. And before you say it, you can kill me if you want, but I'm not the only one who knows what you've done. Plus, Thea would never forgive you, and if she survives this, I think you'll care about that someday."

"Do you know where your wife is right now?"

Torrez blinked.

"*I* know," Harold continued. "She's standing in the kitchen and pouring herself a glass of wine. She looks sad. Her husband has disappointed her."

"You don't touch her," Torrez snarled, getting to his feet. "You don't look at her. You don't even think about her. Are we clear?"

"You don't have the power here. You never did, and you never will. If I wanted to, I could have someone at your door in less than five minutes. I could have your wife killed in a robbery gone wrong or maybe an unfortunate house fire, or I could have one of my men draw it out, toy with her, make her suffer. I could have her brought here for my pleasure if I wanted to—"

"I will kill you if you go anywhere near her," said Torrez. He had to force the words out; the fury invading every cell in his body was rendering him almost speechless.

"I'm not saying that I will—I like my paramours willing. I'm just saying I could...if I wanted to."

Torrez vaulted the desk, his injuries forgotten, but before he could take more than a few steps towards Harold, the older man had pulled a gun from his jacket and levelled it at Torrez's heart.

"And you," he went on with a sneer, "Couldn't stop me because that's what having real power is. The ability to do what you want, to take what you want. So, no. I don't think you will go public, and I don't think you will do anything to save Thea from her fate because if you do, the beautifully delicate Marielena Torrez will pay the price."

Torrez didn't know what to do; he was panting as he stood, overcome with impotent rage.

"From now on, when I call, you come running, when I say jump, you say… Well, you get the point."

Torrez had no idea what to do and no way to expel the anger that was causing him to vibrate.

"You may go," Harold said, waving a dismissive hand.

Torrez made his way to the door, but before he knew what had happened, he was on the ground, an uncomfortable hot sensation spreading across his stomach.

"Zhao," Harold called through the open door. "Be a dear and call Medicus for Mr Torrez; there's a good man. We wouldn't want our newest asset bleeding out on the carpet."

EATSLEEPRAVEREPEAT

"And you wonder why nobody trusts the police. This is harassment. Man, I am sick of this shit."

"Benny?"

"Who else? And if you are gonna come in here and accuse me of shit I didn't do, it's 'Mr Pickford'. We may have crossed paths, but we ain't close."

"How did I get here?"

"You kicked my damn door in, that's how!"

Thea was standing in the atrium of Ward Eight. It was red and filled with posters and catalogues as usual, but how had she gotten there? And why was she there? She couldn't remember.

"Look, lady, you have no proof and no grounds for arrest, so get the fuck off my premises."

"I'm watching you," she said because it was what she usually said, wasn't it?

"Yeah, yeah."

In a dream-like daze, Thea turned away from Benny and left Ward Eight.

"This is getting ridiculous," Benny shouted, slamming his fist on his desk and causing the lamp that sat there to shudder.

"Benny?"

"Who else? And if you are gonna come in here and accuse me of shit I didn't do, it's 'Mr Pickford'. We may have crossed paths, but we ain't close."

"This is..." Thea said, looking around the office.

"Bullshit? I'm glad we agree. You can show yourself out."

In a dream-like daze, Thea turned away from Benny and left the office.

"Bitch, I am gettin' real sick of this shit," said Benny as he put the playing cards and poker chips back into the attaché case that housed them. "There ain't no laws against private games."

"Benny?"

"Who else? And if you are gonna come in here and accuse me of shit I didn't do, it's 'Mr Pickford'. We may have crossed paths, but we ain't close."

"I'll be—"

"Watching? I get it, now piss off."

In a dream-like daze, Thea turned away from Benny and left the basement poker room.

The fifth floor of Ward Eight had a much more clinical aesthetic than the others for those who just wanted to do the deed and weren't fussed with romanticising the experience or employing any particular fetish. Aptly, the sign on the stairwell said: "Business as Usual Floor".

Thea ran as fast as her legs could carry her; she could see Benny just ahead of her, sprinting away.

"Benny," she shouted, delighted to see him alive. She had suspected that O'Malley was lying, but she had still worried that he wasn't.

Benny ignored her, making for the stairs. Thea followed.

Always just too far behind to catch up, Thea pursued Benny down stairway after stairway, corridor after corridor.

"Benny," Thea called again. "You're in danger!"

Benny came to an abrupt halt at the top of a flight of stairs. The sign posted there announced that they were on the "Business as Usual Floor".

"Is that a threat?"

Benny's whole aspect changed; he became taller somehow, fiercer. He seemed to radiate a danger and malevolence that Thea had never known him to before, even at his worst. For the first time ever, when faced by Benjamin Pickford, Thea felt the first subtle flutter of fear.

"No," Thea said warily. "The Gold Legion is coming for you."

Benny came to an abrupt halt at the top of a flight of stairs. The sign posted there announced that they were on the "Business as Usual Floor".

"Is that a threat?"

Benny's whole aspect changed; he became taller somehow, fiercer. He seemed to radiate a danger and malevolence that Thea had never known him to before, even at his worst. For the first time ever, when faced by Benjamin Pickford, Thea felt the first subtle flutter of fear.

"No. Benny, it's Thea! What's happening? Where have you been? Something's wrong. The Gold Legion—"

Benny came to an abrupt halt at the top of a flight of stairs. The sign posted there announced that they were on the "Business as Usual Floor".

"Is that a threat?"

Benny's whole aspect changed; he became taller somehow, fiercer. He seemed to radiate a danger and malevolence that Thea had never known him to before, even at his worst. For the first time ever, when faced by Benjamin Pickford, Thea felt the first subtle flutter of fear.

Benny lunged for Thea. She backed away as far as she could, but it wasn't enough to stop his hands from clasping around her throat. His grip was so tight she knew she would be unconscious in seconds if she didn't act.

She raised her elbow above her head and brought it down on the crook of his arm, twisting as she did to bring him within range of a headbutt that momentarily stunned them both. Before either had fully recovered, Thea pushed Benny away, both of her hands on his chest.

He teetered at the top of the landing for a moment, and then, unable to regain his balance, he was crashing down the stairs and out of sight.

"Benny!" Thea yelled, running to the top of the stairs, but it was too late. Benny lay broken and bloody at the bottom.

"How…? This isn't real." Thea said to herself, stepping back from the stairs.

She blinked, and then she was running down the corridor again, chasing after Benny.

"This never happened. This isn't real!" Thea bellowed.

Benny was running towards her, a gun in his hand, firing blindly. A pulse round hit her squarely in the chest, she felt cold, and then she was falling.

"And you wonder why nobody trusts the police. This is harassment. Man, I am sick of this shit."

They were in the atrium of Ward Eight again. Thea couldn't breathe; it was all too much. She was hyperventilating, but no matter how hard she tried, she couldn't draw breath into her lungs. Her head pounded, and her lungs screamed.

"This isn't real," she choked out.

A booming voice so loud it seemed to shake the very foundations of reality erupted all around Thea, forcing her to her knees as she clutched her ears.

"She's stronger of mind than you gave her credit for. You'll have to go deeper."

Thea was enveloped in darkness; she screwed her eyes shut, drawing in ragged gulps of breath.

"Thea?"

She opened her eyes.

She was resting with her head on the tabletop in the interrogation room, Walt looking down at her, clearly concerned and perhaps slightly rattled.

"Walt! Thank god."

Thea bounded out of her chair and hugged him fiercely.

"You never could keep your hands off me," Walt sneered.

Thea dropped her arms at once and stepped back.

"What?"

Walt's face was contorted in disgust. She didn't understand.

"What?" he mocked with a cruel smile. "You followed me around like a pathetic little puppy dog; how could I say no? You made it so easy; I didn't even have to try. You were just giving it away. Thing is, sweetheart, I'm bored of you now. It was fun at first, but you're old news. The bloom is off the rose. The fire is out. All that stress is starting to show on your face, and kid, it ain't a good look."

"Walt is many things," Thea said, recovering herself and talking directly to the man in front of her. "But he isn't this."

The room dissolved around her, crumbling in upon itself. The mean-spirited caricature of Walt waved as he came apart like a stack of cans in a grocery store.

"It must be nice to have someone so wrapped around your finger,"

Thea was still inside the TPD, she realised it now, and as she recognised the room she stood in, she knew exactly what had happened to her.

She had been inserted into the Virtual Evidence suite not to look over archived footage, but to run possible scenarios of Benny's death. Except she wasn't the one running the simulation; it was completely beyond her control, which was dangerous and, as far as she was aware, illegal, due to the damage it could do to a person's mind.

"I went too far too soon, didn't I?" O'Malley asked casually from where he stood behind the control panel near the door. "It was fun to watch you squirm, though."

"You son of bitch."

But before she had finished the sentence, she was standing in a rain-soaked snicket between two foreboding buildings.

ADDICTED TO LOVE

Walt felt oddly out of place where he sat on Bastion's handsome porch. He had been before, but the opulence had always made him feel uncomfortable.

"Want one?" Bastion asked, noticing that the undrunk glass of wine he had discarded on the side table was drawing Walt's eye. "I'm losing track. Are you on the sauce or off?"

"Off," Walt said stiffly.

"Tell your breath," Bastion said, taking the undrunk glass from the sideboard and placing it in front of Walt.

"It's been a rough couple of days."

Walt sipped gratefully at the wine. He was not a connoisseur by any means, preferring his liquor hard and brown, but the wine was damn good.

"You must find yourself using that excuse almost daily." Bastion said.

He sat back down in his chair and observed Walt much like a psychiatrist would.

"Save it. You don't get to dish it out and then judge me for taking it."

"I do, actually. On any other day, I'd be dragging your ass, kicking and screaming into sobriety. Again. But if you're going to face the DA, I don't suggest you take the DTs with you."

"That's really your advice?"

"After everything you've told me, I don't see another option. The only way to get the charges dropped is if the District Attorney wills it so. You'd think, as his daughter's head is up on the block, he would have done something by now, but he's staying quiet, which means he wants something, and we both know exactly what that is."

"And there is nothing you can do?"

"Like what? I can get you in to see him without a fuss and keep the OL off your back when you do, but I don't have any pull in the legal system."

"What about the case? The victims, those who still stand to get hurt?"

Walt already agreed with Bastion, there was only one way to help Thea, but he was doing it for selfish reasons. With Thea in danger, he cared very little about the Gold Legion, but he also knew it would weigh on him later. He needed his conscience talked into it.

"These people are dangerous and dirty. There will always be more evidence, more opportunities to catch them. There are always more leads."

"She'll never forgive me."

"She'll be alive to hate you. You love her."

"I—"

"I wasn't asking. Give him what he wants; save the world later."

"You really are the worst friend."

"I know, buddy. I know."

AND AGAIN

Thunder rolled, and lightning cracked the smog-laden sky. Rain clattered against the windows of the tall buildings that surrounded, and bounced off the concrete underfoot. Blood dripped from her hands and the knife she held there, mingling with the rain. Benny lay dead at her feet, sightless eyes staring up at the chaotic sky.

"This never happened," Thea said quietly, but firmly.

"You can't trust him," Walt said, dragging her by the arm into the supply closet.

"What?" Thea asked him distractedly. She couldn't remember arriving at the TPD.

"Benjamin Pickford, you can't trust him," Walt said, clearly agitated.

"I don't, but we need him," Thea said, giving Walt her full attention.

"He has a very good reason to want to fuck with me, and I seriously doubt he's above using you to do it."

"Wow, charming sentiments, but his life is on the line here. It doesn't make sense that he would screw us, at least not right now."

Thea reached for the doorknob, but Walt pulled her back.

"I killed his uncle; the guy was an evil sonuvabitch, but he was like a father to Pickford."

Lighting split the sky like a spear. Thea shivered as the rain seemed to soak through her clothes to her very bones. The alley was quiet, but for her and Benny.

"I have been waiting for this," he sneered, brandishing the knife he pulled from his jacket. He lunged for Thea, who jumped back. Benny raised his arm and slashed at her, she brought her arm up to her face just in time to avoid a killing blow, but the blade left a bone-deep slash on her forearm.

Searing pain broke over her as her blood splattered to the ground, where it joined the puddles created by the never-ceasing rain.

Benny readied himself for another attack, and he thrust the knife at her. Thea reached out and grabbed him by the wrist, forcing the knife off course. Using her free hand, she grabbed Benny's thumb and twisted until he lost his grip on the weapon. It dropped from his hand. Thea caught it before it hit the ground, and without hesitating, she plunged it into Benny's chest.

Shock flickered across his face as he fell to the ground. Thea dropped to her knees beside him and plunged the knife into his chest over and over until he stopped crying out and convulsing, and the light behind his eyes went out.

Thunder rolled, and lightning cracked the smog-laden sky. Rain clattered against the windows of the tall buildings that surrounded, and bounced off the concrete underfoot. Blood dripped from her hands and the knife she held there, mingling with the rain. Benny lay dead at her feet, sightless eyes staring up at the chaotic sky.

"This never happened," Thea screamed.

"Are you ready to confess?"

The voice seemed to surround her. It was excruciatingly loud and sent shockwaves through her body. It felt like she was trying to swim through a pool of glass.

"Fuck you!" Thea screamed.

The disembodied voice let out a peal of laughter that caused Thea to fall to the ground. She covered her head with her hands in a vain attempt to block it out.

"Another tack then."

DANCING WITH THE DEVIL

With Bastion's help, it hadn't taken Walt long to pack up all the evidence he and Thea had collected. They took everything from crime scene photos to scribbled notes. The chip had already been stolen; it was just one less thing they had to find.

The obelisk of obsidian that was the District Attorney's office was quiet as the Jonk landed on the pavement in front of it. It was getting late, and the unmistakable signs of tightening security were easily visible.

The usual singular doorman was now three doormen in red three-piece suits, with guns holstered conspicuously at their sides.

Walt and Bastion stepped out of the transporter in unison and marched with an equanimous air towards the door matching each other's strides perfectly.

"Halt," said one of the doormen, holding a hand out to Walt. "You are not cleared for entry, sir."

"Stand aside," said Bastion in a clipped, businesslike tone. He pulled his ID card from his wallet, though Walt doubted anyone could mistake his 6-foot-6 frame.

"Mr Tyrus. Detective James is not permitted entry."

"It's Officer now, actually, and he's my guest. Stand aside." The subtle shift in his tone was enough to stop any other protestations the doorman may have been considering.

"Very well," the red-suited man said. "But I will have to enter this into the official log."

"You do that," Bastion said, striding past the doormen.

Smiling slightly, Walt followed suit.

Several levels of security checks, and an elevator ride that was stopped twice by yet more DA employees demanding that Walt not be allowed in the building later, the two men stepped out into the waiting area of Harold Williams' office.

The door into the office proper was open. Just inside, there was a Chinese man in his mid-thirties on his hands and knees scrubbing a patch of blood on the carpet.

"Jesus, Harry," Bastion said, looking over the young man to Harold, who was sitting on one of his impressive couches surrounded by legal papers. "Zhao is the assistant DA, not a cleaner."

"That's what I said," grumbled Zhao, getting to his feet.

He was lean and neither tall nor short. His hair was cut closely at the sides. The longer top portion was slicked back and bright orange. His waistcoat and trousers were grey-and-green check, his shirt black.

"Think of it as dues paid. Expect a bottle of scotch on your desk tomorrow."

"I should have listened to my mother and become a doctor," Zhao said, giving Harold a sardonic bow and exiting.

Bastion led the way into the office, Walt closely behind him.

"You've brought company, Bast. I usually request they make an appointment," Harold said pointedly, his brow furrowing as he eyed Walt.

"Well, I thought, considering what you did to my face, that you owed me one."

Walt had never thought to ask how Bastion had gotten so bruised and felt a pang of regret for his attitude towards Bastion of late.

"It clearly didn't have the intended effect."

"Thea is in trouble," Walt said loudly.

"So I've heard," Harold said, turning his attention back to his papers.

"Are you really willing to let her die to protect yourself?" Walt demanded.

"That's cold, even for you," Bastion said, moving away from the other two to perch on the edge of the DA's desk.

"I thought I had made my priorities abundantly clear."

"You're a liar," Walt said, his voice rising. "I saw you at the hospital when you thought she wouldn't wake up; you were devastated!"

"There are more important things at play."

"Than the life of your daughter? You already lost Cora."

"And I survived. Proof I will survive this."

"You would think someone around here would have noticed how soulless you are," Walt spat.

"Save your indignity, Mr James. We both know that if I was going to pardon her out of the goodness of my heart or fatherly love, I would have done so already. This back and forth is just you trying to make it abundantly clear that you hold the moral high ground, a concept that I find ridiculous, but there we are."

"What do you want?"

"More pretence, how fun," Harold said with mock enthusiasm. "You know I had the chip removed from your apartment. Give me all you have, end your investigation once and for all, and I will have Thea released. If you don't, I will allow the police to do their jobs, and I think we can both agree that does not bode well for Thea. We have a deal, I assume."

"No." Walt said firmly.

"No?" Bastion said incredulously.

"I give you everything you want, and you let Thea off the hook, resisting arrest charges and all. I want Cleo to be free of you, too. No trying to hurt her, or put her away, and you give me the drugs I need to keep her *her*. That's the deal, or I take everything I still have and put it on every desk in the city, every police captain, every politician, every news network, even you can't silence the whole city."

"Fighting for your lover and your wife, how noble. Fine. One of my men will accompany you to collect the remainder of the evidence you have gathered, and once I am satisfied, Thea will be released, and I will personally ensure no one touches your wife."

FREE?

The walls of Thea's mind were crumbling in on themselves. She felt disconnected from her body, her consciousness adrift. It was painful, yet she couldn't place exactly where it hurt. She and Benny had been caught in an endless loop of death and violence for so long, she couldn't be sure if she was still alive. She would have believed she was in hell if someone had told her that it was so.

But still, there was a tiny part of her brain that retained a small semblance of reality. She was in virtual evidence, and her mind was dangerously close to shattering. Once that happened, she was as good as dead. Lost forever.

Thea wasn't aware of waking up. The harsh white of the virtual evidence suite was making her eyes water, but the cold white glass of the floor soothed her aching body. She didn't look up when the door opened gently. Her head felt like someone had taken a drill to her temple and numbly absent all at once. She was having trouble focusing. She kept momentarily forgetting where she was and how she had got there, expecting to be somewhere in the city with Benny only to remember that he was dead and she had been accused of killing him.

She had mixed feelings about the death of Benjamin Pickford. She hadn't liked him; he had been a thorn in her side as long as she had been a detective. He had been brutal as a pimp, and he had tried to have her killed; he had owned people and turned them into ghouls for the pleasure of his over-privileged clients, but latterly, he had been on her side. He had been willing to fight against the corruption of the city, and he had seemed to want to change. He wasn't a good man by any means, but perhaps, had he been given the chance, he could have been a better one. It was the ally in the fight for justice that she would mourn, and the potential of a man willing to change.

"Thea," a familiar voice said, reminding Thea that someone had entered the room and bringing her back from the depths of her own addled thoughts.

"Drew?"

"Let's get you out of here, Querida."

"Are you better?"

Vague images of blood seeping between her fingers as she pressed gauze to his stomach floated hazily across her mind.

"I went to the hospital...after a fashion," he muttered. "Up you get."

Torrez pulled Thea to her feet and with his arm fastened securely around her waist, he guided her from the room.

Thea's release was somewhat of a blur to her. She only vaguely remembered signing the correct papers and the captain bestowing her with a rare hug, but perhaps she imagined the last as it seemed unlikely.

Before she knew it, Torrez was setting her down, like she was a delicate vase, in the chair behind his desk. She looked around the room, searching for a particular face.

"He isn't here. He tried to be, and he is the reason you're out, but I told him to give you some space."

"Thank you," Thea said, and she meant it.

Her brain was slowly regaining its usual level of function.

"He protected Cleo too," Torrez said quietly, not looking at her.

"How did he—"

"I'll tell you later," Torrez said, gently placing his hand on her cheek; she leant into the warmth. "I have one more thing to do, and then I'm taking you home."

"Ok," Thea said, pulling the jacket that she couldn't remember being draped over her shoulders tighter around herself.

She curled up on the chair and was asleep before Torrez was out of sight.

LOVE AND OTHER DRUGS

It was with a strange feeling of buoyancy that Walt walked up the six flights of stairs to Cora Williams' apartment. He hadn't realised the toll the investigation had been taking on him until he was free of it. Thea would continue to investigate, and though he knew it made him terribly selfish to think that way, it let him off the hook. He had made a deal to save the people he loved, and he didn't know a single person, other than Thea perhaps, who would have behaved differently.

Cleo was nowhere to be seen when Walt entered the living room. It showed signs of having been dusted, but it was far from tidy. The curtains were drawn, and the artificial sunlight that blazed against them bathed the room in a soft orange glow. The coffee table had been upended, throw pillows were scattered around the room, and several of the photo frames lay smashed on the floor.

"Cleo," Walt called softly, his scalp tingling.

Silence was the only reply.

The short corridor that led to the bedrooms and the bathroom was almost completely obscured by shadow, but Walt could just see that the farthest door was ajar.

"Cleo," he called again.

Still, there was no reply.

He walked carefully down the corridor, stopping outside the door. He held his breath as he stood there listening. There was the smallest sound of movement from within, like the shifting of weight from one foot to another on creaky floorboards.

"I'm coming in," Walt said, and he pushed the door open.

The room was dark and apparently empty. The bedding was balled up in the corner, and books had been pulled from the shelves.

Walt stepped inside.

He had known that an attack was coming, but he hadn't expected it from behind. With a feral snarl and surprising strength, Cleo leapt out from behind the door and wrapped her arms around Walt in a bone-crushing bear-hug that pressed her into his back. Walt tried to shake her off, but he was afraid of hurting her. He paid a steep price for his concern as she viciously sank her teeth into his neck. Walt cried out, feeling the warm blood dripping down his front.

He grabbed one of her arms and, torquing his hips, threw her over his shoulder. She landed sprawled at his feet. She was on her haunches in seconds, growling like a caged animal.

"I'm really sorry about this."

Walt dived on top of Cleo, flattening her. The weight of his body pinning her down as he frantically searched his pocket for one of the syringes he had purchased from Dillard Kelly. He placed his other forearm to her chest, holding her down as his fingers finally closed on what he needed. Walt jabbed the syringe into Cleo's chest and held on for dear life as she tried to buck him off. Slowly her protests became feebler and feebler until she fell unconscious.

Panting slightly, Walt rolled off her. He quickly checked her for any obvious signs of injury, then he lifted her carefully and placed her on Cora's bed. He picked the duvet from the floor and covered Cleo with it, making sure to tuck her in neatly.

Next, he pulled the case from one of the scattered pillows and held it to his bleeding neck. He didn't think the bite was deep enough to be dangerous, but it was painful, and he was starting to feel light-headed.

With a final check on Cleo, Walt made his way into the main living area. He made a cursory search of the kitchen cabinets, but they were poorly stocked; the only useful item he could find was a roll of silver duct tape. Walt ripped the pillowcase to make shorter strips and used the duct tape to affix them to his neck as make-shift dressing. It wasn't pretty, but it would do.

He poured himself a glass of water then set to work cleaning the living room. He didn't want Thea to come back and see it trashed, and he didn't want to think about what had just happened.

The sun was starting to set when Cleo stirred. She appeared timidly in the hall, the remnants of his blood dried on her face.

"Are you okay?" Walt asked, looking up from next to the bin, where he had been disposing of the last of the glass from the broken picture frames.

"I'm so sorry. I would never hurt you, never."

"I know," Walt said, standing up and moving towards her.

"Your neck..." Cleo moaned.

"It's fine."

"We have to talk."

"Okay, but not here. I've got plenty of the drug you need now, and no one is searching for you anymore. We can go home," Walt said, holding out his hand to her.

"How? And what about Thea?"

"We'll talk at home."

Cleo took his proffered hand and interlinked her fingers with his; together, they left the apartment.

The Jonk ride home was quiet, but pleasantly so. It was comfortable as it had been in the past.

"I'll clean this up tomorrow," Walt said, waving a vague hand as they stood looking at the aftermath of the intruder in their home.

"I lied to you," Cleo said, righting one of the dining room chairs and sitting down.

"About?"

"My job, the things I did."

"I know."

"No, you don't."

Walt dropped on the couch then jumped back up immediately; something sharp had made contact with his rear end. He lifted the offending remnants of a broken vase and placed it on the floor, then sat back down.

"I don't know where to begin. I can't believe this case came to you. Gin Ricky told me," she added in reply to Walt's questioning look. "Did you know that before he was a bootlegger, he was a Pharmaceutical Researcher?"

"No, I didn't," Walt said, shaking his head.

"He helped develop new drugs, usually recreational ones," Cleo said, using her thumb to spin her wedding ring. "He was good, and sometimes he worked on our studies. That's how we met."

"If you are trying to tell me that you two were having an affair—please don't. This is our new start; the past doesn't matter," Walt said, holding his hands up as if in surrender.

"No, no. Though, that would be simpler," Cleo said with a wistful smile. "I was researching new weight loss drugs."

"I remember."

"I was bored, so damn bored, and one day Chester came into my office."

"Maxwell?" Walt interjected.

"Yeah, I think you're starting to understand. It was like he knew exactly what I wanted to hear. He said he saw my potential. I knew he was flirting, but I was sure I could keep him at bay. He never tried anything; he just liked to flirt with flattery. He told me they were working on cutting edge drugs to rehabilitate offenders. The power of suggestion to treat killers, rapists and paedophiles, to make them malleable and forget their urges, he said we were working to neutralise evil. Second chances for all. The longer I worked on the project, the more curious I got about where all the money was coming from. Even a facility as big as Medicorum doesn't have an endless supply. I heard rumours about the Gold Legion, and when I asked Chester, he called it his 'little club'. He said that they believed in our work. I would notice small things, the kind of things you can brush off individually, but together —it painted a scary picture. But I ignored my gut until I couldn't anymore. They took a kid. I snuck into his office, and I read what he wanted to do to the people of this city. He caught me, we struggled and... that's it."

Walt didn't know what to say. Cleo had known, at least in part, about the Gold Legion's plans all along.

"Did you read about the chips?"

His emotional brain was in freefall; he let the cop in him take over.

"They called it the Morpheus Project; the chips were the final stage. They weren't created by Chester, but he told his superiors that they were."

"What was Styxx supposed to do?"

"Are you interrogating me, detective?"

"I think so."

Cleo nodded. "It was supposed to promote suggestibility, but the side effects included violent tendencies, and as far as I can glean from what I read, they decided to try to test it as a way to eliminate undesirables."

"The people in the Poor Quarter, and then?"

"After my time, but I'm assuming as it provided an extreme high, that it wasn't so easy to keep it to the Poor Quarter."

"And Quietus?"

"We already have psychomimetic drugs, but the results of their use vary, and it's temporary. Styxx produced the same kind of effect at first, but it wasn't permanent, and it turns people into rabid husband-biting monsters." Cleo smiled weakly, and when Walt didn't return the sentiment, she went on. "Quietus is Styxx reversed. You take it, and you're fine, it's a fun high, and if you keep taking it, you won't even know what's happened to you until you stop... that's when you become like me—when you stop taking it. I think the plan is to use it to control anyone in power they can't buy."

"What does the Gold Legion want? Who are they?"

"Chester Maxwell is the head of the chapter here, and I don't know—anyone in power, I guess. They see the poor as a plague, and they want the city."

"I gave up all the evidence we had to save you and Thea, so everything you just told me is moot now."

"What happened to Thea's sister? Does it have something to do with this?"

"The murders that led us to the chips and the Gold Legion were similar to Cora's disappearance. She was a pro, they were pros, but we never worked out why they were picked. She went missing shortly after the first murder, and she'd moved and worked in the same circles. Seemed a logical step to connect the two."

"Chester always talked about the lodge. I eventually asked what it was, and he told me that he and some of his friends rented a place once a month and invited their favourite sex worker along."

"The only two people you tell the truth to, you priest and your pro."

"I don't understand."

"I bet every one of the pros we have found dead visited the lodge. Men like to sound impressive. I bet they chatted and boasted about their GL ties, and while sex workers are, by nature, discreet, it meant they knew too much."

"How are you going to prove any of this if you gave away all the evidence?"

"I'm not. I can't. It was part of the deal; I have to step away. I'll tell Thea what you have told me and hope that it will bring her some answers."

"What are you thinking?"

"I feel relieved and not. I have the answers I wanted, but justice is much farther away. There is a fight coming. I don't know when, but I doubt we can sit it out."

"I meant about me."

"Nothing's changed. We are not perfect people. I know I'm not."

"You could always forgive me, no matter what I did."

"You're my wife." Walt shrugged.

"I knew, Walt. Deep down, I knew that what we were doing was wrong— that they were lying about the whys and the whos. But we had limitless funds to experiment with and endless test subjects. It was challenging, and worst of all, it was fun. I thought testing on death row inmates was fun. I told myself that because of their awful crimes, they were less than human, but how am I any better than them?"

"I have done a lot of terrible things in the last two years, and the way I figure it, you have paid your dues. I'm supposed to stay out of this, but I'm not sure I can watch the city burn. I thought for a second there that I could, but..."

"It's not who you are. I want you to fight the good fight and make Maxwell pay, but I need something else from you," Cleo said seriously.

"Anything."

"Maxwell has Gin Ricky's son. He's the kid Maxwell took. It's why he helped me. He hoped I'd know something, or be able to get him in the building. I owe him. We have to help him."

"And we will."

DID YOU REALLY WANT TO KNOW?

Thea's disorientation had resolved, and her headache had lessened to the amount of a minor migraine by the time she found herself curled up on her own couch, wrapped in the blankets Torrez had pulled from her bed.

She had spent less than two days confined in the Virtual Evidence Suite, but she felt aged, like she had lived several decades longer than her twenty-eight years. She had experienced real torture, both mental and physical, and it had shaken her, setting her adrift from the safety and sure footing of mental dry land.

She was more tired than she could remember being in her life and still felt the slight fracturing in her mind that meant she couldn't be sure she really had been released, but Torrez's reassuring presence went some ways to setting her at ease—he had not featured in the torture.

"I know you don't like wine, but it's a wine sort of day. How I got it is a tale for another time," he said, setting two overly full glasses on the table and climbing back under the duvet. "How you feeling?"

"Better," she lied.

"How are you really feeling?" Torrez said, putting an arm around her shoulders.

"Like I've had a lobotomy or a really bad trip," Thea said with a commendable effort at levity. "I'm angry, Drew. Furious. I have been hunted like an animal, beaten, and tortured. Benny is dead, Chowdhary is in the wind, and Walt gave up everything we had."

"To save your life. And Cleo's," Torrez said reasonably.

"I know. He did the right thing, but now we know that the city is in danger; we know who created the ghouls and who killed all those sex workers in the abstract anyway. We know a war is coming, and we can't do anything about it, and now I know first-hand what the Gold Legion and all the people like my dad are willing to do to get what they want. Ignorance was bliss, as it turned out. We are right back where we started, but it's worse because now I know. I know what's out there. Trust me; we were better off in the dark. I feel like I'm drowning."

Thea placed her head on Torrez's shoulder and closed her eyes.

"Yet. We can't do anything about it yet, but we will. We will find more evidence; we will bring these fuckers down. I promise," he said, lifting her chin so she had to look at him.

"Nearly dying has turned you into an optimist."

"I'm just holding the fort until you get back."

"Thank you for being here." Thea paused. "You have done awful things, you have been an idiot, and you have been selfish and cruel. You've been a terrible person, and I know I should be pissed, but I don't have the energy. Cora is gone, and Walt is as good as gone. You are all I have left."

"I have one friend, and you're it. You're stuck with me, Querida. I am ashamed of myself. I betrayed you, I betrayed myself, I betrayed everything we stand for, but I will make things right." Torrez opened his mouth and shut it again. "While we are talking about this, I have something to tell you. I know I've stretched your forgiveness already, but I went to threaten your father to release you, and it was a bad idea, and if you hadn't been in a hell of O'Malley's design, you probably would have told me not to, but I had to do something."

"My father has proven himself to be the devil; you make a deal with him—you lose your soul. Tell me you didn't."

"I didn't deal. I threatened him, and he threatened Marielena. I know I am a terrible husband, but I love her. Thea, I love her. I didn't realise how much until it was too late. If she died or was hurt, it would destroy me. He told me that I am to be his spy, and if I refuse, she dies. So, when you solve this puzzle and save the city, and you will, you can't tell me because, after today, you can't trust me. I have to put her first. I'm sorry."

"We do what we have to."

"I'm not abandoning you," Torrez said, kissing the top of her head.

"I know."

"That's not everything," Torrez said hesitantly.

"How bad is it?" she asked. She could tell by his face that he didn't want to say whatever he was about to, but felt he must.

"I'm not telling you this to hurt you," Torrez said

"The last few days have been a real shit show. I don't think you can make it any worse."

"Walt knew."

"Walt knew what?" Thea said, sitting up straighter.

"Walt knew that Cleo was alive. He's been trying to find her, to bring her back. He knew about Quietus—that's why he tried to buy drugs from Benjamin Pickford."

Thea's scalp tingled, and her insides knotted.

"For how long?"

"The whole time," Torrez said. His lips barely moved. "He knew she was alive all along."

It was like she had been hit by a train and submerged in ice-cold water all at once.

"I don't think he knew exactly where," Torrez ploughed on. "But he's known this whole time."

"So... when he would disappear for days at a time, he was looking for her," Thea said numbly. "When he told me he loved me, he knew she was out there and had every intention of getting her back." Thea laughed, though there was nothing funny about it.

"I'm sorry, Querida," he said. "You deserve so much better."

Torrez tried to pull her into a hug, but she pushed him away. She didn't want comfort. She wanted to scream. She wanted to rage. She needed to be away from Torrez. His comforting presence now felt like a burden. She stood, but there was nowhere to go.

Walt had known all along.

Walt had known all along.

She had felt sorry for him. She had looked the other way and covered for him because she, like he, had felt responsible for what happened to Cleo. She had allowed so many things to slide until she couldn't anymore, all because she had lost someone too and had thought that in that shared loss, no matter what the truth, they were together. She had forgiven him so many things because she thought he was grieving and drowning in guilt—but it was a lie. She couldn't bear it.

"He let me carry the guilt of what we did alone." The words burst from her because she couldn't keep them in.

Hot tears streamed from her eyes.

"How could I have been so stupid?" she said, looking up to the ceiling as if expecting to see answers there.

"This isn't about you; this is about him. All you did was love him, and there is no shame in that. You aren't weak or stupid for falling in love with the wrong man."

"I am not the person that lets their guard down. I'm a sceptic by nature, so why am I always so blind when it comes to Walt? Why do I keep letting him back in?" She could feel herself spiralling.

"You're rational; love isn't."

Thea sat down on the edge of the coffee table and put her head in her hands. Torrez patted her gently on the knee. "Could you leave? Please?" she said, moving her leg out of his reach.

"Not a chance," Torrez said, shaking his head.

"Drew, I just need to be alone. I'm not angry with you—"

"You have been through hell; alone is the last thing you should be," his tone made it clear he couldn't be swayed. "Did I ever tell you how I met my Marielena?"

"No, never," Thea said, wiping her nose on the back of her hand. "Is this important?"

"Come on." He grasped her hand; she didn't push him away. She knew he could sense how close she was to the precipice. He gave her hand a gentle tug, and Thea let herself be pulled back down onto the couch. When Torrez was satisfied that Thea was comfortable, he began.

"I met her brother Salvador in a gay club when I was about twenty-one. He was the most beautiful man I had ever seen. His smile was slightly crooked; it was unbelievably sexy. I knew I wasn't gay because I had loved women and still found them attractive, but I had thought for a while I might be bisexual; the second I saw him—I was sure. I was relatively innocent then," he gave Thea a roguish smile. She laughed softly and brushed a tear from her cheek. "He saw me watching him on the dance floor. He walked right up to me and said, 'If you are nervous about being with a man, I can teach you.' I think I fell in love with him right then. We had sex in the bathroom of the club. I hadn't known it could be that good, but I assumed it was just a club hookup—true love for one night only, but then, I saw him in a bar a couple of weeks later. From that point on, he became my everything; I was so in love that it was almost painful. We were together for nearly seven years, and then I made a mistake."

"What did you do?"

"I proposed. His family didn't know he was gay, and he wanted to keep it that way. I told him that nobody cared if a person was gay anymore, and he said he wasn't worried about what other people thought; he had always imagined himself marrying a woman and having kids 'as God intended'. I told him that even the church didn't care if he was gay, hell, the president's gay, but it was no good. He walked out of our apartment and never looked back. He left me, still on one knee holding a ring, and slammed the door."

"I'm sorry, Drew," Thea said, squeezing his knee.

"Don't be. Weirdly, it all worked out. About a month later, I met him at a friend of a friend's birthday party. He pretended he had never met me, that I was nobody, but he had brought his sister—Marielena. At first, I flirted with her to make him jealous, and it worked but not enough to bring him back to me, so I started dating her to make him mad, and it did; he was angry and jealous, he turned up at my door in the middle of the night telling me he loved me, but nothing had changed, and I refused to be closeted. I slammed the door in his face, but I was still bitter—I kept dating his sister, knowing it was making him miserable."

"Jesus, Drew."

"I know; it wasn't my finest moment. But then, I realised, somewhere along the way, I had fallen in love with her. I didn't mean to, but I did, and as she smiled at me across the table in some shitty little restaurant, I realised I loved her more than I had ever loved him, and I wanted to ask her to marry me, but I didn't want to lie, so I told her about Salvador, and she said, 'Do you still love him?' I said, 'No', she said, 'Do you still love me?' and when I said, 'Yes', she said, 'Get on with it then, propose.' Unlike him, she loved me completely, and she still does despite my faults. Things might have worked out for me in that regard, but my point is you can't help who you fall for, and you shouldn't punish yourself for it either. Relationships are messy, people are shitty, they do bad things, and they hurt each other; it's all part of life and love. You aren't broken because you fell in love with someone who is."

"Marielena is a wonderful woman; you should treat her better."

"I will." Torrez picked up the glasses of wine and handed one to Thea. "You get today."

"What?"

"You get today to feel sorry for yourself and mourn the loss of Walter; then tomorrow, you pick yourself up because you are far too brilliant to be handcuffed to a drowning man. It might not seem like it, but he has set you free, and when you see it, you'll know that I'm right."

"Thank you for being here," Thea said, taking a glug of wine. She screwed up her face at the unpleasant taste and rested her head on his shoulder.

A CHANGE IN THE TIDES

A thin-bladed knife pinned the little white card to Bastion's front door, leaving a deep gouge in the dark lacquered wood. Bastion had known what it would say before he had read it, and he knew exactly why he had received it. The small red "X" was a chit and what was owed was his life.

He turned the card over in his pocket as he walked between the tables inside Bavarder. It was the most expensive restaurant in the city by far. It was a wide and open space; the kitchen was visible to the dining room and monopolised the entirety of the east wall. The floors were polished olive stone, and the walls were such a pure white that they seemed to reflect the greenish hue. The tablecloths were white silk, and the chairs that surrounded them were dark wood upholstered with brownish-purple velvet. Large light bulbs hung over each table, casting a copper glow upon the diners.

Bastion spotted his prey at the chef's table right next to the kitchen. The waiters seemed to melt away when they saw where he was heading.

"Please, do join me," Harold Williams said sarcastically as Bastion dropped inelegantly into the chair opposite him. "This is bold, even for you."

"Oh, I don't know," Bastion said, taking the chit from his pocket and placing it on the table between them.

"I gave you that as a courtesy. We were friends of sorts before we became enemies. You should have run, Bastion." Harold sipped his wine.

"You no longer have the authority to dole out marks. So, this," he picked the bread knife from the table and stabbed it into the red "X". "Means nothing."

"Explain." It was a command in a tone seasoned by use.

"There has only ever been room for one of us. Sooner or later, you would have made a move to get rid of me; I made mine first. Benny Pickford is dead, the TPD's investigation is halted, and we have several moles within the department. Your daughter is disgraced, and Walter James has far more important things to worry about than our plans for the city. I know that you ordered Thea's torture and trial to give Walter time to come to you. I also know that you had planned for her escape should he refuse you. You have a father's love for her, and it's clouding your judgement. I know you told Cora to run when last you spoke, but thanks to you, she won't listen to either of us. Chester agrees that you have the potential to become a liability, and as such, you are on probation and shall answer to me from now on."

"You?" Harold laughed derisively. "You're barely more than a child playing at being a man. You play checkers while we play chess. You think you have mated me, but you're wrong. The chit may not be sanctioned, but I'd glance over my shoulder from time to time if I were you; you never know who could be coming at you from behind."

"Your purpose is ceremonial at best."

Bastion tossed the breadknife carelessly back down onto the table, it clattered mutedly.

"And what do you offer the cause, hmm? What makes you the man to depose me? You think because you whisper in Chester's ear that you are safe? You are naïve. He will cast you aside long before he does me. You might afford him an army, but I am the real power in these parts. Take your idle threats and leave me to my lunch, boy."

"Thea trusts me."

"Speak plainly."

"I know your pressure points, and as I bide my time pretending to be her friend and making sure her investigation stays shelved, just remember that with me around, she will always be moments from death. Think about that before you make a move on me. In short, I own you, bitch."

Bastion leant over the table and stuck his forefinger into the sauce on Harold's plate. He brought it to his lips and let out a moan of satisfaction as the sumptuous sauce danced across his tongue.

"This place is almost worth the price."

Bastion sauntered from the restaurant, but not before he had seen Harold down his cutlery in disgust and push the nearly full plate of food away from him.

HETAERA

Thea jerked awake as Torrez snored beside her. They had talked and laughed for hours; it had been exactly the kind of catharsis she had needed. Now, she was thirsty. She carefully got to her feet, trying not to wake Torrez as he slept with his head lolling on the back of the couch and his mouth hanging open.

She pulled a mug from the cupboard over the sink and noticed the discarded remains of the wine glass she had shattered when Walt had left her. A lot had happened since then; it made it all seem oddly distant. A soft but insistent knocking stopped her descent down the rabbit hole of miserable thoughts.

On tiptoes, she walked to the door and opened it. Cleo stood in the hallway in a long camel coat tied at the waist.

"Can I come in?"

"Sure."

Thea ushered her inside and beckoned her to follow. She led them into her bedroom and closed the door, leaving Torrez still fast asleep in the living room.

"Sorry, Drew has had a rough couple of days; best let him sleep."

"You and Torrez?" Cleo's eyes widened almost imperceptibly.

"Um, no. He's just a very good friend."

"I didn't mean anything..." She trailed off, embarrassed.

"It's fine...Do you...Need something?"

Thea was extremely uncomfortable; the air between them seemed to be filled with all her misdeeds.

"Yes, right...May I?" Cleo gestured to the bed.

"Please."

She took off her outerwear to reveal a beautiful pearl coloured silk dress. Thea got the impression that she was dressing like her old self in the hope it would make her feel it. She folded her coat neatly and placed it on the bed, then sat down beside it. The moment Cleo made contact with the mattress, Thea's mind was plagued with thoughts of Walt naked upon it, his face contorted in ecstasy. She forced the images from her mind as guilt bubbled uneasily in her stomach.

"I want to thank you for what you did. You risked your life for me. You didn't have to do that."

Thea flushed. She could only nod as she backed away slightly to lean against her dresser.

"I'm just going to be straight with you if that's all right. I know you suspect that I know something about your case and the Gold Legion, and you're right—I do."

"What do you know?" Thea said quickly.

"That's not why I'm here. I've told Walt everything. I'll let him tell you the details as he sees fit."

"I'm not sure he and I are on speaking terms," Thea said evasively.

Cleo looked around the room. Her eyes fell upon a man's shirt draped over the nightstand. Thea's insides froze.

"When did he leave you?"

Thea said nothing. She wanted to melt into the wall and disappear.

"After Gin Ricky's, right?"

Thea nodded reluctantly, her eyes downcast.

"How long were you together?"

"Not long."

"And before?"

"Cleo, I'm sorry. There aren't enough apologies in the world...But this is a conversation for you and Walt."

"He doesn't know that I know, and I'd like it to stay that way."

Cleo reached over to the shirt on the nightstand and pulled it onto her lap. Her fingers traced the wispy pieces of thread left by the missing buttons.

"Will you keep my secret?" Cleo asked when Thea failed to reply.

"He asked me the same thing."

"And I'm sure you have no desire to be in the middle of our marriage, ironic as that may sound."

"None."

"Will you sit with me?"

Thea thought for a moment. She wanted to be further away, not closer, but she understood it was an olive branch, a clear sign that this meeting was not supposed to be hostile.

Slowly she moved over to the other side of the bed and sat down.

"I didn't come here to torture you; I just need to understand, and I can't ask my husband. The embarrassment would eat him alive."

Thea considered this for a moment; how odd it was that after everything Cleo had been through, she was still concerned about Walt, even though she knew what he had done.

"I'll tell you whatever you want. I owe you that at least."

"Thea, you saved my life; you owe me nothing."

Thea flushed again; she couldn't handle the grace Cleo was displaying. It felt like she was staring at the sun.

"How did it start?" Cleo asked, almost business-like.

"There was no one moment, we had a connection, and the more we fought it, the less we could deny it."

"It's that simple, huh? You know, looking back, I think I knew. He had what I called his "Thea look" whenever he spoke about you, and even though the signs were there, I tried to ignore it; I remained wilfully ignorant." Her tone was detached and a little sad. It made Thea more uncomfortable than tears or anger ever could. "When did you start sleeping together?"

"Cleo, I don't think I can do this."

"Please, I need to talk to someone about it, but I don't have anyone. My friends are strangers now or still work for Medicorum, and I can't talk to Walt because it would shatter the illusion he's painstakingly cultivating and I love the 'us' he is inventing for us, but I still need to know, understand. Does that make sense?"

"Two years. We were…for two years."

Cleo blanched. Thea's skin crawled.

"I see," Cleo said faintly. "I can see he loves you. It's obvious. Do you love him?"

"Yes," Thea said, her eyes stinging.

"Why haven't you been together until recently?"

Thea let out a sigh that could have been a sob or a laugh.

"So much has happened. The guilt warped him, I think. He became someone neither of us recognised. It was like the man I knew had disappeared. The Walt I… cared for is different from the Walt he is now. I thought we could…but I was wrong." Thea could feel tears pooling in her eyes; she willed them away. "He and I are done, and we would be whether you were here or not. Please believe me; I'm not trying to take him from you—I never was."

"I do believe you. I don't think either of you thought about me at all."

"I'm so sorry," Thea said helplessly.

"I don't need your apologies; your honesty is enough."

Cleo stood folding her coat and Walt's discarded shirt over her arm.

"Wait," Thea said, standing, too. "If you know something about Medicorum and the Gold Legion, you could be the key to bringing it all down. You could be a witness—"

"No," Cleo said succinctly. "My hands are not clean in this, but I have paid enough. I'm just starting to get my life back, and I'm not willing to do anything to jeopardise that. Thank you for being honest with me. I'll show myself out."

Thea could only watch as Cleo walked out of the room. She waited for the soft snap as the front door shut. When it came, her legs gave way, and she dropped back onto the bed, tears flowing silently down her face.

Torrez appeared in the bedroom a moment later.

"Was that—?" he broke off when he saw Thea's face. "Come here, Querida."

He sat down beside her and pulled her into a warm hug. She cried against his chest as he gently stroked her back, muttering platitudes in Spanish that she didn't understand; they were soothing, nonetheless.

TRANSCRIPT OF RETURN TO DUTY INTERVIEW
Subject: Det. Thea Williams Date: July 17th 2425 Case: #27932-MP-34
Commanding Officer: Captain Betty Charles
Transcribed by: Officer William Fenske

OFFICIAL INVESTIGATION INTO DEATH OF BENJAMIN PICKFORD

Written Transcript as follows:

```
BC: The Purpose of this meeting is to discuss your return to
active duty.
TW: I understand.
BC: While you have been cleared of the murder charge in
relation to the unlawful death of Benjamin "Benny" Pickford,
you remain a material witness to the final days of his life.
TW: I understand.
BC: With this in mind, it is inappropriate for you to return
to your active duties as a Detective Second Class.
TW: But—
BC: As such, you will be assigned desk duties until such time
as the case is resolved.
TW: And what if it's never solved?
BC: You will retain your badge, rank, gun, and all related
privileges, as well as full pay and compensation for the
treatment you received while in the custody of the Tenebrium
Police Department.
TW: I was subjected to mental torture by one of our own;
quantify those damages for me. Please.
BC: You will assist your fellow detectives in their
investigations within the confines of the TPD. Do you
understand the parameters of your new duties?
TW: I understand that I am being punished for something I had
no part in.
BC: You will retain 1 of the 3 strikes that you received.
TW: What? Why?
BC: Resisting arrest and assault of a law enforcement officer.
TW: They were trying to kill me.
BC: Do you understand? [PAUSE] Detective Williams, do you
understand?
TW: I understand.
BC: There will be no suspension or disciplinary action
accompanying this strike as the department recognises the undue
stress caused.
TW: Is that all?
BC: This concludes your official "Return to Work" interview.
Thank you for your time.
[Door slam]
```

Elanor Miller

NOTE: The rest of the official record was destroyed during the fire of September 2427. Summarised copies can be found in the virtual evidence archive.

THREE MONTHS LATER

KEEP CALM AND CARRY ON

The days and weeks that had passed since Thea's return to duty were a blur of late nights, dead ends, and caffeine induced jitters. Thea had engulfed herself in the search for Benny's killer, but as her investigation was not sanctioned, she was only able to investigate off the clock. During her work hours, she was relegated to her desk, filling out forms and completing the paperwork of her colleagues.

By day she was a glorified secretary, and by night she was only a few short steps away from vigilante. Not only had she continued to search for Benny's murderer long after the official investigation had been shelved, she had found a new obsession that went far beyond a desire for justice—searching for evidence of the Gold Legion's grand plans for Tenebrium City. This was far more difficult than even she had imagined, however.

Not a single person, cop, civilian, user, or dealer had come across any trace of Styxx or Quietus since her release. There had been no more murders, no errant ghouls, and as far as tangible evidence was concerned, the Morpheus chips might never have existed. Moreover, the Onyx Legion patrols had all but disappeared; the only place they could be found now was at the SubLevel gates, marching their usual patrol roots and helping the pop-up clinics, donated by Medicorum, hand out free medical supplies.

All in all, the city was quiet, far too quiet.

Walt had kept his distance; in fact, Thea hadn't seen more than the back of his head as it ducked into the officer's lounge in weeks. She preferred it this way; while at work, she could pretend he didn't exist. It was only in the lonely hours of the night that she let herself dwell on thoughts of him.

"Could I trouble you to complete this report on the burglary at the National Museum?" asked Detective Diontae Fischer, a tall and burly Black person who worked Bunco, with bright pink cornrow braids that fell all the way to the middle of their back.

"Sure, I loves me some paperwork."

"Desk duty getting you down?" they asked sympathetically.

"It's a nice change of pace, sitting back and letting someone else get stabbed or shot at," Thea said. She had spouted this lie so often that she had almost convinced herself it was true.

"Are you sure?" Diontae pressed. "You don't look so good."

"The apartment above mine is being renovated around the clock, so I haven't been sleeping so good." Another lie she told automatically when the toll of her out of office investigations showed under her eyes.

"Earplugs will save your life," Diontae said sagaciously.

"I'll try that."

Since her desk designation, Thea had become known for speedy and efficient work. This hadn't been achieved due to her inherent diligence, but rather out of necessity; the quicker she completed her reports, the more time she had to spare with the TPD's resources.

To that end, she completed Diontae's paperwork at lightspeed, allowing her to return to the task at hand.

To the untrained eye, her desk was a mess, but to Thea, it was perfectly organised. She knew exactly what lead or case each pile of papers and data tablets corresponded to and had managed to successfully camouflage her investigation into Benny and the Gold Legion with files on the active cases around the department.

Her current point of focus was the knife that had killed Benny. It was an expensive blade; only a few stores in the city stocked it, but none would admit to having sold one recently. Of course, it could have been purchased from an off-colony supplier and delivered to the culprit, but it should have gone through checks before it was delivered. If it had been mailed, there was no record of it, but a knife couldn't materialise out of thin air. She suspected one of the suppliers within the city limits was lying and was spending a lot of her time trying to link one of the five possible weapons merchants to Medicorum and any of its innumerable subsidiaries.

When she wasn't trying to trace the elusive knife, she was trying to detect a hint of the illegal drug trade that seemed to have completely shut up shop. Even the commonplace illicit substances that were easily purchased and barely monitored by law enforcement had become impossible to procure, leading to violence between users who were desperate for their fix and dealers who had found themselves without product.

Cleo, wishing to distance herself from her past, had gifted Thea the search for Gin Ricky's son, but that too was a bust. While Thea had devoted much of her time to looking for the young man, with no leads to follow, she could find neither hide nor hair of him.

And if all else failed, she returned to Cora's disappearance. She had looked over the so-called evidence more times than she could count. She had read the reports and re-interviewed all the witnesses mentioned on her own time, but still, she had uncovered nothing.

At the end of every day, she went home to stare at the east wall of her apartment. The floor to ceiling windows were covered with bits of paper, data chips, and tablets, all leading nowhere.

Clearly worried about her, she had dinner with Torrez every second night. He turned up without fail no matter how many times she told him she wanted to be alone.

"How long has that been going on?" Torrez asked on one particularly cold night. He had bumped into Bastion, who was leaving as he was coming in.

"I don't know what you're talking about," Thea had lied.

Torrez looked unconvinced, but didn't push the point.

In truth, Thea had been sleeping with Bastion for about a month. He had become a welcome distraction to the trials of her life. Her time with him was meaningless, and they both knew it, but during the hours in which they enjoyed each other, she could briefly forget the downward trajectory she was stuck on.

In short, Thea was spiralling.

MACK THE KNIFE

Around two weeks after discovering Thea's tryst with Bastion, Torrez found himself on his way to the District Attorney's office. He was giving reports on Thea's wellbeing just as often as he was performing grunt work or passing information. He had no idea what had wrought this bout of fatherly care, but he was sure that it didn't bode well.

As had happened on several occasions previously, he ran into Bastion in the lift, and as usual, they shared a curt nod and awkward silence before parting ways when Torrez reached Harold's floor.

Torrez was shown into the DA's office by the ever-colourful Zhao, who had dyed his hair electric-blue since Torrez had seen him last. He looked as he always did, mildly disgruntled.

"Close the door," Harold ordered from where he stood at the window, staring out at his empire.

"I know you've made me your bitch," Torrez said, doing as he was bid. "And I'm suitably intimidated, but I'd appreciate more notice in future. I can't keep abandoning my actual police work if you want me to continue to be an effective double agent."

"Noted," the DA said. The impatience in his voice was clear.

"Good, because—"

"Shut up, Andrew. We don't have much time."

Torrez pulled his fingers across his lips as if zipping them shut. A vein in Harold's temple twitched.

"Before I tell you what I am about to, I need you to understand that I am still a man of considerable means and you, and by extension, your wife, are still at my mercy."

"I understand," Torrez said through clenched teeth.

"There is a coup happening, and I am the object of its ire. You think me cold and cruel, and you are correct to believe those things, but I have been keeping Thea alive. If these usurpers have their way, I will be in a position to protect no one. You think I am an evil man..."

"But better the devil you know? Your replacement won't know I exist, so if I let you be ousted, I'm off the hook."

"You think so? Thea and Walter will be dead as they know too much, and you, and anyone who has come in contact with the case, will follow quickly after. Just ask Benjamin Pickford...oh, wait."

"Cute," Torrez said, irked. "What do you want from me? I'm just a pawn, as you love to remind me. I don't see how I can help you thwart a deposition."

"These waters are far too deep for the likes of you. I'm not asking you to wade into legion business; there are far more expedient ways to kill you."

"And so, I ask again—"

"There is going to be another murder. Another prostitute's body will be dumped in the city. Get there before O'Malley or anyone else. Take the chip, take the evidence you need to have the Pleasure Quarter murder case re-opened."

"You had it closed; why would you want that? How does this help you?"

"I act by proxy, moving my pawns," he looked pointedly at Torrez. "Where they need to go. I have kept to the shadows, and as such, my hands appear clean. I will burn the house down; it may take my empire with it, but the fall of my enemies shall be much harder than mine."

"Clean, huh?"

This would have been a good plan if Bastion hadn't been just outside, listening at the door. Had it not been for that slight snag, it might have worked.

DÉJÀ VU

"Williams. My office, now."

"No thanks, Captain. I'm good here."

The change in the atmosphere was palpable. The usual hustle and bustle of the bullpen died instantly, all conversation stopped, and the officers nearby stood as if they had been petrified.

"Detective Williams—"

"Don't you mean 'Desk Jockey Williams'?"

The collective intake of breath from the spectating detectives was clearly audible.

"Do not make me ask again, Detective, because if I have to, you will find yourself in need of another job."

Thea glanced around her co-workers; their expressions ranged from humour and admiration to disdain and indifference.

"Just go, Thea," said a quiet voice near the lifts.

For the first time since she had been released, Thea made eye contact with Walt. He was beseeching her. It wasn't until she found herself staring into those beautiful blue eyes that she realised; she hated him, completely and without exception.

Thea drew her eyes away from him with as much contempt as she could muster. She stood so quickly that her chair toppled over. The resulting clatter echoed in the silence.

With poise that put Thea to shame, the captain turned and walked towards her office, making it clear that Thea was to follow.

She did.

"This city will eat you alive if you let it. I told you that on your first day, and it holds true now."

The captain walked deliberately around her desk and took up the seat behind it.

"Well, thanks. I'll be sure to log that away." Belligerence came easy to Thea these days; it was a by-product of feeling like she had nothing to lose.

"I know you are having a hard time, but if you continue to talk to me like that, I will dismiss you," the captain said sternly. "People are worried about you, Thea."

"By 'people', you mean Torrez. I don't have 'people' anymore; I have 'person'."

"Yes, I mean Torrez and sit down. I won't have you shouting at me from the doorway."

"I'm not shouting."

"You will."

While Thea knew she had a cheek to think it, but the captain looked tired and put-upon. She had lost some of her ultra-professional manner in favour of a candour that Thea respected even though she tried not to.

The chair facing the captain should have had her name on it, Thea thought as she sat down. She had spent just as much time there as at her desk of late.

"I'm suspending you," the captain said without preamble.

"Excuse me? For what?"

"I was sketchy on the whys—I was thinking misappropriation of resources. Now, I'm suspending you for insubordination." The captain's tone was baiting; Betty had something to say.

"You told me when you made me release Benny that as long as it didn't interfere with my work, you didn't care if I investigated on the side."

"It is affecting your work, and I never said I didn't care; I said that I doubted I'd be able to stop you. It's not the same."

"I haven't gone near a crime scene, I haven't stepped out of bounds, I do the paperwork I'm given, and I do it in a timely manner."

"Don't try to play me. I'd put you on leave if I thought you'd go, but you won't, so I'm suspending you. Don't look at me like that. You aren't yourself. You are bored and frustrated. I understand that, but there is more going on here. You don't want to talk to me, that's fine, but I can't ignore your behaviour. You are obsessed with Benjamin Pickford's murder, and it's not healthy. You need to step back. You have been scrabbling around in the darkness so long I think you've forgotten that there is light out there."

"Inspirational. Truly."

"Detective Williams, you are hereby suspended for a period of two weeks. You are not permitted to set foot on TPD grounds unless summoned, and you are not permitted to take part in any activities directly or indirectly related to your duties as a detective."

"Two weeks?"

"You have been through a lot; you need a break. You need time to come to terms with what happened to you."

"I'm fine."

"No, you aren't. You were stabbed and poisoned, attacked in your own home, hunted by the police, arrested for a murder you didn't commit and subjected to a kind of mental torture that would be illegal anywhere but here.

And that's just recently. You think I'm above it all, but I see. You sister's death—"

"She's not dead," Thea cut across her vehemently.

"What happened to Cora," the captain went on. "Things with your partner—"

"Walt has nothing to do with this."

Thea jumped up from her chair. She didn't want to talk about Walt, or Cora, or Benny, or anything else.

"Get some help, Thea. No one could cope with what you have been through on their own." The captain sounded so sincere that Thea couldn't look at her. She stormed out of the room, slamming the door behind her.

There was a tiny part of her brain that knew she was behaving poorly, that pushing the captain was stupid, that not doing as she was commanded would make her investigations nearly impossible, but it was buried deep beneath her new reckless streak borne out of hurt and loss, loneliness, and a feeling of defeat so acute it was painful.

Walt was waiting for her outside the captain's office.

"What happened?"

Thea ignored him.

"Thea," he called to her retreating back. "What do you need?"

"I need you to stay away from me—that is the only thing I will ever need from you."

She didn't look back to see the effect of her words. She made it all the way to the elevator before he caught up with her. He slipped inside just as the doors shut, trapping them together.

"Don't say a word. You and I have nothing to say to each other," Thea growled.

"You aren't acting like yourself."

"You're right. I'm acting like you."

Walt made a face that said, "Fair point".

The elevator stopped to allow a group of people in Hazard suits to enter. Thea stepped out, not caring that she was still nearly a hundred floors from the lobby. Again, Walt followed.

"Thea, talk to me. I'm worried about you."

"You gave away everything we had."

"To save you," Walt said angrily.

"I never asked you to. I asked you to protect Cleo."

"I did. I protected you both."

"A man who protects his wife and his mistress? Lucky us. What a gentleman. You gave away everything we had. My father and all those like him think they can get away with the things they have done, and now because of you, they're right."

"You would have been killed."

"They had nothing; they were trying to scare you, and it worked. Walter James thinking with his dick again."

"What the hell has gotten into you?"

"They've won, and that's on you."

Thea made for the nearest stairwell and began her arduous descent; Walt, for once, didn't follow.

THE DEVIL WENT DOWN TO GEORGIA

"You should cut the guy some slack," Torrez said as Bill left the canteen looking forlorn.

"He's a traitor," Walt said, sipping at his triple espresso.

These days, Bill never spent more time in Walt's company than it took to leave the room. Walt seemed perfectly content with this arrangement. Torrez felt it was a tad unfair.

"Right, because you're a saint."

"Don't start with me, Torrez."

The two men were sitting opposite each other at one of the many circular tables inside the TPD's canteen, Walt drinking his fourth consecutive coffee while Torrez nursed a dubious-looking berry smoothie. They had come to an uneasy understanding of late; while they were unlikely to be friends, they were capable of being allies.

"Why did you ask me to meet you?" Walt asked, grimacing as the bitter coffee touched his tongue.

"The DA," Torrez looked around the room to check if he and Walt were alone—they were. "Told me that there is going to be another victim with a chip."

"Why would he tell you that?" Walt asked shrewdly.

"Seems he might not be the DA for much longer. Apparently, he's an 'if I can't have it, no one can' kinda guy."

"You're sure this isn't a trap?"

"Of course, I'm not sure. We don't really have a choice, though. It could be our only chance to get the evidence we need."

"Fine." Walt heaved a heavy sigh. "Give me a shout when the call comes in."

"What is the matter with you, Cabron?" Torrez asked, correctly interpreting the furrow of Walt's brow. "If you say 'Thea', I will smack you."

"She's not herself."

"You're not supposed to care anymore, remember?" Torrez said, waving away the conversation.

"You need to talk to her before she burns out," Walt said, disregarding Torrez's jibe.

"First of all, I'm not getting in between you two; that is a sure-fire way to get burned and secondly, no, she won't. Captain Charles suspended her for two weeks for her attitude."

"She's not just gonna sit at home."

"No, but at least she won't be here in harm's way."

Torrez gulped down his smoothy with a shudder; it was vile. Even though the DA had afforded him the best treatment money could buy, he was still having trouble with solid food.

"Right. Well, you know where to find me," Walt said, standing up. There was a suspicious clink as his coat hit the edge of the table.

"The nearest bar?"

"Fuck you, Torrez."

"Fuck you, too."

The call came in five days later. Torrez had been about to go home to sleep on the couch as he had been for the last few months, when Walt came charging into the TPD locker room.

"Where?" Torrez said at once.

"Georgia Peach."

Georgia Peach was a bordello that specialised in fetish play. It was one of the most well-respected brothels in the city, not only for its services, but for the way it treated those who worked there. It was an employee-owned company with a notoriously clean record. Torrez had frequented the establishment once or twice and had enjoyed his visits thoroughly. Tonight's visit would be different, however.

The Ninth Circle was the largest "Dungeon" playroom that Georgia Peach offered. Everything inside was in shades of black and red, except for the bondage furniture, which was made from handsome East Indian Rosewood. Drawers and shelves lined the walls, kitted out with all manner of sex toys and fetish implements. Different shaped racks were free-standing in the centre of the large space, allowing for various levels of restraint. There were also leather-clad benches that to a layman might have looked fit for weight-lifting and a humongous bed to the north drenched in black satin.

Torrez found he had no time for the BDSM equipment, drawn as his eyes were to the body. A short wooden cross that came to chest height was placed in front of the large bed. On it was one of the most horrific sights Torrez had ever seen. Before the unknown female victim had died, she had been kneeling naked facing the cross, her hands raised above her head and held there by supple leather cuffs. Now, she slumped against the restraints. There was a large and sickening hole in the side of her head that had blown so much of her skull away that Torrez could see her tongue from the back at the bottom of the fatal crater. Blood and brain matter had been splattered far and wide.

"I see the devil in the flesh on days like this," Torrez said to Walt, who was stepping carefully around the body, placing evidence markers, his face a mix of anger and revulsion. He nodded.

Torrez took a deep breath and blew it out.

"All right," he called to the forensic team. "I want this place scoured, we don't leave until we find every skull fragment, and if you find anything metal, you bring it to me or Walter immediately."

"Torrez, c'mere," Walt said as he examined the cuffs attaching the victim's body to the cross.

"No way, you c'mere."

Shaking his head, Walt delicately made his way over to Torrez.

"Where's her client?"

"What?"

"She didn't tie herself up, so someone must have been here when she died."

As if on command, a man wearing an open white shirt over a latex jumpsuit sprung out from under the bed and bolted for the door.

Torrez sprinted after him, Walt closely behind.

They chased him out into the street. The neon lights refracting off the rain made for good camouflage, but Torrez saw the man as he darted seemingly undetected into an alleyway between the cinema and yet another brothel.

"TPD!" Torrez yelled from the mouth of the alley.

It was gloomy and, for all intents and purposes, a dead-end due to the chicken wire fence roughly halfway down. Torrez knew the man must be there somewhere, the fence was far too high for him to have completed the climb before he had arrived, but there were multiple dumpsters and piles of rubbish that provided ample hiding spots.

"Would you stop hiding?" Torrez called exasperatedly. "We know you didn't kill her."

For a moment, there was nothing. Then the man crawled out from a rain-sodden cardboard box, hands held above his head.

"You don't think I killed her?" he asked unsurely, stepping into the light. He was a young Black man wearing red contact lenses and with clear signs of blood all over him. Now that Torrez could see him properly, he had obviously grabbed the shirt to cover his latex suit, which was part of a devil costume.

"I know you didn't, but I do need you to tell me what happened to her."

"We were in a scene. That's a—"

"I'm familiar."

"Right, we were in a scene—a corrupted by the devil sorta thing—and she starts saying that her head hurts. I offer to end our session, but she's all, 'No, no, you'll get your money's worth', so I tie her up, and we start...doing our thing, and she starts to moan. I think she's having a good time, and then she starts to scream. Horrible, pained screams, like nothing I'd ever heard. I stop what I'm doing, and I'm trying to untie her, but she's thrashing around, and then her head exploded. Her head fucking exploded. I called the cops then realised I was covered in her blood, and well, they aren't always so understanding, so I hid under the bed. I know it was dumb—but I panicked—her head exploded."

Torrez rubbed his eyes.

"Did you notice if she had a small metal disc on her temple?"

"She did! It was a weird little glowing thing, but I thought maybe it was something to do with her job."

"All right, thank you for your time. You're going to need to come with us back to the TPD; you're covered in evidence, but after that, you'll be free to go. Excuse me," Torrez said, holding a hand up and stepping a small distance away as a call came into his Cicada. "Yeah, what's up?"

"I think we found what you were looking for, Sir."

"Great, give it to Walt."

"He's not here."

I PUT A SPELL ON YOU

Walt burst out of Georgia Peach moments after Torrez. The rain outside was torrential, and he quickly lost sight of the running man, but he could see Torrez's pale trench coat flapping behind him as the detective ran a small distance ahead.

Walt was halfway across the crowded street when he heard the soft *thwip* sound and then felt a slight sting on the side of his neck. He stumbled, unable to control his legs. His vision began to blur. Hands grabbed him under the arms and began to pull him away from Torrez, who had just ducked into an alley. He protested feebly, but had no strength to fight against whoever was guiding him away from his duties.

Flashing lights.
A searing pain.
Muttered words.
Paralysis.
Cold.
So cold.

Water was pooling in his ear. No, it was raining. Rainwater was pooling in his ear; the sensation was horrible. He was soaked to the bone. Walt opened his eyes. There was a milky white haze obscuring his vision. He blinked rapidly until it cleared, and he could see his surroundings.

He was lying on his side on a park bench. The park itself was small and dark. A patch of grass in the centre sported five trees, and there was a gravel path encircling it. There was only one wooden bench to admire the flowers planted here and there, and Walt was lying across it.

He tried to sit up, but couldn't. He tried again, but felt a powerful wave of nausea that made the world spin. He lay back down.

How had he gotten there?

"Walt? Walter? Are you here, asshole?"

He recognised the voice; it was smooth and agitated. Torrez. It was Torrez's voice.

Walt called out, except all that escaped him was a strangled sort of moan.

"Bill, you search the alley across the street. I'll give the park a quick sweep. Walter?"

"Dr...oooo..."

"Walt?"

Footsteps. Feet pounding gravel. Then hands, taking his pulse, shaking him. Were his eyes closed again, or was it really so dark?

"Walter? Can you hear me? Are you hurt? What happened?"

Torrez's concerned face swam in and out of focus as it loomed over him.

"How...did I...get...here?" Walt's words were slurred.

"Are you drunk? Are you fucking kidding me?"

Torrez began to mutter angrily in Spanish, but Walt was too drowsy to follow.

"Not...drunk," Walt garbled.

"Bullshit, you stink of whiskey. You're lit!"

With shaky and uncoordinated hands Walt fumbled around for his hip flask. It was empty, but it didn't hold anywhere near enough booze to get him drunk. His mind was so foggy he could hardly focus. Maybe he was drunk.

"Can you stand?"

Walt tried. He could not.

"For fuck's sake," Torrez spat.

He leaned down and grabbed Walt. Supporting the majority of his weight, Torrez pulled Walt to his feet.

As soon as he was upright, Walt vomited, splattering the ground with a clear foamy fluid. The purge did nothing to settle his stomach or clear his head.

"That's just fucking wonderful. Liquid lunch, was it?"

Torrez half dragged him to the street, where he thrust Walt unceremoniously into a Jonk and climbed in after him. They must not have been far from his home because the Jonk ride was mercifully short. The movement of the transporter had Walt wanting to vomit again.

Torrez hauled Walt from the transporter into the lift, then heaved him along the corridor. Walt flinched as Torrez hammered on his front door. Walt closed his eyes, too discombobulated to keep them open anymore. His world was spinning.

"I'm sorry about this," Torrez was saying to Cleo. "I'm sure he'll be fine once he sleeps it off. Do you need help putting him to bed?"

"The couch will be fine."

More movement, then Walt felt himself being shoved. He landed on something soft and squishy, then fell asleep.

JOLENE

It was a bright morning, or so the artificial lights of the city made it appear. The faux sun beat through the huge windows, causing the spotless counters of Thea's living room to gleam like it was a show home.

Thea paced nervously, checking and rechecking her clothes and hair. She arranged and rearranged the plates of food on the kitchen island and used her Index to check the time over and over.

At precisely nine o'clock, there was a soft knock at the door. Thea forced herself to walk calmly. She waited, hand outstretched, took a deep breath, and then opened it.

Cleo stood before her, dressed in a copper jumpsuit, the pearls she had always worn in the past hanging neatly on her chest where they belonged. Thea and Cleo had barely crossed paths in the last few months, but every time they had, Cleo was immaculate. Yet, something seemed off, like she was trying and failing to capture her pre-Quietus self.

"Thank you for coming," Thea said, slightly breathlessly. "Please, come in."

Cleo looked at her with what Thea thought might be curiosity, then stepped inside. She glanced at the food on the kitchen counter then moved into the living room. She took off her white coat and perched herself on the armchair, which she had no way of knowing had often held her husband.

"Are you all right?" Cleo asked, placing her coat neatly over the arm of her chair.

"I'm fine. There's just a lot going on," Thea said, sitting on the couch opposite.

There was something a little too sympathetic about Cleo's gaze. Thea had to look away.

"Walt finally told you everything," Cleo said matter-of-factly.

"Torrez," Thea corrected succinctly.

"I see. You must have questions," Cleo said, with the air of someone about to jump into ice-cold water.

"Just one, actually. Will you testify? I know you don't want to, and you are worried about the impact it could have on your life, but we—"

"Yes," Cleo said simply, stopping Thea in her tracks. "On one condition."

"Anything," Thea said excitedly. This was going far better than she had hoped.

"He came home drunk last night. He calls me Thea without meaning to, and doesn't even notice; it's as natural as breathing."

Not for the first time, Thea felt the awful mixture of frore fear and guilt roil her insides.

"What I'm asking is unfair," Cleo continued. "You saved my life knowing it would destroy your happiness."

Thea shook her head. "It wasn't a kindness. Walt would have died of guilt."

"I think that's the first lie you've told me since our reunion. I'm begging you, Thea—"

"You don't need to do this."

"When he comes to you," Cleo ploughed on, ignoring Thea. "And he will come; I need you to say 'no'."

"He won't come," Thea said quietly. "He made his choice."

"No matter how hard you push him away, he will try to come back to you. He can't help it. It's always been you." Cleo kept going, seemingly unaware of how uncomfortable she was making Thea as she herself flushed with embarrassment. "I forgive you for the past. I'm here to ensure my future. I came to ask you to let me keep him, to lie, to tell him you don't want him."

"I don't," Thea said a little too loudly.

"I remember everything, Thea. Everything." Cleo got to her feet and paced like she was giving testimony in court. "I remember seeing you underneath him; your bodies joined, that burning look on his face that he has never had when looking at me. I know he doesn't love me. He wants to, he tries to, but he can't. He is sweet and kind and caring, and if I didn't know him, really know him, I would believe that he loved me, but I can see that he's miserable underneath the façade, and so are you."

"I'm fine," Thea lied.

"No, you aren't," Cleo all but shouted. She stopped for a moment to calm herself before continuing. "You're crumbling, and woman to woman, I can see it. It pains me to add to your burden; it truly does. I've been there. I know what it feels like to fall apart at the seams. I know he loves you, and I know you love him, but I love him, and I can't let him go. He is my anchor. He's the thing that reminds me of who I was before this. It's selfish, but I need him. I don't have anyone else. I'm sorry to ask you this cruel thing. You saved my life, but when he comes to you, please say 'no'. Lie, hurt him, tell him anything, but I am begging you, please say 'no'."

There was a wild glint in her eye as she waited for Thea to speak, but Thea found she couldn't. After a moment, Thea nodded.

"Thank you," Cleo said soberly.

Thea felt another pang of guilt as she saw the humiliation of what Cleo had just had to do wash over her face.

"It's not because of him," Thea whispered. She didn't know why, but she felt a strong urge to justify herself, to prove that her troubles didn't begin and end with a man. "It's because of Cora and Benny and everything that has happened. I'm not crippled by the loss of him."

"Then you are a stronger woman than I am." Cleo pulled a tissue from her handbag and dabbed it gently under her eyes. She grabbed her coat and folded it neatly over her arm. "Let me know when you would like to take my statement. I wish you well, I really do."

HAIR OF THE DOG

Walt's mouth was dry, and his head ached. He was uncomfortable. Something was cutting off the circulation to his right arm. He had been awakened by intense pins and needles. He opened his eyes. Nothing changed. It was still dark. It took him a moment to realise he was lying face down. With difficulty, he pushed himself into a sitting position and disentangled himself from his trench coat and suit jacket, both of which had been wrapped awkwardly around his arm.

He didn't remember falling asleep on the couch. In fact, he didn't remember coming home. He was managing his drinking, a sip here, a sip there, just enough to keep him level. He couldn't have gotten blackout drunk, and yet, he was definitely hungover.

The urge to be sick came upon him without warning, and he had no choice but to let himself expel on the rug at his feet. When he was done retching, he got up and grabbed a rag from the kitchen. Unsteadily, he mopped up the acrid mess, barely managing not to let the smell cause him to vomit all over again.

In the bathroom, he peeled off his filthy clothes and started the water running in the shower. He turned to look at the state of himself in the mirror, and a searing pain like an ice pick being lodged in his frontal lobe brought him to his knees. Blood poured from his nose, splattering the pristine floor. He felt dizzier and dizzier, then collapsed on the cold tile.

LET THE BODIES HIT THE FLOOR

"Detective Torrez, I never got the sense you enjoyed the morgue, but this will be your third visit this week. At this rate, you could apply for an internship," Flynn said, looking up from his desk with uncharacteristic confidence.

"I don't think anyone likes the morgue as much as you do, Doc," Torrez shot back from where he stood at the entrance. He was pleased to see Flynn's face fall slightly.

"There have been more murders this week than in the last two months; there is a backlog. I will get to Mr Pickford when I get to him." Flynn turned back to his note-taking.

"He was murdered over three months ago, so don't try to peddle me that bullshit. I ain't buying. But this isn't about what I want, or think is just; this comes from the ivory tower."

Flynn laughed, it was clearly meant to convey derision, but in reality, it showed his nervousness; he had never been able to pull off bravado. "And you have a line to the gods, do you?"

"Hail Khrysos."

Flynn let out a little yelp and all but fell out of his chair.

"Do not utter those words here," he hissed.

Unconcerned, Torrez picked up a binder at random from the nearby counter and began to flick through it.

"You have twenty-four hours," he said, dropping the binder on the floor, causing papers to scatter across it. "I'll be back to check up on you soon."

FRIENDS WITH BENEFITS

Panting, they separated to lay side by side on their backs. Thea pulled the thin sheet up to cover her breasts while Bastion stretched out, still too warm to join her under the bedclothes. They stared at the ceiling letting the high dissipate.

"Walt left a crime scene to get drunk last night. Torrez had to carry him home; he was so out of it," Bastion said after a while.

"Why are you telling me this?"

"I thought you'd care."

"I don't."

Bastion pulled a sweat-soaked lock from her forehead and brushed it back away from her face. "I have no illusions about what we're doing here," he said. "But are you sleeping with me to hurt Walt?"

"If I wanted to hurt him, I'd tell him that we're sleeping together."

"He doesn't know."

"Exactly. Not everything I do is about Walt."

Thea rolled onto her stomach and propped herself up on her elbows.

"You and he are done?"

"Yes," Thea said, leaning over and brushing her lips against his.

"But you still care about him?"

"Does it matter?" Thea sat up and threw a leg over Bastion's waist so she was straddling him.

"No, but—"

"Do you really want to talk about Walt right now?" Thea planted soft kisses along his jawline before making her way up to his lips.

"No, Ma'am, I do not."

EVERYBODY'S FOOL

Torrez never enjoyed dealing with Flynn; the man made his skin crawl. It was with great relief that he left the morgue to make his way to Jasper's office.

As ever, it was cluttered in the extreme. Only Jasper could find his way between the isles created by accumulated possessions.

Today, Torrez found Jasper behind his desk using his index to read the news. He was grateful he didn't have to search through the detritus to find the resident tech expert.

"Did you take a look at the chip I gave you?" Torrez asked, perching reluctantly on the edge of what he thought might be a desk, but with all the books and machines covering its surface, it was hard to tell.

"Yup," Jasper said, not looking up.

"Where is it?"

"Tossed it."

"What?"

"It's fake. The chip you brought me is nothing like the one Walt brought me. It's fake. It's not even a chip. It's a solid metal disk with nothing on it."

"Son of a bitch. The bastard set us up."

"What does that mean?"

"It means Walter wasn't drunk."

"I don't understand."

But Torrez was already hurtling from the room.

JUST A DAME

It felt like the fall had re-broken his nose. It was a miracle that it was still straight-ish, Walt thought as he stared at his reflection in the bathroom mirror. He had awoken from a brief dalliance with unconsciousness in a small puddle of blood with his nose throbbing. Since then, he had been staring at himself in the mirror, wondering what had happened.

He was sure now, as he stepped under the warm torrent of the shower, that he hadn't been drunk. He was starting to remember snippets from the night before, and there was the small red dot on his neck that proved he hadn't imagined the dart that had stolen his wits.

The warm water seemed to cleanse his mind as much as his body, and as he washed his back, he made a startling discovery. There was something stuck there. It was small and cold. He slipped on the floor in his haste to get from the shower to the mirror above the sink. He contorted around to look at the small of his back. There was a metal disk glowing a faint blue.

"No, no, no," Walt muttered.

He twisted his arm around and tried to pull it from his back. A jolt of electricity shot up his spine, and he collapsed again onto the cold tile.

When he awoke, Walt was standing in the corridor outside Thea's apartment, fully dressed. He couldn't remember travelling there. He remembered the chip. He touched it through his shirt, hoping that he had imagined it, but the metal disk was as it had been.

Palms sweating, he knocked on Thea's door.

"I think that's the pizza," he heard Thea's muffled voice through the wood.

"I hope they take credit cards," Bastion said over his shoulder as he opened the door.

Walt's insides disappeared, leaving a void of numbness in their wake.

Bastion's long dreadlocks, which were usually tied back into a ponytail, fell over his back and bare chest. He wore only a pair of tight-fitting black boxers and a smile. His face fell when he saw Walt.

"Walt, this isn't—"

"Save it," Walt said mechanically.

"I'll go get Thea," Bastion said, beckoning for Walt to stay put.

"Don't bother," Walt said, turning on his heel and making for the elevator.

"Wait," Bastion said, chasing after him.

Walt pummelled the call button with his fist.

"Walk away, Bast. I'm not kidding."

"I'm sorry, brother. I didn't plan it, it just sort of happened," Bastion said, reaching out a hand intended for Walt's shoulder.

Walt wanted to leave, to erase the sight from his mind. He told his limbs to work, to shrug off Bastion, but they didn't. A small voice inside his head told him to stay. To act out his darker impulses, to attack. It was like a red rag to a bull. Walt lunged for Bastion, slamming him into the wall and holding him there with his forearm.

"I'm not gonna fight you," Bastion said, in a calm and reasonable tone that only added fuel to the fire raging inside Walt.

Their faces inches apart, Walt glared at Bastion, straining against the urge to attack, as Bastion stared defiantly back.

"Do it," Bastion goaded.

The elevator arrived and the doors opened with a happy little *ping* that brought Walt back to himself. He let go of his oldest friend.

"Just a dame, huh?" he snarled as he stepped into the lift.

THE PAST
Two years ago...

Cora had never been in a place like it. Everything she had always wanted was here in this single room. Clothes, food, jewellery like she had never seen before.

The walls were pure gold, real gold. It was cold to her touch. The furniture was hand-carved from the most exquisite African Blackwood, and the bed with its sheets of the softest and most luxurious silk could have fitted twenty people comfortably.

Cora would have been in heaven if it were not for the overwhelming sense of fear that gripped her. Her memories were in pieces. She remembered leaving Old Fashioned and walking home. She remembered calling her sister to complain about Ajay, the man she was attempting to date. She remembered opening her apartment door and then nothing. She had woken up in this unknown place sometime later with no idea how she ended up there. She had been kidnapped; that she knew for sure.

She drew back the thick velvet curtains, but instead of the window she hoped to escape by, she was greeted by brick.

"You like?"

Cora jumped; she hadn't noticed Bastion enter. "Where am I?"

"Home for the next little while," he said, closing the door and locking it behind him.

She knew Bastion well enough to say "Hello" to him on the streets, but their acquaintance was minimal. He may be a friend of Thea and Walt's, but she could tell, in this situation, that he was the enemy.

"What do you want?" Cora asked, moving slowly to the side so the bed was between them.

"Me personally? Nothing. I didn't take you. You were given to me."

Bastion moved over to one of the several beautifully crafted chairs and sat down, completely at ease.

"What do you mean I was 'given' to you?" Dread was unfurling in her insides now.

"I'll explain everything in time."

"Let me go," she said quietly, trying to hold back tears. "I won't tell anyone. I'll say it was all a prank. Please, just let me go."

"No," Bastion said simply.

Cora threw herself over the bed towards the door. Strong arms caught her around the waist and dragged her back, throwing her onto the diamond inlaid floor. Unable to catch herself, Cora's face was first to hit the polished stone. She felt her teeth shatter as blood poured into her mouth.

"You're not going anywhere. You might as well get used to it." Bastion picked her up and tossed her unceremoniously onto the bed. "Eat some food if you can. Enjoy the finer things. Here you can have whatever you want, as long as you stay put. I'll have someone see to your teeth tomorrow." Bastion left, locking the door behind him.

Cora curled in a ball on the bed and cried.

GLASS HOUSES

Thea pressed her forehead against the cool glass of her living room window and stared out at the vibrant neon city below. It was hypnotic watching the Jonks dance around each other like mechanical birds as they soared through the sky. The tiny glimmering specks of the Tenebites on the street below were so distant, all completely oblivious to the dangers lurking in the shadows just out of sight, waiting to claim anyone who strayed but a little from the light.

Bastion had feigned being tired and gone to bed hours ago, but Thea couldn't bear to lay beside him only to stare up at the ceiling as sleep eluded her.

She thought she would feel something when Walt found out about their relationship, but it was as if she had used up all her emotions. There was nothing left. She had been miserable and afraid, lost and in pain, felt fleeting happiness, but now she was just numb. All her efforts were focused on finding her sister and stopping the Gold Legion. That left no room for guilt or lost love.

She was dragged from her reverie as she so often was by a call coming through her Cicada. "French 75" flashed at the corner of her eye and in the communication panel on the window.

Slightly confused, she answered, "Detective Williams, here."

"Detective Williams, this is Jonathan Stanwick, the manager of French 75," said a precise and professional voice with just a hint of stress. "There has been an incident at the bar, and we require your assistance."

"Mr Stanwick, I'm not sure how you got this number, but it's my personal line. I suggest you call triple seven, and officers will be able to help you."

"Eh...no, ma'am, I think it's better that you come yourself and that you come alone."

"Why me?" Thea asked. She was irritated now by his vagueness.

"Will you come? It's urgent."

"Fine. I'm on my way."

French 75 was a short walk away, doubly so as Thea's gate was more of a march. She stormed through the streets taking in nothing and no one she passed. This was just one more thing in a sea of one more things, and Thea felt like she was drowning.

She stopped outside French 75, and all her irritation vanished at once to be replaced with practised professional caution. The large glass window that was the face of French 75 was smashed, and one of the barrel-shaped tables lay broken on the cobbled street outside.

Thea eased her gun from its holster and stepped through the portal created by the broken window.

The inside of the bar was a wreck. Tables and chairs were overturned, the mirrors were cracked, and the bottle rack behind the bar had been ripped from the wall. To Thea's horror, as the staff cowered in a corner, Walt stood behind the bar pouring shot after shot and throwing them back one after the other. His movements were odd, robotic; they seemed unnatural to him.

"Thea!" he called drunkenly as he spotted her. "Here to join the party?"

"This is a new low."

"What do you care?"

Thea holstered her gun, the temptation to use it was something she wasn't proud of. She held her hand out to the staff and said, "My name is Detective Williams. You're safe now. You can go."

At her ushering, the waiting staff and bartenders hurried from the bar, except for a tall blonde, White man in his thirties with heterochromia, whom Thea assumed was Jonathan Stanwick.

"You should leave too," Thea said.

"Look at the state of my establishment, I will not leave, and I will be pressing charges."

"Bill me," Thea snapped. "Now go."

"You are going to cover the damages here? Personally? In full?"

Thea imagined for a second that she could see credit symbols in his eyes.

"If you don't press charges."

"Deal."

Jonathan held out his hand to shake on the agreement. Thea stared at it with an eyebrow raised, and the proprietor wisely withdrew it. With a curt nod in Thea's direction, he too followed his staff out.

"Swooping in to save the day," Walt said, knocking back yet another shot. "It makes me feel all warm and fuzzy."

"What the hell is wrong with you? Do you really want to die over this?" Thea gestured to the mess. "You got your feelings hurt, boohoo. Is that really worth your last strike?"

"Oh, good. I was wondering when you would bring up dear Bastion," Walt sneered.

"You're pathetic."

Walt picked up a bottle of vodka, and Thea was sure he was going to start drinking that too, but instead, he hurled it at the counter where it smashed, sending hundreds of tiny shards flying through the air. Thea brought up her hands to cover her face, then used them to shake free the slivers that had become lodged in her hair.

"I can picture his hands on you," Walt muttered as he stared at the glass littering the bar top.

"You left me, remember? Twice."

"I didn't have a choice," Walt said quietly.

"All you've ever had is choices. You chose to have an affair, and you chose to end it. You chose not to tell me that your wife was alive. Did you think I wouldn't help you? That I wouldn't want to find her too?"

"It wasn't your burden to bear."

"I am not doing this. I am not having this conversation again. I don't have the energy for another Walter James pity party. We're done, and it's none of your business who I spend my time with."

"Anyone but him." Walt splayed his hands out on the counter, paying no attention to the broken glass that must have been cutting into his palms. Sure enough, when he lifted them, drops of red followed. "Thea?" he said, sounding confused as if the pain in his palm had awoken him from a deep sleep. "What's happening? How did I get here?"

"The bourbon is destroying your brain; that's what's happening."

Walt watched the blood from his hand drip onto the countertop, mesmerised.

"You need to go home." Walt didn't move. He just stared at his hand. "Walt!"

Walt's head snapped up again. "I can see it in my head. I can see him kissing you and touching you, and I can't stand it. I can't stand knowing that he knows the feel of you like I do. You wanted to get back at me? It worked."

"Not everything I do is about you," Thea said stiffly. "Bastion and I have nothing to do with you. Sober up, and go home."

"He's like my brother, Thea!"

"You do not own me. What did you expect? That I would just be alone forever? That you were the only one for me, and if I couldn't have you, I'd have no one?"

"Anyone but him," Walt said again through gritted teeth.

"Go home to your wife, Walt."

Thea turned away from him and made for the door, but not before she saw the wide-eyed look of shock on his face.

Outside, Mr Stanwick was waiting for her.

"He's still inside," he stated unnecessarily.

"He'll leave soon."

"And my bar?"

"You have my details. Send me an invoice."

"It's been a pleasure doing business with you, detective."

Feeling drained in more ways than one, Thea headed home.

SPLISH SPLASH

Gin Ricky had loved a hot bath. It had been his happy place before his life had crumbled. He had loved nothing more than a cigar, a glass of wine, and a good book, while he soaked away the chill of Tenebrium's cold winter days.

Since the disappearance of his son, he had found little joy in anything and had resorted to a "fake it 'til you make it" attitude in the hopes of alleviating the ever-growing pit of fear and worry in his stomach.

To that end, the bathwater was run. It steamed, blurring the imperfections of the shabby bathroom. All that was left was to pour himself a glass of La Morte Jace's finest red, and he would be on his way to his own personal heaven, he hoped. Unfortunately, when he opened the cabinet in which he kept his small wine stock, Gin Ricky found it bare. Cursing, he grabbed an overcoat from the hooks by the door and left for the nearest store that carried bootlegged wine. If he was going to do the thing, he was going to do it right.

It was late, but the streets were still filled with people. A thin fog had settled itself on the cobbles; it shifted slightly, furling like smoke, as countless pairs of feet moved through it.

SeeWoo was a stone's throw from Gin Ricky's building. It was a Chinese supermarket, but it carried an extensive wine collection from vineyards all over the world—a secret it shared with only a lucky few due to neo-prohibition.

Gin Ricky slipped through the automatic door, keeping his head down. He had heard nothing from the Gold Legion in weeks, but he was still keen to pass undetected whenever he left the relative safety of his own home.

The inside of SeeWoo was brightly lit by fluorescent lights that gave everything and everyone within a sickly greenish tinge. Without stopping to browse, Gin Ricky made his way to the back of the store, to an archway of hanging beads.

Beyond the beads was a much darker room, filled with wooden shelves which held nearly every brand and vintage of wine imaginable in dark glass bottles. Gin

Ricky perused the shelves, spoiled for choice. Behind him, the gentle rattling of the beaded curtain told him he was no longer alone.

"I would never have pegged you for a Sommelier."

Gin Ricky whirled around. That voice sent chills down his spine. "How did you find me?"

"I never lost you, Ri Jin-woo," said Chester Maxwell. He was tall, thin, and imposing, like a scarecrow deterring birds.

"Where is my son? What have you done with him?"

Gin Ricky was not a brave man in the conventional sense. He didn't like to fight, and he wasn't skilled in the art of violence. Nonetheless, he gripped the bottle of wine he had been examining tightly, ready to strike.

"Nothing permanent," Maxwell said, examining the many bottles of wine with disinterest. "I want information; that's your bread and butter, isn't it?"

Gin Ricky said nothing. His fight or flight reflex was heavily weighted towards flight, but the exit was barred.

"I'll do anything you want. Please, just give my son back to me."

"How did you know Cleo James was still alive?"

"I—"

"I can tell you are about to lie to me. Be warned, that is unwise. I always know, and it's little Joshy who will pay for daddy's lies. Now, tell me what I want to know. I don't want to spend a minute more in this cesspit than I have to."

"It was Benjamin Pickford," Gin Ricky said, his eyes darting all around. He took an involuntary step back into one of the shelves.

"That wasn't so hard now, was it? I love when a loose end takes care of itself."

"Give me back my son!"

A smirk and derisive head shake were all Maxwell offered.

When he left, it was like a malevolent spirit had been exorcised. Gin Ricky sagged against the shelves, breathing heavily as if he had just run a marathon. Maxwell rarely left his ivory tower; if he was making personal visits in the poorer areas no less, something big was happening.

Gin Ricky hurried home sans wine, determined to hunker down and wait out the brewing storm, praying that Joshua would survive it.

THE THRONE OF DIONYSIUS

Even though it was well after midnight, it was never dark in Tenebrium City. The ever-glimmering lights of the metropolis shone through the window of the District Attorney's office, illuminating the man himself as he sat pensive behind his desk.

The office in which he sat was more than just a room; it was a symbol of all he had achieved, of the power he had fought for and his determination to succeed, yet he could feel it all slipping away from him, and as he sat surveying his kingdom, he found himself wondering something he never had before; was it worth it? Was everything he had gained worth all the dark and dirty things he had done? A month or so ago, he would have said yes. Now, with his destruction looming, he wasn't so sure. He wished he had been a better father and a more faithful husband, but could he honestly say that if he could go back, he would do anything differently?

He was saved from resolving his existential dilemma by the flickering light on his call portal. It was a slim black panel that sat on his desk and allowed calls to be filtered before they were transferred to his Cicada. "Zhao" flashed on the small screen.

"What?" Harold snapped.

"Your transporter is on its way, sir," said Zhao's voice over the portal, clearly nettled by Harold's tone.

"Thank you," He added with a touch more courtesy.

Harold took his time leaving the office. In the waiting room, he ignored Zhao's evening greeting as he stepped inside the elevator and pressed the button for the roof. He tapped his foot impatiently as he ascended. When the doors opened with a high-pitched *ding,* a rush of cold air washed over him. He shivered as he stepped out onto the roof.

It was dark. The District Attorney's building was one of the tallest in the city and, as such, rose above the usual light pollution. Red strip lights were all that stood between the edge of the building and the concrete miles below. The roof was a labyrinth of fencing and cables, huge pipes and heating vents. The heat from the building created a dense mist that obscured most of the landscape.

Harold's transporter was nowhere to be seen. He wrapped his arms around himself against the chill wind.

Something moved in the gloom, catching his eye.

"I wasn't sure you'd come." Walt said, stepping forth from the shadows, his hands behind his back. "You've been working late these days."

"What do you want?" Harold demanded.

Walt's smirk was a threat Harold knew well; he had given it many times himself.

"Ah," Harold smiled. "How fitting that you are to be the instrument of my destruction."

"I don't have a choice," Walt said, his eyes suddenly wild. He turned this way and that as if unsure of where he was, but then a dark shadow passed over his face and the eerie grin returned.

"I bet you don't. But would you stop yourself even if you could?"

"We'll never find out," said Walt, as he pulled a dagger from his waistcoat. "How would you like to do this?"

"The hard way, I think," Harold said with a nod to himself. "I've fought all my life. Why do death any differently?"

"You could run," Walt offered.

"You'd catch me, and even if you didn't, if not today, it would be tomorrow. There's something to be said for accepting one's end with a modicum of grace. That being said, I won't make it easy for you. You understand, I'm sure."

Harold threw aside his jacket and unbuttoned his waistcoat. He slipped off his sleeve garters and rolled up his cuffs. While he did this, Walt waited patiently, his hands clasped in front of his body, holding the knife.

When Harold undid his top button and threw his tie aside, Walt said, "Are you ready?"

Harold lunged for the younger man by way of reply, but Walt sidestepped his attack with ease. Harold lunged again, and again Walt evaded effortlessly; he didn't even unclasp his hands.

Harold ran at Walt, but Walt didn't step aside this time. He turned to the side and brought the knife across Harold's ribs, leaving a bloody slash in its wake. Harold cried out in pain as he felt the warm blood wash over his stomach and doubled over, clutching his side.

"Have you had enough?" Walt asked, patting Harold on the shoulder.

Harold elbowed Walt hard in the face as he straightened up. The detective staggered back as blood poured from his nose. He smiled, and the blood coated his teeth, but Walt made no effort to stem the flow. Instead, he thrust the dagger forward. Harold avoided a killing blow by inches, but the tip of the blade made contact with his chest, and again Harold felt the burning sting of steel on his skin.

"It needn't be this hard," Walt said as if he were bored.

"At least I know Thea will never forgive you for this," Harold sneered, trying desperately to unbalance Walt, to regain the upper hand.

"I don't care what she thinks anymore. Perks of the job."

"Maxwell will be pleased. It seems he has perfected his creation at last."

Walt slashed at Harold, who brought his arms up to protect his face. The cut was bone-deep; it severed muscle, nerve and tendon; Harold's left arm fell limp, numb and useless to his side. He backed away, but Walt pursued him like a predator stalking its prey.

Harold turned to run, no longer willing to accept his end with grace. He cried out as he felt a sharp impact on the back of his thigh. He fell forward, and his chin crashed into the concrete. The eruption of pain around his lower face told him his jaw was broken. He reached his thigh with his remaining hand and found that the dagger was lodged there, but he couldn't pull it out. He began to crawl towards the roof's edge, but a hand dragged him to his feet by the collar of his shirt. Walt yanked the dagger free of Harold's leg and, in one smooth motion, drew it across the District Attorney's throat.

Harold barely felt it. As the blood poured from his neck down his body, it was like being under a tepid waterfall. He was only dimly aware of his feet leaving the ground, and then he was soaring through the air, or was he falling?

WE ARE NEVER EVER GETTING BACK TOGETHER

With tired eyes, Torrez watched the police feed on his Index as he sat at the live wood dining room table. He hadn't bothered to talk to Marielena as he usually would when he arrived home; she had made it perfectly clear she wanted nothing to do with him. The thought made his chest feel empty, but there was nothing he could do about it now; he needed time to decide whether or not they had a future, and he had to respect that.

He had seen neither hide nor hair of Walt since he had accused him of being drunk and was starting to worry that something far more serious had taken hold of the detective. He longed to call Thea, to fill her in on his findings and to tell her about Walt, but he couldn't. She needed to get as far away from Walt and the investigation as possible. For now, Torrez was on his own.

The police chatter emitting from his wrist implant had quieted to hum, and Torrez was on the verge of a gentle doze when he heard the low tones of a hushed conversation coming from the hall.

"Marielena?" he called.

The secretive talk stopped at once.

"Marielena?" Torrez said again a little louder.

When he got no reply, he walked out into the hallway. His heart dropped into his stomach. There were suitcases, full to bursting, piled next to the front door, but his wife was nowhere to be seen.

"Mi Amor?"

His heart beating fast, he darted towards the stairs. Taking them two at a time, he bounded onto the landing and into the master bedroom.

"What are you doing here?"

With his back to the door, Salvador was taking clothes from Marielena's wardrobe, folding them and placing them in neat piles on the bed, ready to be packed.

"My sister is coming to stay with me for a while," he said without looking up from his task.

He was tall and slim. His tanned skin had a golden glow that highlighted his delicately handsome face. His dark hair was loosely slicked-back; it gave the man an air of effortless elegance.

"Where is she?" Torrez demanded of his former lover.

"In a Jonk, waiting downstairs. She didn't want to see you." Again Salvador had not a glance to spare for Torrez.

"When is she coming back?"

"She isn't," Salvador said curtly.

Torrez ran for the stairs, Salvador close behind him. He grabbed Torrez's arm before he could descend even one step. "She doesn't want to see you," Salvador said, this time looking Torrez full in the face imploringly. "You lied to her and took her for a fool. You were unfaithful time and time again. She deserves more." They hadn't been so close in years, and Torrez found the closeness almost too intimate. Salvador could feel it too; he leaned forward and kissed Torrez, chastely at first, then passionately.

It was over as abruptly as it had started. Salvador stepped away from Torrez and moved back into the bedroom.

"See, you can't help yourself," he said.

"Tell her I love her," Torrez said dismally.

"I will, but it changes nothing. We loved each other once, remember. Some things just aren't meant to be."

And with that, he gathered up the last of his sister's clothes and left Torrez standing on the stairs feeling like the world as he knew it was ending.

IF I HAD A HEART

Thea cursed herself for how unkind she had been to Bastion as she moved around the kitchen, clearing away the remnants of their dinner. He had left moments before, after an almighty row that she had started. It wasn't his fault Walt had found out about their friends with benefits arrangement, and it wasn't his fault that Walt had acted as Walt tended to.

Behind her, she heard the door open and sighed with relief.

"I'm glad you came back. I'm sorry. This isn't your fault; I had no right to take it out on you."

But when she turned to greet her visitor, it wasn't Bastion, but Walt.

He stood just inside the apartment, drenched in blood. It flecked his face and covered his clothes. He was shaking. He looked lost and scared, childlike.

"I don't know how I got here," he whispered. He looked down at his hands and his scarlet clothes with wide eyes. "I don't know whose blood this is."

"What do you mean?"

"I don't remember. It's like there's a void inside my head. Thea, I think I killed someone."

"Okay," Thea said, taking a towel from the kitchen counter and wetting it under the tap. "It's gonna be okay."

Slowly she walked to him, afraid she might spook him. She took him gently by the hand and led him over to his armchair. Steadily she kneeled in front of him and began to tenderly wipe the blood from his face. "I think at least some of this is from your nose," she said quietly. "Where did you go after French 75?"

"I wasn't at the bar," he said, shaking his head slowly. "Was I?"

"You...we talked there. You hurt your hands." Thea said carefully. "You don't remember?"

"I haven't seen you since you were suspended," Walt said, looking at his palms, which were indeed cut.

"You were here earlier, Walt. You saw Bastion." Walt shook his head. "We need to get you cleaned up."

Gently Thea eased his coat from his shoulders. Walt allowed her to manipulate his arms as she pulled his suit jacket from him next. His outer clothes were still damp with blood. Whatever had happened had happened recently.

"I think I've killed someone," Walt said numbly. "But I don't remember."

"It's okay. We'll figure this out."

Thea undid the buttons on Walt's waistcoat, but when her hands moved to his shirt, he stopped her. He lifted her hand from his chest and pressed his lips to her fingers; she snatched them away.

"Don't," she snapped.

"Why not?" he said, grabbing her hand and pulling her close. Something had changed within him; he no longer seemed at sea. It was like there was a beastly animal lurking behind his eyes.

"Let go of me," Thea said warningly.

"Make me."

Walt encircled her in his arms, one hand on the back of her head, the other holding her to him. He kissed her hard; it was almost painful.

"Stop," Thea said, slapping him across the face with such force her hand stung. "What is wrong with you?"

She stood up and stepped away so that the coffee table was between them. Walt stood too with an eerie litheness that gave him a wolf-like quality. Lighting fast, he kicked the table aside, and it clattered loudly as it landed upturned on the cold wooden floor. "You want this," he jeered, moving ever closer.

Never taking her eyes off him, Thea stepped backwards around the couch. He stalked after her like she was prey. Something was very, very wrong here.

Suddenly Walt dropped to his knees, clutching his head. He writhed in pain. "Get away from me," he bellowed.

"What's happening?"

"Run!"

She watched as his muscles seemed to coil, and before she could react, he sprang for her. Grabbing her by the shoulders, Walt forced her up against the kitchen counter and began to nip at her neck. Far from pleasurable; it hurt. She yelled as his teeth found the tender skin of her throat.

Thea kneed him hard in the groin and pushed him backwards at the same time. He groaned in pain and toppled over one of the stools that sat along the kitchen island, landing sprawled on the floor. Thea turned to the counter, where she had discarded her gun when she came home from French 75. If she had to stun him, she would, but before she could reach it, a hand clasped around her ankle and dragged her to the floor. She yelped as her knees collided with the solid wood. Desperately, she reached out for anything to anchor her, but she couldn't help but slide on her front along the floor as Walt dragged her towards him. She kicked out behind her blindly and heard a nauseating crunch that told her she had made contact with her target. His grip slackened, and she scrambled out of his reach, but when she looked back at him, she saw that he was facedown and seemingly unconscious.

Leaning over him, Thea pulled his handcuffs from his back pocket and used them to secure his arms behind his back. As she did this, her hand passed over something at his waist. Curiously, Thea lifted his shirt and peered under it.

"Shit."

Nestled neatly in the small of Walt's back, embedded into the skin, was a hexagonal metal chip that emitted a soft blue glow. Thea ran her fingers over it, wondering if she should try to remove it. No, she thought. If it was attached to Walt's spinal cord as it appeared to be, removing it could paralyse him or, worse, kill him.

She settled on dragging Walt's armchair into the centre of the room. With difficulty, she removed his shirt and heaved him into the soft seat and, using his handcuffs and hers, fastened his arms to it.

Next, she filled a glass with water then proceeded to throw it in Walt's face.

Spluttering, he roused, confused at first to find himself tied up and half-dressed, then horror-struck as he clearly remembered what he had just tried to do.

"Thea, I'm sorry, I'm so sorry. I could see what I was doing, but I wasn't in control."

"Are you really you?"

"Yes."

"And you remember what just happened?"

"...Yes."

"But you don't remember how you got here covered in blood?"

"I have no idea. I don't know what's happening to me."

"I think I do."

Thea circled behind him and knelt down. The gap in the armchair's back was perfectly placed to allow her to see the chip nestled snugly against Walt's spine. It was still emitting a faint blue glow, much like the devices that had been attached to the ghouls who had attacked her what felt like an aeon ago.

"Thea, say something."

Thea ignored this and traced the chip with her fingertips. Walt shuddered. She pushed on it slightly.

"Ow!" Walt yelped. "What was that?"

"You've been chipped," Thea said, moving back around to face him. "Like the sex workers and the ghouls."

"What? No. That's not..." his voice trailed away.

"What?"

"I was at a crime scene with Torrez. I ran after a suspect and then nothing until Torrez found me on a bench in Buchanan Park. He thought I was drunk."

"And *you* thought you were drunk? You thought that it was possible you might have gotten blackout drunk at work as opposed to being attacked?"

"I'm handling it."

"Of course you are. And you don't remember French 75? Or anything about Bastion and me?"

"You and Bastion?" There was an uncomfortable pause. "Oh." He closed his eyes. "No, I don't remember that. What happened at French 75?"

DADDY ISSUES

Torrez hadn't moved from where Salvador had left him standing at the top of the stairs, gazing into his empty bedroom. It was almost fitting, he thought, that his past was robbing him of his future. He had wanted to run out into the streets, to find Marielena, to beg her to stay with him, to tell her that he loved her, but he knew, deep down, that he didn't deserve her and that she would be better off without him.

He had never been more grateful to receive a call from the TPD than he was at that moment. The call gave him a start, which was quickly followed by selfish relief. The only reason he would be being called this late was a crime scene.

As it turned out, it was a rather grisly murder, though Bill was quite sketchy with the details.

When Torrez arrived on the scene, he was surprised to see that the cordon covered a four-block radius surrounding the District Attorney's building. Jonks and tactical vehicles were staked out around the perimeter, and what looked like every uniformed officer in the city was standing sentinel.

"Who's the stiff?" Torrez asked a tall Asian officer with a neat moustache, who was leaning against a police issue Jonk.

"No clue. It's a messy one. Pushed from the roof of the DA building. But I'll tell ya this, some schmuck is gonna fry for this one," the man said as he lifted the caution tape to allow Torrez access to the scene. Torrez nodded his thanks.

Though there were people everywhere, it was oddly quiet. All conversation was hushed, and security was tight.

It took Torrez nearly ten minutes to get to the scene proper, and what a scene it was.

Torrez pulled a handkerchief from his pocket and covered his mouth and nose, not against the smell, but in case he lost his battle with his gag reflex.

There was what must have once been a human body splattered on the pavement. Blood and organs formed a gooey pulp that mixed with the dirt and the rain on the street. The fall had shattered both the victim's legs with such force that the left leg was no longer attached to the rest of the body. The skull had cracked open, and brain matter was leaking out onto the street; it looked like congealed strawberry yoghurt.

Captain Betty Charles was standing over the body, her nose wrinkled with disgust.

"Andrew," the captain said by way of a greeting.

"Captain." Torrez inclined his head deferentially. "Do we know who the vic is?"

"District Attorney Harold Williams."

Torrez looked back at the mess of bone and ichor on the ground, trying to find something remaining of the man he knew and loathed. "Does Thea know?"

"No," the captain said gravely. "I don't want to tell her until we have more details. He wasn't just her father. All eyes will be on us from here on out."

"It's not like you to play the game," Torrez observed shrewdly.

"I'm not blind to what's going on in this city," the captain said quietly. "But I am the only thing standing between you and the commissioner, and she is no longer on our side."

"She's one of...them?" Torrez glanced quickly around.

"Everyone has a price."

"What's yours?"

"I don't know; they haven't found it yet." There was a spark of defiance behind the captain's eyes that Torrez respected the hell out of.

"Captain. We have the footage from the building tops," a gruff voice said. Bill stepped out from the District Attorney's office, his wrist held aloft, ready to project what he had found.

"He definitely fell from this building?" she pointed at the shard of onyx.

"Yes, and there's more." Worry creased Bill's face.

"Show me." The captain beckoned for Torrez to join them.

"Eh...I think we should do this somewhere more private, Captain," Bill said.

"Lead on."

Torrez, Captain Charles, and Bill walked quickly over to the captain's transporter and got inside. With the doors shut, Bill raised his index, and the red uplit roof of the DA building was projected into the space between them.

"No," Torrez said as he watched the footage in horror. "No."

"Issue a warrant," the captain said. Her face was stony, but Torrez saw that her hands were shaking.

"Captain..."

"There's nothing I can do for him now."

THE DEVIL'S BACKBONE

"Don't," Walt said, doing his best to squirm out of Thea's reach as she tried in vain to uncuff him.

"We need to get that thing off you," Thea said, redoubling her efforts.

"No. What if you let me go, and I try to hurt you again?" Using his feet, Walt pushed the armchair back a few inches. "I've already killed someone today."

"We don't know that," Thea said firmly.

"No? Then where did all the blood come from?" The lost look he'd had when he arrived crept back over Walt's face for a moment before it was replaced with stubbornness.

"That chair won't hold you for long if you really want out of it, so you might as well let me release you. We need to get you to Chowdhary; he's the only one who can help."

Very reluctantly, and to Thea's great relief, Walt allowed her to remove his restraints which she did so deftly.

"Get dressed," Thea said, for he was still shirtless.

Walt did as he was told, taking the clean shirt Thea handed him and replacing his suspenders on top. When he reached for his trench coat, however, Thea said, "No, leave it."

"Why?"

Thea held up the handcuffs, and Walt presented his wrists without protest. She cuffed his hands in front this time, and once they were secure, she draped the trench coat over them to hide the fetters.

"Smart," he said with a nod. "Listen, Thea, if something happens, if I—"

"I'll put you down if I have to."

They held each other's gaze for a moment. When Walt seemed satisfied that she had meant it, he said, "Let's go."

Perpetually busy as the city always was, no one paid them any mind as they made their way to Chowdhary's clinic. They swapped Jonk taxis twice to avoid being followed and, when they were near enough to walk, disembarked to continue on foot.

The chip gave Walt the affectation of a drunk person. He was unsteady on his feet and periodically felt the sting of brief migraines. Nonetheless, they managed to make their way through the streets, though they had to take a diverted route to the clinic's door due to a large police cordon. Thea wondered idly what had happened, but all thoughts of the crime were pushed from her mind when Walt grabbed her arm in an effort to stop himself from slumping against the nearest building.

"Not much further," Thea said, hauling him to his feet.

When they arrived at the clinic, it was shut. It was a ramshackle place, Thea thought as she took in the chipped paint, barred windows, and the neon sign above the door, which flickered only dimly.

"Dr Chowdhary?" Thea called, hammering on the glass with her fist. "Dr Chowdhary? If you are in there, we need your help."

Thea heard the sounds of hurried movement inside and stepped back from the door. It opened moments later to show a harassed looking Indian man in his fifties, with jet black hair streaked with grey. He wore a long nightshirt, but it didn't appear they had woken him. He seemed fully alert and extremely suspicious.

"We are closed," he said, trying to pull the door shut.

Thea put her foot in the gap, and the doctor clattered the door painfully against her shoe a couple of times before he gave up and stepped back to grant them entry.

"What do you want?" Chowdhary said mulishly.

"My name is Thea Williams—"

"I know who you are. I asked what you want?"

Walt stepped forward. He shook off the coat to reveal his handcuffs.

"I need you to fix me, Doc." Walt turned his back to the doctor and, with difficulty, restrained as he was, lifted his shirt until the small metal disk was visible.

"Is that what I think it is?" Chowdhary said, clutching at his chest.

"You created the originals, right?" Thea asked urgently.

"Does it work?" There was a glimmer of scientific curiosity not completely obscured by the doctor's clear abhorrence for the chip.

"Well, he's my...friend, and he attacked me, so yeah, I'd say so."

"Follow me."

Chowdhary led them into a backroom that was kitted out like an auto-shop and operating theatre equally.

"Release him," he said to Thea. "Lie down there," he said to Walt, indicating the operating table. "And strip to the waist."

Walt made quick work of his clothing and lay face down as the doctor had asked. He shivered as his bare chest touched the cold leather of the table. He was slightly too tall for it, and both his head and feet dangled off the edge a fraction. Thea took up a chair in the corner, watching on apprehensively.

"You've rather been through the wars of late, haven't you?" Chowdary asked, noting the scars on Walt's back that Thea knew must have happened when he was thrown through her bathroom window.

Walt grunted noncommittally. Thea noticed he was tapping his fingers rapidly on the underside of the table.

"I'm going to examine you now," the doctor said, affixing a headlamp to an old-fashioned pair of magnification glasses. "Sometimes low-tech is better," he said in response to Thea's look of surprise. "Now, Mr James, is it? Try to keep still."

The examination took around fifteen minutes. Dr Chowdhary used several implements and devices to inspect the chip, all the while mumbling to himself.

"All right," he said finally. "I think I can help you, but it won't be easy. Medications are in short supply here."

"What does that mean?" Walt asked.

"We are out of anaesthetic. This is going to hurt."

"Do it," Walt said, gritting his teeth.

"There are risks…"

"What risks?" Thea asked quickly.

"The chip is attached to the nerves at the bottom of his spinal cord. Damaging those nerves could paralyse him. He might lose the ability to walk or worse, the ability to breathe on his own."

"You gave Benny a new arm," Walt said, a slight tremble in his voice. "Even if you did…paralyse me, you could fix it, right, Doc?"

"Theoretically… but—"

"Good enough for me," Walt said firmly, but Thea could tell he was scared. "Get that thing off of me."

"Miss Williams, find something for him to bite down on, on the counter over there."

Thea searched and found a padded piece of leather that looked like it was used to make prosthetics more comfortable.

"That will do nicely," Chowdhary said with an approving nod.

Thea sat down cross-legged on the floor at Walt's head. She could feel his fear; though he tried to hide it, it rolled off of him in waves. She carefully folded up the leather and placed it in his mouth; he bit down hard, his breathing ragged. Thea offered him her hand, and he gripped it tightly.

"You're gonna be fine."

Walt nodded and swallowed hard.

"With your leave, I'll begin. I'm going to strap you down, this will be painful, but it is essential that you do not move." Chowdhary pulled ratchet straps from under the table and fastened them over Walt's chest, hips, knees and ankles. "I hope you pass out, my friend."

The tension was insufferable as Chowdhary set to work. He spent what felt like an age examining the chip with various instruments, but he seemed determined not to cut until he was good and ready. Thea thought that the wait must be worse than the operation itself. She was wrong.

Finally, Chowdhary picked up a scalpel and made the first cut. Walt groaned in pain, every muscle in his body tensed, and his hand crushed Thea's, but she held on.

Horrible as seeing Walt in pain was, things didn't get bad until the doctor reached his vertebral column and the nerves protected within. Walt screamed and screamed in intolerable agony, but the doctor never slowed. Over and over, he cried out as sweat soaked him, mingling with the tears of pain that flowed freely down his face. Thea couldn't help but cry herself. She couldn't bear to see Walt in this type of pain; it was like watching him be tortured.

"Please pass out, please pass out, pass out. Pass out. Pass out," she whispered as her tears mingled with his where they fell on their interlocked hands. "Stop, please, stop," Thea shrieked as Walt let out his most harrowing shout yet.

"I can't," the doctor said calmly. "I'll kill him if I stop now. I can't leave his spinal cord exposed, and if we keep going much longer, his heart may give out. I have to finish, and it has to be soon. There is no stopping."

On and on it went until finally, Chowdhary said, "Got it." He held up the metal disc, and Thea was surprised to see jellyfish-like tentacles hanging from it.

"I can't feel my legs. Doc, Thea, I can't feel my legs," Walt said, his voice rising.

"A temporary mercy; this next part won't be pleasant. I had to remove a section of your vertebral column—the bone that protects the spinal cord—in order to successfully remove the chip. The nerves are exposed, and that's dangerous, so I'm going to place a metal cage around the exposed cord to stabilise it and keep it protected."

The doctor picked up what Thea thought looked like a many-legged metal spider from the tray next to him. He tapped it, and the legs flexed and relaxed like a fist opening and closing. Walt's eyes were closed as Chowdhary placed it, and while Thea knew he was awake, he didn't stir as the doctor set to drilling the cage in place.

"You doing okay?" she whispered to him.

"Oh sure, I'd be clicking my heels if I could."

Thea laughed feebly. "Feel anything yet?"

"Not yet."

"Well," Chowdhary said loudly. "I'm afraid that is about to change."

Thea watched as the doctor picked up a twisted rectangular instrument and carefully ran it over the cage.

"Fuck me!" Walt yelled.

"That is a very good sign," the doctor said happily. "Now, If I close with the C02 laser, it will be extremely painful, but you'll be on your feet again in minutes. Shall I proceed?"

"Do it," Walt said, screwing up his face.

Chowdhary made quick work of the closure, and while Thea was sure Walt was still in great pain, he didn't cry out or moan; he just kept his eyes shut, and his jaw clenched.

When the doctor was finished, he undid the straps that had been holding Walt to the table and told him to sit up. Tentatively, Walt did so. He was soaked in sweat and shaking as if he were cold. He looked tired in the extreme, drained both mentally and physically.

"How do you feel, Mr James?"

"Good, I think."

"Stand for me, please." Walt did so, his movements no different from how they had been. "Excellent. Now one last thing. The cage protecting your spine is biomechanical; it's powered by the body it's resting in. However, if something were to disrupt this, an electric shock, for example, the device would reset."

"What does that mean?" Walt asked

"You would be temporarily paralysed. The device will reset once the current is gone, but I'd imagine the use of your legs isn't something you'd like to lose even for a short period."

"Right," Walt said. "No stun weapons."

"Or non-lethal pulse rounds," Thea added.

"The lethal ones might not disrupt the device, but as your doctor I recommend you avoid those, too."

Thea watched as Walt tested his mobility. He stretched his legs and squatted on the spot; he seemed satisfied.

"Where's the chip?" Thea asked, looking around.

"Here." Chowdhary handed her a small, lidded glass specimen jar. The jellyfish chip floated in a clear fluid.

"Thank you for your help," Thea said, taking the jar and then offering the doctor a hand. He shook it warmly. "How can we thank you?"

"Just make a donation for the clinic, if you can. It's why we're here."

"Thank you," Walt said, clapping the doctor on the shoulder.

Ten minutes, a sizeable donation, and several more thank yous later, Thea and Walt stood on the street outside the clinic.

"Thea—" Walt began glancing around the deserted street.

"Go home, lay low. I'm going to see if there were any homicides or attacks called in."

"Right."

"We have the chip as evidence now. Whatever you did, it wasn't you, and we can prove it."

"Be careful."

"You, too."

They turned away from one another, each heading in a different direction.

EXPRESSIONISM

Maxwell was painting when Bastion arrived at his penthouse. The atrium of the huge space was more like an art studio than a grand entrance, but it was no less opulent. Easels were free-standing here and there, and huge canvases, some blank and some etched with colour lined the walls. Jazz blared from a gramophone in another room as Maxwell painted a distorted scene that showed a man with a gun to his head staring out over a huge and oppressive city.

"You didn't tell me you wanted Harold dead," Bastion said without announcing himself.

"I wasn't aware I had to," said Maxwell, slashing at the canvas with his brush.

"And how did he incur your wrath?" Bastion asked stiffly.

"As you thought, he cared too much about his daughter, something you should avoid."

"She means nothing to me."

"She isn't your problem. You want her, you may even like her, but you'd kill her if you had to. I can tell. The real reason you keep failing and dealing in half measures is Walter James."

"If we get rid of Thea, he'll no longer be a problem."

"I don't like loose ends. I'm giving you a choice. It's you or him. Fail again, and I'll take you both."

There was silence for a moment as Maxwell continued to paint.

"Is that all?"

"No, follow me."

Maxwell led Bastion into an adjoining room. The walls were covered in grotesque portraits of the same figure. It was more monster than man, leering down at Bastion from all sides with its small eyes and pointed nose.

"My therapy room," Maxwell said airily. "Do you know how I learned to paint?"

"Boarding school?"

Maxwell laughed, "If only. No, I learnt to paint with my own blood." That brought Bastion up short. "My father was an impressive man," Maxwell went on, a dark edge to his light voice. "He expected much, and his children often disappointed. When we did, he would beat us and lock us in the wine cellar for days on end, bloody, starving, and cold. I would draw the paintings in my room from memory in my own blood and excrement. I hated my father, but he did teach me something—standards. I also expect much, and I am also often disappointed, but I don't beat my children; I erase them like I erased my father. Like it or not, I am his son. Think about that when you make your choice. You may go."

As always of late, Cora was dressed in lingerie, waiting for Bastion when he arrived home. She smiled when he entered, oblivious to the maelstrom in his mind. She stretched out on the large bed, legs wide, a clear invitation, but Bastion wouldn't take her like this. He was tempted for a dark moment to lose himself in her as he had before, but it would be a betrayal of what they shared. The relationship that blossomed between them had grown out of the darkness of their circumstances, but the comfort they had been surprised to find in each other was as lost to Bastion now as Cora was. He had paid dearly for his mistakes.

"What's wrong," she asked shrewdly.

"Maxwell asks too much of me," Bastion said heavily, sitting on the edge of the bed.

Cora crawled across the sheets and began to rub his shoulders. Bastion shrugged her off.

"What does he want?"

"It doesn't matter. I don't have a choice because they won't stop getting in the way."

"What are you going to do?"

"Kill Walt and Thea."

"Finally." The broad grin that split Cora's face was not the response Bastion had hoped for.

BREAKOUT

Nina Carraway was a beautiful White woman in her early forties, with honey blonde hair and bright green eyes. She was the lead anchor of TCN, Tenebrium Central News, and she was preparing for yet another early morning broadcast.

Having been through hair and make-up, she joined her co-anchor Thomas Wilson, a young Hawaiian man, behind the news desk set in the studio. Her chair was slightly taller than his and had a set of steps leading up to it due to her Achondroplasia. As ever, Thomas offered her his hand, and she took it gladly, using it to balance herself as she got situated at his side.

"A breaking story has just come in," Thomas said, tapping his fingers on the desk. This would mean they would have to go on unprepared, and he didn't like that.

"What happened?" she asked curiously.

"No idea. I just got told to be ready."

"All right, is everyone in place?" the director called from behind the auto-prompter. A general muttering of accent filled the room. "We are live in five," the lights around the studio blared. "Four," words began to fill the large screen beside the camera, "Three," the studio credits played, "Two," the breaking news banner appeared on the displays behind the news desk. The director mimed "One."

"Good morning, Tenebrium City. I am Nina Carraway, this is Thomas Wilson, and we are Tenebrium Central News."

"This just in," Thomas went on, paling as he read. "The streets of Tenebrium have been flooded by ghouls. There have been numerous reports of the addicted population causing havoc in and around the city."

"So far," Nina continued. "There are eleven confirmed dead and twenty-four injured. While there has been no official comment from the Mayor, the police, or the Onyx Legion, we have heard that the gates of the SubLevel appear to be intact and closed. No word yet on how these ghouls have found their way onto the streets."

"We urge Tenebites to stay home and lock their doors until this threat has passed. More after these messages."

"Cut to ad break," called the director.

SOLDIER KEEP ON MARCHING ON

Thea felt like her head had barely touched the pillow when the vibrations from her Cicada woke her.

"What?" she muttered groggily.

"Querida," Torrez said in a hushed voice. "You need to come to the station right now."

"What happened?" Thea asked, instantly alert. "Is it Walt?"

"Why would you say that?" Torrez sounded suspicious.

"Something happened to him, he thinks he might have hurt someone, but it wasn't his fault. I can explain."

"Just get here quickly. We'll talk then. Be careful outside. There's ghouls everywhere. The city has gone mad. Bring your gun."

Torrez hung up.

The nights of poor sleep were starting to weigh on Thea, and even though she knew she needed to go to the precinct, she had to drag herself out of bed. She dressed quickly and grabbed her gun on her way as she stepped from the docking bay in her living room into the Jonk.

She saw instantly what Torrez had meant. The Jonk's interior was covered in blood, and the news streams that blared on all sides shared account after account of ghoul attacks throughout the city. As she soared between buildings, Thea looked down at the streets below and saw violence and panic had taken hold. The Onyx Legion were out in force, and the looting had begun.

The Jonk docked on the detective's floor of the TPD. The airlock doors opened with a low mechanical grumble. Thea was surprised when she alighted to be greeted not only by Torrez, but the captain and the detestable O'Malley, too.

"I was called in," Thea said, misinterpreting the captain's sombre expression.

"I know. Let's do this in my office."

Everyone they passed averted their eyes, and Thea felt the familiar sense of foreboding churn her stomach.

Once inside her office, the captain shut the door and drew the blinds.

"All right, this is starting to get on my nerves. What's going on?"

"Take a seat," the captain said gently.

"I think I'll stand."

"Querida," said Torrez, putting a hand on her shoulder. He had a sympathetic look on his face that worried Thea. She did as he asked.

"What the hell is going on?"

The looks of concern on Torrez and the captain's faces were at odds with the smug grin O'Malley wore as he hovered by the door, present, but not part of whatever was about to happen.

Torrez sat down next to Thea and took her hand, she tried to pull it away, but he held on firmly.

"Detective Williams. Thea," the captain said kindly. "There is no easy way to say this. Your father is dead. We recovered his body outside his office an hour or so ago. We believe he was murdered."

"What?" Thea blinked uncomprehendingly. "I don't understand."

She couldn't breathe.

"There's more."

"Show her the tape," O'Malley snapped impatiently.

"What tape?" Thea said, fighting the growing torpor that was threatening to strangle her like creeping vines.

"You don't need to see this," Torrez said. "She doesn't need to see this."

O'Malley pushed between Thea and Torrez's chairs, separating their hands. Thea barely noticed. He tapped the captain's desk, and instantly the data stream sprang to life. He tapped on his Index, and a video began to play.

It showed the roof of the DA building, dark and unforgiving. Thea watched as if from far above her body as Walt stepped out of the lift onto the roof. He stood at the very edge, staring out over the city. It was like she was standing with him on the edge of a precipice.

Moments later, her father joined him. They spoke, though Thea didn't take in a word of what was said. Her father lunged for Walt, who slashed at him with a long knife that left a bloody trail in its wake.

Thea felt sick.

Again and again, her father attacked Walt and every time, Walt rebuffed him and followed up with a vicious attack of his own. As her father fell to the ground and Walt advanced, Thea couldn't watch anymore; she already knew the outcome.

"Turn it off." It was barely more than a whisper.

"We have already issued a warrant for Walt's arrest, but we thought under the circumstances you should know before we take him in," the captain said. She looked more human than she ever had before, not a superior, but a mother fearing for her children.

"Well, that's that then. I'll bring back James. Dead or alive," O'Malley said, rubbing his hands together.

"No," Thea said, getting to her feet. "Let me. I'll do it. He won't fight me. No one else dies tonight."

"Yeah, no. I don't think so," O'Malley said superciliously. "Conflict of interest, and it appears he is armed and dangerous and you're suspended...So... I'll take this one."

"Last time I checked, I'm the captain, not you, O'Malley." The captain's voice dripped with dislike. "Thea, I'll give you twelve hours to bring him in alive. After that, all bets are off."

"Thank you."

"Tick Tock," O'Malley sneered.

Thea swept from the office without a backwards glance, Torrez closely behind.

"Thea," he said, grabbing her arm and pulling her to a stop just before she reached the bullpen. "Are you okay?"

"I'm fine."

"Your dad just died. You're not fine."

"He tried to kill me. He blackmailed you. He nearly killed Walt. How am I supposed to feel?"

"Thea, you're crying. I think it's pretty clear how you feel."

Thea touched her face; it was wet.

"You're in shock," Torrez said, rubbing her arm. "You need to call your mom."

He had said the magic words, and the dam broke.

Thea began to tremble, overcome by the emotions that she was trying so desperately to suppress. Hot tears spilled from her eyes, and then she was in Torrez's arms holding on for dear life as sobs wracked her body. He lowered them both gently to the ground as wave after wave hit her, and she could do nothing to stem the tide. She cried and cried for her father, for herself, for her sister, for her mother. He hadn't been a good father, but he was the only one she had known. The thought of having to tell her mother sent her spiralling again, and it was a long time before she came back to herself.

"My dad is dead," Thea whispered, lifting her head from Torrez's chest and wiping her face. "Walt killed my dad."

"Let O'Malley take him."

"It...wasn't his fault."

"I know you love the guy, for better or worse, but—"

"He was chipped. Someone in the Gold Legion made him kill my dad. He's a victim here too, and holding onto that is the only thing that is holding me together right now. I need to call my mom, and you need to rally every ally we still have here, or Walt's going to die, and I don't think I can handle that today."

Torrez kissed her on the forehead, then got to his feet and made his way to the officer's mess while she made for her desk.

Thea's call with her mother was one of the worst experiences of her life. Athena Williams was a proud woman, who showed no fear nor weakness, but it was not the time for that, and she came apart at the news of her husband's death. She wailed like a wounded animal, and it was all Thea could do not to dissolve into her own grief once more.

"Who did this?" her mother yowled.

"It's complicated," was all Thea could muster.

"Complicated? My husband—your father—is dead."

"There is so much you don't know, mom. Things dad did—"

"Don't you dare blame your father," her mother bellowed, cutting across her.

"Dad was not a good man. He made a lot of enemies and hurt a lot of people. And I loved him anyway, but his death, like his life, isn't as black and white as victim and villain. I promise I'll explain it all to you soon, but right now, I need to go."

"If you can't even bother to pretend to mourn your father, I think I can do without you for a while."

Athena hung up.

Thea pinched the bridge of her nose to stop the stream of fresh tears that were threatening to fall.

Thea watched as Torrez emerged from the Officer's Lounge, followed by Bill and six others. "Are you ready?" he asked as he reached her.

"Bill? Really?" Thea said, not troubling to keep her voice low. Bill had the good grace to look ashamed.

"Cut him some slack. He was just doing his job," Torrez said.

"You would have done the same, would you?"

"No, but I did let Dill Kelly try to destroy you, and you forgave me."

"Fine."

The journey to Walt's apartment was a blur. Thea, Torrez and their entourage of unis were separated between three armed transporters. Once docked in the lobby, they split up as was protocol. Torrez and Bill took the elevator while Thea and the remaining officers filed up the stairs. They reunited on the dimly lit landing.

Standing in front of the door, Thea saw it still bore the marks of the many times it had been battered and pried, kicked and shoved open. There were huge gouges on its face, and the frame was bent.

Taking a deep breath, Thea knocked once.

"Walter James," she said. "Police, open up."

Almost instantly, Walt appeared at the door. He looked like hell. He reeked of bourbon, and it was obvious he hadn't slept.

"It's bad, isn't it?" It was aimed at Thea only.

"Is Cleo here?"

"She's with Gin Ricky."

"Walter James," Thea croaked. "You are under arrest for the murder of District Attorney Harold Williams."

"No," Walt shook his head in disbelief. "Oh, no."

"Turn around."

Thea's hands shook as she placed Walt in handcuffs for the second time in as many days.

"You have the right to remain silent. Anything you say can and will be used against you in a court of law. You have the right to an attorney. If you cannot afford one, one will be appointed to you by the Tenebrium Criminal Court. You will be transported back to the TPD, where you will be detained and questioned. Do you understand?"

"I understand."

"Let's go," Torrez said, reminding Thea he was there. He took Walt by the upper arm and led him to the elevator.

They sat in absolute silence as they travelled back to the TPD. Thea wanted to spare Walt the perp walk, but as they approached the precinct, they were ordered to bring Walt in through the main entrance, another humiliation for them both.

The Jonk landed in front of the building amid a crowd of press and on-lookers. They were everywhere. Cameras flashed and recorded as journalists shouted questions and watchers jeered.

Thea heard "Breaking news; one of the TPD's own has been arrested for the murder of District Attorney Harold Williams," echoed over and over again. Walt didn't try to avoid being filmed or hide his face. He held his head up and stared straight ahead as she and Torrez walked him into reception and booking.

The press had been bad enough, but the atrium was alive with noise and bodies, more like a circus than a police station. It was filled with officers who had come to see if the rumours were true or perhaps hail the fall of a man they didn't like. More than this, ghouls were shackled to benches and railings along with petty criminals who wrestled with their arresting officers.

They marched Walt up to the long smooth reception desk.

"You've to take him into the chambers," the receptionist said. "There is a judge waiting."

"Already?"

"It's a hanging case."

Torrez took hold of Walt again, who had reacted to nothing since his arrest and began to walk him towards the judge's chambers.

"Who is it?" Thea snapped at the receptionist.

"Judge Wolfsheim."

Judge Everard Wolfsheim was a white man in his mid-sixties. He was tall and bat-like in his black robes. His heavy dark eyebrows, in contrast to his wispy grey hair, only added to the impression, as did the way he perched on his chair, arms held close like wings.

The judge's chamber was cold and unforgiving, carved from glossy beige stone, much like the man himself.

"All rise," he said, though no one but himself was seated.

Thea hadn't been surprised that this particular proceeding would take place in front of an audience. The room was crammed with people. The captain, Torrez, Bill, Orion Martin, and O'Malley were among the many who had come to watch the show. Some of the homicide detectives looked solemn, but most looked expectant, excited even.

"State your name for the record," the judge said to Walt in a terminally bored voice. A slight woman of advanced years began to type in mid-air, taking notes.

"Walter James," Walt stated blandly.

"Have you been made aware of your rights?"
"I have."
"This is your third strike, is that correct?"
"You tell me."

The judge glowered at Walt, but continued, "As this is a sentencing hearing, not a trial, you forfeit your right to legal counsel, do you understand?"

"This isn't right," Thea said loudly. Muttering erupted on all sides. "His first two strikes were misdemeanours."

"Silence," the judge called lazily, and a hush fell once more. "This is Mr James' third strike, which means, no matter how petty the previous crimes may seem to you, there is no need for a trial, only a sentencing. All of which I would hope you, as an officer of the law in this fine city, would know. Are you stating for the court that you are unaware of the law?"

"True and right aren't the same," Thea said defiantly. Torrez tried to pull her back, but she shook him off.

"Admirable as your ideals are, this is not a public forum, Detective Williams; this is a court of law. We uphold justice here, not personal moralities. Hold your tongue, or I will find you in contempt of court."

"This is not how we help him," Torrez whispered in her ear, and this time, she allowed him to pull her back from the fore.

"With your leave, we shall continue, Detective Williams," the judge said with awful mordacity. "Mr James, you stand accused of murdering District Attorney Harold Williams. This offence constitutes a third strike. In the face of overwhelming and irrefutable evidence, you are found guilty and sentenced to death."

Thea's shout of protest was drowned out by a general uproar around the room. The noise was such that it was impossible to tell whether the crowd yelled in jubilation or disgust.

"Enough!" Judge Wolfsheim thundered, and the room fell silent at once. "In light of the severity of the crime and the persons involved, the right to appeal has also been revoked."

"What?" Thea and Walt said together.

"And," Wolfsheim overrode them, "the sentence of death shall be carried out by way of hanging in three hours time."

"You can't do this," Walt shouted. "I have the right to appeal regardless of the victim, and you haven't given me an opportunity to speak in my own defence."

"The video evidence supplied by the DA building security office is incontrovertible. You clearly state that it is your plan to kill Mr Williams and then can be seen carrying out the deed."

"I wasn't in control. I was forced to act that way by a chip that was placed on my person without my consent, with the sole purpose of having me commit murder against my will."

"Do you have any proof of this?"

"I do," Thea said.

"Bring it forth," the judge said, holding out a hand.

"It isn't here. It's at my home," Thea said quickly.

"Well then, Detective Williams, you have three hours to present the supposedly exculpatory evidence. If it is not presented within that time, Mr James' death sentence will be upheld and carried out as mandated by the Three Strike Rule. In the meantime, Mr James shall be remanded in custody. Take him away."

Two uniformed officers served as bailiffs. Each took Walt by the arm and began to lead him away into an antechamber. Thea broke through their ranks and took Walt's hand.

"I will fix this," she said with conviction.

"I'm not worried," he smiled weakly.

One of the bailiffs jerked Walt's hand out of her grip, and Thea watched as he was moved from the chambers to death row.

"Drew," Thea yelled, trying to find him in the crowd that had formed in the centre of the room to discuss the verdict.

"Come on," Torrez said, appearing at her side. "You really have a chip? That's all true?"

"It is."

Together they made a path through those still milling around and ran for the atrium. When they burst through the magnificent carved doors, they were confronted by a most unwelcome sight.

O'Malley and a small squad of Onyx Legion Soldiers stood in a semi-circle in front of them, barring any progress.

"Where do you think you're going?"

"Move," Torrez threatened.

"You have no right to detain us."

O'Malley smiled wide and malicious. "Take them," he said with glee.

Thea and Torrez fought and struggled, but in the end, outnumbered as they were, there was nothing they could do to stop themselves from being dragged into the lock-up.

O'Malley's goons didn't bother to put them in a cell; they just tossed them into the holding cell block and shut the door tightly behind them.

THE LAST TO KNOW

Never again would she leave it that long between doses of Quietus, Cleo promised herself. With all that was going on with Walt, she hadn't realised the extra strain her condition was putting on her until she felt the sweet relief of the drug that kept her lucid.

Her husband was not home when she arrived there, and for the first time in her memory, she was glad. He was pretending for her, and the obvious unhappiness that he tried so valiantly to hide was worse than any affair he could have. Knowing that the one constant in her life was in love with someone else wasn't something that could be ignored. She knew in her heart of hearts she would have to let him go, but she wasn't ready yet. She was going to hold onto him for just a little longer.

Unable to stand rattling around in her own head for a moment longer, Cleo tapped the button on the side table next to Walt's armchair. A slim glass screen descended from the ceiling and positioned itself perfectly in front of the couch.

"News," Cleo said, slipping off her shoes and dropping onto the couch. "TNC."

Nina Carraway appeared on the screen. Cleo had always liked the woman and was pleased to find that when she returned from the SubLevel that she was still on the air.

"And in a shocking turn of events," Nina said. "Walter James has been named as the officer arrested for the murder of District Attorney Harold Williams. We are hearing reports that the officer of over twenty years already has two strikes. If this is the case, then we should expect a death sentence to be handed down at any moment. More updates after these messages."

Cleo sprang to her feet, grabbed her shoes from where she had discarded them on the floor moments ago, and raced from the apartment, not even bothering to close the door behind her.

MERCY

Chowdhary tore around the clinic like a tempest, grabbing only the bare essentials in his hurry to disappear; anything else would have to be destroyed. He had thought about calling his husband and son, he longed to, but he didn't want to endanger them; they would recover from his disappearance in time. Better alive and sad than dead and gone.

He didn't hear the footsteps as they approached in his hurry, nor did he see the one who made them leaning against the counter watching.

"Going on holiday?" The silkily dangerous voice of Chester Maxwell inquired.

Chowdhary dropped the bag he was holding. Its contents spilled out over the floor.

"Or perhaps you're fleeing the city," Maxwell said, stepping in front of the exit. He must have seen the urge to run on Chowdhary's face.

"I have no reason to run. I did what you asked."

"Did you? I think I asked you to chip Walter James and put him under my control."

"I did that. I did what you asked me to," Chowdhary spluttered, looking wildly around for any means of escape.

"True, that part you accomplished. But once he had disposed of Harold Williams, he was supposed to kill Thea Williams before the chip killed him. Strange then that I should be watching a news stream and see that he has been arrested, alive and well, by none other than Miss Williams."

"I tried. I hit the kill switch; perhaps the chip was damaged in the struggle, or perhaps it doesn't work as well as we had hoped," Chowdhary invented wildly.

"Considering we have already rolled them out, I'd hope they work correctly." The threat in his voice was overt. "And I know they do because I've been watching you." Maxwell pulled back his cuff to reveal his Index and projected into the air an image that chilled Chowdhary to the bone.

He watched in silence as a holographic version of himself removed the chip from Mr James' back and handed it to Detective Williams in a clear glass specimen jar.

"I think someone has been fibbing," Maxwell said, without a trace of irony. "Let's test these chips of ours."

He lunged forward like a cobra and snared Chowdhary's arm. Using it as leverage, he forced the doctor face-first into the wall. Out of the corner of his eye, Chowdhary saw Maxwell pull a pentagonal disk from his pocket. Chowdhary struggled hysterically, but Maxwell's grip was herculean. He could do nothing but sweat as Maxwell placed the chip on the back of his neck.

For a moment, nothing happened, and then Chowdhary was overcome with agony. He could feel the tiny tentacles burrowing their way into his skin, worming their way into his nervous system. As quickly as the pain came, it was gone.

Chowdhary watched as Maxwell touched a forefinger to his Index. He felt a wave of energy shoot from his neck to his brain and then—

He felt nothing ever again.

THE MILE

Thea and Torrez moved through the concrete passageways that stood among the rows of glass-fronted cells in the TPD's lock-up, searching desperately for any means of escape. Each small cell contained multiple ravenous ghouls. Snarls and howls ripped from their throats as they tore at each other and hammered on the glass with clawed hands and bloodied fists.

They watched in horror as a young man in the cell nearest, newly addicted to Thea's eyes, hurled himself at the glass over and over. She was sure she could hear bones cracking.

"That's not gonna hold," Thea said as she searched for another exit, but she already knew there wasn't one. The lock-up had been designed to have one door serving as both entrance and exit in case of a riot.

"Did they take your gun?" Torrez asked. Thea could tell he was nervous.

"No, you?"

"No. But we are outnumbered in a big way."

"Breach imminent," the tinkling voice of the TPD's mainframe informed them. "Engaging Lockdown protocols."

The young ghoul catapulted himself at the glass with a sickening crunch.

"Computer," Thea yelled. "Detective Thea Williams and Andrew Torrez. We're stuck in the lock-up. Open the door."

"Negative, Detective Williams."

"Computer, cancel the lockdown, override code 1708."

"Lockdown is building-wide and cannot be overridden."

"This can't be happening," Torrez said as the young ghoul launched himself at the glass once more. This time, Thea was sure she saw it bend outward just slightly.

"Full lockdown in five."

The lights overhead began to flash, and the ghouls all around screeched and clawed at their cells.

"Four."

The lights went out, and Thea and Torrez were plunged into semi-darkness.

"Three."

The shutters ground into place over any exposed windows, and the pitch-blackness pressed against Thea's eyeballs as she listened to the baying of the ghouls growing louder and louder.

"Two."

Red emergency lights came on overhead, bathing everything they touched in an eerie crimson glow and making the ghouls look like nightmarish monsters, all desperate to tear them apart.

"One. Lockdown complete."

CRACK

The young ghoul came bursting through the glass. It grabbed Torrez and dragged him to the ground, trying to bite and gnaw at his flesh.

With practised reflexes, Thea pulled her gun from its holster and fired once. The pulse round hit the ghoul square in the back, centre mass. It fell, stunned, on top of a panting Torrez.

"Madre de Dios," he breathed as Thea pushed the ghoul from him and pulled him to his feet.

All around, the growls, howls and groans were punctuated by the sound of glass straining against the onslaught of rabidity.

"Computer," Torrez shouted in panicked fury. "Let us out of here."

"Opening cell doors," the sing-song voice intoned.

"No," Thea said. "No, Computer, do not open the cell doors. Do not open the cell doors."

But it was too late. The soft beeping that served to announce the opening of a single cell was echoed over and over again throughout the gridded room.

"Run," Thea said, pulling Torrez towards the door.

The snarls grew louder and fiercer, and hands began to snatch at their ankles as the glass walls raised inch by inch.

They sprinted to the main door, pressing their faces against the glass as they called for help.

"Call someone," Torrez yelled.

"Cicada's don't work in here—" She broke off; her tragus implant was buzzing. There, next to the door, they must have been close enough to the rest of the station to allow the signal through.

"Hello?"

"Thea? Where are you?"

"Captain," Thea could have cried with relief. "We're stuck in lock-up."

"They are taking Walt to the execution chamber as we speak. You need to get to him."

"We can't; the lockdown has trapped us here, and we are seconds away from becoming ghoul chow."

"God-fucking-dammit." It was the first time Thea had ever heard the captain curse. "Fine, I'll try to get to Walt, but they are keeping me under watch. You survive until I can send someone to get you."

"Deal," she said, ending the call. "What?" she shot at Torrez exasperatedly, for he had been tugging at her sleeve.

"They're out."

Thea turned from the door and saw a horde of advancing ghouls creeping disjointedly towards them like drunk contortionists. It was like being circled by wolves.

She and Torrez raised their guns in unison.

"Don't miss," she said, with a confidence she didn't feel.

Together they fired into the mass, but the ghouls' numbers were so great it was like they were absorbing the pulse rounds. Every time a ghoul fell, another shambled forward to take its place.

The grasping hands of a ghoul Thea hadn't noticed creeping up beside her, grabbed her by the hair and dragged her back into the rabble. Cocooned by undulating bodies, excruciating pain erupted on her shoulder as she felt teeth sink into her skin.

"Drew!" she yelled, but she couldn't see him now immersed as she was in the mass of writhing bodies.

Thea kicked and elbowed anything she could reach until she managed to free her gun arm. She fired over her shoulder and felt the toothy grip on her skin release. She pushed forward and used her shoulder to shunt the nearest ghoul out of her way. The ghoul fell back, taking several of its fellows down with it. Thea used the gap as her escape route and forged her way back to the door, all the while firing blindly behind her to keep those who would pursue her at bay.

"Torrez! Drew!" she yelled as a ghoul threw itself at her. She took aim just in time and caught it full in the face. The ghoul dropped limply to the ground, its outstretched hands caressing her skin as it fell.

Thea pushed, shot, kicked, and shoved her way back to the door, but there was still no sign of any would-be rescuer or Torrez.

"Drew!" she bellowed again, afraid now that he had fallen prey to the ravenous cannibalistic mob.

Then she heard it, a strangled cry from somewhere to her right.

Torrez, who had backed himself into a corner and had, until that point, managed to keep himself just out of the reach of the squirming mass, was dragged to the ground. He thrashed and kicked as ghoul after ghoul piled on top of him.

Stunning another ghoul who had tried to bite her, Thea ran forward and fired at the mass, dragging back each ghoul she had stunned as she fought to thin the pile that was surely crushing Torrez.

More ghouls were creeping up behind her as she struggled to free him, and she knew that if she wasn't successful soon, she too would be lost to the sea of the addicted. She grabbed yet another ghoul by the scruff of its neck and, with all her might, hauled it free.

Under where the ghoul had been lying, Thea saw a bloodied hand, with a large chunk out of it that had almost severed the pinkie finger from the rest of the palm, but unlike the ghouls crawling hands, that were greying and pale with black dead-looking nails, it was tanned and twitching.

Thea grabbed it. She wrapped both her hands around the adjoining wrist and tugged, using her legs to kick out at anything that would stop her. By degrees, bellowing Spanish profanities, Torrez emerged from the mass.

As soon as his shoulders and arms were free, Thea let go of him, and they both worked to loosen Torrez's legs. Once liberated, Torrez scrambled to his feet. He pulled his tie from around his neck and made quick work of wrapping it around his injured hand.

They had stunned or killed nearly half the ghouls in the lock-up, but they were getting tired, and they were still vastly outnumbered. Thea didn't like the idea of harming the ghouls, but she also didn't like the idea of being eaten alive, and while she had opted for non-lethal force, she wouldn't judge Torrez for his lack of it.

"Get in here," she said, darting into the nearest cell.

"Are you crazy?" Torrez shouted, but he followed nonetheless.

Once inside the small cube-shaped cell, Thea called, "Computer, close the cells."

"Closing cell doors."

The glass started to lower into place as Torrez said, "They broke out, they can break in, and we'll be trapped."

Thea ignored him. She used push kicks to stop the ghouls trying to impede the descending glass.

With a last shove to a final ghoul who had gotten down on its stomach to scratch at them, the glass clicked into place.

It was an odd and exceedingly unpleasant site. Stuck behind the glass, like animals at a zoo, Thea and Torrez watched as the crush of ghouls pressed themselves up against the glass, clawing and thumping their uncoordinated fists against it.

"Well, now we're fucked," Torrez said, regaining his usual nonchalance.

"I have a plan," Thea said placatingly.

She pointed upwards.

The cells in the lock-up didn't touch the ceiling. In fact, there was a good ten feet between the top of the walls that formed the square cells and the ceiling proper. In place of any roof, there was a mesh of blue-tinged light that, when touched, provided a shock strong enough to kill.

Torrez's eyes looked to where Thea pointed. "So?"

Each of the wall's top corners had a cylindrical metal stake embedded into it. The beams seemed to bounce off and between them. Thea raised her gun and took aim at each of the cylinders in turn. When she struck the first, the beams flickered, but then readjusted themselves. When she struck the second, the same happened; the beams flickered madly, bouncing between the remaining stakes in its attempt to reform the mesh. When she struck the third with a well-placed pulse round, the mesh disappeared. She shot the fourth for good measure.

"I'll give you a boost," she said, taking a knee.

Torrez placed his foot on her thigh and used the leverage it provided to get on top of the nearest wall. He leaned down, extending a hand to Thea, and pulled her up beside him.

"And now?" he asked, swinging his legs.

"We wait for the captain to get us out."

TENEBRIUM

It didn't take long for the ghouls to notice them, but they were at such a vantage point they were well out of reach. When the glass of the cell eventually broke and the ghouls swarmed in, it was to disappointment as their prey was no longer there to be devoured.

They waited in silence, Thea's sense of dread growing larger and larger the longer they sat there. She hated the act of not acting.

"What if the captain can't get to him in time?"

"Querida, there is no point dwelling. We have to worry about us right now."

The yowling snarls of the ghouls' feet below them blended into white noise as Thea imagined all the possible outcomes of their predicament. Perhaps they would be rescued, and they would be able to save Walt, but there were also much darker and equally possible end results. The longer they stayed quiet and still, the more time Thea had to think, and it was the worst thing for her. It allowed her to dwell on the yawning chasm inside that was the loss of her father. To remember that the man she loved and hated in equal measure had killed him.

Before Walt had turned up at her door, only to discover Bastion there, half-naked and so clearly fresh from frequenting her bed, she had truly hoped never to see him again. He had caused her so much pain, and they had done so much irreparable damage to each other that her continued love for him only served as a reminder of her mistakes, but she hadn't wanted him dead. Gone, out of her life, unable to cause more harm, but not dead. She had imagined him somewhere else, living his life as she hoped to do. Alive and well, but out of sight and reach. Yet the growing prospect of a world without him in it scared her. She felt it would be a colder place, lacking in some way.

"Do you hear that?" Torrez said, squinting to the door.

"No, what?"

"Listen."

She heard it now. Shouts beyond the lock-up walls, and then the door was wrenched open, and a tall Chinese man with orange hair entered. He held his palm aloft, and Thea could just make out a small orb nestled there.

"Run," Thea shouted as the ghouls rushed towards him. "Get out of there," but he paid her no mind.

He closed his fist around the orb, and a blast of energy burst forth, engulfing every part of the room. At first, it seemed to have no effect, and then the ghouls began to drop one by one until they all lay crumpled on the cold metal floor.

Thea jumped down, careful not to step on any of the fallen.

"You," she said when she reached the man. "You worked for my father."

"Yes, unfortunately, I did. My name is Zhao. And I was under your father's control—he threatened my mother. Now I'm not, and I'd like to right some of his wrongs, especially the ones he forced me to facilitate. Let's get you out of here."

"Why should we trust you?" Torrez asked, his eyes narrowed.

"I don't care if you trust me." Zhao shrugged. "But your captain is a very good friend of mine, and she called in a favour."

Torrez opened his mouth to retort, but Zhao pushed on, "Don't you have an execution to halt?"

The precinct was in chaos. The emergency lights flashed red, white, and blue as the lockdown sirens blared. The atrium floor was covered in papers, and the benches that lined the walls and were usually occupied by those waiting to be booked had been ripped from their brackets. Several officers were trying to restrain criminals who had seized the lockdown as their opportunity to escape, fruitless though it would be as huge metal shutters barred any chance of egress.

With Zhao and Torrez in tow, Thea raced towards the staircases, knowing the elevators wouldn't be working, but when Thea opened the fire door that concealed them, she was barrelled out of the way by a flood of people frantically fleeing some unknown threat.

What had caused them to panic became clear at once. Three ghouls, blood dripping from their mouths, were tearing down the stairs, frothy white spittle flying in their wake. Without hesitation, Thea fired, and before the ghouls had even hit the ground, she was sprinting off up the stairs.

Her legs ached, and her thighs burned when she finally came to a halt on the fifth floor. Two Onyx Legion soldiers, clad head to toe in black, stood guard at the entrance to death row.

"Excuse me," Zhao said, pushing in front of Thea to address the guards. "I am the acting District Attorney Jian Zhao. I am representing Walter James, and I am here to provide Judge Wolfsheim with exculpatory evidence. Let me pass."

"Too late for that," the guard on the left said dismissively.

"The execution has already taken place?"

Thea's breath caught in her chest.

"No, but they are taking him in now."

"Then there is plenty of time to save a man's life. Now, move aside, or I shall have you both given a strike."

The guards glanced warily at each other and then parted to let them pass.

Death Row, or The Mile as most within the TPD called it, was a narrow brick corridor with six cells, three on each side, and a long green paint line on the outdated linoleum floor. It was cold and unwelcoming, like it had been created to ensure anyone who was unlucky enough to find themselves there knew that death was all that awaited them.

The execution chamber was situated at the very end of the thin corridor behind a huge cast iron door that wouldn't have looked out of place in a bank vault. The closer they got to it, Thea saw that it was engraved with various depictions of death personified from cultures all over the world.

"Bit on the nose," Torrez muttered.

Zhao pushed the door open and strode inside, projecting an air of irrefutable authority. Thea and Torrez followed on tenterhooks. Neither had ever witnessed an execution. Thea was vehemently opposed to capital punishment, and Torrez had never enjoyed the sight of death.

The death chamber was dimly lit by faux hooded lanterns that made Thea feel like she had stepped back into the past. The room was split into four quadrants, one for each execution method available. A row of tall wooden posts stood in the quadrant nearest the door. Exactly ten feet in front of them on the floor was a painted white line, and just in front of that were the words, "HOLD STEADY. AIM TRUE".

Next to the firing posts was a glass cube. Inside it, there was a metal chair with leather straps hanging from the arms and legs. The headrest was draped with electrodes that were linked to a small lever just on the other side of the glass. Opposite was a gurney, also with leather straps. It was unpadded and looked extremely uncomfortable. An IV stand stood next to it.

The furthest quadrant from the door held the gallows. Thea couldn't help but gasp when she saw Walt. He was blindfolded and gagged, with his hands bound behind his back and standing atop a raised platform, the noose already around his neck, his feet resting on the trap door.

"A word, Judge Wolfsheim, before you proceed," Zhao said in a commanding voice that echoed around the large room. "I have no grounds to stop this," he added in a whisper to Thea. "So, you'd better do something quickly."

The judge raised a careless hand to signal to the execution party of O'Malley, the executioner, and a priest, to wait as he stepped forward to meet Zhao.

"Judge, they're stalling," O'Malley said impatiently.

He stood next to the masked executioner beside the lever that Thea knew would open the trapdoor at Walt's feet. The hungry look on his face made her feel queasy.

Throwing caution to the wind, Thea stunned the executioner. The pulse round hit him in the face, and he seemed to topple back in slow motion taking the priest with him. They both hit the ground with a thunderous clang. The executioner was knocked out cold; the priest scrambled back, clearly shaken.

It took a moment for everyone to realise what had happened.

"Thea!" Torrez yelled incredulously before throwing himself at the judge, who looked as though he was about to call for help and tackling him to the ground. "No, you don't."

O'Malley dived for the lever, and Thea fired again, the pulse round narrowly missing its target, but it was enough to make him jump back from the switch.

"Bitch," he snarled.

"This is madness," the priest uttered.

As Thea ran up the gallows' steps, O'Malley ran down. He struck out at her with his foot. She dodged to the side, and he overbalanced. As he fell, he grabbed hold of her, and they both tumbled to the ground. Thea sprang to her feet just in time to body-swerve the bullet that left a smouldering hole in the concrete wall behind her. O'Malley was shooting to kill.

"I've wanted to do this for a long time," O'Malley sneered. He continued to fire at Thea, and she took refuge behind the viewing gallery as he made his way back up the gibbet steps towards the lever.

Darting out from the relative safety of cover, Thea flung herself under the platform. She stowed her gun in her waistband and started to climb.

Leaning over the railings, O'Malley continued to take pot-shots at her, but none came close.

There were no footholds, and the metal was cold and harsh on her hands, but Thea managed to clamber up and onto the platform.

O'Malley stood next to the lever again, his hand resting upon it, a villainous grin contorting his face.

"Do it, and you're dead," Thea snarled, pointing her gun at his chest.

"So's he."

"If watching Walt swing would mean a life well lived for you, do it, but you will be following him into the afterlife."

"Sorry, sweetheart, but it just don't ring true. You're not a killer. You ain't like me or him." O'Malley nodded to Walt. "You quite literally don't have the stones."

"Pull it and find out."

Thea saw what he was going to do before it happened. He fired his gun with one hand and pulled the lever with the other. Thea dropped low, firing a shot of her own, but hers, unlike his, didn't miss. It hit the rope around Walt's neck, where it was tied to the rafters causing it to fray and snap. Walt fell through the trapdoor that opened underneath him with a muffled yell, but he was spared a broken neck and suffocation.

Thea dove, following Walt through the trapdoor.

They hit the ground in a heap. Thea removed the black cloth that covered Walt's eyes and untied his hands.

"Are you okay?"

Walt pulled the gag from his mouth, "I'd started to think you weren't coming back," he said.

"She might as well not have," O'Malley said.

Thea whirled around, searching for O'Malley. He was standing next to a red crank handle that sat just behind the gallows. He grabbed hold of it and turned.

A sound like an air raid siren blared from all sides.

"That panic button goes straight to the OL. We need to get out of here," Walt said, getting to his feet.

"The building's in lockdown. You're trapped," O'Malley jeered.

Walt made to go after O'Malley, but Thea grabbed his arm and dragged him to where Torrez and Zhao were standing over Judge Wolfsheim, who was sitting on the floor looking thoroughly disgruntled, though not particularly perturbed by the events that had unfolded in front of him.

"Stay here," Thea said to the judge. "And you should be fine. Follow us or attempt to have us stopped; I will put you down."

"You leave here, and you can kiss your career goodbye."

"I wish my career was the only thing on the line."

EXISTENTIALISM

It wasn't hard to go unnoticed in the pandemonium that had consumed the police station. Thea, Walt, Zhao and Torrez had left O'Malley and the judge in the execution chamber and hadn't looked back.

Next on Thea's list was the captain. Betty Charles had always pulled through for her. She had sent Zhao to help them on top of countless other things she had done through the years, and Thea, no matter their differences, wasn't going to leave her at the mercy of the Gold Legion and their Onyx siblings.

The journey to the detective's floor, however, was not as clear cut as the one to The Mile had been. Staircase after staircase was blocked by officers fighting criminals and ghouls, often both. If they weren't waylaid by brawling, it was makeshift barricades made from tables, chairs, and filing cabinets blocking doors, corridors, and walkways.

"It's like everyone's gone mad," Torrez said as they rounded into yet another blocked off corridor.

"Let's go through the morgue," Walt said, setting off again. "Take the service stairs down to the bullpen."

The service stairwell was gloomy. The dim emergency lights barely made a dent in the shadows. The stairs themselves were narrow and made from Dunbar floor plates. Their footsteps on the embossed metal echoed eerily as they descended single file.

At the bottom of the staircase was a thick wooden door with a bar that stopped it from being opened from the other side. As she was first down, Thea lifted it and pushed, but the door wouldn't budge. She tried again. The door moved slightly, but stopped shy of opening.

"What's the holdup?" Torrez said from behind her.

"It won't open; something on the other side is blocking it."

Torrez stepped down into the slender space at the bottom of the staircase. It was so small that he and Thea couldn't comfortably stand side by side.

"On three?" he said.

Thea nodded. Together they threw themselves at the door, and it opened an inch or two, letting in shafts of blue and red light. They threw their shoulders into it again, and it opened just wide enough for Thea to slip through into the corridor that held the officer's lounge.

She saw immediately what had been blocking the door.

Pale, with eyes staring blankly and the ghost of shock still etched on his face, the medical examiner Cecil Flynn was slumped against the door. There was a tiny bullet hole in his forehead and another on his neck. Blood splattered the walls, but it was already dry. He had been dead for a while.

Grimacing, Thea grabbed his feet and dragged him away from the door to allow the others to enter.

"Oh," Walt said indifferently when he saw the body.

"He's been shot," Thea said.

"The Gold Legion abhors loose ends," said Zhao. He wrinkled his nose at the sight.

"Let's go," Torrez said.

Turning into the bullpen, they were confronted by an eerie sight. In the semi-darkness created by the emergency lights, Thea saw every one of her colleagues standing upright and statuesque in a circle facing inwards, with their heads bowed low. They twitched infinitesimally, eyes wide and unblinking.

"What the shit?" Torrez muttered.

As one, the detectives looked up mechanically. Their heads turned on straining necks to see at the new arrivals.

Thea heard a whimper from the middle of the circle; she shifted slightly to see the source. Captain Betty Charles was sitting in her desk chair that had clearly been dragged from her office. Sweat glazed her face, and Thea noticed that her lip was bloodied. This hadn't been what she had imagined when the captain said they were keeping her under watch. The captain raised a shaking finger to her lips, begging them to be silent, but the detectives had seen them now. With the practised precision of military personnel on parade, the detectives turned about.

"Don't move," Thea whispered.

She took a step forward so that she was in full view of the captain. The detectives held their ground.

"Thea..." Walt warned. She ignored him.

"Chipped?" she asked the captain, keeping her voice as low as possible.

The captain nodded.

"What are their orders?"

The captain tapped her eye.

"To watch you?"

The captain nodded again.

Thea raised her hands as if in surrender and took a step towards the circle. Nothing moved.

"Thea, be careful," Walt said.

She took another step closer. The detective's eyes moved in unison to focus on her, but their forms stayed still.

She took another step, then another, and another, until she was inches from the circle of bodies. Being careful not to touch any of them, Thea sidled in between Orion Martin and Deandra. The detective's heads turned back to face her in the centre.

Thea reached out a hand to the captain, who shook her head. "They killed Fischer and Hoffmann." The captain pointed to one of the nearby desks. Thea let out a small gasp. Crammed underneath the desk were two bodies; both had had their necks snapped with such ferocity their heads were facing in the wrong direction; Fischer's lips still quivered.

"We can't stay here," Thea said to Betty.

"I can't move."

Thea took a step closer to her, and so did the detectives.

"Take my hand."

"No."

"Yes. Stand up. We are going to run—all of us."

A tear fell from the captain's eye, and she shook her head again. The detectives each raised a hand. Orion Martin was closest to Thea and he collided with her shoulder. It was gentle; had they been in any other situation, it would have been nothing, but this small touch changed everything.

"Stop," the detectives screeched together.

Thea grabbed the captain's hand and pulled her to her feet. She dragged her through the circle and back to Walt, Zhao, and Torrez.

"Run!"

A hail of screeching, thrown furniture, and bullets followed them back to where Flynn's body lay.

"Hijo de puta!" Torrez yelled.

They had forgotten to prop the service stairwell door, meaning they couldn't escape back the way they had come.

"What now?" Zhao asked, his voice shaking slightly.

"Interrogation," Thea said, and they set off again.

The interrogation rooms were unoccupied, seemingly untouched by the madness that had overtaken the rest of the precinct, but they were a dead end. They linked to no stairs nor exits, and there were no fire escapes outside as there were no windows.

Torrez and Walt quickly grabbed tables and chairs from the nearest interrogation suite and made a reasonably sturdy barricade while Thea searched for any means of exit. Zhao put a consoling arm around the visibly shaken captain.

Torrez and Walt hadn't finished the barricade when it was tested for the first time. An almighty *CRASH* caused it to shake as the furniture they had piled against the door shunted forward by inches.

"We had better find a plan B fast," Walt said as he and Torrez ran to push the barricade back into place.

Thea searched each interrogation room in turn, but they were all bare.

"The vents," The captain said as Thea returned to tell them the bad news. "If you can remove the ceiling tiles, they should reveal the heating vents."

"All right, let's do it."

Thea pulled a table from one of the rooms not ransacked to create the barricade and placed it against the wall.

"Wait, wait, wait, haven't any of you watched a movie?" Torrez said, holding his hands up to emphasise the fact he wanted them to stop. "This is a terrible idea. What if the ghouls have gotten into the vents? We would be trapped in a tiny space with a ravenous monster, and they're pure steel, so we can't use our guns; the ricochet could kill us."

"How would they have gotten in there?" Walt said reasonably. "The shafts are hidden behind walls and ceilings, and they only cover the older parts of the building."

The barricade was shaken again by another thunderous assault. Several of the chairs piled on top of it came crashing to the ground.

"I don't think we have a choice anymore," Thea said.

She stepped onto the tabletop. It was only just high enough to allow her to reach the white ceiling tiles. They were thin and light and came away easily. Thea only had to remove a few before the square silver ventilation shafts became visible.

There was a grate set into the side, but it was bolted shut.

"Here," Walt said, and he threw Thea a small device that looked like the blade of a knife.

She passed it over the screws, and they came loose at once. The grate fell to the ground with a sonorous clang.

"You first," Torrez said, but he climbed up on the table beside her.

Thea jumped and caught the thin and slick edge of the vent. With enormous strength, she pulled herself inside. It was pitch-dark and uncomfortably warm. The metal of the shaft was hot to the touch. The space was narrow and only just tall enough to allow her to crawl. She scooched away from the opening to allow Torrez to follow her up. Once he was inside and she could hear the others climbing up behind her, she set off.

It was slow and gruelling. The heat made it hard to breathe, and her sweaty palms kept slipping. They could hear the shouts, shots, bangs and impacts in the rooms they were travelling over.

"We can't stay in here forever," Walt croaked. His throat sounded painfully dry.

"Just a little further," Thea said, wiping her brow on her sleeve. "We have to make it to the other side of the building, or we have no chance of getting to a fire escape."

"Fire escape?" Zhao wheezed.

"The building is locked down, that means all exits are sealed, but if we can get to one of the upper windows, we should be able to climb down a fire escape."

On and on, they crawled in darkness, backs aching and lips cracking. Thea knew it must be particularly jarring for the captain and Zhao, who, unlike the detectives, didn't have Seer implants that provided night vision. Although, she thought, fuzzy green wasn't much better than blinding darkness, it did, however, allow her to catch a glimpse of a grate up ahead.

"I think we should get out there."

There was a general murmur of agreement.

Thea slid right up to the grate and peered through the gaps between the sharp metal slats. They were above the evidence store. Thea could see the rows and rows of boxes and filing cabinets filled with contraband and samples set against the faux wood grain wallpaper. The weapons store in the corner appeared untouched.

She took the any-tool Walt had given her and ran it over the screws. They made delicate tinkling noises as they hit the floor below. She kicked the grate with no real force, and it fell into the evidence store. The landing had been loud, but nothing stirred.

Awkwardly Thea manoeuvred herself to the edge and jumped. She grimaced at the shooting pain in her shins as she landed.

"Here," Walt said as he landed beside her and held out his hand for the tool.

He disappeared between the rows for a moment before returning with three pistols. He kept one for himself and handed the other two to Zhao and the captain.

"It's been a while," Betty said, checking the barrel. She had regained her usual composure.

"If the corridor isn't barricaded, there should be a fire escape right outside," Thea said. She moved over to the door to listen for any commotion on the other side. All was quiet.

Outside the evidence store, the hallway was empty and still. Papers littered the floor, and there was a smear of blood on the wall opposite, but no sign of the person it had come from.

Slowly, they crept along towards the window at the very end. It was a wooden framed single hung window with a rusted latch. With difficulty, Thea pulled back the catch; it came away in her hand. She threw the twisted remnants to the ground and lifted the bottom sash.

She looked out over a burning city. Smoke rose in billows and plumes, the smell invading her nostrils and scratching at her lungs.

"My god," Zhao uttered behind her.

There were fires everywhere and panic on the streets. Far below, Thea could see the officers who had escaped the lockdown fighting desperately against hordes of ghouls. She stepped out onto the fire escape. From there, high above, she could see the gates of the SubLevel—they were open.

"I think the Gold Legion just made their move," she said.

Nobody replied; they just stared out over the city that was their home, taking in the devastation.

"We have to go," Walt said uneasily, as he looked over the edge at the long drop between them and the concrete below. Thea had forgotten he was afraid of heights.

They were around 200 stories up. The air was thin and mixed with the noxious smoke; it made breathing very difficult. They started their descent. It was slow work, taking each ladder single file, floor by floor. Some of the windows they passed were shuttered, some broken, and some had filing cabinets pushed up against them.

"Wait," Torres shouted when they were halfway down.

Thea was already a ladder below and had to climb back up to see what the problem was.

"It's Jasper," Torrez said, pointing through a window.

Sure enough, just beyond the dusty glass, Thea saw Jasper crouching behind a stack of boxes as three OL soldiers prowled the corridor.

Carefully Torrez opened the window, but focussed as he had been on Jasper, he didn't notice the ghoul crouching just below the sill. It erupted up and out of the window, knocking Torrez down the nearby ladder and tumbling after him.

"We'll get Torrez," the captain said, nodding to Zhao. "You get Jasper."

"Meet us at Ward Eight. Benny's apartment will be empty now."

With a brief nod and surprising vigour, the captain slid down the ladder, Zhao climbing quickly after her.

Thea and Walt took cover on either side of the now open window.

Thea listened hard. She heard a door snap shut and hoped that the soldiers had moved on. She peaked into the corridor; it appeared empty but for Jasper.

"Jasper," she whispered.

His head whipped around. Thea motioned to him to come to the window, to them, but he shook his head, raising his hands. He was handcuffed to the radiator he was leaning against.

"Shit."

Carefully, Thea stepped through the open window. Inside she was struck by how quiet it was.

"What happened?" she said, kneeling next to Jasper.

"Flynn," he said bitterly. "The captain sent me to get you and Torrez from lock-up, and well, he caught up with me on the way."

Thea examined the handcuffs. They weren't the usual magnetic bracelets, but rather the old-fashioned kind, with a chain running between each cuff.

"We'll need to find something to pick them with."

"Do it quickly," Walt said from near the window where he was acting as sentry.

Thea rummaged around in the boxes piled along the corridor. Most were filled with papers and evidence files. Grabbing the nearest file, Thea removed the paperclips then threw the loose sheets haphazardly back into the box.

Thea took two paper clips and stowed the spares in her pocket. The first paperclip she straightened out completely, then folded it in half and twisted the ends together to form a tension wrench. The second, she only uncurled halfway, leaving a curve at the end that she could hold on to. Thea took the straightened end and bent it slightly until it resembled the lines on a heart rate monitor forming the clip into a rake pick.

Kneeling down beside Jasper, she inserted the tension wrench into the bottom of the keyhole and applied pressure, attempting to use the rake pick to open the lock. It was harder than she'd hoped.

"Hurry it up," Walt muttered, and Thea knew exactly why, for she had heard it, too.

Footsteps belonging to multiple people were approaching the T-junction at the top of the corridor.

Thea redoubled her efforts, and with a final wiggle, the lock sprang open.

"Leave her," said a gruff voice close by. "We've to find Williams and James. That's all HQ cares about now."

The three of them froze in place as if they had been turned to stone. The passing group was composed of five Onyx Legion soldiers and two of the chipped detectives. They passed the mouth of the corridor without seeing Walt at the end, or Thea crouched halfway along next to Jasper.

They were so focused on their task that they did not see, but for one. The last soldier stopped just before he would have stepped out of view and turned his head to the side. Thea was running at him before he had time to raise his gun. She speared him into the wall. His fellows turned sharply about, but couldn't attack, for she was using the soldier she had caught off guard as a shield. She pushed him roughly into his comrades, and they scattered like bowling pins.

One of the detectives, Thea thought his name might be Hector, was first to his feet. He struck out at Thea with a heavy fist, but she ducked underneath it. He swung again, and she dodged to the side, causing him to hit the wall. Maybe Hector cried out in pain, clutching his hand. She landed a heavy round kick on his thigh, then another to his head, and he crumpled to the ground.

By this time, Walt had joined the fray. He grabbed the rifle of the nearest OL soldier and wrenched it from his grip. Walt used it like a hammer as he brought it down on the top of the soldier's head. The soldier dropped like a stone, joining Maybe Hector on the shabby grey carpet.

Shooting in such close quarters was sure to result in friendly fire, but that didn't stop the soldiers. As soon as they got to their feet, the air was filled with lead and pulse rounds.

Shots flew everywhere, bouncing off the walls. Walt grabbed Thea and dragged her around the corner; face to face, he pressed her against the wall. He gave a little start, and they both looked down. Blood was blossoming on the left side of his stomach; it was already soaking through his shirt.

"Damn," Walt said blandly, and he dropped to his knees.

"Jasper, help me!"

Jasper ran forward, seemingly awakened from his stupor, and dragged Walt further back from the fight, propping him against the wall and putting pressure on his bullet wound. Walt groaned in pain.

Thea took careful aim around the corner and managed to take out a soldier and the remaining detective with one well-placed shot.

"Three left," she muttered to herself.

She rolled out from cover, hoping to surprise them by keeping low. She fired three times; two shots hit their targets, the third missed. If at that exact moment, the last soldier's gun hadn't jammed, she would have been dead.

Cursing in frustration, the soldier cast his weapons aside and ran for Thea. Staying low, she twisted herself around one of his legs so she was behind him. She then threaded her legs through his and caught his ankles with her heels. Bending her knees sharply caused him to fall to the ground. Thea sat up quickly, gripping his foot. He cried out as the pressure she put on his knee threatened to wrench it from its socket. She pulled with all her might, and there was a loud pop, then the soldier's leg was disgustingly malleable in her grip. She stood up. The soldier groaned into the floor, incapacitated. Thea kicked him in the head, knocking him unconscious as she passed. She didn't want him calling for help.

"How bad is it?" Thea said, running to Walt's side.

He was panting, and a thick sheen of sweat covered all the skin she could see.

"It was a pulse round, not a lead bullet, so it cauterised a lot of the major damage on the way through, but he needs medical attention."

"No worse than almost being hung." Walt smiled weakly, a touch of blood on his lips.

"Help me get him to the window," Jasper said.

"He can't climb down a hundred stories worth of ladders," Thea said incredulously. "We need to get to the elevators."

"They've been deactivated because of the lockdown."

"Are you kidding? You're the tech guy. This is literally your job."

"Right," Jasper shook his head as if to clear it.

"I don't mean to sound pushy, but could we hurry this up?" Walt's voice was thin and breathy.

"On the count of three," Thea said, taking one of Walt's arms. Jasper took the other. "One, two, three." They hauled him to his feet and, supporting his weight between them, began to make their slow way along the corridor.

"I don't even know where we are," Thea said as she and Jasper half-carried Walt.

"Same floor as my office. The elevators are on the other side. In fact, if we can get to my office, I might be able to help Walt."

"Sounds good to me," Walt said weakly.

They had difficulty traversing the hazard strewn halls with the injured Walt in tow. He could barely stand as blood seeped from his stomach and down the front of his trousers. While his legs shambled with their guidance, his head lolled on his shoulder, and his eyelids drooped.

"Still with me?" Thea said.

"Ready to go ten rounds." His words were slightly slurred.

"We can cut through here," Jasper said, leading them over to a covered walkway.

The glass tunnel was long and wide, connecting the admin block they had come from to the tech wing. It looked over a communal area and office cubicles. Thea saw soldiers, police officers, and ghouls engaged in a violent and bloody struggle far below them. She watched as the soldiers were pushed back by the tide of ghouls. A soldier cornered in a cubicle by a mob of ghouls rummaged around a supply crate that had been placed there. Thea watched in horror as he pulled out an RPG.

"They've lost their minds. We have to get back," she yelled, but they had crossed too far.

The soldier fired the rocket; it missed the horde by miles. With a monumental explosion, it hit the underside of the walkway. The next thing Thea knew, she was flying through one of the glass panes and plummeting to the ground.

When Thea awoke, she was in the open-plan area below the now collapsed walkway.

TENEBRIUM

Water was falling on her face, and smoke filled her lungs. Her ears rang, making all the noise around her sound distant as if she was hearing them via a bad phone line. There was rubble and debris everywhere. The sprinklers had come on to tackle the fires that had broken out all around, adding a thick mist of vapour to the smoke and dust that obscured her view.

"Walt? Jasper?"

Thea coughed; it made her ribs ache. She got shakily to her feet. There was a sharp pain in her calf. She looked down. A large shard of glass was sticking out of her leg. She gripped it carefully and pulled; it came out without resistance. The gash it left wasn't that deep, and as Thea tested her weight on it, while painful, her footing held.

"Walt? Jasper? Walt?"

The more of the space she explored, the more carnage was revealed. She scrambled over bodies and body parts, unable to tell whether they were friend, foe, or ghoul. The survivors paid her no mind as they collected themselves and searched for friends and colleagues. The OL soldiers didn't trouble her either; they were more concerned with the wounded and dead.

Thea found her way to the remnants of the walkway. It had split in the middle so that each side was like a steep and perilous ramp. Hoping that Walt and Jasper had made it across, she chose the side that was closer to the tech expert's office.

The climb was not an easy one. It had been a very long day, and her muscles were throbbing long before the explosion, but she pushed on regardless.

When she reached the top, she was pleasantly surprised to see that other than some cracking where the walkway had come away from the walls, the corridor was relatively intact.

Thea had taken only a few steps when she heard a low moan.

"Th..ea..."

She ducked into the nearest room and found Walt lying on top of a long conference table in a meeting room that, explosion notwithstanding, had seen better days. He didn't look good.

"You...hu..rt?" It sounded like every word sapped his limited energy.

"Nothing serious. Where's Jaz?"

Thea lifted Walt's shirt. There was a small hole around the size of a dime just under his rib cage on the left-hand side. There was dark purplish bruising around the edge, and blackish-red blood oozed sluggishly from the wound.

"Gone to...get...needs...office."

Thea stroked his damp hair. If they didn't do something soon, Walt wouldn't survive.

"I'm going to look for Jasper."

She didn't have to look for long. As she stepped back outside the conference room, Jasper came jogging towards her carrying a small canister.

"He hangin' in there?"

"Just about. What's that?" Thea nodded to the canister.

"It's a polyurethane liquid foam that is used to dress wounds. You inject it into the wound, and it expands and helps stop bleeding and infection, but this one is special because I modified it by adding nanites that actively rebuild the cells,

441

meaning if he survives that long, he will be good as new in a couple of days; assuming his body doesn't reject the nanotech," he added quickly.

Thea kept guard just outside while Jasper set to work. The fires seemed to be contained on the level below thanks to the fire suppression system, but the building had taken a large hit, and she had no way of satisfactorily quantifying the structural damage. She didn't like staying still. Despite the tumult, they were all fugitives now, and at some point, someone would begin to look for them again.

"What's your blood type?" Jasper asked, sticking his head out into the corridor.

"O negative."

"Perfect."

The blood transfusion took about half an hour. Thea was sure Walt could have used more blood than he took, but they had remained in the same place for too long. Walt's colour was better, and he was able to speak breathily, but in complete sentences. He wasn't able to walk on his own, but he could sit up, and that was enough.

"We need to move. If we stay here much longer, we'll never get out," Thea said to Jasper. "You ready?" she added to Walt. He nodded grimly.

Each taking an arm, she and Jasper helped Walt to his feet. He was unsteady and in great pain, but he could move, and he wasn't bleeding anymore.

"Nearest elevator?"

"Next to my office, it's not far. We can cut through the lecture hall."

The lecture hall was large and deep and, in Thea's opinion, the perfect place for an ambush. More than this, it was all stairs. While Walt was slightly better, he was still in bad shape, and it took them some time to get him down the stairs, across the podium, and up the stairs on the other side. But soon enough, they were next to Jasper's office facing the elevator.

There was one problem—Orion Martin.

Dishevelled and dirty, his usually pristine clothes ripped and a graze on his pate, Orion stood like a menacing troll barring their path.

"I'm sorry, youngblood, but I can't let you pass."

Thea disentangled herself from Walt and Jasper.

"You're not yourself," she said, holding her hands out in front of her. "You're being controlled. You have to try to fight it because Ri, I don't want to hurt you."

Orion laughed uncharitably. "Ah, the arrogance of youth. You're barely grown. Still having high school romances and acting out. You are a disgrace to the badge. I tried to take you under my wing, but you're too caught up in your own cleverness. You've been skating by the seat of your pants since day one."

"You've been chipped against your will. These thoughts—aren't yours. You are a kind man, an understanding man. Not some bitter and jaded has-been. Fight it, Orion. Fight. It."

"Why? When I could just kill you?"

A shot whizzed past Thea, and for a moment, she thought Orion had fired and missed, but then he fell to the ground.

"Jasper!"

TENEBRIUM

"I've never fired a gun before. Is he dead?"

"No, it was a stun round. Let's go. You can get the elevator working now, right?"

"I shot someone."

"Now, Jasper."

Jasper moved over to the elevator and opened the metal panel on the wall next to it to reveal a small screen and keyboard. Thea had no idea what he was doing or how he was doing it, but his fingers moved at lightning speed across the keys. Within minutes, he had the elevator up and running.

The three of them stepped inside, and Thea pressed "L" for Lobby.

"What's the plan?" Walt said.

"I have no idea."

The elevator let out a small *Ding*. Thea took a deep breath as she readied herself for whatever would be on the other side of the doors. When they slid apart, the atrium was flooded with people. The lockdown had lifted, and emergency personnel rushed in and out. A triage had been set up to treat the injured, and OL soldiers marched in groups of six. It was clear the TPD was being used as a disaster base. Thea could only imagine how bad the rest of the city must be if a building on fire in places and swarming with ghouls was the safest location to take refuge.

"What now?" Jasper whispered.

"We walk right out the door."

Thea put her arm around Walt's waist, and catching on, he let go of Jasper and put an arm around her shoulders. Keeping close and avoiding eye contact with anyone they passed, they made their way through the crowds. No one noticed as they stepped through the revolving door out into the courtyard.

It was even busier than the atrium. Armoured transports, Medicus, fire engines, and police Jonks all blared their sirens, as more responders carried supplies in, while those needing more medical care than could be provided on-site were carried out.

A TPD Jonk sat abandoned with its doors open just beyond the ring of emergency vehicles. Just as they had walked out of the precinct, they walked among the rushing bodies to the transporter and got inside. Not a single person saw as they rose into the air.

HE FOOLED US ALL

Benny's penthouse was exactly how Thea had imagined it; leather and animal print, with silk sheets, fur pillows, and faux pelt rugs. It was gold, everywhere gleaming gold.

Torrez, Zhao and the captain had been waiting for them when they arrived. Bruised and battered, but relatively unharmed. All except Torrez, who had a nasty ghoul bite. Thea felt a pang of regret as she raided Benny's cupboards for something to dress Torrez's hands with. Benny, as it turned out, kept his home well-stocked. There was no shortage of food, first aid, and recreational drugs, not to mention an impressively stocked bar.

"The city has gone mad," Torrez said as Thea wrapped a clean bandage around his mangled hand. She was kneeling in front of him while he sat on a bright red couch the size of three king-sized beds stuck together.

"Can you move your fingers?"

He wiggled them to show he could.

"What now, Querida?"

"I don't know. Walt needs to rest; I put him on Benny's bed. We could all use some food and some sleep. After that? I have no idea. We can't go back to the precinct. We have officially gone rogue. I have no idea what our next move is."

"Get a couple hours sleep. We can think of a plan when our heads are clearer."

Thea placed a final piece of tape on his hand to secure the bandage, then joined him on the couch. She put her head on his shoulder and was asleep within seconds.

The smell of food brought Thea back to consciousness.

Through the archway that separated it from the living room, Thea could see that the captain and Zhao were working away in the kitchen like a well-oiled machine. Whatever they were concocting smelled heavenly. Walt was up and about, talking in hushed voices with Torrez at one end of the long dining table while Jasper monitored the news streams at the other.

She wanted to check on all of them to see how they were holding up before she told them what she had decided. It has seemed to come to her in a dream. As soon as she opened her eyes, she knew exactly what they had to do.

Thea ambled into the next room.

"What are you making?" she asked the captain.

"Fried chicken. Zhao here is no stranger to soul food." She bestowed a warm smile upon him. "I've been teaching him how my grandmother used to make it."

"Where's Ruth and the kids?"

The captain smiled sadly. "With my parents on the mainland. I sent them there a couple weeks ago. It was only a matter of time before this city erupted, and I couldn't bear for them to be caught in the crossfire. I miss them like crazy, but we are lucky. Not everyone will make it out of this."

"And you?" Thea asked Zhao.

He put down the spoon which he had been using to stir the macaroni cheese. "My mother has cancer. She's in a hospice in Atene on Colony Five. My partner...is an Onyx Legion soldier. I have no idea where he is."

"I'm sorry," Thea said, and she meant it.

"He picked his side, and it was the wrong one."

Zhao sniffed and began to stir the mac and cheese again. Thea took this as a sign that he didn't want to talk about it, and she didn't press. She hardly knew the man, yet in the few hours they had spent together, he had proved a valuable ally. It was strange, she thought, the kind of relationships that are forged through fire. She trusted Zhao, and that was that.

"What's the latest?" she said, moving over to Jasper.

"Nothing good," he said succinctly. "Ghouls. Carnage. The mayor declared a state of emergency, giving the Onyx Legion 'executive power', whatever that means."

"I think it means the Gold Legion is in control."

"Speaking of, I think I know how the detectives were chipped."

"Oh?"

"The blood drive. No one here was chipped because no one gave blood. And I managed to snag a chip from someone who was hurt in the explosion. It's nothing as advanced as the one you described on Walt or the ones that were killing the sex workers. I think they were cheap versions. Maxwell and his goons don't care if the people wearing them live or die, and they aren't worried about covering their tracks anymore. He thinks he's won."

"He's wrong."

"You are in your element. You thrive on this."

"What do you mean?"

"This. The hunt. The search for justice."

"It's my job."

"It's more than that. Look at what happened when you were relegated to a desk. Were you feeling lost because you've been through a lot? That's understandable. Or because you were bored without the danger? You're the bravest person I know, but you're also the most reckless. Something to consider before you do whatever it is you're planning to do."

"I'll keep that in mind."

Jasper was another person she didn't know well. They had had conversations in the past, both professional and personal, but he had never been in her circle until now. He was shrewder than she had previously thought. Skittish and excitable as he usually was, it was easy to miss the sharp intelligence buried beneath. Was he right? Was she reckless? Addicted to the life and death of it all? Her life had certainly been high stakes of late, but she didn't want it to be like that all the time, did she? She wasn't having fun; in fact, she was miserable almost perpetually, but didn't that make her feel alive?

"Can we talk?"

Walt's voice brought her back to herself.

"Not yet."

She was pushing the grief of her father's death down, trying to ignore it, but it was so close to breaking the dam, and she couldn't let it.

"I killed your dad. I came this close—" He held up his thumb and index finger to indicate the distance. "—to being hanged for it."

"I know. I saw the tape. I watched you, but not you, toy with him, and I watched you cut into him. I know exactly what you did to my father. I'm sorry you feel guilty, but I don't want to talk about it. I can't because if I do, I'll have to feel it, and I am not ready for that." Walt looked as though he was going to say something more on the subject but Thea cut him off. "What were you and Drew talking about?"

Torrez, who had remained silent and statuesque for the duration of their short conversation, looked visibly relieved.

"I can't get a hold of Cleo. She could be anywhere. I don't know when her last dose was. For all we know, she's running around outside with the ghouls. She could be dead."

"We were trying to figure out the best way to find her. There is no way to safely search ourselves, so we are trying to search street cams, but a lot of them are out of action," said Torrez

"And Marielena?"

"With her brother."

"Okay. I'm going to check in with Bastion, then we all need to talk."

Something passed over Walt's face, but it was gone as quickly as it appeared. Thea left the dining area and moved back into the living room to call Bast.

He answered on the second ring.

"Thea? Thank God. Are you all right? Is Walt?"

"Things got hairy, but we're okay."

"I'm sorry about your dad."

"Thanks. Trying not to think about it. Listen, we're holed up in Benny's penthouse at Ward Eight."

"Who's we?"

"The captain, Walt, Torrez, Jasper—the TPD tech, and Zhao."

Silence.

"Bast, you there?"
"The assistant DA?"
"Zhao? Yeah. Why?"
"Nothing, it's good that he's on our side. Look, I'm nearby. Can you meet me downstairs?"
"Why?"
"You might trust them, but I don't. I found something at your father's office that I think you are going to want to see. It could be what we needed, but I'm not ready to share with the group. Will you meet me?"
"Sure. How long?"
"Twenty minutes? At reception?"
"See you then."

When Thea returned to the main group, food had been served. She ate quickly and made her way to the elevator that would take her to the brothel below.
"Where you going?" Walt said, catching up to her.
"To meet Bastion downstairs. I'm not leaving the building. I'll be back."
"Just a dame," Walt muttered to himself.
"What?"
"Nothing. Be careful."
Thea nodded and stepped into the lift.
The brothel was deserted. It was eerie without the music, porn videos, and catalogues blaring. It seemed bigger somehow, but in a way that made Thea feel isolated. She hoped that those who worked there had gotten out safely, a thought that was bolstered by the lack of destruction to the building. Nothing was out of place, rather, just out of service.
Bastion was waiting for her when she arrived at the reception that usually housed Mary Pickford. As soon as he was close enough, Bastion took Thea in his arms and kissed her.
"I was worried you'd got yourself killed," he said, holding her a little too tightly.
"Not yet. How did you get here?" Thea said, stepping out of his embrace.
"With difficulty." There was something off about his demeanour.
"What do you have?"
"Can we talk first?"
"About what?" Thea said suspiciously. She took a step back. "You said you have something that could end this."
"About...us. Everything that's going on has made me realise what's important." His words sounded sincere, but his eyes were cold.
"Is this really the time? Tell me what you know, and we can talk about 'us' after."
"I need you to know how much I care about you." It sounded more like a threat than a romantic admission.
"I care about you too, but we have more important things to worry about."
There was a scuffling sound from the street outside.
"Did you hear that?" Thea said, reaching for her gun.

"Why did I think this would be easy?"

"What?"

"Your sister is far more compliant. Your father should have given you up instead. If he had, he'd probably still be alive."

It was like being struck by lightning. Thea's heart burst and disappeared entirely, all at once.

"Where is she?" Her words shook.

"Where she wants to be. She, unlike you, does as she's told. The thing is. I didn't even want to kill you. I really do care about you, but if it's a choice between you and me, I'll choose me every time. That's what this is. I ran out of time. I have to prove myself."

"Where is she?" Thea raised her gun and pointed it at Bastion.

"That's what's so great about you. I tell you I'm going to kill you, and you are worried about someone else. I wish I could be as selfless as you. I don't hate anyone. I love Walt like a brother, but you've chosen badly—you both have. You picked red, and it's black all the way. That's all this is."

"You sound like you're trying to convince yourself, not me. Tell me where she is."

"I thought you should know she's alive before...well. I'd take you with me, but if I've learned one thing about you, it's that you never pick what's easy."

"You've been working for Maxwell this whole time, and he took Cora?"

"Yes and no. Your father was required to prove his commitment to the Gold Legion. I worked for your father until recently, and he gave me Cora for... safekeeping. She was supposed to keep us in line, someone to threaten. Nobody ever realised that the threat would be you."

"Where is she?" Thea snarled, her gun still pointing at Bastion, who seemed not to care.

"Even if you could reach her, she doesn't want to leave. She's happy where she is. She's clean—no drugs, no booze. She wants for nothing."

There was a muffled yell from beyond the entrance.

Bastion used the momentary distraction to full effect. He grabbed Thea by the hair and threw her to the ground. Her gun went skittering away as it fell from her grip. White-hot pain burst across her chest as he stood on her collarbone, holding her down.

"I can't let you do that," Bastion said, pulling a stray strand of Thea's hair from his hand and tossing it aside.

With as much force as she could muster, Thea punched Bastion hard in the side of the knee. He yelled in pain and withdrew his foot, and Thea sprang to her feet.

"You're no match for me, kiddo."

Bastion kicked her in the stomach with such force she crashed into the wall behind her. Before she could register the nauseating pain rippling across her abdomen, he punched her in the chest. He punched her again, this time in the face. Dazed and coughing, she slid down the wall. A single large hand grabbed her by the neck. He lifted her so that only the tips of her boots were touching the tiled floor.

Thea couldn't breathe, blood was pumping desperately in her ears, and black spots were flickering before her eyes. There was a tremendous *SMASH,* and something came crashing down on Bastion's head. He dropped Thea, who fell to the floor in a crumpled heap, before he too toppled over. Cleo stood behind him, arms still raised—she had smashed a vase over his head. Thea had no idea where Cleo had appeared from, but she was eternally grateful she had.

Thea crawled over to Bastion. She climbed on top of him and began to punch him in the face over and over. At first, he tried to cover his head, but then he sat up, throwing her onto her back. He reached for her throat again, and Thea grabbed his wrist with both hands. She wrapped one of her legs around his head and hooked it under the knee of the other, trapping him in a triangle choke. He punched every bit of her, but she held on. With herculean strength, he managed to stand up with Thea still dangling from him, cutting off his airway. He lifted her high and slammed her back down on the reception counter, but she didn't let go.

"Aaaaahhhh!" he howled in pain. Cleo had scooped one of the shards of porcelain from the floor and thrust it between his shoulder blades. He flailed blindly behind him, catching Cleo across the face and sending her spinning to the tile.

Bastion lifted Thea high again and slammed her onto the counter once more. The impact winded her, and she could hold on no longer. She released her grip on his arm and neck and slumped to the ground.

Cursing as he tried to pull the sliver from his back, Bastion fled through the front door and into the night.

"Cleo? Are you okay?"

Thea crawled towards her on all fours, unwilling to stand just yet.

"Walt? Did they execute him?" she said wild-eyed.

"No. No, he's upstairs. He was shot, but he's fine. He's fine." Thea said again when Cleo didn't look convinced.

"Thank God. I was outside the station. They wouldn't let me in to see Walt, and then Bastion grabbed me. He said he would take me to Walt, but he tied me up and shoved me in a transporter."

"I trusted him," Thea said, shame reddening her face.

"He fooled us all," Cleo said resolutely, reaching out to Thea and giving her hand a squeeze.

"Let's get you to your husband."

When they arrived in the penthouse, Cleo ran into Walt's arms. He winced as she squeezed him.

"You were shot," Cleo said, looking worried.

"I'm fine. What happened? How did you get here?" Walt touched the bruise blossoming on her cheek.

"Bastion kidnapped me, and he tried to kill Thea."

"You were right," Thea said, not meeting his eye.

"I'll kill him," Walt said fiercely. "Did he hurt you?"

"I'll live. They think they've won," Thea said, looking at each one of them in turn. "But they're vulnerable. The city is overrun, and they still want us gone, which means we still have the power. Or some of it at least."

"What do you propose?" the captain said.

"We go public. We tell the world everything we know. They can't kill us all. They can't make the whole city disappear. This isn't a couple of rogue detectives with a story anymore. Millions of people are looking for answers, and we're going to give them some."

THE PAST
Seven years ago...

The TPD lecture hall was full. Sitting alone in the back of the auditorium, Walt watched on disinterestedly as the academy cadets graduated to active-duty officers. It was mandatory for the detectives to attend the ceremony to make the rookies feel welcome, but Walt couldn't care less. To him, it was a distraction from the real police work that none of those down below receiving their call numbers would be capable of for a couple of years at least.

"You really need to lighten up, buddy."

Walt smiled and turned to the row behind him. Bastion sat there lounging casually across three seats.

"What're you doing here?"

"I came to visit my brother, of course."

"Uh huh." Walt turned back to the ceremony. "You just want to get a look at the new recruits. Particularly the ones with breasts."

"That makes me sound creepy," Bastion said, feigning offence.

"That's because it is creepy."

Bastion looked as though he was considering this for a moment, then he shrugged and reached into his pocket for a hip flask. He took a swig then offered it to Walt.

"I'm on duty."

"I'm not." Bastion shrugged again. "That's her. The DA's daughter." He pointed to a woman in her very early twenties who was next in line for the podium.

"Who cares. Having a rich dad can only get you so far."

"I heard her scores are off the charts. I watched her final combat test. Man, that is a dame I would like to get to know better."

"Yeah, I watched her, too. I'm not convinced. Training isn't like being out in the field. That's the real test, and my bet is she'll crumble. When in her privileged little life will she have been in a brothel, or back alley, or mobster's den? She's about to get the shock of her life."

"No way. She's tough. You can see it in her eyes. There is something about that broad."

"I just don't see it."

"You will."

BREAKING NEWS

"The biggest challenge is getting people to believe you," Cleo said.

"Actually, the biggest challenge is not sounding crazy."

"Torrez is right, Thea," the captain said. "It's all about spin. You want to tell the truth, but it's going to be a lot for people to swallow."

It had taken a lot of discussion to convince everyone that telling the public everything they knew and letting the chips fall where they may, was the best plan. It was, in Thea's opinion, the only plan.

Thea had been surprised by how readily Gin Ricky had agreed to the plan when she called him and even more so by the fact he was willing to meet them. It appeared that as he had exhausted all other avenues in the attempt to rescue his son, he was willing to do just about anything in hopes of his safe return. Another less surprising benefit of having a known bootlegger and snitch on her side was that Gin Ricky came with contacts.

Nina Carraway, a well-respected news anchor, frequently used Gin Ricky to research her stories and was more than happy to host an interview with Thea on the show. She had wanted Thea to come into the studio, but Thea had nixed that, feeling it was better to remain out of reach.

Within an hour of Gin Ricky's arrival, they were ready to go on air, just in time for the six o'clock news.

Thea's palms were sweating as she sat behind the large desk in Benny's study.

"You'll be fine," said Walt from where he stood behind the camera Jasper had erected with Zhao and the captain.

"We're here to help you," Cleo said. She, Torrez, and Gin Ricky were standing just out of shot, waiting to be called on, having finally been convinced to tell their stories.

Thea fiddled nervously with her Cicada. She had an open line to the news studio, but nothing had happened yet.

"Can you hear me, Detective Williams?" came the pleasantly bright voice of Nina Carraway.

"Loud and clear."

"Okay, we can see you here, but we are just making sure the feed is okay to broadcast. Before we go on, are there any topics you don't want to answer questions on? Gin Ricky said this was a tell-all, but I like to make sure."

"I'll answer anything."

"Great. That's our ten-second warning; are you ready?"

"Yes, I think so."

"Okay, we are live in five, four, three, two... Good evening Tenebrium City. I am Nina Carraway, and this is TNC. Tonight, our city is under siege as ghouls and violence overtake the streets reminding us of the chaos caused by the drug Styxx nearly three years ago. Officials have remained silent, and at the time of reporting, there has been no statement from the Mayor's Office or Law Enforcement addressing the pandemonium outside or the murder of the District Attorney, Harold Williams. The Onyx Legion, previously under the control of the late DA, has said in a short statement that the release of the ghouls from their quarantine in the SubLevel was due to a hacked computer and that they are actively searching for the culprit, but refused to take questions.

"With me today, to discuss this ongoing issue is one of Tenebrium's finest, a decorated detective and the late Harold Williams' daughter. You may remember her for her heroic efforts to rid the now-closed brothel Ward Eight of sex trafficking. Please join me in welcoming Detective Thea Williams to the show. Thank you for joining me, Detective."

"Thank you for having me."

"I'd first like to offer my condolences for the death of your father."

"Thank you."

"What can you tell me and the viewers at home about what's happening in our city tonight?"

"I believe that the ghouls were released from the SubLevel as a distraction."

"Released by who? And to distract from what?"

"There is an invisible coup happening in our city. A sect called the Gold Legion has resurfaced, and they have been insinuating themselves into positions of power for nearly three years. They created Styxx in an effort to control the public. When that didn't work, they used it in an attempt to eliminate the poor. They think that they are above the law, that anyone who isn't part of the elite is a drain on their privilege. I have proof that they have been creating devices, that we have been calling chips, that can manipulate nerve impulses making the wearer suggestable."

"Sorry, can you clarify what you mean by suggestable?

"The chips allow them to control the wearer's actions."

A deafening silence followed this pronouncement.

"Do you mean they are capable of mind control?"

"That's exactly what I mean."

"And who is behind this plot?"

"The Gold Legion."

"And who leads this 'Gold Legion'?"

"Dr Chester Maxwell. Head of Medicorum Medical services."

The interview lasted well over an hour, and Thea held nothing back. She told Nina everything from the murdered sex workers to the attack on herself. She told of her father's misdeed, the things Benny had revealed to her, and the many attempts to silence her and Walt. Torrez told of his introduction to Dill Kelly and his own transgressions thereafter, while Cleo laid bare all that had taken place at Medicorum with Gin Ricky's help.

All in all, Thea thought that they had painted a convincingly vivid picture. Maybe they would be believed, and the city and those in power still loyal to it would rise up and take back what was theirs. Maybe they would be heralded as lunatics and cast out. All they could do now was wait.

GOD'S GONNA CUT YOU DOWN

It was like an earthquake. The sound reverberated with such ferocity that it caused the building to shake. Windows cracked, and ornaments on shelves toppled to the floor.

Thea sprinted down the stairs and out into the alley, the others close behind. She sidled onto the main street. It was packed with people all staring at the sky. Projected there, titan sized, was Dr Chester Maxwell.

There was no direction that the image could not be seen from or that his booming words could not be heard.

"People of Tenebrium City. You have been lied to. You have been told that you are under siege. This is not true. No one wants to hurt you. I am the head of the Gold Legion, and we have taken control, but this is not martial law. I am not your enemy. I am your saviour."

"You have got to be kidding me," Walt said from behind Thea.

"This is gonna be bad," Thea said.

"We are not trying to control you. We are not interested in taking your free will. My fellows and I have not poisoned you; we have not tried to eradicate those of you who are living in poverty. We are here to elevate you. We are here to protect you. We are here to restore Tenebrium to its former glory. To do this, the Gold Legion will be taking command of the city for the time being. We know this is confusing, but in time, we are confident that you will see us as a positive force for change.

"In conjunction with Law Enforcement and the Mayor's Office, the Onyx Legion will patrol the streets day and night to ensure your safety. All communications in and out of the city, as well as media outlets, have been temporarily suspended to prevent lies and scaremongering from spreading in these already difficult times.

"The police, while still vital, will no longer be your first port of call. For any crimes, we ask that you report to the Onyx Legion, who are better equipped to deal with our shared situation. Trials will be suspended, and lawbreakers will be punished severely. Ghouls are to be rounded up and returned to the SubLevel. While we endeavour to complete this task, we ask you to remain indoors temporarily when you see the OL engaging. We would hate any civilians to get caught in the crossfire should more violence erupt.

"I urge you not to fight this change or our transition to power. We have begun to recapture the ghouls, as evidenced by the fact you are all standing here before me, protected. We are already making good on the promises I make to you here. We are dedicated to showing you a different, better way of living, and we trust that in time you will come to see how much we care about each and every one of you. The Gold Legion, Medicorum, and I work for you, not the other way around."

The image disappeared.

It was like the whole city had been stunned into silence. No one moved. They just stood in the streets staring at where Maxwell had been in the sky.

After a moment or two of nothing, smaller images began to pop up in the sky; wanted posters featuring Thea, Walt, Torrez and Cleo.

"We need to get inside," Walt said, tugging gently on Thea's arm.

Thea paced Benny's living room, paying no attention to the worried conversations happening all around her.

"We're fucked," Torrez was saying.

"You're fucked," Gin Ricky said, pointing at Torrez. "They didn't mention me. Or Betty. Or Zhao, is it?"

"Noble," Walt said derisively.

"I have my son to think about!"

"This isn't helping," Cleo said, stepping between them. "Thea, would you stop that and talk to us."

"What do you want me to say? We *are* fucked. My dad's dead; your husband killed him. The man I was seeing tried to kill me and kidnapped my sister, and we just became public enemy number one. And that's just the last couple of days."

"I know you've been through a lot, but you don't get to freak out. We don't have the time. We are stuck here, and there is no way they will allow us out of the city. We have to do something."

"Do you have something in mind? Or are you just hoping I'll have all the answers? That's what I thought."

"This was your fight."

"It stopped being my fight a long time ago. This is everyone's fight. Every person in the city is in this now. That includes you. I know you didn't want to be part of this, and I'm sorry I made you, but with or without me, you're in."

"We need to contact the federal government outside the city, the president of the colony," Zhao said. "Exactly what they are trying to stop us from doing. They might have bought the mayor here and the DA and the commissioner, but they are only powerful in this city."

"You're right," Thea said. There was an idea forming in her mind. "You're right. We act like Tenebrium is all there is. Jasper, could you hack into Medicorum?"

"If I was inside, sure. Not from here, though; their servers are far too heavily protected to access from the outside."

"Then let's get inside. Gin Ricky, you stole Quietus, right? You could get us in?"

"That was before," Gin Ricky said, seeming alarmed to have been brought into the conversation again. "Now, they will be on high alert."

"Let's arrest Maxwell. Let's walk in and arrest him."

"That's insane," Jasper said.

"Is it? Going to a city news station wasn't thinking big enough. We just need to get inside. If I get you to the server room, could you expose everything? The city might be able to be controlled, but the rest of the colonies and countries won't stand for this. They can cover up a murder here and there, silence a cop who's too nosy. But they can't hide from the world."

"It could work. If they are blocking external communication, they're probably doing it from there. If I can get in…yeah, I could probably air their dirty laundry to the world."

"Then let's do it. I and anyone else who's willing will protect and distract, and you can destroy them."

"I'm in," Walt said at once.

"I'm game." Torrez shrugged.

"Zhao? Captain? Cleo?"

"I will go back to the DA's office and distract the OL. I want to help, but I'm no fighter," said Zhao. "I'm a bureaucrat, but that doesn't mean I can't be useful."

Thea nodded her approval. "Captain?"

"There must be officers and even soldiers still loyal to the city. I'll rally them in case you get into a tough spot."

"Cleo?"

"Where Walt goes, I go. I owe you, and you're right. I helped cause this; I should help fix it. I know my way around, where the cameras are."

"Great. Gin Ricky." Thea turned to him. "Can you get us inside? You don't have to fight."

"I helped rescue Cleo, and I helped her remember everything she forgot."

Walt looked sharply from his wife to Thea. Neither looked at him.

"I know," Thea said uncertainly.

"My son is in there. I am not useless. I'm coming with you. You all promised to help me save him, and you've done a piss-poor job so far."

"We'll find him. I promise," said Thea.

"So, this is it?" Torrez said with a smile. "For better or worse, going for the head of the snake."

"How long do you need to prepare?" Thea asked Jasper.

"Depends what kind of equipment Benny has stashed here, but if he's got what I need? Maybe a few days? I need to familiarise myself with their system."

"All right, get ready, everyone. This would be the time to check on your loved ones. If you can."

SIEGE

An eerie calm had fallen over Tenebrium. While the citizens continued to go about their daily business, the constant and oppressive presence of the Onyx Legion lining the streets ensured that no one could forget the fact that they were now prisoners in their city, ever watched and ever monitored.

In the days that followed the Gold Legion's take over, the ghouls were rounded up and re-imprisoned in the SubLevel. Protesters were arrested and subjected to violence if they didn't cease and desist from "disrupting the peace". The TPD was closed to the public, and the mayor made several press appearances with Maxwell, who seemed keen to project an air of benevolence.

"Why hasn't Bastion come back?" Torrez shot at Thea for what felt like the hundredth time. "Why hasn't he told them where we are?"

They were sitting in Benny's kitchen, which had quickly become their "spot". Thea nursed a coffee while Torrez chewed on an apple.

"He's hurt," Thea said yet again. "Cleo got him good."

"Okay, but he hasn't sent any of his many goons after us either."

"The way he was talking, I think he and the GL are on the outs. I think letting Cleo escape and not killing me might be the failure that gets him excommunicated. I think he's afraid to tell them that he had us and lost us. I'm sure we'll see him again."

"I feel like we've had this conversation a hundred times."

"That's because we have, Drew."

Torrez lapsed into silence. Thea drained her mug while he picked the apple clean.

"I'm sorry. Querida," he said, throwing his apple core into the trash.

"You're nervous. I get it. We all are."

"I mean, for everything."

"You don't need to—" Thea began, but Torrez cut her off.

"Yes, I do. I'm sorry for the hurt I caused you. For being selfish and stupid. I'm sorry that I lost sight of what's important. Before we do this, I need you to know that I love you and that I'm so proud of you. There is no one on this planet that I trust more. Whatever happens, wherever you lead, I'll follow."

Thea leaned forward and hugged him tightly. "I love you, too."

The longer the group spent holed up together as fugitives from the Gold Legion, the tenser the atmosphere became. Jasper, in particular, had become snappish and downright rude if anyone disturbed him while he worked, even if it was to insist that he eat something. The more time Thea spent with him, she wasn't sure she liked him very much.

"I think I'm ready," Jasper said four days after the GL takeover, just as Thea had been about to ask, aware she was risking a scolding.

He was sitting at Benny's dining room table, which he had set up much like his own office. It was a cluttered mess of screens and cables, with the data stream constantly hanging in the air, keeping track of current events and testing Medicorum's security.

"Explain this to me again," Walt said, holding a slim gadget that Jasper had dubbed a "Trojan", just as Cleo returned from the bathroom having taken her latest dose of Quietus.

"I will get into their Data Centre. It should house their communications hub, servers, and archives, too. I'll remove all the blocks they have put on coms and release any files I can. I'm sure there will be plenty of sketchy shit stored there, but for the real goods, someone will need to get the trojan to Maxwell's computer in his office. It should give me access to everything, including any personal servers he may have locked off from the mainframe. With that, I can make all of their dirty laundry public for the whole world to see."

"Then what are we waiting for?" Walt asked.

"Nothing, Thea said. "Is everybody ready?"

"I'd follow you into hell, Querida," Torrez said with a sad smile. He, like Thea, wasn't betting on all of them surviving their assault on the Gold Legion's ivory tower.

The sewers of Tenebrium were dank, dark, and pungent. Much like a rat, Gin Ricky seemed to navigate with some other sense that neither Thea nor Walt, Cleo, Torrez, or Jasper possessed. Like the city above, the sewer was composed of a network of entangled passages.

Thea kept close to the walls avoiding any of the deeper puddles in the centre of the narrow tunnel they were traversing. The flashlights they had brought could only illuminate so much, and Thea heard frequent curses from those behind her who had tripped or put their foot in something unpleasant.

"I was right," Jasper said quietly.

He walked in front of Thea, running his hand along the wall.

"What about?"

"If this isn't reckless, I don't know what is."
Jasper stopped abruptly, and Thea walked into him.
"What's wrong?"

They had come to the end of the tunnel. The channel of water that had run beside them now poured over the edge into a deep pool far below. Without hesitation, Gin Ricky jumped. He landed with a splash and began to swim, disappearing from view through an archway leading into another flooded tunnel.

Thea caught Cleo's eye; she shrugged in a resigned sort of way. Thea knew that the sewer tunnels must be reminding her terribly of the SubLevel, but she showed no signs of it outwardly. Together they threw themselves into the water. The fall was higher than they had bargained for, and Thea started to panic before she hit the water. She relaxed instantly as she disappeared under the surface. She rose just in time to see Torrez and Walt plummeting. She had already started to swim after Gin Ricky when Jasper joined them.

The water was cold, and her clothes and weapons made swimming difficult and tiring work. She followed the ripples Gin Ricky left in his wake as they swam further into the tunnel. The waterway curved to the left, and as Thea made her way around, she saw that it opened up into a much larger passage with a long ladder against the far wall. Thea struck out towards it with renewed vigour.

The relief she felt being out of the water did little to warm her numb fingers and chattering teeth as she waited for the rest of the party to catch up. Jasper was the furthest behind, making slow progress due to the bag of equipment clinging to his back, but he joined them shortly after Walt and Torrez had left the water.

"This ladder will take you into the basement on the south side of the complex," Gin Ricky said, placing his foot on the bottom rung.

"You aren't coming with us." Thea said. It wasn't a question.

"The hell I'm not. My son is in there!"

"You're scared. Really scared, and I get it. You never wanted to fight, but they took your son, and now you have no choice. But if you die, what will your son do then? Someone needs to stay behind, to make sure that if we fail, there is still someone out there who knows the truth."

"I will bring your son back to you," Walt said. "I promise, but Thea is right. Up there, you'll get yourself killed."

"I can't abandon him," Gin Ricky said. His voice was strangled.

"You aren't."

Very reluctantly, Gin Ricky nodded. Thea could see guilt and worry mingling with relief. She watched him as he swam back down the passage, around the corner and out of sight.

The ladder was coarse, pitted and rusted. Flakes of russet metal came away each time she moved her hand up a rung, and her footfalls echoed around cavernous stone walls. At the top was a heavy iron manhole cover. There were no bolts or handles; it wasn't locked.

Thea climbed another rung so she could press her shoulders into it and pushed, using her hands to steady the round metal slab. It was heavy, but lifted easily. Thea pushed it aside and pulled herself up through the opening.

The basement of Medicorum was a far cry from its gleaming upper floors.

Twilit and composed entirely of concrete, the bowels of the medical giant were much more in line with Thea's idea of the place.

The room they had stepped in seemed to be designed for the disposal of anatomical waste. There was a furnace to the north and several large troughs covered by clear plastic containing a soup of organs and bodily fluids. Each trough was linked to a chute that allowed it to be filled from above. The smell, even with the vacuum seal, burned the inside of Thea's nose.

"Follow me," Cleo said, pinching her nose.

She led them to a long set of steeply ascending stairs which led to another basement level of bare brick and concrete. Unlike the floor below, this level was in use as storage. Doctors and nurses, research staff, cleaners and porters moved from room to room collecting equipment and supplies.

It was nothing short of a miracle that they made it another floor up without being noticed. After clearing four of the numerous basement levels, they finally found themselves in one of the clinically white corridors that Thea had come to associate with the medical service.

"Where are we?" Torrez asked Cleo quietly.

They were huddled at a dead end next to the communal bathrooms, having ducked around the corner to avoid a doctor in a crisp white lab coat.

"The research wing. It has a lobby just like the medical wing. The lifts and stairs are on the other side from here, though."

"The data centre?"

"Right in the middle of the building. It's a tower that starts on the fiftieth floor and ends around the hundredth."

There was a smash and then a blaring siren. Walt had tripped the fire alarm.

"What the hell?" Thea yelled over the noise.

"We will never make fifty floors without getting caught, but maybe we can use the panic as cover. They think they are untouchable. They are too arrogant to think we would come for them so soon. Besides, it minimises the chance of innocents getting caught in the crossfire. This is going to end ugly."

"I hope you're right, asshole," said Torrez, shaking his head.

One at a time, they joined the tide of subjects and staff running for the fire escapes. The sheer volume of people within the research wing was staggering. They were buffeted and bashed as they ran. Thea was blindsided by a man exiting an office. He bowled her over and didn't look back as she scrambled to her feet.

The research lobby was similar to the medical services. Vast and open with large pillars, all white and glass. The reception desk sat in front of a transparent elevator that led to the mezzanine above, with stairs running up either side.

Thea grabbed Walt and pulled him back behind a pillar just in time. The shot that was meant for him whizzed past and left a smouldering gouge in the floor. Standing atop the mezzanine, gun in hand, and a look of determination on his face, was Bastion.

The gunfire caused those fleeing to scramble and panic further. They waited until the lobby was empty.

"No," Thea said, trying to pull Walt back behind the pillar, but he shook her off.

"He's mine. You take them," he nodded to Cleo and Jasper. "To where they need to be."

"You take them. He knows where Cora is—"

"This was your plan. You did this. You are going to save this city and everyone in it. Follow it through to the end. I'll be fine. I'll find out where he's keeping Cora, but he and I have business. Go. Thea, Go."

Walt's eyes seemed to pierce her; it was clear he had made up his mind. Cursing, Thea beckoned to Cleo and Jasper.

"You, too, cowboy," Walt said when Torrez showed signs of staying put.

"C'mon," Thea said, and they left Walt walking out to meet Bastion.

IT'S EASY TO LOVE HER, ISN'T IT?

Bastion Tyrus stood on the mezzanine overlooking the lobby. He watched with a trained eye as the last of the staff exited through the double doors to the east.

The shot he fired at Walt had been a warning, meant to graze, not kill, but as Thea and her friends ran for the doors without him, he knew that his best friend, the man he loved like a brother, had other ideas.

Bastion and Walt had never had to compete with each other. They had always been formidable in their own rights, top of their own chosen fields. He had never thought of Walt as a rival, as competition, and that hadn't changed now.

He trained his gun on Thea as she crossed the floor, never intending to fire, but knowing he could if he needed to. When she was clear, he refocused on the pillar he knew Walt was concealed behind.

"I never thought it would come to this," Bastion said. Even though he hadn't spoken loudly, his voice carried thanks to the acoustic properties of glass and marble.

"I never thought you would betray me."

Still, Walt stayed hidden.

"I haven't betrayed you. I don't want to do this, but I'm practical. The Gold Legion are the only possible winners here, and you know how I hate to lose."

"You've killed people, Bast. Innocent people. You've gone against everything we stood for."

"And what do you stand for? You're a cheater and a drunk. You're reckless and self-sabotaging. Hell, there's a suicidal edge to you, but that's not new, is it? You've always had it. That's the secret that Cleo and Thea don't see. Even at your happiest, you are always chasing death; it's the only way you feel alive."

Keeping his guns ready, Bastion sidled to the stairs trying to get a clear line of sight. He took three steps down, just enough to see where Walt should have been hiding, but he wasn't there. He had moved without Bastion seeing.

TENEBRIUM

The glass bannister in front of him smashed, and Bastion crouched down on the stairs. He caught just a flash of the hem of Walt's coat as he disappeared behind another pillar.

"Impressive," Bastion muttered to himself.

"Did you think, because it's you, that I wouldn't try?"

Plaster and crumbling mortar filled the air as Bastion's shot hit the pillar opposite Walt and ricocheted on target. Bastion heard a faint cough and moved to the bottom of the stairs.

A single foot stuck out from one of the marble columns, unmoving.

"Walter? You wouldn't be fucking with me, would you?"

The foot disappeared, and Walt leaned out from the other side of the pillar. Bastion dropped to the ground avoiding death for a second time. He too, took up residence behind a pillar.

"I care about her, you know? But between her and me, there's no choice. Once I'm done with you, Walter, I'm going after Thea again."

"That's cheap, even for you."

Another shot whizzed through the air, closer than Bastion would have liked. Walt had always been a good marksman.

"You don't want to compare notes?"

"Sure, you first."

Walt dove out from behind his pillar to another closer to Bastion, but he was too fast to target. Bastion followed suit. Now, the only thing between them was a single column. Bastion stepped out from cover, gun levelled at Walt's chest. Walt did the same.

Both men stood out in the open; both had a clear line of sight for a kill shot, but neither moved. It was harder than Bastion had thought it would be to point a gun at the one constant in his life.

Their relationship had been rocky of late, but he never doubted that if he had needed Walt, the man would come running without question. Walt's family had all but adopted Bastion. They had grown up together, started training for the military and the TPD together, they had even been promoted within weeks of each other. The only thing Walt had done alone was get married, and even now, they both cared for Thea.

"I can't let you go," Bastion said, gripping his gun more tightly.

Walt was in the way. He couldn't let Walt stop him, but still, he couldn't pull the trigger. With a snarl of rage, Bastion threw his gun aside.

Walt kept his gun raised. Perhaps he could do what Bastion couldn't. But then, he tossed the weapon aside and pounced.

Walt ran at Bastion, a life's worth of disappointment on his face. He was a brawler driven by emotion; he was easy to read.

Bastion slipped the punch Walt threw with ease, landing a devastating uppercut of his own on Walt's jaw. Walt fell to the ground, arms and legs akimbo. He stayed down.

As Bastion had predicted, Walt's lack of control was his downfall. But then, Walt was on his feet, and he was running at Bastion again. Bastion punched him hard in the face before Walt grabbed him around the waist. Bastion brought his knee up with bone-crushing strength, and it connected perfectly with Walt's nose.

Walt reeled back. He teetered the way a drunk person does before they fall. Out of nowhere, a ruinous fist collided with Bastion's temple. He backed off, surprised by the strength and accuracy. His ears rang, and his vision blurred.

When he mastered himself, the Walt he saw had changed somehow. He had always thought of the man as good to his great. Skilled, but never a threat. Now, there was something behind his eyes, in his stance, in his relentlessness that set Bastion on edge.

It was his turn to close the distance, but Walt was so much faster. Bastion felt rather than saw the blow to his stomach, then another to his chin, and finally, a cataclysmic strike to the side of the head sent him to the floor.

He tried to stand, but couldn't. His equilibrium was shattered. The best he could manage was all fours. Walt wasn't the kind of man to kick someone when they were down, and that was his mistake.

Bastion seized a handful of plaster dust from the floor and hurled it at Walt's face. Walt coughed and grunted in pain as it stung his eyes.

Bastion half crawled, half ran to the elevator. Walt had wiped the dust from his eyes just in time to see the doors close as Bastion ascended to the mezzanine. Bastion watched as Walt sprinted up the stairs to meet him, and when the elevator doors opened, Walt was waiting for him, red-eyed.

Abandoning his calculated demeanour, Bastion threw himself at Walt, and they both tumbled to the floor. Like school kids wrestling, they rolled around on the ground, punching any bit of the other they could reach before Walt finally succeeded in throwing him off. Bastion used the momentum to spring to his feet.

He had ended up back in the tiny elevator, Walt barring the door.

It was like time slowed. Bastion ran forward as Walt brought a leg up to meet him. He hit Bastion hard in the chest, slamming him onto the back wall. The elevator shook, and the glass behind Bastion shattered. He pushed off the rail and watched as Walt jumped and threw out both legs.

The dropkick sent him through the glass wall and tumbling to the ground far below. He landed in a sea of glittering shards. Nothing hurt, really, but he couldn't move. His legs wouldn't listen. Something warm was dripping from his nose into his mouth; it tasted like liquid metal. He was sleepy, and it was hard to breathe.

Walt skidded to a halt next to him.

"Bastion? Bastion?"

"It's easy, isn't it? Loving her."

He closed his eyes.

I LOVE YOU SO MUCH I HATE YOU

The Data centre was a hugely tall circular space, all in blue. Thea couldn't see the ceiling as it rose into darkness high above. The room itself had a round glass desk in the centre with enough terminals for twenty people. Around the walls and placed in rows throughout were huge rectangular server stacks with blinking orange and blue lights. They were slightly hypnotising to watch as they flickered in their hundreds. A spiral staircase ran around the walls, with small platforms to access more of the stacks housed on demi-floors that looked out into the centre.

The Onyx Legion and their Gold masters knew they were there. Watching one of the large monitors in the data centre, Thea saw soldiers arriving in droves, all heavily armed.

"Work quickly," Thea said, watching the soldiers file through the corridors searching for them room by room.

"It takes as long as it takes," Jasper snapped.

"They're going to be here before we're finished," Torrez said, watching the screens.

"Then we'll have to distract them," Thea said.

She grabbed one of the chairs from the circular desk and took it to the elevator, and used it to prop the doors open. The elevator had brought them straight to the Data Centre from the lobby; they didn't want the OL doing the same.

"At least, that's one way they can't get in." But there were several others. There were two fire exits and a door that led to each wing, as well as the sets of spiral stairs linked to every other accessible floor in the building.

"Walt's been gone too long," Cleo said, speaking for the first time in nearly fifteen minutes.

"He'll be fine. He's always fine," Thea said comfortingly.

"You shouldn't be here," came an achingly familiar voice from between the stacks.

Thea whirled around, searching for her.

"Over here, little sister."

Cora stepped out from behind a stack. She had changed, but it was still her. Her hair was much longer now, and she had dyed it blonde. Her clothes and jewellery were expensive, far beyond the things even their father had provided, but her face was the same. It was as it has always been, like looking into a mirror.

In spite of where they were and what they were attempting, Thea wanted to cry with happiness. She ran to her sister and embraced her tightly, but Cora stood stock still, cold even. After a moment, she pushed Thea away.

"You shouldn't be here," she said again.

"I'm going to get you out of here," Thea said.

"This is where I belong. You always knew what you wanted; I never did until now. Bastion showed me the way."

"Cora, these people killed dad—"

"Dad gave me away as an entry fee to a cult. I'm glad he's dead." Cora's face was contorted with spite. She looked so unlike the person Thea had known in that moment. Her features were the same, but it was a new expression and one that didn't suit her.

"They've taken over the city."

"They? Who's they? I don't care about any of that. I'm owed, Thea; I deserve a good life, and Bastion can give me that."

"Cora—"

"And you brought Drew. He and I had a couple of good times, but he always preferred you. Never in that way, but he'd rather have you as a friend than me as anything more. They always choose you. Why? What's so special about you? I bet she's been asking herself that," Cora pointed at Cleo, who didn't flinch. "We are identical, yet you're the pretty one, the smart one, the together one, and I'm just a mess. Everything that went wrong in my life is because I was sick of being compared to you."

"This isn't you."

"But it is me. It always has been."

"You're my best friend. You're my sister. I know you."

"I've always hated you. Always. Did you know that? Even when we were kids, I was sick of living in your shadow. You'd call me to talk about your day, and I wanted to scream. I was so sick of listening to you whine about your perfect little life—I was glad when they took me—anything to not have to hear about Walt. 'I think I love him, Cora...I feel so guilty, Cora,' and still, all everyone did was praise you. Your perfect test scores, your perfect record. Best in your class, youngest rookie to make detective. You're a tough act to follow, sis. You never gave me a chance."

"What have they done to you?"

"They're here, in the data centre." Cora spoke into her Cicada. "You have less than a minute. It was great catching up. Goodbye, sister mine."

She turned away. Thea grabbed her arm. Cora wheeled around and slapped her in the face in one motion. The shock of it stung more than the hit itself.

"Don't touch me. I relish the thought of being rid of the plague on my life that is you." Cora wrenched her arm from Thea's grip and ran between the stacks.

"Thea, we can't stay here," Torrez called. "This place will be flooded with soldiers any second."

"I'm going for Maxwell. Protect them. Make sure that you're ready when I use the trojan."

"There's too many," Torrez said. "You can't go alone."

"Protect them." she pointed to Jasper and Cleo. "This was never supposed to be a walk in the park."

Thea turned on her heel and ran after Cora. As she darted between the stacks, Thea caught a glimpse of her blonde waves as they slipped through a door at the far end of the data centre. Thea burst out into a long corridor just in time to see Cora disappear around a corner.

She chased Cora into an empty ward. Six beds enclosed in ovoid pods faced each other in rows of three. Dormant machines connected to each of the beds through a tangled mass of wires.

Cora leaned uninhibited against the nearest pod. Now Thea saw her in the clean clinical light of the ward, she could see the change the last two years had wrought. Cora has been an optimist and a hedonist, a pleasure seeker unconcerned about consequences. Now, there was the shadow of something darker on her face. A splenetic rancorousness gained by a life hard-lived. What had been done to her during her captivity that could have snuffed out a light so vibrant?

"They sent me here to distract you. Mission accomplished, it seems." She was dripping in pearls and feathers, but even the material things she had loved so much before seemed to bring her no joy. "You're so predictable, Tee. You never could let someone go, not if you thought you could save them."

"I don't understand," Thea said. "This can't be who you are now."

From under the silver silk of her dress, Cora pulled a small handless dagger. She threw it at Thea; it hit her in the thigh.

"Ah!" Thea shouted as the sharp burning pain turned to a wet warm one. She winced and pulled the dagger out as Cora reached for another.

"I'm not gonna fight you."

"Fine, makes this a lot easier for me."

Cora threw a second dagger. This time Thea was ready for it; she brought her leg up in a graceful arc, knocking it out of the air. It clattered to the ground and skittered under one of the nearby beds.

"Cora! Stop!" Thea yelled.

Ignoring her, Cora lunged.

Thea picked up a thin metal chair from beside the nearest bed and threw it. Wholly unprepared for the attack, it hit Cora in the body, and she fell back into the pod she had been leaning against. Finally, Thea saw it. A little silver disk on the base of her sister's neck. Thea marched forward and grabbed Cora by the arm. She hit, slapped and scratched at Thea, but she didn't have the strength or the skill Thea possessed, and it served her little.

Thea pulled open the ward's bathroom door and glanced around to check it was windowless, which it was. She thrust Cora inside and slammed the door shut before jamming the thrown chair under the handle, trapping her sister.

"I will come back for you. I will get that thing off you, I promise."

Shakily, she sat on the cold, sterile floor and put her head on her knees. She had imagined finding her sister so many times in the past. It had never gone like this.

Cora screamed and raged behind the barred door as Thea got to her feet. She wanted more than anything to take Cora and run. To go straight to Chowdhary and get the damned chip removed. She wanted her sister back, but she had a job to do. She wasn't going to give up now.

Thanks to Cleo, she knew the labs were on the floor above, and from there, she would be able to make her way to Maxwell's office and end the Gold Legion once and for all.

PROTECTION DETAIL

Torrez stood behind Jasper, watching the red-headed man work at one of the many terminals in the data centre, while Cleo monitored the progress of the soldiers into the building on the screens surrounding them.

"How much longer?" Torrez asked tensely.

"I'm nearly there," Jasper snapped. "The first round of files is out into the world, but there is so much more here than we had ever imagined, and some of it is behind some serious firewalls."

"Drew," Cleo said, pointing at the screen. "Six soldiers coming up the north stairs."

Torrez ran to meet them. He burst into the stairwell and fired expertly over the railings, killing two soldiers before they even realised he was there. The remaining four held back, each trying to see who had attacked them. Torrez jumped over the bannister, landing on the flight below. He raised his gun, but the first soldier he encountered kicked it from his hand. Torrez lunged for the soldier pinning him to the wall. He grabbed the man's sidearm from his belt and let loose three shots into its owner's stomach before turning it on his comrade, who had rushed in to help.

Torrez leant down and scooped up one of the rifles. He fired it into the flight below; the thumps and yells he heard told him he had hit his targets.

Danger abated, for now, he made his way back to Cleo and Jasper.

"I'm in. Everything stored here is out in the open," Jasper said. "The rest is up to Thea."

Torrez threw the handgun to Cleo. "More on the way."

HIGH VOLTAGE

Walt sprinted between the desks and cubicles of the large open office, ducking the hail of bullets that followed him. He had gotten turned around while evading the flood of legionaries who were pursuing him mercilessly.

He burst from the office into the stairwell. Six corpses in black armour littered the flights. Quickly Walt dragged four of them to the door and piled them up against it, it wouldn't stop their fellows for long, but it would slow them down. He continued on upwards.

The barrel of a rifle was all he saw when he opened the door at the top of the stairs.

"It's me," he yelled.

Torrez grabbed him by the shirt and pulled him into the room, slamming the door behind him.

"There are hundreds of them out there."

"We know. Bastion?"

"Dead," Walt told Torrez bluntly. "Are you okay?" he asked his wife.

"Fine. Drew kept us safe."

Walt nodded his thanks to Torrez, who nodded once in return.

"Jasper, are you done here?"

"I'm connected to the system. I can access it remotely now."

"Drew, get them out of here, up the spiral staircase. Find a way to the roof. You can call the captain, and she'll send someone to get you." He stopped and looked around the room. "Where's Thea?"

"She went after Cora," Cleo said.

"Cora?"

"Go," Cleo said, nodding to the door Thea had left by. "Help her."

"I'll get them out," Torrez said.

TENEBRIUM

Without looking back, Walt raced through the door and into the maze of corridors beyond.

He stopped in a disused ward. It seemed empty, yet there was a small smattering of blood on the floor. The further in he stepped, he noticed a chair pressed against a heavy wooden door.

"Is someone out there?" The voice was so familiar and yet not quite right.

"Cora?"

"Walt? Is that you? Please get me out of here!"

Walt pulled the chair away from the door and flung it wide.

Cora tumbled out and into his arms. "Thank god you found me."

"Are you all right?" Walt asked, setting Cora on her feet.

"Sure am," she said, all traces of fear gone.

Cora stepped in close, placing her hands on his shoulders. She lifted her chin as if intending to kiss him.

"What're you doing?"

Something hard, under her palm, pressed into his chest. He felt a sudden jolt that caused him to spasm and then crumpled to the ground. His legs went numb, and even though they were bent awkwardly underneath him, he couldn't move them.

"They told me that electricity would incapacitate you."

"Where's Thea?"

"It's only her, isn't it? For you. No one else comes close. I tried to kill her, but she got away."

"Why? She loves you."

Walt struggled to sit up, his legs were starting to tingle, but he couldn't move them yet. He had never felt more vulnerable.

"And if that were enough, you two would still be together."

Walt's leg twitched.

"Oh, I don't think so," Cora said, leaning down and shocking him again.

He clenched his teeth as the convulsions rocked him. His legs were numb and useless once more. He began to drag himself away from her, but she kept pace with ease, strolling beside him as he crawled using only his arms. She shocked him time and time again. Each time the pain grew more intense, and the time it took for the feeling to come back to his legs lengthened.

"You haven't pulled your gun yet." She shocked him again. "Afraid if you hurt me, Thea will never forgive you?"

He wasn't willing to kill Cora, but that didn't mean he wouldn't hurt her.

He rolled onto his back and waited for the next shock. When she leaned down, he grabbed her ankle. She screamed as the shock meant for him only coursed through her body, too. She fell on top of him. He pinned her arms down and held her in a tight bear hug.

She kicked and screamed, but benumbed as his legs were, he couldn't feel it. When he was finally able to stand, he threw her from him and got to his feet. She hit the wall and slid down to the ground.

"Stay down," he warned. "I don't want to hurt you, but I will."

She lunged for him, and he saw that it was a ring that administered the shocks.

He grabbed her by the wrist and pressed her own hand to her temple. Her teeth snapped together as she convulsed. Her eyes rolled into the back of her head, and she slumped to the ground. Walt checked her pulse; she was unconscious, but otherwise unharmed. He took the ring from her, dropped it on the floor and stamped on it then continued on to the lab.

A STUDY IN WHITE

The lab was a study in white. The walls, the floors, and the furniture were all pristine and gleaming. A central walkway led to a platform lined with medical equipment and computers. On each side of the walkway was a large glass cube suspended over a vast drop. On the right-hand side, the cube hung over a pit filled with some gel-like material that bubbled and oozed. On the left, an abyss so deep Thea couldn't see the bottom.

The screens on the platform came to life; the images they showed reflecting all around her. She watched as, on every floor, the legions clashed with the police. The captain had made good on her promise. Unmasked soldiers and what was left of the TPD, along with citizens who fought for the only home they knew, battled against the sect's forces.

On the top-right screen, Thea saw Walt, a floor below, taking a group of legionaries to task. On another, Torrez and Cleo beat back the tide, dodging and dancing between bullets. The captain wrestled with Orion Martin, nearby O'Malley, who was cornered by Bill. The battle for Tenebrium City had begun.

"They'd die for you."

Thea's head whipped around so quickly it hurt her neck. She hadn't noticed the doctor sitting below the many screens in his white lab coat that blended in so perfectly with his surroundings.

A PROMISE KEPT

Chaos surrounded Walt. The fighting had spilled out into the ward behind the Data Centre and beyond. He could hear that battles raged on every floor as gunfire filled the air and explosions shook the building's foundations. There was no way he could follow Thea to the lab now that the Gold and Onyx Legions had joined the fray. He had no choice but to trust she would do what was needed.

"Cleo," he shouted as he fired at a soldier who was determined to end Torrez. "Where are the cells?" His shot caught the woman between the shoulder blades, and she dropped like a bag of bricks.

"Two floors up," Cleo shouted back, ducking under a table to avoid falling debris.

Walt bowled allies and enemies out of the way as he sprinted towards the stairwell. A soldier wearing a gold mask tried to halt his progress on the first landing, but Walt barely broke stride as he grabbed the man by the shoulders and threw him over the bannister.

He burst into the cellblock and was surprised to see that the fighting hadn't made it that far. The block was cold and impersonal, all transparent plastic and glass. Only one cell was occupied by a young Asian man in a prison-style striped grey uniform.

"Joshua?" Walt called to him as he searched for a way to open the cell door.

"Where's my dad?"

"Waiting for you to come home. How do they usually open these?"

"A key fob."

As he had no idea who would be in possession of such an item, Walt moved over to the fire suppression unit. It was a large red cabinet that contained a foam extinguisher, a fire blanket and exactly what he had been looking for, a small black glass breaker.

Walt used his elbow to break the safety glass. Immediately a siren blared overhead. Ignoring this, he pulled the tool from its housing and placed its pointed end delicately against the glass of Joshua's cell. He pushed and heard the click as the spring mechanism released and then the muted crack as the glass shattered into a thousand tiny pieces and fell to the floor like rain.

"C'mon, kid. Let's get you out of here."

THE ECSTASY OF GOLD

The fire alarm clamoured, reverberating around the cavernous room.

"I had hoped it would be you," Maxwell shouted over the noise, smiling as if with genuine pleasure. He looked at Thea, where she stood near the door as if she were a curio. "The thorn in my side. You are a worthy adversary. But you are too late; the city is mine."

"Not while there are still those willing to fight for it."

There was a soft whirring sound, and then the sprinklers in the ceiling high above spun into life. Cold water fell like heavy rain, drenching the room.

"I want them to fight this impossible battle. I want the unworthy among them to fall at the hands of my soldiers," Maxwell said, turning his face upwards to let the faux rain engulf him.

"You have no right to this city or its people. What can you possibly gain? You can't think that you could hold onto the power here. It's insanity. How long before the armies of the world march in to find out why the city has gone dark? At the behest of families missing their loved ones. You can't just disappear millions of people."

"Can't I? It's already done. This city is sick. It is plagued by the average, the normal, but it was built for the great. To house the genius, the most influential, the minds capable of shaping centuries to come, but instead, it's filled with human rats running around a city built for kings. People like you and your friends scurrying around out there. They were never meant to be here; you were never meant to be here. The colonies were supposed to be a symbol of status, and Tenebrium was to be their jewel. Only the most worthy deserve this city of plenty. The plague of the everyman was one thought to be without a cure—until now. It was my vision, my foresight. Why can't we prune the undesirable from our population and restore this city to its past glory?"

"You're mad. That's the big secret," Thea said, shivering and soaked to the skin.

"You're a lunatic. Your privileged lifestyle is propped up by those you call average; with them gone, who will supply the things you value over human life? You've been driven mad by the ecstasy of gold."

"Is that what this feeling is?" Maxwell asked, his arms wide. "'The ecstasy of gold?' I like it."

"Why did you make the drugs?"

"To create the perfect workforce, unfeeling and obedient, but it didn't work. Drug manipulation can only go so far, and the effects are usually temporary. But the high it created, the rats are addicted to it."

"You knew it would create ghouls, didn't you?"

"The first step of my goals was achieved—nearly a million of those draining our resources, removed from the supply chain. The loss of them eased the food shortages. I saved lives."

"You are raving," Thea said with as much contempt as she could muster. "Why did you kill the sex workers?"

He seemed unable to stop talking, given the opportunity to gloat over his vile misdeeds.

"I'd give them to my men to let off some steam. They are cheaper than therapists, you know. Clients, even clients among my ranks, tell their by-the-hour lovers more than they tell their priests. Lost souls no one would miss, loose ends tied up and a supply of test subjects all in one. Whoever thought of selling sex was a genius."

"And Henshall?"

"Ahh, poor Henshall. He was the one who designed the implantation methods for the chips, but he got cold feet. He fell for the hooker and told him everything. I had no choice but to silence them both. Richard was the first successful trial of the Morpheus chip. He fought me so hard, but he still killed the man he loved. Mr James fought when he killed your father. He tried so hard to hold back, and when I made him attack you, well, no one had ever been able to wake up before, but we made sure that's not an issue now."

"What did you do to my sister?" Droplets dripped from the end of Thea's nose and clung to her eyelashes; she blinked them away, trying to clear her vision.

"The delightful Cora. Nothing. Bastion didn't hurt her either. In fact, I think he may have loved her in his own way. He gave her whatever she wanted, no matter what she asked for. He treated her like a queen."

Thea knew that she should leave him to his ranting and find his office and end the tyranny, but this might be her only chance to get answers.

"Why did you kill my father?"

"Another case of cold feet. He would sell his own mother to get ahead, but he just couldn't bear to see his precious daughter hurt. If only he had loved poor Cora as much."

As Thea's mind chewed over what she had been told, her eyes flickered to the screens. Torrez was cornered in an office, fatally outnumbered. Bill lay unmoving at O'Malley's feet next to Jasper, who was slowly bleeding out. Walt was nowhere to be seen.

"Enough. This ends now."

Cleo had told her that Maxwell's office was connected to the lab by a small corridor that housed a personal lift. She turned and ran towards it, her feet slipping on the slick floor. She could hear his quick splashing footfalls behind her, but Thea didn't care. She would get to his office before he could stop her.

She tore through the corridor, past the lift and finally found herself inside Maxwell's office. Artwork covered the walls. A single computer terminal sat atop a large desk.

She had already inserted the trojan at the workstation when he burst through the doors. His neat hair mussed, a gun held aloft.

"What are you doing?"

"We talk about Tenebrium like it's all there is. But it's just a city; there is a whole wide world out there. Are you ready to face them?"

"What are you talking about?" There was an ill-concealed note of panic in his voice as he eyed the trojan where it was nestled.

"It's over."

The trojan let out a small *ding* and began to decrypt the files held on the terminal, sending them out into the world.

"Step back," Maxwell screamed. "Pick up that thing!"

"You're too late."

"I will destroy you."

"Go ahead. Changes nothing now."

Thea walked around the desk and passed Maxwell, who ran to his workstation to see what she had done. She heard his shriek of fury as she made her way back to the lab.

There was a loud bang, and something hot and hard hit Thea in the back, sending her to the ground. She landed in a shallow puddle, her warm blood mixing with the cool water.

"I will kill you," Maxwell screeched. He looked like he was falling apart at the seams. "I will not be undone by the likes of you."

He fired at Thea again, but crazed as he was, he missed every time. Out of bullets, he threw the gun aside with a howl of rage. Maxwell ran at Thea and began to kick her in the stomach over and over. The pain seemed dull and far away, distanced from her by the knowledge that she had done it. She had exposed them. In time the city would be free.

As he raised a foot intending to stomp on her face, she grabbed his ankle and kicked at his other leg. He tumbled forward towards the edge of the walkway, headed for the unknown gel, but as he fell, he grabbed Thea, taking her over the edge with him.

The gel was warm and thick and, now she was in it, she realised, full of body parts. The bullet wound in her back was robbing her of her strength, but she struggled to the edge of the disgusting pool. She saw feet on the artificial shore. An immaculately manicured hand reached out to her, and she grasped at it gratefully.

Captain Betty Charles pulled her onto the catwalk over the pool as two uniformed officers dragged a still clamouring Maxwell from the depths.

"Would you like to do the honours?" the captain asked.

"No, this one is all you."

"Dr Chester Maxwell, you are under arrest for perpetuating a coup against the establishment, illegal human experiments, the creation and mass distribution of a highly destructive drug…"

As water continued to fall on her face, Thea closed her eyes and drifted. The pain would come later, but for now, she was content.

SOLE SURVIVOR

The battle at Medicorum raged on for days before those loyal to the legions realised it was over, and the survivors allowed themselves to be rounded up by the authorities sent in to aid what remained of the TPD.

No one paid any mind to Bastion, where he lay on his bed of glass, broken and in pain. Slowly over the course of several days, seemingly invisible, he dragged himself to the outside, where he was finally spotted by a Medicus.

They loaded him in an ambulance, not caring if he was friend or foe and carted him off to Tenebrium General.

The weeks he spent there recovering gave him time to think and time to plan.

BETTER DAYS

Though Tenebrium City had only been under the complete control of the Gold Legion for two weeks, its people had felt the effects of the sect's influence for two long years as life in the city grew more and more restricted. Families had been torn apart by Styxx, and many who didn't deserve to be executed were killed. Tenebites had lived through some of the darkest of days.

With the arrival of the Colonial Military and Federal Investigators, the first true sign of their liberation, the citizens of Tenebrium took to the streets to show their gratitude and joy. Loud and raucous parties erupted all over the city and lasted for days after the abolition of the Three Strike Rule and the removal of the Onyx Legion's presence on the streets. The people of Tenebrium were free to express their relief however they wanted for the first time in far too long.

Thea spent the week that followed her meeting with Maxwell in The Rice Medical Institute, where she was being treated. Lying in the large comfy bed was the most relaxed she could remember being. There were still so many things that needed to be done, but now she had the time to do them. All Thea had was time.

She was visited frequently by Walt and Cleo, the captain, Torrez, and even Gin Ricky once, who thanked her for her part in the safe return of his son. Zhao had sent a card, wishing her well and leaving her to wonder if he had found his partner after the chaos had died down. When she was better, she would visit him and thank him for everything he did for her and the city.

"You look better," Torrez said with a smile. It was evening now, and even though he had visited that morning, he still came back to check on her. He too had healed from most of his injuries. Though his hand was still recovering, the doctors had told him he would regain full function in time.

"Honestly, I'm ready to go home, but not quite ready to face my responsibilities yet."

"They can wait," he said firmly. "Things are good out there. Did you see they arrested Mayor Howell?"

While Thea had lain in the hospital, there had been many reports of wealthy business owners being arrested, of high-ranking officials resigning, and of new appointments in all facets of the establishment. The cavalry had well and truly arrived, and they were taking no prisoners when it came to the Gold Legion coup.

"I did, and Zhao is officially the DA. He pardoned Walt as his first act."

"That could have been awkward otherwise."

"Any line on O'Malley?"

"Nah." Torrez shrugged. "He's either dead or underground. I think we are rid of him either way."

"And what about Marielena?"

Torrez shifted uncomfortably in his chair. "She's safe with Salvador. She won't talk to me, and I think I'm going to stop calling."

"Drew, she's your world."

"Yeah, she is, but I've treated her so badly. I've cheated too much, lied too much. I've hurt her too much. I don't think there's a way back for us. The things she would have to forgive me for or let slide...I think that would be asking more than any one person could offer. It took me longer than it should have to realise what was important. What's the saying? You don't know what you've got 'til it's gone." He brushed a tear from under his eye. "I ruined the best thing that ever happened to me, and I'm going to have to live with that."

"I'm sorry."

"Don't be. I did this to myself. After everything I've done, I got off easy, and besides, I still have you, right?"

"Always."

"That's something. Not much, but it's something."

They both smiled.

There was a knock on the door, and they both looked up to see a small Costa Rican woman in a crisp suit. "Could I have a word, Detective Williams?"

"I'll come back in the morning, Querida."

"Be good."

"Never."

The woman watched Torrez leave and closed the door behind him.

"How can I help you?"

"My name is Natalia Vargas. I work for the Augmentation Regulation Committee, and I'd like to offer you a job."

HAPPINESS IS AN INSIDE JOB

Walt dropped his keys in the bowl next to the door as he entered and hung his coat on the rack nearby. He was stuffed. He and Cleo had decided to go out for dinner as neither particularly wanted to cook. The food had been amazing, and while dessert had him wishing for an elasticated waistband on his trousers, it was more than worth it.

They had laughed and talked for hours. Now they were home, Walt was ready for a shower and then bed.

"We should go back to that place again soon," Walt said. He glanced over at Cleo. She had been quiet on their walk home.

"Yeah, sure," she said absently.

"Is everything okay?"

"I think I know what I want to do now."

"Oh, yeah?" Walt moved over to the dining table and sat down. Cleo followed.

"I want to help the ghouls. There's no cure yet, and I helped create Styxx. I think it's my duty to help fix it. To help the people I've hurt."

"I think that's a great idea. If anyone can do it, you can."

"Thank you." Cleo paused. "It's not the only thing I've been thinking about. Can we talk? I mean, can we really talk?"

"Sure," Walt said, sitting up straighter.

"You're trying so hard, and it means so much, but you're miserable."

"I'm fine."

"No, you aren't. I know you. We were friends long before we were anything more, and I think if I kept my mouth shut, we could probably muddle along just fine together for the rest of our lives, but I want more. I want more than nice and fine. I want the kind of love you and Thea have."

"Cleo..."

"I should have said something before Medicorum. I've known all along, and what's worse, I told Thea I knew. I put our marriage on her, and that wasn't fair. I thought I needed you. Everything I knew disappeared when I became a ghoul—except you. I thought if I clung onto you, I could claw my way back. But I don't want to go back anymore. I need to move forward. It was all I could think about when we were surrounded by those soldiers. I didn't want to die your wife. I didn't want to die living that lie. The thought that my gravestone might have said 'loving wife' felt so damn wrong. I'm still in love with you, but you aren't in love with me. And I deserve better than that."

"I never meant to hurt you. I just…"

"Fell in love." Cleo smiled wistfully.

"I thought I loved you more than I could ever love anyone. Thea… she blindsided me. I'm so sorry. There's no excuse for what I did."

"I was so angry and so hurt. I wanted to destroy you both. I played the memory of that night over and over in my head. I wanted to know what she had that I didn't, but it doesn't work like that. It was never about something I lacked, it was about something you two found in each other, and it doesn't matter anymore. So much has happened. Watching you together, I get it. I didn't at first, but I do now. I was gone for two years; anything before that feels like it's from another life, and we can't keep living in the past. I forgive you; I'm just done competing for you."

"I'm sorry," Walt said again. There were no words adequate.

"Don't be," Cleo leaned across the table and took his hand. "Go be happy. That's what I'm planning to do. Life's too short; the last few weeks have proved that."

"I don't know what to say."

"Be happy, Walt."

"If you need me for anything, I will always be here for you."

"I know. This is the end of our marriage, but I think in time, our friendship will be just fine."

COLD STORAGE

"She'll be happy here," Athena said, taking Thea's hand and giving it a reassuring squeeze.

They were sitting in the family room of the Rampling Psychiatric Centre. It was a bright and airy place painted in pastels and filled with plants.

"I feel like I'm abandoning her," Thea said sadly.

"She isn't well. This is the best place for her."

"I don't know how we got here." A tear escaped Thea's eye and rolled unbidden down her cheek.

"She's not in her right mind. What your father did to her...it would traumatise anyone. They played with her psyche. You heard what the doctor said; when the chip was removed...It did something to her brain. She may never be who she was, but she's still my daughter, and she's still your sister, and we will love her no matter what."

Thea nodded.

"She's asking for you, Mrs Williams."

Cora's doctor was a tall Black man with several face piercings. His short hair was bleach blonde, and he had a tattoo that said "Truth" under his right eye. Thea's sister had taken to him immediately, and he had shown himself to be kind and understanding. Knowing that he would be in charge of Cora's care put Thea's mind at ease.

The facility had settled Cora into a long-term room. While they had been able to choose which hospital she would stay in, a minimum stay of three months had been mandated by the Federal Investigators while they investigated her involvement with the Gold Legion. Thea was sure her sister would be cleared, she was a victim, but it would be a lot longer than three months before Cora was fit to be on her own.

Cora's room was plain, but beautiful. She had a single bed, her own bathroom, a desk, and large windows that looked out onto the grounds of the facility, but that could also be changed to look like anything she wanted. There was a squishy couch under the window and a projector screen that could be used to take in media. Her access to the data stream was to be limited and supervised.

Cora herself was wearing a long purple dressing gown made of the finest silk. It had been a gift from Bastion she had refused to part with.

"Hey," Thea said uncertainly.

"Thea," Cora smiled widely. "Hey, Mom."

"How are you feeling today?" Athena asked gently.

"Good, a little bored. I was painting earlier. They don't give us brushes, so it's messy, but kinda fun. I feel like I'm back in kindergarten."

"Can we get you anything?" Athena reached out to take Cora's hand, but she shrunk back from her touch.

"Don't touch me, nonbeliever. When Khrysos returns, he will burn you all."

Cora lunged for her mother, but Thea caught her and held her in a restraining hug. After a moment, Cora went limp.

"Mom, you okay?" Thea asked over Cora's head.

Athena nodded shakily, clutching her hands to her chest.

"You know," Cora said, as Thea led her over to the bed. "Some cultures believe that twins are a single soul that gets split. Maybe as you were destined to be good, I was destined to be bad."

"You aren't bad. You're just a little lost right now, but we're here for you. We aren't going anywhere."

Outside Cora's room, Thea leant against the wall giving herself a moment to recover. She exhaled slowly and rubbed her face with her hands. Cora had a long way to go, but Thea could wait.

The captain was waiting for Thea on the sidewalk outside the Bedford Institute. It had taken many meetings and assurances to convince the powers that be of this course of actions, but they had agreed in the end that it was a punishment befitting the crime.

"Are you sure about this?" Betty asked, watching Thea closely.

"Jail is too easy. He killed thousands and hurt millions."

"It's just that this shows a bitter streak I never knew you had."

"He had my father killed and my sister locked up. He's responsible for the death of so many innocent people. Jasper and Bill. He's the reason Benjamin Pickford is dead and all those sex workers. We haven't been able to identify them all. They and so many more deserve justice."

"I'm glad you're back to your old self; that attitude didn't suit you."

"I'm sorry for how I behaved; it was childish."

"You were lost, hurting. We all act out when we're in pain."

"Thank you for your understanding."

"Here he comes."

Thea looked to the sky. A gleaming transporter, all in silver, was descending

TENEBRIUM

towards them. It landed smoothly, and when the door opened, Thea was surprised to see Zhao stepping out.

"Thea," he said, stepping in and giving her a warm hug. "I'm glad you have recovered."

"It's wonderful to see you. I just wish it was under better circumstances."

"I'm sorry I didn't visit; I needed some time to process...things."

"Did you find your partner?"

"I did. He didn't take part in the battle at Medicorum, but he could still face some jail time for his misplaced loyalties. It's complicated, but what relationship isn't? We're working through it as best we can. Betty," he said, turning to give the captain a hug and making it clear he would say no more on the subject.

"Shall we?" the captain said after they had exchanged pleasantries.

"Yes, let's." Zhao nodded to two guards who opened the rear doors of the transporter and pulled out a coffin-shaped gurney.

Strapped to the anthropoidal trolley, his mouth covered by a piece of leather, was Chester Maxwell. His eyes darted around madly as they readjusted to the bright outdoor light.

"Take him in," Betty said with a jerk of her head.

The Bedford Institute of Cryogenics was named after the first-ever person to have their body preserved. It provided preservation via liquid nitrogen for the notable in the scientific world. It was not a facility used for punishment regularly, but in the case of Dr Maxwell, they had only been too happy to oblige.

The institute staff took the small party into a room called a Cryosuite, where the body was prepped and frozen before being stored in the vaults with the others who had opted to be cryogenically preserved.

The room was clinical. Fittingly, its white décor reminded Thea uncomfortably of the lab in Medicorum.

The Bedford doctors placed Maxwell in a slim capsule. "When we close the capsule, the process takes around ten seconds. It's relatively painless. From there, he will be placed in storage. You can visit whenever you like, but we need a week's notice if you wish to revive someone from preservation."

"How often are they revived without injury?"

"In the last five years, we haven't had a single case where the recipient didn't revive at full capacity, with full function, and no memory damage."

"Good. I want him to remember," Thea said, looking Maxwell straight in the eyes.

"Captain Charles, shall I begin?"

The captain nodded.

"Everything is ready for you. You just have to push the button there, and the preservation will happen automatically. We will be in the control room if you need us. Take as long as you like."

"Thank you," Betty said, and the doctor left.

Thea strolled over to the capsule savouring the moment. She leaned down and pulled the gag from Maxwell's mouth.

"I will end you," he spat. "I will destroy everything you hold dear, and only then, when you are broken, will I kill you."

"I'll be long dead before you're in any position to make good on that threat. You are going to wake up in a few centuries with nothing. No one will remember you, and you will know what it feels like to be just like everyone else. Privilege is all that sets you apart, and I'm taking it from you. Dream of me while I forget you."

She pushed the button, and the lid of the capsule slit shut. Maxwell struggled against his restraints, screaming empty threats of vengeance. Slowly a delicate mist filled the air around him; his movements became slower and slower until he was still, his face frozen in a mask of malice.

"It's over," the captain said.

There was a pleasant finality to the end of Maxwell. His removal from society was like closing a particularly bloody chapter in history.

"You had better get back to the precinct, Detective. We have a lot of paperwork to do."

"Gladly."

They left the Bedford Institute without a backward glance.

WE RUINED EACH OTHER, YOU AND I

Walt flipped his one-month sobriety chip over in his hand. It was a small achievement, but it was his. It was the first step. He felt better than he had in a long time. He could picture the future now. It was nice to feel like he had one.

Cleo had moved out the week before, and he had helped her get settled into her new place. They had talked, and he had done his best to make amends. He had a long journey ahead of him, but it was one he undertook willingly.

He flipped the chip in his hand one more time for luck and slipped it back into his pocket. He hadn't been back to the TPD since his near execution, but it felt good and right to walk back in as a Detective. That had been his reward for his part in the city's liberation. It was more than enough.

There was a nervous flutter in his stomach as he rode the lift upwards. When the doors opened, the bullpen looked as it always did. There were fewer detectives now, but the clean-up crew had erased any trace of the violence that had happened within.

It would be a while before those who worked there found their version of the new normal. It would be a while before they regained each other's trust and moved past the things they had seen and done.

Thea sat behind her desk with her back to him. He watched her for a moment, drinking her in. She was filling in paperwork, he couldn't see her face, but he could imagine a subtle smile on her lips.

He called to her as he walked, not wanting to surprise her. She turned to look at him and smiled.

"You're back!" She sounded pleased.

"Given the all-clear."

"That's great."

"I got my one-month sober chip today." He showed it to her proudly.

"Congratulations. That's wonderful."

"It's been hard, but worth it. Listen, can we talk? Somewhere else?"
"Ehh...sure. Wanna get some coffee? I saw Gin Ricky outside."
"Yeah. Yeah. I'd love that."

They exchanged small talk on their way to the coffee cart. When they had bought their drinks and thanked Gin Ricky, they moved over to a vacant bench to enjoy the fake sun, which was beating down upon them warmly.

"So," Thea said, waiting for him to speak.

"So," Walt repeated. He was nervous. "Cleo left," he blurted.

"Oh," she said, caught off guard. "I'm sorry."

"No. No, it's a good thing. We've been separated for a few weeks now. She didn't want to live a lie; neither of us did."

"Oh," Thea said again, her face inscrutable.

"I got my badge back. I'm single. I'm sober."

"Walt..."

"Just let me say it. I love you. I love you, and I want to be with you if you'll have me. I have made so many mistakes, and I have hurt you—"

"I forgive you," she cut across him. "But I can't be with you."

"If you forgive me, why not?"

"We ruined each other, you and I," she said wistfully. "We ruined each other."

"The things I did—"

"We ruined each other long before any of this happened. And we just kept on ruining. Taking piece after piece of each other, things we can never get back. Some things can't be fixed. You're an alcoholic. You. Because of the things we did."

"It isn't your fault I'm a drunk, Thea."

She paused to watch the people around them for a moment before going on. "I was your mistress, and I let it happen because I didn't care that it was wrong. I just wanted any part of you. I was always yours, but you...you were never mine. Not really."

She was crying. So was he.

"But there's nothing standing in our way now."

"There's always something."

"You died in my arms. You saved me from being executed."

"You killed my dad, Walt. I don't blame you, but it was your hands."

"I..." There was nothing he could say to right that wrong. "Thea, please."

"I love you so much, but I am worse when I'm with you. The things we do... I don't want to be madly in love anymore. I want to be sanely, happily and healthily in love. I love you, I really love you, but loving you means hating me, and I'm not gonna do it anymore."

She leaned forward and kissed him gently. It was a goodbye with no words.

She stroked her thumb over his cheek once, stood, and walked away.

NEW START

Thea laughed as she watched Torrez examine the frankly insane amount of throw pillows she had bought.

They were standing in the living room of her new apartment. It was full of boxes, but it was hers.

"This is a nice place, Querida. Smaller than your last, but nice."

"Couldn't live on daddy's dime forever." Her smile flickered and faded.

"It was a nice service," Torrez said, moving over to her and rubbing her arm.

"People told so many kind lies."

"That's what funerals are for; you lie, you say so and so was great, while inside, everyone thinks about how much of a dick the dead person was."

Thea smiled reluctantly. "You should bring Joseph over; I'd love to meet him."

"I don't think we're there yet. I have had two long term relationships in my life, and I destroyed them both. He and I haven't really talked about what we are, and meeting you would be like taking him to meet my mom."

"I think that was a compliment."

"It was. You're family. So you have to wait."

"Okay," Thea chuckled. "I'll wait."

"When do you start your new job?"

"Monday. I'm nervous."

"Don't be. Agent Thea Williams has a nice ring to it."

"What about you?"

"As of today, I am officially no longer in the employ of the Tenebrium Police Force."

"Drew, I'm sorry."

"Nobody forced me to do the things I did, and I knew the tribunal would rule against me. I'm lucky not to be in prison. That's why..." He fished a slip of paper out of his pocket and handed it to Thea. It was a Private Investigator's License.

Elanor Miller

"Andrew Torrez, Private Eye."
"Sounds good, doesn't it?"

LEFT BEHIND

Walt had thought it would feel strange when the captain had told him that he could have his old desk back, but as he sat there opposite Thea's empty chair, it didn't feel strange at all. There was a comforting familiarity about it. He imagined doing his job like he had in the past, and it felt good. He wondered idly if he and Thea would still be partners; he couldn't see why else he would have been put back in his old spot—partners often shared desks. The thought gave him hope. He wouldn't pressure her, but maybe in time, they would both get to a place where they could try again. He would like that.

Thea hadn't arrived yet when Walt got to work that morning. When she didn't arrive by midday, he thought she must have been on the night shift. But by six in the evening, he knew something was amiss.

"Torrez," he called as the man entered to collect the last of his things.

"Yeah? What's up?"

"Where's Thea? She hasn't come in yet."

Torrez looked surprised, and then something else crossed his face. Pity.

"She left," he said quietly.

"What? What do you mean 'she left'?"

"She left Tenebrium. She got another job in Caligo City. I'm sorry, man. She's gone."

EPILOGUE

There you have it, my tale from Tenebrium. I hope it has shed some light on the events of the year 2425. More than this, I hope it provides answers to those of you and your families who were affected by the events of that time. The official records are still sealed, and most likely, they always will be, but I'll say once more that I believe what I have written here to be true.

Tenebrium and its citizens have found some semblance of normality in the intervening years. The system is still broken, and much still needs to change, but there are those who see it now and who want to make a difference. Progress is undeniably a slow process, but the wheels are finally in motion and that in and of itself, is a victory. There are more who should have been held accountable who never can be now, but things are undeniably better. It is cold comfort for most, but leaves a glimmer of hope for the future.

Acknowledgments

I'd like to begin by thanking my 'gals'.

Kerry, for always being my best and loudest cheerleader. Over the shield.
Rachael, for her support and ability to read faster than anyone I have ever met in my life.
Lu, for her willingness to deep dive into every project, and her never-ending patience and ability to talk, ad nauseum, about the people I make up in my head.

To my parents, you have done so much for me over the course of my life it seems almost silly to thank you for taking the time to read Tenebrium, but your support and continued belief in me means everything.

To my sister, thank you for the distraction when writing is too hard.

To Gage, this book is dedicated to you because without you, it wouldn't have happened. My life is infinitely better because it has you in it.

Special Thanks:
To Stephanie Francis of The Abundant Word

Printed in Great Britain
by Amazon